TIGER WOODS

Recent Titles in Greenwood Biographies

TIGER WOODS

A Biography
Second Edition

Lawrence J. Londino

GREENWOOD BIOGRAPHIES

 GREENWOOD

AN IMPRINT OF ABC-CLIO, LLC
Santa Barbara, California • Denver, Colorado • Oxford, England

Copyright 2010 by Lawrence J. Londino

All rights reserved. No part of this publication may be reproduced, stored in a retrieval system, or transmitted, in any form or by any means, electronic, mechanical, photocopying, recording, or otherwise, except for the inclusion of brief quotations in a review, without prior permission in writing from the publisher.

Library of Congress Cataloging-in-Publication Data

Londino, Lawrence J.
    Tiger Woods : a biography / Lawrence J. Londino. — 2nd ed.
        p. cm. — (Greenwood biographies)
    Includes bibliographical references and index.
    ISBN 978-0-313-38050-1 (hard copy : alk. paper) —
    ISBN 978-0-313-38051-8 (ebook)
1. Woods, Tiger.   2. Golfers—United States—Biography.   I. Title.
    GV964.W66L66   2010
    796.352092—dc22
    [B]   2010008863

ISBN: 978-0-313-38050-1
EISBN: 978-0-313-38051-8

14   13   12   11   10   1   2   3   4   5

This book is also available on the World Wide Web as an eBook.
Visit www.abc-clio.com for details.

Greenwood
An Imprint of ABC-CLIO, LLC

ABC-CLIO, LLC
130 Cremona Drive, P.O. Box 1911
Santa Barbara, California 93116-1911

This book is printed on acid-free paper ∞

Manufactured in the United States of America

To my wife Cathleen, who has lovingly supported my passion for playing, watching, and talking about the game of golf for lo these many years. To son Jonathan, whose copyediting and style suggestions are chiefly responsible for whatever clarity this work possesses. To son James, my caddie for the only A Flight Championship I ever won. And to son Paul, my last best hope for a Father-Son trophy.

CONTENTS

SERIES FOREWORD

In response to high school and public library needs, Greenwood developed this distinguished series of full-length biographies specifically for student use. Prepared by field experts and professionals, these engaging biographies are tailored for high school students who need challenging yet accessible biographies. Ideal for secondary school assignments, the length, format and subject areas are designed to meet educators' requirements and students' interests.

Greenwood offers an extensive selection of biographies spanning all curriculum related subject areas including social studies, the sciences, literature and the arts, history and politics, as well as popular culture, covering public figures and famous personalities from all time periods and backgrounds, both historic and contemporary, who have made an impact on American and/or world culture. Greenwood biographies were chosen based on comprehensive feedback from librarians and educators. Consideration was given to both curriculum relevance and inherent interest. The result is an intriguing mix of the well known and the unexpected, the saints and sinners from long-ago history and contemporary pop culture. Readers will find a wide array of subject choices from fascinating crime figures like Al Capone to inspiring pioneers like Margaret Mead, from the greatest minds of our time like Stephen Hawking to the most amazing success stories of our day like J.K. Rowling.

While the emphasis is on fact, not glorification, the books are meant to be fun to read. Each volume provides in-depth information about the subject's life from birth through childhood, the teen years, and adulthood. A thorough account relates family background and education, traces personal and professional influences, and explores struggles, accomplishments, and contributions. A timeline highlights the most significant life events against a historical perspective. Bibliographies supplement the reference value of each volume.

INTRODUCTION

The first edition of this book left off at the end of the 2005 season, Tiger Woods's eighth full year as a professional golfer. At that time he had already amassed a most incredible record as a professional golfer, winning 63 professional tournaments, 10 of them major championships. For all but one golfer (Jack Nicklaus) that book would have sufficed as a chronicle of the most productive career in the history of the game. But Tiger Woods has always set his sights on the career record of 18 majors set by Nicklaus, and so his quest has continued. Since 2005 he has continued his dominance of professional golf, winning 30 times, including 4 more major championships bringing his total to 14. He has won an amazing 33 percent of the professional tournaments he has entered over his career, a feat that is unapproached in the game. In 2007 he compiled a streak of seven consecutive PGA Tour wins that challenged the standing record amassed by Byron Nelson in 1945.

And he accomplished all of this while encountering his share of upheaval in his personal life. In 2006 his father Earl passed away after a long battle with cancer. As this book will explore, Tiger's relationship with his father was a foundation for his life. And Tiger proved to be human when he missed the cut in a major for the first time at the 2006 U.S. Open, his first tournament after his father's death.[1]

Woods also became a father twice.[2] And in addition to dealing with the challenges of fatherhood, Tiger also had to contend with speculation that his interest in golf would wane because of the distraction of his children. So far fatherhood has not significantly altered his dedication.

Just as this edition was going to press, the image of Tiger Woods suffered a substantial blow when it was disclosed that he had been involved in a series of extramarital affairs with several women. How this disclosure has and will affect the career of Tiger Woods will be dealt with in the Epilogue, due to the timing of the events.

This edition will look at how Tiger's relationship with the PGA Tour has evolved as his reputation has grown. Television ratings swell by at least 50 percent when he is competing, and the number of spectators at tournaments increases when he plays.[3] While most of his fellow professionals appreciate what he means to the PGA Tour, there has been some resentment aimed at Woods because of the amount of influence he yields over the organization. His corporate sponsors make it possible for him to host his own tournament as part of the regular schedule of the PGA Tour. And there has been some grumbling from some observers that tournament directors tend to look more favorably at donating to Tiger's foundation in hopes of getting him to play in their event.

The Tiger Woods Foundation has prospered in the last four years. In February 2006, The Tiger Woods Learning Center was officially opened in Anaheim, California, where former President Bill Clinton was an honored guest. We will examine exactly what the objectives of the foundation are, and how Tiger has managed to capitalize on his celebrity to steadily increase the resources available to it.

On June 24, 2008, Tiger underwent surgery to repair the anterior cruciate ligament (ACL) in his left knee in Park City, Utah. Earlier in the month, in what was probably one of the most engaging sports stories of the century, Tiger won the 2008 U.S. Open playing on his bad knee, winning on the first sudden-death hole after an 18-hole playoff against veteran golfer Rocco Mediate. Mediate, himself plagued by back troubles throughout his career, battled Woods right down to the last putt. We will describe this epic David and Goliath battle and how it generated tremendous interest among golfers and nongolfers alike.

I have been a fanatic about golf for over 50 years. I remember vividly the black-and-white television images of the first coverage of golf, the 1956 Masters. Ken Venturi was a promising amateur and was leading the tournament after three rounds, only to shoot an 80 on Sunday to finish second to Jackie Burke. I didn't know who Arnold Palmer was, and Jack Nicklaus was not yet a student at Ohio State.

I first heard of Tiger Woods in 1985 while doing research for a television documentary about the history of African Americans in golf. Whenever one of my colleagues at New York University asked me what I was working on, and I told them, the standard chiding response was "That will be a pretty short documentary." Eventually I discovered evidence of African Americans playing the game of golf all the way back to colonial days. So while Tiger Woods is not the first person of color to master the game of golf, nobody, of any color, has garnered as much attention. An informal Internet search for Tiger Woods yields some 22 million hits—Arnold Palmer warrants 2 million. But still, a central question has to be posed and answered: Why write a biography of a person who is, as of this publication, 33 years old, and still very much alive?

Tiger Woods was a golf prodigy. By the age of three, he had already mastered the rudimentary skills of the game, was regularly covered by local and national media, and had appeared on the *Mike Douglas Show*, where he demonstrated his remarkable skills. But unlike many child prodigies, he delivered on his early promise, winning an unprecedented three consecutive United States Golf Association Junior championships, and eventually duplicating the feat at the USGA Amateur Championship, the most prestigious amateur title in golf. He won the NCAA Championship (individual) as a student athlete at Stanford University.

Woods made the transition to professional golf seamlessly. To date, he has won over 95 professional golf tournaments, including 14 major championships, which are universally accepted as the most coveted titles. His mixed African American/Thai/Chinese/Native American/Caucasian racial heritage further underscored his achievements in a historically segregated sport.

He grew up in a very normal middle-class suburban Northern California neighborhood, attended public schools, and, while competing in professional tournaments as a teenager, was a regular member of his high school golf team.

These reasons alone would justify this book. However, the phenomenon of Tiger Woods goes beyond his extremely high profile in the world of golf and sports.

After signing his first contract with the Nike Company he began to apply his superstar celebrity status and fortune to a variety of philanthropic activities that, because of his high profile, could eventually have significant impact on American and world culture. And he has accomplished all this as a racially mixed man in a predominately white society, in a predominantly white sport.

There is a tendency to be a little cynical about these vaguely messianic prophecies when talking about Tiger Woods. It's hard not to be. The media wants to mythologize our sports heroes. Tiger Woods is no exception. There are times when the public, through the media, will expect him to be perfect. If he shows any temper or is caught swearing, the commentators will take him to task.

This book will endeavor to examine this short but extremely accomplished life. The role of parents is always an important element of any biography. But when an individual is so young, his parents will necessarily be major elements in the story. His father, Earl Woods, had the greatest influence on the evolution of Tiger Woods. This is also the story of how Earl grew up in the middle of the United States in the time before the Civil Rights movement and how that shaped his life; and of his mother, Kultida, who was born in Thailand and came to this country as the wife of a black man.

A significant part of this story has to do with the game of golf. The unique characteristics of this truly international game, the intense individual adherence to the rules, and its generally elite origins all played a role in the evolution of Tiger Woods.

As with any pioneer, there are always others who made sacrifices and endured hardship to make it possible for others to succeed. So this book will introduce some of these early African American golfers who were not allowed to join the Professional Golfers Association until 1961, and explore how their achievements paved the way for Tiger Woods.

Tiger Woods has had an impact on popular culture, and this edition will examine what the effects of the Tiger Woods "brand" is on society.

Because of his exposure on television, the Internet, and a variety of other media (e.g., video games), he has altered somewhat our perception of celebrity.

This is not, strictly speaking, a sports biography. It is the story of a sports prodigy who accomplished unimagined records in the sport of golf in a very short time span. But at its heart it is a story about a middle-class family and its next generation struggling to assimilate into a majority culture, and along the way how it produced arguably the greatest golfer of all time.

NOTES

1. Most tournaments cut a number of players over a certain score.

2. Sam Alexis Woods, born 2007, and Charlie Axel Woods, born 2009.

3. Richard Sandomir, "Absence of Woods Could Cost Networks," *The New York Times*, June 19, 2008.

CONCISE HISTORY

Eldrick "Tiger" Woods is a professional golfer who has achieved a record of accomplishment that has approached the most historically significant players of the game of golf. At a relatively young age for golfers, he is well within range of establishing records in terms of regular PGA Tour tournaments and the all important major championships. However, he has also had a significant impact on the marketing of sports celebrities and, combining prize money and corporate sponsorships, he is the most highly compensated athlete in the world. As a person of considerable wealth, he has established a growing philanthropic legacy in the form of an educational foundation and other efforts to help the underprivileged. Woods has the distinction of being of mixed racial heritage in a sport not traditionally hospitable to people of color.

Born on December 30, 1975, in Cypress, California, Tiger Woods is the son of Earl and Kultida Woods. Earl Woods grew up in Kansas and graduated from Kansas State University, where he was one of the first African Americans to play varsity baseball. After graduating from the university, Earl Woods was commissioned as a 2nd lieutenant in the U.S. Army and enjoyed a successful career in the military. He served two tours of duty in Vietnam, the second as a member of the elite fighting unit, the Green Berets. After retiring from the military, Earl Woods settled in Northern California with his wife, Kultida, a Thai woman he met while on one of his tours in Asia, and their young son, Tiger, nicknamed after a Vietnamese colonel Earl served with in combat. Tiger grew up in a middle-class community, attending public schools and developing an interest in golf, after observing his father, who took up the game at the age of 38, practicing his swing. Exhibiting an unusual talent for the sport, Tiger was featured on several television programs, including the *Mike Douglas Show* in 1978, when as a three-year-old he appeared with entertainer Bob Hope. He played for his high school golf team and began what was to become one of the best records ever as a junior golfer.

He won the Junior World Golf Championship a record six times, four in a row from 1988–1991. He won the prestigious USGA Junior Championship three times, the youngest multiple winner of this event. He was designated Amateur Player of the Year by both *Golf Digest* and *Golfworld* magazines in 1991. That same year he competed in the PGA's Nissan Los Angeles Open, as an amateur.

The amateur career of Tiger Woods is matched only by legendary golfer Bobby Jones. He became the only golfer ever to win three consecutive USGA Amateur Championships from 1994 to 1996. Woods was a member of the 1994 Eisenhower Trophy World Amateur Golf Team that won the championship, and the 1995 Walker Cup team.

In 1994 he was recruited by Stanford University, where he enrolled as an economics major. In 1995 Woods was voted Pac-10 Player of the Year, NCAA First Team All-American, and Stanford's Male Freshman of the Year (encompassed all sports), and in 1996 he won the NCAA individual golf championship. Woods left Stanford after his sophomore year and turned professional.

In what was the most lucrative sponsorship deal in sports history, Tiger Woods received $6 million from the Nike Company to represent them. Primarily known for sports shoes, Nike was anticipating entry into the golf equipment market, and they were counting on the Woods sponsorship to pave the way.

Faced with the challenge of qualifying for his PGA Tour card without waiting for the Qualifying School the following fall, Woods had to earn enough prize money to break into the top 125 on the money list. Securing sponsors' exemptions to play was not a problem. With all the anticipation of Tiger Woods on the tour, every tournament director was more than willing to have him play in their event. His first professional tournament was the 1996 Milwaukee Open. He shot 67 in the first round, but his 73 in the second round made the 36-hole cut, and he was out of contention. However, in the second round he gave some indication of the appeal he would have to the fans when he had a hole-in-one on a 202 par three hole, sending the crowd into frenzy. He finished in a tie for 60th, earning $2,544. For all the endorsement deals, Tiger would savor that check, the first he had earned strictly on the basis of his own accomplishment.

Through the B.C. Open, Tiger had earned $58,000, placing him 128th on the PGA money list, thus insuring that he would earn enough to qualify him for the 1997 Tour. However, he assured his exemption for the next year by winning the Las Vegas tournament two weeks later. He defeated seasoned professional Davis Love III in a sudden death playoff.

In 1997 Woods began to fulfill the expectations of the press and the public. He won the Masters, his first major championship. And he won it in style, setting the scoring record in his first major as a professional. After shooting a 40 on the first nine of the first round, he rebounded with a sizzling 30 on the back nine. He then went on to shoot 271, 18 under par, breaking Jack Nicklaus's record by a stroke, and winning by 12 strokes.

Over the next 13 years he has continued to build on this unprecedented beginning. He has won just over a third of the tournaments entered worldwide, a figure that is unrivaled in tournament golf history. After 12 years on the Tour, Nicklaus, the only player who compares to Woods at this point in his career, had won 20 percent of the tournaments he entered by the same age.

His record in the major championships is eclipsed only by Jack Nicklaus.[1] Woods has to date won 14 Majors to Nicklaus's 18. And Woods is 34 years old. At the same age Jack Nicklaus had won 12 Majors. He is one of only five players to have won all four majors at least once in his career. He holds (or is tied for) the scoring records in relation to par in all four of the majors. Tiger Woods has led the PGA Tour Money List nine times. He has won the Vardon Trophy (low scoring average) eight times, and ten times he has been the PGA Player of the Year.[2] He has competed for the American team in the Ryder Cup competition five times and the Presidents Cup five times. In 1996 Woods was named *Sports Illustrated* Athlete of the Year, and again in 2000. He was designated as "Male Athlete of the Year" by the Associated Press in 1997, 1999, and 2000.

Tiger Woods has had an unparalleled impact on the PGA Tour, as well as sports marketing in general. His appeal to an audience has been demonstrated by the significant increase in television ratings when he is playing in a tournament. Between 2003 and 2008 Woods finished in the top five 54 times in 88 tournaments, with television ratings averaging 4.4. The average ratings in the 34 other events was 3.4. In 2007, ratings were 58 percent higher on weekends in tournaments in which he played.[3] His endorsements have made him the highest compensated athlete ever. At 33 he is on track to become the first athlete to earn over a billion dollars.

Woods, in collaboration with his father Earl, established the Tiger Woods Foundation in 1996. The main focus of the foundation is to provide supplemental educational programs for students 4 to 12 years old. In 2006 The Tiger Woods Educational Center was dedicated in Anaheim, California. The opening was the culmination of a $25 million campaign to build this state-of-the-art educational center. The building houses 100 computers and a 1,200-square-foot multimedia center.

Despite his considerable accomplishments as an athlete, Woods has come under some fire from the press and some other athletes about his lack of commitment to social causes, particularly regarding discrimination against minorities in American society. In 2003 the press tried to elicit a comment from Woods about the National Council of Women's Organizations' protest against the discrimination of the Augusta National Golf Club's prohibition of women members. He was quoted as allowing that the private club had the right to determine membership criteria. There have been other issues dealing either directly or indirectly with golf that have been presented to Woods. He has tended to avoid involvement.

His level of concentration tends to be so intense at tournaments that he has been accused of not being crowd-friendly enough. He rarely signs autographs, and, other than tipping his cap after applause, he does not interact with crowds at tournaments. However, despite the criticism of the press, his popularity has not diminished.

The public has an insatiable appetite for information about Woods, and even nongolfers take an interest in golf when he is in contention at a tournament. And to date he has managed to maintain a level of excellence in his sport that has not been matched. The only question is whether he will be able to eclipse Jack Nicklaus's record of 18 major championships.

NOTES

1. The major championships include the Masters, the U.S. Open, the British Open, and the PGA Championship.

2. In 2009, Tiger Woods was named PGA Player of the Year and won another Vardon Trophy.

3. Richard Sandomir, "Absence of Woods Could Cost Networks," *New York Times*, June 19, 2008.

TIMELINE: EVENTS IN THE LIFE OF TIGER WOODS

Born: December 30, 1975

1978–1981 Guest appearance on *That's Incredible* television program. Shot 48 for nine holes at Navy Golf Club in Cypress, California.

Guest appearances on *CBS News* and *Mike Douglas Show* putting with Bob Hope.

1982–1989 Guest appearances on *Today Show, Good Morning America,* ESPN, CBS, NBC, and ABC.

Second-place finish at the Insurance Youth Golf Classic (Big "I") National at age 13.

Winner of the Optimist International Junior World at ages 8, 9, 12 and 13.

1990 The youngest winner of the Insurance Youth Golf Classic (Big "I") National.

Winner of the Optimist International Junior World.

1991 *Golf Digest* Junior Player of the Year.

Titleist-*Golfweek* National Amateur of the Year.

Named First Team, Rolex Junior All-American.

Named American Junior Golf Association Player of the Year.

Participated in U.S. Amateur Championship.

Named Southern California Player of the Year.

1992   Top 32, U.S. Amateur Championship.

Selected to First Team, Rolex Junior All-American.

Southern California Player of the Year.

Named *Golf Digest* Player of the Year.

Competed in Nissan Los Angeles Open on PGA TOUR and U.S. Open Sectional Qualifier.

Named Titleist-*Golfweek* National Amateur of the Year.

1993   Received golf scholarship to Stanford University in November 1993, to join freshmen class of 1994.

First Team, Rolex Junior All-American.

Made top 32 at the U.S. Amateur Championship.

Won the U.S. Junior Amateur Championship.

Played in three PGA Tour tournaments, the Nissan Los Angeles Open and the Honda Classic, and the GTE Byron Nelson Classic.

Played in the U.S. Open Sectional Qualifying.

1994   Winner of the Western Amateur Championship.

Winner of the U.S. Amateur Championship, played at TPC Sawgrass in Ponte Vedra Beach, Florida.

Winner of the Southern California Golf Association Amateur Championship.

Golf World Man of the Year.

Winner of the Pacific Northwest Amateur Championship.

Member of the United States Team at the World Amateur Team Championships in Versailles, France.

1995   Winner of the U.S. Amateur Championship, contested at Newport Country Club, Newport, Rhode Island.

Tied 67th in the British Open at St. Andrews, Scotland.

Tied as an amateur for 41st in the Masters Tournament, the only amateur to make the 36-hole cut.

Selected as a member of the U.S. Team in Walker Cup Match in Porthcawl, Wales.

Stanford's male Freshman of the Year.

First Team All-American.

1996   PGA Tour Rookie of the Year.

Named *Sports Illustrated* Sportsman of the Year.

Won the NCAA Championship, The Honors Course, Chattanooga, Tennessee.

Winner of the U.S. Amateur Championship, Pumpkin Ridge Golf Club, Cornelius, Oregon, the only golfer ever to win three consecutive Amateur titles.

Named the Fred Haskins College Player of the Year.

Selected unanimous First Team All-American.

Tied British Open 72-hole record for an amateur with total of 281 at Royal Lytham and St. Annes, England.

Finished tied for 82nd in U.S. Open.

1997   Leading money winner on PGA Tour.

Named Associated Press Male Athlete of the Year.

Qualified for U.S. Team for Ryder Cup Matches.

Named ESPY Male Athlete of the Year.

Won the Masters Tournament 72-hole record with a total of 270 and set Masters record with 12-stroke victory margin, becoming the youngest champion and first major champion of African or Asian heritage.

1998   Won $4,561,494 on PGA Tour ($5,300,204 worldwide) with seven victories and 26 top-10 finishes in 47 events (9 victories and 30 top-10 finishes in 55 events worldwide).

Won $2,927,006 worldwide in 26 events to surpass 1997 earnings of $2,440,832.

Held current PGA Tour record for most consecutive events without missing the cut (17). Has missed only one cut in 48 events since joining PGA Tour 1996.

Qualified for U.S. Team for Presidents Cup.

1999   ESPY Male Athlete of the Year and ESPY Golfer of the Decade.

Player of the Year as selected by PGA Tour, PGA of America and Golf Writers Association of America.

Leading money winner on PGA Tour with $6,616,585.

Mark H. McCormack Award winner as the No. 1 player on the 1999 Official World Golf Ranking.

Qualified for U.S. Team for Ryder Cup Matches.

Won four consecutive PGA Tour events, the first to do that since Ben Hogan in 1953.

His eight PGA Tour victories and 11 overall were the most in one year at such a young age since Horton Smith had eight PGA Tour victories in 1929.

Named the Associated Press Male Athlete of the Year for the second time in three years and the seventh man—and the second golfer—to earn the award twice since it was begun in 1931.

2000   *L'Equipe* (France) World Champion of Champions.

Reuters Sportsman of the Year.

Winner of the PGA Championship, setting the PGA Championship record for the lowest score in relation to par, 18 under par, 270.

Lowest actual scoring average (68.17), breaking Byron Nelson's record from 1945.

Lowest adjusted scoring average (67.79) for Byron Nelson Award (PGA Tour) and Vardon Trophy (PGA of America).

Leading money winner on PGA Tour with $9,188,321 (most ever won in a single year).

Sports Illustrated Sportsman of the Year, and became the first person to win the award more than once.

The Associated Press Male Athlete of the Year.

ESPY Male Athlete of the Year for the third time in four years.

Player of the Year as selected by PGA Tour, PGA of America, and Golf Writers Association of America.

Mark H. McCormack Award winner as the No. 1 player on the 2000 Official World Golf Ranking.

Winner of the U.S. Open Championship, tying Open record with 272 total (65–69–71–67).

Qualified for United States Team for Presidents Cup.

Became the first ever to have won the U.S. Open, U.S. Amateur, and U.S. Junior Amateur titles.

With British Open victory, became the fifth ever and the youngest to complete the career Grand Slam of professional major championships.

Winner of the British Open Championship, setting British Open and Major championship records for the lowest score in relation to par, 19 under par, 269.

With PGA Championship victory, became the first since Ben Hogan in 1953 to win three major championships in the same year. Hogan won the Masters, U.S. Open, and British Open.

2001 Selected as Player of the Year by PGA Tour, PGA of America, and Golf Writers Association of America.

Mark H. McCormack Award winner as the No. 1 player on the 2001 Official World Golf Ranking.

Lowest adjusted scoring average (68.81) for Byron Nelson Award and Vardon Trophy.

Leading money winner on PGA Tour with $5,687,777.

Winner of the Masters Tournament to become the first golfer ever to hold all four professional major championships at the same time.

2002 Leading money winner on PGA Tour with $6,912,625. Winner of the Masters Tournament.

Selected as Player of the Year by PGA Tour, PGA of America, and Golf Writers Association of America.

Second player to be leading money winner on PGA Tour for four consecutive years.

Qualified for U.S. Team for Ryder Cup Matches.

Became the first ever to have won two or more titles each in the U.S. Open, U.S. Amateur, and U.S. Junior Amateur.

2003 Won $6,673,413 on PGA Tour.

Mark H. McCormack Award winner as the No. 1 player on the 2003 Official World Golf Ranking.

Qualified for United States Team for Presidents Cup.

First player to win at least five events on PGA Tour every year for five consecutive years.

Selected Player of the Year by PGA Tour, PGA of America, and Golf Writers Association of America.

2004   Career money leader on PGA Tour with $45,142,737.

Set record with 334 total weeks as No. 1 on the Official World Golf Ranking, through the list of August 29, 2004. (Previous record was 331 weeks by Greg Norman.)

Mark H. McCormack Award winner as the No. 1 player on the 2004 Official World Golf Ranking.

Qualified for U.S. Team for Ryder Cup Matches.

Married Elin Nordegren on October 5, 2004.

2005   Winner of the Buick Invitational.

Winner of the Doral Open.

Winner of the Masters Tournament.

Winner of the British Open Championship at St. Andrews.

2006   Winner of his third British Open with an 18-under-par score.

Earl Woods, 74, dies of cancer in early May.

Winner of the Buick Invitational at Torrey Pines.

Winner of the PGA Championship.

Winner of Dubai Classic.

Winner of Ford Championship.

Winner of Deutsche Bank Championship.

Misses the cut for the U.S. Open by three strokes, breaking streak in 39 consecutive Majors.

Winner of the Buick Open becoming the youngest player to win 50 PGA Tournaments.

Player of the Year as selected by PGA Tour (Jack Nicklaus Award), PGA of America, and Golf Writers Association of America.

Career money-leader on PGA Tour with $65,712,324.

Leading money-winner on PGA Tour (Arnold Palmer Award) with $9,941,563.

Qualified for U.S. team for Ryder Cup Matches.

2007   Winner of the British Open.

Winner of the PGA Championship.

Winner BMW Championship.

Winner of the Buick Invitational.

Winner of The Tour Championship.

Winner of the WGC-CA Championship.

Winner of the Wachovia Championship.

Winner of the WGC-Bridgestone Invitational.

Winner of the Target World Challenge.

Player of the Year as selected by PGA Tour (Jack Nicklaus Award), PGA of America, and Golf Writers Association of America.

Lowest adjusted scoring average (67–79), equaling record Woods set in 2000.

Award (PGA Tour) and Vardon Trophy (PGA of America).

2008   Becomes father in June 2008 with the birth of Sam Alexis.

Winner of the U.S. Open Championship.

Winner of the Buick Invitational.

Winner of the Dubai Desert Classic.

Winner of the WGC-Accenture Match Play Championship.

Winner of the Arnold Palmer Invitational.

Winner of four of six PGA Tour starts, including the U.S. Open before season-ending knee surgery in June.

Winner of the fourth consecutive Buick Invitational at Torrey Pines.

Tied Arnold Palmer (62 victories) with his first win of the year, and ended his season one ahead of Ben Hogan (65–64) for third place all-time.

June 16 Official World Golf Ranking marked his 500th week ranked Number 1.

2009   Winner of Buick Open.

Winner of the Arnold Palmer Invitational.

Winner of the Jack Nicklaus Memorial Tournament.

Winner of AT&T National.

Winner of the WGC-Bridgestone Invitational.

Winner of the BMW Championship.

Winner of four or more tournaments in 11 out of 14 years on Tour.

Winner of BMW Championship.

Winner of the FedEx Cup.

5-0-0 record in Presidents Cup Matches.

Injured in minor automobile accident outside his Windermere home on November 27.

February 19, 2010 From PGA headquarters in Ponte Vedra Beach, Florida, publicly apologized for infidelities and reported that he was participating in therapy. Fielded no questions from reporters.

March 21, 2010 Interviewed on ESPN and The Golf Channel. Announced that he would return to competition for the 2010 Masters.

Chapter 1

EARLY LIFE

Golf in America has not historically been a sport for the common man. In spite of the fact that golf, as we know it, was first played by Scottish shepherds and soldiers in the 13th century, by the time the game made its way to America at the end of the 18th century, only people of means played it. It was not until Francis Ouimet, a scrappy amateur and former caddy from the other side of the tracks in Brookline, Massachusetts, upset two of England's best professionals in a playoff for the 1913 U.S. Open that the game began to capture the fancy of the masses. However, golf has always been associated with wealth and privilege.

All the more ironic that, during the writing of this book, the number-one ranked golfer in the world is an American of color—in fact, of many colors. Eldrick "Tiger" Woods is an amalgam of five different races: African American, Native American, Caucasian, Thai, and Chinese. And it's hard to resist judging his accomplishments against the stereotypical characteristics of these races. In many ways he represents them admirably: determination, physical prowess, mental acuity, and spiritual calm. But just as no stereotype holds completely faithful, the same can be said of him. Ultimately, the story of Tiger Woods is not a simple analysis of his genetic makeup.

Tiger was born Eldrick Woods on December 30, 1975. His father, Earl Woods, nicknamed him "Tiger" in honor of a Vietnamese officer with whom he served in the Vietnam War. When Tiger was born his father was 44, recently retired from the military, divorced, and not particularly anxious to start another family. He already had three other children from a previous marriage and had purposely sought to locate somewhere close to these children in Northern California. Tiger's mother, Kultida Punswad, had met Earl while he was serving in Thailand during the Vietnam War in 1967 and had quickly adjusted to life in America. Thai culture does not recognize a marriage as fully consummated until there are children, and Kultida persisted in her desire to have a child and ultimately persevered.[1]

Even in the mid-1970s in one of the most ethnically diverse states in the Union, Earl and his new wife faced instances of discrimination in Southern California. After several incidents where house prices suddenly increased when Earl appeared in person, he was convinced that there was a reluctance to sell to African Americans. The Woods were able to rent his broker's condominium temporarily. There were instances of Kultida being shunned by other wives at the condominium pool. An ugly incident occurred when Earl's 18-year-old son from his first marriage, Earl Jr., who was living with Earl Sr. at the time, was harassed by the local police for trying to park his car in the Woods's garage. Eventually they were able to purchase a house in Cypress, California, where Tiger was raised.

INTRODUCTION TO GOLF

Earl Woods developed an interest in golf while stationed in Fort Hamilton in 1973. Given Earl's innate competitiveness, he wasn't satisfied playing the game simply for exercise and recreation. He approached the game with the same dogged determination that he had demonstrated throughout his life. Since he had retired from the Army and started working as a consultant for McDonnell Douglas, he had had limited time to actually play or practice golf, so when he did, he wanted to make the most of those opportunities. By the time Tiger was born, Earl had become a single-digit handicap golfer, which meant he was among approximately eight percent of excellent recreational players.[2] He set up a net in his garage and began regularly to go back there after work and pound golf balls to perfect his golf swing. In an effort to relieve his wife from the daylong rigors of watching the baby, he began taking Tiger out to the garage and putting him in a baby seat to watch Earl while he practiced. A fairly accomplished athlete in his own right, Earl possessed a decent swing. There were indications even before Tiger was born that this child would have a special affinity for the game. Earl tells of playing in a golf tournament in Lake Shastina in Northern California when his wife, who was pregnant with Tiger, walked along with him on the course. He claims that the "in vitro" Tiger was noticeably agitated in his mother's stomach every place on the golf course except when his mother approached a green. For some unexplained reason he seemed to stop moving when the players were putting.[3]

Earl has described the unusual fascination with the golf swing that his baby son exhibited.[4] He notes that the small child very rarely let his concentration waiver as he watched for hours while his father hit golf balls into a net. Earl was surprised when at the age of nine months, barely able to walk, Tiger picked up a club, swung, and hit his first golf ball. By the age of 18 months, Tiger was accompanying his father to the driving range and hitting golf balls.

As a veteran, Earl had playing privileges at the Navy course at Los Alamitos where he played regularly.[5] He brought Tiger with him to play on a regulation-length golf course at an early age. When eventually Tiger began to play without his father, the authorities at the clubs selectively enforced a rule that young players had to be at least 10 years old to play without adult supervision—despite the fact that Tiger and his father observed other kids regularly violating this rule. But access to a golf course at this early age undoubtedly precipitated his rapid improvement. By the age of four he managed to shoot 48 for nine holes.[6] He scored his first birdie on a regulation golf course before he was five years old.

There is no evidence that Earl Woods had a master plan for creating a golf superstar before Tiger was born. It was not until both of Tiger's parents began to observe his unusual interest in the game that they began to indulge his passion for the sport. In the early years of Tiger's development, Earl served exclusively as his coach. Earl was able to teach him the fundamentals of the game—grip, stance, and the basics of the swing—so that Tiger had a solid grounding from the beginning. But his more significant contribution to his son's evolution as a champion golfer was in the mental aspect of the game. Earl would play little games with young Tiger to test his ability to eliminate mental and physical distractions. For example, Earl would wait until his son was in the middle of his backswing and drop a golf ball, or rattle some change in his pocket, to try to disrupt his concentration. Sometimes Tiger would get annoyed, but, indicative of the unique relationship the two had forged, Earl would leave it up to Tiger to determine when he had gone too far. Tiger has talked about his father's early techniques: "It was pretty tough but, it was never in a bad-natured way. It was always in a way that he never degraded you as a person, just what you did and your actions. He would never get into your personality."[7]

Games like these were part of a program to prepare Tiger for not only the physical challenges of golf, but also the psychological obstacles to winning. Tiger was constantly and understandably trying to challenge his father, to test his skill against his teacher's. They would have driving contests during which Tiger would routinely out-drive his father by 20 yards. However, Earl would insist that the ball had to stop in the fairway to be counted, sometimes a matter of inches. Both Tiger's parents intentionally contributed to what Earl has referred to a "dark side, a coldness" in his son.[8] His mother reinforced that idea. While she would not tolerate him losing his temper on the golf course, she made it clear that the objective was to win. "I tell Tiger, 'When you are ahead, don't take it easy, kill them,'" she said. "'After the finish, then be a sportsman.'"[9]

By 1979, stories of Tiger's precociousness began to circulate, and eventually Tiger's mother called Jim Hill, a former football player and local Los Angeles sports television reporter, and asked him to come out to the Navy course to watch Tiger play. Hill brought along a camera crew and produced a news piece featuring the four-year-old Tiger. Subsequently Tiger appeared on *That's Incredible* with Minnesota Vikings quarterback Fran Tarkenton, *The Mike Douglas Show* with comedian Bob Hope, and *The Tonight Show with Johnny Carson*. When he was seven he played an exhibition match with Sam Snead. The first notable mention of him in a national magazine was a one-paragraph item in the November 1981 issue of *Golf Digest* entitled "5-Year-Old

Tiger: He's Incredible."[10] This kind of publicity and adulation for a five-year-old might have been a problem for many kids. However, the constant nurturing of Tiger's parents apparently kept him immune from developing a large ego. And he did not appear at all intimidated by the pressure of talking in front of large groups of people, let alone by the cameras broadcasting to a national audience. When Bob Hope asked the young golfing prodigy if he had any money, jokingly implying that they were going to bet on their competition, two-year-old Tiger cleverly moved his ball closer to the hole and tapped it into the cup.

Earl Woods tells the story of the four-year-old Tiger coming off the golf course with a pocket full of quarters. He had won them by putting for quarters with some older boys. His father reprimanded him and told him that he shouldn't be gambling for quarters anymore. Later his father saw him with a fistful of dollar bills and asked where they came from. Not wanting to disobey his father, the young golfer had been playing a skins game, for folding money—not putting for quarters. His father told him to cease playing for money in the future—unless he was his partner.[11]

While he was an accomplished amateur golfer, at a certain point Earl Woods felt that he was no longer able to provide the advanced training Tiger required. So he tried to find a professional who would work with Tiger, and who would not be too expensive. Kultida Woods, in search of a course where Tiger would be allowed to play without his father, found the Heartwell Golf Course in Long Beach, a par-three public course. When she approached Rudy Duran, an assistant professional there, and asked about someone who could teach her son, he asked to see the boy swing. Duran was amazed: "I felt he was like Mozart. He was a little shrunken touring pro. If I could have taken Jack Nicklaus and shrunk him down to that size, that's what you would have had. It was genius."[12] Duran agreed to work with Tiger and devised a special "par" for the short course that took into account the limited distance the four-year-old Tiger could hit the ball. Since Tiger was able to play below the adjusted par even at this young age, it significantly bolstered his confidence. Ironically, the apparent discrimination at the Navy course, which led Tiger to the par-three Heartwell course, did not hinder his development, but instead forced him to concentrate on his short game at a very early age. Eventually Duran used the young Woods to help him when he did teaching clinics. Tiger had an uncanny under-standing of the golf swing, and even at his age he was able to point out flaws in the swings of other golfers.

Subsequently Earl would expose Tiger to a series of professional teach-ers and advisors—later nicknamed "Team Tiger"—each supplying a vital element at the appropriate time in his development. John Anselmo had once been an aspiring tournament golf professional until he lost his peripheral vision after being struck by a golf ball. He turned to teach-ing golf and was working at the Meadowlark Golf Club in Huntington Beach, California, when Earl Woods sought him out to teach his son in 1986. "I saw so much rhythm and balance, even when he was ten. I was awed by it. I knew even at the time he was special. It's like destiny. I was so excited to have been a part of the Tiger team."[13] Anselmo would be actively involved in Tiger's instruction for about seven years.

When Tiger was 14, he met another golfer who contributed crucially to his training: Jay Brunza. Earl Woods had met and played with then-Commander Brunza, USN, at the Navy course in Cypress. Brunza, a sports psychologist who had worked with Naval Academy athletes to help them concentrate, and himself an avid golfer, would play an im-portant role in the developing Tiger's unprecedented power of concen-tration on the golf course. Through hypnosis and other mind tricks, Brunza was able to sharpen Woods's ability to focus on the task at hand even when faced with the most intense pressure. He also occasionally caddied for Woods through his junior career.[14]

Despite the fact that Tiger was considered special by so many people, his parents tried to instill in him a sense of proportion regarding his talents. On his first day of kindergarten in September of 1981, at a school with relatively few minority students, he experienced his first brush with overt racism. He was confronted by a group of mostly older white boys who tied him to a tree and taunted him with racial slurs. The incident was handled by the school authorities and the guilty par-ties were identified and punished. Despite this incident, and due in no small part to economics, his parents were committed to sending him to public schools, and overall his experience in school was positive. During kindergarten, his teacher recommended that he skip a grade because she thought he was clearly ahead of most of the class. After considering the prospects, his parents decided that they should leave it up to Tiger to decide. Because he was already competing mainly against older kids in golf, Tiger told them he wanted to stay with his own classmates in school.

No one has been able to provide an explanation of why, even before he was born, Tiger Woods exhibited an almost mystical passion for the game of golf. While even he cannot explain it, there are numerous examples of Tiger's obsession with the game. His mother tells how, when he was growing up, the ultimate punishment was to take away his golf clubs. If he had homework to do, he could not play golf until it was done. It is tempting to assume that his parents were either openly or subtly exerting pressure on him to practice. But various observers have concluded that they saw no evidence of such pressure. Jay Brunza commented, "Tiger was pursuing something from intrinsic passion for the game, and wasn't forced to live out somebody else's expectations. If he said, 'I'm tired of golf, I want to collect stamps,' his parents would say, 'Fine son,' and walk him down to the post office."[15] He participated in a variety of sports and exhibited exceptional skill in many of them, including baseball, basketball, and cross-country running. But inevitably he dropped any other activities because it was taking time away from practicing and playing golf.

By the time he turned 10 years old, at 4'9" and 81 pounds, he had already won two Junior World Championships (under 10 years old division). He continued to maintain an unprecedented competitive record as a child golfer. In addition to a host of local tournaments in and around his home, he won the Optimist International Junior Championship six times, from the ages of 8 through 13. At 13 he finished second in the Insurance Youth Golf Classic National Tournament. By the time he was 14 he had accumulated over 200 trophies.[16] He carefully constructed a chart with a list in the left-hand column of all the major championships (U.S. Open, British Open, Masters, and PGA Championship). In the right-hand column he pasted a cutout picture of Jack Nicklaus, and his age when he first won each of these tournaments. It was not only his goal to win all the major championships, but also to do it at an earlier age than his idol.

In interviews, Tiger has repeatedly emphasized his relatively normal teenage years. However, there are countless examples of how his adolescence deviated from the norm. He refused to participate in Little

League baseball because it would take too much time away from practicing and playing golf. During the summer between the seventh and eighth grades, one of his female classmates asked him out on a date; he declined for the same reason. The only consistently normal aspect of his teenage behavior was his diet. He exhibited a great interest in McDonald's, Taco Bell, and pizza. He also watched his share of television, favoring *The Simpsons* and professional wrestling.

TIGER IN SCHOOL

Tiger Woods attended Orangeview Junior High School in Cypress, and then Western High School in Anaheim, where Don Crosby was his coach. Crosby recalls the first time he saw Tiger practicing at the Navy course at Los Alimitos, where his high school golf team practiced. He was fascinated by this young, slight, junior high school boy hitting golf balls at the practice range by himself for hours. He tried to use the young Woods as an example to his team of the value of practice. Their response was that they preferred to practice while they played. He would see Woods on the practice tee when they teed off and he would still be there when they finished several hours later. He describes his feelings when he learned there might be a chance that Tiger Woods would enroll at Western High:

> One day in 1990, my number-one player casually said to me, "Coach, Tiger Woods lives in my neighborhood." I stopped cold. "Same housing tract as you?" I said, afraid to even think what I'm thinking. "Yeah," he said, "he lives right around the corner from me." "Same Tiger Woods as we saw at Los Alimitos, not some other kid coincidentally named Tiger Woods?" I asked, just to make sure this wasn't some cruel joke. "Yeah, coach, the Tiger Woods." Well, he might as well have told me Johnny Unitas, Mickey Mantle and Michael Jordan were going to play for Western High. This was a coach's dream.[17]

Barring a last-minute redistricting, owing to declining enrollment occurring during the late 1980s and early 1990s in the district, Crosby allowed himself the luxury of contemplating the impact of Tiger

Woods on his golf team's fortunes. The impact was instantaneous and unprecedented.

Tiger played varsity golf all four years at Western High, despite the fact that by his senior year he was being invited to and occasionally did play in PGA tournaments that precluded his participation in the high school matches. He won the Southern Section California Inter-scholastic Federation Championship four times, culminating with a 30 on the back nine of the final round in his senior year. High school golf matches are usually nine-hole medal (stroke) play competitions, with points awarded for each of the two-player matches. Over his four-year high school golf career, Tiger Woods managed to score an amazing 36 strokes under par for over 100 nine-hole matches.

During his sophomore year, Western High lost the conference team championship to Valencia High by one stroke, after Tiger, unaware of its importance, nonchalantly missed a two-foot putt. Coach Crosby reminded Woods's teammates that Tiger had not lost the title; it was a team loss. However, the experience was undoubtedly an important lesson about maintaining concentration for the young Woods.

The unprecedented attention this young golfer received throughout his life had hardly been missed by college golf coaches throughout the country. *Sports Illustrated* featured Tiger in its "In The Crowd" feature on September 24, 1990: "Tiger Woods, Cypress, Calif. Tiger, 14, shot a two under 286 for 72 holes to win a national junior golf tournament at Ridglea (sic) Country Club in Forth Worth. He has won five Junior World Titles, including the Optimist International in San Diego last July."[18]

Wally Goodwin, the coach of the Stanford University golf team, no-ticed the article and sent a letter indicating his interest in having Tiger consider attending Stanford. He was considerably impressed when he received a return letter from the 13-year-old seventh-grader himself, thanking him for his interest and telling him that his junior high school GPA was 3.86, and that he was starting an exercise program to help fill out his 5'9", 120-pound physique. Goodwin was somewhat taken aback at the composition of the letter and the quality of the prose that clearly seemed beyond the skills of most 13-year-olds. He told some of his players that this letter was from a minority kid in Los Angeles and they could learn something from his example.

Tiger was recruited by dozens of colleges and universities, but most intensely by Stanford, Arizona State, Virginia, Arizona, and Nevada–Las Vegas. Eventually he narrowed his college choices down to the University of Nevada–Las Vegas and Stanford. His high school coach, Don Crosby, described the first press conference ever held at Western High School to announce Tiger's collegiate intentions. There were two baseball caps on the table in front of Tiger, and finally he placed the UNLV hat under the table. There was a rule that students could only wear Western "Pioneer" hats in school to avoid potential conflict between gang affiliations. The photographers clamored for Tiger to put on the Stanford hat, and finally the principal made an exception to the rule for that one day.[19]

Tiger had the choice of virtually any college he wanted to attend, since, in addition to his golfing prowess, he had always been a good student. He owed this academic success mainly to the influence of his parents, particularly his mother. He was regularly on the honor roll and belonged to the National Honor Society. In his senior year he was named the 1993 Dial High School Athlete Scholar of the United States.

The unremarkable backgrounds of Tiger Woods's parents certainly did not foreshadow the creation of a prodigy. Both had endured considerable hardship in arriving at the point in their lives when their only son was born. And while there is clearly not any single influence that led to the phenomenon that is Tiger Woods, the special bond between Tiger and his parents early in his life cannot be minimized when trying to discover the reasons for his success.

NOTES

1. Earl Woods, *Playing Through* (New York: Harper Collins, 1998), 60.
2. National Golf Foundation, http://www.ngf.org/cgi/whofaqa.asp#5.
3. Ibid., 67.
4. Ibid., 70.
5. Tim Rosaforte, *Tiger Woods: The Making of A Champion* (New York: St. Martin's Press, 1997), 17.
6. John Strege, *A Biography of Tiger Woods* (New York: Broadway Books, 1998), 14.
7. "Golf Talk Live," The Golf Channel, December 18, 1996.

8. Quoted in Strege, 37.

9. Quoted in Rosaforte, 21.

10. *Golf Digest,* November, 1980, 15.

11. Strege, 15.

12. Quoted in Strege, 16.

13. Quoted in Strege, 34.

14. Rosaforte, 25.

15. Quoted in Bill Gutman, *Tiger Woods: A Biography* (New York: Pocket Books, 1997), 28.

16. Nicholas Edwards, *Tiger Woods: An American Master* (New York: Scholastic Inc., 1997), 18.

17. Don Crosby, *Tiger Woods Made Me Look Like a Genius* (Kansas City, MO: McMeel Publishing, 2000), 11.

18. *Sports Illustrated,* September 24, 1990, 10.

19. Crosby, 132–133.

Chapter 2

PARENTS

Tiger Woods has what is probably the most recognized nickname in the world of sports. His real name, though, is Eldrick Woods, and it is worth noting that his mother insisted on that name starting with the letter E for Earl, and ending with the letter K, for Kultida, so that "he would always know that he was surrounded by his parents."[1] In an age when most references to parents' involvement with their talented offspring are negative, Tiger Woods and his parents have certainly managed to convey a very positive example of how to nurture a sports prodigy. There is no evidence, however, that they started out with that objective.

EARL

While both parents were influential and contributed some element to the overall development of Tiger Woods, there is no doubt that Earl Woods provided the more visible presence both with Tiger and with the public through the media. It was because of Earl's interest in golf that Tiger was introduced to the sport, and he has by far been more accessible to the press than his wife. There seems little doubt that all of Earl's experiences before the birth of Tiger Woods had a significant impact on how he dealt with this potential superstar athlete.

Pinning down exact events and dates in the life of Earl Woods is not easy, considering this man was born and raised in the middle of America in the middle of the 20th century. He has demonstrated a colossal inability to remember specific dates and times of what most people would consider significant events in their lives. For example, when asked when he got married to his second wife, Earl couldn't remember the date.

Luckily, because of the overwhelming interest in his son, and the universally acknowledged impact Earl had on his son's development, many reporters have devoted countless hours tracking down confirmation of some of Earl's exploits. The influence of the army on Earl's life is undeniable, especially the two tours of duty that he served, but when *Golf Digest* reporter Tom Callahan asked when he served in Vietnam, Earl could not remember the dates. For any veteran, this seemed implausible, so Marine veteran Callahan embarked on a journey into Earl's military files, compliments of the Freedom of Information Act, and discovered that he had in fact served in Vietnam at two different times.[2] Because of this, although this book will contain ample references to Earl's autobiography, *Playing Through*, specific information about Earl's life has been confirmed or corroborated as much as possible.

Kansas Years

Earl Dennison Woods was born in Manhattan, Kansas, on March 5, 1932, into a family of six children. As the youngest child of Maude and Miles Woods, he grew up in what would today be called modest circumstances. While Earl does not recall being poor, he remembers the local Rotary Club delivering food baskets to his family on Thanksgiving days. He describes his childhood as being happy, despite having been aware that they did not have plenty. One enduring memory he has is of the best Christmas present he received, a 25 cent kite. Earl Woods grew up in Kansas at a time when blacks had not yet gained, even technically, the full rights of citizenship in America.

Earl's own father was a brick mason who once had aspirations to play professional baseball and taught Earl the value of hard manual labor.

In addition to his primary job, he worked part-time as a gardener and ran the scoreboard at a local baseball field on weekends. Earl occasionally accompanied his father to help him work the scoreboard. Not incidentally, the field was reserved for white teams only, namely teams from the Ban Johnson League, which tried for a time to challenge the American and National Leagues. From all descriptions of Earl's father, their relationship was more dependent on their love of baseball than on conversation and intellectualizing.

Maude Woods was a college graduate who spent her entire life doing domestic work, because there were few opportunities for educated black women in Depression-era Kansas, or anyplace else in America, for that matter. According to Earl's recollection, it was his mother who instilled in him most of the values that today are ascribed to his youngest son Tiger. Apparently Tiger's grandmother was a soft-spoken woman who nevertheless had strong opinions and stated them. There seems to be no question that her own education had a great effect on her children in their early life. She valued education and demanded that her children study and attain good grades. Earl talks about how he once had several bad conduct reports from school, and how his mother went in to see the teacher. Rather than challenging the teacher, she implored him to give Earl more work. Earl distinguishes between the phrases his mother used, such as "pride" and "being responsible for your own actions" and our contemporary emphasis on "positive self-image" and concern about children's "damaged egos." Undoubtedly her training in education provided both the will and ability to teach her children to speak and write properly, and she would not tolerate sloppy grammar. Earl tells a story of how, when he was a child, he and the black community looked up to heavy-weight boxing champion Joe Louis. Coincidentally, Joe Louis was a close friend of one of the Woods's neighbors, Mr. Fred Harrison. Louis was stationed at Fort Riley and would occasionally visit the neighborhood, and Earl got to meet him personally. He recalls his mother's comments after that meeting, "Don't you dare talk the way Joe Louis talks when you grow up! I want you to get an education, and I want you to speak properly."[3]

Interestingly, Earl's father was a Baptist and his mother was a Methodist, and while he participated actively in religious events throughout his early childhood, there was apparently never any pressure to commit to one or the other sect. So while there is no question that religion played a role in his upbringing, there was not any hard emphasis on which religion was "right."

The considerable influence exerted on Earl by his parents is very apparent in light of the fact that they died when he was relatively young and he was, for the most part, raised by his oldest sister, Hattie. When Earl was 11, his father died of a stroke. At around the same time, Earl's older brother Miles enlisted in the air force, leaving Earl as the oldest male in the house. Earl refers to this moment as a significant turning point in his life, from childhood to manhood. He was forced to watch his mother grieve over the loss of his father, and die herself of a stroke two years later. He describes his mother's funeral, when distant relatives gathered and spoke in hushed tones in corners of the funeral home, trying to determine what would become of Earl and his sisters and brothers. He notes with obvious pride when his 29-year-old sister Hattie stated to the relatives, "We are not going to be separated. We will stay in this house. I will raise everybody."[4]

Despite the nontraditional arrangement in Earl's family, he had a fairly normal upbringing through high school. He notes in his book that the responsibilities in the house were delegated pretty much along gender lines, which led to his lifelong ideas about male/female roles, asserting that "...today I could have 10 vacuum cleaners and I still wouldn't touch them."[5] As a teenager he played American Legion baseball on a white team, and his family traveled all over the state to watch him play. Earl was a catcher and was close to the stands, where bigots would shout insults, frequently racial epithets. His family had to endure these indignities and remain composed.

One incident in high school exemplifies the general racist environment of postwar Kansas: Earl was a finalist for the prom king contest, and school administrators were anticipating the prospect of a black king having to kiss a white queen. According to Earl, the results were rigged against him and the so-called problem was averted.

Graduating high school in 1949 presented the young Earl Woods with a dilemma about what direction he would go in his life. Earl was offered a scholarship to play baseball at the nearby Kansas State

University. His mother had always hoped throughout her brief life that he would graduate from college. So Earl enrolled and rode his bicycle the four miles to the university every day. He diligently tried to maintain his studies while he devoted most of his time to his real love—playing baseball. Miles Woods had aspirations of Earl playing baseball in the Negro Leagues, specifically for the local Kansas City Monarchs. Despite the fact that the Negro Leagues would soon be on the wane (Jackie Robinson broke the color line in major-league baseball in 1947), Earl was offered a contract with the team during his first year in college, which would have been the fulfillment of his father's dream. It was becoming increasingly more difficult for Earl to study and play baseball, and accepting the contract with the Monarchs would have eliminated any possibility of his finishing college. A decision had to be made. Apparently, Maude's voice from the grave was the stronger, as Earl decided to bypass the baseball contract and dedicate himself to finishing college.

While continuing to play baseball for Kansas State, he majored in psychology. Earl was a better-than-average baseball player, and while at Kansas State he established some racial firsts of his own. He was not only the first African American baseball player at Kansas State, but also in what was then the Big 7 Conference.[6] Playing baseball and going to college were important choices; however, another decision he made would eventually have an even greater impact on the rest of his life.

Earl's sister Hattie married a World War II veteran, Jesse Spearman, who was a premed student at Kansas State. As an officer, he sent all his pay home to be put away to help finance his medical education. When he returned from the war, he found out that his brother had spent all the money. In what must have been an extraordinary demonstration of discipline and dedication, considering the prevalent racial discrimination of the times, Jesse somehow managed to work his way through college and medical school, eventually becoming a gynecologist. Jesse served as the major male figure in Earl's life when he was in college. It was Jesse who convinced Earl to consider signing up for advanced ROTC at Kansas State, and even though he had missed the deadline, the officer in charge, recognizing Earl as the only black player on the baseball team, made an exception and accepted him.

Army Years

After graduating from Kansas State in 1953 and accepting a commission in the U.S. Army, Earl played semiprofessional baseball while waiting to be called to active duty. His first assignment took him to Germany, where he encountered his first personality conflict with a superior officer that had clear racial overtones. After answering a question in what the officer obviously considered a flippant manner, Earl was confronted by the following outburst: "You're one of those smart niggers. We don't have any place for people like you in the army. I'm going to make damn sure that you don't stay."[7]

In the military there is a distinct delineation between Regular Army Military Academy graduate officers and reserve officers commissioned by other means (ROTC, Officer Candidate School, direct commissions). Non-academy officers tend to be looked down upon by the West Pointers, and even though President Harry Truman had officially outlawed discrimination in the military in 1948, the reality of the newly integrated units was not fully accepted by every officer. Early in his career, Earl mainly served in administrative positions, and, at least partially because of the racial situation, he was not put in positions that would enhance his opportunities for promotion. In order to facilitate promotions, particularly in the infantry branch, an officer must serve time as a unit commander. A lieutenant is usually designated a platoon leader, a captain serves as company commander, and so on up the line.

The Vietnam War represents a significant period in the life of Earl Woods. It was during this war that he met two people who would influence him greatly and would come to contribute immeasurably to the evolution of Tiger Woods. While Earl himself could not exactly pinpoint when he served in Vietnam, the records indicate that he served two tours of duty there, first from February 12, 1962, to February 24, 1963, and then again from August 15, 1970, to August 13, 1971. His first duty in Vietnam was as a regular infantry officer, and from what information is available, he served in administrative positions. He subsequently returned to the United States, and, after an assignment to Thailand, he made the unorthodox decision to volunteer for Special Forces training at the age of 35.

Beginning in 1961, when President John Kennedy authorized the adoption of the green beret as the official headgear of all Special Forces, this elite unit of the army became associated with the highest levels of courage and achievement in the U.S. military.[8] The qualifications for Special Forces training were very strict, and the prospects of a 35-year-old officer meeting those standards were slim. However, Earl Woods had determined that Special Forces units were the one place in the army he felt he would be judged completely on his ability to complete his mission. As a former athlete, Earl had little trouble with the physical aspects of training. He first completed airborne jump training at Fort Benning, Georgia. As the ranking officer in the jump school class, he was called upon to serve as an example to the other soldiers. Earl tells of an incident when he led his class in a pull-up exercise in sub-freezing cold, being the first to jump up and take the ice-covered metal bar.[9] After jump school Earl was briefly assigned as the briefing officer at the Vietnam Village at Fort Bragg, while the John Wayne movie *Green Berets* was being filmed. Indicative of the intensity of the training, Earl recounts an exercise at survival school in Alaska when the candidates were required to make a forced march across 20 miles of frozen tundra. One of the soldiers couldn't make it and told Captain Woods that he needed help. Earl told the soldier that he had two choices: keep up with the rest of the party, or be found frozen in the snow—because there was no way that a truck was going to come out to get him. The soldier caught up.[10]

Tiger "One"

After completing Special Forces training, Earl served a second tour in Vietnam in 1970. This time he would not be behind a desk in Saigon. As a Special Forces commander, he would be in charge of a Special Forces team made up of 12 soldiers. Earl had a number of brushes with death and was awarded the Vietnamese Silver Star for unspecified acts of bravery.[11]

More importantly, Earl met and befriended Lieutenant Colonel Vuong Dang Phong, Deputy Chief of Binh Thuan Province, to whom Earl was assigned as an advisor. Their assignment was to visit relocation villages in which the United States was intent upon convincing the "hearts and minds" of the Vietnamese people to reject the communist ideology in favor of democracy. Earl experienced the same fears as the rest of the American soldiers assigned to Vietnam: it was impossible to determine who the enemy was. In these villages it was impossible to know which Vietnamese had malicious intent toward the Americans and which collaborated with them. Children as young as eight or nine were trained to plant munitions, and it was not uncommon to find young boys selling pure, powerful heroin for 50 cents to GIs with the goal of getting them hooked on the drug.[12] It was a new kind of war, and the North Vietnamese army and the insurgent Vietcong represented an entirely new kind of warfare.

Under the extreme pressure of the situation, Earl Woods developed a strong bond with this slight (5'5" tall) South Vietnamese officer. Beyond his deep respect for Col. Phong's innate intelligence and thoroughly professional competence as a military officer, Earl credits Phong with several instances when he literally saved his life. While Earl has occasionally justified these brushes with death as some kind of cosmic plan preparing him for his eventual role as the father of Tiger Woods, there seems to be no question that these incidents helped strengthen the relationship between these two men, and, for the purposes of tracing the impact they would have on his son, they are worth recounting.

Earl recounts an incident on a mission when he asked Col. Phong to call in helicopter fire support for his South Vietnamese troops. The mission was beyond the capabilities of the South Vietnamese units, so only Earl could request the support. The ground was dusty, and while completely engaged in coordinating the gunfire from the helicopters, he noticed Col. Phong hollering at him from a ditch beside the dike of a rice paddy. Oblivious to anything but his mission, he noticed a pile of dirt to his right as it was blown away by a shell. There was also a pile of dirt to his left and suddenly it was gone, too. Phong continued to holler, but Earl, unable to understand what Phong wanted, continued to direct the gun ships. The helicopters finished their mission, and Earl finally joined Phong in the ditch and asked what he wanted. Phong replied, "You are the coolest adviser I have ever had in my life. A sniper bracketed you. The first shot went to your right. The second shot went to your left. And I expected the third shot to go right through your chest. That's what I was trying to tell you."[13]

A little while later Earl found a quiet bamboo thicket to get some much-needed rest. He was awakened by Phong, who told him to stay perfectly still. The bamboo viper is apparently one of the most poisonous snakes in the world, and one had made his way down the bamboo to hang inches from Earl's face. In what Earl later described as another unexplained reason for his life being spared, the viper retreated back into the bamboo thicket.

Because of his tenacious reputation on the battlefield and his unrestrained commitment to the mission and his troops, Earl nicknamed Col. Phong "Tiger," the most feared and courageous animal in the jungles of Vietnam. These two men from widely different cultures were able to forge a relationship that went beyond professional respect. In their off hours, Earl introduced Phong to the world of jazz music, chili, and tennis, and Phong taught Earl the rudiments of Eastern philosophy and religion. The two men spent many hours drinking in Earl's quarters, nicknamed the "Blue Room," painted infantry blue, the color of Earl's service branch. When Saigon fell in 1975, Earl vowed that if he ever had another son (by this time he was remarried), he would name him "Tiger" in honor of his comrade in arms.

Except for the fact that Earl would father the most heralded professional golfer in the world, the relationship between these two men would probably have been forgotten as one of the many cross-cultural friendships precipitated by war. Earl lost all contact with Phong when he left Vietnam in 1971. In subsequent years he made attempts through missing-person services in New York City to find out what happened to his friend after the fall of Saigon in 1975. But it was not until Tiger became an international celebrity that he was able to make any serious progress toward determining Phong's fate. Earl enlisted the services of several detective agencies to try to find out what happened to Phong after they lost touch. Ultimately, it was not until Tom Callahan, a reporter for *Golf Digest* magazine, went on a journalistic adventure to find out what happened to Tiger One, that the true story emerged.

Callahan, skeptical about Earl's fuzzy memory with regard to his military career, in particular his service in Vietnam, began research on an article for his magazine in 1996. Under the guise of doing an article on a new golf course in Vietnam, designed by prominent international golfer Nick Faldo, Callahan managed to acquire a visa to visit Ho Chi

Minh City, formerly Saigon. He had been warned to bypass the Ministry of Foreign Affairs if he didn't want to be "handled" by the local bureaucrats, so he hired a driver, Thanh, and his sister Thuy, who suggested that they start the search at the Pagoda of Vinh-Nghiem. Callahan was unable to acquire any concrete evidence about the fate of Phong, but he did gather information that eventually led to the answer. It turned out that the ostensible reason for the trip, an article about the new golf course, reaped the most fruitful benefit of the trip to Vietnam. While he was playing the course, one of his playing companions, a North Vietnamese businesswoman named Flower, suggested that Callahan place an ad in a Vietnamese-American newspaper asking for information about Earl's friend. It was apparent that the government was not going to help him; he was reprimanded during a call from the ministry in Hanoi for not reporting to the ministry in Ho Chi Minh City.

After returning to America and placing some ads in the local Vietnamese-American press, Callahan received a phone call from a man who connected Col. Phong's name with those of Earl Woods and the Blue Room. Despite the language barriers, several calls to Vietnam revealed that Earl had been mistaken about Phong's first name—it was "Vuong," not "Nguyen." This was understandable, since "Nguyen" is comparable in frequency to the name "Bob" in America. Through Callahan's golf mate Flower, the journalist made contact with the family of Vuong Dang Phong, also known as Tiger One.

The story that emerged confirmed the legacy of Tiger One. He surrendered to the Communists on June 15, 1975, and was sent to a re-education camp in Vinh Phu. During the first year, he managed to send a letter to his family of nine children. For the next 10 years, his family received no word from Phong, until the government finally informed them that he had died in the camp on September 9, 1976.[14]

Ironically, Earl was subsequently to learn that Phong's widow, Lythi Bich Van, had been living in the United States in Tacoma, Washington, since 1994, and had no idea who Tiger Woods was. Tom Callahan, through the courtesy of *Golf Digest* magazine, arranged for the two families to meet at Earl's home in Cypress, California. Phong's wife and two of her children met Earl, his wife Kultida, and Tiger, who flew in from Florida to join them. It was an emotional and tearful occasion, as Earl and Phong's family recalled the life of Col. Phong. The friendship

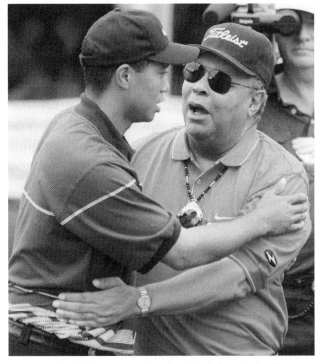

Tiger Woods, left, receives a hug from his father, Earl, after win-
ning the Tour Championship on October 31, 1999, in Hous-
ton. Earl Woods—who was more determined to raise a good
son than a great golfer and became the role model, architect,
and driving force behind Tiger Woods's phenomenal career—
died on May 3, 2006, at his home in Cypress, California. He
was 74. AP Photo/David J. Phillip.

between these two military officers had made an indelible impact on
both of them. Colonel Vuong Dang Phong's story brought some much-
needed attention to the fate of thousands of other South Vietnamese
citizens who vanished when America withdrew from Vietnam, and it
inspired one of the greatest nicknames in all of sports.

Earl's First Family

Divorce in 20th-century America was not an unusual phenomenon, so
it is not especially significant that Earl Woods was married twice.

However, in order to thoroughly examine the forces that shaped
Tiger Woods, it is important to explore the factors that led Earl to

marry right out of college and father three children, then divorce and remarry a woman of a completely different cultural background, and, most importantly, father a son at the age of 43.

As with other aspects of Earl's life, it is difficult to pin down exact dates and sequences for various events. This is also the case regarding his marital history. Earl admits in his autobiography that he made a number of mistakes regarding the choice of his first wife, Barbara Hart, whom he married in 1954.[15] Eventually they had three children, two boys (Earl and Kevin) and a girl (Royce). Several different sources give evidence of different dates for their divorce, but it appears that the date was in 1966. Earl openly admits that many of the factors that led to his divorce were his own fault. He notes that the pressures of being a new officer at a new post in Germany were only exacerbated when he decided to bring his new wife along. The army made no accommodations for housing junior officers' families, and consequently they had to pay rent from his modest lieutenant's salary. Undoubtedly adding to the stress was the racial situation in Germany at the time. The Germans were not used to seeing black men, and certainly not black women, and some white GIs had told outrageous stories about black people, thereby causing the locals to look with curiosity at this young black couple.

After they returned to the United States, things did not get any better. Earl was constantly away from his family, and he admits that he didn't pay enough attention to the children from his first marriage, and that he considered it a second chance to be able to make up for his past mistakes with his new son. Through the years, Earl has managed to maintain contact with his first family, and from time to time the children have all lived with him. He notes an incident involving his son Kevin, a natural left-handed batter. Earl returned from an assignment overseas to find Kevin batting right-handed. He told his father that since everybody else seemed to be batting right-handed, he decided to switch.[16] Earl felt that it would not have happened if he had been around to play a more significant role in the children's upbringing.

He refers to the final chapter of his first marriage when he was served with papers filed by his wife in 1996 suing for half of his military retirement pay, retroactively and in the future. In light of the fact that she had remarried, the case was thrown out of court.[17]

KULTIDA

Just as difficult to pin down as the date of Earl's divorce is the date that he met Tiger's mother Kultida. At some point between his first and second tours in Vietnam—between 1963 and 1970—he was assigned to Bangkok, Thailand. It was there, as a special services officer, that he was working at a civilian personnel office attempting to hire four thousand civilian workers. Earl was accompanied by a white junior officer. The attractive, petite Thai receptionist asked the white officer, "Can I help you?" But it was Earl who answered "Colonel Woods." When Earl returned to talk to the young woman, Kultida Punsawad, she was immediately embarrassed to have wrongly assumed that the white officer was Colonel Woods.[18] So their first encounter foreshadowed some of the racial assumptions that would someday mark their son. They made arrangements for a date at nine o'clock. Earl waited at the agreed-upon location, since it would have been impolite for him to go to her house. Kultida never showed up. The next morning Earl was roused out of bed at nine o'clock by Kultida and her chaperone. She had assumed he was talking about morning, since it would not have been appropriate for her to go out that late at night. They eventually did go out to visit a Thai church.

Kultida Punsawad came from a family with considerable commercial standing. Her father owned a tin mine, and the family owned a fleet of buses in Bangkok. Tida (as she is known) was brought up in a boarding school because her parents had separated when she was five.[19] Like her husband-to-be, she was the product of a several races and cultures: she was a mixture of Thai, Chinese, and Caucasian, and was a practicing Buddhist.[20] Young women of her social class were not encouraged by their families to fraternize with American soldiers, much less black soldiers, so Earl and Kultida's relationship faced cultural obstacles in her native country, even before those they would face in the United States. There is no question that this was an unusually self-directed young woman who had her own modern ideas about relationships, despite the fact that many in her family ostracized her. Some of these same qualities become apparent in her role as Tiger's mother, and she must have experienced some form of revenge when she returned to Thailand in 1997

Golf sensation Tiger Woods shows his gold Buddha image to reporters at a press conference during the Asian Honda Classic in Bangkok on February 6, 1997. Woods, who wears the image at all times, was raised as a Buddhist by his Thai mother. AP Photo/Charles Dharapak.

to watch Tiger win the Asian Honda Classic Tournament at the Thai Country Club by 10 strokes. Kultida and her son were hailed as royalty.

Kultida Woods is certainly the least publicized member of what has become known as Team Tiger, the people who now cater to the golfer's needs in all aspects of his life. This quiet woman combines a stern single-mindedness with a spiritual calm that has undoubtedly been a significant influence on her son. Buddhism is the state religion in Thailand, even though there is religious freedom in the country. The philosophy of Buddhism stresses three principal aspects of existence—suffering, impermanence, and nonsubstantiality. Without reading too much into the impact of Buddhist philosophy on the eventual ability of Tiger Woods to hit a golf ball, his mother's religious history has certainly had an effect on his personality. So it is probably not too much to assume that since the objective of Buddhist philosophy is to overcome all desire and thereby reach a state of inaction that assures the end of a cycle of rebirth or reincarnation,[21] this emphasis on self-discipline, unfettered determination, and calm has seeped into the psyche of Tiger Woods. When Tiger was nine, Kultida took him to Thailand to introduce him to her native country, and to a part of his culture. She brought him to a Buddhist monk to analyze a chart she had kept on Tiger's life. Unaware as the monk was of the game of golf, or the accomplishments of Tiger, he told Kultida that Tiger was special child who was destined for leadership. If he went into the military, she was told, he would become a four-star general.[22]

According to one source, Earl and Kultida married sometime in 1969.[23] There is some question as to that exact date, but by 1973 they were living in New York City, where Earl was assigned to Fort Hamilton as a public relations officer. It was around this time that he seriously took up the game of golf.

Earl had been challenged by a fellow officer, and considering himself a pretty decent athlete, he took up the challenge of a golf match. He was soundly defeated, but rather than shun the game, he embraced it. He dedicated himself to perfecting his golf swing and devoted most of his leisure time to practicing golf. He made a commitment to a rematch with this officer before he left the service less than a year later. Earl requested a rematch and shot a career best round of 84 to win the match.[24] More than any natural physical ability, it was this indomitable will to win that was the most lasting legacy Earl Woods imparted to his son Tiger.

Following Earl's retirement from the Army in 1974, Earl and Kultida moved to California, ostensibly to be closer to his three children. With the birth of Tiger, both parents devoted all their energies to their new son, and Earl admits that this unbridled dedication to the well-being of Tiger had its effects on the marriage. They lived in separate residences and lived separate lives, except for Tiger. Kultida has not spoken publicly about their relationship, but Earl summarized the state of their marriage in his autobiography: "Today, we are the best of friends, have a beautiful amicable relationship and ardently follow Tiger's development and progress every step of the way, still fully supportive. She has her home, I have mine."[25]

Each parent played different roles in the raising of Tiger Woods: Earl provided the early introduction to both the physical and psychological rudiments of the game of golf, while Kultida provided the environment of discipline and strong work ethic and made significant sacrifices to make sure Tiger was able to display his prodigious gifts on the golf course.

EARL'S DEATH

Tiger Woods lost his best friend and role model when his father, Earl Woods, died at his home in Cypress, California, of cancer on May 5, 2006. He said:

> My dad was my best friend and greatest role model, and I will miss him deeply. I'm overwhelmed when I think of all of the great things he accomplished in his life. He was an amazing dad, coach, mentor, soldier, husband and friend. I wouldn't be where I am today without him, and I'm honored to continue his legacy of sharing and caring.[26]

Probably more than any other athlete, the relationship between Tiger and Earl Woods has been written about and speculated over. Therefore when Earl died there was concentrated focus on how Tiger would react, both personally and in his golf game. Earl had been ill for several years, so when he finally died Tiger certainly was anticipating the death. His death motivated many journalists to go back and review the relationship, while trying to weigh the effect it would have on Tiger Woods. Adding to the frustration of these journalists was the relatively vague nature of Tiger's interaction with the press. This wariness was grown out of some initial missteps he took early on in his career (referred to later in this book). Consequently Tiger began to cover up his real feelings with the standard cliché responses to virtually any question. This style applied to questions about his golf game—and about his personal feelings. So the chances of a reporter getting any substantive response to personal questions are bleak. Instead Tiger issued standard press release quotes about how much his father meant to him and how much he would miss him in the days ahead. Jack Nicklaus has said that one of the most difficult periods of his life was when his father died in

1970, ironically when Nicklaus was 30, the same age as Woods. And there is no evidence that the death of a parent in any way affected Jack's performance on the golf course over any period of time.

It is interesting that there has been virtually nothing written about the at best unusual relationship between Earl and Kultida Woods. One cannot help feeling that journalists have been reluctant to go there, for fear of angering either Earl or Tiger, and thus cutting off access to Team Tiger, and clearly the great golf story that Tiger represents. In fact, getting any information about Kultida is an impossible job. To my knowledge she has not been interviewed in any depth about herself. Most quotes from her are comments on Tiger's performance or how he was raised. Consequently it is difficult to get a read on what Tiger's relationship was to her husband, particularly in the last years of the marriage, to shed some light on the impact of Earl's death on Tiger.

Given the dearth of personal reflections from Tiger about what his father meant to him, we only have his record in golf to glean whether or how it affected him. The year before Earl's death, during the presentation of his fourth green jacket for winning the Masters, Tiger broke down when he said that he was dedicating the victory to his father, who was deathly ill and unable to be there. However, overall, Tiger's record did not suffer during what must have been Earl's worst days before he died. At the 2006 Masters, Tiger lamented the fact that he didn't win, because he knew that this would probably be the last major championship Earl would experience.

In 2005 he won two majors in addition to six other tournaments. However, during that season he did finally end his streak of not missing the cut for the first time in seven years and 142 tournaments. Starting in 1999, until the 2005 Byron Nelson Championship, he did not get eliminated for weekend play. Whether or not this happened because of him worrying about his father cannot be determined. Tiger said, "I just had a tough day. Things I don't normally do, I did today." He made no reference to his father.[27]

However, in the first tournament he competed in after his father's death, Tiger failed to make the cut in the 2006 U.S. Open at Winged Foot Golf Club in New York. Woods had not missed a cut in a major since the 1996 Masters, as an amateur, and his stretch of 39 tournaments over the ensuing nine years tied him with Jack Nicklaus for the record of most consecutive cuts in major championships. Woods finished three strokes over the cut line. Once again he didn't offer up the excuse that his poor play was as a result of the loss of his father. "When you don't execute, you're not going to be happy either way," Woods said. "I don't care if you had what transpired in my life of recent or not. Poor execution is never going to feel very good."[28]

NOTES

1. Quoted in Earl Woods, *Playing Through* (New York: HarperCollins, 1998), xi.

2. David Owen, *The Chosen One* (New York: Simon & Schuster, 2001), 57.

3. Quoted in ibid., 57.

4. Quoted in Woods, 4.

5. Quoted in ibid., 13.

6. This conference became the Big 8 in 1959 and the Big 12 in 1996.

7. Quoted in Woods, 26.

8. "History of Special Forces, 1961–1971," Department of Army Publication, 1989, http://www.specialoperations.com/Army/Specialjorces/default.html.

9. Woods, 30.

10. Ibid., 31.

11. Tom Callahan, *In Search of Tiger* (New York: Crown Publishing, 2003), 2.

12. Woods, 33.

13. Quoted in ibid., 36.

14. Callahan, 2.

15. Woods, 44.

16. Ibid., 47.

17. Ibid., 50.

18. Ibid., 54.

19. Gary Smith, "The Chosen One," in *Chasing Tiger,* ed. Glenn Stout (Cambridge, MA: Da Capo, 2002), 59.

20. Curt Sampson, *Chasing Tiger* (New York: Atria, 2002), 6.

21. Thanapol Chadchaidee, *Buddhism in Thailand*, December 28, 2004, http://sunsite.au.ac.th/thailand/buddhism/.

22. John Strege, *A Biography of Tiger Woods* (New York: Broadway Books, 1998), 25–26.

23. Ibid., 9.

24. Ibid., 11.

25. Woods, 63.

26. Tiger Woods Web site, May 6, 2006, http://web.tigerwoods.com/index.

27. "Tiger Misses Cut for First Time in Seven Years," May 16, 2005, ESPN Golf Web site, http://sports.espn.go.com/golf/news/story?id=2059700.

28. Larry Fine, "Tiger Woods Misses the Cut at U.S. Open," Friday, June 16, 2006, Red Orbit Web site, http://www.redorbit.com/news/sports/540859/tiger_set_to_miss_cut_at_us_open/index.html.

Chapter 3

EARLY COMPETITION

JUNIOR CAREER

Tiger Woods was not the first sports child prodigy to capture the imagination of the American public. What made him unique was the fact that he was a child of color, competing in a sport that was generally reserved for white children who had the advantage of early access to facilities and coaching, usually in connection with a private club or public courses in exclusive neighborhoods. Golf is the last American sport to actively seek and embrace minority players. Tennis, another sport born of privilege, had already had several black stars by the 1960s, due mostly to the relative accessibility of public courts, the international appeal, and the somewhat blurred line between the amateur and professional versions of the sport until 1968. As will be examined in detail in chapter 4, it was not until 1961 that black golfers were allowed to play regularly on the PGA Tour. Consequently, the motivation for minorities to pursue a professional career in golf before then was limited.

Baseball, basketball, and football had a head start in organizing youth sports because of the great number of young people playing those sports. What amounted to a minor league system developed, which would start children as young as seven not only learning the rudimentary skills of these sports, but also giving them the opportunity to compete locally, regionally, and eventually on a national scale. The high visibility of professional leagues in these sports, showcasing an increasing number of minorities, motivated young minority athletes and their parents to gravitate toward these sports.

When Tiger Woods began at age seven to participate in the junior golf program in Southern California, there were already enough highly organized tournaments to constitute what could only be called a "tour." This tour consisted of 30 tournaments, with upwards of 100 youths playing in each.[1] By the mid-1980s junior golf had expanded to provide a circuit of highly organized tournaments that attracted talented young golfers from all over the world. The American Junior Golf Association (AJGA) is the organization that controls most of those tournaments.

While there were many national junior tournaments of varying degrees of importance, each summer Tiger geared up for the U.S. Junior Championship, staged by the U.S. Golf Association. The USGA is the preeminent golf organization in America. In addition to writing the Rules of Golf in collaboration with the British Royal and Ancient Golf Club, the USGA conducts national championships at all levels. Because of the long history and tradition of the organization—it was formed in 1894—and the normally high-quality field of players their tournaments attract, the USGA events are considered to be the most prestigious in golf. The U.S. Amateur Championship and the U.S. Open were first conducted in 1895, and players from all over the world attempt to qualify for this tournament. Before he graduated from junior golf, Tiger would become the only male ever to win three U.S. Junior Championships, and each time in dramatic fashion on the 18th or 19th holes.[2] However, being a major success on the junior golf circuit is not an automatic indicator of future success in professional golf. For example, of the six players who won the U.S. Junior Championship before Tiger, only three—Gary Koch, Jack Renner, and Willie Wood—ever went on to win a PGA tournament.[3]

The evolution of what could now be called a youth sports culture paralleled a significant change in parenting. Where once young people were left to their own devices to entertain themselves, many parents now feel it is necessary to provide a never-ending series of options to occupy their children. Whereas young people used to climb trees, run, and make up their own games, they are more and more reliant on technology for entertainment. The physical activities they do participate in tend to be more specialized, so that rather than seeing good athletes, we are getting good baseball players or good gymnasts or good swimmers.[4] But beyond the physical consequences of this new trend, it is still to be determined how such changes will affect the emotional development of this generation of athletes.

It is interesting that one of the most significant and arguably most insidious examples of this new emphasis on early development of athletic talent was prompted by a company that would play a significant role in Tiger Woods's adult career. International Management Group (IMG) was the brainchild of the late Mark McCormick. In the early 1960s, McCormick, an attorney, was doing some legal work for Arnold Palmer. Up to this time, athletes had business managers, not agents. McCormick, convinced of Palmer's earning potential, became his agent and made him a multimillionaire, above and beyond whatever he earned playing golf. McCormick is generally considered to be the first true sports agent. In short order he enlisted Jack Nicklaus and Gary Player as clients and eventually developed IMG into an international business that not only represented athletes but also created and ran major sports events. Beyond that, IMG formed IMG Academies in Bradenton, Florida. Originally dedicated exclusively to tennis, under the watchful eye of Nick Bollettieri (who coached Andre Aggasi and Maria Sharapova, among others), the Academy now provides training for young athletes in other sports such as golf, baseball, basketball, and soccer. Parents of these promising athletes move to the Bradenton area, where the Academy sells condominiums on the grounds for $310,000, and combines athletic training with an academic program for middle and high school students. The cost is $30,000 for students who board on campus.[5]

These parents are attracted by the possibility of college scholarships, and the lure of a professional career. Today there is considerable money to be made in every sport beyond the multimillion-dollar salaries, in the form of product endorsement. But it was golf that paved the way for the other sports because of IMG. The reason is that while the audience for golf is relatively small in comparison to those of other major sports, it is also relatively educated and wealthy, and it has corporate connections. Also, except for tennis, there is little opportunity to sell equipment to a fan of baseball or football, whereas golf has a gigantic market.

Parents of children with the desire and physical abilities to compete in sports must always face the question of whether they are encouraging participation for their child's sake or for their own. In the case of Tiger Woods, there seems little doubt that he wanted to play golf.

Much has been written and speculated about the extent to which Tiger Woods's parents imposed their will on his to produce such a prodigy. The situation has been somewhat clouded by the fact that most of the journalists and writers who have stated opinions on the subject are only witness to the creation of the Tiger Woods phenomenon, while those people who actually participated in his development, it can be argued, have a vested interest in presenting and perpetuating a positive image of that history. In reviewing the material that has been written about the upbringing of Tiger Woods, there is a general consensus that he was a model junior athlete. Trying to ascertain what made him that way is another question. From his earliest years he not only demonstrated unusual skill at playing golf; he developed a competitive desire that cannot be ascribed to any one source.

EARLY TRAINING

From the start, it must be stated that Tiger was not an ordinary child when it came to golf. As was noted in chapter 1, even the baby Tiger had an unprecedented attraction to the sport, and, unlike most youths, eschewed what would be considered normal diversions. Comparisons have been made to other child prodigies such as Wolfgang Amadeus Mozart, and it is hard to resist the temptation to ascribe supernatural characteristics to this young child. Both had strong father figures who had to strain to support the creative activities of their sons.[6] Admittedly, we are talking about golf, not the symphonic music that has remained in the public consciousness for over two hundred years, but the characteristics are similar, and given the amazing accomplishments of the young Tiger Woods, there is no question that he possessed motivation that was well beyond what his or any other parents could create.

His precociousness on the golf course was surpassed only by the maturity he demonstrated even as a junior golfer.

From all information that the author has been able to review concerning the junior golf career of Tiger Woods, there seems to be no indication that his parents put any undue pressure on him to excel in golf. While at times it is difficult to separate what are the wishes of the son and the wishes of the father, it seems impossible that anyone, even Earl Woods, could have been persuasive enough to make this young child want to play golf at such a competitive level. Nevertheless, there is no question that Earl and Kultida made great sacrifices to nurture the career of Tiger Woods.

Early on, when it became apparent that the young Tiger had unusual talent and desire to play competitive golf, his parents realized that it would involve a considerable time commitment as well as substantial financial resources to allow him to compete. Earl talks about how he and Kultida decided that, whatever it would cost, they would make the sacrifices to allow him to develop his God-given talents in golf.[7] Earl describes his method of financing Tiger's junior career by taking out a series of equity loans on his house every summer, which he would pay back during the winter. He estimates it cost about $25,000 to $30,000 a year to pay for expenses related to junior golf tournaments.[8]

While Earl was still working, it was Kultida's responsibility to get Tiger from tournament to tournament, and she quickly became a fixture on the Southern California junior golf circuit. She tried to stay as far in the background as possible, often following Tiger's matches from a distance. Despite her unquestioned loyalty to her son, she always recorded the scores of all the boys in the group and cheered for all the golfers if they made a good shot. There was an incident in one tournament when Tiger missed a short putt and lightly tossed his putter in the air in disgust. This was against AJGA rules. This rule, which was instituted mainly to eliminate swearing and overt demonstrations of temper, was generally not enforced for minor infractions. However, two of the boys in Tiger's group reported him at the end of the round and he was penalized with disqualification. Even though Kultida was convinced that there was some racial motivation on the part of the parents of the boys who reported Tiger's actions, she refused to let Tiger protest the disqualification. Her message to him was clear: Let your clubs speak for you.[9]

It wasn't until Earl retired from his job as a buyer for defense contractor McDonnell Douglas in 1988 that he devoted himself full-time to Tiger's junior golfing career. Because of limited funds, Earl and Tiger usually arrived the night before a tournament and stayed in a motel. Once, Tiger asked his father if there was any way that they could get there earlier so that he might be able to play a practice round before the tournament, like most of the other players did. That was when Earl and Kultida decided to borrow money to give Tiger the optimum opportunity to compete. Earl decided that he would "go broke if he had to."[10]

The Woods were not like other families who would go on family vacations during holidays and the summer. They would always be traveling to the various junior tournaments. At Christmas, Earl would travel with Tiger to the Junior Invitational Tournament in Miami. At Thanksgiving it was a junior tournament in Tucson, Arizona. Easter was the Woodlands Tournament in Texas. Their lives revolved around Tiger's golf schedule.

Fairly early on Kultida recognized the celebrity potential of her young son and convinced him to have his eyes examined for contact lenses. The young Tiger was vehemently opposed to the idea and vowed not to put anything into his eyes. She was finally able to convince him that they would be less trouble than glasses, especially on the golf course, and he relented. The future celebrity was also fitted with braces that at least helped perfect the now famous Tiger smile. Earl was quoted as saying, "A million-dollar smile that cost me four thousand dollars."[11]

There were a number of instances when Tiger and his parents confronted one another in the course of his junior playing career. Tiger was leading the Orange Bowl Junior Classic in Miami when he missed a short putt and exploded. He then proceeded to give up for the rest of the match, playing in a disinterested fashion—he quit. Following the match, his father, a former military officer and no stranger to dressing down a subordinate in colorful fashion, could be heard over most of the golf course reprimanding his young son. The object of his ire was not the fact that Tiger missed the putt, but that he had given up. Earl reminded Tiger that the game did not owe him anything, and that he owed it to the game to keep trying, however hopeless the circumstances. Earl Woods referred to Jack Nicklaus, the gauge by which Tiger measured his own accomplishments, and how many times the great golfer continued to grind even when he was not in contention.[12] There is ample evidence that this advice took hold of the young golfer and carried through to his subsequent amateur and professional career. Even the harshest critics of Tiger Woods admit that he continues to try to play his best even when not in contention. In fact, throughout his career, some of his best rounds have come after some of his worst. During the British Open in 2002 at Muirfield, he shot an 81 during the rainy, windswept Saturday round—his worst professional tournament round at that point—only to come back the next day and shoot 65, finishing the tournament at even par.[13]

There has been much written about how Tiger dazzled the adults as a young child with his virtually perfect golf swing, and the images persist of this little American child smiling and swinging a golf club like a professional. However, when Tiger began competing in junior tournaments, both he and his father agreed that he would not compete on a level that was beyond his capabilities. When he was 12 and competing in the Yorba Linda (CA) Junior Invitational, he was the overall leader going into the final round, which for 14-, 15-, and 16-year-olds would be played from the blue tees (the longest distances). Tom Sargent, the tournament director, asked Tiger if he wanted to play from the blue tees and thus be eligible for the overall championship. Tiger declined, saying "there'll be plenty of time for that later."[14] So he played from the white tees (shorter distance) and only competed for his age bracket. He did the same thing the next year. Sargent was so impressed with Tiger's maturity that he contacted his friend Wally Goodwin, the golf coach at Stanford, and told him he should start recruiting this young golfer.

There are numerous examples of parents of accomplished developing athletes encouraging them to seek the highest possible levels of competition, despite the possible negative effects. In the National Basketball Association, high school graduates are occasionally given a special exemption to be drafted by NBA teams. While there have been cases when an athlete has been able to make the physical transition from high school to the NBA, it is not possible to know what the emotional and psychological effects are. So while Lebron James seems to be prospering in professional basketball, it is difficult to gauge the long-range effects. In tennis, so many young players have skipped leagues in this way that the World Tennis Association has imposed minimum age limits and restricted the number of tournaments in which young players can compete.

A good comparison in golf is the emerging career of Michele Wei, the teenage prodigy from Hawaii, who has generally avoided playing the junior golf circuit in order to compete in as many LPGA tournaments as sponsor's exemptions would allow. Both Michele and her father have stated that she will learn more competing against professionals than playing in the more traditional junior girls' tournaments. One of the many criticisms of Wei in the press, and from other LPGA touring professionals, has been that a young player has to learn to win, and the experience of winning in the junior events would be better preparation for Michele.

Earl developed the idea of enlisting a carefully selected group of people to work with his son to help him perfect all aspects of his golf game, psychological as well as physical. When Tiger turned professional, the media quickly picked up on the idea and began referring to this growing group, not always flatteringly, as "Team Tiger." One of those early members of the group was Dr. Jay Brunza, a clinical psychologist for the navy and occasional caddie for Tiger during his junior and amateur career. In addition to carrying his clubs, Jay also worked with Tiger to help him control his mind. He hypnotized Tiger once and told him to hold out his arm straight. Earl, unaware of the hypnosis, tried in vain to move his young son's arm. On another occasion Brunza presented Tiger with a series of focusing techniques, and then arranged a 12-player match, including Tiger. Tiger was five strokes under par, and one of his frustrated opponents drove back to the seventh hole to confront Brunza, claiming he had created a golfing monster.[15] There has been speculation about whether or not Brunza ever hypnotized Tiger before a match. While not indicating that Tiger was ever playing golf in a hypnotic state, he did say that as a professional, "He's now mature enough, too, to put himself into a zone of intense concentration during a round of golf."[16]

Given the relatively small number of junior golfers who ever compile particularly significant professional or amateur records, it would normally not be significant to track the accomplishments of a junior golfer. However, in light of the later success of Tiger Woods as both an amateur and a professional, a summary of his junior golf accomplishments is illuminating. Also, much of what he represents today as a professional golfer, businessman, philanthropist, and husband had its foundation in his junior career.

When reviewing Tiger's junior career, it is sometimes difficult to keep in mind that we are talking about a boy, albeit one with exceptionally advanced skills on a golf course. And while he was generally able to compete at a level beyond his age, he was constantly learning and developing his personality under the increasingly intense scrutiny of the sports media. When he was four years old he had his first exposure to some young people cheating in a junior tournament.[17] Tiger observed one of the golfers touching the sand in a bunker (which is punishable by a penalty of two strokes) and not counting those strokes. It is impressive that this four-year-old was so knowledgeable about the rules of golf, and observant enough to be aware of the violation. More importantly, he told his father and vowed that he would not cheat even if others cheated. Golf is probably the only popular sport played for money in which competitors actually call penalties on themselves, even if no one else observed the violation.

Since Tiger was still small of stature when he began playing competition golf, he sometimes had to overcome feelings of inferiority. An incident occurred at the Junior World Championships in San Diego when Tiger was 12, before he began to grow and fill out physically. He played a six-foot-tall golfer who drove the first hole. Tiger was intimidated by his size and strength. Earl reminded Tiger that golf is a game that does not depend on size and strength. Tiger eventually defeated the larger boy and vowed to his father that he would not be intimidated again.[18]

In 1989, 13-year-old Tiger competed in the Insurance Youth Golf Classic, a unique tournament in which junior golfers are paired with professionals. Tiger, paired with future star John Daly, beat eight of the professionals, and while he eventually lost to Daly on the last few holes after a brilliant performance, he clearly demonstrated that he could compete on a professional level. He was not yet in high school when he received his first recruiting letter from Stanford University.

In 1990, when Tiger was 14, he won the Optimist International Golf Championship for the fifth time, and he established a record by winning the Junior World Championship six times. As a result of his outstanding record, when he was 15 he was selected as the American Junior Golf Association's Player of the Year, as well as the Southern California Player of the year, and was named to the First Team on the Rolex Junior All-American list.[19]

The relationship Tiger had with his parents during his junior career was a sensitive balance between trying to please them and learning to compete. Tiger lost the 1990 U.S. Junior Amateur semifinals to Dennis Hillman, and he was severely disappointed. In the car before going home Tiger leaned over, hugged his father and said, "Pop, I love you."[20] Earl also tells of an incident when the 10-year-old Tiger was competing in a junior tournament. Faced with a situation that called for the selection of one of a number of possible shots, Tiger chose a shot that seemed odd to Earl. After the round Earl asked him why he decided to use that particular shot. Tiger told him he thought that was what his father wanted him to do. Earl impressed upon Tiger the fact that he was not playing for his father, he was playing for himself, and since he had to live with the consequences of his decisions—in life and on the golf course—he alone could make them. While the media created an image of a happy little boy, unfazed by the outside world, Earl has recounted how Tiger had some recurring nightmares centered around racial bigotry, including one in which he dreamed he was playing in a tournament in the South and was the target of an assassin. Despite the pressures Tiger might have felt, he continued to excel on the golf course.

In 1991, he attempted to qualify for the Nissan Los Angeles Open at South Course at Los Serranos Golf Club in Chino Hills, California. There were two qualifying spots for the 132 players. When he reached the par-five 18th hole, his father, who was caddying for Tiger, mistakenly told him he needed a birdie to get one of the two spots. It would not have mattered, since Tiger had every intention of going for the green in two shots when he left the tee. The ball was on a down slope, the lie was bare, and when he swung he did not catch the ball squarely. The ball landed in the pond in front of the green, thereby dashing any hope of qualifying. The two professionals who did qualify, Mac O'Grady and John Burckle, each shot 66. Tiger, after holing out a bogey, shot 69. Several of the professionals watching the performance of the 15-year-old were impressed, not only by his physical skills, but also by his

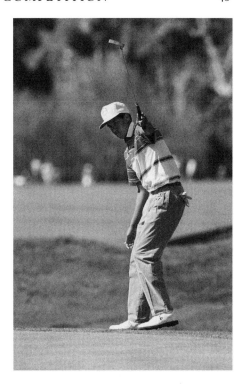

Amateur Golfer Tiger Woods urges a putt toward the seventh hole during the opening round of the Los Angeles Open at Riviera Country Club in Los Angeles, California, on February 27, 1992. The 16-year-old Woods was the youngest player ever to compete in a PGA event. AP Photo/Bob Galbraith.

"go for broke" attitude that would eventually characterize his career on the PGA Tour.[21]

On the basis of all the attention he was receiving through the press coverage of his junior record, Tiger was invited to play in the 1992 Los Angeles Open PGA Tournament, and while he ultimately missed the cut by six shots, he learned a number of valuable lessons about playing on the professional tour. Apparently not everyone playing in the tournament knew about the exploits of the new phenom, so when Sandy Lyle was asked what he thought about Tiger Woods, he asked if that was a new golf course.[22]

As a consequence of winning the Junior Amateur, Tiger was exempted from the local qualifier for the 1992 U.S. Open and competed in the sectional qualifier held at Lake Merced Country Club in Daly City, California. There were 10 spots for the 77 professionals and exceptional amateurs. Trying to qualify while studying for exams and preparing for his driver's license test took its toll, and he missed by four shots. His father noted that this was a good experience for Tiger: since he really had no chance to qualify, there was little pressure on him. But he felt it was a worthwhile experience for him to get a feel for the U.S. Open.[23]

Winning the USGA Junior Amateur automatically qualified Tiger to compete in the 1992 USGA Amateur. The competition consists of a two-day 36-hole stroke play event from which the 64 lowest-scoring players are allowed to proceed to a match play format. On the first day of the qualifier, Tiger had one of his worst rounds as an amateur, not only shooting poorly, but also losing his temper and storming off the course without talking to the media. This was uncharacteristic and ironic since he was certainly not a favorite to qualify; there were plenty of other players in the competition with better records than his. However, it did not take the 16-year-old long to recover from the bad experience. When asked how long it took him to "cool down" after the round, Tiger was quoted as saying "Dinner," going on to say that he ate 10 tacos. After his emotional recovery, he went out the next day and shot one of his best competitive rounds. He and his father had anticipated needing a score of 69 in order to make the match play rounds. He scored a 66, hitting all but two greens in regulation and scoring four birdies, an eagle, and 13 pars. Despite the fact that he was eliminated in the second round of match play, this experience once again demonstrated his incomparable ability to rebound after adversity and not allow his emotions to dominate his game.[24]

By 1993 Tiger was finding it difficult to maintain his concentration during rounds, which could have been attributed to the fact that the level of competition in junior golf was not challenging enough anymore. However, he had one more challenge in junior golf, and that was to win his third consecutive USGA Junior Championship, to be played at the Waverly Country Club in Portland, Oregon. Tiger made it to the finals, where his opponent was Ryan Armour. Armour was dormie two (meaning two holes up with two holes remaining in the match). This meant Tiger had to win both remaining holes to send the match to extra holes in order to have a chance at winning. Tiger birdied the 17th but hit his second shot on the 18th into a sand bunker some 40 yards from the green. This is one of the most difficult shots in golf under any circumstances, let alone on the final hole of a USGA championship. Tiger hit a spectacular shot to within eight feet of the hole and sunk the putt. His opponent bogied the hole, sending the match to extra holes—in essence, sudden death. Woods defeated his opponent on the first extra hole.[25]

Once again, because he had won the USGA Junior Championship in 1993, he was eligible to play in the U.S. Amateur, which was held at the Champions Club in Houston, Texas. Tiger was again eliminated in the second round of the match play, but it was at this event that he was introduced to Butch Harmon, who would become one of his most trusted teachers and a crucial member of Team Tiger during his transition from amateur to professional golf. Butch was the son of Claude Harmon, the 1948 Masters Champion. After Harmon watched his swing, he told Earl and Tiger that despite his unprecedented accomplishments as a junior golfer, it would be a three-year project to make the complete transition into top-flight amateur and professional golf.[26]

The more celebrity Tiger gained, the more he was placed in the spotlight, and the more he was subjected to increased scrutiny. Ironically, his fame resulted in a kind of reverse discrimination. Tiger was offered an honorary membership at Big Canyon Country Club in Newport Beach, California. Earl Woods, very cognizant of the strict rules concerning amateur status in golf, contacted the USGA to find out if Tiger could accept the membership and still remain an amateur. They told Earl that he could, but that Earl should get in touch with the National Collegiate Athletic Association (NCAA), since they might have other stipulations. Earl was somewhat confused about this advice since Tiger was still in high school, but he contacted the NCAA and at first was told that Tiger could not accept the membership and still remain eligible for college golf. Eventually the NCAA granted permission, but this was to be the first in what would become an ongoing series of conflicts and misunderstandings between Team Tiger and the governing body of collegiate sports.[27] Indicative of the difference between golf and other sports, here was Earl Woods assiduously protecting his son's amateur status despite his own strained financial situation. It has been written, albeit cynically, that Earl was hanging on to Tiger's amateur status because there would be a larger payoff down the line. Whatever the reasons, Tiger retained his amateur status. However, it was becoming apparent that even as an amateur the public would demand more from him than his golf game.

Tiger was 14 when an incident at Shoal Creek Country Club in Alabama threatened to cancel the 1990 PGA Championship. In a pre-tournament press conference, Hall Thompson, the president of Shoal Creek, was asked about the lack of any black members in the club. He responded that the club would not be pressured into accepting black members because "that kind of thing isn't done in Alabama."

He exacerbated the situation by stating that the club accepted women, Jews, Lebanese, and Italians. A number of community groups and civil rights groups demonstrated and planned to picket the tournament. However, it was not until several of the tournament's corporate sponsors began to feel the financial pressure that anything was done. Eventually, the PGA, and subsequently the USGA, instituted policies that prohibited staging any of their sanctioned tournaments at clubs that discriminated. Suddenly this teenager became the great black hope, and as such the press expected him to have opinions about the racial situation in America. While Tiger was keenly aware of his racial heritage, he did not want to become the greatest black golfer, he wanted to become the greatest golfer ever.[28] However, as his career evolved he would face more and more pressure to take on the role as spokesman for his race(s), and for oppressed minorities in general.

NOTES

1. Earl Woods, *Playing Through* (New York: Harper Collins, 1998), 88.

2. Ibid., 92–93.

3. John Strege, *A Biography of Tiger Woods* (New York: Broadway Books, 1998), 48.

4. Michael Sokolove, "Constructing A Teen Phenom," *New York Times Magazine*, November 28, 2004: 80.

5. Ibid., 82.

6. Curt Sampson, *Chasing Tiger* (New York: Atria, 2002), 7.

7. Woods, 99.

8. Ibid., 100.

9. Strege 25.

10. Quoted in ibid., 24.

11. Quoted in ibid., 27.

12. Ibid., 34.

13. Henry Blauvelt, "Woods Finishes with a Good Score, Good Spirits," *USA Today,* July 21, 2002, http://www.usatoday.com/sports/golf/2002–07–21-britishwoods.htm.

14. Quoted in Strege, 23.

15. Ibid., 35.

16. Quoted in John Andrisani, *Think Like a Tiger* (New York: The Berkley Publishing Group, 2002), 43.

17. Woods, 81–82.

18. Ibid., 91–92.

19. Edwards, 27.

20. Quoted in Strege, 33.

21. Ibid., 41.

22. Ibid., 50.

23. Ibid., 54.

24. Ibid., 56–57.

25. Ibid., 59.

26. Ibid., 61.

27. Ibid., 53.

28. Ibid., 39.

Chapter 4

PIONEERS

In 1995 Tiger Woods received an award from a little-known nine-hole golf course in Indianapolis, Indiana. Douglass Park Golf Course was one of the prominent stops on what represented a segregation-induced black golfers' tour until the PGA of America eliminated its racial exclusion from its constitution in 1961. A month later he played in his first Masters Tournament, as the reigning U.S. Amateur Champion. Commenting later on the significance of his predecessors, he said, "I have a great deal of reverence for the Masters tradition, especially since my victory in 1997, but I must admit, the first time I drove down Magnolia Lane I was not thinking about Bobby Jones or all the Masters stood for: I was thinking about all the great African American players who never got a chance to play there. That I was able to win there, I believe, brought a little bit of vindication."[1]

It is important to trace a brief history of the game, because part of the intense interest in Tiger Woods is due to the fact that he is of mixed race and playing a game that throughout most of its history excluded minorities. In order to fully appreciate the accomplishments of Tiger Woods, one must understand the tremendous obstacles that have prevented people of color from establishing a presence in the sport of golf, both in the professional ranks and in most of the private clubs and courses throughout America. It is not without some irony, given the history of the game, that there is ample evidence that the first American-born professional golfer was an African American.

DEVELOPMENT OF THE GAME

No other sport has stratified social classes like the game of golf. Golf as we know it was first played by shepherds in Scotland, who probably observed Roman soldiers playing a game called *paganica*, which was played with a bent stick hitting a leather ball stuffed with feathers.[2] So the game was not originally a gentleman's game. By 1457 the game was popular enough to be banned by the parliament of King James II because it took too much time away from archery practice. Between the lifting of the ban in 1502 and the mid-19th century, the game was played by British gentleman amateurs on courses throughout the country and wherever the empire spread.

The first generation of professional golfers, not unlike the first boxers, used the game to raise themselves up out of poverty. The golfers we remember are not the gentleman amateurs who played the game in Stuart Scotland. Between 1830 and 1860, three Scots pioneered the sport: Old Tom Morris, Alan Robertson, and Old Tom's son Tom Jr., who dropped dead of grief at the age of 24, hours after his wife died in childbirth. The British Open Championship—or, as the British prefer, the Open Championship—was first played in 1860.

In 1877, Harry Vardon's family was evicted from its shanty to make way for the Royal Jersey Golf Club. Vardon would become the first golfer to gain an international reputation and, as such, would be the precursor to Tiger Woods. It should be pointed out that though he was otherwise typical of the golf professionals of the day, he was probably the first who was able to capitalize on his playing prowess financially beyond the prize money, through exhibitions and challenge matches. At this time golf was a game for gentleman amateurs, who played golf in their spare time as a leisure activity. People who made golf their living were not well respected by civilized society, were largely uneducated, spoke with thick regional accents, and lacked social graces. Their main role was to make and repair golf clubs, tend to the care of the golf course, and teach the members how to improve their games. If they were good enough they would occasionally compete in tournaments. When they did, they were rarely allowed to even change their shoes in the clubhouses, let alone eat lunch in the club dining room.[3]

Bobby Jones was the true embodiment of the ideal of amateurism when he won the so-called Grand Slam of golf in 1930: the U.S. Open, the U.S. Amateur, the British Amateur, and the British Open. Jones would later gain fame as the founder of the Masters Golf Tournament and the world-renowned Augusta National Golf Course. On display at the USGA headquarters in Far Hills, New Jersey, are the four medals he received, in lieu of the cash prize he would have been awarded for winning the two Open Championships. Jones, a lawyer, never turned professional, and to this day he represents to some the quintessential amateur. Of course, it must be pointed out that in 1930 there was little money to be made in golf by today's standards. The connection between the sport and commerce had not yet been made. Most significantly, the media was in its infancy and had a limited ability to create much mass interest in the game.

In comparison to other sports, the game of golf does not on the surface generate much passion. It is one of the only sports in which spectators must remain completely quiet during play. It is the only sport in which the match takes place simultaneously over a 20-acre tract of land. Most of the competitors themselves exhibit little emotion. So how has this sport managed to periodically capture the imagination of the sports public and gain large audiences and mass media coverage? Every so often there emerges a player who, by virtue of their personality and flair, captures the public's imagination. Vardon and Jones were early examples this phenomenon; Tiger Woods is the latest incarnation. Players with this kind of appeal transform the game from a slow, plodding test of endurance to a dramatic performance. We relate to golfers because they play a sport that is conducted in open space with no walls or barriers between the spectator and the player. They wear clothes that roughly approximate our own—no helmets, or funny socks, or shorts. It is the sport that most closely reflects the style of the period and place in which it is played, and while the game began in Britain, it adapted well to America.

The South Carolina Golf Course, established in 1876 in Charleston, South Carolina, is arguably the first golf club in America.[4] However, it was not until the 1890s that golf was played in earnest in the United States. Willie Dunn, a Scotsman, came to America in 1891 and built the first incorporated, formally designed golf course at Shinnecock Hills, on Long Island.[5] The game was imported from Britain by wealthy American businessmen who had the reason and means to travel to Europe. While the game was played principally by the wealthy, African Americans played an important role in the early development of the game in America.

AFRICAN AMERICANS AND GOLF

African Americans have been involved with the game of golf since it was first played in America. While that connection was almost exclusively as caddies, they inevitably developed the skills to play the game. However, it would be a long time before blacks would be able to play the game legitimately on a golf course.

By the early 1920s, there was a golf boom that fueled an unending need for caddies at both private and public courses. Traditionally, clubs allowed caddies to play on the one day a week when the courses were closed to members for maintenance, and it appears that caddy masters were fairly color-blind when it came to letting the caddies play. Consequently, many young black teenagers were able to play on courses that would not allow them as members even if they could have afforded it. While the caddies did earn some playing privileges, they were still shown little respect. A former black caddy at Augusta liked to tell the story of a black caddy who grumbled when the Great Emancipator's son tipped him a dime after a round. "Northern gentlemen usually give me a quarter," he said. Lincoln glared, "Didn't my father do enough for you people already?" "I don't know," he responded, "I never caddied for your father."[6]

Despite the limited opportunity to play golf, enough black people developed an interest in the game that a number of black-owned golf clubs were founded as early as the 1920s. Although these were not posh layouts and many were poorly maintained nine-hole courses, they did provide a way for interested black people to play golf regularly. One such club was Shady Rest Golf Club in Westfield (now Scotch Plains), New Jersey, established in 1921. The members consisted of "prosperous Negro merchants, lawyers, doctors, Pullman porters, waiters and janitors."[7]

Shady Rest

Shady Rest started out as the all-white Westfield Country Club, which was established in 1900 and featured a nine-hole golf course north of the Westfield train line on Jerusalem Road in Scotch Plains, New Jersey. On either side of the club was an African American community of small houses, and the residents would routinely cut across the golf course to get to the train line or to socialize. Over a period of years, a "right of travel" evolved, which came to affect the legal rights of the private club. In 1921, when it considered plans to expand the course to 18 holes., this legal condition was likely a factor in their ultimate decision to sell the club and merge with the Cranford Golf Club to form the Echo Lake Country Club in Springfield. The former Westfield club was mortgaged to the Progressive Realty Company, an organization created by a group of prominent African Americans, and became the Shady Rest Golf and Country Club, considered to be the first African American golf and country club in America.[8]

There were other black-owned and/or operated golf courses before and during this period, but only Shady Rest had combined golf with the club house, restaurant, lockers, tennis courts, horseback riding, skeet shooting, croquet, and other social activities that were generally associated with country clubs of the era. Shady Rest was run by and for blacks and became an important social and economic institution in the local community and the New York metropolitan area.

In 1925 a fight for control of Shady Rest erupted over mismanagement of the club's finances, between forces representing a New York contingent, headed by Henry Parker, and a local group from New Jersey. The local group managed to vote out the New York slate of club officers, but the New York group was reinstated after the election was challenged in the courts. Following this controversy it was rumored that Parker and another New York member, John E. Nail, left Shady Rest along with money collected to pay off the mortgage, leaving the club in substantial debt.[9] It was at this point that William Willis Sr. assumed control of the club.

William Willis Sr. ran Shady Rest for the remainder of its history. In many ways he represents the struggle of African Americans entering the mainstream of middle-class America. He served in the Army during World War I and became a supply sergeant. Upon returning to the United States he started a taxicab company and began dealing in real estate in the Scotch Plains area. However, sometime in the early 1930s, because of the rising tax levies, Shady Rest was forced to change ownership and became the property of the township of Scotch Plains.[10] Through an informal agreement, the municipality committed to retain the club for the African American community, and Willis agreed to continue running it.

In 1963, the gentlemen's handshake between William Willis Sr. and the township of Scotch Plains came to an end. Shady Rest became the Scotch Hills Country Club and was opened to the public. While the end of Shady Rest as a private club is linked to the rise of integration in public facilities in the 1960s, there is ambivalence over the inevitable deterioration of African American institutions.

Shady Rest provided a forum for some of the most prominent African Americans of the period, from all spheres of influence. Because of its proximity to New York, many famous musicians performed regularly at the club. Ella Fitzgerald, Count Basie, and Duke Ellington all made appearances at Shady Rest. The late Althea Gibson learned to play tennis and later golf at Shady Rest. On Memorial Day of 1923, over five hundred automobiles from all over the Northeast jammed the parking lot at Shady Rest as an overflow crowd gathered to hear a lecture by W.E.B. DuBois, the distinguished activist-scholar.[11] The club boasted a membership of working-class and professional men and women and their families and provided an atmosphere of civility and belonging in what could otherwise be a hostile and unfriendly world.

The story of Shady Rest represents a symbol of black achievement during a period when African Americans were suffering even more than Depression-era white Americans. The club offered the evolving black middle class a social and economic institution with access to activities not associated with a minority community.

John Shippen

One person intimately connected to the Shady Rest Country Club, and relatively overlooked until recently, was John M. Shippen. During the ABC telecasts of the 1981 and 1984 U.S. Open tournaments,

Jim Thorpe was referred to as the first Native American to lead the U.S. Open in its history. Jerry Izenberg, a syndicated sports columnist for the New Jersey's *Newark Star Ledger,* wrote a column challenging that statement and telling the story of John Shippen.[12]

Shippen was born in December 1878 in the Washington, D.C., area, and his family came to Long Island in 1888. Shippen's father was a Presbyterian minister, and his ministry was with the Shinnecock Indian Reservation. Shippen recounted that by 1893 he was caddying and playing golf at Shinnecock, and that he was party to a number of matches with the members of Shinnecock (who would put up $50 purses). He said he played Shinnecock golf professional R. B. Wilson four times and beat him three times.[13]

Shippen, then 18 years old, competed in the 1896 Open along with Shinnecock Indian and fellow caddie Oscar Bunn, and a racial incident occurred that has led to some question and controversy concerning the racial identity of John Shippen. Shippen, then an assistant to Willie Dunn, the professional at Shinnecock Hills, almost did not compete, because a group of mostly foreign-born professionals and amateurs threatened to boycott the tournament if Shippen and Oscar Bunn were allowed to play. Theodore Havemeyer, the president of the newly formed U.S. Golf Association, is reported to have informed the disgruntled golfers that the tournament would be run even if Shippen and Bunn were the only two competitors. According to this story, the other golfers relented, and they competed in the tournament with Shippen and Bunn. Different versions of the story have survived. One has Havemeyer telling the other players that Shippen was not a Negro, but an Indian, and this supposedly quelled the uprising. This version of the story is less plausible in light of a reference in a now-extinct British publication of the period, *The Golfer,* in which there is a reference to "John Shippen, a sixteen-year-old coloured caddie attached to the Shinnecock Hills course."[14]

This incident has relevance here since we are examining the life of certainly the most prominent golfer of mixed race in the history of the sport of golf, and it is important to point out that as far back as the turn of the century there were overt examples of discrimination based on race in the sport of golf. And, historically, the fact that an African American was competing for the national golf championship of the United States in 1896 is significant.[15]

To the extent that African Americans' or anyone's race in America can be definitively ascertained, it seems clear that John Shippen was the child of predominantly African American parents. Two of Shippen's daughters contributed their recollections to a book written by Paul E. Sluby in which they say, "Milton Winfield Lee, our great grandfather, was the first of our Lee lineage who was of Shinnecock heritage."[16] And Shippen himself identified his father as a "Negro" and his mother as a Shinnecock Indian.[17] The question of Shippen's race has taken on increased significance since the fight for civil rights in the 1950s and 1960s, and particularly with the arrival of African American professionals on the PGA Tour.

There are several factors that have clouded the ethnic origins of John Shippen over the years. The principal point of confusion is the fact that John Shippen married a Shinnecock Indian woman, so his children were of mixed ethnic background. Among the Shinnecock tribe there are many examples of intermarriage with African Americans, but apparently it was not always easy for disinterested Shinnecock members to distinguish the ethnic origins of the help. From photographs of Shippen it is evident that his ethnic origins could have been mistaken. The fact that there is a debate about the ethnic heritage of John Shippen is a significant indication of the status of American blacks during this period. Furthermore, it is interesting to speculate about the controversy over whether or not Shippen and Bunn would be allowed to play in the 1896 Open. As the name implies, the tournament was open to both professionals and amateurs. Given the humble station of virtually all golf professionals of the period, it is unlikely they would have cared who competed in the tournament. It is much more likely that the amateur golfers would have taken exception to these ethnic outcasts being included. In the final standings Shippen tied for fifth place in the Open competition with H. J. Whigham of Onwentsia, the player who had won the amateur competition the day before.

Shippen left caddying and took his first professional job teaching golf to the wealthy Cromwell family of Bernardsville, New Jersey.[18] For the next two years Shippen served as the golf professional at the Maidstone Golf Club in East Hampton. After working at several Metropolitan-area clubs in New Jersey (Spring Lake) and Brooklyn (Marine and

Field Club—which became the Dyke Beach Club), Shippen returned to Maidstone, where he worked from 1902 until 1913. He was next employed for a year as a private professional for steel tycoon Henry Clay Frick. In 1916 Shippen returned to Shinnecock to serve as green-skeeper for two years, after which he served in a similar capacity for the National Golf Links, which is adjacent to Shinnecock. He then moved back to his hometown of Washington, D.C., left golf, and worked for several years for the Department of Public Grounds.

Shippen returned to golf and worked for the National Capital Golf Club, a black club in Maryland. In 1932 he went to back to New Jersey and became the professional at the Shady Rest Country Club. He would work there until he died in 1968.

During the time Shippen was playing competitive golf, the only significant tournament in which professionals could compete was the U.S. Open Championship. So it is worth listing his accomplishments in that prestigious event, despite the many obstacles that faced an African American golfer during this period:

1896:   July 18 (36 holes played the same day), Shinnecock Hills. 78–81 = 159. Tied for 5th. Affiliated: Shinnecock Hills.

1899:   September 14–15, Baltimore Country Club. 86–88–88–88 = 350. 27th. Affiliated: Aronimink (Philadelphia).

1900:   October 4–5, Chicago Country Club. 181–89–83 = 353. Tie 25th. Affiliated: Marine & Field (Brooklyn).

1902:   October 10–11, Garden City Golf Course. 79–82–76–81 = 318. Tie 5th. Affiliated: New York.

1913:   September 16, 17, 18, 19, The Country Club, Brookline, MA.[19] (165 qualifying score) 81–73–87–87 = 328. Tie 41st. Affiliated: Maidstone Golf Club (Long Island).

It seems that during this period the USGA only listed the players who completed the competition and handed in a scorecard, because the records indicate more entries than final scores listed. So it is possible that Shippen participated in more Opens but did not finish. However, considering his financial situation, it is unlikely he competed in many other tournaments. During this period there were few other opportunities to compete since there was not a golf tour.

The Professional Golfers Association was not formed until 1916, so technically there was no such thing as a golf professional when Shippen played the game competitively. He worked in the game for over 70 years and fulfilled the responsibilities of what a golf professional did during the period—keeping the course in good playing condition; supplying and repairing equipment; teaching; serving as starter and scorekeeper for tournaments; and occasionally playing for prize money—so although he would never become a member of the PGA, it is safe to refer to Shippen as the first American-born golf professional.[20] By the time Shippen took the job at Shady Rest, he was 54 and his competitive golfing days were over.

Shady Rest was not the first, nor the only, golf club exclusively for African Americans. At about the same time, black golfers in Washington, D.C., found it increasingly difficult to gain access to courses in the area. Because of the federal government's growing sensitivity to equal rights, there were probably more emerging middle-class blacks in Washington, D.C., than in any other area of the country. Blacks there had better jobs, more leisure time, and access to municipal courses, so this area produced the most African American golfers. In 1938 a coalition of men and women black golfers petitioned the Secretary of State, Harold Ickes, to desegregate Washington's public golf courses, and one of the results was the building of Langston Course in 1939.[21]

So strong was their interest in the game that several of these Washingtonians rented summer cottages in Stow, Massachusetts, where Dr. John Ritt Randall, a wealthy, Harvard-educated doctor, had constructed a golf course on his family's estate.[22] The Mapledale Country Club would play a significant role in the development of black golf in America.

Other early black-owned clubs were Sunset Hills Country Club in Kankakee, Illinois; Lincoln Country Club of Atlanta, Georgia; Freeway Golf Course in Sicklerville, New Jersey; and the Asbury Park Course in Asbury Park, New Jersey. As more golf courses became available to blacks throughout the country, the desire for competition increased.

In 1925, the first National Colored Golf Championship was held at Shady Rest. The winner of the inaugural event was Harry Jackson and the runner-up was John Shippen, both from the Washington, D.C. area.[23] This championship was organized by a group formed earlier that the year in Washington, D.C., called the United States Colored Golfers Association. B.C. Gordon, president of Shady Rest, was elected the president of the association. Two years later the group was renamed the United Golfers Association, an organization that served as the governing body of black golf until desegregation opened up many public courses to blacks in the mid 1960s.

The United Golfers Association

By 1926 there were enough black clubs across the country that Robert Hawkins, a resident of Stow, was able to invite the known black clubs throughout the United States to a tournament at his Mapledale course. On Labor Day weekend of 1926, 35 black golfers came to play the 72-hole medal (stroke) tournament. The winner of the professional division was paid $100; the amateurs received medals. The men's and women's winners of that inaugural event were Harry Jackson of Washington, D.C., and Marie Thompson of Chicago. John Shippen finished fourth and won $25.[24]

The United Golfers Association consisted of regional organizations of black golfers, such as the Eastern Golfers Association, which would periodically stage competitions for individual members and interclub matches. The UGA coordinated the scheduling of these events and sponsored an annual national championship held at various black clubs throughout the country. These events usually consisted of an amateur competition and an open competition. As the number of tournaments increased, the prize money available also increased, thus luring more and more black golfers to play golf professionally. The first president of the UGA was Dr. George W. Adams Jr., who was also founding member of the Royal Golf Club of Washington, D.C., which led to a proliferation of local clubs organized into regions across the country. He was reelected in 1929.[25] Two important women in the history of the UGA were Ms. Paris Brown and Ms. Anna M. Robinson, who served as historian and tour director.

There is ample evidence that African American women took a more active role in establishing opportunities to play golf than their

Caucasian counterparts. The first formally organized women's golf club, the Wake-Robin Golf Club, was started in Washington, D.C., in 1937. It should be noted that this club was not an auxiliary of a men's club. Several months later, the Chicago Women's Golf Club was established. It is important to explain that these clubs did not own golf courses. They usually had access to a public course on certain days and times when they were permitted to play their tournaments.[26]

Black women faced all the same obstacles presented to the men, yet the UGA was able to nurture several outstanding women golfers, some of whom went on to compete in the Ladies Professional Golf Association and distinguish themselves. Ann Gregory of Gary, Indiana became the first black woman to compete in a USGA Amateur Championship in 1957 at Meridian Hills Country Club in Indianapolis, followed by Eoline Thornton of Long Beach, California in 1958. Althea Gibson, who played golf at Shady Rest, took up golf after her highly visible championship tennis career and became the first black woman to compete on the LPGA circuit in 1967. Renee Powell, whose father William built and operated the Clearview Country Club in Canton, Ohio, had a successful college career at both Ohio State and Ohio Universities. She played for several years in the late 1960s on the women's tour.

Throughout the years when black professional golfers were unable to compete on the PGA Tour, the UGA served as the only opportunity for these golfers to showcase their abilities and, for some, to earn at least a modest living playing golf. It also represented a social network for middle-class blacks who were otherwise excluded from the social institutions associated with the game.

While the UGA provided an opportunity for black club pros and amateurs to test their skills against other club players, it had little success in promoting black golfers into the major white golf establishment. The United States Golf Association did not reserve any places in its annual championship for members of the UGA—as the U.S. Lawn Tennis Association did for the American Tennis Association (the UGA's tennis counterpart). There was very little interaction between the USGA and the UGA. It wasn't until 1959 that any USGA championship was won by a black person, when Bill Wright won the Public Links Championship. Subsequently, Charles Duhon won the 1982 USGA Senior Amateur Championship in 1982. After winning consecutive

USGA Junior Championships, Tiger Woods became the first amateur golfer ever to win three consecutive USGA Amateur Championships in 1994, 1995, and 1996.

While many accomplished black golfers were spawned by the activities of the UGA, because of the limited national media coverage of their tournaments, many went unheralded. Robert "Pat" Ball from Chicago won UGA professional titles in 1927, 1929, 1934, and 1941. Howard "Butch" Wheeler, who was Bobby Jones's favorite caddie at the Brookhaven Country Club, was known for his long drives. He was the UGA professional champion five times between 1933 and 1958.[27]

The military service and black colleges were two other avenues for the development of black golfers. For some, the army offered the only opportunity to play on 18-hole courses that approached championship caliber. Pvt. Calvin Searles (who subsequently died in World War II) played in the 1944 Tam O'Shanter All American event. This was the only mainstream tournament that allowed blacks to compete during the war years. The only black college with its own course was Tuskegee Institute: a three-hole course was built there in 1920, which was eventually expanded to nine holes in the 1930s. Tuskegee sponsored the first black intercollegiate tournament in 1938, and they established a National Intercollegiate event in 1940.[28]

The Fight for Equality

African Americans were also making efforts to increase access to public courses. The opportunity to play these courses offered the only real chance to improve the overall skills of the growing number of black golfers. In several cases around the country blacks were suing to gain either access or increased access to public facilities, along with other civil rights efforts of the period.

A black dentist, Dr. P. O. Sweeny, sued the Louisville (Kentucky) Parks Department in 1947 for the right to play unrestricted on the public courses there. The decision ruled, in essence, that the courts could not enforce social equality, and the suit was dismissed.[29] Other lower court cases yielded similar results or, in some cases, modified rules for access. There followed a host of court cases, which eventually led the Supreme Court, in 1955, to reaffirm its rejection of "separate but equal" accommodations for public golf and recreational facilities. In the relevant case, the Court vacated a ruling by a lower court that allowed Atlanta to legally segregate blacks and whites if the facilities were of equal quality. However, the ruling did not immediately open up public golf courses to black golfers.

The struggle of black professionals took to the courts as well as the national media. In 1948, Ted Rhodes, Bill Spiller, and Gunter Madison, accomplished black golfers, forced the PGA to rethink its exclusionary rule. These golfers brought suit against the PGA for discrimination when they were not allowed to compete in the Richmond Open in Richmond, California.[30] The case was settled out of court in September 1948 when "the PGA, through attorney Dana Murdock, declared...that it would not discriminate or refuse tournament playing privileges to anyone because of color."[31] However, discrimination on the professional tour continued.

At the 1952 San Diego Open, Joe Louis, himself an accomplished amateur golfer, was invited by a local Chevrolet sponsor to participate in the tournament.[32] A PGA committee notified Louis that he was banned from participation. While the PGA constitution prohibited non-Caucasians from membership in the PGA, Louis had been invited, according to the rules, by the local sponsor as one of five amateur golfers allowed, without the need for qualification.

Horton Smith, PGA president, eventually polled the members of the executive committee to gain an exemption for Louis to compete. The PGA added a clause to their by-laws that allowed one PGA-approved "Negro" amateur (under 5 handicap) and one PGA-approved "Negro" professional of "recognized standing and ability" to be designated by local sponsors to compete in PGA events. Despite the national attention generated by the San Diego Open racial controversy, it would be nine years before the PGA would officially rescind its "Caucasian only" clause.

Charlie Sifford was the most prominent black professional golfer between 1945 and 1970 and was also the black golf professional most discriminated against. Aside from John Shippen, he accomplished the most "black firsts" in golf. After dominating the annual UGA professional championship, winning a record five in a row between 1952 and 1956, he became the first black player to win a significant title in a predominantly white event, the Long Beach (California) Open in 1957.[33] While Pete Brown, another early black professional, helped pave the way for other black professionals, as the first black pro to win a PGA tournament (the 1964 Waco Turner Open), Sifford became the first black player to win a major PGA event, the 1969 Los Angeles Open. Sifford began playing golf as a caddie in Greensboro, NC, where he won several local events. He then moved north to Philadelphia where he worked as a teaching professional.

In 1960, after receiving a letter of protest from Charlie Sifford, the attorney general of California, Stanley Mosk, announced, "We intend to take every step available to us, both in and out of the courts, to force the PGA either to eliminate this obnoxious restriction or to cease all activity of any kind within our state."[34] Eventually the executive committee of the PGA voted to eliminate racial restriction for membership. The full membership of the PGA ratified the committee's decision in November 1961.[35] Charlie Sifford eventually received his Class "A" PGA card in 1964.

In the 1969 Greater Greensboro Open, Sifford missed an opportunity to qualify for the 1970 Masters, the most exclusive invitational event on the professional golf tour, when he encountered heckling from several white spectators. Coming into the tournament, Sifford was in 10th position on a point list to qualify for the Masters; the top six would qualify. Four white men began heckling Sifford, prompting this comment from George Walsh, the tournament supervisor: "I followed them for four holes. I told them we wanted everybody to have a good time and asked them to stop it. But they didn't and I had the deputy detain them until a state patrolman arrived to arrest them."[36]

The black golfer who played the most prominent public role in bringing black golf to the attention of the sporting world was Lee Elder. After competing mainly in UGA tournaments, Elder earned his PGA card in 1967.[37]

Elder is best known as the first black golfer to compete in the Masters. This tournament, played on Augusta National Golf Course in Augusta, Georgia, is the ultimate symbol of the exclusivity of golf. The club has one of the most restricted memberships among all private clubs, and over the years, the tournament represented the inability of African American golfers to gain equality in major tournament golf.

Unlike most PGA events, only invited golfers are allowed to compete in the Masters. Most other PGA events were open to any golfer who finished the previous year in the top 60 money winners on the tour or was able to qualify for any remaining open spots. No black had ever been invited to the Masters.

Throughout the early 1970s, Elder was the focal point of an effort to force the officials who ran the Masters to establish permanent criteria for a golfer to obtain an invitation to the tournament. In 1971 the Masters changed earlier policies that invited players on the basis of a complicated point system and by ballot of former Masters champions. The new policy granted an invitation to anyone who won a PGA tournament in the year prior to the Masters.[38] Finally, in 1974, Elder won the Monsanto Open, which qualified him to compete in the 1975 Masters.

The most successful black golfer before Tiger Woods was Calvin Peete. Ironically, Peete did not come to golf by a traditional route. Born in Detroit in 1943, Peete was one of 19 children. His family moved south after the war, and he grew up in Pahokee, Florida. He made a living selling trinkets to migrant fruit pickers up and down the East Coast. On one trip to his northernmost stop of Rochester, New York, friends tricked him into playing golf. He was 23 years old.[39]

In addition to his late start, he was further hampered by a left arm he could not straighten out due to a childhood injury. But he persevered. By 1971 he had turned professional and earned his tour card by 1975. Since then, he accomplished what no black golfer had before. He won his first PGA tournament in 1978, the Greater Milwaukee Open (coincidentally Tiger's first professional win) and became the first black pro to earn $100,000. By the end of 1984, Peete had won more tournaments on the PGA Tour over the preceding four years than any other player.[40]

In 1982 he became the first black multiple winner, capturing the Greater Milwaukee Open (for the second time), the Anheuser-Busch Classic, the BC Open, and the Pensacola Open, and he had his best finish of an African American golf professional in a Grand Slam event, placing third in the 1982 PGA Championship.

The accomplishments of early black golf professionals were instrumental in creating interest in the game among the African American community, and making the career of Tiger Woods possible.

Undoubtedly the emergence of Tiger Woods as a dominant figure in professional golf has further helped popularize the sport in the minority communities, in particular the proliferation of minority junior golf programs. The organizations that control the sport of golf also have clearly made a commitment to eliminate discrimination. However, despite the phenomenal spotlight that the success of Woods has shone on black golfers, and all the policy changes with respect to host clubs for PGA and USGA events, there has been limited progress in the increase of the number of minority members at local private clubs. While the historic legacy of "separate but equal" continues to manifest itself at the recreational level, the amateur and professional career of Tiger Woods has dispelled any question of the ability of minorities to excel at the game.

NOTES

1. Quoted in Pete McDaniel, *Uneven Lies: The Heroic Story of African-Americans in Golf* (Greenwich, CT: American Golfer, 2000), 9.

2. "Golf," in *The World Book Encyclopedia* (Chicago: Field Enterprises Educational Corporation, 1976), 255.

3. Mark Frost, *The Greatest Game Ever Played* (New York: Hyperion, 2002), 12.

4. Calvin Sinnette, *Forbidden Fairways* (Chelsea, MN: Sleeping Bear Publications, 1998), 4.

5. Tom Flaherty, *The U.S. Open (1895–1965): Complete Story of the United States Golf Championship* (New York: E. P. Dutton & Co., 1966), 18.

6. Flaherty, 39.

7. "Only Negro Golf Course in U.S. Is Thriving in Suburban Jersey," *New York Sun*, July 11, 1922: 22.

8. *A Place For Us: The Story of Shady Rest and America's First Golf Professional*, dir. Larry Londino, WNET Channel 13, December 19, 1996.

9. Lester A. Walton, "Shady Rest Club Ends Big Fight in Jersey Courts," *Pittsburgh Courier*, July 18, 1925, 9.

10. William Willis Jr., personal interview, October 14, 1991.

11. "Thousands Motored Out to Shady Rest Country Club Decoration Day," *Amsterdam News*, June 6, 1923, 5.

12. Jerry Izenberg, *Sunday Star Ledger,* June 17, 1984, 28.

13. Frank Strafaci, "Forgotten Pioneer Professional," *Golfing Magazine,* March 1957, 11.

14. *The Golfer,* August 5, 1896, 109.

15. In the course of my own research for a documentary about John Shippen and the place where he spent most of his professional golfing life, the Shady Rest Country Club, I was able to meet and interview a number of people who knew him and caddied for him. I met his grandson, Hanno Shippen Smith.

16. Paul E. Sluby Sr., *The Family Recollections of Beulah A. Shippen and Mabel S.(Shippen) Hatcher* (Self-published, 1994), 43.

17. Strafaci, 12.

18. Ibid., 12.

19. This is the Open that established American golf. Francis Quimet, a 21-year-old former caddy and amateur who had never won any national championship, staged a heroic quest and defeated British professionals Harry Vardon and Ted Ray in a dramatic 18-hole playoff at the Country Club in Brookline, Massachusetts. The story of Quimet's quixotic journey is brilliantly chronicled in Mark Frost's 2002 book, *The Greatest Game Ever Played* (New York: Hyperion).

20. Lawrence Londino, "Shady Rest: Itself a Strong Ship," *Golf Journal,* Spring, 1996, 17.

21. Ron Lux, "Golf Pioneers by Necessity," *Golf Leisure,* fall 1989.

22. Richard Porter Preiss, *Mashies at Mapledale: A Black Country Club in Massachusetts during the 1920's.* Paper presented at North American Society for Sport History Convention, Vancouver, British Columbia, Canada, May 24–25, 1986, 1.

23. *Baltimore Afro-American,* July 18, 1925: 6.

24. Preiss, 7.

25. Guilford Jones, "Past Greats," *Black Sports,* July 1973, 65–66.

26. Calvin Sinnette, 99–100.

27. Arthur Ashe Jr., *A Hard Road to Glory: 1919 to 1945* (Victoria, Australia: Warner Books, 1988), 67.

28. A. S. Young, *Negro First in Sports* (Chicago: Johnson Publishing Company, 1963), 164.

29. Ibid., 166.

30. Bill Mardo, "2 Negro Golfers Sue PGA for $250,000," *Daily Worker,* January 16, 1948: Back page.

31. "Will Not Bar Negroes: P.G.A. Revises Attitude, Suit by 3 Pros Dismissed," *New York Times*, September 22, 1948, 45.

32. "P.G.A. Committee Votes to Ease Tourney Ban on Negro Players," *New York Times*, January 14, 1952, 25.

33. Young, 163.

34. "Will Not Bar Negroes," *New York Times*, November 23, 1960, 163.

35. "P.G.A. Will Shift '62 Tourney Site," *New York Times*, May 18, 1961, 45.

36. Lincoln A. Werden, "4 Men Removed after Heckling Sifford, Negro Golf Pro, in Greensboro Open," *New York Times*, April 5, 1969, 35.

37. "Elder Denies He Made Charge of Race Bias in Pensacola Golf," *New York Times*, June 6, 1969, 49.

38. "Masters Policy Change Seen As Aid to Blacks," *New York Times*, June 13, 1971, Sec V, 5.

39. Ashe, 154.

40. Ibid., 157.

Chapter 5

THE RECORD

AMATEUR CAREER

While Tiger Woods is statistically the most successful professional golfer in the shortest period of time, his amateur record—in particular his three consecutive victories in the U.S. Amateur Championship— was a definitive forecast of what was to come. Even though today the public's attention is clearly focused on the professional game, the early popularity of the game originated with amateur golf. The fabulous amateur career of Tiger Woods helped rejuvenate the public's interest in the amateur game, and in order to fully appreciate the career of Tiger Woods we should first understand something about the origins of the game, and the role amateur golf played in that history.

The U.S. Golf Association (USGA) is the preeminent governing body of golf in America. The championships conducted by them are important because they represent the national championships of the United States. Considering the lofty reputation of American golf in the world, the USGA Amateur Championship is arguably the most important amateur title to win. And while American culture values monetary accomplishment, there has always been prestige attached to people who play only for the title and a medal, not cash. Call it romantic, but there is something to be said for the golfer who is not sullied by the taint of commercialism, retains his amateur purity, and plays the game just for the joy of competition. While golf was first played in Scotland by the peasant classes, by the time it came to America, only people of means were able to embrace the game.

It was played recreationally by people who did not have to depend on golf to earn a living. By 1894 there was enough interest in the game of golf in America to justify two so-called national amateur championships. In an effort to create a governing body that would oversee one championship, Charles MacDonald, prominent businessman and amateur golfer, and who himself was runner-up in both championships, called for a meeting of the representatives from prominent existing golf clubs. The result of that meeting was the establishment of The Amateur Golf Association of the United States on December 22, 1894. Reflecting the increased number of non-amateur golfers, the name was soon changed to the U.S. Golf Association. There were five charter member clubs: Newport Golf Club, Shinnecock Hills Golf Club, The Country Club (Brookline, Massachusetts), St. Andrew's Golf Club (Yonkers, New York), and Chicago Golf Club.[1]

The first USGA Amateur Championship was held at the Newport Golf Club in Rhode Island, a nine-hole course, in October, 1895. The original date was changed because of a conflict with the America's Cup Yacht races, which gives some indication of who the competitors and interested spectators would be. It should be pointed out that the Open competition was held the same week but was merely an afterthought of the main event, which was the Amateur. Author Mark Frost explains the attitude of most Americans toward golf's national championship:

The USGA's National Amateur Championship received the lion's share of attention America paid to the sport of golf during the first decade of the twentieth century. It was the main event played by the sport's founding fathers, upper-crust captains of industry. They and their social equals who could afford the time–consuming sport still looked slightly askance at the U.S. Open as a Masonic cloister of lower-class, foreign-born professionals, gathering like an annual tradesman's guild convention. The truth was neither the press nor the public could get that worked up about a bunch of hard-faced immigrant Scotsmen wrestling amongst themselves not simply for honor, but for a negligible pile of cash.[2]

In fact there was relatively little interest in the sport at this point, since it was remote from the majority of Americans' daily lives. It was not until the 1913 U.S. Open was won by a scrappy former caddie named Francis Ouimet that the general public began to follow golf. Ouimet played the role of David to Scotland's dual Goliaths, in the persons of Harry Vardon and Ted Ray, seasoned, veteran professionals who dominated the sport. It was during this upset that the British-dominated sport finally caught the attention of the American public, who were rooting for one of their own.

If Francis Ouimet put the sport of golf on the map in America, it was an unassuming young man from Atlanta, Georgia, Robert "Bobby" Tyre Jones Jr., who kept it there. While there are many parallels between the junior and amateur careers of Jones and Tiger Woods, their family and social backgrounds are worlds apart. Jones was born March 17, 1902, but his father, Col. Robert Purmedus Jones, was a prominent Atlanta lawyer. As distinctly different as their backgrounds are, there are some interesting similarities between the relationships of the fathers and sons. Both fathers were accomplished baseball players and considered careers in professional baseball. Bobby Jones's grandfather, Robert Tyre Jones, threatened to disown Robert P. Jones if he signed a minor league baseball contract; just as Earl did, Jones stayed on and graduated college instead.[3] Both fathers had close relationships with their sons, functioning both as friends and mentors. While Robert P. Jones was a colonel in nickname only, Earl actually attained the rank of lieutenant colonel.

The Jones family spent summers across the street from the Atlanta Country Club's East Lake Golf Course; the young Jones learned to play golf copying the swing of East Lake's professional, Stewart Maiden, who had emigrated to America at the turn of the century.[4] By the age of six Jones won the East Lake Children's Tournament. He graduated from Georgia Institute of Technology with a mechanical engineering major, then from Harvard with a graduate degree in English, and after only one year at Emory University Law School, he passed the Georgia State Bar and joined his father's law firm.

Over the seven-year period between 1923 and 1930, Jones competed in 52 tournaments and won 23 of them, culminating in what
was then referred to as the Grand Slam. In 1930, as an amateur, Jones
won the U.S. Amateur, the British Amateur, the U.S. Open, and the
British Open Championships. At the time, these were the most prestigious golf championships, referred to as the majors. Over the course
of his career, he would win 12 major championships, second only to
Jack Nicklaus, who won 20 majors during his career. It was this record
of Nicklaus's that first inspired Tiger Woods as a child. The modern
Grand Slam consists of the U.S. Open, the British Open, the American PGA Championship, and the Masters.[5] Amateurs can compete in
all of the majors except for the PGA Championship, and they are all
contested under a stroke (or medal[6]) play format.

There are two principal types of competition in the game of golf:
match play and medal play. The former is played by comparing the
score of each player after each hole—the lower score wins the hole.
The winner is the player who wins the most holes in an 18-hole match.
When one player is ahead (or "up") by more holes than there are remaining to play, that person is declared the winner, for example three
holes up with two holes to play, or three and two. If a player is up
as many holes as there are holes remaining, the player is said to be
"dormie."[7] Throughout the early history of the game, match play was
the most popular method of scoring, both in competition and in social
matches. Today, virtually all professional competitions are played as
medal, or stroke play, events.

There are some different rules applying to match play that do not
apply to medal play competition. For example, the score in match play
is only kept for the individual holes, not for the entire 18 holes. So
in match play a player may shoot a significantly lower score than his
opponent for 18 holes and still be defeated. A good analogy is the elec-
toral college for the American presidential elections. It is possible, as
was the case in the 2000 election, for a candidate to have a smaller
popular vote across the country and still be elected president, as long as
he wins the most populous states.

It was the advent of televised golf that changed the format of professional tournaments. While the head-to-head competition of match play
truly tests the skill of one golfer against another, medal play assures that

most of the players will be playing for the full four days of a professional tournament. This guarantees the commercial sponsors of tournaments a sufficient number of so-called marquee players on Sunday afternoon, and usually higher television ratings. It is regularly demonstrated, for example, that when Tiger Woods is competing in a tournament, the television ratings for that tournament will increase significantly. If these tournaments were match play and Tiger was eliminated, the ratings would drop and the sponsor would have to be compensated. It was the monumental appeal and charisma of Arnold Palmer, who gained popularity just as televised golf was evolving in the late 1950s, that sounded the death knell for match play in major championship golf. The U.S. Amateur remains one of the few televised championships to be contested using the match play format.

Anyone with a handicap index of 2.4 or below is eligible to apply for the Amateur competition. Golf handicaps are determined by taking the 10 best scores of a player's most recent 20 scores and, based on a mathematical formula, assigning a handicap index. It allows players of widely different abilities to compete fairly against each other. There are regional qualifying sites for the Amateur throughout the country. A certain number of players from each of the regional qualifiers advance to the medal play competition of the Amateur. Those players play a two-day, 36-hole medal play competition, and the lowest 64 players advance to the match play rounds. The players are seeded according to their medal play score, so the lowest score plays the highest score, and the second-lowest score plays the second-highest score. To become the Amateur Champions, players must qualify for the match play rounds and then win six matches.

By virtue of winning the USGA Junior Championship, Tiger qualified for the 1992 and 1993 USGA Amateur Championships. He managed to make the 64-player field through medal play both years but was eliminated in the first and second rounds of match play respectively. While he did not advance very far in either of these tournaments, he did gain experience that would be valuable in his subsequent attempts for the title.

Tiger had to qualify for the 1994 Amateur like any other golfer. The site he was assigned was in California, and circumstances had him and his father in Chicago the day before the qualifier. Earl and Tiger were late getting to the airport and missed the flight. They were put on a standby list for the next flight, which was oversold. They were mistakenly given tickets that should have gone to a couple with the same last name, and when Tiger and his father politely gave up the seats, even though it meant it would be virtually impossible for Tiger to have a chance to qualify for the Amateur, the airline personnel were so impressed with their attitude that they moved them to the top of the standby list. They eventually got on a plane and Tiger was able to make the qualifier—which he did as the medalist (low qualifier), after very little sleep.[8]

1994 AMATEUR

The 1994 Amateur was played at Tournament Players Club (TPC) at Sawgrass, in Jacksonville, Florida. This golf course is one of a number of courses designed and run by the professional golfing community. The Professional Golfers Association of America is the governing body of all professional golfers in the United States. When it was established in 1916, both touring professionals and club professionals belonged to the PGA. But by the late 1960s it was becoming increasingly apparent that the needs of the touring pros and the club pros were often at cross purposes. Consequently, in 1968 the Tournament Players Division split off from the PGA and became the Tournament Players Tour, a sister organization that is made up exclusively of touring professionals. The TPC courses are owned and run by the Tournament Players Tour, and they are characterized as being fan-friendly (with plenty of vantage points from which spectators can view tournament golf), and as being the ultimate test for the highest caliber of golfer. The 17th hole at TPC Sawgrass is the signature hole that represents the challenge of all TPC courses. A short par three (up to 156 yards, depending on where the hole is placed), the hole requires players to shoot to a green completely surrounded by water. The relatively small target, coupled with the ever-changing Florida winds, make this hole one of the most entertaining on the PGA Tour. This was the venue that Tiger would face as he attempted to win his first U.S. Amateur.

Tiger's first opponent in the matches was Vaughn Moise, a 46-year-old rules official, whom he defeated easily two and one. He then met

Michael Flynn and had little trouble defeating him six and five. Tiger's next opponent in the round of 16 provided the closest match so far in the tournament. His opponent, Buddy Alexander, was an older player and a coach of the University of Florida golf team. Alexander was three up after 12 holes, and considering his experience and the psychological advantage he had over Tiger, there was every reason to believe that Tiger could lose. However, the mental training that Earl had drilled into Tiger as a boy allowed Tiger to overcome all disadvantages. Alexander had a short three-foot putt to go "dormie" on the 14th, but the putt lipped out of the hole. By this time a large crowd of clearly partisan Gator fans were following the match, and the press scrutiny of this young African American's career was increasing every time he played. Even though consideration of his race had been largely accepted by the public, this was still about an hour and a half from the university campus in Gainesville, Florida. A man in the crowd was overheard saying, "Who do you think these people are rooting for, the nigger or the Gator coach?"[9]

They arrived at the famous 17th hole all square. Rather than playing for the safe portion of the green, as most players, including Alexander, had done, Tiger hit his nine iron into the breeze right at the hole. The ball hovered over the water before settling on the fringe of the green, within three feet of the bulkhead guarding the water hazard. Alexander three-putted from twenty-eight feet, and Tiger chipped to within two feet and sank the putt to win the hole. Both players double-bogeyed the final hole and Tiger won the match one up.

The quarter-final and semifinal matches were relatively easy for Tiger. In the quarter-final his opponent was Tim Jackson from Tennessee, and in the semifinal, Tim Frishette of Ohio. Tiger defeated them both five and four. Between these two matches, Tiger, uncertain about the consistency of his driving, contacted his coach, Butch Harmon, who was able to give him advice over the phone to solve the problem.

In his first U.S. Amateur final match, Tiger faced Trip Kuehne. Tiger and Earl were friends of the Kuehne family, and Tiger was good friends with Trip's younger sister Kelli (who was to become a standout college golfer, and later LPGA touring professional). Trip's younger brother Hank Kuehne also became a professional golfer, and at one time he was one of the longest drivers on the PGA Tour. Tiger was down by six holes after the morning 18-hole round, and five down with 12 holes remaining. He managed to get the match all square after 16 holes. On the 17th hole (the 35th of the match) Tiger hit a soft wedge shot to the 138-yard par three hole. It stopped eight inches from a bulkhead guarding the water. He holed a 14-foot putt and was one up going to the final hole. Tiger won the 18th and became the youngest winner in the history of the Amateur.

His victory generated significant national attention. Tiger received letters from then-president Bill Clinton, Gary Player, Jesse Jackson, and entertainer Sinbad. Jay Leno and David Letterman wanted him to appear on their programs; he declined. He also received a congratulatory letter from Phil Knight, president of Nike—who apparently did not mind the fact that Tiger wore Reebok golf shoes during the Amateur final.

1995 AMATEUR

The year 1995 marked the 100th anniversary of the U.S. Golf Association, and in tribute the U.S. Amateur was staged at the Newport Golf Club in Rhode Island, one of the charter members of the organization, and the site of the first Amateur. Only eight players had won the Amateur two years in a row, and Jack Nicklaus was not one of them. This fact was extra motivation for the defending Amateur champion. For Tiger, this tournament represented another goal: the opportunity to win five consecutive USGA championships in a row—only Bobby Jones had won more.

After a good opening round of 68, which could have been lower if he had putted better, followed by a second round of 75, Tiger nearly didn't make the 64-player field to continue in the match play competition. Of the next five matches, Tiger had trouble only in the semifinal, when he played Mark Plummer. The competition in the Amateur is a mixture of well-coached college players, former college players, occasional former professionals who have regained their amateur status, and some golfers who were pretty much self-taught and schooled on less-than-glamorous golf courses. Plummer, a 43-year-old with a swing that NBC commentator Johnny Miller said "only a mother could love,"[10] had failed to gain a PGA card and regained his amateur status. But

Amateur Golf Champion Tiger Woods of Cypress, California, holds his trophy on August 27, 1995, at the Newport Country Club in Newport, Rhode Island. Woods defeated George Marucci to win the championship two years in a row. (AP Photo/ Matt York.)

despite Plummer's uncanny ability to get up and down from any place on the golf course, and eight one-putt greens, Tiger won this semifinal match two up on the 18th hole.

George "Buddy" Martucci was Tiger's opponent in the final match. Martucci was a 43-year-old Mercedes-Benz dealer and member of Pine Valley, Merion, and Seminole, three of the most exclusive American country clubs. He was an experienced match play player, and not likely to be intimidated by Tiger's reputation. Tiger was two down when they broke for lunch after the morning 18. By the 26th hole Tiger was leading, but Martucci evened the match at the 29th hole. Woods was one up going into the 36th and final hole. Martucci hit his approach shot about 20 feet from the hole. With the pressure squarely on the young Tiger, he hit a shot that significantly contributed to his growing legend. The previous spring, Tiger had been criticized by the press for his modest performance at the Masters. While he impressed everyone with his prodigious drives, the general consensus was that he was unable to control the distance of his approach shots—that he lacked finesse. Partially in response to the criticism, but mostly because of his obsessive desire to improve his game, he had practiced many hours to develop more control over how far he hit his iron shots. This 140-yard shot, to an elevated green, was exactly the kind of shot he had been practicing. Now it was time to hit under excruciating pressure. He did. The ball came off his eight iron club and floated on the breeze, traveling exactly 18 inches farther than he calculated, and directly at the hole. Martucci conceded the putt, and the match was over.[11]

1996 AMATEUR

In the history of the Amateur nobody had ever won the championship three consecutive times. Bobby Jones had won the tournament five times during his career, but never three times in a row. So the stakes were already established as Tiger prepared once again to make history at the Ghost Creek Course at Pumpkin Ridge, Oregon, site of the 1996 U.S. Amateur.

This would be the first Amateur that Tiger's mother would see him win. Because of the anticipated crowds, tournament officials allowed Kultida to go inside the ropes, which made it possible for her to watch her son compete. Throughout his amateur career, Tiger and his parents had maintained fairly good relations with the USGA. As early as the 1896 Open, when USGA president Theodore Havemeyer insisted that an African American player should be allowed to compete, the organization had championed the rights of minorities in golf. During Tiger's junior career, the USGA had also loosened some restrictions on travel expenses, allowing for a child and a parent to travel to junior competitions and still retain amateur status. However, some critics of the Woods family complained that these changes were done specifically to allow Tiger to compete in more tournaments. The USGA denied this.

Earlier, Earl had been peeved when he'd had to pay $300 extra to change the dates for airline tickets he had purchased, because the scheduled starting date for the Amateur was changed, and neither he nor Tiger had taken notice. As it turned out, this would be the last time Earl or Tiger would worry about the price of airline tickets, or any other expenses, for that matter.[12] This would be Tiger's last amateur competition.

There were 311 golfers trying to qualify for the 64 match play slots. Tiger shot 69, 67, and was the medalist. As if there was not already a considerable amount of pressure, only once in the previous 55 years had the medalist gone on to win the Amateur championship (Phil Mickelson accomplished the feat in 1990).

It has been well documented that Tiger Woods had a diet similar to most young men of his age, and fruits and vegetables did not make up a substantial percentage of his calories. In Oregon, he would make a nightly stop at the local McDonald's on the way back to his hotel. Aware of his celebrity presence, the staff put up a picture of Tiger and began to list his daily intake of Big Macs and Egg McMuffins for the entire McDonald's clientele to peruse.[13]

Tiger faced J. D. Manning in his first match. Manning was a senior at Colorado State University. Tiger was in control of the match throughout, but undoubtedly the highlight was a shot he fashioned on the eighth hole. Tiger's ball was on the fringe of the green right up against the collar, making it virtually impossible to get the face of the putter on the ball. Indicative of his ability to create shots as the need arose, he took a pitching wedge, a very lofted club, struck the ball with the sole of the club in the center of the ball, and holed out the shot. Tiger went on to win three and two.

Tiger's next match was with Jerry Courville, the reigning Mid-Am Champion[14] from Milford, Connecticut. A 37-year-old coordinator for Pitney Bowes, Courville had accumulated an impressive number of amateur golf titles, both in Metropolitan Golf Association (MGA) and USGA competitions. As with many of Tiger's previous opponents, Courville's vast tournament experience should have put Tiger at a distinct disadvantage; however, Woods birdied six of the final nine holes to defeat Courville four and three.

The next match featured Tiger against 14-year-old Charles Howell, the first opponent who was younger than Woods. In his short career Howell had demonstrated considerable promise, prompting Earl Woods to comment that he, if anybody, could match Tiger's Junior Amateur record. His age and sense of humor were reflected in response to a question on his Amateur application. Howell wrote that he had a superstition about walking under moving cars.[15] At the conclusion of the match, which Tiger won three and one, Howell said that he didn't lose ten and eight (the maximum margin of defeat possible in an 18-hole match), so he considered it a good day. Charles Howell would never win the Amateur, but he has gone on to play professional golf and to date has won three tournaments on the PGA Tour.

In the quarter-final match, D. A. Points, a sophomore at Louisiana State University, was Tiger's competition. On the 12th hole, a par three with the hole cut dangerously close to a pond adjacent to the green, Points played the prescribed shot that dictated he hit his ball to the fat portion of the green, away from the trouble. Tiger aimed and hit his shot at the hole, and it wound up leaving him a six-foot putt, which he made to go three up in the match. He eventually won three and two. This win set up a semifinal match between Tiger and his Stanford teammate and friend Joel Kribel.

Kribel was certainly not awed by Tiger. Kribel had been playing well during the summer and had won two of the most prestigious amateur tournaments, the Western Amateur and the Pacific Northwest Amateur. He and Tiger competed on the same college team and had roomed together when the Cardinal team traveled to matches. Despite their close off-course relationship, Tiger virtually ignored his opponent, an indication of his unique ability to concentrate on the matter at hand. In reviewing comments by his teammates at Stanford, there is clearly a sense that they were uncomfortable with this side of Tiger's personality, but they all agree that it is the reason he was able to win so consistently.

At first Kribel showed no signs that Tiger's concentration was bothering him. He birdied the first hole and went two up through 10 holes. However, he was unable to persevere. The combination of outstanding play by Tiger—he didn't bogie a hole, in fact he went 116 holes without a bogey during the tournament—and less than stellar play from Kribel, meant that Tiger was able to take control of the match. The only birdie Kribel scored, on the 14th hole, was countered by an eagle from Tiger. Woods defeated his teammate three and one, to set up the historic final for the Amateur Championship.

Up to this time, the final of the U.S. Amateur generally was not considered a marquee event on television. In 1981, the late Bing Crosby's son Nathaniel won the Amateur final defeating Brian Undley, and this attracted some national television attention. Normally, the event was carried for the hardcore golf fans and was usually part of a package that helped ensure a network's bid to the USGA to obtain the rights to carry the more ratings-friendly U.S. Open Tournament. Tiger's opponent, Steve Scott, was a 19-year-old college sophomore from the University of Florida who suddenly found himself in the middle of a national spectacle. And to add contrast to the match, Scott's girlfriend, Kristi Hommel, caddied for him. So on one side there was Team Tiger with Butch Harmon working with Tiger on the practice tee, and on the other Scott's girlfriend massaging his neck between shots. There were a considerable number of people pulling for the couple—against great odds.

But Scott's David was up to the challenges of Tiger's Goliath. The challenger was five holes up after the morning eighteen. Scott continued to put on the pressure with some miraculous shots to win and halve holes. It came down to the 17th hole with Tiger one down. He was feet from the hole and, despite the immense pressure, rolled the putt in to tie the match. On the 18th hole, both players made pars, so the match went into a playoff. After matching pars on the 37th hole, Scott stumbled and missed a six-foot putt to bogey and Tiger stroked in a short par putt to win.

Beyond the interest in Tiger's record-setting performance, the story that got more attention was whether this would be Tiger's last amateur competition. At this time there were rumors that he was planning to leave college and turn professional after the Amateur. But before considering the implications of that transition, it is necessary to examine the circumstances surrounding the college recruiting process and the impact of Tiger's two years at Stanford University.

COLLEGE GOLF

Tiger Woods had good grades in high school; he could have gone to college pretty much anywhere he wanted. In addition to his solid academic record and golfing prowess, he was a member of the National Honor Society. He was recruited by a number of colleges, but it ultimately came down to University of Nevada-Las Vegas and Stanford. Stanford's golf coach Wally Goodwin had contacted Tiger before he was in high school to tell him about the golf program at Stanford. In addition to a reputation for excellence in Division I athletics, Stanford ranks in the top echelon of America's competitive academic universities. It annually ranks among the top institutions for graduation rates of athletes.[16] These factors were all important, not only to Tiger and Earl, but also to Kultida, who was adamant that Tiger get a college degree, and she influenced his decision in his senior year at Western High School to select Stanford.

Having won the U.S. Amateur before college, Tiger was already a celebrity before entering Stanford, but the university was not at a loss for highly talented students. In his class were actor Fred Savage, who starred in the long-running television series *The Wonder Years*, and Olympic gymnast Dominique Dawes.[17] His team was not without some talented golfers as well. Two of his teammates, Casey Martin and Notah Begay, have gone on to significant careers, and both have garnered their own degree of celebrity.

Martin was an upperclassman when Tiger came to Stanford. Winner of 17 junior titles in Oregon, Martin suffered from Klippel-Trenaunay-Weber Syndrome, a rare circulatory disease that made it difficult for him to walk. After graduating from Stanford, Martin pursued a career in professional golf. However, due to tournament rules against riding in a golf cart during competition, he couldn't compete in PGA or USGA tournaments. Martin challenged the rules and the case went ultimately to the U.S. Supreme Court. The high court ruled seven to two in his favor in 2001.[18] Martin was granted an injunction and was allowed to use a cart on the PGA Tour, and he has otherwise been successful on the Nationwide Tour, made up of a series of smaller tournaments for players who have not earned PGA Tour playing privileges.

Notah Begay, the most successful Native American golfer, with four PGA Tour victories, is half Navajo, one-quarter San Felipe, and one-quarter Isleta. After a successful start on the PGA Tour, Begay was arrested in January 2000 and pled guilty to charges of driving while intoxicated. He subsequently talked openly about his problems with alcohol and how he dealt with them. He is currently on medical exemption from the Tour because of chronic back problems.[19]

Despite an unprecedented buildup to his arrival at Stanford, Tiger functioned as any freshman would. He was regularly relegated to the back of the line by the upperclassmen on the golf team. When they traveled on road trips he would inevitably be assigned the rollaway bed in the hotel. Tiger pledged for Sigma Chi fraternity and participated in the normal schedule of parties. One of his fraternity brothers was quoted as saying, "Tiger Woods is probably the greatest golfer of all time, but he is probably the worst dancer."[20] He more or less blended in with the student population and was able to gain a certain amount of anonymity at Stanford. Freshmen at the university are assigned roommates at random, and it happened that Tiger's roommate knew nothing about golf. He once told Tiger he had a phone call from somebody with a funny accent. It turned out to be Australian Greg Norman calling to arrange for a practice round at Augusta National.[21]

From the beginning, Tiger showed that he would not be intimidated by collegiate competition. He won the first college tournament he entered (it actually took place a week before the fall term started), the William Tucker Invitational. He placed fifth in the NCAA Championships, and he was named Stanford Male Freshman of the Year. He was selected as a preseason First Team, All-American by *Golfweek* magazine and then was named to their First Team, All-American (at the end of the season).[22] Probably the most satisfying victory in Tiger's collegiate career occurred at the Jerry Pate Invitational tournament, at the Shoal Creek in Alabama.

The club had been at the center of the controversy described earlier when, on the eve of the 1990 PGA Championship at the club, Hall Thompson, the club's president, stated that there were no black members in Shoal Creek, and there would not be. Tiger was only 15 at the time, and was not fully aware of the controversy. However, even as a college freshman, he understood completely the opportunity he had to score a symbolic victory for racial tolerance. Ironically, an African American group threatened to protest Tiger's participation, claiming that he should not play at this club that had only allowed an honorary black member in order to host the PGA tournament in 1990. Tiger did compete, and in a growing body of evidence that he was able to completely filter out outside distractions when he was on a golf course, he shot 67 and won the tournament by two strokes.[23]

Only Jack Nicklaus and Phil Mickelson had ever won both the U.S. Amateur and the NCAA Championships—Mickelson in the same year—so this goal was clearly in Tiger's sights. However, due to some illnesses and injuries earlier in the spring of 1995, Tiger had not practiced with the usual intensity, and his game was not its sharpest. In the NCAA Championships he shot four respectable rounds but finished fifth. Assuming that he stayed in school for four years, he would have three more opportunities to join Nicklaus and Mickelson as Amateur-NCAA winners.

His second year confirmed that he was the dominant amateur player in America. The big college tournaments were the Pac 10 Championships, the NCAA Regionals, and the NCAA Championships. All three were to be played at courses that Tiger had played on and become familiar with.[24]

It was at the Pac 10 Championships where Tiger had one of his finest days on a golf course. In the morning 18-hole round he broke the course and Pac 10 records, and he equaled the NCAA record when he shot 61. After a 15-minute rest in the 90-degree heat, he went out and shot 65. He won the individual title by 14 strokes, and Stanford placed eighth. But the culmination of his college career was to be the NCAA Championships held at the Honors Course at Ooltewah, Tennessee. Tiger trailed by one stroke after shooting 69 in the first round, when Pat Perez of Arizona State University broke the course record with a score of 68. By the end of the day, that record was shattered when Tiger shot 67, giving him a five-shot lead. A third round of 69 gave him a nine-shot lead, and even though he faltered and shot 80 on the last day, he won the individual title by four strokes.

In addition to being selected to every All-American college golf team, Tiger won the Jack Nicklaus Award for the top male collegiate Golfer of the Year and the Fred Haskins Award, and was named Pac 10 Golfer of the Year.

But his experiences at Stanford were not all positive. One night when returning from a campus party he was mugged by a man with a knife. The assailant took his watch and a gold chain and struck him with the handle of the knife. He was not hurt, but the fact that the perpetrator used Tiger's name during the assault was unsettling to both Tiger and Earl.[25] And he continued to get letters that could only be called hate mail. One anonymous letter read, "You can take the nigger out of the jungle, but you can't take the jungle out of the nigger."[26] This kind of letter seemed to indicate that despite the general acceptance of

African American athletes in most other sports, there was something different about golf.

Tiger and Earl also continued to have problems with the governing body of intercollegiate athletics, the NCAA, and by default the Stanford athletic administration. As indicated earlier, two years before Tiger attended Stanford he had had a run-in with the NCAA when Tiger was offered an honorary membership in the Big Canyon Golf Club. The NCAA first said that he couldn't accept, and then they relented. Another incident that further defined the relationship between the Woods family and the NCAA involved a controversy over Tiger's having dinner with Arnold Palmer. Tiger had the opportunity to meet Palmer when he won his first Junior Amateur Championship in 1991 at Palmer's Bay Hill course in Florida. They had communicated by mail and phone over the years, and when Palmer was scheduled to participate in a senior tournament in California, Tiger contacted him to see if they could meet to talk. Tiger sought advice about the ever-increasing speculation that Tiger would some day assume Palmer's unofficial role of ambassador of golf. Arrangements were made for Tiger to drive to Napa Valley to have dinner with Mr. Palmer. They met at a restaurant, ate dinner, and had a most valuable exchange of information about Palmer's career and its parallels to Tiger's. When the bill came, Palmer picked up the check, despite Tiger's offer to pay for his portion of the bill.

Tiger was shocked when someone showed him a newspaper with a headline indicating that the dinner was apparently a potential violation of NCAA rules. Wally Goodwin, Tiger's coach, immediately suspended him pending a reply from the NCAA. Both Earl and Kultida were surprised and angered. They wondered why the coach did not attempt to find out more about the circumstances that led to the dinner and Palmer's largesse. The situation was exacerbated by the fact that Tiger's parents could not talk directly with the NCAA, whose rules required them to deal with a compliance officer at Stanford, who could tell them nothing. In frustration, Kultida finally contacted some members of the press to explain what had happened. It is difficult to determine exactly why, but eventually the NCAA determined that since Tiger had known Palmer as a friend before the dinner, he would not be suspended. Earl wondered why these facts could not have been gathered before Tiger was suspended from the team.[27]

Throughout his junior career, Tiger had regularly staged instructional clinics, coordinated by Earl, and generally in areas where there were few opportunities for kids to have access to golfing facilities or instruction. When Tiger came under the sanctions of the NCAA, he was prohibited from individually conducting clinics farther than 30 miles from Stanford. Earl Woods sarcastically notes in his book that these rules were probably formulated when the farthest one could travel in a day was by horse and buggy.[28] The rules, however, did allow for individual institutions to sponsor clinics anywhere, so Tiger did a number of clinics with the Stanford golf team. During the 1995 Masters Tournament, Tiger had written a series of diary entries published in the *Golf Week* and *Golf World* magazines recounting his experiences as an amateur at the Masters. Even though he was not paid for the writing, he was suspended by Stanford for one day.

While Tiger was at Stanford, Earl began writing his first book, *Training a Tiger*, and he tried to contact both the NCAA and the USGA to find out what Tiger could do in connection with the publication and promotion of the book. According to Earl, the USGA informed them that in order for Tiger to retain his amateur status, he could not appear on the cover of the book or make promotional appearances, but he was allowed to pose for instructional photographs and to write the book's foreword. The NCAA, through Stanford's compliance officer—since technically Earl could not communicate directly with the NCAA—said pretty much the same as the USGA, but Earl's perception of their abuse of power drove Tiger closer and closer to his decision to turn professional.

Tiger's parents were not the first to question the almost dictatorial power of the NCAA, which made member institutions afraid of even the threat of a sanction. Since his problems with the NCAA, the organization has instituted a series of reforms to try to grant more local control to the member institutions. However, an inextricable bond has been forged between intercollegiate athletics and commerce, and mere adjustments in the system have not significantly alleviated the problem. Given the immense financial benefits reaped by academic institutions from intercollegiate athletics, there is little incentive to change the system. The time has come to deal honestly with student-athletes as part of the public relations/development arm of academic institutions. Just as accommodations are made for special students (e.g., older students returning to school, students with learning disabilities, handicapped students), athletes should be granted similar accommodations. They should have classes only when they are not in season, and they should be paid enough to eliminate the attraction of unauthorized cash and amenities.

But to be fair, Tiger Woods presented a unique situation for amateur athletics in general. Never before had there been such interest and commercial potential anticipated for an amateur athlete. So while Earl's frustrations are understandable, both organizations defining amateur status were operating in uncharted waters. And the fact that Earl had been contracted by the International Management Group early in Tiger's career to scout junior golf prospects didn't help the situation. Regardless of the right and wrong on both sides, for the purposes of the fate of Tiger Woods's amateur career, the damage had already been done.

THE PROFESSIONAL

It was apparent by the summer of 1996 that Tiger Woods was ready to play professional golf. Even though he had not yet contended in any of the professional tournaments he played as an amateur, he was physically mature and, at least as far as golf was concerned, emotionally ready to compete on a higher level. But both Tiger's parents were adamantly committed to his finishing college, since both their families recognized the value of education. Butch Harmon, his coach, was against Tiger turning pro at this time. Harmon told him he should have fun in college; the opportunity was once in a lifetime. And Tiger enjoyed his years at Stanford. He enjoyed the camaraderie of his teammates and was fully engaged in both his academic studies and the social life of a college campus. He had spoken to many of his teammates throughout the year about the possibility of turning pro, but he would never disclose his future plans. It is difficult to say whether he would have stayed in college and graduated had he not encountered so many problems with the guidelines of the NCAA, and to a lesser extent the USGA.

Tiger's mother and father made him promise that if he left Stanford he would finish college at some time in the future. Jack Nicklaus never went back to finish his degree at Ohio State University when he left to become a golf professional, and since Tiger was constantly comparing himself to Nicklaus, this fact undoubtedly influenced his ultimate decision to leave college early. Nicklaus had declared Tiger to be the "next Nicklaus." However, some speculated that Nicklaus made the pronouncement to exert pressure that might prohibit his prophesy. After all, Tiger was not the first "next" Nicklaus. There had been many promising young golfers who never lived up to the hype—Tom Weiskopf and Andy Bean among them.

Tiger's performance at the 1996 British Open demonstrated that he was ready to make the transition. He shot 75 the first day of the Open, and afterwards, Jack Nicklaus gave him a stern talking-to that impressed Tiger. Nicklaus told him that he had to put the same intense concentration on the first day of a tournament as the last. Tournaments are not won on the first day, but they are lost.[29]

In retrospect, Tiger's decision to become a professional seems like a foregone conclusion. However, in the 17 professional tournaments he competed in as an amateur, he only made seven cuts. So there was still a question as to whether he would make the transition successfully. There was no such doubt among potential agents and corporate sponsors. Early in Tiger's junior career, International Management Group had exhibited interest in Tiger as a client. During that time, Earl Woods was hired by IMG to serve as a scout for potential talent in the junior golf ranks. A cynic might see this arrangement as an early guarantee that Tiger would sign with the company as his representative. Hughes Norton was one of the principals at IMG and early on he had befriended Earl.[30]

Immediately following his victory at the 1996 Amateur, rumors began to circulate that Tiger would turn professional. While Tiger wanted to make a formal announcement at a press conference at the Brown Deer Park Golf course, site of the Milwaukee Open, where he was scheduled to play as an amateur in the Wednesday Pro-Am, a secret like this inevitably would be leaked, and it was. So on the Tuesday before the start of the tournament Tiger was forced to issue a press release with the following statement: "This is to confirm that, as of now, I am a professional golfer. I will not answer any questions, or have any further comment until tomorrow at 2:30 P.M. at my scheduled press conference. I would appreciate the media respecting my wishes to practice without distractions today. I will be available to answer your questions tomorrow."[31]

There were, of course, many corporations that were interested in snagging Tiger Woods to endorse their products. Speculations about the size of potential deals were in the $5-million-a-year-for-five-years category. The final major deal was with Nike for $40 million for five years, including a $7.5 million signing bonus. Phil Knight, the CEO of Nike, was questioned about the prospects of spending that much money on a golfer who had never teed up a ball as a professional, but he said that the preprofessional promotion had been so overwhelming that it was not such a gamble.

A deal was also cut with Titleist, manufacturer of golf balls and other golf equipment. Tiger was paid $3 million to play the Titleist golf ball and other Titleist equipment (e.g., gloves, golf bag). Eventually Titleist began manufacturing golf clubs and paid Tiger additional money to use their clubs, but for the time being he was able to stay with the Mizuno irons, the clubs he had used throughout most of his amateur career.

Once again Tiger had bested Jack Nicklaus. In 1961 when Nicklaus left Ohio State to become a professional golfer he received $450,000 for five years from the MacGregor (golf equipment) Company. The deal included a $100,000 signing bonus, $100,000 in guaranteed royalties, and $50,000 a year for five years. Adjusted for 1996 monetary standards, Nicklaus's package was about $500,000 a year. Tiger's deal produced just under $9 million a year. In addition to signifying Tiger's tremendous appeal, these figures are also indicative of the tremendous increase in interest in sports (brought on largely by television) and the sport of golf in 47 years.[32] ABC golf producer Jack Graham pointed to the 5.3 overnight rating garnered at Tiger's dramatic win at the Amateur, against a rival network's golf telecast featuring PGA stars Greg Norman and Phil Mickelson.[33] These deals made Tiger among the highest-paid professional athletes. Michael Jordan remained the highest-paid athlete, at about $40 million for 1996, while Tiger (before the Titleist deal) was ranked 25th. An indication of the rapid transition from amateur to wealthy professional is demonstrated in an incident described by Butch Harmon, who had to lend Tiger the money to

pay the entry fee to the Milwaukee Open because he hadn't yet opened
a checking account.[34] Another time Harmon and Tiger went out to
buy some clothes at a mall. When the salesperson rang up the total
Tiger handed her a credit card. It didn't go through, so he handed her
another credit card, and it didn't go through. Harmon asked him if he
had activated the cards, and Tiger asked, "What's that?"[35]

The much-anticipated press conference in Milwaukee had to be
moved to a larger venue as the requests for media credentials had
doubled from the previous year. There were representatives from *Time*,
People magazine, and television's *Extra*. Tiger read from a statement:

> Several weeks ago I spoke with some very special people, my par-
> ents, and told them after a frustrating and painful process, I was
> struggling with the decision to become a professional golfer. Then
> I spoke with a few very close friends, whose advice and counsel
> I trust and respect, and told them of my thoughts. The reaction
> of both my parents and friends were similar...they asked seri-
> ous questions, offered their views, then, after heated debate, es-
> pecially by my dad, told me they would fully support any decision
> I made.[36]

After Tiger's press conference Earl stayed and talked to the press,
who were understandably anxious to get some quotes. Unfortunately,
Earl was obliging. He stated that there was no comparison between
Tiger and Muhammad Ali or Arthur Ashe since Tiger would have an
impact beyond sports. He boasted that if Tiger was not playing golf
he would be a premier 400-meter runner, who would beat the then
current Olympic champion (Michael Johnson, whom Earl referred to
as Michael Jackson). Finally, in describing Tiger's killer instinct, he
drew an analogy between Tiger and a Western black gunslinger.[37] Putting aside a father's obvious pride in his son's accomplishments, Earl's
quotes made it no easier for Tiger, who was already facing some resistance from his fellow professionals.

The reception for Tiger Woods as a newcomer by his fellow professionals was, at best, mixed. Generally the established stars accepted
him and recognized that his presence would reinvigorate the public's
interest in the game and eventually lead to higher television ratings

and more prize money. However, there were less-recognizable names who resented the fact that all this money was going to a player who had yet to pay any dues to the tour.

Not all the press was buying the supposed impromptu coming out of Tiger Woods on August 27, 1996. Writer John Feinstein questioned the spontaneity of Woods's opening line at the press conference in Milwaukee—"Well, I guess it's, hello world." Less than 48 hours later the line was part of a sophisticated ad campaign featuring Tiger, already filmed, using the line as a theme.[38] The subsequent ad campaign featured a three-page ad in *The Wall Street Journal* that pictured Tiger and the copy:

> I shot in the 70s when I was 8. I shot in the 60s when I was 12. I won the U.S. Junior Amateur when I was 14. I played in the Nissan Los Angeles Open when I was 16. I won the U.S. Amateur when I was 19. I am the only man to win three consecutive U.S. Amateur titles. There are still golf courses in the United States that I cannot play because of the color of my skin. I'm told I'm not ready for you. Are you ready for me?[39]

Woods shot a 67 in the first round at Milwaukee and 69 the second round. That put him eight shots behind the leaders. This was the beginning of Tiger's initiation into the world of the professional ranks. By the third round, the events of the previous week finally caught up with him. He was clearly exhausted and shot a 73, putting him out of contention. During the third round, he gave a preview of the impact he would have on the PGA Tour when he made a hole-in-one from 202 yards. He went on to shoot 68 and finished tied for 60th, earning $2,544. Tiger was pleased with his first attempt at professional golf. Despite the fact that he had just signed a $40 million endorsement deal, Tiger treasured this first check as the only money he had earned completely on his own.

There are several ways for a golfer to qualify to compete full-time on the PGA Tour. While it was a virtual certainty that eventually Tiger Woods would qualify for the PGA Tour, the question was how he would do it and how quickly. As has been stated, the PGA Tour is a relatively recent phenomenon. It was not until Walter Hagen quit his job as head professional at Oakland Hills Golf Club following his victory in the 1919 U.S. Open that anyone could conceive of making a living playing tournament golf.[40] In fact Hagen made the most money playing exhibition matches throughout the world. The tour in Hagen's day consisted of a schedule of local and regional tournaments for small prize money. There was very little corporate sponsorship, and there was no television to generate mass interest in the sport. Most professional golfers of the period maintained some connection to a golf club for their main livelihood. For the really accomplished players, their responsibilities to the home club were minimal, because if they won, it brought publicity to their home course. The less talented players had to serve as club professionals, giving lessons to the members, running club tournaments, and selling golf equipment. So in the early days on the Tour anybody who could come up with the entrance fee could play in the tournament. That has changed dramatically. It was not until the confluence of televised golf and the arrival of Arnold Palmer in the late 1950s that most of the players on the PGA Tour could earn a living playing in professional golf tournaments exclusively.

Since there are so many golfers who want to play on the PGA Tour, a special tournament qualifier is held every year to determine who will have the right to participate. To begin with, a player must have won at least two legitimate tournaments at the local level, either through their local or regional golf association, or the PGA Section in their part of the country. That allows them to register, after paying a $2,500 registration fee, to compete in a regional qualifier from which a designated number of the players with the lowest scores advance to the Qualifying School Finals. "Q" School Finals consist of six rounds and 108 holes. First the players must survive a 72-hole cut, from which the low 90 players advance to the final 72 holes. Only the top 26 finishers and ties are fully exempted to play on the PGA Tour the following year. The players scoring from 27th place to 77th place are qualified to play on the Nationwide Tour, which is a smaller tour with less money, prestige, and television coverage. Qualifying through "Q" School only exempts a player for one year. Only the top 125 players on the PGA Money List earn an exemption for the following year. If a player does not make the Top 125 on the PGA Money List, they must go back to the Qualifying School. It is probably the most demanding selection process of any professional sport, and even if a player gains his tour card he is not guaranteed a salary.

Another way a player may participate in a PGA Tournament is by sponsors' exemptions. If a player gets enough sponsors' exemptions and is able to earn enough prize money to get into the top 125 list, he is declared eligible to compete on the tour for the year. This was the way Tiger would first try to qualify for the 1997 PGA Tour. However, he had a limited number of opportunities since there were relatively few tournaments left on the schedule. It wasn't a problem of getting sponsors' exemptions, since every tournament director was more than anxious to get Tiger to play in their tournament.

After tying for 60th place at the Milwaukee Tournament, Tiger was 334th on the PGA Money List. He would need to win about $250,000 more to gain exemption for the 1997 season.

The next event on the PGA Tour was the Canadian Open, played at the historic Glen Abbey Golf Club. Although this is the national championship of Canada, the prize money from this tournament counts toward the PGA Money List. The tournament was shortened to 54 holes because of inclement weather, but with the help of a tournament-low round of 68 on the last day, Tiger was able to finish in 11th place and collect $37,500. He was now 204 on the money list.

The Quad City Open is held annually at the Oakwood Country Club. Four cities sponsor the event (Davenport and Bettendorf, Iowa, and Rock Island and Moline, Illinois), and that was the next stop on the PGA Tour. The tournament director was beside himself that Tiger was going to compete, and despite all the preparations they wound up using magic markers on people's hands because they ran out of tickets. Before the tournament, in an interview with Forrest Sawyer on ABC's *Nightline*, John Feinstein (as he had written in a *Newsweek* article) compared Earl Woods to then-fallen tennis prodigy Jennifer Capriati's father, Stephano. He noted that Earl had not had a job since 1988, and that he was living off his son.[41] This criticism overlooked the fact that Earl Woods had retired after what could only be called a distinguished military career, and that despite Earl's propensity for hyperbole, he was certainly capable of providing for himself and his family. Despite the distraction of this negative image, the Quad City Open proved to be a significant lesson for the emerging superstar.

Tiger was leading after the third round by one stroke over Ed Fiori, a journeyman pro, who was about to achieve the greatest moment in his professional career. Tiger hooked a ball off the fourth hole, a 460-yard par four, into a pond. Rather than dropping a ball, taking the penalty, and punching out onto the fairway to try and salvage a bogey, Tiger chose to try a virtually impossible shot through a narrow opening in the trees. The ball hit a tree and wound up in a swamp. Later in the round he was on the par-four hole in two strokes, eight feet from the hole, and, unbelievably, he four-putted for a double bogey. But he didn't give up. He finished tied for fifth and won $42,150, vaulting him up to 166th on the money list. Despite all his amateur triumphs, it was obvious that Tiger had to adjust to the rigors of PGA competition, where the depth of talent in the players was formidable. Also, the field at the Quad City tournament was not particularly strong, because it was scheduled against the Presidents Cup Tournament, where most of the top PGA players competed. The young golfer learned that over 72 holes, you sometimes have to cut your losses.

Most people unfamiliar with golf would assume that the B.C. Open, the next stop on Tiger's quest to gain his tour card, was played in British Columbia. Instead, the now-defunct tournament was played in Endicott, New York, and was named in honor of the comic strip B.C., whose creator, Johnny Hart, lived in the town and was an avid supporter of the game, both in his cartoon and in real life. It too was hampered by bad weather and resulted in a 54-hole winner, Fred Funk, who finished three strokes ahead of Tiger, who came in third. When asked what Tiger needed to be successful on the PGA Tour, Funk responded, "A good accountant."[42] The third place finish added $58,000 to his earnings and put him at 128th on the money list, virtually assuring that Tiger would be able to compete on the tour in 1997.

He withdrew from the next week's tournament, the Buick Open, which caused a considerable furor. This incident demonstrated that more would be expected of Tiger Woods than to play golf, and this will be addressed in chapter 6.

The next tournament was the Las Vegas Invitational, played at three different golf courses. This tournament was unique in that it was contested over 90 holes rather than the normal 72. Tiger started steadily, shooting 70 in the opening round and a brilliant 63 in the second round. His good play continued on Friday and Saturday when he shot 68 and 67 respectively. The extra day allowed Tiger to stay in contention despite the mediocre opening round. In the final round Tiger came to the last hole needing a par to tie Davis Love III, who was still on the course. He made par and then had to wait and see if Love would be able to birdie to win. From the practice range, where Tiger refused to do any interviews, he struggled to maintain his concentration in case there was a playoff. Over one of the official's walkie-talkies, Tiger and his caddie "Fluff" Cowan heard that Love had an eight-foot birdie putt to win, and they listened as the voice on the other end informed them that the putt was missed. A playoff ensued.

Because of television contracts, the tradition of 18-hole playoffs had long ago become history. Television requires a drama, and the prospect of clearing lucrative afternoon network time on a Monday is not an option. Consequently most tour events stage a sudden-death playoff immediately following completion of play. The only tournament that retains an 18-hole playoff on the following day is the U.S. Open. The tradition-minded USGA has not yet given in to the pressure of television. Because the cameras traditionally cover the last few holes best, sudden-death playoffs usually take place on those holes. This playoff at Las Vegas was to be held on the 18th hole, and if the players tied again they would go to the 17th hole and then back to the 18th.

Davis Love won the honors with a toss of a coin and used his driver, hitting the ball in the middle of the fairway. Tiger reached for a three wood, a more lofted club that would undoubtedly leave his ball farther from the hole than Love's. In golf, the player farthest from the hole plays first, and it was suggested later that Tiger used this tactic so that he would play first and try to get his ball on the green to put more pressure on his opponent, who was a much more experienced tournament golfer. Once again Tiger demonstrated that he had the instincts of a much more mature player. After hitting an eight iron about 18 feet from the hole, it was Love's turn to play. He swung too hard and his ball landed in a bunker past the green. Love played the bunker shot to within six feet of the hole, and Tiger lagged his putt to within inches of the hole, thereby insuring a par for the hole. Love needed the six-foot putt to tie the hole and prolong the playoff to the next hole. He missed and Tiger Woods, after only seven weeks on tour, at 20 years old, was the winner of his first championship on the PGA Tour. Tiger embraced his mother, who was at greenside.

Unfortunately for Earl, who was not in Las Vegas for the momentous occasion, ESPN opted to go back to the studios to start their pregame NFL football coverage, promising to show updates of the playoff during the football game. It was just not the same as seeing it live. It was probably the last time Tiger was preempted.[43] Tiger finished third at the following week's Texas Open, and if he won again he would be eligible for the Tour Championship, a $3 million event with a $540,000 first prize.

It was on to Florida and the Disney/Oldsmobile Classic. This was now Tiger's home—he had recently moved into the exclusive Iles-worth Community in Orlando. The tournament director of the Disney Classic, Michael McPhillips, had been courting Tiger to play in their tournament since he turned pro. He had been in constant touch with Hughes Norton, at one point phoning from his car that he was driving around Orlando with six strawberry milkshakes from McDonald's trying to find a drop point near Tiger's home.[44] Initially Tiger had said he wasn't going to play at Disney, but McPhillips continued to press, setting up newspaper copy announcing the arrival of Tiger, and even promising to allow Tiger to use a normally locked back gate of the golf course that would cut off 15 minutes from Tiger's daily commute to the tournament. When it was finally known that Tiger was going to play in the tournament, a whole new operational plan had to be put into effect. More programs had to be printed, additional security had to be enlisted, additional bleachers had to be constructed behind the practice area, and more buses had to be added. The usual suspects from the press were joined by an influx of national media writers—*Sports Illustrated, Golf Magazine*, the *New York Times*, and probably the biggest of all, the Golf Channel, which had the rights to televise this tournament. The producers could only have speculated that Tiger Woods would turn professional before this event, and they certainly didn't know whether or not he would play in the tournament. The reason the Golf Channel secured the rights to this event in the first place was because it was normally a year-end attempt by the lesser-known professionals to try and make the Top 125 Money List, and not of interest to the broadcast networks. The Golf Channel became the beneficiary of the ratings bonanza.

In what was becoming his trademark slow start, Tiger shot 69 in the opening round. While he was well down the leader board, he was playing well and felt confident. The Disney tournament was played on several of the park's courses, so on Friday Tiger played the Lake Buena Vista course and shot 63, which put him two shots from the leader. Tiger shot 69 on Saturday and three-putted on the 18th hole to lose a share of the lead by one stroke. The final round of the tournament resulted in another Tiger win but did not end not without some unusual incidents.

Tiger was paired with former U.S. Open Champion Payne Stewart, and the crowds following them were tremendous. As the twosome was going from the sixth hole to the seventh, the crowd, en masse, cut across a wooded area between the holes and startled a young deer who ran toward the swamp, whereupon a local alligator was apparently roused with the prospects of an early dinner. The deer didn't know which direction posed the most danger and skittered off into the fields to escape the whole situation.

Unaware of the deer's plight, Tiger was busy on the golf course finishing his round in 66 strokes; Stewart shot 67, and it appeared Tiger would win his second tournament in eight weeks. But out on the course, Taylor Smith, a relatively unknown young professional, still had a chance to tie Tiger. Earlier in the round, Smith's playing partner, Lennie Clement, had noticed that Smith was playing with a putter that had an illegal grip, and he reported the infraction to the PGA officials. Smith asked if he could continue playing while the Committee considered the situation, and they allowed him to do so. Smith eventually birdied the final hole to apparently tie Woods, but the Committee ruled that he be disqualified. Tiger expressed disappointment that Smith and he were not able to compete in a playoff.[45] The win boosted Tiger's winnings to $734,790 and gained him a spot in the Tour Championship the following week in Tulsa, Oklahoma. This tournament was restricted to the top 20 money winners on tour.

It was inevitable that comparisons with Jack Nicklaus would continue to be made. Tiger had finished in the top 10 in five of his first seven professional tournaments, winning two; Nicklaus had finished in the top 10 only once and had not won a single tournament in his debut on the tour. Woods had managed to achieve the most promising start of any golf professional in the history of the sport.

During this euphoric period, Tiger's closest friend on tour, Mark O'Meara, had indicated that the time to judge the true greatness of Tiger Woods would be when he was not playing at his best and winning tournaments, but when adversity struck. That prediction was made reality during the Tour Championship in Tulsa, Oklahoma, on October 25, 1996. After a serviceable opening round of 70 he was two strokes off the lead, anticipating his Friday 2:51 P.M. tee time for the second round. That night Earl Woods was admitted to the St. Francis Trauma Center, across the street from the hotel where Tiger and his family were staying, complaining of chest pains. Tiger didn't get to sleep until 5:00 A.M. and the following day went through the motions on the course, opening with par, double-bogey, and then proceeding to bogey five of the last six holes. But he didn't quit. Somehow he managed to shoot 35 on the back nine for a 78. His playing partner, the veteran John Cook, said,

> He showed me a lot today and it wasn't golf. You can lose your mind out here, and he didn't. To hold his demeanor like he did was more impressive to me than some of the drives he tried to hit. In a situation like that you could stomp off and complain, moan and act like a 20 year old but he didn't do that. He tried to make the best of a difficult day.[46]

It was not determined whether Earl was suffering from a mild heart attack or from a bronchial problem. He had had bypass surgery 10 years earlier and had not made any serious attempts to curtail his unhealthy heart behavior—he still smoked and was overweight. Tiger managed to shoot 72 and 68 for the final two rounds and finished tied for 21st.

Tiger completed his abbreviated season 24th on the money list with a total of $790,594 in prize money. His average winnings-per-tournament was the highest on the tour, surpassing Tom Lehman, who at the time held the season-earnings record of $1.78 million. In 10 weeks Tiger had two victories.

Tiger continued his great play to begin the 1997 season. At the Mercedes he shot a 65 on Saturday, birdying the last four holes to tie the 1996 Player of the Year, Tom Lehman. The following day a torrential downpour caused the officials to cancel the final round and stage a sudden-death playoff between Woods and Lehman. The playoff would be at the seventh hole, a par three with an elevated green, and about the only hole playable on the course. It required a shot completely over water. Lehman had the honor and, obviously not fully warmed up, hit his six-iron shot into the water. The stunned crowd expected Tiger to play a conservative shot, since he could probably make a four and still win the tournament. In what was fast becoming a characteristic of his style of play, he proceeded to hit a shot that came within six inches of going into the hole. After a penalty stroke Lehman dropped his ball and hit a shot that almost went in the hole, but even if it had, it was still only three. Tiger tapped in his birdie to win his third tournament. In spite of his amazing start on the PGA Tour, Tiger's professional career was only just beginning. All eyes were on him as he prepared to play in his first major championship as a professional. Winning regular tour championships assures a good living; winning major championships assures a place in golf history.

THE MASTERS RECORD

Although the Masters Tournament is the youngest of the four golf tournaments considered majors, it is arguably the most significant, because its founder was the legendary career-amateur Bobby Jones, and because it is played every year at the same golf course, Augusta National. As one of the most exclusive country clubs in the world, the Augusta National club has had a long history of discrimination and has resisted attempts to change its policies. Leading up to the 2003 Masters, the president of the National Organization for Women, Martha Burk, challenged the officers of Augusta to admit its first woman member. Burk threatened to call a boycott of the companies sponsoring the tournament because of Augusta's discriminatory policies. Indicative of the financial clout of the club and its members, the club announced that it would sponsor the telecast itself, and it provided coverage without any commercial interruptions.

CBS first televised the Masters in 1956 and has retained the contract ever since. And while the network covets this perennial ratings leader, it has had very little control over many of the aspects of the event, unlike most other tournament telecasts. The club dictates the number of commercials (no more than four per hour), and, whether directly or not, they have the final say over the selection of announcers. There have been several situations when the club has flexed its muscles in this regard. During the 1994 telecast, for example, one of the commentators, Gary McCord, suggested that the greens had been "bikini-waxed" (the closer the greens are cut, the more difficult they are to putt). The following year Gary McCord was replaced for the Masters broadcast.

The Masters is different from the other majors also in that the field is determined by invitation, and the criteria for invitations are determined by the Augusta members. This fact has contributed to the feeling among minorities that they have been systematically excluded from the Masters because of discrimination. The most bitter example of this was the situation of black golfer Charlie Sifford. Sifford was one of the first black players to secure a PGA card and to win a tournament on the PGA Tour. During the period from 1961 to 1974 he was the only black golfer who played at a level that would qualify him to play in the Masters. Sifford described an incident in 1962 when he was leading the Canadian Open after the first round. Traditionally, a Masters invitation had gone automatically to the winner of the Canadian Open. At the conclusion of his round, Sifford noticed someone had posted on the clubhouse bulletin board a note indicating that this year an invitation to the Masters would not be offered to the Canadian Open winner.[47]

At one time the top 16 finishers at various tournaments would automatically get an invitation to the Masters. In 1960 at the U.S. Open, Sifford was in contention on the final day. The late sportswriter and commentator Dick Schaap related a conversation in *Sports Illustrated*:

> "If Charlie Sifford has a real hot round," a writer said, "he can finish among the top 16. Now that would be interesting. That would mean he would automatically qualify for the Masters tournament next year." "Y'all crazy?" said a reporter from Georgia. "If Sifford makes the top 16, they'll change the rules so only the top 15 qualify. If he finishes 11th, it'll be the top 10. And if he finishes second, then it'll be the top one."[48]

The top 25 money winners automatically got a Masters invitation at one time. In 1967, Sifford had one of his best years and was high enough on the money list to be invited; however, the criteria were changed and a point system was devised to determine who would be invited. Not surprisingly for Sifford, he did not have enough points to qualify.

Lee Elder is best known as the first black golfer to compete in the Masters in 1975. Throughout the early 1970s Elder was the focal point of the effort to obtain equality in entrance to the Masters. By 1971 the Masters changed earlier policies, which invited players on the basis of a complicated point system and by ballot of former Masters Champions. The new policy granted an invitation to anyone who won a PGA tournament in the year prior to the Masters.[49] In 1973, a group of 18 members of Congress, led by Representative Herman Badillo, sent a letter to Clifford Roberts, chairman of the Masters, urging that Lee Elder be invited to compete in the tournament.[50] Roberts refused the request. Elder himself rejected the idea and publicly responded, "There is only one [way] left for me to get into the Masters field this year, that's if I can win either at New Orleans or Greensboro. That's certainly what I'm going to try to do."[51] The following week Elder shot a 65 in the first round of the New Orleans Open and led by two strokes, but he faltered and did not win. The following spring Elder won the Monsanto Open in Pensacola, Florida, and thus qualified for the 1975 Masters—the year Tiger Woods was born.

Tiger Woods faced none of the problems of Sifford and Elder as he prepared to play in his first Masters as a professional. By virtue of his U.S. Amateur victories he had already played in two Masters, and as a result of his place on the money list and his Tour wins, Tiger had easily secured an invitation to the 1997 Masters; however, by this time the public interest in Tiger Woods guaranteed him an invitation by any set of criteria.

With expectations running high at the Masters, Tiger Woods prepared to tee off with his fellow competitor, Nick Faldo, a three-time winner of the Masters and defending champion. It is a Masters tradition that the defending champion be paired with the Amateur champion, in this case Tiger Woods. Despite the fact that Tiger had turned professional since his Amateur victory, the tradition was honored. It was apparent from Tiger's opening drive that he was not yet in his rhythm. He bogeyed the first hole and finished the first nine holes at four over

par—40. Throughout the press corps, murmurs of overinflated expectations were prevalent. But suddenly, on the 10th hole, Woods regained
control of his game when he rolled in a birdie putt. Then, in famous
Amen Corner,[52] he made a shot that maintained his momentum and
probably saved the round and the tournament: Tiger had overshot the
green on the 12th hole, a par three, and faced a difficult chip shot to
save par. He boldly chipped the ball into the hole for birdie and went
on to shoot a near record-tying 30 on the back nine. At a score of
70, two under par, Tiger was only three shots behind the leader, John
Huston.

Tiger played with Paul Azinger on the second day, and he was clearly
more confident as he walked to the first tee. He had proven that he
could put up a good score at Augusta. He proceeded to shoot a score
that vaulted him into the lead. His 66 gave him a three-shot lead over
Scotsman Colin Montgomerie. By the end of the third round he had
increased the lead to nine shots. Colin Montgomerie had earlier in the
season commented to the press that Tiger's reputation had been forged
on what he referred to as "resort courses," and that he looked forward to
facing Tiger at the Ryder Cup matches (a biannual competition between
American professionals and European professionals) later in the fall. At
his press conference after the third round at the Masters, Montgomerie
was beside himself in describing the play of Woods: "I appreciate that
he hit the ball long and straight, and I appreciate his iron shots were accurate. I do not appreciate how he putted. When you add it all together,
he's nine shots clear, and I'm sure it will be higher tomorrow."[53]

The final round of the 1997 Masters had little to do with who would
win the tournament. The previous year, Greg Norman, perennial con-
tender for the Masters, held a six-shot lead over Nick Faldo at the start
of the final round and wound up losing by five strokes. The general
wisdom is that the Masters does not really begin until the back nine
on Sunday. The only question was whether the pressure would get to
Woods. It didn't.

After playing even par for the first nine, he birdied three holes on
the back nine that had him standing on the 18th tee needing a par
to break the 72-hole scoring record for the Masters. A photographer
rapid-fired three quick shutter clicks at the top of Tiger's backswing,
which caused him to pull his drive left onto the adjacent fairway. After

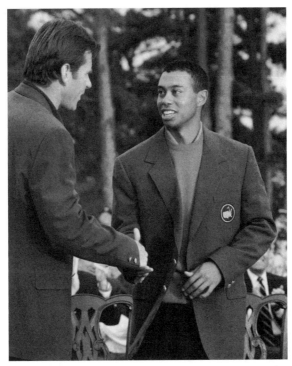

The 1997 Masters champion Tiger Woods receives his Green Jacket from the previous year's winner Nick Faldo, left, after winning the Masters at the Augusta National Golf Club in Augusta, Georgia, on April 13, 1997. AP Photo/Amy Sancetta.

sufficiently reprimanding the guilty party, he proceeded to hit the second shot on the green and calmly sank a four-foot par putt to break the record and win his first major championship.

This would be the first of many major championships, but the significance of Tiger's win reverberated throughout the African American community. Lee Elder had been invited to the final round and was at greenside when Woods sunk the last putt. Charlie Sifford rejoiced from his home in Kingston, Texas. This win was a vindication for all the African American players who had toiled simply to make a living playing golf, never mind playing in, or winning, the Masters Tournament. And beyond the social significance of Tiger's win at Augusta, this event had gained importance well beyond the golf community. The ratings for CBS's final round coverage were 15.8. This represented about

15.3 million television sets tuned to the Masters to watch this young black man play golf. That Sunday night only *60 Minutes* had a higher rating, and the lead-in for that program was the Masters broadcast.

By sinking a 15-foot putt on the 72nd hole of the 2001 Masters for a two-stroke victory, Tiger completed what became known as the Tiger Slam. He became the first golfer ever to hold all four major championships at the same time.[54] Purists complained that the feat was not accomplished in the same year, but Tiger and his supporters pointed out that he did in fact hold all the trophies.

In 2002 Tiger won his third Masters. Due in part to the general improvement in golf equipment and the overall improved fitness of players, traditional golf courses had become considerably easier for professional golfers to play. In 2009 the average driving distance for PGA professionals was 283 yards, with Bubba Watson averaging slightly over 311 yards, compared to the average drive in 1992 of 260 yards.[55] This trend led the "fathers" of Augusta golf to implement renovations to the Augusta Golf Club, due in no small part to Tiger's success at the Masters. The story goes that Hootie Johnson, the president of Augusta National, was sitting in a golf cart watching Phil Mickelson playing the 11th hole, a par four dogleg. Mickelson boomed a drive around the corner, leaving him merely a wedge to this 455-yard hole. Johnson is supposed to have decided that the hole had to be lengthened the next year, along with other renovations to toughen up the course. In 2002 the 11th hole measured 495 yards and has since has been extended to 505 yards. So the course Tiger faced in 2002 was considerably more difficult than the year before. As defending champion, Tiger started slowly on the first round, shooting two under par 70. However, by the third round he tied for the lead with South African Retief Goosen. A one-under-par 71 secured a three-shot victory for Woods, only the third golfer to repeat in the Masters, and he set a scoring record for a repeat victory.

Maintaining a tradition of not scoring well in the first round of the Masters, Tiger shot a two-over-par 74 in round one of the 2005 Masters. His poor play was highlighted when a question arose about his stance on a short putt he holed on the 14th green. In the act of tapping in the putt, there was a question of whether or not he had straddled the line of putt. It was determined subsequently that he had not.[56]

Woods's play steadily improved over the next two rounds, finding him leading going into the final round, three strokes ahead of journeyman pro Chris DiMarco. The final round was close all afternoon, coming down to the par three 16th hole. Leading DiMarco by one stroke, Tiger hit his tee shot over the green, leaving a difficult chip to secure his par. DiMarco was safely on the green with a birdie putt. What followed was an amazing shot by Woods that remains one of the iconic images in Masters' history. He chipped the ball onto the green some 20 yards left of the hole and allowed the slope of the green to carry the ball toward the hole. The ball seemed to stop right on the edge of the lip—just long enough to provide the Nike logo to be clearly observed by the tight close-up on television—then tumbled into the hole. The roar was deafening. DiMarco missed his birdie putt, and, even though Tiger bogeyed the 17th hole and 18th hole that led to a playoff, he was able to birdie the first playoff hole and win his fourth Masters.

THE OPEN CHAMPIONSHIP

The most prestigious of the Major championships is the British Open, or as the Brits call it simply, the Open. As the oldest golf championship, the first Open was played at Prestwick Golf Club in Ayrshire, Scotland in 1860. That first Open was technically closed, since it was only open to professional golfers. However, the following year, the tournament was open to amateurs. For the first 10 years the winner was awarded, in addition to a modest purse, a belt emblematic of the championship. However, when Young Tom Morris won for the third consecutive time, he was given the belt, and in its place the winners were given a Golf Champion Trophy—now commonly referred to as the Claret Jug.[57] The only one of the major tournaments played outside the United States, the Open is played on one of nine links courses in Scotland and England and provides a unique experience of watching golf being played as it was originally intended; not on lush manicured fairways and greens, but rather subjected to the linksland conditions that can render Open courses dry and brown, as well as the wind and regularly inclement weather.

Bobby Jones was among the first American golfers to pay homage to the birthplace of golf and regularly compete in both the Open and the British Amateur Championship. However, after Jones retired from golf on the heels of his Grand Slam,[58] American golfers did not as a matter of course make the trip to England to play in the Open. It was the confluence of Arnold Palmer recognizing its historical significance and playing in the 1960 Open, and his appeal heightened by television coverage of golf, that reestablished the Open to its rightful place in the pantheon of golf championships. Palmer won the Open in 1961 and thus encouraged a steady stream of American winners, including Jack Nicklaus and Tom Watson. Tom Watson held the Claret Jug more than any other American, with five Open Championships.

Tiger has always cherished the history and traditions of the game of golf and has played in every Open since turning professional, after competing twice as an amateur. He has won three Opens, two of which occurred at the home of golf, St. Andrews. Jack Nicklaus said, "If a golfer is to be remembered he must win the Open at St. Andrews."[59] Tiger's victory in the Open in 2000 made him only the fourth and the youngest golfer to have won all four major championships in his career.[60] In 2006 Tiger competed in the Open at St. Andrews in his first major since the death of his father, Earl. When he sank the last and winning putt on the 18th hole, he broke down and sobbed on the shoulder of caddy Steve Williams.

The 2009 Open Championship was contested at the Turnberry, and as usual Tiger was the favorite, handicapped at 2:1 odds by the British bookies. However, what transpired turned into one of the most fascinating stories at a major championship ever. To begin with, Tiger was not in contention in the final round. In fact, he missed the cut after 36 holes for only the second time in a major as a professional golfer. With consecutive rounds of 71 and 74, he was one stroke out of the final two rounds.

The story of the 2009 Open was Tom Watson, the 59-year-old five-time winner of the Claret Jug. Watson needed only a par on the 18th hole to win his sixth Open Championship by a stroke over Stewart Cink, an American pro who had never won a major. However, Watson's approach, shot to the 18th green, skipped over the green, and he was unable to get up and down and was forced into a playoff with Cink. Despite the overwhelming support of the British crowds, Watson was simply out of gas during the four-hole playoff and Cink won handily.

THE U.S. OPEN

Arguably the most challenging golf tournament to win is the U.S. Open. It is truly an open competition. Anyone with a 1.4 or lower handicap index who has the entry fee has a chance to qualify for the U.S. Open. Local qualifiers are held at designated courses around the country, in a two-stage process. Players must enter a local qualifier and be among a designated number to continue on to a sectional qualifier. Golf professionals are exempt from the local qualifiers, as are some 34 other categories of golfer, such as all past winners of the Open and the winner of that year's U.S. Amateur. There are 18 categories for full exemptions from qualifying. So while the field of the U.S. Open includes the best professional and amateur players from all over the world, there are always a few players who qualify that are not household names. In addition to the quality of the field, the U.S. Open is generally played on very challenging golf courses that are set up to play at their most difficult. The rough is traditionally considerably longer than the rough at regular PGA Tour events. The hole placements are also designed to provide players with the greatest challenge to get the ball close to the hole on their approach shots. Finally, the greens at the U.S. Open are cut very low, making it difficult to judge the speed of putts. The stimpmeter readings at the U.S. Open can be upwards of 13 feet.[61]

Tiger's first victory in the U.S. Open was the first leg of the Tiger Slam. The 2000 event was held at the Pebble Links Golf Links on the Monterey Peninsula in Northern California. Pebble Beach is always rated among the best and most beautiful courses in America. Tiger led after the first day of competition by a stroke, after which he left his fellow competitors in the dust. By the end of the tournament he was 15 strokes ahead, becoming the first player in the 106-year history of the U.S. Open to finish in double digits, and he tied Jack Nicklaus's record for the lowest score, 272.

In 2002 the U.S. Open came to New York, for the first time staged at a public golf course, Beth Page. A sprawling golf facility in Long Island, Beth Page actually boasts five different courses. The most famous and most difficult is Beth Page Black, one of the last courses designed by A. W. Tillinghast. For the U.S. Open, the course was lengthened to over 7,000 yards. After the first round, Tiger led over Sergio García by a stroke and extended that lead to three strokes by the second round. Tiger shot an even par 70 on the third day but picked up two shots on the field as principal challengers García and Phil Mickelson were not able to contend with the rainy conditions. The final round was suspended because of inclement weather, but despite spirited challenges by García and Mickelson, Tiger prevailed. He finished at three under par and won the $1,000,000 first prize.

Tiger had suffered from knee problems back to his amateur days. In 1994 he had a cyst removed from his left knee, and in 2002 he had a tumor removed. While these were both relatively simple procedures, he continued to have knee problems into the beginning of the 2008 season. After finishing second in the 2008 Masters, thus precluding any chance of a Grand Slam, he decided to undergo arthroscopic surgery (called a scope) to repair cartilage damage that was found during the procedure. Woods planned to return to golf for the U.S. Open, being played in 2008 at Torre Pines, a public golf course outside of San Diego, where Tiger had played as a youngster, and where he had won the Buick Invitational earlier in the year. He had won there six times as a professional. So it was with great anticipation that the golfing world looked forward to this U.S. Open and the return of Tiger Woods to competition.

Playing in a threesome made up of the three top players according to the World Golf Rankings (Phil Mickelson and Adam Scott), Tiger shot a first round 72, leaving him four shots behind the leaders. It was during this round that a relatively unsung journeyman golf professional, Rocco Mediate, surfaced to become part of one of the most dramatic scenarios ever to be played out at the U.S. Open.

Rocco Mediate joined the PGA Tour in 1985. He had grown up in rural Greensburg, Pennsylvania, and after a somewhat undistinguished high school golfing career, he got serious about golf. Unable to get into a class at the Bob Toski golf school, he was directed to talk to Jim Ferree, a disciple of the Toski-Jim Flick teaching method. Eventually Ferree became his mentor, and under his tutelage Mediate improved and was accepted to California University, a Division 2 Pennsylvania teacher's college, on a golf scholarship. While he had problems with some of his teammates early on at California, Rocco began to establish himself as player. After playing well enough to qualify for the Division 2 National Championships, Rocco was paired with a player from Florida Southern College. Impressed with the player as well as his coach Charlie Matlock, Mediate approached the coach and told him he wanted to transfer. Because the NCAA frowns on coaches recruiting players from other colleges, coach Matlock deflected Rocco's advances. It was not until the following spring that Rocco was able to transfer to Florida Southern.[62]

After a solid collegiate career, making the Division 2 All American team, he prepared to qualify for the PGA Tour through the Q-school. At the time, there were two qualifying school opportunities. He failed to qualify the first attempt but did so on the second. He had promised his mother that if he failed the second time he would go back and finish school. He never did go back to get his degree.

Despite the fact that he didn't win enough money on the tour the first year to qualify for a return the following year, he requalified through Q-School and settled into a fairly successful career. He got married to a local Greenburg girl and started to put on some weight. The weight apparently was a contributing factor to the beginning of his chronic back trouble. In an effort to alleviate the pain he adopted the long putter[63] and was the first player to win a PGA event using the long putter in 1991. He would go on to win four more tournaments but was always plagued by intermittent back trouble. So the last name on anyone's list of contenders for the 2008 U.S. Open was Rocco Mediate.

Mediate shot 71 in the second round, and that score tied him with Woods, who shot 68. It was apparent to everyone that Tiger was hurting. He started slow for the third round, but despite the pain from his knee, he played an amazing back nine, featuring two eagles and a chip-in birdie from thick rough on the 17th hole. Due in part to the difficulties encountered by most of the leaders, Woods carried a one-shot lead going into the final round. In his 13 major championship victories up to this point, he held or was tied for the lead going into the final round in every one.

Tiger double bogeyed the first hole and bogeyed the second. Playing with Lee Westwood, immediately behind Rocco Mediate, both Woods and Westwood came to the 72nd hole needing birdies to tie Mediate. The relatively easy par five 18th hole found both players driving into fairway bunkers. Westwood laid up on the fairway with his second shot, while Tiger hit his second shot into the rough, leaving a difficult lie for him to get his third shot near the hole. However, both players hit their third shots onto the green, leaving Westwood with about a 20-foot putt and Tiger about 12 feet. Westwood missed his putt, setting the stage for Tiger to attempt a putt that would tie him with Mediate, forcing an 18-hole playoff the following day. The putt started out down the hill and seemed to be considerably right as it approached the hole. Then, in what seemed to be the product of the collective energy of both Woods and the thousands of people around the green and the millions watching on television, the ball caught the right lip of the hole and was going just slow enough to dive into the hole.

A collective gasp was followed by an uproar from the crowd. Tiger clenched both his fists and screamed and then embraced his caddy, Steve Williams. He had somehow managed to play just well enough to get into a playoff despite, he was later to divulge, a stress fracture of his left tibia, which had occurred during rehabilitation from his earlier surgery. The question was now whether or not he would be able to hold up well enough to take the title over 18 holes the following day.

The combination of stories—Rocco Mediate, the 45-year old every-man golf professional vs. Tiger Woods, the wounded icon, presented sports writers with a field day. The playoff saw Tiger play well on the front nine, building a two-stroke lead by the turn (9th hole). But Mediate continued to impress, birdying three holes and taking the lead from Woods by the 15th hole. Both players parred the 16th and 17th, thereby requiring Woods to birdie the last hole and hope that Mediate did not do the same. After Tiger reached the par five hole in two strokes he two-putted for birdie, leaving Mediate with a birdie putt, which he missed. After 18 holes of playoff golf, the two players would continue play until one of them scored lower on a hole. They started the sudden death[64] playoff on the 7th hole. In what was a somewhat anticlimactic end to this epic battle, Rocco Mediate bogeyed the hole and Tiger parred it to end the competition.

THE PGA CHAMPIONSHIP

The PGA of America was incorporated on January 16, 1916. Later that year they held the first tournament at the Siwanoy Country Club in Bronxville, New York, and the competition was won by Jim Barnes.

For the first 42 years the tournament was played, it was a match play competition. In 1958, due in large part to television, it was converted to a medal (or stroke) format.

Tiger's first PGA Championship victory in 1999 took place at Medinah Country Club and featured a duel with up-and-coming 19-year-old rival, Sergio García. Despite an outstanding charge by the young Spaniard, Tiger was able to hold on and win by one stroke.

The following year Tiger won his second PGA Championship, held at the Valhalla Golf Club. It was the third leg of his Tiger Slam, to be completed the following spring when he won the 2001 Masters and was the first golfer ever to hold all four major championships at one time. He persevered and won despite pressure from Bob May, a relatively unknown pro who forced a three-hole playoff, the first in PGA history. Woods needed to sink a tricky 6-foot putt to even get into the play-off. Holding a one-shot lead over May going into the final hole of the playoff, Woods pulled his drive well left of the 18th fairway. His second shot left him in deep rough short of the green on the five-par hole, followed by a third shot that landed in a bunker fronting the green. May was safely on the green in three shots but 40 feet from the hole. Tiger hit his bunker shot two feet from the hole, thereby assuring a par five. Bob May then hit a magnificent putt that ran slightly by the hole, securing Tiger's victory.

In 2006 the PGA Championship was played again at the Medinah County Club. This was a different Tiger Woods than the one who had met the challenge of Sergio García. He had undergone a complete reworking of his golf swing, but leading up to the PGA his putting seemed to have abandoned him. However, over the four days at Medinah in 2006, he made just about every putt he looked at. In the third round Geoff Ogilvy finished and glanced back at the green, where Luke Donald had a putt on the final hole to take a one-shot lead going into the final round. Ogilvy said, "We need Luke to make this putt so Tiger doesn't have the lead. Because when he has the lead, he wins."[65] Donald missed and Tiger did not disappoint the next day, tying his own record for the lowest PGA total score.

The 89th PGA Championship, played at Southern Hills Country Club in 2007, was the first major that Tiger won as a father. As he strode to the scorer's tent after posting a final round 69, he was greeted by his wife Elin and new baby daughter Sam, appropriately dressed in Tiger's traditional Sunday red T-shirt. Despite a spirited challenge from South African Ernie Els and fan favorite pro Woody Austin, Woods was able to fashion a two-shot victory.

Expectations were high as Tiger prepared to compete in the 2009 PGA Championship, held at Hazeltine Golf Club in Minnesota. Having missed the cut at the British Open earlier in the summer for only the second time as a professional, he proceeded to win consecutive tournaments at the Buck Open and the WGC Bridgestone Championships.

The week before at the WGC tournament, Woods had battled with Padrig Harrington, an Irish professional and winner of three of the last six majors, until Harrington scored an 8 on the 15th hole to drop out of contention.[66] So the press was geared up for another epic confrontation between Woods and Harrington, especially since they were paired to play together on the first two days at the PGA. Going into the final round, Woods led Harrington by two strokes, but a totally unknown Korean golfer, Y. E. Yang (110th in the World Rankings) had somehow managed to get into the final pairing with Woods. The consensus was that Yang would wilt under the pressure of being in the final pairing of a major championship with Tiger Woods.

However, in what was to become one of the most shocking upsets in golf history, Yang managed not only to stay in touch, but he chipped in for eagle on the 14th hole to take a three-shot lead over Tiger. Tiger got the deficit down to one stroke going into the 18th hole, where Yang was faced with a difficult shot to the green. He hit a towering iron over a tree guarding the green that plunked down within eight feet of the hole. Yang had won.

Interestingly, Tiger received more publicity losing than he would have if he had won. What would have been just another sports story, and a fairly standard one at that, "Tiger Wins Another Major," became a front-page news story. In addition to defeating the heavily favored Woods, Yang became the first Asian to ever win a major, and given the significant impact of Korean women golfers on the LPGA, his victory would signal increased interest in world golf.

Significant also was the comparison of television ratings between the 2008 PGA (without Tiger) and 2009, with Tiger in contention. The 2008 ratings were 3.0 compared to 7.5 in 2009.[67]

THE RECORDS

Over the course of 13 years as a professional golfer, Tiger Woods has compiled a record that remains unparalleled in the history of the sport. He entered 203 tournaments, worldwide, and finished 145 times in the top 10. He won 55 times and finished second in 23 tournaments. He won over $45 million in prize money. Among his many records accomplished on the PGA Tour, his run of six PGA tournaments in a row stands out. Starting with the PGA Championship on August 15, 1999, Tiger won six consecutive PGA tournaments, ending with the AT&T Pebble Beach National Pro-Am on January 9, 2000. During this streak, considerable attention was paid to the historical significance of Tiger's quest to replace the legendary figure, Byron Nelson, who in 1945 set the record, winning 11 consecutive tournaments. However, it should be noted that when Nelson set the record he was playing on a tour with relatively few full-time professionals. Consequently the depth of the competition could not be compared with the PGA Tour of 1999–2000, when virtually every player on the tour was a full-time tournament golfer. World War II was just ending, and the quality of the tour was further depleted because of the potential professionals who were in military service. For winning 11 tournaments, Nelson won $52,000, which has no comparison to the monumental purses on the modern PGA Tour. Finally, in 1945 the media exerted considerably less influence on the American public than the high-powered newspaper, magazine, radio, Internet, and international television coverage of contemporary tour events.

It looked to all that the streak would come to an end at the AT&T Invitational at Pebble Beach as Tiger trailed by five shots going into the final round. On the 15th hole, he was still four shots behind the leader, Matt Gogel. Woods hit his approach shot to the par four hole and the ball bounced on the green, spun to the left, and rolled into the hole for a rare eagle two. He trailed by two strokes. He birdied two of the final three holes and was declared the winner. When Tiger finally lost the next week to Phil Mickelson in the 2000 Buick Invitational, he had tied the streak of Ben Hogan, who won six consecutive PGA tournaments in 1948.

But while his record in regular tour events is impressive, it is Tiger's ability to win major tournaments that has separated him from any other golfer playing today. Sports writers had coined the term "Grand

Slam" in 1930, when Bobby Jones won the U.S. Open and Amateur, and the British Open and Amateur. Since the two amateur championships became less important with the evolution of a legitimate professional tour, the writers invented a professional Grand Slam, which included the U.S. and British Opens, the Masters, and the U.S. PGA Championship. Only five players, over their careers, have ever won all four champion-ships. At the age of 24, Tiger Woods became the youngest player to achieve this feat, beating out Jack Nicklaus (at age 26), Gary Player (age 29), Gene Sarazen (age 33), and Ben Hogan (age 40). While the professional career Grand Slam had been done before, golfers and the press had only speculated on the possibility of a player winning all four tournaments in the same year.

Only one player had ever come close. Ben Hogan had a promising career in 1949 when he was injured in a near-fatal automobile accident, after which doctors said he would never walk again, let alone play tournament golf. After tortuous rehabilitation and by virtue of his indomitable will, Hogan resumed a professional golf career. In 1953, at age 41, Hogan won five of six tournaments he entered, including three majors: the Masters, the U.S. Open, and the British Open.[68] That is as close as anyone had come to winning pro golf's Grand Slam, the four majors in the same year, until Tiger Woods. In 2000 the U.S. Open was held at Pebble Beach in California. Tiger Woods became the fifth person to lead the Open start to finish and set a record for the lowest score in relation to par. This victory was the first of Tiger's two U.S. Open Championships, and no one was even thinking about a Grand Slam yet.

Later that summer the British Open was conducted at the birthplace of golf and home of the Royal & Ancient Society, St. Andrews. Tiger shot 67 for the first round and was in second place. In the second round he scored 66. He had played 36 holes without a bogey. In the third round Tiger finally scored a bogey, but by the conclusion of the round he held a six-stroke lead over fellow American and friend David Duval. They were paired together on the last day. Duval got to within three strokes of Tiger on the front nine, but he faltered on the 17th hole, when he took eight shots after failing to get out of the famous road hole bunker. Tiger finished with a 68, and his winning total, 19 under par, won by eight strokes, which established a record for the British Open in relation to par. Suddenly the possibility of Tiger holding the four major championships simultaneously, albeit over two seasons, was a possibility. The press was roughly divided on whether or not such a feat would be a true Grand Slam. The fact that there was even speculation that Tiger would be able to do it, let alone what it would be called, testifies to the monumental scale of his reputation.

The Vallhalla Golf Club in Louisville, Kentucky was the site for the final major of the year, the PGA Championship. Tiger opened with a 66 and followed with a 67 to lead by one stroke going into the weekend. On Saturday, Tiger birdied the final hole to maintain his one-stroke lead over Bob May. May held the lead until the 17th hole, when Tiger drew even. On the 18th hole, a par five, Tiger was forced to sink a curling six-foot putt to tie May and trigger a sudden-death playoff. On the third playoff hole, both Woods and May hit errant tee shots, and neither reached the green in two. Tiger hit a brilliant shot from a bunker short of the green, forcing May to make a long putt over an undulating green, which he missed by inches. Tiger was the PGA champion for the second year in a row.

Now the debate started in earnest. If Tiger was able to win the 2001 Masters the following April, would it be a Grand Slam? He would hold all four championships within a one-year period—albeit not the same year. The press and the sports-minded public would have eight months to discuss it. The sports talk radio programs had a field day.

Tiger started slow in the first round of the Masters the following spring. He shot 67, but the course was ripe for low scores and he found himself five shots off the lead. On Friday he rebounded and shot a 66 to take a one-shot lead on the field. On Saturday he maintained the one-shot lead and set up another confrontation with his ever-present rivals David Duval and Phil Mickelson. The three golfers battled throughout the Sunday round. By the 15th hole, Duval was tied with Woods, and Mickelson was one stroke behind. Both Mickelson and Duval bogeyed the critical 16th hole while Tiger parred. A definitive birdie putt on the 18th hole concluded the round for Tiger and assured his victory and claim to at least a form of a Grand Slam.

When asked if he considered this the Grand Slam at the press conference following the presentation ceremony, Tiger said that the press could call it whatever they wanted, but he had all four trophies in his

Tiger Woods chips to the green on the 15th hole during the second round of the Players Championship on March 26, 2004, in Ponte Vedra Beach, Florida. AP Photo/Phil Coale.

possession at the same time. Ironically, the debate over defining the feat overshadowed the sheer brilliance of it. Considering the immense amount of public attention focused on Tiger, the 12 months of building pressure, and the level of competition he faced, the Tiger Slam, as it came to be known, represents, to date, the single most exceptional accomplishment in modern golf history.

RYDER CUP COMPETITION

While Tiger has mounted an unprecedented record of accomplishment in individual events, he has not fared as well in the two major team-play competitions: The Ryder Cup Matches, and the relatively recent addition, the Presidents Cup Matches,[69] which pit the best American professionals against the best international players (excluding Europe).

The Ryder Cup is a competition that was initiated in 1927, when Samuel Ryder put up a trophy as a prize for the competition that would match American professionals against the best British professionals, alternating between the two countries. Ryder, an Englishman from St. Albans in Hertfordshire, made his fortune selling penny seed packets. Initially the press paid little attention to the matches, since the American professionals dominated the competition until the 1960s. It was not until 1977 when the British team was expanded to include European players in an effort to upgrade the Ryder Cup competitive level that the event started to attract an audience. The United States had won all but one match from 1959 to 1977, that one being tied, 16 to 16, in a memorable duel in 1969 at Royal Birkdale in Southport, England.

Since the British team was expanded to include all European players, the matches have become much more competitive and have taken on importance both in Europe and in America. Of the last nine matches, the American team has won only three. In addition to the inclusion of new players from all European countries, several factors have contributed to this reversal. The European tour is less affluent than the American tour, and American pros tend to travel alone and stay alone on the road. The European tour is also smaller, and the players tend to socialize together more than in American professional golf. Since members of the European team tend to be less-recognized players, they have more to prove than the star-filled American team. In part because of Tiger's outstanding amateur record in match play tournaments, and the tremendous amount of publicity his debut on the PGA Tour had generated, expectations were high that Tiger's presence would significantly enhance the Americans' chances of winning.

The Ryder Cup competition consists of a three-day event alternating every two years between the United States and Europe. It starts on Friday, when there are five matches in the morning. Two players on each team do not compete, so the captains must determine who will play and the order of the matches. The format is called foursomes, in which the players alternate shots, using one ball. The team with the lowest score on a hole wins that hole. The team that wins the most holes wins the match. When one team has won more holes than there are remaining, that team wins the match and gets a point. If the teams tie, a half-point is awarded.

The afternoon matches play a "four ball" format. This is the most common form of competition among recreational golfers. In it, each player plays his own ball. The lowest score of one team is compared to the lowest score of the other team, to determine the winner of that hole. The team that wins the most holes wins the match. On Sunday there are 12 individual matches, involving the entire team. There are potentially 32 points to be won. So to win the Ryder Cup a team must win at least 16½ points. If a tie occurs, the team currently holding the cup retains it.

Tiger Woods has competed in four Ryder Cup matches since joining the professional tour. His overall record in those matches is 7 wins, 11 losses, and 2 ties. It should be noted that he has fared better in the singles matches than in the team play, but overall the American team has only won once with him on the team. There has been considerable speculation as to why he has not dominated the Ryder Cup as he has all other competitions he has attempted. While it is impossible to pinpoint the reason for his less-than-outstanding performance in the Ryder Cup, there have been several incidents relating to the Ryder Cup that highlight an aspect of Tiger's career that has evolved as his golfing reputation has grown: the higher his celebrity profile, the more the press and the public have expected him to speak out on issues.

In 1997 the PGA, which conducted the Ryder Cup matches, would not pay for Earl Woods to accompany Tiger to the matches in Vallderama, Spain, a perk afforded the wives of married players on the team. At the time, Tiger questioned the logic of this policy. Then, several months before the matches in 1999, to be held at the Country Club in Brookline, Massachusetts, David Duval was quoted in a *Golf Digest* article complaining about what he called the hypocrisy of the Ryder Cup. Players were not paid to compete on the team; only their expenses were paid. Duval complained that since the PGA made a considerable overall profit on the matches ($23.5 million according to the article),[70] and the players put their reputations on the line at these matches, he thought that there should be some compensation for the players, even if it was in the form of a contribution to the charity of the player's choice.

Even though many players had privately voiced similar concerns, Tiger was the only member of the team who spoke up publicly in support of Duval. At a press conference at the PGA Championship at Medinah, outside of Chicago, Tiger agreed with Duval that the players should derive more benefits from playing in these matches. There was subsequent furor over his remarks, as the media generally sided with golf's establishment, in this case the PGA of America and the PGA Tour. Eventually the PGA acquiesced and devised a plan whereby the players would have the right to donate a certain amount of money to a charity. However, this incident is the first of many that would represent the pressures confronting Tiger Woods once he established his position as the number-one golfer in the world.

Interestingly, Tiger did not compete in the 2008 Ryder Cup competition due to his knee injury, and the Americans won for the first time since 1999. Held at the Valhalla Golf Club in Kentucky, the 2008 team led after every session for the first time since 1979.

PRESIDENTS CUP

Due in large part to the ever-growing worldwide appeal of the game, in 1994 the PGA Tour initiated the Presidents Cup. The competition features an American team against a team made up of professionals from any country other than ones in Europe (The Ryder Cup). The format is similar to that of the Ryder Cup, with the chief exception that the Ryder Cup can end in a tie, and the Presidents Cup lasts for one day longer. In individual matches of the Presidents Cup competition, as long as the overall competition has not been decided, players continue tied matches until a winner has been determined. If all the matches have concluded and the team score is tied, a sudden-death match is played until a winner is declared. Before the competition begins, the captains of both teams decide which player will represent their team in the event of a tie.

Through 2009, the American team has won the cup for seven of the eight competitions, only tying once with the International team. Like the Ryder Cup, the Presidents Cup is held every two years (alternating with Ryder Cup years), and since players represent all countries outside of Europe, the Presidents cup is played in a variety of golfing venues around the world. The format is match play, both team and individual competitions.

Tiger has participated in every Presidents Cup as a professional and has a record of 18 wins, 12 losses, and 0 ties. His record in the singles matches is six wins and two losses. Once again, the press and the public place pressure on Tiger to match his PGA tournament record in these team competitions.

Probably the most exciting performance by Tiger Woods in the Presidents Cup occurred in 2003 in South Africa. Originally scheduled for 2002, the competition was delayed for a year in the wake of the terrorist attack on the World Trade Center. Jack Nicklaus and Gary Player served as captains of their respective American and "Rest of the World" teams. America held the Cup and only had to tie in the overall competition to retain the cup. Tiger was partnered with Charles Howell III for the opening foursome competition. This format requires the two-man team to play one ball, alternating shots. Tiger and Howell easily defeated South African Tim Clark and Korean K. J. Choi, as the American team held a one-point lead, 3½ to 2½. The International team evened up the team score after the Friday morning four-ball matches. This format has both members of the team playing their own balls, comparing their best score against the other team's best score. Howell and Woods again teamed up but were defeated by two South Africans, Ernie Els and Tim Clark. Woods and Howell narrowly defeated another South African team, Clark and Retief Goosen, one up, as the American team forged a 9½ to 6½ point lead. The American team was shut out on the Saturday foursome matches, losing all 6 points, including a two-and-one loss by Tiger and Charles Howell. So going into the Sunday singles matches the International team only needed five points to win the cup.

There are 12 singles matches on Sunday, and the Americans started out solidly, winning five of the first six matches. The International team came back and won three matches. When Tiger defeated Ernie Els four-and-three in the penultimate match, it all came down to the last match, Australian Robert Allenby vs. Davis Love III. Love was one up going into the last hole. He only needed to halve the hole to win his match and the Presidents Cup. Allenby won the 18th hole. Their match was halved and the competition was deadlocked at 17–17. Captains Nicklaus and Player, before the competition started, placed the name of the player who would represent their team in case of a tie.

There was little surprise when it was disclosed that Tiger Woods would play for the Americans and Ernie Els would represent the International team.

The playoff would be sudden death. They would play the 18th, 1st, and 2nd holes. Both parred the 18th and the 1st holes. The 2nd hole was a par three and both players hit poor tee shots, leaving Tiger a putt of over 100 feet and Ernie about 50 feet. Woods putted to within 12 feet, and Els left himself about 6 feet for his par. It was getting dark and difficult to read how the putt would break, but Tiger calmly stroked his putt and, to the delight of his teammates, it rolled into the hole. Ernie Els now needed to make his putt to continue the match. Despite the excruciating pressure, Els holed his putt and the match was to continue.

However, both Captains and their teams decided that the diminishing light would make continuing impossible and, given the commitments of most of the players, staying over until Monday was not possible. It was declared a tie: both teams would share the Cup until the 2005 competition. But once again Tiger had demonstrated his uncanny ability to seize the moment and perform at his best when the pressure was greatest. Unfortunately, and due in part to the time difference between South Africa and the United States, the results of the dramatic finish had been widely reported several hours before it was shown on tape delay.[71]

The 2009 Presidents Cup was played in San Francisco at the Harding Golf Course, a public course. As the number one player in the world and winner of the recent FedEx Cup competition, Tiger Woods became the unofficial leader of the American team. As has been noted, this is a role that Tiger has not always felt comfortable with. Unfortunately (or fortunately), the early success in his career thrust him into this role at a very young age, and as he has aged he has managed to take on a more mentoring nature. Phil Mickelson was also on the team, fresh from his dramatic victory at the Tour Championship two weeks before. He relished the opportunity to help some of the less experienced team members, and in fact was paired with four different players throughout the partner competition. Tiger played all four team rounds with Steve Stricker.

The American team was heavily favored to retain the Presidents Cup, since five of the American team's players were ranked in the top 10 of the World Rankings, including numbers 1, 2, and 3. The first day featured foursome competition and, as was the case for all the partner formats, Tiger's partner was Steve Stricker. The American captain, Fred Couples, decided to pair Woods and Stricker mainly on the basis of their having been paired together some eight times over the final five tournaments of the 2009 season. Stricker won the Deutsche Bank Championship, the second in the FedEx Cup playoffs, and was ahead of Woods in the FedEx Cup standings going into the BMW tournament. Woods and Stricker proved to be a formidable team throughout the week. Together they won all four matches by substantial margins.

Tiger finished his 2009 season with a 5–0 record at the Presidents Cup. He was the only player to win all five of his matches. However, it was during the morning foursome matches on Saturday that he added to his growing reputation for the dramatic. Woods and Stricker were one down playing the 17th hole. Stricker drove the ball well, but Tiger hit the second shot short of the green and into a bunker. Stricker proceeded to chunk the third shot from the bunker, leaving Tiger with a 22-foot putt for par. Meanwhile Tim Clark, the gritty South African, hit his approach shot to within five feet, leaving his partner Mike Weir a relatively easy slightly downhill putt for birdie. The chances of Tiger making his putt seemed grim, and even if he did there was little chance that Weir would miss his short putt. Woods putted and the ball started to the hole and seemed to come to a complete stop on the lip of the cup. Almost defying gravity the ball somehow took one last roll and tumbled into the hole. The partisan crowd erupted. They were all even going to the 18th hole.

The 18th hole was a relatively short par five, and several of the teams had reached the green in two shots. Stricker left Tiger with about 204 yards to the green. Tiger selected a four iron and launched the ball toward the green. In what has become a signature move of Tiger's after he knows he has just hit a good shot, he spun the club in his hands and then, almost like a maestro conducting an orchestra, held up both hands as the ball settled onto the green, about 10 feet behind the hole. Weir and Clark could only manage a par, and they conceded Woods and Stricker the eagle putt and the match one-up.

Tiger capped off his perfect week the next day, defeating Y. E. Yang handily. The announcers were trying to build some drama into this match, billing it as Tiger's revenge against the only player to have defeated him when he was leading a major after three rounds. The drama never materialized. Fittingly, it was Tiger's five-foot putt on the 13th hole that actually clinched the cup for the Americans.

FEDEX CUP

In 2007 the PGA Tour collaborated with the Federal Express Company to establish a playoff system for the first time in professional golf. Members of the Tour can earn points throughout the regular golf season (January through August) by placing high enough in the tournaments. Based on the totals during the regular season, the top 125 point earners qualify for the four playoff events. The golfer with the most points after the four playoff events wins $10 million.[72] Tiger won the initial FedEx Cup in 2007, and Vijay Singh won in 2008. Even though Singh finished in 22nd place, 15 strokes behind the leader in the Tour Championship (the final event) in 2008, he won the FedEx Cup. It was in part because of this somewhat embarrassing development that the PGA revised the point system for the FedEx Cup in 2009.

The new point system resets after the regular season with the top 125 point winners being invited to play in the first of four playoff tournaments.[73] The field is successively reduced until the top 30 players compete in the final playoff event, the Tour Championship. If any of the top five point-getters win the Tour Championship, they win the FedEx Cup.

Tiger was ranked number one after the regular season in 2009 and competed in all four playoffs. He finished 2nd at the Barclays, tied for 11th at the Deutsche Bank, and won the BMW Championship. By winning the BMW, Tiger led in FedEx points going into the Tour Championship. Tiger battled with Phil Mickelson on the final day, but, plagued by an inability to make any significant putts inside 20 feet on Sunday, he finished second in the tournament. There were several players who could have overtaken Tiger for the Cup, but it would have required Tiger to finish lower than second. Woods had to finish no better than eighth for Mickelson to claim the Cup, and Steve Stricker, second place in Cup points going into the Tour Championship, needed to finish ahead of Tiger to take the Cup. "I'm sure I would probably be more happy tomorrow than I am right now, because you're in the

Tiger Woods holds up his trophy on March 25, 2007, after winning the CA Championship golf tournament in Miami. AP Photo/ Wilfredo Lee.

moment trying to win this event," Woods said. "Winning takes care of everything. But when you're in the moment out there, I'm trying to win a golf tournament. I'm trying to beat Phil, he's trying to beat me . . . we're all there, and it was just a great leaderboard."[74]

NOTES

1. U.S. Golf Association, "USGA History," http://www.usga.org/aboutus/usga_history/usga_history.html.

2. Mark Frost, *The Greatest Game Ever Played* (New York: Hyperion Books, 2002), 107–108.

3. Mark Frost, *Grand Slam: Bobby Jones, America, and the Story of Golf* (New York: Hyperion Books), 17.

4. Atlanta History Center, "Down the Fairway with Bobby Jones," http://www.atlantahistorycenter.com/cms/Down+the+Fairway+with+Bobby+Jones/107.html.

5. John Feinstein, *The Majors* (Boston: Little, Brown and Company, 1999), 13–14.

6. The term refers to the early custom of awarding a medal to the winner of the amateur competitions. In medal competition the player with the fewest number of strokes during the entire round wins.

7. The term is generally considered to be from the French verb *dormir*—to sleep. In essence, the player would have to fall asleep to lose the match.

8. John Strege, *A Biography of Tiger Woods* (New York: Broadway Books, 1998), 69–70.

9. Quoted in Strege, 71.

10. Quoted in ibid., 123.

11. Ibid., 126.

12. Ibid., 168.

13. Ibid., 174.

14. The Mid-Amateur Championship was created in 1981 for amateurs over 25 years old.

15. Ibid., 176.

16. Joe Drape, "New Study Shows Gap on Court and in Class," *New York Times*, March 16, 2005, D5.

17. Strege, 81.

18. U.S. Department of Justice, "Faces of the ADA—Casey Martin Continues His Professional Golf Career," July 17, 2000, http://www.usdoj.gov/crt/ada/fmartin. htm.

19. PGA Tour, "Notah Begay-Media Guide," http://www.pgatour.com/players/ bio/149683.

20. Quoted in Strege, 82.

21. As quoted in Strege, 83.

22. Nicholas Edwards, *Tiger Woods: An American Master* (New York: Scholastic Inc., 1997), 136.

23. Strege, 88–89.

24. Strege, 135.

25. Earl Woods, *Playing Through* (New York: Harper Collins, 1998), 122.

26. Quoted in Strege, 85.

27. Woods, 128–129.

28. Ibid., 133.

29. Strege, 157–160.

30. Woods, 141–152.

31. Quoted in Strege, 188.

32. Ibid., 189.

33. Ibid., 194.

34. Ibid., 191.

35. Quoted in Tim Roseforte, 91.

36. Quoted in Strege, 192.

37. Tim Rosaforte, *Tiger Woods: The Making of a Champion* (New York: St. Martin's Press, 1997), 64.

38. John Feinstein, *The First Coming* (New York: Ballantine), 10.

39. Quoted in Strege, 194.

40. Frost, *Grand Slam*, 99.

41. Roseforte, 72.

42. Quoted in Strege, 202.

43. Strege, 212.

44. Roseforte, 92.

45. Strege, 216.

46. Quoted in Roseforte, 100.

47. Quoted in Charlie Sifford, *Just Let Me Play* (New York: British American Publishing), 175.

48. Ibid., 176.

49. "Masters Policy Change Seen as Aid to Blacks," *New York Times*, June 13, 1971, sec V: 5.

50. Lincoln A. Werden, "18 in House Demand Masters Invite Black Golfer," *New York Times*, March 18, 1973, 1.

51. Lincoln A. Werden, "Special-Bid Idea Disliked by Elder," *New York Times*, March 20, 1973, 45.

52. So named because of the abrupt change of the hole directions and the difficulties of the 11th through 13th holes, often forcing players to rely on divine intervention.

53. Quoted in Rosaforte, 127.

54. The 2000 U.S. Open, the 2000 British Open, the 2000 PGA, and the 2001 Masters.

55. Erik L. Heiny, "PGA Tour Pros, Long, but Not So Straight," *Chance Magazine*, Winter 2008, 11.

56. In fact, this rule was changed in 2008.

57. Wikipedia, http://en.wikipedia.org/wiki/The_Open_Championship.

58. Winning the U.S. Open and Amateur and the British Open and Amateur in the same year.

59. St. Andrews Links, "The Open," http://www.standrews.org.uk/News/Events/The-Open.aspx.

60. The so-called Career Slam.

61. The stimpmeter is a device used to measure the speed of a golf course putting green by applying a known force to a golf ball and measuring the distance traveled in feet.

62. Rocco Mediate and John Feinstein, *Are You Kidding Me?* (Little, Brown and Company, New York, 2009), 72.

63. Traditional putters are approximately the same length as the other clubs. The long putter is considerably longer, and most players anchor the club with one hand on the stomach and the other under the chin.

64. Some would question the use of this term since it is anything but death for the winner of sudden death.

65. Alan Shipnuck, "All Business," Golf.com, August 28, 2006, http://www.golf.com/golf/special/article/0,28136,1717327–1,00.html.

66. Both Woods and Harrington were warned about slow play on the 15th hole, and Tiger was reprimanded by PGA Tour officials for complaining that the warnings probably affected Harrington's play on the hole.

67. Sandomir, Richard. "Woods Presence Gives PGA a Rating Boost," *New York Times,* August 18, 2009, B10.

68. This was the only time Hogan played in the British Open. The PGA Championship in 1953 was scheduled during the British Open, thus making it impossible for Hogan to even attempt the Grand Slam.

69. The Presidents Cup was initiated in 1994. It is a three-day series of matches featuring professionals from the United States against international players (excluding Europe).

70. Rosaforte, 152.

71. Brent Kelley, "An Amazing Day at the Presidents Cup," November 23, 2003, http://golf.about.com/b/2003/11/23/an-amazing-day-at-the-presidents-cup.htm.

72. The money is placed into their tax-deferred retirement accounts, not given in cash.

73. The Barclays, the Deutsche Bank Championship, the BMW Championship, and the Tour Championship.

74. "The Daily Wrap-up, Round 4: The Tour Championship," PGA Tour.com, http://www.pgatour.com/2009/tournaments/r060/09/27/recap_round4/index.html.

Chapter 6

IMPACT

There is no question that during his short career Tiger Woods has had a significant impact on the game of golf and the PGA Tour. However, his life so far has had influence beyond the realm of sports. While he is certainly not the first athlete or celebrity to endorse consumer products, the scale of his compensation and the variety of products he has endorsed have ramped up the standards within the advertising industry. As a minority celebrity he is expected by some to not only excel on the field but also represent the interests of all minorities on issues that have nothing to do with sports. It is impossible to separate his growing celebrity from the media-saturated environment we occupy. Without the media—especially broadcast television—there would not be a Tiger Woods phenomenon.

SPORTS AND BROADCASTING

The first regularly licensed commercial radio station is generally considered to be KDKA, which began broadcasting on November 2, 1920.[1] Within six months the first sports broadcast occurred on KDKA when Florent Gibson, a sportswriter for the *Pittsburgh Post*, was enlisted to provide what we now call a blow-by-blow description of a prize fight on April 11, 1921. The station began broadcasting the Pittsburgh Pirate baseball games on August 5, 1921. The marriage of sports and broadcasting grew out of the broadcasters' desperate need for programming once they went on the air. They needed programming that didn't cost much and had some mass appeal. Sports provided the perfect solution to their problem. In the early days of this relationship, sports team owners were wary of this new technology, but since there weren't enough receivers to have much impact, they didn't object.

As the number of listeners grew, team owners began to worry that prospective customers, who would normally attend games and pay for tickets, would stay at home and listen to the game on the radio for free. So immediately the question of the value of rights for a particular sporting event had to be settled. Several court cases eventually confirmed that sports teams owned the rights to their games. In one case a team would not allow the broadcast of its games, so the broadcasters, KGHI in Little Rock, Arkansas, erected a platform in a tree a few hundred feet from the stadium, hooked up a telephone line, and began describing the game over the air. In 1934 the local court told the station to get out of the tree. The federal courts further confirmed the principle in 1938 when KQV in Pittsburgh was sued for recreating Pirates games[2] stolen from two stations that had paid for broadcast rights. The stations were joined in the suit by the sponsors of the legal broadcast, since by this time the idea of selling advertisements to sponsors to underwrite the cost of production and make a profit was firmly entrenched.

On April 30, 1939, a television broadcast from New York City featured President Franklin D. Roosevelt opening the World's Fair. The broadcast was carried on the National Broadcasting Company (NBC), which had established the first station to provide sporadic television programming to a few receivers owned mainly by NBC executives. Less than a month later, on May 17, NBC broadcast the first television coverage of a sporting event, a baseball game between Columbia University and Princeton University.[3] The coverage was limited, as they used only one camera for the game and interviews. World War II significantly slowed down the evolution of commercial television, as virtually all research and development was dedicated to the war effort, and after the war the Federal Communications Commission (FCC) imposed a two-year freeze on the issuance of any new licenses. However, the Nielsen Media Research Company found a jump in television households from 9 percent in 1949 to 64.5 percent in 1954.[4] Television was firmly established as a principal means of providing information and entertainment to the American public.

Just as with radio, sports provided television a staple programming product that attracted a mass audience and cost relatively little to produce. In the early days, boxing was the easiest sport to broadcast, and consequently it dominated early television schedules. It took place indoors in a relatively small area and could be covered with very few cameras, hence low production costs. As it was not seasonal, the sport was a natural for television. The DuMont television network was the first network to televise boxing, along with a number of other firsts in broadcasting, such as the first professional football game and the first daytime drama (or soap opera). Early on, baseball became by far the most popular televised sport—especially the World Series. In 1947 NBC first televised the World Series, and fortunately for the network the two competing teams were both from New York,[5] as had been the case when NBC had made the first radio broadcast of a World Series 26 years earlier.[6]

The appeal of broadcast golf took much longer to catch on. In 1938, Dave Garroway, who would later gain fame as the avuncular host of NBC's *Today* television morning show, carried a bulky remote radio transmitter on his back as he competed in a celebrity golf tournament. He reported on his stroke-by-stroke progress for his audience listening on KDKA. The unwieldy equipment hampered his swing and he played poorly (fortunately for Garroway there is no record of his score).[7] As stated earlier, golf at this time was not a sport for the masses, and it attracted little attention from a mass audience. It was not until the election of Dwight Eisenhower to the American presidency in 1952 that the game began to gain wider appeal.

Eisenhower, the popular leader of the Allied Forces during World War II, was an avid golfer and was responsible for popularizing the sport beyond the country club set. He played golf regularly and even had a putting green installed on the White House lawn for occasional practice between meetings. He was a member of Augusta National Golf Club, home of the Masters and Bobby Jones, and undoubtedly his membership called attention to the annual staging of the Masters.

In the late 1950s there was an explosion of golf coverage on television. In addition to the influence of the Eisenhower presidency, remote television equipment became smaller and made it possible to televise an event over a five-acre playing field with action occurring simultaneously. There was also more money to spend on leisure during this period, and more people were playing golf. Even though the audience for golf is relatively small in comparison to the big three television sports— baseball, football, and basketball—it is a demographic that is coveted by advertisers: people who are interested in upscale products like luxury automobiles, business systems, investment companies, travel, and the golf equipment the pros use. Interestingly, golf delivers 35 percent more people who vote than an evening network news broadcast.[8]

But by far the most important factor in popularizing the game of golf was the arrival of Arnold Palmer as the most popular and telegenic personality in golf before Tiger Woods. Palmer was born and raised in Latrobe, Pennsylvania. His father, Milfred J. "Deacon" Palmer, worked at the Latrobe Country Club as the golf professional and course superintendent. However, Palmer did not enjoy a country club upbringing. He was solidly blue-collar and worked hard for his father on the course; along the way he developed a strong golf game. He possessed rugged good looks and had the kind of flair that just lent itself to television. He withdrew from Wake Forest University during his senior year and, after serving a three-year tour in the Coast Guard, he won the 1954 U.S. Amateur Championship. He met and married Winifred "Winnie" Walzer and embarked on a career as a professional golfer.

At a time when golfers, along with most professional athletes, were generally considered dull, Palmer was a revelation. In a game that was perceived as boring by all except those who played it, Palmer brought a new element that made golf tournaments exciting: he didn't just *win* tournaments, he charged out and overwhelmed them. With the ability to cover multiple holes simultaneously, and to be up close and personal, television amplified Palmer's style of play. He began to win tournaments, usually coming from several strokes behind on the last few holes—the media began to call it a "charge." Legend has it that during one of his charges at an early Masters, one of the uniformed soldiers from the nearby Ft. Gordon (then Camp Gordon) Army post who were manning scoreboards raised a sign that said "Arnie's Army," and that's what the television commentators started calling Palmer's fans. It stuck. Palmer and the Masters would be forever linked.[9]

The first Masters was televised in 1956. While Palmer was not a factor, Jackie Burke made up eight strokes on the final day to overtake amateur Ken Venturi by one stroke. In 1958 Palmer won his first major championship at Augusta. A situation occurred on the 12th hole: Palmer's ball embedded in a bank behind the green. Due to heavy rain the night before, a local rule was in effect that allowed players to lift and drop embedded balls, but the official on the hole was not sure if the rule was applicable where Palmer's ball was embedded. He informed Palmer that he could play the ball as it lay, and play a second ball (also allowed under the Rules of Golf). Palmer made a five with the first ball and a three with the second ball. Three holes later, after he holed a long putt for an eagle, Palmer was informed that the second ball counted. He defeated Ken Venturi by one stroke. In 2004 Venturi revisited the 1958 Masters incident when he raised a controversy in his autobiography, *Getting Up and Down: My 60 Years in Golf*, where he stated that Palmer had violated a rule when he didn't announce that he intended to play the second ball until he scored double bogey with the first. Irrespective of the intricacies of the Rules of Golf, the interest in Palmer and golf was growing to a larger and more diverse national television audience.

Palmer needed to birdie the final two holes of the 1960 Masters to once again defeat Ken Venturi by one stroke. Winning his fifth tournament for the year, Palmer made a 30-foot putt on the 17th hole and a 6-foot putt on the 18th hole. Two years later, Palmer participated in the first three-way playoff with Gary Player and Dow Finsterwald, winning by three strokes for his third Masters title. In 1964, Palmer, after tying for the first round and leading the remaining three rounds to win by six strokes, won his last Masters Championship, and in doing so became the first player to win four Masters.[10] Palmer's exposure on the PGA Tour (especially in the Masters, which garnered exceptionally high television ratings for any program, let alone the sport of golf) led to many business opportunities beyond the golf course.

Between his discharge from the Coast Guard in 1954 and the start of his professional golf career, Palmer worked as a salesman in Cleveland, where he had been stationed. During that time he became reacquainted with a young lawyer he met when he competed in college golf.

Mark McCormack graduated from Duke University and began working for the Cleveland law firm Arter, Hadden, Wykoff, and Van Durzer. That relationship developed into one of the most lucrative business arrangements in sports and led to the start of an industry.

THE MARKETING OF TIGER WOODS

Palmer was not the first sports star to endorse products. As early as 1905, Honus Wagner, "The Flying Dutchman," signed a contract giving J. F. Hillerich & Son permission to use his autograph on Louisville Slugger bats. Not only was Wagner the first of countless baseball stars to sign a contract with the Hillerich, but he was the first known professional athlete to endorse a retail product. Perhaps the greatest baseball player of all time, Ty Cobb, signed a contract with the same company for autographed Louisville Slugger bats in 1906.[11]

When Arnold Palmer began on the PGA Tour, most of the extra money he or any other pro made beyond prize money was from exhibition matches that were usually played on the Monday before the tournament began later in the week. In 1958 Palmer asked Mark McCormack and his partner Dick Taylor to act as his representative to make the arrangements for these matches. That year McCormack formed National Sports Management and represented Palmer and golfer Dow Finsterwald. The following year Palmer asked McCormack to represent him in all his business matters, and thus McCormack became the first sports agent.[12] National Sports Management soon became International Management Group (IMG).

IMG has since evolved into a multinational corporation with clients well beyond the sports world.[13] The firm represents celebrities, mostly athletes, and in addition has become involved in actually running events that are created so that their clients will have a platform on which to perform and earn money—which in turn earns commission money for IMG. The company has expanded into virtually every facet of the entertainment industry. An example of the extent to which the tentacles of IMG reach is a deal in which "The writer of a book agented by IMG Literary and printed and distributed by IMG Publishing interviewing golfers who are IMG clients at an IMG-created golf tournament for which they receive appearance fees from the tournament organizer—IMG. The agency earns fees from sponsors, and sells the television rights, and God knows what else."[14]

It was Mark McCormack, through IMG, who originated the idea of world rankings of golfers, thus internationalizing professional golf. Recently IMG expanded its interest in developing junior sports talents when it bought Nick Bollettieri's tennis camp in Bradenton, Florida, and converted it into IMG Academies, where precocious young athletes with well-off parents pay hefty tuitions in the hopes of earning college scholarships, if not a professional career. Many of the parents purchase $310,000 condominiums and live on the IMG campus with their children.[15]

In 1960 Jack Nicklaus won the U.S. Open and also became a client of IMG. Both Palmer and Nicklaus represent a model that was the standard for athletes until Tiger Woods. Eventually IMG was representing Arnold Palmer, Jack Nicklaus, and Gary Player, the South African golfer who, along with Nicklaus, was to become one of the five golfers to have won the four major championships. These three players were the most sought-after on the tour and commanded the highest appearance fees, although their fees were small in comparison to those received today by Tiger Woods.

The image that IMG was trying to foster for their clients was one of success beyond the tournaments they won, and the products they endorsed reflected that success. However, in 1960 their clients had to rely on many, relatively small endorsements. These athletes had to continue working, and while IMG clients were wealthy, they had to invest their own money to create more wealth. Both Palmer and Nicklaus had several investment deals that were unsuccessful. Palmer invested in a network of Cadillac automobile dealerships that eventually had to be sold off at a loss. Similarly, Nicklaus had ups and downs in his own various business ventures.

There are other factors that balance the comparison between the commercial potential of today's celebrity athletes and early IMG clients. The change in the social climate has helped increase the potential market appeal for Tiger and his contemporaries. Compared to the early days of the civil rights movement in 1960s America, today's virtually universal acceptance of multiculturalism expands the commercial possibilities for a young athlete, particularly of mixed racial background.

Finally, the performance of today's athletes is clearly superior to that in the days of Palmer and Nicklaus.

While there is no question that Palmer and Nicklaus pioneered the concept of sports marketing, the marketing of Tiger Woods reflects the change in the business climate for successful athletes. He averages about $10 million per endorsement deal and, more importantly, rarely invests his own money. The difference between the cultural climate in 1960 and today is significant. The saturation of media now is overwhelming compared to the early 1960s; there are more outlets and many more opportunities for synergies—the magic concept that drives corporations, particularly in media, to buy up parallel businesses and cross-promote their products at reduced costs. So it is not mere coincidence that a network television morning show does multiple stories about a movie produced by their parent or sister company. Modern advertising campaigns are built on product branding: if the product brand matches the athlete's so-called brand, the campaign is successful. Nike assembled the outstanding performer in basketball (Michael Jordan), soccer (Mia Hamm), track (Michael Johnson), and now golf (Tiger Woods).

Despite the universal acceptance of advertising, there is the ongoing question as to whether or not the advertising money spent is reflected in the sales of products. In August 1996, Nike stock sold for $35 per share; it soared to $75 per share at the peak of Tigermania; and it dropped back to $35 per share in 2001. How much Tiger had to do with those numbers is not clear. The value of celebrity endorsement is an inexact science. Professor Russ Ackoff from the Wharton School at the University of Pennsylvania conducted an exhaustive study to determine which factors influenced the purchase of beer, and he concluded the most reliable determinant was the weather; the hotter it got, the more beer people bought.[16] But scientific evidence to the contrary, advertisers were eager to attach their products to Tiger Woods.

The road to that attachment was through IMG agent Hughes Norton. A Harvard and Yale graduate, Norton joined IMG in 1972 and, after an initially solid relationship with IMG client Greg Norman soured, he rescued his career by convincing Earl and Tiger Woods to sign with IMG. He had begun to court the Woods family early on and was responsible for hiring Earl to act as a scout for IMG early in Tiger's junior career. There has been inevitable speculation about Norton's motives, and although there was little doubt that Tiger would become an IMG client, there have been a number of situations in which the press has been critical of Norton's handling of Tiger's affairs, particularly early in his career.

John Feinstein is a respected writer and media commentator who early on was critical in articles and interviews of Earl Woods and the handling of Tiger by IMG. He wrote that he thought IMG would, in a rush to capitalize on Tiger's instant fame, overschedule him with corporate outings and various other nontournament events. He warned that Tiger should be left to concentrate on winning golf tournaments rather than pile up endorsement money and corporate commitments. But when he compared Earl Woods to Stefano Capriati, the quintessential self-interested sports parent, whose daughter Jennifer had burned out after a brilliant start in tennis, Feinstein was effectively banished by Team Tiger.

At about this time IMG was considering which golf magazine Tiger should affiliate with as a playing editor, *Golf Digest* or *Golf World*. Feinstein wrote for *Golf World*, and his editor, George Peper, arranged for a meeting with Norton to try and clear the air and possibly give his magazine a chance at securing the services of the young professional golfer. Norton implied that if Feinstein would be less critical of Tiger and Earl they would seriously consider *Golf World* as Tiger's magazine home. Feinstein announced that if his writing was toned down by editors he would quit. That didn't happen, and Tiger signed on with *Golf Digest*. If there was any doubt, it was very clear how Norton would represent his new client.[17] Whether incidents like this were examples of mismanagement, or the product of normal interpersonal conflict and misunderstanding present in any business transaction, by 2000, with Earl's health deteriorating, Tiger was beginning to call his own shots. That had not been the case when the first Nike campaign was conceived.

The idea for the Nike Company grew out of a term paper by Phil Knight, speculating on the creation of a company that would sell running shoes. Knight was a runner at the University of Oregon under track coach Bill Bowerman (later, Bowerman's protégé would be distance runner Steve Prefontaine, who died tragically at a young age of cancer). Knight's interest in Tiger was fueled when the young star won his third U.S. Junior Amateur at the Waverly Country Club, which was Knight's home course in Oregon. Nike was one of the first new age companies. Its headquarters in Beaverton, Oregon is called a campus because "Isn't everybody a college junior at heart?"[18] In addition to offices it features dry cleaners, a gym, barber shops, and a cafeteria with scales to weigh your sliced turkey.

This was the company that designed the campaign to produce the television spot that featured Tiger talking directly to the camera: "There are still courses in the U.S. that I am not allowed to play because of the color of my skin. Hello, World. I've heard I'm not ready for you. Are you ready for me?"[19] The commercial immediately caused an uproar within the golf community and the press. Columnist James K. Glassman of the *Washington Post* questioned in a column exactly which courses Tiger would not be able to play. David Faye, the executive director of the USGA, contacted Nike to point out that the golf shirt Tiger was wearing in the commercial had the logo of Butch Harmon's home course, Lochinvar Golf Club in Houston, which did not allow women members.[20] The general consensus was that the theme of the ad was somewhat disingenuous. Granted there were golf courses in America where African Americans could not play, but they certainly did not exclude Tiger Woods. Critics questioned why, after not concentrating on his color before the campaign—he had in fact asked that reporters refer to him not as African American or Asian, but as an American—race was suddenly a primary issue. Tiger responded to questions indicating that he had approved the copy, and that he wanted the message of the commercial to stoke controversy and get people talking about the issue, and he added that while he is no longer the target of discrimination, when he was growing up he was. Finally, some golf traditionalists felt uncomfortable with the in-your-face style of the spot, which conjured up images of urban macho rather than country club golf chic. There is little question that, regardless of the appropriateness of this spot, the reaction of the golf community represented the ambiguity it was feeling toward this new personality. There was more to come.

Whether planned or not, the "Are You Ready for Me?" campaign quickly disappeared from the airwaves and was replaced by a softer Tiger image. The ad featured a series of shots of children of various ethnicities identifying themselves as Tiger Woods. The clear message: Tiger represents all people. Once again the ad sparked controversy. Most of the criticism by the press centered more on Nike, and the fact that Tiger Woods was being manipulated by the corporate image makers, than on the golfer himself. Nonetheless, the initial attempts to define the public persona of this new star were tentative at best.

By far the most successful ad produced early in Tiger's career was the one in which he ad-libbed remarks while bouncing a golf ball off the face of a club while talking to the camera. He performs a series of tricks while bouncing the ball and finally bounces the ball above his head; just before it strikes the ground he takes a full swing and drives it down the fairway. Commentators speculated whether the commercial involved special editing effects, but it subsequently came out that Tiger was able to accomplish the feat on only the fifth take while filming. He later explained to kids during a golf clinic that he developed the technique while waiting on the usually crowded tees at the par-three golf course he grew up on, Heartwell, back in California.[21]

During these initial campaigns, the by-now famous Nike logo was in evidence in virtually every frame of film and photograph. Nike had become aware of the possible dangers of oversaturation of their logo, especially in light of the fact that the company had been the target of criticism about the working conditions of foreign workers who actually made their products. They were starting to get comments from focus groups that referred to their ubiquitous logo as a "swooshstika."[22] Consequently they began developing individualized logos for some of their superstar endorsers, like Michael Jordan, who was identified with a jumping man symbol. In Tiger's case, they developed a stylized logo that merged his TW initials, which began to replace the Nike swoosh.

A good example of how important product endorsement is in sports marketing is Tiger's association with the Titleist company. Titleist manufactures the largest-selling golf ball. One of the main reasons for this is that more top golf professionals use Titleist than any other golf ball. Consequently, more good amateur golfers and recreational golfers use Titleist's ProV1 golf ball. Player endorsement in golf marketing is serious business, unlike most other sports. In golf, even recreational players have the opportunity to play on the same golf courses as the professionals, and use the same equipment. It would be like a NASCAR fan getting the opportunity to take a lap at the Daytona Speedway, in a professional stockcar. So when a particular golf ball is used by most of the winning professionals, recreational golfers can purchase that ball to play their weekend games. Through the Tour Championships in November 2004, winners of 152 tournaments worldwide used Titelist gold balls, nearly 100 more than the nearest competitor. Consumers clearly took notice.[23]

So when Tiger turned pro and signed on with Titelist to use their golf balls, wear a Titleist golf glove, and use a Titleist bag, for which he would be paid $3 million for three years,[24] the company benefited every time he teed up their ball in competition. However, in 2000, partly because of Tiger's overwhelming successes, Nike began to manufacture golf equipment, notably their own golf balls. Actually, Nike does not manufacture golf balls; Bridgestone in Japan and Wilson in the United States make golf balls for Nike. Titleist was concerned that, since Nike was now in the golf ball business, it would lead consumers to think Tiger was using a Nike golf ball in his many successful Nike commercials. They sued and as a result restructured their deal with the superstar, paying him only when he used their ball in a tournament. Soon Tiger switched to the Nike ball and eventually began using Nike clubs as well. The competition became so heated that Nike produced a commercial with Tiger in which he described his contract with them that stipulated that he could use whatever equipment he chose, intended to show both confidence in their products, and the stature of Tiger to be able to warrant such liberty. In 2003 this liberty was exercised when Tiger announced that he was going back to his Titleist driver.

Another initial corporate relationship arranged for Tiger by IMG was with the American Express Company. Tiger represented the ideal spokesman for the financial institution. In one television ad we see Tiger playing golf in an urban landscape, negotiating obstacles to reach his goal, with the somewhat belabored implication that AmEx cardholders will be able to overcome the same obstacles. Despite the surrealistic style of the commercials, the connection between Tiger and the good life was made.[25] Tiger's relationship with American Express points out another area of potential conflict with competing sponsors on the PGA Tour. Tiger only competed once in the MasterCard Colonial Tournament, in 1997. In subsequent years he chose to play in the Deutsche Bank German Open in Europe. Not coincidentally, this tournament was run by IMG, and Tiger received appearance money for his efforts. Paying players to compete in your tournament is allowed in Europe, but not on the PGA Tour. Similarly, Tiger took exception with promotional material for the 2001 Mercedes Championship, after he won the 2000 event. There was some concern that consumers might conclude that Tiger actually drove a Mercedes rather than his corporate sponsor Buick.[26]

Nowhere in advertising is product branding more important than in automobiles. So it was surprising to advertising-industry observers that Tiger wound up endorsing a Buick, a modest car aimed at a middle-class consumer, rather than a Ferrari or Lamborghini. The general rule is that celebrities cannot improve their image after developing an association with a down-scale brand. Fellow professional Fuzzy Zoeller had become the spokesman for K-Mart earlier and had never really risen above the so-called bargain image. Zoeller suffered severe criticism from PGA club pros who make a living selling brand-name golf clubs, and who did not want consumers getting the idea that you could buy clubs without the advice of a golf professional.[27] But the strong market appeal of Tiger Woods has defied all the general rules of marketing.

His appeal derives from a number of factors that converged to make Tiger Woods a marketing bonanza. He is young in a culture that idolizes youth. Nobody has accomplished what he has done in golf at his age. Consequently he is able to appeal to a coveted demographic while also reaching teenagers' parents. He is strikingly good-looking. His combined genetic makeup produces a broad range of appeal that is not limited to one segment of the population. The fact that an African American has been able to succeed in a sport that has a long history of discrimination, at a time when racial discrimination is universally denounced, only reinforces the popularity of his accomplishments. Finally, his Asian mother has both physically and spiritually influenced Tiger to respect her Thai roots, and he has endeavored to play golf around the world. His presence has contributed to the overall evolution of golf as an international sport. Starting with the institution of the Sony World Rankings of golf professionals, the game has steadily grown as an international attraction. With the creation of the Golf Channel in 1980, international golf has become a regular feature in American homes. Interest in the Ryder Cup competition has also spawned the

Presidents Cup, further fueling interest in international competition. Tiger Woods has been a contributing factor to this increased interest, while he has benefited financially as well.

Golf Magazine recently reviewed the financial worth of athletes and, not surprisingly, Tiger Woods stands as the number one compensated athlete in the United States Woods's total annual income was estimated at $127,902,706, with $22,902,706 in winnings (2007) and $105,000,000 in endorsements. He has earned over $800,000,000 during his 13-year career, and at age 32, he should become the first athlete to earn $1 billion in his career.[28]

What follows is a summary of the sponsorship arrangements Tiger has with various companies.

Nike

Tiger continues to represent the Nike Company. He wears their clothing as well as using their golf equipment. The first company to commit to Woods before he turned professional in 1996, Nike, with Tiger as their spokesman, has staked itself to a substantial portion of the golf marketplace. The terms of Tiger's most recent five-year deal (December 2006) were not disclosed, but the 2001 arrangement was reported as $100 million. What the sponsor gets for that money is evident in the meticulous planning that goes into what exactly Tiger will wear in which tournament. It is particularly important for the major tournaments, since by far they attract the largest television audiences and press coverage. For example, at the 2009 British Open, his wardrobe was anticipated almost 17 months before the tournament. Unfortunately for Nike, Tiger only had the opportunity to display two of the outfits designed since he missed the cut and therefore only played two days. The reason that the planning is done so far in advance is so that Nike can insure that the clothes will be available in retail stores immediately after they are seen on television.[29]

Gatorade

Gatorade is the first licensing agreement for Tiger. That means that he will not be simply endorsing their products but will actually have a say in the development of new products. In fact, he supposedly selected the first flavors (cherry blend, citrus blend, and grape). It became apparent that Tiger was leaning toward going to Gatorade when he started drinking it while playing on the tour, even at places where Gatorade was not available. During the 2009 U.S. Open at Bethpage, a series of new commercials was unveiled that featured a cartoon character of Tiger frolicking in the woods with cartoon animals, giving a strong indication of the marketing strategy, which is obviously to sell Gatorade to young people (or at least through their parents who might be watching the tournament).[30] Interestingly, the voiceover on the commercial is that of Kelly Tilghman, whose comments during a Golf Channel telecast sparked a controversy that will be covered later in this chapter, which indicates that Tiger does not hold a grudge against her. This deal is estimated at $100 million over five years.

Gillette

This arrangement highlights three dominant athletes in their respective sports, all appearing in ads with their faces covered with shaving cream. It is a good example of an attempt by an American company to appeal to an international audience. Most Americans would not recognize Thierry Henry as a soccer champion in the English Premier League, but tennis fans would certainly know Roger Federer as the winner of 15 major championships in tennis. And virtually everyone, golf fans or not, will recognize Tiger Woods. The deal is estimated at from $10 to $20 million.

EA Sports

Woods has made a significant entry into the world of video games. No stranger to video games himself, Tiger has expressed a preference for Sony's PlayStation line over Microsoft's consoles. He has told of growing up playing *Socom*, a series of military Special Forces simulations, in honor of his father's career as a member of the Green Berets. He has also admitted to being a fan of *Killzone 2* and of the Resident Evil series, and to not being aware of the minor controversy concerning the game's killing of African zombies. In spring 2009 Tiger became immersed in the promotion of his new video game, *Tiger Woods PGA Tour 10* from Electronic Arts.[31] Woods appeared on ABC's *Good Morning*

America with cohost Robin Roberts and played one hole, each scoring a par.[32]

Woods appeared with Late Night host Jimmy Fallon in a press event to promote the Wii version of his game in Times Square. Woods needed a hole-in-one on the last of the three-hole tournament to catch Fallon, but he didn't get it. ESPN host Scott van Pelt was quoted as telling Tiger, "You stink. No offense."[33]

The details of his deal with EA are unknown.

Accenture

This arrangement is a good example of corporate involvement with an athlete that goes beyond his simply endorsing their product. Accenture sponsors a series of international tournaments, the World Golf Championships, and it gives exposure for their international company to a world golf community. In addition to sponsoring the tournaments Accenture also airs commercials featuring Tiger, further associating the company with his winning brand. Tiger has been involved with Accenture since 2003. According to a study of business executives, since initiating the "Go on. Be a Tiger" campaign, Accenture's brand identity increased significantly.

James E. Murphy, Accenture's chief marketing and communications officer, gives some idea of why athletes in general, and Tiger Woods in particular, are excellent corporate images: "Tiger continues to be the ideal representative for our High Performance Business strategy. The world associates Tiger with high performance. He embodies the relentless pursuit of perfection, and we are delighted to continue our relationship with him."[34]

Target Corporation

In 1999 the Tiger Woods Foundation partnered with the Target Corporation to establish "Start Something," a scholarship program that encourages young people (8–17) to identify a goal and work toward achieving that objective. Target sponsored the first World Challenge tournament that first year. The event, which Tiger hosts, takes place in December after the regular golf season and is an invitational event with only 18 professionals competing. The prize money ($1.35 million to the winner) is comparable to regular season tournaments, even though the winnings are not calculated in the PGA Money List. In 2009 the Chevron Oil Company took over the principal sponsorship of the tournament.

The World Challenge is an example of the clout that Tiger exerts on the business community as well as the PGA Tour. In addition to this tournament, Tiger also hosts the ATT National Tournament, a regular tour event. Most of the proceeds from the tournament go to the Tiger Woods Foundation, in addition to some local charities. The PGA Tour gives more money to charity than the NBA, Major League Baseball, and the NFL combined.[35]

TAG Heuer

In 2003 Tiger began wearing TAG Heuer watches and representing the company, allowing this very high-end product to capitalize on the Woods phenomenon. Jean-Christophe Babin, TAG Heuer's president and chief executive officer, stated, "His personality, which is very close to TAG Heuer's values—such as his obsessive quest for superior achievements and perfection, his ability to withstand pressure, his commitment to live up to expectations and then surpass them, and also his passion for his discipline—seemed to make this a natural and appropriate partnership."[36] Despite this rather hyperbolic rhetoric, the company did produce a memorable television commercial early in the relationship, featuring Tiger hitting a golf ball in some Monte Carlo–type city as a Formula One race car speeds off on the course to beat the golf ball. The ball wins the mythical race.[37]

Tatweer: The Tiger Woods Dubai

Arnold Palmer and Jack Nicklaus were the first professional golfers to go into the business of designing golf courses. Other pro golfers have also, on a somewhat smaller scale, dabbled in the design business. Nicklaus's firm has 341 courses open for play in 34 countries and 39 states. Jack Nicklaus himself has actually been directly involved in the design of 271 of those courses. According to USA Today, a Nicklaus course has a $2.5 million price tag.[38] Despite Nicklaus's reputation as the most accomplished professional golfer of all time, so far he has had financial difficulties on two separate occasions—both times when he delegated too much responsibility for running his businesses to other people. In both instances Nicklaus came back to fiscal stability, and since he retired from competition he has taken much greater control over his business affairs.

Tiger established his own design company in 2006 and has several projects currently in the preliminary stages. The project is called the "Tiger Woods Dubai." It includes 100 villas, 75 mansions, 22 palaces, and a 360,000-square-foot boutique hotel. It is also to feature a 139,000-square-foot clubhouse and a golf academy.[39] The course and development were originally scheduled to open in fall 2009, but because of the downturn in the economy it looks like it will open in the summer of 2010. The houses in the development will range in price from $12 million to $23 million. Cognizant of Nicklaus's past financial problems, Tiger has steadily increased his involvement in the running of his various business deals. However, the worsening economy has had an impact on virtually all sports sponsorships, and Tiger is not immune.

Buick

Tiger has had a contract to represent the Buick car company since he came out on tour. Automobile companies have long been a regular advertiser at sporting events, and as our media environment diversifies and splinters, and audiences can record programming and fast-forward through commercials, sporting events provide a large, devoted audience that normally watches events live. Products like razor blades, beer, and automobiles seek this audience and have been a staple source of advertising dollars for sports stars and leagues.[40]

But in December 2008, after 12 years, Tiger and Buick parted ways, just before parent company General Motors filed for bankruptcy. It is estimated that the deal was worth $7.5 million per year for Tiger.

Over the past several years, as the economy has deteriorated, sponsors are rethinking their commitments to advertising at sporting events. The sporting world in general is constantly facing the challenges of securing and maintaining the sponsors who, in better economic times, are the underpinning of the funding of professional sports teams and leagues. The LPGA lost corporate sponsorship of two tournaments in

2009. Thus far the PGA has not lost any sponsorships, and they apparently have enough reserve funds to maintain their current schedule.

Tiger is criticized for not playing in enough PGA Tour events, which certainly has an effect on the general strength of the PGA Tour. However, his record is similar to that of Jack Nicklaus when he was in his prime. A PGA Tour member must compete in a minimum of 15 tournaments to keep his card. In 2005 Tiger played in 21 events. In 2006 he played in only 15, and he generally gears his schedule around the major championships. For obvious reasons his presence translates into more interest in the tournament, both in ticket sales and television ratings. The Golf Channel, which recently contracted with the PGA Tour to carry the Thursday/Friday rounds of most PGA tournaments, estimates their ratings drop between 18 and 33 percent when Tiger is not playing. From 2003 to 2008 Tiger competed in 88 tournaments. When he finished in the top five (54 times) the average ratings were 4.4. In the other 34 tournaments the rating was 3.4. In 2007, weekend tournament ratings were up 58 percent when he played.[41]

BEING TIGER WOODS

Being Tiger Woods is certainly not without its challenges. Early on he and his original team experienced problems establishing his image. The fact that he had a team was a problem in itself. Before Tiger was a teenager, there was a group of people who, along with his parents, provided support for the budding superstar. Irrespective of who these people were and how much they contributed, his parents were always the final authority—especially Earl Woods. In addition to Earl and Kultida, the original team consisted of Hughes Norton, Butch Harmon, Fluff Cowan, Jay Brunza, and John Merchant. Since turning professional the team has not remained the same.

The most significant change in Tiger's advisors was Mark Steinberg, who replaced Hughes Norton as Tiger's IMG agent at the end of 1999. Steinberg was young, 30, and had a background in athletics. He was a backup player for the University of Illinois and sat on the bench during the 1989 NCAA Championships. Replacing Norton was a delicate situation. Norton had initially convinced Earl to consider signing up with IMG during Tiger's junior career and arranged for Earl to work for IMG.

There had been growing discontent with Hughes's over-scheduling Tiger in nontournament activities, which paid off in dollars (and commissions) but took their toll on the golfer.[42]

Claude "Butch" Harmon Jr. was the son of Claude Harmon, who defeated Dr. Cary Middlecoff by five strokes in the 1948 Masters. Claude was the father of four sons, all of whom were great teachers of golf, although none of them could beat their father. After attending the University of Houston for one year, Butch dropped out and joined the army. He served in Alaska, where he won the Alaska State Amateur, and eventually spent six months in Vietnam. He competed for two years on the PGA Tour and then went to Morocco, where he was King Hassan II's personal golf professional. It was at the Champions Club in Houston, after Tiger had lost in the second round of the 1993 U.S. Amateur, that Earl Woods had lunch with Harmon and asked if he would work with Tiger. Harmon was Tiger's coach from then until 2004.[43]

Throughout most of Tiger's junior career, navy psychiatrist Jay Brunza served as Tiger's caddie and sports psychologist. He was replaced on Tiger's bag at the 1996 U.S. Amateur by Byron Bell. Brunza held no grudges, saying, "I trust Tiger's judgment about what he needs to win."[44]

When Tiger announced he was turning professional in 1996, Mike "Fluff" Cowan was his caddie. Cowan was loaned to Tiger by Peter Jacobson, who was recovering from a back injury. Eventually Fluff stayed on, and some in the golf community felt that this was a breach of professional etiquette. Nonetheless, Cowan established a persona for himself with the media. He did his own commercials and was generally media friendly. By the 1999 Nissan Open, Tiger told Cowan that he was replacing him on his bag temporarily. Reportedly the reason was the overexposure Cowan was receiving in the media. In a *Golf Digest* interview Cowan disclosed his pay scale, saying he "...made $1,000 a week, plus standard percentages for wins [10%] and top ten finishes,"[45] and finally when Tiger observed him doing television interviews, he was replaced.

Tiger's new caddie was in many ways the antithesis of Fluff. A New Zealander, fit and not at all conversant with the media, Steve Williams was working for Raymond Floyd when Tiger contacted him. He carried Tiger's bag for the first time at the March 1999 Bay Hill Invitational in Florida. Tall, trim, and athletic, and a fairly accomplished golfer on his own, Williams often played practice rounds with Tiger. While Fluff enjoyed interacting with the fans and the press, Williams was nowhere to be found after the round. And there was little chance of seeing Williams in any television commercials.

John Merchant was the first African American to be named to the USGA Executive Committee, and he was involved in some of the decisions concerning Tiger's amateur status during his amateur career. A Connecticut lawyer, Merchant had worked with Earl in the mid-1990s in an organization called the National Minority Golf Foundation.[46] This group met annually and tried to encourage the growth of golf in the minority community. Several corporations helped underwrite the organization, including *Golf Digest* and Titleist. At one time Merchant served as the first head of the Tiger Woods Foundation. But in December of 1996 he was fired. Tiger has said he made the decision, but Merchant says he was fired by Earl: "I haven't talked to Tiger since. I was puzzled by it. But lawyers come and go, so I got out of Dodge."[47]

Another new member of Team Tiger was Greg McLaughlin. Earl and Tiger had first encountered McLaughlin when he was a tournament director and granted sponsor's exemptions for Tiger at the 1991 Nissan Open and the Honda Classic in 1992. Later he served as director of the Western Golf Association. Indicative of Tiger's increasing assumption of control of his own affairs, McLaughlin commented, "I see a huge difference [in attitude] between 1997 and 1999. The swing changes are one thing, but he seems to be much more 'with it.' He manages the whole thing a lot better now than he did a couple of years ago. That comes with experience, age, maturity, whatever you want to call it."[48]

Earlier in Tiger's career, there were a series of incidents that could only be called public relations disasters. The first involved an award that was to honor his amateur play and occurred as Tiger was scheduled to play in the 1996 Buick Challenge tournament. Following his unprecedented third U.S. Amateur victory in August, Tiger had played in four consecutive tournaments as a professional and had climbed to 128 on the money list, virtually assuring his place on the 1997 PGA Tour. He was exhausted and decided not to accept the sponsor's exemption for the Buick Challenge. However, he had committed to attend the Fred Haskins Award Dinner on the Thursday night during the tournament to be honored as the College Player of the Year. Given the tremendous interest Tiger had generated in his first days as a professional, the dinner was immediately sold out in anticipation of his presence.[49] When the news of his withdrawal from the tournament leaked out there was obvious disappointment, and when it was learned that he had declined to attend, the dinner was canceled. The press savaged Tiger and his team.[50]

Immediately Tiger realized that he had made a mistake. Two weeks later he was scheduled to compete in the Las Vegas Open. He sent a letter of apology to each person who was to attend the dinner. In a column he wrote for *Golf World*, he said:

> I am human...and I do make mistakes. The decision to miss the Fred Haskins Award Dinner being held in my honor two weeks ago was one of them. Wow, did I get blasted for that and withdrawing from the Buick Challenge...I didn't realize how tired I was after the U.S. Amateur...I never got a chance to rest. I kept playing...I didn't even think about the dinner. I realize now that what I did was wrong. But hindsight is 20/20.[51]

The following year on tour there were other decisions that resulted in bad press. After winning the Masters in May, Tiger was invited to participate in a ceremony scheduled to honor the 50th anniversary of Jackie Robinson's breaking of the color line in baseball. President Clinton was to participate in the event at Shea Stadium. The invitation went through IMG and Tiger said no. Even before the fallout from this snub of the president had subsided, another controversy erupted.

There is a tradition at the Masters that the defending champion hosts the Champions Dinner and chooses the menu on the eve of the tournament. That meant Tiger would select the menu for the 1998 dinner. During an interview with CNN, 1979 Masters Champion and tour kibitzer Fuzzy Zoeller made an offhand remark that immediately was picked up by every news organization. Concluding his complimentary remarks about Tiger's record-setting performance at the Masters, Zoeller added, "The little boy's playing great out there. Just tell him not to serve fried chicken at the [Champions] dinner next year," but then added, "Or collard greens or whatever it is they serve."[52] As a result of the comments, Zoeller took a terrible beating in the press, culminating in K-Mart, his corporate sponsor, dropping him as their spokesman. He was unable to talk to Tiger directly to apologize and finally publicly asked Tiger to call him to discuss the incident. Several players represented by Nike called and implored Tiger to make some kind of comment to defuse the situation. It was not until three days after the second apology that Tiger finally made a public statement accepting Zoeller's apology. The incident did little to endear Tiger to a number of his fellow tour professionals.

Another misunderstanding further strained Tiger's relationship with his golfing colleagues. Several weeks after the Masters, Tiger was scheduled to play in the Byron Nelson Classic in Dallas. Billy Andrade was an outgoing golfer who had befriended Tiger when he first came on the tour. Andrade and Brad Faxon run a charity golf tournament in Delaware every year, and as a fundraiser they ask fellow pros to sign golf balls to be auctioned. They wanted to assemble a dozen balls each signed by a Masters Champion, so they asked Tiger to provide them with a signed ball. Tiger refused. Jack Nicklaus had signed and Arnold Palmer had signed. Nick Faldo and Tom Watson had signed. When two young boys read about the story, they donated a ball Tiger had signed when he was an amateur. The actor Joe Pesci bid $50,000 for the dozen balls and gave the Tiger-autographed ball back to the two boys; the publicity about the incident resulted in a record auction for charity. Eventually Tiger donated a signed lithograph, but once again he had exhibited poor judgment, not atypical of a 20-year-old.[53] But Tiger was not a typical 20-year-old.

His youth also led to another problem when, according to an Associated Press report, Tiger was able to get into the Lucky Lady River Boat Casino in Iowa, using fake I.D. When the bouncer was informed that this was Tiger Woods, he was quoted as saying, "I don't care if it's the Lion King."[54]

An article in the March 1997 issue of *Gentleman's Quarterly* provided another lesson in Tiger's education in dealing with the media. Writer Charlie Pierce accompanied Tiger on a photo shoot that would appear in the magazine. Under the assumption that he was speaking off-the-record, Tiger let his guard down and told several slightly off-color jokes with racial and gay-bashing themes. The reaction to the

GQ story varied. Some felt it humanized Tiger, while others felt it was just reward for limiting his interviews to a select few reporters who tended to sanitize their subject for public consumption.[55]

Despite the occasional bad press, Tiger's public image did not suffer. As he matured and began to take on more responsibility for his actions, he relied less on handlers. The result was generally better press. But famous athletes always maintain a love/hate relationship with the reporters who cover them. The reporters need access to the athletes, and so they are necessarily reluctant to criticize these people who can make or break their careers. A reporter who writes negative stories about an athlete generally loses access to that athlete, and conversely, generally the negative stories come from reporters who have been denied access to that athlete. That has been the case with Tiger.

Despite his unprecedented accomplishments on the golf course, when *Sports Illustrated* made Tiger the Sportsman of the Year in 1996, Mike Lupica (*Daily News*) said, "Tiger Woods was one of the best sports stories of the whole year. His first month on the PGA Tour was one of the most exciting things to ever happen to the PGA Tour. But he was not the Sportsman of the Year. Unless you can win Sportsman of the Year on spec these days."[56] In the cover story, Earl could not restrain himself from expressing his understandably inflated predictions for his son. He claimed that Tiger would eventually have a greater impact on society than Nelson Mandela, Gandhi, and Buddha. His reasoning was that because of modern means of communication, Tiger would have a larger forum. While his reasoning was sound, it was not the sort of thing that one should actually say out loud. The reaction of the press pretty much reflected the access the respective reporters had to the Woods camp: the closer you were to the team, the less likely you were to pan Earl's comments.

But such comments only put more pressure on Tiger in his dealings with the press. It was only natural that the press expected him, as a minority, to weigh in on issues beyond the world of golf. The most uncomfortable situation occurred during the 2003 Masters tournament. Several months before the event, Martha Burk, the president of the National Organization for Women, wrote the president of Augusta National demanding that the all-male club admit a woman member. In the months leading up to the tournament the story made front-page news, culminating with the *New York Times* recommending in an editorial that Augusta should admit women and suggesting that Tiger Woods should boycott the tournament.[57] As defending champion, it was inevitable that Tiger Woods would be drawn into the controversy. Pulitzer Prize–winning columnist Dave Anderson's column encouraging Woods to play was initially suppressed by the *Times* editors. Burk called for a boycott of the tournament and urged CBS to cancel the telecast. Burk also called for Tiger to refuse to compete in protest. Opinions in the media were split. Everyone wanted a statement from Tiger. He finally spoke out on the issue, saying that he felt Augusta should allow female members, but that as a private club they should be able to deal with membership policies themselves. Not surprisingly, nobody was interested in the opinions of other golfers competing in the Masters.

It became apparent that Tiger Woods would be expected to do more than play golf. Other black athletes had established reputations for speaking out on racial issues. Jackie Robinson, Arthur Ashe, and Muhammad Ali were no strangers to controversy and spoke out on issues of race, the Vietnam War, and discrimination. The press wanted Tiger to follow in that tradition; Tiger just wanted to play golf. However, the 24-hours-aday/7-days-a-week saturation of media makes it increasingly difficult for a public person, regardless of his sphere of influence, to remain silent.

Despite his reluctance to insert himself in every political or social issue demanded by the press, Tiger, with strong support from his parents, has been committed to helping less fortunate people beyond the world of golf. Even before Tiger was making an income from playing golf, he was giving back. As a junior golfer he was offering clinics for young people, particularly minority youth. After completing his second round in the 1995 Masters, Tiger left Augusta immediately and traveled across town to the Forest Hills Golf Club, a municipal course. He conducted a clinic for a group of black children and some of the black caddies from Augusta National. Following the Masters, Tiger sent a letter to the Augusta officials thanking them for inviting him to play in the Masters. Several of the more cynical reporters dismissed his letter and the fact that he did the clinic as propaganda engineered by Earl. While questioning the motivation for Tiger's actions, one writer for the

San Francisco Chronicle made a point that had eluded other reporters: "The letter and the clinic smack ominously of a father instilling values in his son. Almost 900 golfers have played in 59 Masters tournaments, and only one of them has taken the time to give a clinic at that frumpy muni course."[58]

As he matured and his career flourished, the public wanted more information about Tiger and his personal life. The first public relationship with a woman became evident when Joanna Jagoda began attending Tiger's tournaments occasionally with Kultida. Jagoda was a former college cheerleader who went on to law school at Pepperdine University, and she fit the physical stereotype for the women of most touring professionals—tall, blonde, and attractive. At the 1999 Ryder Cup matches, Justin Leonard sank a crucial putt on the 17th hole of his match with José María Olazábal that virtually assured America would retain the cup. When the European press witnessed the invasion of American players' wives and girlfriends streaming onto the green in celebration, they wondered, "How is it possible they all married the same cocktail waitress?"[59] The press speculated about how marriage would affect Tiger's dedication to the game. Even Jack Nicklaus questioned whether Tiger would be able to maintain his unwavering concentration when he was also responsible as a husband and father. The relationship with Jagoda lasted for two years.

In 2004 Tiger married former Swedish model Elin Nordegren in a guarded ceremony in a Caribbean resort. The couple had met two years earlier when she was serving as nanny for golfer Jesper Parnevik's children. As with any aspect of Tiger's personal life, the press had a voracious appetite for details, and Tiger and his representatives were just as diligent in trying to maintain his privacy. The lavish wedding took place in an exclusive resort in Barbados and reportedly cost $2 million; and the 150-person guest list included celebrities such as Michael Jordan, Oprah Winfrey, and Bill Gates. A small army of security personnel was enlisted to provide security for the guests, who were ushered onto a $57 million yacht. By this time, Team Tiger had become much more comfortable working with the media.

It is interesting to reflect back on how Tiger was raised and how it will be difficult for him to repeat the process with his own children. As has been stated, Earl was determined not to repeat the mistakes he felt he

Elin Nordegren looks to her husband, Tiger Woods, following the opening ceremonies for the 2005 Presidents Cup on September 22, 2005, at the Robert Trent Jones Golf Club in Gainesville, Virginia. AP Photo/Rob Carr.

had made in raising his first family. The vast amounts of time he was away from the family, in part because of his military commitment, clearly not only had an effect on his relationship with his children, but also was a critical element of the divorce. So Earl devoted himself to his child from the second marriage. When Tiger was born, Earl had left the Army and was working at Graumann and had normal working hours. Therefore he was able to devote more time to Tiger and how he was raised. Ironically, Tiger probably will not get such a chance with his own children.

Despite his stated commitment to take his family along with him when he travels, it will remain to be seen how long he will be able to continue to do this.[60] In John Feinstein's book,[61] written with Rocco Mediate, he alludes to the deterioration of Mediate's marriage of 21 years. For all the media build-up of Mediate as the jocular common everyman, he succumbed to the same pressures that plague many professional athletes.

How Tiger will deal with balancing his family life with his profession remains to be seen. While the children are young it is obviously easier to accomplish. As they get older and need to attend school, they may not want to travel away from their friends. Of course, unlike the journeyman professional golfer, Tiger will be able to afford any level of accommodation when his family travels with him.

During Tiger's long recovery period from knee surgery, between June 2008 and April 2009, he had the unusual opportunity to be around his family more than ever before. He has publicly stated that he enjoyed his time at home with his family. It remains to be seen whether that extended time at home will affect his approach to playing competitive golf.

Thus far he has embraced fatherhood with the same dedication and determination he applies to his golf game. Wife Elin gave birth to their first child, a daughter, Sam Alexis, on the early Monday morning of June 18, 2007. Tiger had finished second the day before in the U.S. Open at Oakmont. There was some notice taken of the name Sam, which is somewhat gender nonspecific. There was of course speculation as to whether or not the name had any significance. This is not the name associated with frilly pink dresses. Was Tiger disappointed that she was not a boy? Did the name predict how she would be raised? Was she destined to take up the game of golf? Tiger was quoted as saying, "Yes, she clunked me on the head once. She has this cut down little putter she likes to drag around and that's neat."[62] So it seems that she will at least be introduced to golf.

On Sunday, February 8, 2009, Tiger's wife Elin gave birth to their second child, a boy, Charlie Axel Woods. The middle names of both children are derivatives of "Alex," the name of Elin's brother, which the parents wanted to keep in the family. The first son of Tiger Woods will of course be the subject of much speculation by the press. As the sons of other famous athletes have found out, it is difficult, if not impossible, for the son to live up to the father's accomplishments. While there have been a number of professional golfers who have had sons follow in the father's footprints and go on to play professional golf, there has not yet been one who has matched the father's records.

Jack Nicklaus is the most famous such father—he had two sons who were fairly accomplished golfers. Son Gary actually made it to the PGA Tour in 2000, but he finished 169 and 218 on the money list the succeeding two years and, after playing on various minitours, applied for and was granted his amateur status in subsequent years. Jack's other son, Jack Jr., was a creditable golfer but was most remembered as father Jack's caddie when Nicklaus won his last major at the Masters at the age of 46. "People always ask, 'How does it feel to be Jack Nicklaus, Jr.?' And he'd say, 'Well, I've never been anything else. What difference would it make? That's what I am.' And that's what his answer used to be when he was a kid, so he never really had a big issue with it. It is what it is."[63] Both sons are now involved with their father's golf design business and they are fashioning good careers.

Probably a good indication of how Tiger will handle his own children when and if they intend to participate in golf is his relationship with his niece, Cheyenne. The daughter of Tiger's half brother, Earl Jr., Cheyenne Woods is an accomplished golfer who competed for Wake Forest University's golf team as a sophomore. She has more than 30 amateur championships, and she was the second-lowest scorer for Wake Forest when they finished tied for 13th in the 2009 NCAA women's championships. Earl Woods Sr. served as her advisor and mentor when he was alive. Since Earl's death, Tiger has stepped in as a sounding board for Cheyenne. When Tiger competed in a tournament in Charlotte in May 2009, he left tickets for Cheyenne and her teammates to attend the final round of the competition.[64]

In June 2009 she was granted a sponsor's exemption to compete in Wegman's LPGA tournament outside of Rochester, New York. Beyond the burden of her family name, she also is attempting to become only the fourth African American woman to earn an LPGA card, and the first since LaRee Sugg played on the tour in 2000.[65] Cheyenne missed making the cut by four strokes but played well on a difficult golf course.

In comparison to any famous professional athlete in the past, Tiger Woods is entering the prime of his career, and based on his current success in professional golf, he may be destined for other accomplishments beyond the world of sports. He began as a child prodigy, and the problem with prodigies is that they do not always fulfill the public's elevated expectations. And the public's expectations are being fanned by an ever more incendiary media. During his junior and amateur career, Tiger was promoted by the media as both a model golfer and a model young man. But while he was once able to concentrate his entire being on the perfection of his golf game, he now faces the challenges of balancing the rest of his adult life with the game he plays. He is a businessman, a husband, a son, and a role model. He is a man with an exceptional ability to play the game of golf, but the media has created a situation in which he has to live up to some imaginary standard, ironically one he established—not only in golf, but also in his personal life.

After his brilliant and unprecedented introduction to professional golf in 1997, Tiger decided to completely rework his golf swing in 1998 and 1999, and though he won a major championship and nine tournaments overall, the media began to ask the question: was Tiger in a slump? The answer in 2000 was the first three legs of his Grand Slam, completed at the 2001 Masters. He went on to win the Masters and U.S. Open Championships in 2002. For the next three years he did not win a major championship, and the press again began to wonder if Tiger had lost his desire to compete. Speculation became more intense as he became more involved in outside corporate projects, devoted more time to the foundation, and became engaged and subsequently married. During the 2004 season, Tiger did not win a stroke play tournament[66] and finished no higher than ninth in any of the majors. However, he extended his streak of consecutive cuts[67] made, a PGA Tour record, and continued to work on his game. In early 2005 he won twice and gave every indication of a new dedication to his game. Then in April he won his fourth Master championship, finished second in the U.S. Open, won the British Open for a second time at St. Andrews, and finished tied for fourth in the PGA Championship. But the media and the public, as reflected by the press, want perfection.

It is impossible to examine the life of Tiger Woods without observing the growing and inexhaustible need the public has for more personal information about interesting, accomplished, and beautiful people. Media executives argue that it is the public that creates the need and that the media simply satisfies the need, but that is an oversimplification. The question should be: How accurate is the information the media is dispensing? With the ever-growing number of media outlets, there is an increasing need for more information to fill the increased

time and space, but there is less and less time for reflection. Print journalism was always controlled by a deadline, but the electronic media
have virtually eliminated the chance to check facts. Because of the
printing process there was some opportunity for editors to review copy,
check facts, and verify sources. With instantaneous modern media distribution, the practice of editing before distributing information on a
media outlet is a luxury that competition renders obsolete. It is becoming more difficult for even the most concerned, careful, and conscientious reporter to take a sufficient amount of time to complete even
rudimentary research. There was a time when the book was the most
reliable source of information. It was a cumbersome process and cost a
great deal of money to write, print, and distribute, but these very factors
assured an element of veracity. Today the Internet makes it possible to
get access to millions of sources without leaving one's study. And while
conducting research on the Internet in and of itself is not bad, it does
pose the danger of relying on information that may be of questionable origins. Ultimately the most reliable sources for reporters are the
people they cover. But the closer reporters get to the source, the less
objective they become.

Tiger Woods is a good example of this catch-22. John Feinstein, an
excellent writer and commentator, has been the most critical of Tiger,
and more particularly the influence IMG exerted on him early in his
career. Feinstein, presumably because of his negative articles, has had
little access to Team Tiger. Reporters who have good things to say about
Tiger and Earl tend to be allowed to get closer to Tiger and his team.
Those that don't, aren't. If reporters are denied access to the source,
then what we know comes either directly from the source or a reporter
who is close to the source. Most of what the public knows about Earl,
for example, comes from his own books.

Earl Woods was clearly a man who felt he had done a good job raising his son and wanted some credit. But he alluded to the fact that no
matter how good a parent he might have been, Tiger's development as
a person and as a golfer was driven by something beyond his parents.
Earl made the mistake of saying that very thing out loud, and the press
jumped on him. He talked candidly about his first marriage publicly,
and the problems with his former wife after Tiger became successful.
He had a decent relationship with his kids from his first marriage, but

he admitted he had not been a very good father to them. He was even quite forthcoming about his relationship with Kultida. So it is hard to accuse him of having tried to sugarcoat his life. It is difficult to take to task the man who raised Tiger Woods.

The question then becomes: can we not just appreciate excellence for what it is? Does Tiger Woods have to do anything other than excel at golf? Does he also have to speak for all people who have been or ever will be discriminated against? Is it not enough that he has succeeded as a minority in the professional sport that most epitomizes privilege and exclusion? Most professional golfers on the PGA Tour went to college on golf scholarships and when they graduated went directly into a job that afforded luxuries not normally associated with the masses. They operate as independent contractors or entrepreneurs, and they tend to be conservative in their politics. Tiger Woods is the closest thing to diversity in the upper echelons of touring golf professionals.

Tiger Woods continues to be measured by a different yardstick than are other golfers on the PGA Tour. Most professional athletes scoff at the idea that they have a responsibility as role models. Tiger Woods has the opportunity to become the greatest golfer ever, and along the way provide a role model for young people, especially minorities. By any account, so far he has done a pretty good job.

THE TIGER WOODS FOUNDATION

Whether calculated or not, immediately upon Tiger's turning professional in 1996, Tiger and Earl established the Tiger Woods Foundation. The foundation has grown in direct proportion to Tiger's accomplishments. Virtually every one of the corporations Tiger represents has some program that is connected to his foundation. His association with Target Corporation has been the most visible example of these philanthropic relationships. In addition to sponsoring a golf tournament, the Target World Challenge, the corporation has created a program designed to help young people, called "Start Something." Unlike many charity tournaments, this one gets network coverage because Tiger Woods competes in it, along with a host of other prominent pros. Recently the Woods Foundation was awarded a grant from Orange County in Southern California to build the Tiger Woods Learning Center. The Center will be an educational resource to young people of diverse backgrounds, aimed at improving reading, math, and science skills.[68]

On February 10, 2006, Tiger Woods officially dedicated the Tiger Woods Learning Center in Anaheim, California. The event attracted a large audience and featured remarks from Tiger as well as former President Bill Clinton and California first lady Maria Shriver. It is significant that the center opened in Anaheim, next to Cypress, the place where Tiger grew up. And it was not coincidental that the music was provided by the Western High School band—the public high school that Tiger attended, located next to the H. G. Miller Golf Course where he played on the golf team.

The opening was the culmination of a $25 million campaign to build this state-of-the-art educational center. The building houses 100 computers and a 1,200-square-foot multimedia center. It is important to point out that this center is not a golf academy. The center provides children in grades 4 to 12 access to supplemental educational programs.

Tiger Woods and his mother, Kultida, smile next to a bronze statue bearing the likeness of Tiger with his late father, Earl Woods, during its unveiling inside the Tiger Woods Learning Center in Anaheim, California, on January 21, 2008. AP Photo/Damian Dovarganes.

President Clinton said, "I'm glad Tiger Woods decided to do this when he was 30 instead of when he was 60. It's hard to have great gifts and bring them to bear in the public eye under enormous pressure when you're young."[69] He went on to say that it was difficult to accomplish what he has on the golf course and still start giving back at this point in Tiger's life. Unfortunately Earl was too ill to attend the opening, but his presence was certainly felt through Tiger's remarks. Originally the Woods Foundation was planning to convert the vacant Hine Junior High School into the educational center, but recently those plans changed and the foundation is still looking for a suitable site.[70]

Charity Navigator, an organization that reviews financial records of various charities, gives the Tiger Woods Foundation four stars— its highest rating. One reason is that the foundation in 2005 reported spending $1 million, a relatively low percentage of revenue, on management and fundraising expenses.[71]

RIVALRIES

The media tend to build up their own stories, particularly when it comes to sports. It was not lost on the press that interest in the game of golf was significantly heightened in the 1960s and 1970s when Jack Nicklaus challenged Arnold Palmer as the best golfer. And in fact there are a number of parallels between the phenomenon of Tiger Woods and that of Jack Nicklaus. When Nicklaus first came out on the tour in 1960, he was a slightly pudgy golf machine. Arnold Palmer had the reputation of the people's choice. He wore his emotions on his sleeve. You always knew whether Palmer hit a good shot or bad; he reacted viscerally. Nicklaus was much more businesslike. Eventually by dint of his exceptional golf game, he did earn the respect of the golfing public. But to this day, even though Nicklaus's record far outshines that of Palmer, Arnold Palmer is still considered "The King."

So it is not surprising that the media have tried to establish rivalries between Tiger and anybody they could. One of the biggest problems Tiger has faced in his career is that there is no individual who has consistently challenged him throughout his career. There have been individuals who have defeated him, but no one who consistently challenges him on a regular basis. So the media have desperately tried to create rivalries. First there was Sergio García.

García is an accomplished professional in the tradition of his Spanish countryman Seve Ballesteros. Seve lit up the golfing world during the 1970s and 1980s when he won five major championships. But it was not just that he won, but rather how he won. He is probably the most creative shot maker in the history of the game. His scrambling[72] ability made him one of the most colorful golfers of all time. Ballesteros was chiefly responsible for the resurgence of the European Ryder Cup teams during this period.[73] Because of Seve's success in Europe and on the American tour, golf became a popular sport in Spain. As a high-spirited teenager, his younger countryman Sergio García challenged Tiger in the 1999 PGA Championship. After sinking a putt on the 17th hole that put him one stroke behind Woods, Sergio turned to the tee and signaled Tiger to "bring it on." Eventually Tiger defeated García by one stroke, but the media smelled a rivalry.

When he first came on the tour, Sergio was a breath of fresh air. His youthful exuberance was highlighted in the 1999 PGA when he was faced with an impossible lie after his tee shot wound up against a tree, virtually eliminating any opportunity to go for the green in two. However, Sergio took a wild swipe at the ball, recoiling from the shot, protecting himself from the possibility of the ball ricocheting back to hit him. The ball amazingly wound up on the green, as Sergio vaulted up the fairway, jumping up to be able to see the elevated green. It was these kinds of shenanigans that endeared Sergio to fans early in his career. However, as time went on, he has arguably not lived up to his potential, and he has tended to turn sullen as a player. Sergio is the latest player to be saddled with the designated title of "best player never to have won a major." This moniker has soured many a professional golfer. Sergio did beat Tiger in the 2000 edition of Battle at the Bighorn, a made-for-TV event after the regular golf season.

The second media-generated rivalry was between Tiger and David Duval. Duval, the son of a golf professional, actually was ranked number one in the world in 1999. Duval was one of only two golfers to shoot the magical score of 59 in a regular PGA event, in his case the 1999 Bob Hope Desert Classic. Duval had a kind of a Darth Vader image on the tour. He always wore reflector sunglasses, even sometimes during television interviews. He also displayed a sour demeanor both on the course and off. So the media tried to generate controversy between him and Woods. But after the 2000 British Open, Duval virtually disappeared from the professional golf scene due to a series of injuries. After getting married and starting a family, however, he began a comeback, which culminated in a dramatic performance at the 2009 U.S. Open. Ranked 829th in the world, he finished third overall in the tournament, coming back from a triple bogey early in the final round. In an effort to capitalize on the interest in Tiger and whoever his competition was, the ABC Television Network started a made-for-TV competition featuring Tiger and David Duval at the Canyons course at Bighorn Golf Club in Indio, California, in 1999. In this match play competition Tiger defeated Duval one-up.

Most recently the media glare has settled on the competition between Tiger and Phil Mickelson. Phil Mickelson was probably the most celebrated example of "best player not to have" for many years before his breakthrough victory at the 2004 Masters. He has since gone on to win three majors. Unlike the relationship with David Duval, Tiger and Phil Mickelson have never been the best of friends. The difference in their backgrounds probably had something to do with their cool relationship. Phil, like Tiger, was brought up in Southern California. While Phil did not enjoy a "country club" upbringing, he was the product of a white middle-class family. He went to Arizona State University on a golf scholarship after a fairly anonymous junior golf career. Mickelson has the distinction of being the fourth amateur to win a PGA Tour event, the Northern Telecom Open in 1991.

Mickelson's career has not been without its downside. While he has won 43 tournaments, including, finally, a major championship, he has been unsuccessful in winning the U.S. Open, undoubtedly the most coveted crown for an American player. In fact, Mickelson has finished second a record five times in the national championship. In all five of those tournaments, he has had the chance to win on the last few holes but has always had some disastrous occurrence. At the 2007 Open at Winged Foot Golf Club in New York, he was leading by one stroke with the 18th hole to play. Needing only a par to win, he used a driver and drove the ball into trees, ultimately double bogeying the hole and losing to Geoff Ogilvy. Over the past seven years, the

Open has been held at New York area golf clubs, and Phil Mickelson has been the clear crowd favorite in New York. He has had three of those second-place finishes happen in New York, which probably has something to do with the empathy the New York fans feel toward Phil. This was especially the case at the 2009 Open at Bethpage. Several weeks before the tournament, Phil's very popular wife Amy Mickelson was diagnosed with breast cancer, and the golfing community and the public reached out to Mickelson and his family. Unlike Mickelson, who enthusiastically courts the public by signing autographs liberally and acknowledging the public even when competing in a tournament, Tiger tends to be so lost in concentration during a tournament that he rarely signs autographs or interacts with the crowds. At the 2009 U.S. Open, Mickelson was in contention during the final round. He was seen giving high fives to spectators lining the walkways between holes. Tiger's demeanor on the golf course is all business. He rarely acknowledges the fans.

The relationship was further damaged by an incident in 2008 when Tiger's caddy, Steve Williams, was quoted in an article in the British newspaper *The Guardian*, referring to Mickelson with an expletive and saying that "he didn't consider Mickelson as a great player."[74] Mickelson subsequently issued a statement taking exception to the Williams remarks, and Tiger was forced to issue his own statement: "I was disappointed to read the comments attributed to Steve Williams about Phil Mickelson, a player that I respect. It was inappropriate. The matter has been discussed and dealt with."[75] The fact that Williams was involved in this incident certainly could not have endeared him to his boss. As has been noted, Tiger fired his first caddy, Fluff Cowan, for getting too familiar with the press. A few years earlier Mickelson had made remarks about what he called the inferior equipment Woods was using, so the two have not been particularly close.

Human nature roots for the underdog. So in sports, no matter how good someone is, or some team is, eventually public opinion will shift toward the individual or team that is not favored. This phenomenon probably explains why some people absolutely hate the New York Yankee baseball team, and it may explain how the media has tended to cover Tiger Woods over the years of his career. When he first came out on tour he was the media phenom. He won at a pace that had never been seen before, and everybody was on his bandwagon. But eventually when there seemed to be no more real challengers for Tiger, the media started creating these rivalries, almost in an effort to create some competition. In the final analysis, if there is no competition, there is not much of a story.

And one would be naive to think that race was not a factor in the media coverage of Tiger. Wood's ethnicity has certainly affected the coverage, especially in the sport of golf, which, despite the USGA's efforts to diversify the game, for the most part is still associated with people of means. Recently the president of Venezuela, Hugo Chávez, announced that officials of his administration would close down two of the country's best known golf courses. "Let's leave this clear, golf is a bourgeois sport,"[76] Chávez said.

There is undoubtedly resentment at the amount of coverage Tiger gets, even when he is not in contention to win a tournament. Ironically, there are people who feel that the press is prejudiced in favor of Tiger because he is a minority. He is also subject to much different scrutiny than virtually anyone else on the tour. If he swears after a bad shot there is a comment. When he tends to give very pat answers to questions from interviewers, he is criticized. Of course whatever he says becomes big news. This is not the case with other players, unless they say something controversial.

When Kelly Tilghman blurted out in banter with Nick Faldo during the telecast of the 2008 Mercedes Championship that younger players on the tour might want to "lynch him [Tiger]," a furor was unleashed by the media immediately. Ultimately Rev. Al Sharpton called for the Golf Channel to fire her. While the Golf Channel did not fire her—they instead suspended her for two weeks from their telecasts—the incident does shed some light on the uniqueness of Tiger Woods's media coverage. Immediately there was pressure from the press for Tiger to comment on the incident. Tiger's agent from IMG, Mark Steinberg, put out a statement indicating that nobody in the Tiger camp took offense from the remark, and that Tiger and Kelly have known each other for 12 years and are friends. It is worth noting that Tiger himself did not comment directly about the incident, but IMG did not want to repeat the problem that occurred when Fuzzy Zoeller made an ethnic joke earlier in his career. It is worth pointing out the irony that the media has created this very wary Tiger, but they complain about his lack of candor.

Recently Tiger was the object of some harsh criticism for his alleged lack of a social conscience. As part of a profile of former Cleveland Browns running back Jim Brown and Boston Celtic basketball center Bill Russell on HBO's series *Real Sports with Bryant Gumbel*, Woods was singled out as someone who was not doing enough for underprivileged people. Brown said that Tiger was "a monster competitor...he is a killer. He'll run you over, he'll kick your [butt], but as an individual for social change, or any of that kind of [stuff]...terrible. Terrible. Because he can get away with teaching kids to play golf and that's his contribution."[77]

Jim Brown said both Brown and Russell were two outstanding athletes who came of age in the 1960s at a time when African Americans were questioning whether their hard won civil rights would result in any significant changes in their lives. Two incidents in particular exemplify this challenge, and both Brown and Russell took stands. In 1968 both athletes came to the aid of Muhammad Ali, supporting his refusal to be inducted into the military draft. And when Dr. Harry Edwards tried to organize a boycott of the 1968 Olympic Games, Russell and Brown publicly supported the effort.[78]

It should be pointed out that the Tiger Woods Learning Center in California does not teach youngsters how to play golf. It represents a substantial curriculum that prepares lower- and middle-class students, who might not otherwise have a chance to get this supplemental instruction, to go to college. To date the Center has served 20,000 to 25,000 young people. Brown's assertions assume that social change comes about only by confrontation. It should also be pointed out that Jim Brown had already retired from professional football when he became actively involved in social justice causes. As a 33-year-old man in the prime of his career, Tiger Woods seems to be using his leverage to help less fortunate people. It seems that it is no coincidence that Tiger's ATT Challenge tournament is contested at Congressional Club in Washington, D.C., where Tiger intends to build the next Learning Center.

Tiger is even compared to athletes in other sports. All famous athletes are expected to perform at their best when it counts. Michael

Jordan, a good friend of Woods, always seemed to want the ball when the game-winning shot was called for, and he very often came through. So Woods is often called the Michael Jordan of golf. However, it is difficult to compare an athlete in a team sport to an individual performer. About the only real comparison to Woods is Roger Federer in tennis. But this comparison is not completely valid, since in tennis the performance of your opponent has a considerable amount to do with your own performance. Federer has won 15 major championships— the 2009 Wimbledon Championship, going one ahead of Woods, and breaking the record of Pete Sampras.

The comparison is inevitable. Both are clients of IMG, but Woods is far and away a more valuable property than the tennis player. For example, the overnight Nielsen ratings for the final round of the Buick Open in 2006 were 5.6. The ratings for the final match of the Australian Open tennis championship in 2006 were 0.5, which translates to less than 900,000 viewers. Something called a "Q score" measures a performer's awareness and appeal to an audience. Roger Federer had a Q score of 14 compared to a 40 for Tiger Woods. The Davie-Brown talent agency has developed another measurement of advertising appeal called a DBI Score.[79] Once again Woods has more than twice Federer's score (86.1 to 44.8).[80] Advertisers have tried to capitalize on the Woods/Federer friendly rivalry, casting them together in shaving razor commercials.[81]

Tiger's objective has always been the 18 major championships won by Jack Nicklaus. Federer recently eclipsed the record of Pete Sampras, who won 14 major championships[82] in tennis over a 12-year period, when he won the 2009 Wimbledon title.[83] Despite the relative popularity of tennis, golf, with the help of Tiger Woods, far surpasses it in advertising revenue.

AND SO ON

An interesting op-ed article in the *New York Times* by conservative political writer David Brooks mentions, of all people, Tiger Woods. The piece is about what makes a genius. With all the speculation about why Tiger Woods became who he is, whether it was because of his father, his mother, or some mystical force, Brooks notes that what modern science tells us is that what separates genius from the rest of us is not a divine spark, but practice. The simple fact is that IQ and natural talent are not chief factors.

What Mozart had, we now believe, was the same thing Tiger Woods had—the ability to focus for long periods of time and a father intent on improving his skill. Mozart played a lot of piano at a very young age, so he got his 10,000 hours of practice in early and then he built from there.[84]

In another article he further expounds on Woods's ability to control himself and most of what goes on around him:

> As an adult, he is famously self-controlled. His press conferences are a string of carefully modulated banalities. His lifestyle is meticulously tidy. His style of play is actuarial. He calculates odds and avoids unnecessary risks like the accounting major he once planned on being. "I am by nature, a control freak," he (Woods) once told John Garrity of *Sports Illustrated,* as Garrity resisted the temptation to reply, *"You think?"*[85]

When a political columnist is regularly making reference to a sports figure, it is probably a good time to pause and try to put in context all the inflated expectations about Tiger Woods and his place in golf history and American culture. The year 2009 was the first since returning from major surgery on his knee, and also the first year since 2004 that he didn't win a major championship or make the cut in the British Open. It might appear that his career has peaked and that due to these and other factors (family, commercial commitments, the Foundation) we will see his accomplishments diminish. Unfortunately, the statistics belie this prediction. While he didn't win a major, he finished sixth in two majors and second in the third, won six times on the PGA Tour, and won the FedEx Cup. He won seven tournaments through the summer of 2009. He remains number one on the PGA Money List. He stood number one in the Sony Rankings, and his win of the FedEx Cup is emblematic of the best golfer of the year.

Nobody can predict how long Tiger Woods will continue to have the ability to "focus for long periods of time." He has clearly demonstrated that he no longer needs a father "intent upon improving his skill."

Rather than speculating on "whatever happened to Tiger Woods," it seems that the best thing to do is to simply sit back and enjoy his quest to become the greatest golfer of all time, as one might listen to a Mozart piano concerto.

NOTES

1. John R. Catsis, *Sports Broadcasting* (Chicago: Nelson-Hall Publishers 1996), 5.

2. Ibid., 16.

3. Ibid., 27.

4. Ibid., 32.

5. This cut down significantly on production costs since the broadcasters didn't have to travel and their headquarters were in New York.

6. Catsis, 30.

7. Ibid., 16.

8. Ibid., 93.

9. The Masters, "Official Site of the Masters Tournament," http:// www. masters.org/en_US/history/jacket/palmer.html.

10. The Masters, "Official Site of the Masters Tournament," http:// www. masters.org/en_US/history/jacket/palmer.html.

11. Louisville Slugger Museum, http://www.slugger.com/museum/.

12. Curt Sampson, *Chasing Tiger* (Atria Books, 2002), 195.

13. John Feinstein, *The First Coming* (New York: Ballantine, 1998), 17.

14. As quoted in Sampson, 196.

15. Michael Sokolove, "Constructing a Teen Phenom," *New York Times Magazine*, November 22, 2004, 81.

16. Sampson, 208.

17. Feinstein, 58–59.

18. As quoted in Tom Callahan, *In Search of Tiger* (New York: Crown Publisher, 2003), 142.

19. As quoted in Tim Rosaforte, *Tiger Woods: The Making of a Champion* (New York: St. Martin's Press, 1997), 142.

20. John Strege, *A Biography of Tiger Woods* (New York: Broadway Books, 1998), 195.

21. David Owen, *The Chosen One* (New York: Simon & Schuster, 2001), 35.

22. Sampson, 205.

23. Titleist Company, "Titleist," http://www.titleist.com/mediacenter/pressreleases.asp.

24. Strege, 189.

25. Owen, 206.

26. Sampson, 212.

27. Jonah Freedman, "Ranking The 50 Highest-Earning Athletes in the World," SI.Com, http://sportsillustrated.cnn.com/more/specials/fortunate50/2008/index.html.

28. Sampson, 212.

29. "Elite Players Have Their Clothes Laid Out for Them," *New York Times*, July 13, 2009, D1.

30. Bob's Blitz, April 9, 2009, http://njfrogman.blogspot.com/2009/04/video-tiger-woods-cartoon-gatorade.html.

31. "Tiger Woods, Sporadic Gamer," *New York Times*, June 26, 2009, http://www.nytimes.com/2009/06/27/arts/television/27woods.html?_r= 1.

32. ABC News, "Tiger Woods Tees Off with Robin Roberts," June 25, 2009, http://abcnews.go.com/video/playerIndex?id=7926326.

33. Tracey John, "Jimmy Fallon Crushes Tiger Woods Wii Golf, *Wired*, http://www.wired.com/gamelife/2009/06/jimmy-fallon-tiger-woods-wii/.

34. "Tiger Gets New Stripes: Accenture Launches New Global Advertising and Marketing Campaign Based on Three-Year 'High Performance Business' Research," *The Free Library*, http://www.thefreelibrary.com/Tiger+Gets+New+Stripes:+Accenture+Launches+New+Global+Advertising+and...-a0154337605.

35. Quoted from article in Rick Horrow and Karla Swatek, "Pro Golf Holes It for Charity," *Business Week*, May 7, 2009, http://www.businessweek.com/lifestyle/content/may2009/bw2009057_627236.htm.

36. Federation of the Swiss Watch Industry, "Tiger Woods Joins TAG Heuer," http://www.fhs.ch/en/news/news.php?id=193.

37. Metacafe.com, video added November 2008, http://www.metacafe.com/watch/2014527/tag_heuer_v2_tiger_woods_review/.

38. "Woods Following Nicklaus, Launches Own Golf Course Design Firm," World Tournament Golf, http://www.worldgolftournament.com/index.php?option=com_content&task=view&id=86&Itemid=2.

39. Golf.Com, "Woods Says Dubai Golf Course on Hold," June 5, 2009, http://www.golf.com/golf/tours_news/article/0,28136,1903124,00.html.

40. "G.M. and Woods Put Early End to Their Endorsement Deal," *New York Times*, November 25, 2009, B8.

41. Richard Sandomir, "How Big is 'Tiger Effect'? Networks Will Soon Learn," *New York Times*, June 19, 2008.

42. Samson, 210.

43. Rosaforte, 179.

44. Earl Woods, *Playing Through* (New York: HarperCollins, 1998), 185.

45. Tim Rosaforte, *Raising the Bar* (New York: Thomas Dunne Books, 2002), 182–183.

46. The author of this book was also involved with the National Minority Golf Foundation, served on a committee with Earl Woods, and had an opportunity to play a round of golf with him at Doral.

47. L. Price, "Tunnel Vision," *Sports Illustrated*, April 3, 2000, 56.

48. As quoted in Rosaforte, *Raising the Bar*, 185.

49. The problem was exacerbated when Hughes Norton read a statement by Tiger, rather than Tiger making the statement in person.

50. Rosaforte, *Raising the Bar*, 76.

51. As quoted in Strege, 205.

52. As quoted in Feinstein, 64.

53. Ibid., 71.

54. As quoted in Rosaforte, *Raising the Bar*, 81.

55. Charles Pierce, "The Man, Amen," in *Chasing Tiger*, ed. Glenn Stout (Cambridge: Da Capo Press, 2002), 93.

56. Mike Lupica, "Young Act Is Too Old," *Daily News*, December 22, 1996.

57. Richard Baehr, "Thank You Martha," *American Thinker*, April 14, 2004, http://www.americanthinker.com.

58. As quoted in Strege, 108.

59. As quoted in Callahan, 205.

60. Anderson, Dave. "Woods Chases Nicklaus as a Father," *New York Times*, June 21, 2007, B2.

61. John Feinstein and Rocco Mediate, *Are You Kidding Me?* (New York: Little Brown & Company, 2009), 117.

62. "Tiger Woods' Daughter Behind his Comeback," *Thaindian News*, June 11, 2008, http://www.thaindian.com/newsportal/sports/tiger-woods-daughter-behind-his-comeback_10058960.html.

63. Nicklaus Web site, http://www.nicklaus.com/nicklaus_news/news120306.php, Jack Nicklaus transcript at the Del Webb Father/Son Challenge at Champions Gate.

64. "Following a Famous Uncle and Also Her Ambition," *New York Times*, June 25, 2009.

65. Renee Powell and Althea Gibson were the other two.

66. He won the WGC Accenture Match Play tournament.

67. Most PGA tournaments (and the U.S. Open and Masters) cut players above a certain score, usually after the second round of competitions.

68. Tiger Woods Foundation, http://twfound.org.

69. Damon Hack, "A High-Tech Learning Center Is Woods's Way of Giving Back," by *New York Times*, February 11, 2006.

70. Jonathan O'Connell, "D.C.'s plans for Hine School Redevelopment Don't Include Tiger Woods," *Washington Business Journal*, May 22, 2009, http//Washington.bizjournals.com/Washington/stories/2009/05/18/daily93.html.

71. The Sports Philanthropy Project, as quoted from an article by Joe Stephens, *Washington Post*, July 5, 2007, http://www.sportsphilanthropyproject.com/resources/details.php?id=469.

72. Every hole is assigned a par. The par assumes a player will always need two putts on a hole. Therefore on a par 3 hole a player should be on the green in one shot and make two putts. A player who manages to score par without hitting the green in the assumed number of shots is said to be a good scrambler.

73. Starting in 1979 the Americans began playing a team made up of professionals from all of continental Europe.

74. "Woods Left Holding Bag after Caddie's Remarks," *New York Times*, December 16, 2008.

75. Ibid.

76. Simon Romero, "Assuming a Proletarian Stance, Chavez'z Loyalists Push to Close Golf Courses," *New York Times*, August 29, 2009, A4.

77. Washington Post.com from MSNBC.com, http://nbcsports.msnbc.com/id/31674326/ns/sports-washington_post/ (see Tiger's response).

78. The boycott, though largely ignored, precipitated sprinter Tommy Smith and John Carlos to raise their gloved fists (the symbol of black power) at the medal ceremony, leading to both of them being banned from the rest of the games.

79. It measures a celebrity's awareness, appeal, and relevance to a brand's image and the person's influence on consumer buying behavior.

80. Richard Sandomir, "Not All Are Created Equal," *New York Times*, January 30, 2009, D1.

81. Gillette Commercial, http://www.youtube.com/watch?v=q8-bOSEfFWk&NR=1.

82. The four major championships in tennis are Wimbledon, and the French, Australian, and U.S. Opens.

83. Karen Crouse, "A Tennis King Content to Stay Home," New York Times, June 28, 2009, D1.

84. David Brooks, "Genius: The Modern View," *New York Times*, May 2, 2009, A23.

85. David Brooks, "The Frozen Gaze," New York Times, June 17, 2008, A21.

EPILOGUE

On Friday morning, November 27, 2009, at approximately 2:30 A.M., the life of Tiger Woods changed significantly.

Up to that point in time, as has been documented in the preceding biography, Tiger Woods had established a pristine reputation not only as the preeminent golfer of his time, but also as a solid family man and philanthropist, contributing significant amounts of money to help educate children who might not otherwise have had that opportunity. However, in light of the events after that date, it becomes evident that the basis for that reputation was apparently not objective reporting by independent sources. Rather, it appears that it was based on carefully meted out bites of information fed from the Tiger Woods public relations machine, mainly through his Web site.

THE INCIDENT

On that fateful night, a neighbor of Tiger Woods's estate in Windermere, Florida, called 911 and reported an accident in front of their house. They identified the driver, who had crashed his SUV into a fire hydrant and tree in front of the house, as Tiger Woods. From this point on there are conflicting accounts of what actually happened. According to what officers from the Windermere police force said, when they arrived, Tiger's wife Elin had smashed the rear window in an effort to extract the injured Tiger from the vehicle. The neighbor confirmed that Tiger was lying on the ground, already out of the car, and that he was not wearing shoes.

The initial press reports said that Tiger was seriously injured in the crash. However, the same reports also indicated that the vehicle was traveling at a very slow rate of speed since the air bags did not release (under 30 mph). Then the press began to ask questions about why, given the relatively light damage to the car, was Elin bashing out a rear window with a golf club, since it was apparent from pictures of the crash scene that no one could have been trapped in the car. And where was Tiger going at 2:30 in the morning?

Tiger was taken to the Health Central Hospital, treated for facial cuts, and released. It was later learned that both Tiger's mother, Kultida, and Elin's mother, Barbo Holmberg, had been guests in the house when all this took place. Several days later, Barbo was also taken to the local hospital with an undisclosed ailment, after collapsing in the Woods's bathroom.

By nightfall on November 28, what was a sports story began to take on proportions that were, in the next several months, to at least temporarily bring down the most highly paid and well respected professional athlete in sports history. Reports surfaced immediately that the tabloid newspaper *The Enquirer* was about to release a story that Tiger Woods had had an affair with Rachel Uchitel, a New York City hostess. Within the next week a number of women came forward to declare that they too had had sexual relations with Tiger.

Speculation began immediately that Tiger's crash was the result of a domestic dispute between Tiger and Elin when she discovered messages on his cell phone from one of his assignations with cocktail waitress Jaimee Grubbs. From recordings of the calls, which were released to the press, Tiger's voice was clearly heard telling Grubbs to cease calling his cell phone because his wife had discovered the communications and was mad. Over the course of the next several weeks the list of alleged mistresses grew to over 20 and counting.

Immediately following the incident, the Florida Highway Patrol was interested in talking with Tiger to find out exactly what happened, and

Maj. Cindy Williams with the Florida Highway Patrol speaks during a news conference concerning Tiger Woods's accident in Orlando, Florida, on December 1, 2009. AP Photo/John Raoux.

he scheduled a meeting with them for the day after the crash. He then canceled the meeting and rescheduled, only to cancel the second and a third meeting. Tiger was under no legal obligation to meet with authorities, but his refusal only fueled the media's speculation. In the end Tiger was charged with careless driving and was fined $164, and four points on his driving record.

TIGER'S RESPONSE TO THE MEDIA

On December 2, Tiger posted a message on his Web site that said in part, "I have let my family down and I regret those transgressions with all of my heart." He then went on to chastise the media, the tabloid media in particular, for his problems. On December 11 he issued another statement on the Web site: "I am deeply aware of the disappointment and hurt that my infidelity has caused to so many people, most of all my wife and children. I want to say again to everyone that I am profoundly sorry and that I ask forgiveness. It may not be possible to repair the damage I've done, but I want to do my best to try." That was the extent of Tiger's efforts to explain what happened. In that same message he indicated that he was taking a break from tournament golf for an indefinite period of time.

Between the incident on November 27 through January, he was completely out of sight from the public. The speculation was rampant as to where he was and what he was doing. One unsubstantiated report had him in Hattiesburg, Mississippi, in a rehabilitation clinic for sexual addiction. The only picture of him (a grainy shot of Tiger walking with a hood) finally surfaced during the third week in January, and there was some question if it was actually Tiger Woods.

Two months after the fateful night, no one had seen Tiger Woods, either in person or on videotape or photograph. Virtually every public relations person on the planet has chastised his decision to avoid the public. Mike Paul, the president and senior counselor at MGP & Associates public relations in New York said, "...he cannot remain silent, out of sight. He should have done a one-on-one interview within the first 24 to 48 hours. He should have done something like Oprah, and he needs to do it soon."[1]

MEDIA RESPONSE TO TIGER

When a celebrity's character is called into question, does it really matter to the general public? Does it matter to the world if Tiger Woods is cheating on his wife? Clearly, people are interested, but does it have any effect on their lives? Other than the general disappointment of those who have set him up as a role model, the infidelities are a private matter between Tiger Woods and his wife. However, if the magnitude of Tiger Woods's image does qualify this story as a legitimate news story, then why didn't any media outlet provide any inkling that Tiger was not the family man he professed to be but rather a philandering husband? Did the media know about his antics? What about his fellow professionals on the PGA Tour?

As has been documented in this book, Tiger Woods has had at best a tenuous relationship with the sports press, and the press in general. But because he is arguably the best golfer to have ever played the game, the media has had to tolerate his lack of forthrightness. When he competes in a golf tournament, he is the story, whether he wins or not. Despite the raging controversy about his personal life, in December he was voted the Golf Writers Association Player of the Year 2009, and Athlete of the Decade by the Associated Press. When he is not playing in a tournament, the television ratings drop by 50 percent, and sponsors are always vying to get him to play in their tournaments. The average cost of a 30-second commercial for the 10 tournaments that Tiger competed in during the 2009 PGA season was 30 percent higher than the 20 events when he didn't compete.[2]

However, the press, and therefore the public, always wants to know more about athletes than their ability to play their sport. They want to gain insight into the personality of their stars. Tiger has been notoriously stingy with any details about his personal life. Observing Tiger in post-round interviews or press conferences is a study in boredom. He would describe every shot of the completed round and what his thinking was for playing each shot. But any attempt to dig deeper into his personal feelings about anything were always short-circuited by Tiger. There was always a tension that someone would ask a question that would touch too close to who this athlete really is. Compared to a Phil Mickelson press conference, Tiger's "up close and personal" abilities were sorely lacking.

Therefore it is not surprising that when the scandal broke and it became apparent that the image of Tiger was not the real Tiger, the media relished and embellished the story. And Tiger's refusal to surface and face the media has only damaged his reputation further.

It should be pointed out how the relationship between sports reporters and the athletes they cover has changed significantly over the past 40 years. A good example is the mythology that has surrounded the career of 1950s golfer Ben Hogan. A description of Hogan's attitude toward the press sounds eerily like many contemporary accounts of Tiger and the media: "Hogan, in short, had a different standard on the press than any other high profile players. Byron (Nelson), for example, appeared to sympathize with the deadline reporter's plight, often making himself available to the press and rarely criticizing the resulting news copy....Hogan, by contrast, simply couldn't abide anything less than a watchmaker's strict accounting of his words and deeds and found, as a consequence, probing interviews of almost any duration nearly unbearable to take for one simple reason: the more he expressed, the more likely the interviewer was to take his words and use them against him."[3] But it was generally the tradition in this period for reporters to steer clear of the personal lives of the athletes they covered, and consequently there was never any indication until long after Hogan's death that his "ideal" marriage included periods when Ben lived away from his wife when they had conflicts.

The mainstream media has also had a field day with this story. Even people who knew nothing about the sport of golf knew about Tiger Woods. And what they knew was very positive. So when this scandal broke, many commentators took the opportunity to draw parallels between Tiger's downfall and those of other public people who established reputations that were at odds with the real person. Former New York governor Eliot Spitzer, ardent fighter against corruption as attorney general, got caught frequenting prostitutes; South Carolina governor Mark Sanford, a staunch family values Republican, was discovered to have been carrying on an affair with a woman in Argentina. Normally the mainstream media separates entertainment celebrities from political celebrities since there is less at stake when a rock star gets in trouble. However, indicative of the scale of the Tiger Woods image beyond entertainment, Frank Rich, *New York Times* columnist, in an op ed piece, suggested that Tiger should have been *Time Magazine*'s Man of the Year instead of Fed Chairman Ben Bernanke. Rich's point was that Woods's "sham beatific image"[4] symbolized the general malaise of an American society that tolerates the duplicity of its public figures. Arguably the most bizarre comment on the Tiger Woods situation came from *Fox News* anchor Brit Hume on *Fox News Sunday* on January 10: "He's said to be a Buddhist; I don't think that faith offers the kind of forgiveness and redemption that is offered by the Christian faith. So my message to Tiger would be, 'Tiger, turn to the Christian faith and you can make a total recovery and be a great example to the world.'"[5]

The Tiger Woods story also spilled over into popular culture humor. Late-night television hosts feasted on the Woods dilemma. *Saturday Night Live* spoofed Woods, and Jimmy Fallon offered Tiger advice on his late-night program. Conan O'Brien said that "the jokes practically write themselves."[6] David Letterman, alluding to his own personal troubles with "other women," opened one of his monologues referring to Woods, saying "If this had happened three months ago, I would have had material for a year."[7] Jay Leno also contributed: "According to TMZ, a congressman was supposed to award Tiger with the Congressional Gold Medal–our highest civilian honor–and then had to withdraw it because of the scandal... which seems odd to me. What's it up to now? 15 mistresses? That seems like something members of Congress would give you a medal for!"[8] The Woods scandal was even satirized in Gary Trudeau's *Doonesbury* political comic strip.

PGA RESPONSE TO TIGER

There is no question that Tiger Woods's announcement that he was taking an indefinite leave from the tour had to be a blow to Tim Finchem, the Commissioner of the PGA Tour. Given the current economy, all professional sports leagues are facing problems attracting audiences and therefore sponsors. So the news that the PGA's premiere attraction would be missing was certainly bad news for the Tour. Finchem finally responded publicly to the Woods situation on December 17 and, as expected, he minimized the severity of the situation and basically said it was a family matter and he respected the Woods's privacy.

However, another totally separate question was raised in Woods's connection to the Canadian doctor Tony Galea, who is under criminal investigation by the FBI for allegedly providing athletes with the performance-enhancing drugs HGH and Actovegin. Woods had been treated by Galea in the past.[9] Galea's secretary was caught transporting growth hormone drugs across the border from Canada. So while there is absolutely no evidence that Woods took performance-enhancing drugs, the timing could not have been worse for the PGA Tour.

The consensus response from Tiger's colleagues on the PGA Tour has been supportive. Steve Stricker, who finished second to Tiger in the Player of the Year voting last year, has urged Tiger to go before the media and talk about the situation, but that seems unlikely. Stricker added, "It was a little unfair how we have built him up over the years. Obviously on the course, he's one of a kind. But I think it's a little unfair how we judged him."[10] John Daly, a golf professional who knows something about scandals, said, "Take a break, get it together. My heart goes out to both of them. I just hope they can make it."[11] Jack Nicklaus, whose 18 major titles is the goal Tiger is pursuing, said, "Our public is pretty forgiving at times. Time usually heals all wounds. I think the hardest thing is obviously his family. That's a private matter for him and his family."[12]

However, not all the reactions to Tiger's troubles were comforting. Chris DiMarco, who battled Tiger down to the last putt in the 2005 Masters, hedged slightly when he stated, "Contrary to what everybody believes, the tour will go on. Anytime you take the greatest competitor of all time out of the game, it will miss him."[13] But Boo Weekley might have said what many pros actually feel: "The tour isn't all about Tiger. There are 200, 300 guys out here playing to make a living like he did. It isn't just about one player. He isn't bigger than the game."[14] That remains to be seen.

By far, the most pointed comments from a tour player came from Jasper Parnevick. Tiger met Elin when she was the nanny for Parnevick's children. In an interview on ESPN's *Outside the Lines*, which aired on December 13, Parnevick said, "I vouched for this guy. I told her (Elin) this is the guy that I think is everything you want. He's true. He's honest. He has great values. He has everything you want in a guy. And uhh, I was wrong."[15] Another Swede, LPGA golfer Helen Alfredsson, said that other PGA golfers were aware of Tiger's infidelities but didn't talk about it: "I heard it last summer during the British Open," she told an interviewer for Sweden's TV4. "If he just paid for the escorts, I (would) understand a bit more. Then no one needed to know. But now he did everything and a girlfriend and everything."[16]

CORPORATE RESPONSE TO TIGER

In the hours and days that followed the incident of November 27, most of Tiger's sponsors issued statements vaguely supporting him and respecting his family's privacy, but not necessarily enthusiastically pledging their commitment to him as a spokesman. Of all his sponsors, only Nike has unequivocally stood by Tiger and their deal with him.

Immediately following Tiger's statement posted on his Web site that he would be taking a break from golf, Nike signaled that the company would stand by him, announcing, "Tiger has been part of Nike for more than a decade. He is the best golfer in the world and one of the greatest athletes of his era. We look forward to his return to golf. He and his family have Nike's full support."[17]

EA Sports, the producer of the Tiger Woods video games, in a statement said: "We respect that this is a very difficult and private situation for Tiger and his family. At this time, the strategy for our Tiger Woods PGA Tour business remains unchanged."[18] Subsequently the company announced that it was maintaining its relationship with Tiger, speculation being that the video game demographic was probably not all that engaged or interested in the scandal situation.

Gatorade announced on December 8 that it would be discontinuing the heavily advertised Tiger Woods Sports Drink, the commercials for which featured an animated version of Tiger Woods as a child. The company said that the decision had been made before the events of November 27.

The first company to signal some change in the relationship as a result of the scandal was Gillette Shaving Company. At first they announced that they would be temporarily suspending all advertisements featuring Tiger Woods until further notice. Company spokesman Damon Jones issued a statement: "Tiger said I want to take a timeout from being in the public eye. And we think that's right that he takes a timeout," and that Gillette would limit Woods's role in its marketing.[19]

By far the most financially significant damage to the Woods's bank account came when Accenture announced on December 13 that they were severing ties with the golfer. The management consulting, technology services, and outsourcing company featured Tiger Woods in 83 percent of its advertisements. The statement wished Tiger and his family their best, but "After careful consideration and analysis, the company has determined that he is no longer the right representative for its advertising."[20] This company decision was necessary doubtless because of Tiger's possible prolonged absence from the tour. The company might have been able to stay with him if they had some idea of when he would return. This situation points out why companies are reluctant to tie so much of their image with one person, especially an athlete. It signifies that Woods transcended the typical celebrity athlete. Although Mark Steinberg, Woods's agent, will not discuss financial negotiations, it is speculated that Tiger was not paid for the remaining compensation in the contract.

The Tag Heuer watch company dedicated about a quarter of its advertising budget to the Tiger Woods image, and some of the most creative television commercials featured Woods in the Tag Heuer spots. After initially supporting Woods and his family, citing the scandal as a personal problem, the company reversed itself. CEO Jean-Christophe Babin said, "We recognize Tiger Woods as a great sportsman but we have to take account of the sensitivity of some consumers in relation to recent events."[21] They plan to use Leonard DiCaprio as their spokesperson going forward.

On New Year's Eve 2010, AT&T dropped Tiger as its spokesman. Tiger will no longer sport the AT&T logo on his golf bag. So far, the company has not indicated whether or not it will continue to sponsor the AT&T National PGA Tour event that benefits Tiger's foundation. Apparently IMG, Tiger's agent company, did not threaten to require AT&T to honor the remainder of the contract. It is presumed that any litigation against AT&T would require Tiger to testify and bring out more sordid details about his personal situation.[22]

Two University of California, Davis, professors of marketing conducted a study to determine the impact of Tiger's fall on several of his biggest sponsors. Of the nine companies studied, the losses were greatest among three sports-related companies, Tiger Woods PGA Tour Golf, Gatorade, and Nike. They estimated the shareholders would suffer a 4.3 percent loss, or about $6 billion.[23]

WHAT NEXT

The question now is how will Tiger Woods respond to this monumental breakdown of his carefully crafted image? Will he continue to stay in the shell he and his handlers have created for him? But beyond the story of Tiger Woods and whether or not he is the monster that the press has created, there is another more interesting question surrounding this whole Woods incident: How on earth did nobody provide a photograph of Tiger Woods, either while he was engaged in one of his trysts, or since the events of November 27? It was reported that Tiger (or his people) had in essence paid off American Media, Inc., publishers of the *Enquirer,* to not print the original story of Tiger's infidelities in exchange for the rights to an interview with *Men's Fitness,* one of the company's other publications. And while Tiger's ability to pay off select media outlets is unquestioned, it is impossible to pay off everybody. A candid shot of Tiger ducking into a car with an attractive woman who was not his wife was, and is, worth a considerable amount of money. Why has no one to date come forward with this photograph?

The lack of any substantial reports of where Tiger was following November 27 fueled incredible speculation and rumor and only worsened his situation. Finally, on February 19, 2010, Tiger Woods formally apologized, in a rather strained and awkward presentation, to his friends, family, and others gathered at the PGA headquarters in Ponte Vedra Beach, Florida. Only pool reporters were allowed in; two cameras provided a pool feed to other television outlets.[24] No questions were permitted. Woods walked out from behind an almost funereal curtain and read his apology from a lectern. He took full responsibility for his "infidelities" and announced that he was in therapy to address his problems. Kultida Woods sat in the front row, and Elin Woods did not attend. He indicated that he didn't know when he would return to competitive golf.

On March 16 Tiger announced that he would play in the 2010 Masters Tournament, April 8–11. This is not surprising, since he would not forgo the chance of competing for a major championship, and the Masters is one of the most strictly controlled tournaments in professional golf. Patrons are regularly escorted from the premises if their behavior displeases the members of the Augusta Club.

On March 21 Tiger submitted to interviews with the Golf Channel and ESPN Television. Kelly Tilghman[25] conducted the Golf Channel interview with Tiger, and Jim Rinaldi interviewed him for ESPN. Because of a five-minute time limit, the reporters didn't have an opportunity to get more than basic information. In general, the press response to these interviews was negative. Non-golf reporters and commentators chastised Woods and his handlers for restricting the freedom of the press. For the most part, the golf press rejoiced in the story, and especially in Tiger's impending return to golf.

Will Tiger Woods be able to apply the same ability to concentrate that he exhibits on a golf course to dedicating himself to repairing his relationship with his wife and family? Part of that answer lies in the extent to which the prescandal image was based on fact. Certainly only the most fundamentalist moralists will not be willing in time to accept the fact that Woods strayed from the path of marital fidelity. And if no other negative information is forthcoming regarding his character, the American public will undoubtedly be likely to forgive him and buy the products he endorses. It is sometimes hard to remember that this is still a sports story. Tiger Woods remains the greatest golfer of the era and could become the greatest golfer ever. When he comes back to the PGA Tour and if he continues to dominate as he has in the past, he will eventually regain whatever he lost during this ordeal.

NOTES

1. Larry Dorman, "A Star's Persona Slips from View," *New York Times*, December 9, 2009, B15.

2. Michael Buteau and Andy Fixmer, "Tiger's Costly Affairs," *Star Ledger*, December 18, 2009, 57.

3. James Dodson, *Ben Hogan: An American Life* (New York: Broadway Books, 2004), 152.

4. Frank Rich, "Tiger Woods, Person of the Year," *New York Times*, December 30, 2009, 7.

5. David Sessions, "Brit Hume: Tiger Should 'Turn To The Christian Faith,'" *Politics Daily*, posted January 14, 2010, http://www.politicsdaily.com/2010/01/04/brit-hume-tiger-woods-should-turn-to-the-christian-faith/.

6. "Devil Ball Golf: A Video Compendium of Tiger Woods Humor," http://sports.yahoo.com/golf/blog/devil_ball_golf/post/A-video-compendium-of-Tiger-Woods-humor?urn=golf,208617.

7. "Tiger Woods Late-Night Roundup: Will David Letterman's Personal Experiences Help or Hurt Him." *EW.Com*, http://popwatch.ew.com/2009/12/08/tiger-woods-late-night/.

8. Citizens against Pro-Obama Media Bias, http://citizensagainstproobamamediabias.wordpress.com/2009/12/14/jay-leno-humor-tiger-woods-crashers-biden/.

9. Don Van Natta, Jr., Michael S. Schmidt, and Ian Austen, "Doctor Who Treated Top Athletes Is Subject of a Doping Inquiry," *New York Times*, December 15, 2009, 1.

10. Feedback, *New York Times*, December 14, 2009, D7.

11. Ibid.

12. "Golf Legend Jack Nicklaus Says Tiger Woods Scandal 'None of My Business,'" *Daily News*, Associated Press, December 10, 2009, http://www.nydailynews.com/sports/more_sports/2009/12/10/2009–12–10_nicklaus_says_tiger_scandal_none_of_my_business.html.

13. Feedback, *New York Times*, December 14, 2009, D7.

14. Ibid.

15. "Parnevick Still Unhappy with Tiger," ESPN.com: Golf, December 11, 2009, http://espn.go.com/espn/print?id=4733865&type=story.

16. Corky Siemaszko, "Golfer Says Woods' Peers Knew of His Swinging Lifestyle," *New York Daily News*, December 24, 2009, 5.

17. "Feedback: What They're Saying About Tiger Woods," *New York Times*, December 14, 2009, D7.

18. Ibid.

19. Ibid.

20. Mark Williams, "Accenture Cuts Ties with Woods," *Star Ledger*, December 14, 2009, 2.

21. Corky Siemaszko, "Time's Up for Tiger Woods: Ticked-Off Watch Company Tag Heuer Drops Golfer as Pitchman," *New York Daily News*, December 23, 2009, http://www.nydailynews.com/gossip/2009/12/18/2009–12–18_odds_are_that_elin_nordegren_will_divorce_husband_tiger_woods_after_sex_scandal_.html#ixzz0djwX1Gay.

22. Richard Sandomir, "No Payoff for Woods As AT&T Ended Deal," *New York Times*, January 21, 2010, B24.

23. Bill Lindelof, "Tiger's Woes Costing Sponsors $12B," *Star Ledger*, December 29, 2009, 29.

24. Several news organizations refused to accept the places reserved for them in another room at PGA headquarters during Tiger's apology.

25. See Chapter 6. Kelly Tilghman was suspended from the Golf Channel for remarks she made about Tiger that were interpreted as having racist overtones, but she was exonerated by Tiger.

BIBLIOGRAPHY

BOOKS

Andrisani, John. *The Tiger Woods Way*. New York: Crown Publishing, 1997.

Andrisani, John. *Think Like a Tiger: An Analysis of Tiger Woods' Mental Game*. New York: The Berkley Publishing Group, 2002.

Anselmo, John. *"A-Game" Golf: The Complete Starter Kit for Golfers*. New York: Random House, 2001.

Ashe, Arthur, Jr. *A Hard Road to Glory: 1919 to 1945*. New York: Warner Books, 1988.

Callahan, Tom. *In Search of Tiger: A Journey through Golf with Tiger Woods*. New York: Crown Publishing Group, 2003.

Catsis, John R. *Sports Broadcasting*. Chicago: Nelson Hall Publishers, 1996.

Concannon, Dale. *Golf, The Early Days: Royal & Ancient Game from Its Origins to 1939*. London: Salamander Books, 1995.

Cook, Kevin. *Driven*. New York: Gotham Books, 2008.

Crosby, Don. *Tiger Woods Made Me Look Like a Genius*. Kansas City, KS: Andrew McMeel Publishing, 2000.

Dodson, James. *Ben Hogan: An American Life*. New York: Broadway Books, 2004.

Duran, Rudy. *In Every Kid There Lurks a Tiger*. New York: Hyperion Press, 2002.

Echikson, William. *Shooting for Tiger*. New York: Public Affairs, 2009.

Edwards, Nicholas. *Tiger Woods: An American Master*. New York: Scholastic Inc., 1997.

Feinstein, John. *A Good Walk Spoiled: Days and Nights on the PGA Tour*. Boston: Little, Brown and Company, 1995.

Feinstein, John. *Open: Inside The Ropes at Bethpage Black*. Boston: Little, Brown and Company, 2003.

Feinstein, John. *The First Coming, Tiger Woods: Master or Martyr?* New York: Ballantine Publishing Group, 1998.

Feinstein, John. *The Majors*. Boston: Little, Brown and Company, 1999.

Feinstein, John, and Rocco Mediate. *Are You Kidding Me*. New York: Little, Brown and Company, 2009.

Flaherty, Tom. *The U.S. Open (1895–1965): Complete Story of the United States Golf Championship*. New York: E. P. Dutton & Co., 1966.

Frost, Mark. *The Grand Slam: Bobby Jones, America, and the Story of Golf*. New York: Hyperion, 2004.

Frost, Mark. *The Greatest Game Ever Played: Harry Vardon, Francis Ouimet, and the Birth of Modern Golf*. New York: Hyperion, 2002.

Frost, Mark. *The Match*. Hyperion Books: New York, 2007.

Garrity, John. *Tiger 2.0*. New York: Sports Illustrated Books, 2008.

"Golf." *The World Book Encyclopedia*. 1976 ed. Chicago: World Enterprises Educational Corp.

Gutman, Bill. *Tiger Woods: A Biography*. New York: Pocket Books, 1997.

Kearns, Brad. *How Tiger Does It*. New York: McGraw-Hill Companies, 2008.

McCormack, Mark H. *What They Don't Teach You at Harvard Business School: Notes from a Street-Smart Executive*. New York: Bantam Books, 1984.

McDaniel, Pete. *Uneven Lies: The Heroic Story of African-Americans in Golf*. Greenwich, CT: The American Golfer, Inc., 2000.

Owen, David. *The Chosen One: Tiger Woods and the Dilemma of Greatness*. New York: Simon & Schuster, 2001.

Raatma, Lucia. *Tiger Woods*. Ann Arbor, MI: Cherry Lake Publishing, 2008.

Roberts, Jeremy. *Tiger Woods*. Minneapolis: Lerner Publishing Group, 2002.

Robinson, Lenwood Jr. *Skins & Grins: The Plight of the Black American Golfer*. Evanston, IL: Chicago Spectrun Press, 1997.

Rosaforte, Tim. *Raising the Bar: The Championship Years of Tiger Woods*. New York: Thomas Dunne Books, 2000.

Rosaforte, Tim. *Tiger Woods: The Making of a Champion*. New York: St. Martin's Press, 1997.

Sampson, Curt. *Chasing Tiger*. New York: Atria Books, 2002.

Schultz, Brad. *Sports Broadcasting*. Boston: Focal Press, 2002.

Sifford, Charlie. *"Just Let Me Play": The Story of Charlie Sifford, the First Black PGA Golfer*. Lathan, NY: British American Publishing, 1992.

Sinnette, Calvin. *Forbidden Fairways: African Americans and the Game of Golf*. Chelsea, MN: Sleeping Bear Press, 1998.

Sluby, Paul E. Sr. *The Family Recollections of Beulah A. Shippen and Mabel S. (Shippen) Hatcher*. Self-published, 1994.

Smiley, Bob. *Follow the Roar*. New York: Harper Collins Books, 2008.

Stafford, Ian. *In Search of the Tiger*. New York: Random House, 2003.

Stout, Glenn, ed. *Chasing Tiger: The Tiger Woods Reader*. Cambridge, MA: Da Capo Press, 2002.

Strege, John. *A Biography of Tiger Woods*. New York: Broadway Books, 1997.

Venturi, Ken, with Micahel Arkush. *Getting Up and Down*. Chicago: Triumph Books, 2004.

Williams, Michael. *The History of Golf*. Secaucus, NJ: Cartwell Books, 1985.

Williams, Steve. *Golf at the Top*. Ulysses Press: Berkley, CA, 2006.

Woods, Earl. *Playing Through: Straight Talk on Hard Work, Big Dreams and Adventures with Tiger Woods*. New York: Harper Collins Publishers, 1998.

Woods, Earl. *Training a Tiger: A Father's Guide to Raising a Winner Both in Golf and in Life*. New York: Harper-Collins, 1997.

Young, A. S. *Negro First in Sports*. Chicago: Johnson Publishing Company, 1963.

MAGAZINES

Altman, Alex. "The Moment." *Time Magazine*, December 21, 2009, 23.

Bassinger, Buzz. "Tiger in the Rough." *Vanity Fair*, February 2010, 80.

Faces in the Crowd, *Sports Illustrated*, September 24, 1990, 10.

Heiny, Henry L. "PGA Tour Pros, Long, but Not So Straight." *Chance Magazine*, Winter, 2008.

Jones, Guilford, "Past Greats." *Black Sports*, July 1973, 65–66.

Londino, Lawrence. "Shady Rest: Itself a Strong Ship." *Golf Journal*, Spring 1996, 17.

Lux, Ron. "Golf Pioneers by Necessity." *Golf Leisure*, Fall 1989, 32.

Price, L. "Tunnel Vision." *Sports Illustrated*, April 3, 2000, 56.

Sokolove, Michael. "Constructing a Teen Phenom." *New York Times Magazine*, November 28, 2004, 80.

Strafaci, Frank. "Forgotten Pioneer Professional." *Golfing Magazine*, March 1957, 11.

VIDEO

Golf Talk Live. The Golf Channel, December 18, 1996.

A Place for Us: The Story of Shady Rest and America's First Golf Professional. Dir. Larry Londino. WNET Channel 13, New York, December 19, 1996.

Tiger Woods: Son, Hero and Champion. Trans World International, 1997.

Tiger Woods: The Authorized DVD Collection. Golf Channel Documentary, February 2005.

The Tiger Woods Story. Dir. LeVar Burton. Paramount Pictures, 1998.

INTERNET

Atlanta History Center. "Down the Fairway with Bobby Jones," http://www.atlantahistorycenter.com/cms/Down+the+Fairway+with+Bobby+Jones/107.html.

Baehr, Richard. "Thank You Martha." *American Thinker*, April 14, 2004, http://www.americanthinker.com.

"Big 12 Conference." http://www.britannica.com/eb/article?tocId=9079156.

Blauvelt, Henry. "Woods Finishes with a Good Score, Good Spirits." *USA Today*, July 21, 2002, http://www.usatoday.com/sports/golf/2002–07–21-british-woods.htm.

Bob's Blitz. April 9, 2009, http://njfrogman.blogspot.com/2009/04/video-tiger-woods-cartoon-gatorade.html.

Citizens against Pro-Obama Media Bias, http://citizensagainstproobamamediabias.wordpress.com/2009/12/14/jay-leno-humor-tiger-woods-crashers-biden/.

"The Daily Wrap-up, Round 4: The Tour Championship." PGA Tour.com, http://www.pgatour.com/2009/tournaments/r060/09/27/recap_round4/index.html.

Devil Ball Golf: A Video Compendium of Tiger Woods Humor, http://sports.yahoo.com/golf/blog/devil_ball_golf/post/A-video-compendium-of-Tiger-Woods-humor?urn=golf,208617.

"Essays on Thailand. Bangkok Thanapol Chadchaidee." *Thaichareunkanpem*, 1994, http://sunsite.au.ac.th/thailand/buddhism/.

"Faces of the ADA—Casey Martin Continues His Professional Golf Career." U.S. Department of Justice, July 17, 2000, http://www.usdoj.gov/crt/ada/fmartin. htm.

Fine, Larry. "Tiger Misses the Cut at U.S. Open." Red Orbit, June 16, 2006, http://www.redorbit.com/news/sports/540859/tiger_set_to_miss_cut_at_us_open/index.html.

Freedman, Jonah. "Ranking the 50 Highest-Earning Athletes in the World." *Sports Illustrated, SI.Com*, http://sportsillustrated.cnn.com/more/specials/fortunate50/2008/index.html.

Gillette Commercial, http://www.youtube.com/watch?v=q8-bOSEfFWk&NR=1.

Golf.com, http://www.golf.com/golf/gallery/article/0,28242,1811171–7,00.html.

"Golf Legend Jack Nicklaus Says Tiger Woods Scandal 'None of My Business.'" *Daily News, Associated Press*, December 10, 2009, http://www.nydailynews.com/sports/more_sports/2009/12/10/2009–12–10_nicklaus_says_tiger_scandal_none_of_my_business.html.

"History of Special Forces, 1961–1971." Department of Army Publication, 1989, http://www.specialoperations.com/Army/Special_Forces/default.html.

Horrow, Rick, and Karla Swatek. "Pro Golf Holes It for Charity." *Business Week*, May 7, 2009, http://www.businessweek.com/lifestyle/content/may2009/bw2009057_627236.htm.

Jack Nicklaus transcript at the Del Webb Father/Son Challenge at Champions Gate. Nicklaus Web site, http://www.nicklaus.com/nicklaus_news/news120306.php.

John, Tracey. "Jimmy Fallon Crushes Tiger Woods Wii Golf." *Wired*, http://www.wired.com/gamelife/2009/06/jimmy-fallon-tiger-woods-wii/.

Kelly, Brad. "An Amazing Day at the Presidents Cup," November 23, 2003, http://golf.about.com/b/2003/11/23/an-amazing-day-at-the-presidents-cup.htm.

Louisville Slugger Museum, http://www.slugger.com/museum/.

National Golf Foundation, http://www.ngf.org/cgi/home.asp.

"Notah Begay-Media Guide." PGA Tour, http://www.pgatour.com/players/bio/149683.

O'Connell, Jonathan. "D.C.'s Plans for Hine School Redevelopment Don't Include Tiger Woods." *Washington Business Journal*, May 22, 2009, http//Washington.bizjournals.com/Washington/stories/2009/05/18/daily93.html.

Official Site of the Masters, http://www.masters.com/index.html.

Official Site of the PGA Tour, http://www.pgatour.com/players/bio/149683.

Official Site of Tiger Woods, http://www.tigerwoods.com.

Official Site of Titleist Company, http://www.titleist.com/mediacenter/press releasesdetail.asp?id=87.

Sessions, David. "Brit Hume: Tiger Should 'Turn to the Christian Faith.'" *Politics Daily*, January 14, 2010, http://www.politicsdaily.com/2010/01/04/brit-hume-tiger-woods-should-turn-to-the-christian-faith/.

Shipnuck, Alan. "All Business." Golf.com, August 28, 2006, http://www.golf.com/golf/special/article/0,28136,1717327–1,00.html.

Siemaszko, Corky. "Time's Up for Tiger Woods: Ticked-Off Watch Company Tag Heuer Drops Golfer as Pitchman." *New York Daily News*, December 23, 2009, http://www.nydailynews.com/gossip/2009/12/18/2009–12–18_odds_are_that_elin_nordegren_will_divorce_husband_tiger_woods_after_sex_scandal_.html#ixzz0djwX1GayT.

Stephens, Joe. "Raising Millions for Charity, and Even More for Golfers." *Washington Post*, July 5, 2007, http://www.sportsphilanthropyproject.com/resources/details.php?id=469.

Tag Heuer Watch Commercial, http://www.metacafe.com/watch/2014527/tag_heuer_v2_tiger_woods_review/.

"Tiger Gets New Stripes: Accenture Launches New Global Advertising and Marketing Campaign Based on Three-Year 'High Performance Business' Research." The Free Library, http://www.thefreelibrary.com/Tiger+Gets+New+Stripes:+Accenture+Launches+New+Global+Advertising+and...-a0154337605.

"Tiger Introduces New Video Game." ABC Television Network, http://abcnews.go.com/video/playerIndex?id=7926326.

"Tiger Woods Daughter behind His Comeback." *Thaindian News*, June 11, 2008, http://www.thaindian.com/newsportal/sports/tiger-woods-daughter-behind-his-comeback_10058960.html.

Tiger Woods Foundation, http://twfound.org.

"Tiger Woods Late-Night Roundup: Will David Letterman's Personal Experiences Help or Hurt Him." EW.Com. December 12, 2008, http://popwatch.ew.com/2009/12/08/tiger-woods-late-night/.

"Titleist." Titleist Company, http://www.titleist.com/mediacenter/press releases.asp.

"USGA History." U.S. Golf Association, http://www.usga.org/aboutus/usga_history/usga_history.html. *Washington Post.com* from MSNBC.com, http://nbcsports.msnbc.com/id/31674326/ns/sports-washington_post/ (see Tiger's response).

"Woods Following Nicklaus, Launches Own Golf Course Design Firm." World Tournament Golf, http://www.worldgolftournament.com/index. php?option=com_content&task=view&id=86&Itemid=2.

"Woods Says Dubai Golf Course on Hold." Golf.Com, June 5, 2009, http:// www.golf.com/golf/tours_news/article/0,28136,1903124,00.html.

NEWSPAPERS

Anderson, Dave. "As Streaks Go, One for the Books." *New York Times*, February 15, 2007, D1.

Anderson, Dave. "Woods Chases Nicklaus as a Father." *New York Times*, June 21, 2007, B2.

Arango, Tim. "Big Risk in a Brand of One Man." *New York Times*, December 12, 2009, D1.

Barrett, Devlin. "M.D. Who Treated Woods Probed." *Newark Star Ledger*, December 18, 2009, 6.

Brady, Erik. "An Imperfect 10." *USA Today*, December 17, 2009, C1.

Brooks, David. "The Frozen Gaze." *New York Times*, June 11, 2008.

Brooks, David. "Genuis: The Modern View," *New York Times*, May 1, 2009, A23.

Buteau, Michael, and Andy Fixmer. "Tiger's Costly Affairs," *Star Ledger*, December 18, 2009.

Clary, Christopher. "A Decade of Achievement, Marred by Scandal and Suspicion." *New York Times*, December 21, 2009, D3.

Clary, Christopher. "A Weekend Warrior Falls in a Spate of Mistakes." *New York Times*, July 18, 2009, D1.

Crouse, Karen. "All Eyes Are on Tiger Woods, the Father." *New York Times*, June 14, 2009, 1.

Crouse, Karen. "Score Is Too Small a Matter to Matter to Woods," *New York Times*, March 24, 2006, D4.

Crouse, Karen. "Following a Famous Uncle and Also Her Ambition." *New York Times*, June 25, 2009, B1.

Crouse, Karen. "A Tennis King Content to Stay Home." *New York Times*, June 28, 2009, D1.

Crouse, Karen. "Woods Will Return Next Week in Match-Play Event." *New York Times*, February 20, 2009, B14.

"Cruising in Final Round, Woods Wins Buick Open." *New York Times*, August 3, 2009, D6.

Dorman, Larry. "After a Big Victory, a Huge Loss for Golf." *New York Times*, June 19, 2008, D1.

Dorman, Larry. "As Woods Backs Away, So Do Sponsors." *New York Times,* December 13, 2009, 1.

Dorman, Larry. "As Woods Enters Prime, Time Is on His Side." *New York Times,* December 13, 2007, D1.

Dorman, Larry. "As Woods Exits, Watson Finds New Life." *New York Times,* July 18, 2009, D1.

Dorman, Larry. "Even by His Standards, Woods Reaches a Major with a Head of Steam." *New York Times,* August 12, 2009, B10.

Dorman, Larry. "Golf Loses Its Star as Woods Announces 'Indefinite Break.'" *New York Times,* December 12, 2009, 1.

Dorman, Larry. "L.P.G.A. Tightens Schedule and Purses." *New York Times,* November 20, 2008, B13.

Dorman, Larry. "O'Hair Ends Rough Day at Bay Hill Ahead by 5." *New York Times,* March 29, 2009.

Dorman, Larry. "PGA Tour Alters Playoffs in Search of Closer Finish." *New York Times,* November 26, 2008, B11.

Dorman, Larry. "Player to Beat? It's Woods, As Usual." *New York Times,* June 8, 2009, D5.

Dorman, Larry. "Pro-Ams Humble Rich While Rewarding the Tour." *New York Times,* September 4, 2009, B12.

Dorman, Larry. "A Special Place, a Singular Experience." *New York Times,* April 6, 2009, D6.

Dorman, Larry. "A Star's Persona Slips from View." *New York Times,* December 9, 2009.

Dorman, Larry. "Storms on the Horizon." *New York Times,* November 19, 2008, B1.

Dorman, Larry. "This Year, FedEx Cup Is Still Up for Grabs, and Still Relevant." *New York Times,* September 21, 2009, D5.

Dorman, Larry. "Tiger Slam, Tiger Effect, Then Scandal." *New York Times,* January 2, 2010, D6.

Dorman, Larry. "When Woods Goes Missing, So Does the Audience." *New York Times,* December 14, 2009, D1.

Dorman, Larry. "With Typical Drama, Woods Caps His Latest Comeback." *New York Times,* March 30, 2009, D5.

Dorman, Larry. "Woods Announces the Birth of a Son, but Not a Return." *New York Times,* February 10, 2009, B12.

Dorman, Larry. "Woods Displays Top (Interview) Form." *New York Times,* December 18, 2008, B16.

Dorman, Larry. "Woods Has Swing Made for Camera and British Open." *New York Times,* July 15, 2009, B1.

Dorman, Larry. "Woods Left Holding Bag after Caddie's Remarks." *New York Times*, December 16, 2008, B13.

Dorman, Larry. "Woods Makes Jump into Final Pairing, but Cejka's Lead Is Five Strokes." *New York Times*, May 10, 2009, 7.

Dorman, Larry. "Woods Plays Genial Host, Then Responds to Criticism." *New York Times*, July 1, 2009, B16.

Dorman, Larry. "Woods Remains Busy as He Plots His Return." *New York Times*, February 4, 2009, B16.

Dorman, Larry. "Woods Will Appear at Inaugural Celebration." *New York Times*, January 17, 2009, D4.

Drape, Joe. "New Study Shows Gap on Court and in Class." *New York Times*, March 16, 2005, D5.

"EA Sticks with Plans for Online Tiger Woods Game." *New York Times*, January 5, 2010, B15.

"Elder Denies He Made Charge of Race Bias in Pensacola Golf." *New York Times*, June 6, 1969, 49.

Feedback. *New York Times*, December 14, 2009, D7.

Ferguson, Doug. "He's the Athlete of the Decade, Nonetheless." *Star Ledger*, December 17, 2009, 11.

Fredrix, Emily. "Sponsor Gillette Dumps Tiger Woods, for Now." *Star Ledger*, December 13, 2009, 5.

Fredrix, Emily. "Tiger's Fall Likely to Make Sponsors Cautious." *Star Ledger*, December 15, 2009, 38.

Hack, Damon. "A High-Tech Learning Center Is Woods's Way of Giving Back." *New York Times*, February 11, 2006, D8.

Hack, Damon. "Augusta's Payne Has No Plans to Meet Burk." *New York Times*, May 9, 2006, D3.

Hack, Damon. "Mickelson and Woods Are Back in Hunt and Right at Home." *New York Times*, January 28, 2006, D2.

Hack, Damon. "Raising a Child First, Then a Champion." *New York Times*, April 3, 2006, D7.

Hack, Damon. "Woods's Schedule May Aid His Pursuit of Nelson's Record." *New York Times*, February 8, 2007, D1.

Hack, Damon. "Tinkering with Success." *New York Times*, November 4, 2005, D1.

Hack, Damon. "Woods Can Give the Tour What It Wants: More Woods." *New York Times*, February 7, 2007, D4.

Hack, Damon. "Woods Turns 30 and Best Present Is More of the Same." *New York Times*, December 30, 2005, D1.

"Harry Jackson is Leading Golfer," *Baltimore Afro-American*, July 18, 1925, 6.

Hine, Chris. "Tour's Future Clouds U.S. Women's Open." *New York Times*, July 9, 2009, B1.

"Hi, I'm Tiger Woods. I'll Be Your Caddie." *New York Times*, October 21, 2008, B18.

"Influential Figures, '09 Year In Review." *New York Times*, December 27, 2009, 8.

Izenberg, Jerry. *Sunday Star Ledger* [Newark], June 17, 1984, 28.

Kato, Matthew. "Tiger Is Tops; His Coach? Not So Much." *Star Ledger*, September 9, 2008, 16.

Kramer, Andrew E. "They May Say, 'Tiger Who?' but They Like His Sport." *New York Times*, September 8, 2006.

Lindelof, Bill. "Tiger's Woes Costing Sponsors $12B." *Star Ledger*, December 29, 2009, 29.

Manahan, Kevin. "PGA Needs Its Tiger out of the Tank." *Star Ledger*, January 27, 2010, 13.

Manahan, Kevin. "Ryder Cup Watching for Woods." *Star Ledger*, September 16, 2008, 23.

Mardo, Bill. "2 Negros Golfers Sue PGA for $250,000," *Daily Worker*, January 16, 1948, Back page.

"Masters Policy Change Seen As Aid to Blacks." *New York Times*, June 13, 1971, V 5.

Newman, Andrew Adam. "Awkward Timing for a Book by Woods." *New York Times*. December 12, 2009, B4.

"Only Negro Golf Course in U.S. Is Thriving in Suburban Jersey," *New York Sun*, July 11, 1922, 22.

Pennington, Bill. "Cruising in Final Round, Woods Wins Buick Open." *New York Times*, August 3, 2009, D6.

Pennington, Bill. "Elite Golfers Have Their Clothes Laid Out for Them." *New York Times*, July 13, 2009, D1.

Pennington, Bill. "Tiger Woods Is Waiting for You On the 10th Tee, No Need to Panic." *New York Times*, October 26, 2008, 1.

Pennington, Bill. "Woods Embraces Memories of 1997." *New York Times*, April 8, 2009, B11.

Pennington, Bill. "Woods Will Need Help to Make a Run for the Title." *New York Times*, June 22, 2009, D5.

"P.G.A. Committee Votes to Ease Tourney Ban on Negro Players." *New York Times*, January 14, 1952, 25.

"P.G.A. Will Shift '62 Tourney Site." *New York Times*, May 18, 1961, 45.

Politi, Steve. "Tiger's Greatest Loss Will Be Faith of Kids He Once Inspired." *The Sunday Star Ledger*, December 13, 2009, 1.

Riccio, Lucius J. "Match Play Is a Recipe for Mediocrity." *New York Times*, March 4, 2007, 9 (Sports).

Rich, Frank. "Tiger Woods, Person of the Year." *New York Times*, December 30, 2009, Sunday Opinion page.

Romero, Simon. "Assuming a Proletarian Stance, Chavez'z Loyalists Push to Close Golf Courses." *New York Times*, August 12, 2009, A4.

Sandomir, Richard. "In a Downturn, Corporate Ties Have Put a Bind on Sports." *New York Times*, March 22, 2009, 6.

Sandomir, Richard. "Live from the Masters, It's the Also-Rans." *New York Times*, April 14, 2009, B16.

Sandomir, Richard. "No Payoff for Woods As AT&T Ended Deal." *New York Times*, January 21, 2010, B24.

Sandomir, Richard. "Not All Icons Are Created Equal." *New York Times*, January 30, 2007, D1.

Sandomir, Richard. "On Day Filled with Options, TV Watchers Chose the Jets." *New York Times*, September 29, 2009, B17.

Sandomir, Richard. "Woods Plays Beth Page with Coach." *New York Times*, June 10, 2009, B14.

Sandomir, Richard. "Woods Presence Gives PGA a Rating Boost." *New York Times*, August 18, 2009, B10.

Sandomir, Richard. "Woods's Site Becomes Place for Debate." *New York Times*, December 12, 2009, B1.

Schiesel, Seth. "Tiger Woods, Sporadic Gamer." *New York Times*, June 27, 2009, 1 (Arts).

Schmidt, Michael. "Reyes among Ballplayers Treated by Embattled Doctor." *New York Times*, December 16, 2009, B13.

Schmidt, Michael, and Juliet Macur. "Doctor Dispensed Drugs to Athletes, Assistant Says." *New York Times*, December 18, 2009, B11.

Siemaszko, Corky. "Golfer Says Woods' Peers Knew of His Swinging Lifestyle." *New York Daily News*, December 24, 2009, 5.

Silva Laughlin, Lauren, and Una Galani. "Out of the Game." *New York Times*, December 17, 2008, B2.

Stelter, Brian. "At a Company Woods Defined, It's as if He Were Never There." *New York Times*, December 17, 2009, 1.

Swartz, Alan. "'The Greatest': What a Concept." *New York Times*, June 14, 2009.

"Tape Offers More Details." *USA Today*, December 4, 2009, 10C.

Thomas, Katie. "As the Economy Worsens, Is There Money for Play?" *New York Times*, November 16, 2008, 1.

Thomas, Katie. "G.M. and Woods Put Early End to Their Endorsement Deal." *New York Times*, November 25, 2008, B18.

"Thousands Motored Out to Shady Rest Country Club Decoration Day," *Amsterdam News* [New York], June 6, 1923, 5.

"Through It All, He Is Still Tiger Woods." *New York Times*, December 12, 2009, 9.

Van Natta Jr., Don, Michael S. Schmidt, and Ian Austen. "Doctor Who Treated Top Athletes Is Subject of a Doping Inquiry." *New York Times*, December 15, 2009, 1.

Vecsey, George. "In Armstrong, an Example for Woods." *New York Times*, December 17, 2009, B14.

Vecsey, George. "Woods Makes Time for Small Talk but He's in an Open State of Mind." *New York Times*, June 17, 2009, B16.

Walton, Lester A. "Shady Rest Club Ends Big Fight in Jersey Courts." *Pittsburgh Courier*, July 18, 1925, 9.

Werden, Lincoln A. "4 Men Removed after Heckling Sifford, Negro Golf Pro, in Greensboro Open." *New York Times*, April 5, 1969, 35.

Werden, Lincoln A. "18 in House Demand Masters Invite Black Golfer." *New York Times*, March 18, 1973, 1.

Werden, Lincoln. "Special-Bid Idea Disliked by Elder." *New York Times*, March 20, 1973, 45.

"What They're Saying about Tiger Woods." *New York Times*, December 14, 2009, D7.

"Will Not Bar Negroes." *New York Times*, November 23, 1960, 163.

"Will Not Bar Negroes: P.G.A. Revises Attitude, Suit by 3 Pros Dismissed." *New York Times*, September 22, 1948, 45.

Williams, Mark. "Accenture Cuts Ties with Woods." *Star Ledger*, December 14, 2009, 2.

"Woods Finishes with a Flourish to Earn His 7th Tour Win in a Row." *New York Times*, January 29, 2007.

"Woods Will Be Fined for Comments." *New York Times*, August 11, 2009, B10.

PERSONAL INTERVIEWS

Lee Elder, May 30, 1991.

Renee Powell, August 23, 1991.

Charlie Sifford, July 31, 1991.

Jim Thorpe, August 24, 1991.

William Willis Jr., October 14, 1991.

OTHER

Preiss, Richard Porter. "Mashies at Mapledale: A Black Country Club in Massachusetts during the 1920's." Paper presented at North American Society for Sport History Convention, Vancouver, British Columbia, Canada, May 24–25, 1986.

INDEX

About the Author

LAWRENCE J. LONDINO served as head of Undergraduate Film/ Television Studies at New York University's Tisch School of the Arts before coming to Montclair State, where he is currently the chair of the Department of Broadcasting. He holds a PhD from the University of Michigan. He has written, produced, and directed a variety of radio, television, and film projects over a 30-year career, most recently a public television documentary, *Ripple in the Water: Healing through Art*, and *A Place for Us: The Story of Shady Rest and America's First Golf Professional*, which traces the history of African Americans and golf in New Jersey.

BY BARRY UNSWORTH

The Partnership

The Greeks Have a Word for It

The Hide

Mooncranker's Gift

The Big Day

Pascali's Island (published in the United States
under the title *The Idol Hunter*)

The Rage of the Vulture

Stone Virgin

Sugar and Rum

Sacred Hunger

Morality Play

After Hannibal

Losing Nelson

Nan A. Talese

Doubleday

New York   London

Toronto   Sydney   Auckland

Losing Nelson

L O S I N G

Nelson

a novel

B A R R Y

Unsworth

PUBLISHED BY NAN A. TALESE
an imprint of Doubleday
a division of Random House, Inc.
1540 Broadway, New York, New York 10036

DOUBLEDAY is a trademark of Doubleday, a division of
Random House, Inc.

All of the characters in this book are fictitious, and any resemblance
to actual persons, living or dead, is purely coincidental.

Book design by Maria Carella
Flag illustrations by Jackie Aher

Library of Congress Cataloging-in-Publication Data
Unsworth, Barry, 1930–
Losing Nelson: a novel / Barry Unsworth.—1st ed. in the U.S.A.
p.   cm.
1. Nelson, Horatio Nelson, Viscount, 1758–1805—Influence Fiction.
2. Napoleonic Wars, 1800–1815—Historiography Fiction. 3. Great
Britain—History, Naval—19th century—Historiography Fiction.
I. Title.
PR6071.N8L67   1999
823'.914—dc21   99–28757
CIP

Published simultaneously in the United Kingdom by Hamish Hamilton, Ltd., London

ISBN 0-385-48652-9
Copyright © 1999 by Barry Unsworth

FOR AIRA,

with my love

Losing Nelson

I

I had a bad fright that morning. I wouldn't have left the house at all on such a special day if the man at Seldon's hadn't phoned to say they had a piece I might be interested in. It was an oval plate, bone china, frilled at the edges, slightly curved at the sides, pale cream in colour, with a central medallion enclosing his profile in dark blue. There was an inscription of the same colour in slightly worn cursive, running round the upper half of the medallion: *Hero of the Nile.* They had used the De Vaere profile made for Wedgwood in the summer of 1798. Nothing very remarkable about it. But of course I agreed to buy it. It bore his image. It was seldom indeed I could resist that.

I was on my way back home with it, back to Belsize Park. It was a raw day and the sky was darkly overcast. Nevertheless, I decided to walk as far as Knightsbridge for the sake of the exercise. I had time to spare—or so I thought. As I was crossing Pont Street it started to rain, not very heavily. The platform in the Underground was crowded and became steadily more so while I waited. There was a silence among the people there, silence of waiting—they were resigned. I began to feel the first twinges of panic. Then an Asian voice on the loud-speaker: a delay on the line due to security checks at Gloucester Road station.

It was thirteen minutes to twelve. Imagine my feelings. This was February the fourteenth; it was the two hundredth anniversary of the Battle of Cape St. Vincent, Horatio's first great disobedience, the day he became an angel. On this day, at 12:50 P.M.—just over an hour's time—his ship, the *Captain*, went into close action. And here was I among this mute herd, sweating despite the cold, a good two miles from my table and my models. The ships were not even set out. It mattered so much to get the time right, therein lay the whole meaning—how else could I keep my life parallel with his? Before my father died—he died last April—I fought out this battle wherever I could: on my bed, on the floor, one freezing day in the shed behind the house. We never missed, year after year we broke the line at ten minutes to one. Now I had the basement all to myself. The thought that I might fail the appointment now was unendurable, it made me feel sick.

There was no time to be lost. I struggled back to the surface along with numbers of others who had made the same decision. I was feeling distinctly unwell by now; my breath came with difficulty and there was the usual suffusion of blood at the temples, obscuring my vision, making me feel hemmed-in. It was still raining and there were no free taxis anywhere near the tube, nor outside Harrods. I had to walk some way towards Hyde Park Corner before I found one, and even then I was lucky; the previous fare was alighting as I came up.

I gave the address and sat back and concentrated on keeping my face composed and my breathing inaudible. Closing the eyes has al-ways helped me to cope with anxiety, but now I waited two minutes by my watch before allowing myself the luxury. Timing is the key to control, and control is the key to concealment. The driver, if he glanced in his mirror, would think it strange if his passenger were dozing too soon. My father was a master of concealment; he kept it up so well that nobody knew just when he died, nobody registered the precise moment.

We made it with twelve minutes to spare. I was still gasping a little as I went down to the basement. I did not allow myself to be sidetracked by considerations of where among the shelves and cabinets to put my new acquisition; such a decision would involve extensive rearrangement, it could easily have taken the whole afternoon, in these last months I had got steadily slower. I simply left the plate, still in its damp wrapping, on the floor and went straight through to my operations room and began setting out the ships, the Spanish first in their two loose groups, 9 in the van, 18 in the rear, these last headed by de Córdoba in his great flagship, the *Santissima Trinidad*, 4 decks, 136 guns, the most powerful wooden warship ever built. One of the first models I made; I was fourteen, home from school for the summer holidays. Odourless now, the ship in my hands, but still seeming to bear the spiritous, heady scents of its making—glue, paint, freshly cut shavings. The shed had a smell too, dust and hot creosote and the rank weeds that grew against the boards outside. Smells are more intense for solitude and remembered more intensely, as every lonely person knows. Sounds too. But I wasn't lonely, I had him.

Now for the English fleet, under Admiral Sir John Jervis in the *Victory*, Horatio's death-ship at Trafalgar eight years later—eight years, eight months, and one week. In contrast to the disorderly Spanish, our ships are sailing in impeccable close order, fifteen warships in perfect line-ahead formation, approaching from the south at right angles, making for the fatal gap in the enemy fleet, two feet wide on my table, roughly seven miles in actual fact.

The sight of them now, disposed for battle, gunports open and cannon run out, quite restored my calm. In full press of sail, with their flags and pennants and painted hulls, their figureheads picked out in gold and vermillion, they made a fine show. How much care and devotion I lavished on those models, those sloops and frigates and ships of the line, what pride I took in them. Before my father died I had to keep them in cardboard boxes in my bedroom, together with all the other Nelson memorabilia I had collected over the years. My room was full of boxes, you couldn't get the door more than half open, you had to edge your way in. Now my ships had for their manoeuvres the whole surface of the billiard table that had always been a feature of the basement. My brother Monty and I used to play on it sometimes, before he left. I had covered it with dark blue baize and had a sheet of glass fitted exactly over it. In the light of the lamp overhead—no daylight ever entered that room—the surface glinted like dark water and reflected the colours of the ships.

Eight minutes to go. Since first light these stately, deadly vessels have been slowly drawing closer together, approaching in a fashion apparently leisurely the thunder and carnage of a close encounter. Incongruous, and to me entirely fascinating, this dreamlike slowness. Consider the ferocious fire power of those ships, their capacity for destruction, more devastating than anything known before, on sea or land. Jervis is taking well over a thousand cannon into action with him. Now they are 25 miles west of the Portuguese headland of St. Vincent, 150 miles northwest of Cadiz, for which port the Spanish are running with a fair wind.

They would avoid the engagement if they could, but they cannot be allowed to, they must be intercepted. A heavy weight of responsibility lies on Jervis's shoulders today. The French Revolutionary War has reached a crucial phase. The Dutch fleet has joined with the

French at Brest. One attempt to invade Ireland has already been made. Admiral Lord Bridport's Channel Fleet has been driven back to England by bad weather and forced to abandon the blockade of Brest. Only this same bad weather has so far prevented an enemy break-out and an unopposed Irish landing. If the Spanish are allowed to join them, the odds will become impossible. Not only have the English been forced to quit the Mediterranean—a vital sphere of influence—but the whole of continental Europe is now dominated by the armies of France. Drained by the subsidies she has been obliged to pay to keep her allies in the field, her trade routes curtailed, her merchant-men harassed by privateers, England is on the verge of bankruptcy. Ireland is simmering with rebellion. There are rumours of mutiny in the ships of the Royal Navy. It is indeed true, what Admiral Jervis is heard to remark as the weather brightens: "A victory is very essential to England at this moment."

Words that are remembered, recorded, famous words. But this brightening weather has revealed an awesome discrepancy in the strength of the opposing fleets. Jervis has fifteen sail of the line. Six of them are three-deckers, but only the *Victory* and the *Britannia* have as many as a hundred guns. All the rest, including Horatio's, are two-deck ships with seventy-four guns, the standard warship of the Royal Navy at that time. In addition Jervis has four frigates, faster than the line ships, essential for scouting and intelligence. I set them out now, on a diagonal, to windward of the English line. This is the force with which Jervis is proposing to engage the Spanish Grand Fleet, twenty-seven ships of the line, ten frigates, and a brig. Six of the Spanish three-deck-ers are carrying 112 guns, and there is the mighty *Santissima Trinidad* with 136. Altogether they have twice the fire power of the English. But there are compensating factors. The Spanish have put to sea in haste, they are undermanned, their officers are inexperienced.

Everything is in place. It is fourteen minutes to one. One hour and four minutes previously, while I was panicking at Knightsbridge, Jervis had given a bold and unconventional signal. On this occasion he cannot follow the rigid procedures laid down by the Admiralty in London for the conduct of sea battles, procedures that have not changed in a hundred years: You lay alongside, preserve strict in-line formation, and pound away in a duel of broadsides until the enemy is crippled or surrenders or runs. Jervis cannot do this because his force is too inferior; he would be overwhelmed. So he has given the order to put on press of sail and break through the gap in the enemy formation. It is the only tactic possible. Once through, the English fleet can attack to windward, concentrating its fire on the eighteen ships of the rear, disabling them before the van can make the turn into the wind and come to their aid.

A perfect day for sea fighting—calm, with a light breeze, no rolling to disturb the calculation of the gunners. I check that the English ships are in correct order of sail as they pass through the enemy, Troubridge leading the van in the *Culloden*, Collingwood bringing up the rear in the *Excellent*. Third from the rear is Horatio in the *Captain*, flying the Broad Pennant; he is a commodore now—since the previous March.

So they pass through. The Spanish spine is severed. But now Jervis blunders. He cannot altogether break from his conditioning, free himself from the rigid code of line-ahead formation. He hoists his signal: once through to the west of the Spanish, the fleet is to tack in succession and bear down on them. *In succession*. No sir, wrong. It should have been simultaneously. For fifteen ships to make the turn, one after the other, each waiting till the one ahead has completed the manoeuvre, and then to reform in line—this will take too long, the advantage will be lost.

But of course they obey, they are bred to obedience. Here they are now, in a wide inverted V on the ocean as they begin to execute the manouevre, in perfect formation still, the *Culloden* still leading. But the Spanish have the wind. De Córdoba has understood, he alters course northwards, he means to bear over the wind and unite his fleet. Then he can fight or run as he chooses, and he will have time to do it; only the first six English ships have so far completed the turn and they have not yet come up with the Spanish, they are still out of range.

One man sees this, and that man is Horatio Nelson. It is now 12:50 P.M. Without a second's hesitation, disregarding his commander's signal, he veers the *Captain* away from the wind, *he breaks the line*. The audacity of it, the impetuous logic! To recognize absolute necessity and act on that instant of recognition. Now again, in this silent room, as I send the *Captain* into the attack and her colours glint on the dark surface, I feel a constriction in the throat and my heart beats faster at the dash and defiance of it. The move has brought us, at a stroke, across the bows of at least seven Spanish ships, among them the huge *Santissima Trinidad*, the *San Josef*, the *Salvador del Mundo*, and the *San Nicolas*, these four alone possessing 440 guns against Horatio's 74.

At the moment that he swung away from the wind and broke the line, risking the outcome of the battle and his whole career on this one throw, at that moment, in his thirty-ninth year, Horatio became an angel. He entered a different sphere. I will say what I think angels are. They can be dark or bright, but they all have the gift of spontaneity, of creating themselves anew. This is a pure form of energy, and Horatio was winged with it. All the same, angels are not complete, they need their counterparts, the dark needs the bright, the hidden needs the open, and vice versa. Sometimes they meet and recognize each other. Sometimes, as with Horatio and me, the pairing occurs over spaces of time or distance. He became a bright angel on February 14, 1797, during the Battle of Cape St. Vincent. I became his dark twin on September 9, 1997, when I too broke the line.

I had no presentiment of this on that February afternoon, as I moved my model ships about on their glass ocean. Since my father's death I had been experiencing bouts of gloom—not sorrow—and at times a sort of excited restlessness that made it difficult for me to keep still. And I had run into a difficult patch in the book I was writing, *The Making of a Hero*. I had got bogged down in the events of June 1799 in Naples and Horatio's part in them. This book had been going on for more than five years, ever since December 1991. I started it on Boxing Day, the anniversary of his mother's death. The Naples business was worrying me; I could not leap over it. Progress was slow; lately, in fact, there hadn't been any. I kept retreating, rewriting pieces of his earlier life. It was for this reason that I began to feel slightly uneasy now, as I went on with the battle. Because at this point I had to bring Troubridge into the action, and at the time I did not much care to dwell on Troubridge, Horatio's brother officer and friend, closely associated with him in this battle but also in the treatment, two years later, of the Jacobin rebels in Naples—the business that was holding me up with my book.

Certainly there is no doubt of his fighting spirit. Horatio is not left long to fight alone. He is joined by Troubridge in the *Culloden*, the leading English ship, which has now completed the turn ordered by Jervis and come within range. For nearly an hour these two exchange broadsides with the Dons, superior discipline and gunnery making up for inferiority of armament. Now here is the gallant *Blenheim* coming up to give them a respite, passing between them and the enemy, pouring fire as she goes. The *Culloden* is crippled, she falls astern. Collingwood ranges up in the *Excellent*, last ship of the line. He passes within ten feet of the *San Nicolas*, eighty guns, and blasts her in masterly fashion with two broadsides in succession.

Ten feet. The length of this table. That would be about it. Almost jumping distance. These towering ships, fighting so close, hardly more than the length of a man between them, launching their thunderous fire, shuddering from stem to stern with the repeated recoil of the guns—the English gun crews could deliver a broadside every seventy-five seconds. Dismemberment and maiming inflicted almost within range of an embrace. Hard even for a landsman of the time, the notion of such closeness, such promiscuous intimacy of destruction. How much more so for us now, with our concept of war as distant erasure, a button touched, a figure or a thousand figures obliterated on a screen.

The close-quarter fighting gives Horatio his second great triumph of the day. The *San Nicolas*, reeling from Collingwood's fire, falls foul of her compatriot, the huge *San Josef*, three decks, 112 guns. The two Spanish ships, both badly damaged, are inextricably locked together. I set them together here, side by side, to the windward of Horatio. His own ship by now is completely disabled. She has lost her fore topmast; her wheel has been shot away; neither sail nor rigging is left. She is incapable of fighting in line, incapable of giving chase.

Again Horatio demonstrates the promptness of genius. The genius of a hero lies in his extreme readiness to action—which is not the same as rashness. He lays his ship aboard the starboard quarter of the *San Nicolas*. His sprit sail passes over the Spaniard's poop and locks in her mizzen shrouds. Three ships tangled together now; here they are, side by side. Horatio calls for a boarding party. Short of stature—he is only five feet six inches—slight of frame, with one eye more or less useless to him after the wound he suffered in the Corsican campaign two and a half years before, newly fledged angel with bright sword in hand, he leads the way, passing from the fore chains of his own ship into the quarter gallery of the *San Nicolas*. In the exchange of fire that follows, the Spanish commander is mortally wounded. The Spaniards surrender, but while Horatio is receiving the officers' swords, his party is fired upon. Seven English seamen are killed in this fusillade. Where is it coming from? From above and beyond, from the stern gallery of the *San Josef*, still helplessly tangled aloft. Without a flicker of hesitation, Horatio orders his mariners to return the enemy fire, stations sentinels at the hatchway to keep the enemy belowdecks, and charges on. He will board an enemy ship from the deck of another already boarded and taken!

His friend Berry is at hand, helping him into the main chains, keeping beside him during the headlong scramble from ship to ship. But on board the *San Josef* there is no resistance. A Spanish officer hails from the quarterdeck to say that she surrenders. The flag captain, on bended knee, presents his sword. The admiral is dying of wounds below. With his own ship disabled, Horatio has captured two enemy ships, both more heavily armed, using one as a stepping stone to the other. An action without parallel in the annals of naval history.

Luck, some might say—the right man in the right place at the right time. But angels make their own luck. Otherwise, how can it be explained that it was always he who broke the mold? Collingwood was equally well placed to veer out of line and throw himself across the bows of the Spanish. Not a question of courage or skill; Collingwood had plenty of both. But he stayed in line.

Late afternoon; the light is failing. Jervis has only twelve ships now that are capable of fighting. The Spanish have been defeated, four of their ships have been taken. It is time to disengage. Gradually the fire ceases, the fleets separate, the English stand for Lagos, the Spanish for Cadiz. After this terrible local storm, these hours of thunder and slaughter, peace settles down, the ocean comes to herself again and swallows the corpses and the drifting spars.

I sat on there, after the battle. I have never been at sea, except twice on the cross-Channel ferry. That was a long time ago, before my illness. No, I am his land shadow. I have been abroad only once since then, just once in twenty years. That was when I went with my father to Tenerife to see the place where Horatio lost his right arm.

2

I sat for quite a while without moving, sensing the winter dusk that was falling beyond my shuttered room, muffling the streets outside as it had the blank sea after that ferocious encounter. The short duration of these battles has always stirred my imagination. Fifty or sixty miles those ships could make in a day, not more. They had only recently invented instruments that could tell them where they were. For weeks or months they tracked each other across vast spaces of ocean. Then one day the sail on the horizon, the gradual closing of the distance, the routine activity of preparation. Finally the moment that gave this murderous patience its meaning: the twitch on the lanyard, the crash of the guns.

My models sat there, unmarked, immaculate. No decks slippery with blood. The glass showed nothing but the reflection of the hulls. No pools of tar, no wreckage, no swirl of sharks. Silence in the room had been unbroken. No storm of grapeshot, no shrieking tangles of chains and nails and razor-edged splinters of metal and wood, no groans and screams of wounded and dying men, no cheers as the gun crews saw their shots strike home. Cheers and screams, the two conflicting sounds of eighteenth-century sea battle.

I was visited by a sense of desolation, something like bereavement. Could one who had never known it in his own person grieve for the din of battle and the confusion and the blood? The question, coming to my mind in such a form, made me feel restless and somehow awed, a sensation difficult to describe, like a brush of wings, quite unaccustomed at the time, though it became more frequent afterwards. Usually when we fought these battles I had a feeling of fulfilment, they brought me closer to him, I shared in his triumphs. I know now that this first taste of mourning was a sign to me. At the time I thought it was no more than a delayed reaction to my panic of earlier, my fear of failing him.

The feeling of unrest set me walking back and forth from one end of the room to the other, passing between the table and the wall, from the zone of light and the reflections of the ships into the shadowy area at the far corner of the room. I found in my raincoat pocket—I had forgotten to take the raincoat off, so great had been my haste—a cheese-and-cress sandwich, still wrapped in its clingfoil, which I had bought the day before at a Safeway and then forgotten about. Living alone as I did, and preoccupied with my book, I quite often forgot to eat and was only reminded of the need to do so by onsets of faintness. But I never forgot times and dates. Mrs. Watson still came, as she had done in my father's time, only twice a week now, in the mornings. I didn't want her shopping or cooking for me. I used to leave the week's money in an envelope on the kitchen table. Usually I stayed down in the basement, out of her way. She had no key to the basement, naturally; I had changed the lock.

I ate the sandwich as I walked about the room. I was thinking

still about the battle and its aftermath. It had not been an overwhelming victory. The Spanish, though severely mauled, had not been
put out of the war. But there had been a great boost to national
morale, and—of crucial importance—the Mediterranean was opened
to our sea power once again. From that moment, and for the rest of
the war with revolutionary France, we would never allow these waters to be closed to us; our ships would patrol them freely, enabling us
to frustrate French invasion plans and defeat Napoleon's purposes in
Egypt.

For Horatio, of course, an important stage in his career, bringing
the first taste of the fame he longed for. He was no humble hero, a
contradiction in terms in any case. No, he wanted to have his being in
glory and he wanted the world to see it, see the beautiful shine of it.
That is the nature of heroes—they are nourished by fame.

He was cheered throughout the fleet after the battle, wherever
they saw his pendant flying. Crowned with victory, moving through a
rain of cheers—how wonderful to be Horatio at that moment. I felt
my heart dilate with the pleasure of it. Nightfall, the lamps on the
ships, lamplight over the water, cheers raining on him as he passes
through in his launch on his way to the *Victory*, to present his respects
to the admiral.

We have Horatio's account of the meeting, as given some
months later in conversation with his brother-in-law Bolton. He had
come straight from the fighting. His shirt and coat were badly torn, he
had lost his hat, his face was streaked with gunpowder, he was bleeding from a wound in the back made by a shell splinter. Jervis, who
greeted him with outstretched hands, was immaculate in silver and
blue. This was because he had been obliged to change his uniform.
During the battle a marine standing close beside him on the poop had
had his head blown off, and the admiral's face and chest had been
splashed with blood and brains and bits of bone and tissue. An officer,

believing him to be badly wounded, rushed to his side. No, he was not hurt, he said calmly, and he turned aside and asked a midshipman to fetch him an orange. This in the heat of the action. When the fighting was over and the day was won, he went below and washed away the evidence of mortality and changed. *The Admiral received me on the quarterdeck and, having embraced me, said he could not sufficiently thank me.*

This was to be an important friendship for Horatio. He had a gift for friendship. All through his career he won respect from superiors and subordinates alike; not only respect, affection too, he was always loved. On February 20, in the normal course of seniority, Commodore Nelson became Rear-Admiral Nelson. Later, when news of the victory reached England, the Order of the Bath was conferred upon him by a grateful sovereign. Rear-Admiral Sir Horatio Nelson K.B.

It would have been a baronetcy, almost certainly, but he had hinted in a letter to Sir Gilbert Elliot, viceroy of Corsica, who was returning to England with despatches of the battle, that he would be reluctant to accept a hereditary title as he had not the means to support one. Of course, there were some—sneaks and subversives being always with us—who attributed other motives to him. Chief sneak was Sir Gilbert's aide, Colonel Drinkwater, who had a conversation with Horatio on the morning of the battle and afterwards published an account. He suggests that Horatio was really attracted by the very conspicuous nature of the knighthood, which carried with it the right to wear a prominent and glittering star, and that he pleaded poverty in order to obtain this.

According to the colonel, it was he who suggested to Horatio the possibility of a baronetcy, but he was stopped by a hand on his arm: "No, it must not be in that manner." "Oh," Drinkwater reports himself as saying, "you wish to be a Knight of the Bath then?" And Horatio's immediate answer: "Yes; if my services have been of any value, let them be noticed in a way that the public may know me or them." Drinkwater is not sure about that final pronoun, but he professes himself to be sure about the rest and pronounces his judgement with confidence: *I could have no doubt of his meaning, that he wished to bear about his person some honorary distinction to attract the public eye* . . .

I could not take this seriously. It seemed to me unmistakably the voice of the cynic. The two men were alone, Horatio never spoke of this conversation, there is no independent support of it, he was dead when the account was published. Would Drinkwater, whom he hardly knew, have questioned him with such impertinent directness about his wishes and ambitions? Surely not. A radiant light would have been upon Horatio that morning, the morrow of one of the greatest days of his life. Drinkwater was trying to sully that light, as there will always be people ready to do.

It was not the imputation of vanity that I found offensive. I always knew that he prized the trappings and insignia of fame. His decorations killed him in the end, the stars on his breast made him a sniper's target at Trafalgar. The attainment of public honours is a hero's vocation; he bears them for all those who cannot, just as he bears the nation's dignity. No, it is the hinting at ambivalence, even duplicity, in Horatio's attitude, the suggestion that he lied about his means for the sake of the glittering star.

To hold this smear in mind long enough to repudiate it, let alone defend him from it, made me feel I had betrayed him, stirred a feeling of nausea in me similar to that I sometimes felt in those days when I tried to understand the events of June 1799 in Naples. I had devoted myself to a study of his life, I had followed him through the succession of his days and the succession of my own, though sometimes the course had run below ground. I was nine when this started. That was in 1964, the year my mother left us. Chess led me to Horatio—chess and my father and my absent mother and the fact that on that day I broke the rule about not showing what you feel.

I thought my mother had gone because she did not love me and Monty enough to stay. I suppose I already knew, in the way that children know such things, that she did not love my father. He, no doubt intent on setting a good example of not showing what you feel, did not succeed then or later in explaining the matter to us. He did not say she loved us or had been sorry to go. Our mother had gone to India, he said, because she had become besotted with oriental religions. *Besotted.* I did not know what the word meant, but I knew that my father was expressing his loss through contempt.

My form master of that year at the private day-school I went to was a chess enthusiast. He explained the rules to us, he encouraged us to play. He was kind to me, and I admired him, more than admired: I wanted to be where he was. I suppose I was more than usually responsive to kindness just at that time. To please him I tried hard to be good at chess, and I discovered that I was good. I had a natural talent, the master said. Mr. Lyle was his name. I don't remember much about him now. He had glasses. I seem to remember that he wore his hair brushed straight back. Blurred remains of a focus once so intense. I joined the school chess club. I took part in tournaments and distinguished myself. Shining at few things, for a brief season I shone at chess. I see it now, the stark arena of the board, the ruthless game that hung so paradoxically on feelings of love.

I studied the game, I read the accounts of historic encounters, the ploys of long-dead masters, and I played them out alone. I would set out the pieces at random, then sweep them off and try to replace them from memory. At night, crying for my mother, I would picture the chess board, go through the moves of some legendary endgame, and find consolation.

A colleague of my father's was there one Sunday afternoon—my father was a senior official at the Treasury. "Your father tells me you are quite a chess player." On his reddish face an indulgent look. "At least by his own report," my father said. He seemed to suggest I had boasted. Perhaps I had. "Not up to your level, Henry, not yet." Henry, Harry, Humphrey. A chess player of note. "Fancy a game, young man?"

We played and I won. He still had half his pieces on the board when I checkmated him. Pleasure in victory, expectation of praise—face and voice were not yet practised enough, I suppose I showed my feelings too clearly. My father looked at me but uttered no word. He went out, came back with a book from his study, brought it over for me to see. "Look here," he said, the colleague meanwhile looking on. "Look at these people here."

He had opened the book roughly in the middle. There were two faces, one on either side: William Pitt the Younger and Horatio Nelson. Neither name meant anything to me at the time. Later, of course, I knew them for close contemporaries—Horatio was a year older and died three months earlier.

"Take a good look," my father said. "These two men saved our country. They had reason to be pleased with themselves."

He meant it for my benefit, or so I like to think. He did not want me to be jubilant in victory, to overrate small achievements. He wanted to inspire me with worthy ambitions. But in his manner and tone I sensed displeasure; he was not pleased at my success, it had disturbed his sense of the natural order.

Two faces side by side, two lives in parallel. I think I was fascinated by parallel tracks even then. Both plates were in colour, but for some reason the two men were depicted at quite different times in their lives, Pitt dark-suited, close to his end, ravaged by alcohol and the strain of government, Horatio the twenty-year-old captain, in the dark blue and gilt of his full dress uniform, his youthful face severe, intrepid. There was no comparison, none at all. I scarcely looked at the statesman, the architect of victory; my eyes were all for the splendid young fighter, so slender and small-boned, so different from me in physical form, even then. I am on the heavy side, with thick wrists and big hands. Not clumsy, though; I am good with my hands, good at making things.

My interest in chess did not long survive that day; the lesson in humility proved the death blow to it. I continued to play during what was left of the term, but my heart was not in it, I lost the appetite for victory, my game fell off. In the autumn Monty and I were sent away to boarding school. I never saw Mr. Lyle again and I never played chess again.

With Horatio it has been otherwise. My interest in him seemed altogether to disappear, but it had merely gone underground, waiting for another sign. This came when I was thirteen, during a history lesson, when I discovered that Horatio Nelson lost his mother *when he was nine years old*.

It came with the force of revelation, like an assault of light. All the surrounding circumstances were lit up by it, as if by the arc of a flare in the night. The usual darkness descends again, but the print is there forever. My exact position in the classroom, the desktop mutilated by generations of idle inscribers, the look of the blackboard, the gestures of the master's hands. These things were as present to me that afternoon last February as they had ever been. Undimmed, untarnished over the years, the lustre of the kinship so casually discovered then.

I felt the need now to look again at the Rigaud portrait, the picture my father had shown me on my last effective day as a chess player, my first sight of Horatio's face. I got up, went through to the next room. The plate I had bought that morning was still lying there on the floor, but I left it where it was. I crossed to the wall where the portrait hung above a narrow cabinet containing objects commemorating his death: a black silk bookmark with the date of Trafalgar on it, a piece of Staffordshire pottery that showed him dying in the arms of two officers, a model of his funeral car that I made myself when I got interested in Horatio again, after my illness.

The original portrait, of course, is in the National Maritime Museum at Greenwich, a three-quarter-length oil by John Francis Rigaud. My picture was a photograph, blown up to poster size, mounted, and framed. Horatio was an eighteen-year-old lieutenant when it was begun. It was commissioned by his commanding officer, William Locker, who must have seen his distinction even at that age. Before it was quite finished, Horatio had to sail for the West Indies. He didn't return until 1780, three years later, still desperately ill with the yellow fever that nearly killed him and destroyed his youthful bloom forever. But Rigaud changed nothing in the face, merely touched in the background and added the insignia of Horatio's new rank—he was a captain by then, one of the youngest in the navy.

I stood before the portrait for a time I did not measure. He had been through the shadow of death, but the painter had allowed no hint of mortality. No sickness, no lines of pain, mar the confidence of his face. His sword is planted before him, his hands rest on the hilt. In the background, painted on his return, a view of Fort San Juan in Nicaragua, scene of the ill-starred expedition of the year before.

Disasters, fevers, the great victories, and the heroic death—all this was before him, undreamed of, when this impervious face was painted. Twenty years away his crushing defeat of the French at Aboukir Bay, the triumphant entry into Naples, the gratitude of monarchs, the songs and the praise and the abundant love of Emma, Lady Hamilton. Twenty years away his dealings with the Neapolitan Jacobins, which day by day, with oppressed spirits, I was striving to disentangle.

Thoughts of this period in Horatio's life brought the usual vague distress to my mind. I was still standing there before the portrait, but no longer looking at it. My eyes fell on the papier-mâché bust of him standing not far away, more or less in the middle of the floor. It was larger than life-size, three feet high and crudely painted, the eyes jet black and wide open, the cheeks rouged, hectic-looking; but there was a curve of power and authority in the mouth that I liked. I had seen it in the jumbled interior of a curio shop in Camden as I was passing by, and I had gone in and bought it and brought it home in a taxi, muffled up in brown paper. Only a month or so before—I would not have done it in my father's time. Now I found myself looking fixedly at him, at the straight line of the cocked hat that shadowed his eyes, the garish stars and medals on his chest, the gilt letters running along the base. I could not read them at this distance, but I knew what they said: ENGLAND EXPECTS THAT EVERY MAN WILL DO HIS DUTY.

Sublime message, surely the most famous naval signal ever given. Greeted with cheers by every ship in the fleet. Then came the last message he ever gave, his favorite, number 16, the signal for close action, which remained at the top-gallant masthead of HMS *Victory* until it was shot away . . . The trance of admiration that was descending on me was disturbed by the ringing of the front-door bell. I looked at my watch: it was exactly seven o'clock. I knew at once that it must be Avon Secretarial Services in the person of Miss Lily, who came twice a week, Tuesdays and Fridays, to help me with my manuscript— no small task, as I was constantly revising the earlier sections. I could not use a computer myself. My illness had left me with an abiding fear of screens. Twenty years ago, but I had not been able to overcome it. Not mirrors or clear reflecting surfaces, I had no fear of those, but opaque electronic screens from which faces might emerge. Faces with eyes . . .

I had known, of course, that she was coming. But what surprised and rather frightened me was the realization that nearly three hours had gone by that could not really be accounted for. Since the dusk of the battle and of this winter evening in London, since the separation of the fleets, as I sat by my operations table and stood before the portrait, this mass of time had accumulated and then dissolved away.

As I mounted the basement steps and went along the passage to the front door, I felt some return of the terror of that morning. Twinges, no more. But somehow it was always later than I thought, I was constantly striving to keep abreast. So much, so very much, depended on that, keeping abreast, keeping the lines parallel.

3

*M*iss Lily was always on time. I had taken to calling her that, not to her face, only in my mind, though she had none of the aspects conventionally associated with the flower, she wasn't languorous at all or scented much or markedly virginal, she was a steady person, in her early thirties, and her name was Lilian Butler. She had been coming for three months by then and she had never been late. This punctuality was one of the things I liked best about her; without strict timing, our lives are formless. However, Miss Lily was inquisitive, and that was a drawback.

There she was on the doorstep, her little red car parked in the street below. Slung over her shoulder was the case that contained computer and printer. "You have been going up those stairs too quick," she said to me when I opened the door. Even after such a short acquaintance she allowed herself remarks like that. I must have been breathing rather heavily and she had seen it. How could I explain to her that it was not a question of haste? I could never publicly admit to anxiety, any more than I could show tears or give vent to anger. And how did she know I had been down there, in the basement? Only from my breathing? It didn't seem much to go on. It was as if she had somehow been spying on me. She had never been down there, no-one had, I always kept it locked.

We went straight to the room I call my study, which adjoins the sitting room on the ground floor. The room where I sleep is on this floor too. The house is tall and narrow, late Victorian, like all six houses in this short row off England's Lane. It has four floors if you include the basement, but I rarely used the two upper ones.

It was warm in the room, and Miss Lily was clearly grateful for the warmth. Her nose was shiny from the cold air of night and she rubbed her hands together as if they were chilled, though she could have been out of the car only a couple of minutes. It occurred to me, not for the first time, that her circulation might not be so good. "It takes ages for that car to warm up," she said, as she saw me looking at her. "I get here just when it's starting." She only has to come from Camden.

I went to hang up her coat in the little entrance hall. When I returned, she was already seated at the table she uses for these typing sessions. The screen and keyboard and printer were there before her, all connected up and ready to go; the case she keeps them in was stowed neatly behind her, against the wall. All this in the time it had taken me to walk a few paces and hang up the coat on one of the pegs! Not only that, she was sitting there somehow expectantly, as if she had been installed for some time and was wondering where I had got to. I saw that somehow I had fallen behind again. How had I spent the time? Had I studied the pegs, trying to decide which one was appropriate for Miss Lily's dark brown, nylon-fur coat? Had some reorganization been necessary to make space for it? Had I examined the coat itself, the loop at the collar perhaps, to find a clue there as to the right peg or the right way of hanging it? I could not remember. The time was lost, it had sifted away from me.

To disguise the disturbance these thoughts occasioned me, I began to pace about the room, something I often did in any case while dictating pages of my book to Miss Lily. It was for the sake of this dictation that I had employed her. I was constantly revising sections of the book already done, those dealing with Horatio's early life, his marriage, and his career up to his great victory at the Battle of the Nile in 1798, his arrival in Naples in September of that year, his rescue of the royal family and the beginning of his love affair with Lady Hamilton, the wife of the ambassador, in February 1799.

This process of revision had intensified since I had reached the impasse of that June. My text was tangled with handwritten emendations, insertions, crossings-out. No-one but I could have deciphered it. Miss Lily's help had been invaluable; she was patient and efficient and—until that same evening—ventured no comments of her own. She also represented a notable piece of self-conquest on my part. I had hesitated for several weeks before taking the step of applying to Avon Secretarial Services, whose advertisement I had seen by pure chance one afternoon while waiting to have my hair cut. It was a difficult decision to make. I was always reluctant to change my routine, apply to strangers. But I needed someone, and there was really no choice. In the end I took the bull by the horns and phoned. Avon Secretarial Services turned out to be just one person, and that was Miss Lily.

So far it had been a success, we had worked well together. It was rather expensive, at fifteen pounds an hour, but I could easily afford it; my father's death had left Monty and me quite comfortably off. And I considered the money well spent. After such torments of indecision about engaging her, I did not want to lose her services now. We would continue together, or so I thought. With her help I would extricate Horatio with honour from the languors and horrors of Naples, I would accompany him through the final years to his splendid death and sumptuous funeral. My book would be the best account of Horatio ever to appear in print, a profound study of the man and a lasting tribute to the hero.

This evening, however, I could not begin. I made no move to get my papers from the drawer in the desk where I kept them. The restlessness that had been possessing me, the sense of displacement, of tracks obliterated and time somehow running out of control, kept me moving about the room. I found myself speaking in an unaccustomed way to Miss Lily, more freely and directly than I had ever done before. More personally too—talking about Horatio was like talking about myself.

I talked about the Battle of Cape St. Vincent, which I had just been enacting, and its aftermath and in particular about the exchange of letters between Horatio and his wife, Fanny, after the news of the victory had reached her. "Fame had come to him at last," I said. "At the age of thirty-eight he was a national hero, the whole country was ringing with his praises. Difficult to imagine now, but people were really afraid of French invasion. There was intense rejoicing when the news came, but Fanny didn't find much to say. His father wrote to him, full of pride—he was wintering in Bath when he heard the news, he had to go back to his lodgings to hide his tears."

Quite unexpectedly, at this mention of the old man, my voice broke a little and I felt a faint prickling behind the eyes. I have always been easily touched to tears and I have always been ashamed of it—it goes counter to my upbringing and the precepts of my father—but the assault always comes before the defences can be assembled. Was he ever seen to weep? Horatio, yes, on occasion; my father, naturally, never.

I had turned away from Miss Lily's gaze and now fell silent for some moments, trying to think of instances. I hoped she had noticed nothing. It was weakness on my part, yes, but I had found it moving, that pride in his son, those private tears.

"Why was he wintering in Bath?" Miss Lily said.

"His Norfolk parsonage would have been freezing in winter. Anyway, the main point is that everyone was singing Horatio's praises, everyone but her. All she could do was express her own fear and anxiety. That was not the note to strike with a man like him."

"You call him by his first name."

"Yes, yes, I do. An old habit."

Miss Lily permitted herself a smile. She has a wide mouth, rather pale, sharp at the edges, with a general tendency to curve upwards. "It seems funny," she said, "when you think that he is long gone."

"Gone?" I said. "Horatio Nelson is not gone—what an idea. He lives in the memory and gratitude of the whole nation."

"Well, I am British enough," Miss Lily said, this being the first of many cryptic remarks she was to make during our various conversations. I was still not sure what she intended by it when she spoke again. "But if her fear was for him, for her husband?"

"What use was her fear to him?" I was beginning now to regret having opened my mind to Miss Lily; it was obvious that she understood nothing about the nature of heroism. "He told her what he expected of her in a letter after the battle," I said.

"What he expected of her?"

"Yes," I said, and I quoted from the letter—much of Horatio's correspondence I know by heart: *All do me the justice I feel I deserve. You will receive pleasure from the share I had in making it a most brilliant day, the most so of any that I know of in the annals of England.*

I allowed a short silence for this to sink in. Then I said, "There you are, there you have it, that is clear enough, I think."

"Quite clear," Miss Lily said. "He wanted her to praise him."

"He says that he expected her to be pleased at his success." Her obtuseness was beginning to annoy me. "Let us see how she replies."

I went to the shelf where I keep the collections of his correspondence and took down Geoffrey Rawson's compilation of 1949 as being shorter and easier to handle than most. I found Fanny's letter in a few moments and read it aloud to Miss Lily, deliberately dwelling on the more plaintive phrases: *Thank God you are well . . . My anxiety was far beyond my powers of expression . . . Altogether, my dearest husband, my sufferings were great . . .*

This read, I looked rather closely at Miss Lily. "She has a hero for a husband and that is how she writes to him."

However, she returned my gaze firmly, and I could tell that she was not convinced, that she was siding with Fanny. Her eyes are brown and soft in expression but very steady in their gaze. I could feel my annoyance with her turning into rage. "She couldn't give him what he needed," I said. "She let him down."

"Well, after all, she grew up in the West Indies. That was where they met, wasn't it?"

"Yes, they met on Nevis. But what has that got—"

"You said yourself that the parsonage would have been freezing in the winter."

"Parsonage?" Later I was to become more used to Miss Lily's oblique approach to things, so strangely at odds with the directness of her gaze. But now I was bewildered. And my anger grew.

"You probably think I am taking too much on myself. I knew hardly anything about him, about Lord Nelson, when we started this work. History was never my strong point in any case. I have got secretarial skills, that's about all you can say. Most of my work is not historical, it is more contemporary."

"I don't know what you are driving at with this reference to the parsonage."

"Well, she would have been used to something warmer, wouldn't she? As I see it, he left her there alone, or with just her father-in-law for company, I mean disregarding him being a hero and all that side of it, either in a freezing parsonage in Norfolk or in lodgings somewhere she had not chosen to be. Draughty places, those old houses." I saw her hunch herself a little and clutch at her elbows; she was putting herself in Fanny's place. "And I grew up in this country," she said. "He doesn't write to ask her if she is keeping warm enough or anything like that. I mean, it was the middle of February. He was all right, wasn't he, he was down there in the south."

"All right? Good God. He had received a shrapnel wound in the battle that opened his forehead to the skull. He was suffering from attacks of breathlessness due to stress and fatigue, he had—"

"She was alone, she was frightened for him. You would think he would know what it is like to be frightened."

"But he did," I said. "He never showed fear himself, but he understood it in others, and he was always gentle with those who—"

"But that is among men, isn't it?"

I had no idea what she meant by this, but I could not escape the feeling that she was getting the upper hand in this discussion. And she was daring to criticize him, Horatio. The skin on my face felt tight with the efforts I was making not to let my fury show. I was afraid it would show in my eyes, which tend to get suffused with blood when I am upset. I moved round behind her to the other side of the table, where she could not see me without swivelling right round in her chair. The screen was facing me now, but I took care not to look at it. At a distance of about three feet, I found myself studying the back of Miss Lily's head. Her dark brown hair was caught up behind in a ponytail, exposing the nape of her neck, naked, palest cream in colour, surprisingly sturdy-looking, with a tender, faintly gleaming down on it, just below the hairline. Her earlobes looked pink and waxy seen from this angle, somehow improbable; ruby-coloured drops of glass dangled from them and seemed to shiver in the light. Words continued to issue from the front part of this head: "It's just like Scott of the Antarctic, he left his wife alone for months and years while he went looking for the South Pole . . ."

One moment the words were there, in the space before her. Then, quite suddenly, the sound of them diminished, receded. A sort of throbbing hush descended on me, as if something had been pressed over my ears. I was still looking intently at Miss Lily's undefended nape and the shape of her skull under the hair. Then she turned in her chair a little, as if to glance round. I had a moment of giddiness and the hush was broken, sounds started coming again, occupying all the room. I moved round to the side of the table. I felt no anger at all now, only a sort of surprise.

"I read about it in the paper," Miss Lily said.

"I'm sorry," I said, "what was it you read about?"

"This rumour that she had an affair while he was away in the frozen wastes. His son was asked about it and he said it was absolutely untrue and slanderous because his mother was not that sort of woman. What sort of woman did he mean?"

Her voice had risen. I looked at her face and saw that she was flushed. "What did he *mean*?"

This sudden annoyance over an issue so trivial seemed absurd to me and went a good way to restoring my feeling of being altogether on a higher plane than Miss Lily. I could not understand how I had allowed myself to get so upset. After all, from Avon Secretarial Services, what could one expect? She was light-years from appreciating that for a bright angel like Horatio, praise was manna, it was essential nourishment, essential combustion, he fed and blazed, like the sun. No good trying to explain this to her, she was still talking about the wretched explorer. Where did Scott come into it, a person only remembered for the manner of his death? Scott was not a hero. Heroes *succeed.*

"He probably didn't know what he meant himself," she said, more quietly. "Years ago I read it, and it always sticks in my mind."

I decided to let her go early. It was too late now to start dictating. Besides, the mood was wrong. This time when I went to get her coat, the parallels stayed in place: she was still busy when I returned, putting her things into the bag. I waited until we were at the door. Then, quite casually, I put the question to her. "How did you know I had been in the basement?"

"In the basement?" She looked puzzled, but this could well have been a pretence.

"When you arrived this evening, when I came to answer the bell, you said I had come up the stairs too quickly. I have been wondering—how did you know I had come up the stairs? Was it just because I seemed out of breath?"

"Oh, that," she said. "Well, yes, you did seem a bit breathless as a matter of fact, but I would have known anyway. These dark evenings, before you come to answer the door you always put the light on in the passage, and anyone standing on the top step outside, if they look up at the glass panel over the door, they can see a sort of shadow passing over it. If the shadow comes from the right—my right as I am standing there—it means you must have come up from the basement. If it comes from the other side, you have been in your study or the sitting room."

She was standing immediately below me, on the bottom step. Light from the passage behind fell upon her face. She was smiling as she looked up at me. Not a broad smile, just a sort of deepening of her usual expression. "How funny you should remember," she said. She seemed pleased, I couldn't quite see why.

"You are quite a Sherlock Holmes," I said. "Female version, I mean." I realized now, as I looked down at her, that Miss Lily had been tested back there in my study, that she had passed, and that her success had changed things between us.

<h1 style="text-align:center">4</h1>

*A*fter Miss Lily had gone I found in the fridge a covered dish that proved on investigation to contain ravioli with a filling of spinach and cream cheese, which I then remembered buying at a delicatessen near Chalk Farm station two, or perhaps three, days earlier. I sniffed it but could detect no trace of taint. Cold from the fridge like that, it didn't taste of anything much. I washed it down with some claret, about half a bottle, all I had left.

After the various upsets of the day I felt exhausted, but I had no inclination to sleep, in spite of the wine. I returned to my study and began to leaf through the loose pages of my manuscript, coming soon—as invariably happened in those days—to Horatio's fateful arrival at Naples in September 1798 and subsequent events, in particular those of the following June, from the tenth to the thirtieth. I was enmeshed in those twenty summer days.

The preliminary events are not in dispute. I knew them by heart, without needing to look at the pages before me. Horatio arrives in Naples on September 22, some two months after his resounding victory over the French at the Battle of the Nile. He is given a hero's welcome by King Ferdinand, the Bourbon ruler of the Two Sicilies, and his queen, Maria Carolina, who regard him as their saviour. They are terrified of the French, and with reason—Queen Marie Antoinette, Maria Carolina's sister, was guillotined in Paris five years previously. Horatio, though gratified by his reception, is far from well. He is still suffering from battle stress and the effects of a bad head wound received during the action. He needs rest and nursing, and this is provided by Lady Hamilton, the wife of the British ambassador to Naples, Sir William Hamilton, connoisseur and collector, thirty-five years her senior.

The danger of a French invasion by land is not over; in fact, it grows daily greater. Their armies have occupied northern and central Italy; they have taken Rome, expelled the pope, and declared the city a republic. There is a treaty in existence between France and the Kingdom of the Two Sicilies. However, from Rome to Naples is only a few days' march, too close for comfort. Horatio, supported by the queen, urges the irresolute Ferdinand to assume command of the Neapolitan army and march on Rome as defender of the faith against the atheist French. After much hesitation, he is prevailed upon to do so. At the head of thirty thousand troops, under the direction of the Bavarian general Baron Karl Mack von Leiberich, he sets off.

What an army. Described by Mack as the finest in Europe, it consists mainly of peasants in uniform, with an admixture of bandits and released convicts. Mack himself proves both obstinate and hesitant, not the best of combinations in a general. The king shares with his soldiers a strong distaste for personal risk.

At first there are successes. The French withdraw to concentrate their forces. Rome is recovered; Ferdinand rides in triumph through the streets, mounted on a white horse, accompanied by dragoons in glittering uniform. But then comes the counterattack. The Neapolitans break and run, both officers and men; Mack conducts a disorderly retreat; the king bolts back to Naples in civilian disguise, groaning with fear, beseeching his aides not to desert him.

Horatio, it has to be said that your advice was disastrous. The king is humiliated, Naples is left defenceless, the French have been given a pretext for breaking the treaty. The Kingdom of the Two Sicilies will be plunged into civil war, the royal family obliged to quit the mainland and flee to Palermo in order to avoid falling into the hands of the French.

Not Horatio's fault, of course. I was intent on making that absolutely clear in my book. Other biographers have called it a blunder, but this is to misunderstand completely his character and temperament. Attack came naturally to him; he was all fire. How could a man so noble of soul comprehend the baseness of his instruments—a king who had nothing of the kingly, a commander who could not command, an army that melted away?

He is now all that stands between the royal family and the advancing French. The ships are ready to embark the monarchs if need be. He has already vowed British support to the queen; now he is drawn into a personal promise not to desert her. A very different thing . . . I had noted the reference, it was there on the page before me, taken from a letter to his wife, Fanny, dated December 11, 1798: *The poor Queen has again made me promise not to quit her or her family until brighter prospects appear than do at present.*

This promise was troubling to me. Why did you make it? Why did you tie yourself down in that way? Your orders from the Admiralty were to protect the whole Adriatic coast as well as those of Naples and Sicily and to supervise the blockade of Malta, then in French hands.

Ten days later the situation has become impossible. The French are approaching Naples, and many will welcome them with open arms—the educated classes, the liberal aristocracy, united in their hatred of Bourbon cruelty and oppression, ardently possessed with the spirit of reform and republican ideas.

On the night of the twenty-first of December, the royal family is embarked, together with the Hamiltons and various Neapolitan notables. Bad weather prevents them from sailing until the twenty-third. At two on the morning of Boxing Day they anchor at Palermo. It is here, in the following February, that Horatio and Emma become lovers. And it is here that the news is received from Naples that the French army has taken the city, aided by the Neapolitan republicans, crushing an uprising of the *lazzaroni*, the fearsome Naples mob, who are devoted to their king and queen. The royalist forces have been expelled from the castles of Sant'Elmo, Nuovo, and dell'Ovo, and a republic, known as the Parthenopean Republic, has been set up.

Meanwhile, King Ferdinand is approached in Palermo by Cardinal Fabrizio Ruffo, a warrior cleric of ancient lineage, who offers to go to Calabria, where his family's estates are, appeal to the patriotism and religious faith of the peasantry, and lead them in a holy war to recover Naples for the monarchy. The offer is accepted. Ruffo enlists a force of Calabrese irregulars, murderous, ill disciplined, avid for loot. Holding this horde by force of personality under precarious control, he marches on Naples.

This Christian Army of the Holy Faith, as Ruffo calls it, has astonishingly rapid success. By the end of May the French have been forced to withdraw, leaving only a garrison in the castle of Sant'Elmo to support the Neapolitan republican militia—patriots, as they regard themselves; traitors, as Horatio regards them—who now take refuge from the bloodthirsty vengeance of the *lazzaroni* in the fortified castles of Nuovo and dell'Ovo.

So far, so bad. I took up my papers again. We were approaching the last week of June, the days that were causing me so much perplexity. By now Naples is in chaos. Ruffo's troops are out of control, plundering, raping, and killing unchecked. Mobs of *lazzaroni* are roaming the streets, murdering and mutilating anyone, man or woman, suspected of Jacobin sympathies. For the details of this terrible period I was mainly relying on the account of Constance Giglioli, who quotes an eyewitness, Giuseppe di Lorenzo. I glanced over his words now in the calm of my study, which, however, still seemed to have something of Miss Lily's argumentative presence in it. *Heads and mutilated limbs were scattered in the street corners . . . A great number of victims were shot, one after the other . . . This done those butchers, not caring whether they were alive or dead, proceeded to cut off their heads, some of them were borne in procession on the ends of long poles and others served them to play with, rolling them along the ground like balls.*

It is to avoid an indefinite continuation of this bloodshed that Cardinal Ruffo, on June 23, makes terms with the enemy. He accepts the surrender of the French garrison and their Neapolitan allies in the city's forts. The French will be shipped home, the Neapolitans given the option of accompanying them or returning to their homes under a general amnesty. The treaty is also signed, in the name of His Britannic Majesty George III, by the senior British officer in Naples, a certain Captain Foote, Horatio having sailed to the west coast of Sicily in an attempt to intercept the French fleet. The other cosignatories are Baillie and Achmet, for Russia and Turkey, respectively.

A regular treaty then, signed by accredited representatives of all the forces opposed to the French. Horatio, when he hears of it on the twenty-fourth, is violently opposed, not to the terms offered the French but to an amnesty for the Neapolitan Jacobins. There are heated arguments. The cardinal has given his word; the treaty must be

honoured. For Horatio the republicans are vile traitors who have supported an invading force. They must surrender unconditionally and
throw themselves on the royal mercy.

Could they have had any faith in this? Surely they must have
known what to expect. Maria Carolina was frightened and ferocious;
Ferdinand's vindictiveness was notorious. Yet on the afternoon of the
twenty-sixth, the rebels came out of their forts. The fate that befell
them was predictably atrocious.

So why did they do it? In this question lay all my trouble. It was as
far from solution that February night as it had been when I first stumbled on it three months before. Until I found an answer, an *acceptable*
answer, I could not proceed. I had been over the events hour by hour,
as far as I had been able to find reliable authority for them, especially
the forty-eight hours between Horatio's arrival in Naples and the
rebels' quitting of the forts. I had puzzled so long and so earnestly
that it had all gathered to a sort of bruise in my mind; touched even
gently, it would throb and hurt me, driving me always to seek refuge
in the less ambiguous triumphs of his career.

Refuge I found now, as I sat there, in thoughts of his splendid arrival in the city just ten months before, the conqueror, still a sea-
being, still untouched by this corrupt and sensual place. Already, off
Stromboli, in early September, his squadron has been joined by the
Mutine, bringing from Naples the first letters of congratulation on his
victory. Sir John Acton, the prime minister of Naples, expresses the
felicitations of Ferdinand and Maria Carolina addressed to the Saviour of Europe. Sir William Hamilton, on behalf of himself and his
wife, Emma, addresses him as "bosom friend." *You have now made
yourself, my dear Nelson, immortal.* In fact, the acquaintance at that
point was slight; they had met briefly five years previously, when Horatio was a young captain, still whole and unmutilated. Since then
there had been Corsica and the blinding of his right eye, there had

been his exploits at Cape St. Vincent, the fiasco of Tenerife and the loss of his right arm. Now this astounding victory at Aboukir Bay.

In the same batch of letters are two from Emma. All of Naples is mad with joy, she is walking on air with pride at having been born in the same land as he, she is dressed from head to foot *alla Nelson*—even her shawl has blue-and-gold anchors all over it. She urges him to write or come soon. He has written already, expressing the hope that his mutilations will not make him the less welcome.

The British ships are sighted at dawn on September 22 off the island of Capri. A Saturday. I had then never looked across that most famous of bays, but I had imagined it often, that dawn advent of the hero, that slow approach to the jubilant city . . . I knew what it would have been like to see it from the quayside, the faint sails in the half-light, now seen, now lost, drawing nearer as the light strengthens, silhouetted against the tawny cliffs of the island. Then sunrise, a single track of flame across the expanse of pale water . . .

Ten o'clock. The bay is a platter brimming with sunlight. Hundreds of pleasure boats have put off from the shore. I see their sails and hulls reflected in the water, shades of blue, scarlet, dark orange. The boats make ripples in the surface, but to my mind there is no gash of white; it is as if the colours themselves have power to cleave the water. Bands of musicians have come out to meet the ships. The orchestra of the San Carlo Opera, in a barge strung with red, white, and blue bunting from stem to stern, plays "God Save the King" and "Rule Britannia" and "See the Conquering Hero Comes." The martial strains resound across the bay and carry to the approaching ships. The *Vanguard* responds with the boom of cannon.

The quayside is thronged with cheering people. We stand there at the prow. Tier upon tier of houses rise above us, pale yellow, rose pink, parchment colour, terracotta, rising into sun-hazed darker slopes of cypress and ilex. The balconies of the houses are festooned with flags, hung with baskets of carnations and roses. The ambassador's barge comes out to us, greeted by a salute of thirteen guns. It draws alongside. Lady Hamilton, all dressed *alla Nelson*, flies up the ladderway. One of the most beautiful women of her time. She exclaims, "Oh, God, is it possible?" She faints in my arm and falls to the deck.

A left-handed handshake from Hamilton; elderly, thin, distinguished. His words are not recorded. An hour later a further salute, twenty-one guns this time. Ferdinand I, ruler of the Two Sicilies, is approaching in his state galley, painted scarlet and gold, with spangled awnings. Some months away still the fiasco of his expedition, the ignominious flight. Perspiring in his black velvet and gold lace, he makes a speech of welcome. There is gratitude in that big-nosed face as he hails his "Deliverer and Preserver."

As the *Vanguard* moves in stately fashion towards the waiting city, we sit down to an elegant breakfast. Among the illustrious guests is Commodore Caracciolo, Bailli of the Order of Malta, admiral of the Neapolitan navy, who is in charge of the nautical education of the king's nine-year-old son, Leopold. He is only a few months away from court-martial and death at our hands by public hanging as a traitor to his king.

As we step onshore, the air is full of fluttering wings. Hundreds of fishermen with captive doves in wicker cages have been standing at the quayside, waiting for just this moment. They raise the cages aloft, release their captives. As the white birds mount upwards, I try to follow their flight, but my eyes are dazzled by the brightness of the sky, the sunlight hazed with dust, the rain of petals. I am confused by the music and the shouting of the people. We gain our waiting carriage and go clattering away over the black lava paving stones, up towards the British Embassy, Palazzo Sessa, whose façade is draped with red, white, and blue hangings.

Something brought me back from this, perhaps some sound outside. Sitting there in the calm light of my study, my eyes felt this daze, this bewildering assault of sunlight and movement. Half involuntarily, I glanced up at the ceiling, as if to follow those beating wings, those floating petals. But there was only the Victorian stucco, crumbling here and there, of the cornice. Has any man before or since, any conquering hero whatever, made such a triumphant appearance in such a magnificent setting?

I doubt it, really I doubt it. In the carriage clattering up to the embassy, there is not much talk. Fascinating to my mind, that short journey. The whole situation, all that was to happen, already contained there, in the words and glances. Four people in close proximity: Horatio, Sir William and Lady Hamilton, and Miss Cornelia Knight, the authoress, who had accompanied the Hamiltons in their barge and was to relate the details of this historic meeting in her autobiography. Three principals, then. First—always first—the hero, still sick, suffering from the prolonged anxiety of that long pursuit and the stress of the nighttime battle in the hazardous shallows at the mouth of the Nile, lonely, in need of comfort, in need of the mother we lost so young; Emma, the blacksmith's daughter, exuberant, beautiful, excessive, ridden by follies, full of admiration for him, experienced in love; Sir William, aristocratic, cultivated, world-weary, aware of declining powers, prepared if need be (though perhaps not knowing it yet) to lend his wife or even give her, as she had been given by his nephew to him.

So we go clattering uphill in our open carriage, leaving the pleasure boats and the white birds and the thronged quayside behind us, up to the Hamilton residence, easily recognizable at a distance by those vivid hangings of scarlet, white, and blue. After arriving, some hours of repose. While we are resting, darkness falls. The three thousand lamps that have been set in the façade of the palazzo all spring to life, and the words "Nelson of the Nile" blaze out over the city.

We take our places at the dinner table. A distinguished gathering. Among the blue uniforms are those of Troubridge and Ball, constant companions of those Naples days. Your two favourite captains. It was they who carried the note to Ruffo that June morning the following year, the note that seemed to promise so much, that brought the Jacobins out of their forts. Your note. I didn't want to think about this; I wanted to hold on to the scene of our triumph, there in the candlelight, honoured guest, perhaps unsettled by the steadiness of things after so long at sea, perhaps confused by the beauty of full-bodied Emma and the slimmer versions of her that looked down from the walls in a multitude of guises and postures, copies acquired by Sir William before the original was securely his: teenage rosebud Emma in a black hat and pink silk gown; Emma as a bacchante, auburn tresses in artful disarray, flimsy draperies loose about her; Emma as Saint Cecilia, robed in white, palms closed in prayer, eyes looking heavenwards.

Your eyes were bombarded with Emma. Tired eyes, but not too tired to be beguiled. Were there glances already? Was there already something you wanted to repress or deny? Is that why you said you preferred Emma as a saint? Is that why you found occasion to say, with emphasis, there at the table, that the happiest day of your life was not the victory at the Nile but the day you married Lady Nelson?

Your room was on the upper floor. It had a broad semicircular window looking southwards over the bay towards Capri. The entire opposite wall was covered with mirrors. You could see the pale disc of the moon rise from the fiery mouth of the volcano as if exhaled upwards. Below, on the silver water, the ruddy torchlights of the small boats, fishing for tuna. And all this again, this blending of ruddy and pale, reflected in every detail in the glass of the wall. And when, in the days of your sickness, the hot September afternoons when you were feverish and she came to tend you, to see to your comfort, as she moved about the bedside you would see the lines of her body through the light summer clothes. And every movement, the turn of her shoulders, the sway of her hips, would be reflected in the glass. Repeated reflections like a repeated caress. Sweetness of the loins under the bedclothes . . .

All this was to come. But how strange it must have seemed to you as you lay alone there on the first night, in that room of multiple reflections. It was the first time in six months that you had slept away from your ship.

5

*T*hat night my sleep was broken by dreams. As so often, he was with me and there was the accustomed sense of mourning or lamentation, the massed sense of it and somehow the grain of it in the air. I never see his face clearly. I see it only in glimpses, in obscured light, a fleeting impression of the mouth, the brows, the line of the jaw. I am always strongly aware of his presence, shadowy, indistinct, but immensely potent. He knows I am there, he expects certain things from me, but I am not sure what. This time we were together on that ill-fated expedition up the San Juan River in Nicaragua.

I had been reading Pocock's account of it—the fullest there is. Horatio saw a good deal of action on land, a fact that is sometimes forgotten. In January 1780, as a twenty-one-year-old captain in command of the *Hinchingbrooke*, a frigate of twenty-eight guns, he was ordered away from the West Indies to assist the army by landing a force at the mouth of the River San Juan, which rises in Lake Nicaragua and flows into the Caribbean Sea. This was the naval part of a grandiose plan to transport troops up the river, storm the Spanish forts that controlled the upper reaches, and take possession of the lake, thus at one stroke cutting Spanish America in half.

What had not been much studied by the army high command, if at all, was how to get troops totally unacquainted with tropical rainforest, along with their artillery and essential supplies, through the hundred miles of the river's course. No-one knew the position of the enemy strongpoints. No-one knew what conditions were like in the interior. Apart from local Indians, nobody was thought to have navigated the river since the days of the buccaneers, a century previously. Horatio's task was to escort a convoy of troopships to the river's mouth and wait there on guard till they returned.

There were, however, problems. None of the five hundred or so officers and men who had been assembled had the smallest experience of river navigation; many of them were already sickening and should have been in hospital instead of preparing for active service. And the preparations had taken too long. The dry season was already two months old; the river was so low that boats often had to be unloaded and hauled by men wading in the shallows. Now enter Horatio. He does not believe that the soldiers can manage it unaided. So what does he do? As always, he is practical, unhesitating, prompt without rashness. He offers to leave his ship at the river's mouth and lead the way with two of her boats and fifty of her crew. Major Polson, the commanding officer, is delighted to accept.

Offered like that, on his own initiative, fifty men! It had impressed me when I first knew of it, and I had thought often about it since. Even here, even at so young an age, he showed the angelic nature; he disobeyed or at least exceeded his orders, which were simply to await the troops' return. *I'll give you myself and fifty men.* It was the same for him, I tried to explain to Miss Lily when we were revising this section later—in May, I think. He went with them, he led them, he took the same risks. The fangs of the cotton-snake, the sucking of the vampire bats, the hammer stroke of the sun by day and the noxious damps of night. And the diseases, I said, above all the diseases— malaria, bloody flux, black vomit. Before they reached the enemy, before they even knew where the enemy were, a third of the expeditionary force was already dying. Miss Lily couldn't see it—there is a lot she doesn't understand and never will. It wasn't the same for him, she said, it was his idea, not theirs. By that time she was accustomed to make remarks, whether invited or not. What had they to gain? she said, with that very clear and candid look of hers. What was there in it for them? A typical Miss Lily question, difficult to answer and at the same time quite beside the point. Those men had no destiny, I told her, tried to tell her. Horatio had. Destiny is possessed by very few.

Fifty miles upriver, fifteen terrible days; then the first sign of the enemy, a small outpost on an island in midstream. Horatio's sailors take the battery by storm, he leading them barefoot, his shoes having got stuck in the mud. Two days later, just below the lake, they come upon a powerful fort, called by the Spanish Castel San Juan. Horatio urges an immediate assault by storm—when did he ever counsel delay? But the castle is in a strong defensive position, above the fiercest rapids in the river. Major Polson waits to land his men, he waits to take the surrounding heights and position his batteries, he waits for reinforcements to arrive. And while he waits the clouds build up, the rains break. The forest steams; malaria kills the men in droves.

After a siege of eleven days, the fortress surrenders. The surviving Spanish are in even worse shape than the besiegers—gaunt, starving, in rags, living in low sheds made of putrid animal skins. A stink of death hangs over this place, this possession so much suffered for, so much longed for. Spanish and British are now united in misery. The rains have swollen the river to a torrent; the expeditionary force is trapped there in the jungle, unable to get through to the lake. There, in the mud of the riverbank or among the wet leaves, they continue to die.

And Horatio, by a miracle, is not there! He is not there to see the taking of this stronghold and its disease-ridden garrison. If he had remained, he would have died, beyond a doubt, choked on his vomit like so many. He had acute poisoning after drinking from a pool infected by the sap of the manchineel tree; he had contracted yellow fever, fatal in most cases; it is likely he had dysentery as well. Yes, he would have died . . . At the very last moment, before it became impossible for any boat, even a canoe, to struggle up against the flood, a message came from Admiral Parker, his commander-in-chief. Horatio was recalled; he was to make his way down to the sea again, hand the *Hinchingbrooke* over to his friend Collingwood, return to Jamaica, and take command of the *Janus*, a bigger and better frigate, with forty-four guns. Not luck, destiny, I said to Miss Lily, but it was a waste of time trying to explain such distinctions to her. Those fifty men, she said, what became of them? They all died, I told her.

Make his way down to the sea again. Of all the phrases contained in his orders, that one had stayed in my mind. The sea was life, the land was death; these were the parallels on which my book was constructed. His mutilations were suffered on land, a fact I regard as highly symbolic. But that was not the reason these words had stayed with me. It is a question of dates. Horatio's reprieve came on April 28, and that was the date I first started seeing Penhas. True, I was younger by a year, I was only twenty; but that is not important. The date is the same, and for both of us it meant a return to life.

Horatio set out that same day. He could not walk unaided; he had to be helped onto the boat. As those swirling, muddy currents carried him towards the sea, I was seeking help from Penhas, who belonged to the same London club as my father and was a psychiatrist. I am aware of the time difference; in Nicaragua it would have been several hours earlier than in London. But Horatio's journey to the sea took four days and four nights; it is the *parallel* that has to be kept in mind—that full river was still carrying him over shoals and shallows when I began the first of my conversations with Penhas. And it was Penhas who brought me back to him, to Horatio, whose hope lay in the sea, just as mine—guided by Penhas—lay in him.

Of course, this was not apparent either to Penhas or myself on that first meeting between us, which was more in the nature of getting acquainted. I had been dreading this meeting, as at the time I dreaded everything not entirely familiar, which in practice meant everything but the four walls of my room.

It was the end of my second year at Cambridge, where I was reading philosophy. I had been working very hard. I had to give up my rooms in college and find lodgings in the town. Possible reasons. How can one know? It is difficult to know the moment when the world starts to change aspect. It was mainly a matter of suspicion getting out of hand. Twenty-two years ago now. The progression of my illness has become vague to me in its detail. At first merely a daily sense of surviving, of reaching bedtime unscathed—coming through a tutorial, a chance meeting in a café or pub, even, later, just a wave of greeting across the street or a nod to some acquaintance in the library. The days bristled with encounters and my fear of them grew, extending to glances from strangers, especially certain faces, certain eyes. Unpredictable, uncontrollable, always just round the corner, the power to smash my life. Fear of eyes kept me from sleeping. Then one morning I was unable to leave my room. I dragged a cupboard across the door. When they began knocking and calling, I remember pressing back against the wall farthest from the door, pressing hard with my back against the wall—I remember the pain of it. They had to break in, and I soiled myself while they were doing it.

At home in London, here in this house, in my familiar room, the fear receded, but I knew it waited for me outside. I kept my door locked. Monty talked to me, and so did my father—it was my father who wanted me to see Penhas. I had been schooled to trust my father's judgement, and in his judgement what I needed was this fellow member of his club. Even so, I must have been somewhat better by then, or I could not have been persuaded.

Penhas was in his fifties, aquiline of feature, with a short beard lighter in colour than the hair on his head, somber dark eyes, and a smile of disconcerting charm. Some faces grow indistinct in our minds as the years pass, but his has never done so, nor the slow, emphatic gestures he made with his hands as he talked. He talked a great deal. I have often heard since that the psychiatrist's function is mainly to listen, but this was not true of Penhas, at least not at the beginning. He told me a great deal about certain things that had befallen him when he was just my age. He was a Sephardic Jew whose parents had gone from Spain to Turkey in the years before the Second World War. The family had an agency for imported machine tools in Izmir, but this collapsed, leaving them in poverty.

Penhas wanted to get back to Spain and set off in 1952 with almost no money in his pocket. All sorts of things happened to him on the way. He had begged in the streets and snatched washing off a line and even rooted about in rubbish bins. But the stories I afterwards remembered most vividly were the stealing of the bicycle and the adventure with the high-class prostitute, the *poule de luxe*, as Penhas always called her, reverting to French for this salacious interlude.

Both these stories contained a moral lesson in Penhas's view, but the lesson of the bicycle was easier to see. In some hilly region, footsore and penniless, he had seen two bicycles standing outside a lonely farmhouse, one very old and battered, the other quite new. He had stolen one of them. Which one did I think? "The new one," I said, because it was expected, but he shook his head. No, he had taken the other. Now came the lesson: in thievery, as in all else, there were degrees of gravity. This, rather obvious in itself, led to the more important point: the vital need to make distinctions. Sanity depends on our ability to make distinctions, Penhas was fond of saying. The bicycle he took was falling to pieces. The reason he stole the washing was to wrap it round the wheels, the tyres having rotted off. He had done a thousand kilometres on this contraption, he told me.

The *poule de luxe* episode must have happened before this. It seems she took a fancy to Penhas, took him to live with her in her luxury apartment, which he had to vacate whenever there were clients, maintained him for some unspecified period of time—a period he brought to a close by leaving at dawn with the contents of her purse. As I say, the lesson in this case was not so clear to me. It had to do with clarity. Incompatible missions, Penhas said. Hers was to pursue her profession, his was to get to Spain. Sanity depends on clear perceptions of incompatibility.

His adventures were interesting to hear about, and when I did begin talking to Penhas, it was not so much a matter of admitting or confessing anything but of trying to invent a personality for myself capable of responding to the confidences he had made me—the confidences of a fellow twenty-year-old. I think now that this was his deliberate purpose. Otherwise, how could it have been that I knew so much about these youthful escapades of his but nothing at all about his later life, his metamorphosis into a psychiatrist with an office in Brook Street, W1, speaking carefully perfect English, and a member of the same club as my father, about whose doings at twenty I knew nothing at all? I could not match his exploits with any of my own, but I could more than match them with Horatio's.

So it was that in the presence of this talkative psychiatrist I found him again. He had been there all the time but underground, obscured by the stress of A levels and my studies at the university. In the course of time I told Penhas about the chess game, the two faces side by side in my father's book, the luminous moment of my discovery that Horatio and I had lost our mothers at the same age. I told him about my history teacher, the redoubtable Grigson. I told him about the scrapbooks and the model ships.

Once this was avowed, there was no going back. Penhas fastened on it. With gentle questions, he led me along. For months he was the only person I really talked to. I told him about my earlier conviction that there existed some intimate link between this great man's life and mine. Penhas encouraged me. He never reacted immediately. Things I said would lie dormant between us, sometimes for several meetings. Meanwhile, though he never admitted so much, he did some studying on his own. His knowledge of eighteenth-century sea battles visibly increased. He even began to use nautical terminology.

"Think of the mystery of the man, use him as a source of meditation."

"What mystery?"

"The mystery of his courage. Think of him there, in the heat of the action, on the quarterdeck. Think of the tendency to fear there must have been. Men are more likely to be mastered by fear when they are fully conscious of the risks they are running. Everyone else would be too busy manning the guns and so on. Only the officers on the quarterdeck had to stand still and be shot at. Think of that quarterdeck. At the forward end, looking across the waist towards the forecastle, there was only an open rail. That is where your Horatio stood. Think of him there, dressed impeccably—full uniform, cocked hat, silk stockings, buckled shoes. Immaculate. Unoccupied, fully aware of his danger, carnage all around him. Like a rock, Charles, like a rock. That is the way, that is the way forward. Horatio is your lifeline—stay with him, he will get you out and about. Join the Nelson Club, there must be one—in London there is a club for everything under the sun, if you can run it to earth. I'll get my secretary to find the address."

This was towards the end of my treatment. I remember it quite well, an afternoon in late summer. I remember the gesture of his hands as he spoke, a downward movement, with the palms facing inwards, about eighteen inches apart, as though sketching two sides of a box. Dark eyes with their look of sombre sincerity. Sunlight filtered through thin curtains, white or beige. Two parallel lines, the sides of a box. *Horatio is your lifeline.*

There is a club; Penhas was right. It is called the Nelson Club and has premises in Bloomsbury. But I did not become a member then, in spite of his advice. In fact, I did not join until much later. At the time I was not up to joining anything. I did not return to university. For quite some time I could not easily be persuaded to leave the house. Neither Penhas nor anyone else succeeded in explaining how it had come about, how it was that I had stumbled into such terror. It might as well have been some viral infection, like jaundice, for example. You are dreadfully familiar with the symptoms but you don't know why it happened, why it happened to you. However, I stayed with Horatio, who did not know fear, and he with me; we have been together ever since.

The fifty lives he had offered were wretchedly consumed. Many thousands more were to go the same way before Dalling, the governor of Jamaica, and Lord George Germain, the colonial secretary, were to abandon the dream of possessing Lake Nicaragua and opening a route to the Pacific. There was no expeditionary force left by this time. Since the previous February, two thousand troops had been sent to Nicaragua, of whom fewer than a hundred survived, and they were wrecked in health. More than a thousand sailors died in their ships. These are details that make Horatio's escape more wonderful, and I liked to dwell on them.

The final act of this tragic farce was curiously fitting. When, finally, the survivors made their way downriver (the boat they left in was called the *Lord Germain*, after the man who in the remote purlieus of Whitehall dreamed up this costly enterprise), the rearguard of Light Dragoons was left behind with orders to blow up the bastions of the fort before abandoning it. Of these soldiers, recruited in the quayside bars and brothels of Jamaica, a motley assortment of Portuguese, Italians, Negroes, and a few British, nothing more is known. Perhaps the charges were too weak, or the bastions too strong, or they were surprised by the Spanish before they could complete the work. Presumably they died there. All that is known for certain is that by the end of the year the Spanish flag was again flying over the Castle of San Juan. The jungle closed over the corpses just as the discreet silence of government closed over the expedition itself.

How fortunate for Horatio that he was not present at the final stages of this fiasco. Now that is luck, I said to Miss Lily. I was still trying to make her see the difference. He was not associated with the defeat. Because, you see, he had advocated immediate assault by storm, but Polson had chosen to wait. Waiting proved disastrous, so Horatio emerged with credit, his superiors were favourably impressed. Had young Nelson been listened to, they said, the castle would have been taken, the lake attained, and the healthy uplands of Nicaragua occupied before the onset of the rains. It was never put to the test, of course. That is what we mean by luck, I told her. Reputation thus enhanced, skeletonic, dressed in his captain's uniform of blue, white, and gold, he was borne swiftly away, down to the open sea. Heroes have both, I said, they have luck *and* destiny.

However, I did not, that night last February, dream of open skies and sunlit seas and the passage of Horatio to life again, but of that nightmare journey upriver with the fifty doomed men of the frigate *Hinchingbrooke*, the stream narrowing as the forest pressed dense and close on either side. There was no turning back. Horatio at the prow with his narrow back turned to me, I behind him in the same boat. He looks round once, his face is noseless, eyeless, mouthless, just a pale shape of flesh beneath the sharp wings of his captain's hat. But I know it is at me he is looking; we are about to face something terrible together. From the banks on either side a massed sound of lamentation, sorrow falling on us like rain. The river takes a bend and we come upon the Spanish stronghold, fortress of the dead and the dying, open gates, litter of corpses, crawling survivors, the swarming glint of flies. The sound of mourning grows wilder, it fills the air. Suddenly I am alone, he is no longer with me . . .

I woke from this sweating. I was not Horatio in the dream, he abandoned me, I did not take his place. Otherwise, how could I dream of the besieged in their putrid prison, something he never saw? An echo of the Holocaust, filmed images of the heaped dead, the walking dying, central experience of our century whether we lived through it or not, pit into which all our nightmares flow?

For a long time I lay awake in the darkness. The intensity of the dream, that mingling of horror and grief, kept my mind on a gloomy track. I thought again of those dying dragoons, lost between the lake and the sea, fumbling to blow up the fort. No-one will ever know what became of them. That much, at least, we know about Jervis's decapitated marine. Perhaps he was no farther than a foot away. The grotesque *suddenness* of that death, no gasp or cry. And soundless in effect, amidst all that din of battle. Only the brief song of the missile, then the splatter of blood and brain over the face and chest of the crusty old admiral. Why did he call for an orange? To demonstrate unconcern? Or did some stuff splash into his mouth? Probable, yes, though naturally beyond the touch of proof. It must have been a shock. There would have been an intake of breath, an involuntary gasp of surprise. Even so seasoned a campaigner . . . Yes, the viscid substance of the marine's death, some of it entered his mouth, and he called for an orange to get rid of the taste. Naturally he stayed on the quarterdeck till victory was assured, stained with the marine's blood and bits of his brain tissue and spinal marrow and the soft, fatty substances that had sheathed his nerves.

Somewhere that soldier's name will be recorded, though I have never found it; also, just possibly, as an incident in some more general account, how he was standing at the moment of his death, whether loading or firing, and so on. But of course his name does not matter, what he was doing does not matter; he provided an occasion for his admiral, at the height of the battle, to call for an orange. Jervis acquired an extra name, he was created Earl St. Vincent. And Horatio, hero of the day, became Sir Horatio, Knight of the Bath . . .

Sea battle in those days so peculiarly designed for mutilations and maimings. A hail of missiles. Shrapnel from the cannon-shot, razor-edged projectiles from sliced and splintered timbers, whizzed through the crowded decks. Selective, however—death not a reaper but a sort of crazed sniper, here a face shorn off, there a leg carried away. Men rarely died in swaths. Sometimes, of course, when a ship was raked fore and aft—this was the fire Horatio had to suffer at Trafalgar, when he drove into the French line at right angles. But death in daily dress was the gouger, the slicer, lord of eviscerations and lopped limbs. And he, my Horatio, pacing back and forth on the quarterdeck, pausing to observe the progress of the battle, stars and ribbons prominent on his breast, showing no haste, showing no fear, as if he were out on a Sunday morning stroll, looking at birds or clouds through his telescope. What sublime conquest of self he gave proof of, not once but over and over, what shining bravery and quality of command. Nerves of steel, a courage not merely of endurance—that alone is not the hero's brand—but possessing that fierce patience of the fighter who waits to deliver the killing stroke. *The mystery of his courage.* Admiration, the old admiration, flooded over me as I lay there. Ever since my talks with Penhas, I had loved him for this sauntering in the midst of terrible damage. The ugly dream receded, and I felt again that prickle of tears so common with me then and now.

My own first experience of death was on a Sunday morning, during a stroll in the country. It came in the form of one sick rabbit, which my father stamped on. I was five years old—it is one of my earliest memories. My brother, Monty, was with us; he is three years older. We were out on a country walk with my father. This was in Surrey, where we lived then—it was two years later that we came to live here, in this house. We were walking along a footpath, not very wide, clay-coloured, dusty—I suppose there had been no rain for some time. Open, heathy country. I have worked out that it was a Sunday; we were generally taken for walks on a Sunday morning if the weather was fine enough, while my mother, unaided on this day of the week, saw to the lunch.

We met the rabbit, or it met us—it was coming from the opposite direction, hopping slowly towards us along the edge of the path, not seeming disabled or distressed, not at first, though slower than you would expect a rabbit to be in the open and in full view. When we were quite close, it stopped, and I saw the gummy bulge of its eyes and I knew there was something badly wrong with this rabbit. Its head was too big. At the last moment, when we were almost upon it, fear supervened; it made an effort to get away, leaving the path and going off perhaps three yards into the grass. Then it stopped again. I saw now that the rabbit was trembling all over. I looked at my father's face to see what we were to make of this business, but there was no expression on his face at all. A last impression of the bloated head, the swollen, suppurating eyes. Then my father, without a word, stepped off the path, approached the rabbit, raised his right knee well above the horizontal, and stamped down with force—a single, plunging motion. Then he briskly but thoroughly wiped his shoe in the grass.

Strange how clearly I could remember these actions in their exact sequence, yet had no certain recollection of the dead rabbit, nothing I could be sure belonged to the time. Images of pulped or squashed rabbits visited my mind frequently enough afterwards and still sometimes do, but I can never be sure they are authentic. The stamping and the wiping I remember well, however, the gray flannel trouser leg, two or three inches of greenish sock, the stout, cherry-brown brogue; this last could not have been much below my eye level at the time, when raised to stamping height—he was a tall man. He looked at us and I remember his face. *We have put the poor beast out of its misery,* he said.

I don't know what I felt about this or what I feel now. We crave a dominant note, we seek in memory for the single element, one stain to colour the whole. But the tints do not blend, the colour eludes us. There was no balance in the thing. The dreamlike preliminaries, the loping, lolloping rabbit, my father's casual stepping aside, the violence of the plunging shoe, that brisk rubbing in the grass.

We have put the poor beast out of its misery. He included Monty and me in that decisive act. It was true, he had done a merciful thing. A paradox too difficult for a child to appreciate, the intention of mercy expressed in a gesture so seemingly brutal. And then there was the look on his face, a certain look of alertness, almost eagerness, as he scanned our faces to see if the lesson had gone home.

That is the earliest memory I have of my father's face; the latest is the face of his death, that settling of stillness, as if he had answered his own question. But what lesson was it that he was seeking to bring home to us? This is the nature of reality, this is what the world is like, a place of suffering and pain which a man must confront with decision? Something like pleasure on his face, a sort of brightness; not at killing the rabbit, I don't think he took the smallest pleasure in that, but at the stern message implicit in it. He was observing his sons' faces, driving home a moral, making a useful dent on the soft minds of Monty and me. The memory is all violence now, like the springing of a trap in a silent place; the moral side of it has been diluted. In later years my father seemed often to be held in that same incommunicable woe of the rabbit. Not his eyes, not the alertness of his glance, that was unimpaired . . .

I did not want to think about this. Horatio was my refuge, as so often. I felt the impulse to look again at the face of his father. For some minutes I lay there, summoning resolve. Then I got up, put on my heavy dressing gown, and went along to the kitchen, with the idea of making some tea and taking it down to the basement.

6

*I*t was not yet light and very cold. I always turn the heating off before going to bed; it makes the air too dry and gives me headaches. Besides, a cold bedroom is more manly, or so I was brought up to believe. Apart from anything else, it's a long-standing habit and habit is law, habit is safety; without habits we would just flop around and die. I put the heating back on now, however, and began to make the tea.

By then it was taking me a long time to make tea. In fact, everything seemed to take longer and longer. I urgently wanted to look at Edmund Nelson's face, but things had to be done in order, I knew I couldn't take short cuts. I had given up cooking because it took up too much time, all the pondering what to buy and getting lost in supermarkets. And there had been times when it conflicted with some important date in the Horatio calendar—I celebrated all the key events of his life. I didn't mind giving it up, there is no framework in it, no procedure, as an activity it is messy, amorphous, clogged with alternatives. Mrs. Watson would have cooked for me, at least on the days that she came, but I didn't want that, it was too much of an involvement.

Run the cold water for ninety seconds to flush out the pipes, kettle two-thirds full, warm the pot, two level teaspoons of Darjeeling, catch the kettle at the precise moment it rises to the boil, on no account must it bubble or oxygen is lost and then you have to start all over again. Pour from a height of eight inches—I had made a pencil mark on the wall. Tea cosy. Allow to stand a full three minutes. Strainer at the ready, resting on its blue saucer. I believe in procedures. When our world comes crashing down about our ears, when this planet chokes in its own fumes or stings itself to death like a demented scorpion, it will be owing to neglected procedures. Horatio knew the importance of procedures—none better.

I have my own mug, blue and white, with a thin band of silver going round the top. It has my monogram on it in a panel of pale blue, two curly C's twining together, Charles Cleasby. It was a present from my mother when I was six years old, one of a number of things given to me when I came home from hospital after my appendix operation. It seemed to me miraculous that she should have found a mug with just my initials on it, among all the initials and all the children in the world. Only years later, long after she had left us, did it occur to me that she might have had them specially put on. I had been drinking my tea out of that mug for thirty-five years. Apart from the rug in the sitting room, it was all of her I had left.

No milk—I never touch milk. One cube of Demerara sugar. Mug in hand, I went down to the basement. I went through to the small middle room that lies between my collection of Nelson exhibits and the ops room with the model ships. This was my picture gallery, mainly reproductions—original portraits are naturally difficult to obtain even if one could afford them, though I had some good paintings of sailing ships, among them one by John Nathan, R.A., of HMS *Victory* with sails loosed for drying at Spithead.

Fanny Nelson was there, the wronged wife; and Emma Hamilton, the adored mistress; and Sir William Hamilton, the complaisant husband; and Horatio's uncle, Captain Maurice Suckling, who gave him his first chance; and Jervis, he of the orange; and Collingwood, who supported Horatio so loyally at the Battle of Cape St. Vincent; and Hardy, who kissed him when he was dying. Horatio himself was not to be found on these walls. I hung all the likenesses of him that I had collected in the exhibits room; he looked down over the cabinets and showcases that commemorated his wonderful life.

I stood before the portrait of Edmund Nelson, sipping my tea, warming my hands on the mug. He was seventy-eight when Beechey painted this likeness of him. Less than two years to live. A long, fair-browed, narrow face, lugubrious, scraped close to the bone with age; resigned, yes, but not serene. The tones of the painting are sombre; his black habit merges into the dark sepia of the background, his two-tailed clerical stock is tucked close up to his bony chin. Submission in the face, feeling suppressed, something feminine. Not quite the face you would expect in a Norfolk parson of yeoman stock . . . My father's face quite different, all straight lines: square jaw, sheer planes at the temples, level eyes and brows, large, regular teeth—the stem of his pipe had bite marks on it.

The man who begot me, the man who begot Horatio—in death they became contemporaries, as all the dead are. In the face before me now there was no trace of the angelic, no hint of breaking the line. Duty his creed, as it was his son's, but like many of the virtues we extol, this can take forms active or passive. The Reverend Nelson's was the latter sort, finding its reward in sufferance. Not so Horatio, for whom duty was a seeking out, a fulfilment in fame.

His was the ambition of genius. But it was the lesson of obligation, of doing what one is called upon to do, that the father passed down. What Horatio made of it was his own. *Thank God I have done my duty.* Probably the last words anyone heard him say, as he lay dying in the dimness belowdecks at Trafalgar. The surgeon who attended him and recorded the last hours of his life heard him murmur these words some minutes before the voice was lost forever. Duty done, victory achieved—it was the same thing for him, the duty lay in the achievement. And so it is with me; I am the same, in spite of appearances. My doubts and fears, these were his purifying discharge. A medal has two faces; my face was hidden against his breast.

Still looking closely at that eroded face, I thought of the stories of Horatio's childhood that have passed down to us. Courage, leadership, indomitable will, all so precociously shown by this slightly built, pale-faced boy. How, one Norfolk winter, he battled through great drifts of snow to get to school, urging on his faltering—and much more robust—elder brother, because they had promised their father to do their utmost. *Remember, brother, it was left to our honour.* How, at an even tenderer age, he wandered away, got lost in the woods as darkness fell, was found after long search, sitting by the side of an impassable stream. Surprising that fear did not bring you home, they said. *Fear? I never saw fear. What is it?*

Useless to look for clear outlines in this twilight of infancy. These were anecdotes told after his glorious death, after he had become the saviour of his country, memories embroidered into legend. The life of a hero is a grafted tree, rooted in fact, branched with hearsay. And Horatio Nelson is the English hero; he has no rival. No threat of rivals in the future, either—this country will never produce heroes again.

Equally useless to judge by faces. This mild-faced man I was looking at now was capable, when roused, of seizing a housebreaker by the collar and throwing him bodily out of the house. Horatio and his brothers and sisters, when old enough to sit at table, were forbidden to touch with their backs the backs of the chairs. Weak sight was not deemed a reason for spectacles. Yet the rector did not strike his parishioners as a man of forceful character, and he considered himself to be lacking in firmness. "Tremulous over trifles and easily put in a fuss," to use his own words. Always something strange in the progenitors of genius . . . Self-denial imposed on a sensuous and emotional nature—was this the key to both father and son? Quite suddenly, while still formulating the question, I felt that same gathering of tears behind the eyes, but they were more urgent now; I knew that if I allowed my features to relax, I would blub in good earnest. I kept my face stiff and fought it off, knowing the cause quite well. It was the grief of never grasping, never fully knowing. Horatio had occupied my life, I knew more about him than anyone else because I was his heir, I had inherited his being. The conviction of this had grown stronger in the years that had passed since my chats with Penhas; it had been fed by both study and intuition. But still I could not reach to the essential part, the mystery of his courage.

I did not then, that February night, as I clutched my mug and resisted the tears, see myself as an angel like him, a creature of radiant violence. That came later. At the time I thought of myself merely as a repository of his essence, a sort of memorial urn. But I knew that the same forces had moulded us both—thoughts of his childhood led me always back into the labyrinth of my own. For him the lesson had been duty. What lesson did my father give to me, what guiding principle? *Put things out of their misery.* That look of alertness, a brightness on his face. My father was a watcher. Not, I think now—I permit myself to think now—a very kind one. Selective, highly so. Unobservant of many things, unseeing, locked in some cold trance of self-absorption, nevertheless he watched our faces. My mother would hesitate in replying to him, beginning in one way and changing to another, and he would watch her with that same expression, a sort of expectancy, a hope of entertainment, in which there was also, when I think of it now, the ironic certainty of disappointment. Afterwards, long after she had gone, it came to me that she must have been afraid of him, as Monty and I were, though I cannot remember him ever raising his voice.

I looked at my watch: ten minutes past four on the morning after the great victory of Cape St. Vincent. Did Horatio manage to get some sleep in these morning hours? So much can never be known to us—whether he woke or slept, what he thought of in this aftermath of his triumph. The night before the battle he had not slept at all, and in the action itself he was wounded by a shell splinter which, though he described it as of no consequence, gave him acute pain for some days afterwards and must have made sleep difficult. He was still awake at 2 A.M. to receive the note of casualties aboard his ship— sixty dead and wounded. We know that he wrote to his friend Collingwood later that same morning to thank him for his support in the engagement. Perhaps in the space between he was able to snatch some hours of sleep.

The old man was in modest lodgings in Bath when the news came. He and Fanny were spending the winter there, the Norfolk parsonage too miserably uncomfortable in cold weather for his age and frailty. In February, Horatio's promotion to rear-admiral was posted up and his father, in the innocence of joy, posted an immediate letter to him—*My dear Rear-Admiral.* Then, less than two weeks later, came the news of Cape St. Vincent. The rector was in the street when he heard it, heard of his son's part in it. He was obliged to return in haste to his lodgings so as to hide his tears. *The height of glory to which your professional judgement, united with a proper sense of bravery, guarded by Providence, few sons, dear child, attain to, and fewer fathers live to see.*

I know these words of his by heart. They sounded in my mind as

I stood there. Orotund in phrasing, but no mistaking the pride. My father had no pride in me, or at least he never showed any. I suppose I never gave him cause, I was not good at the right things. I was good with my hands, even when quite small, good at making things. For a brief season I shone at chess. Then at fifteen a certain sort of order came into my mind, things began clicking into place, I started to do well at school. But these were not the right things. I think now that for my father there were no right things, but as a child I tried to find out what they were. I suffered when I failed and must have shown it. Better not to show, better to conceal, much better—perhaps that was the lesson, the guiding principle my father gave me.

All the same, it was showing that brought me to Horatio: that and my father's need—I suppose it was a need—to chasten and subdue. I remembered it again as I stood before this meek-faced father, remembered the forced jocularity of that Treasury colleague defeated at chess by a child, remembered the strangeness of my father's displeasure and his words. *Look at these people here—they had some reason to be pleased with themselves.* And the two portraits side by side, the ravaged, dark-suited statesman and the dashing captain in the splendour of full-dress uniform. No comparison, then or now. But there was a shadow on the splendour now, one that I could not dispel, and it came to me in the words of Cardinal Ruffo's secretary Sacchinelli, who wrote a biography of his employer after the latter's death. *The violation was at sea.* He was talking about the violation of the treaty with the Neapolitan republicans.

How could anything Horatio did at sea be wrong? Written years after the events, of course, and partial to Ruffo; but in the silence of that early morning the words were loud in my mind, seeming to defy argument, like a warning bell in a threatened town. No, not at sea. It was in the city that the plan was made and the harm done. Naples seemed to me more than anything else like a carnivorous plant that I had seen years before on a television wildlife program, in the days when I still watched television: a wide-mouthed, pinkish flower, like a frilly trumpet, with a pool of some sweet substance in the depths of it, into which unwary flies went slithering to be dissolved and devoured. Quite unexpectedly, as it seemed from one day to the next, I had lost the bright track of Horatio's life, slithered down into this scented, tainted well of Naples. I felt in danger of dissolving there, ending up as a mere particle of nutriment for this monstrous host of a city, so flaunting and gross and beautiful, which so much changed Horatio's life.

I should have left the basement then, before Sacchinelli's words could work their poison, but I waited long enough to feel the return of nausea, the sense of being caught in the sticky gum of a city I had never seen. Fear followed this close behind, fear of my need and my solitude, made sharper by the vastness and promise of the night outside, where some bird had started singing in the darkness; fear of the eyes and the face before me, from which I could not look away. They were mild no longer, they watched me, they were my father's eyes.

I was saved by a sudden thought of Miss Lily, whose eyes were calm and somehow dwelling on things but not watchful at all. She had felt sorry for Fanny in that cold parsonage with no-one to hold her in his arms. *Better to be warm in bed . . .* The matter-of-fact voice with its dying falls of Essex stayed in my mind as I left the basement, shuffled in my slippers back up the stairs to my room. Slight edge of protest in it, as if borders unquestioned by the decent were constantly being impinged upon, infringed. What borders? Once more in bed, I tried for some time to determine this. There was a slide of light now, very faint, on the plaster mouldings on the wall above the window. With the approach of dawn, the eccentric birds of England's Lane had stopped singing. I passed into sleep without being able to decide what it was that for Miss Lily made life fall short.

7

*O*n the Wednesday of the week following, I went in the evening to the Nelson Club, as I do most weeks. Wednesday evenings are open evenings at the club; there is usually someone giving a talk, and members can invite guests or bring their wives (the membership is entirely male; to the best of my knowledge no woman has ever enrolled, though I have heard talk of an Emma Hamilton Club with premises in Battersea, which boasts a large female membership). There is no Fanny Nelson Club, of course. Who would want to identify with the wronged wife?

I had been a member of this club for eight years now. Making up my mind to join had involved me in much travail; three months of painful hesitation elapsed before I felt able to take the plunge. In fact, becoming a member of the Nelson Club and engaging Avon Secretarial Services were the two most decisive steps I had taken in years, perhaps since choosing to confide in Penhas.

I didn't go there for the company—far from it. I could well have done without that, but I was always hoping to learn something more about him; the smallest fact can be illuminating when it is added to others. It could be anything. Generally, of course, I was disappointed. That evening a man called Robbins, a long-standing member of the club, was due to give a talk on the system of signalling by means of coloured flags, devised by Admiral Sir Home Riggs Popham and introduced into the navy in 1803, not long before Trafalgar.

The premises are on the top floor of a tall, narrow-fronted house off Gray's Inn Road, above an obscure publisher of devotional literature. There is no lift, the stairs are uncarpeted, and the bannisters have a rickety feel to them; but there is a small licensed bar, open on Wednesday and Saturday evenings, a reading room where you can find the publications of the Navy Records Society and back copies of the *Nelson Despatch* and the *Trafalgar Chronicle*, and a lecture room that can accommodate an audience of seventy or so (it is rare indeed to have that many).

They open the bar at half past six. It was about ten to seven when I arrived, and there was no-one there but Hugo, the barman, and a morose, sleepy-looking man called Jimson, sitting on his own at the far end. I was feeling very much on edge, having struggled for hours that day and the one before to disentangle the events of June 1799 in Naples and establish a strict chronology, especially for the period spanning Horatio's arrival in the city on the afternoon of the twenty-fourth, the quitting of their forts by the rebels on the twenty-sixth, and their arrest and imprisonment on the twenty-eighth. It all lay here, in these few fateful days. If I could only get the times right, fix the moments at which things had been said and done, surely I could clear him of blame. How wonderful to be the one to free him from the shadow that has been hanging over him so long. Nearly two hundred years, ever since Robert Southey's scathing verdict of 1812. Those terrible words of his came frequently to my mind these days: . . . *no alternative but to record the disgraceful story with sorrow and with shame* . . .

I asked for a glass of red wine, with a vague idea of fortifying myself, restoring the corpuscles. It came from a Spanish bottle and was roughish but not unpleasant. While I was paying for it, a couple called Barber came in and stood beside me at the bar.

"Here we are again," Barber said. "Half of the draught lager for me, please, Hugo, and a Bloody Mary for Barbara. You ready for Popham's flags?"

This question was put to Jimson, who, however, did not reply. Barber smiled at me and shook his head. He is a shortish, balding, chirpy man with a beakish nose and a thin mouth and a habit of tapping his feet. Upon meeting his eyes and his smile, I at once looked away. For years now I have not been able to sustain eye contact for more than a few seconds, and I found the close proximity of the Barbers distinctly oppressive, especially in a place so nearly empty—I can endure much better the nearness of people in a crowd. I was looking straight before me when he spoke again.

"Your turn coming up soon, old boy, isn't it?"

"Not for some weeks yet," I said. I was sure he already knew the exact date of my talk, which was Wednesday, April 9. They had asked me to do it on the second, but that is the date of the Battle of Copenhagen, last of his great victories before Trafalgar, and I wanted to be at home for it, at my table, with nothing to distract me. "It is up on the notice board," I said. Thinking about it made me nervous—it was my first talk in eight years of membership.

"What is it about again?" Mrs. Barber asked, and she tilted her head a little, like a thrush on a lawn—she is birdlike too, they are both birdlike people. The question irritated me, though of course I showed no sign. There was no interest in it, only a sort of social reflex; she was keeping the conversation going.

"Two Episodes in the Making of a Hero," I said.

"Ooh!" Mrs. Barber straightened her head from its tilt with an exaggerated suddenness, clearly derisive in intention. Why did she come to these meetings? I wondered, not for the first time. What possible interest could she have in Popham's system of naval signalling? Anyone might think she would be glad to see the back of Barber for a while. But no, she always came with him.

A short silence followed this exclamation of hers. To the oppression of their closeness was added that of their mockery. I have no friends in the club. People are jealous of me, they envy my intimate knowledge of his life. I never boast of this, but there is nothing I can do about the aura it creates about me.

"Don't much care for the title," Jimson said, speaking for the first time, as if emerging from some unhappy sleep. "Heroes are born, not made."

"Quite right, good point," Barber said, eager to ally himself against me.

"Well, that is true of idiots," I said.

"I beg your pardon?" Jimson's eyelids fluttered; he was rising to an unprecedented state of wakefulness. It came to me that he had misunderstood, he thought I was calling him an idiot. I felt an impulse to prolong this impression.

"What is the point you are seeking to make, old boy?" Barber said. "We lowbrows need things spelling out."

What could they know about heroes? Jimson was interested in eighteenth-century naval dockyards; Barber dabbled in Horatio's life, as many do, but had no essential knowledge of him. I felt indifferent now to their hostility. "Fools, cretins, morons, blockheads," I said, and I paused long enough for them to suspect that I might be ending here, with these terms of abuse. Then I went on. "These are born, not made. You can't refine on stupidity, can you? But the true hero has to go through the fire, he has to be purified, he has to shed his dross."

My own words moved me, they came close to my feelings about him, too close—I could feel my hands trembling slightly. I rested them on the bar; I don't think anybody noticed. I glanced towards his portrait on the wall behind Hugo, high above the glass shelves and the rows of bottles, one of the earliest of the many likenesses of him painted by Lemuel Abbot.

"What about humble heroes, then?" Hugo said from behind the bar. "People you've never heard of that do something really brave."

Hugo is somewhere round the thirty mark and has a narrow, long-nosed face, rather sensitive. He has a gold band passing through the pierced lobe of his left ear. He is not a member, at least he wasn't then; he just came to do the bar twice a week. What he did with the rest of his time, I had no idea.

"Or what about the people that devote their lives to others?" he said now. "You know, asking for nothing, spirit of service and all that."

"Hear, hear, good point," Barber said.

"I have nothing against them. They are not heroes, that's all. Humble hero is a contradiction in terms. Heroes are public figures, they represent the nation."

Jimson was beginning to say something indignant about lowly privates who won the VC, he wanted to bring it all down to obscure people, but at this point I withdrew from the conversation. I turned away and rested my elbows on the bar and began to look more steadily at the portrait, which was deeply familiar, a rather good copy of the famous one commissioned by Horatio's friend William Locker and painted during the autumn of 1797 while Horatio was convalescing at Greenwich after the amputation of his right arm above the elbow. The stump had not healed yet, he was still in much pain from it.

Sparse grey hair swept back, mouth resigned to the maiming, the right eye not much showing its damage, though virtually sightless by now, three years after the injury on Corsica. A face bleak with pain and the knowledge of glory. He would be scarred a year later by a wound on the forehead at the Battle of the Nile, but otherwise this face would not change in the eight years remaining to him. It would, however, change greatly in the versions of him made by Lemuel Abbot, who died insane in 1803. Abbot did at least forty subsequent portraits of Horatio, slowly slipping into idiocy as he did so. In fact, Horatio was his main source of income during this long decline. Versions were painted for Lady Nelson and Collingwood and many others. In these later Abbot portraits, Horatio loses the severe and drawn expression of a man who has suffered much and made a conquest of suffering. His looks become gentler, better-tempered, like a ruddy, benevolent farmer at first, then gradually plumper, softer, more vacuous. Like Abbot's brain, it occurred to me now. I have always been fascinated by parallel tracks, and this was an almost perfect example. Forty likenesses over the years. Horatio's face softening back into infancy along with Abbot's brain.

Oppressed by this thought, which in some way seemed disloyal to him, I turned my eyes away from the portrait. The bar was more crowded now, though I had not been aware of people coming in. I expected to see Jimson and the Barbers, but there was no sign of them. Standing beside me now was Kismet Walters. My glass of wine was still half full. Through the open door I saw people passing down the passage towards the lecture room, among them the president of the club, a tall, slow-moving man named Pratt-Smithers. I had again the feeling that time had slipped away from me, I had somehow fallen behind.

"Heroism is a form of pure energy," I said to Kismet Walters, and he instantly and fervently agreed, nodding his head so forcibly that his white hair—still thick, though he is well into his sixties—flopped over his forehead. He is the only member of the club who comes remotely near to sharing my feelings for Horatio, but he is a dangerous ally because his notions are very simple, some might say crude. His nickname, which no-one ever uses in his hearing, comes from his life-long denial that Horatio ever said "Kiss me, Hardy" when he lay dying belowdecks at Trafalgar. Walters regards such a request as out of keeping with the heroic character, altogether too unmanly. According to Walters, what Horatio actually said was "*Kismet*, Hardy," this being the Arabic word for "destiny." Basing himself on this premise, he has spent twenty-five years accumulating evidence that Horatio was early attracted to the faith of Islam, was in fact a secret convert, and made incognito trips to Cairo on three separate occasions for audiences with the sharif. He is intending someday to publish the results of this research.

"Fuelled by faith," he said now. "A hero has to *believe*." He reared his head back and fixed me with his small blue eyes. "Valhalla," he said.

"Right enough." I finished my wine in one go. "It's nearly half-past," I said. "Shall we go in and hear what Robbins has to say?"

There were a respectable number of people in there, about thirty-five, I estimated—not too many empty seats. Robbins had fixed up a blackboard so that he could illustrate with coloured chalks the way the system worked, how the same coloured flags or pennants were used for the numbers 0 to 9 and for the letters of the alphabet 1 to 26 and how each ship had a codebook in which common words or phrases were allotted numbers from 26 upwards. Where possible, the ships used these standard forms; any other words had to be spelled out with a flag for each letter. The flags were hoisted to the upper yardarms or the mastheads, wherever they could be seen by the ships they were addressing.

Robbins had faults as a speaker—he was hesitant in delivery and tended to repeat himself—but the miraculous nature of this new form of communication came through all the same, to me at least. He quoted the young Henry Blackwood, commanding the leading frigate, *Euryalus*, in the build-up to Trafalgar, within four miles of the enemy and nearly sixty from Horatio's flagship, yet still, as he later wrote to his wife, "talking to Lord Nelson by means of Popham's signals." In that slow approach, as the British fleet closed in and the French under Villeneuve tried first to wriggle through the Strait of Gibraltar for the safety of Toulon and then made a run for Cadiz, it was the frigates that kept Horatio informed, using Popham's system. And in that last, most famous message to the fleet, the word *expects* was substituted for *confides* because it was in the codebook and the other wasn't, and could therefore be signalled with only one flag instead of eight.

It was after half-past eight when the talk finished. I did not return to the bar or speak to anyone; I got my coat and went straight downstairs and out onto the street. It was a cold night, very clear. In spite of the streetlights, the sky looked black, and stars were visible in it. I went across Mecklenburgh Square with the intention of making my way to King's Cross and getting the tube home. However, when I came out onto Gray's Inn Road, without pausing to think about it I turned south, towards the river.

At the moment it seemed no more than an impulse, though of an unusual kind for me, perhaps no more than a desire to prolong the evening. But by the time I was crossing Holborn and starting down Chancery Lane, I knew exactly where I was going and why. For the first time, consciously and deliberately, I was following in his footsteps. Of course, it was wrong, it was the wrong time of the year. It should have been December. But I was troubled in spirit, there was this obstinate shadow over our relationship, I needed to do it then, I had to violate the calendar.

December 1800. Those closing weeks of the year saw the end of his marriage. The Naples days were over for Horatio, that strange interlude in the unreal city where his passion for Emma grew at a landsman's rhythm in gaudy nights and slow mornings, along with his allegiance to the implacable Queen Maria Carolina. Over for the Hamiltons too. Sir William was recalled to London and never returned. The three came home together in close amity, the husband, the lover, and the mistress-wife, arriving at Yarmouth in early November and reaching London three days later. News of the scandalous liaison, conducted under the husband's roof with his apparent blessing, had preceded them.

It was in London that the historic meeting took place between Fanny and Emma, with Horatio introducing his mistress to his wife. Emma had been carrying his child for six months, but her amplitude of form and the loose clothes she wore perhaps concealed this. Fanny the soul of provincial gentility, angular, reticent, and dutiful; Emma flamboyant and insecure, her Lancashire accent still there after all the years in Naples. Two different sorts of women, divided by temperament and by the traditional roles forced upon them. Each saw in the other her fears and prejudices realized. Below the civilities of the occasion, a palpable detestation that was never to waver. He must have seen it, the instant, inevitable dislike. What else could he have hoped for? Whatever dream of harmony he had, perhaps the hope that the amity of three could merge into one of four, must have gone for good that afternoon, as he watched them together, with the wind bellowing outside and the rain lashing the windows—it was a day of drenching storm, with gales uprooting trees in Kensington Gardens and St.

James's Park. The place of that meeting has long gone, vanished without trace—Nerot's Hotel on the south side of King Street, where the St. James's Theatre later stood and office blocks now rear up their undistinguished façades.

According to James Harrison, one of his first biographers, late one night some three weeks after this bleak encounter, Horatio left the rented house in Dover Street where he was living with Fanny and walked for hours through the streets, quite alone. He went eastward along the Strand and Fleet Street as far as St. Paul's, then down to Blackfriars Bridge, then back via the Embankment and Soho. Slightly built, maimed, wasted in looks, quite unrecognized. Miles of walking in the dead of night.

I came onto Fleet Street and turned eastward. Now I was on his actual route. The streets were quieter in the vicinity of the City. I had the feeling that I was stepping in time with him, my heavier footfalls and his lighter ones making a single rhythm. I knew with absolute certainty where he had lingered, where he had hurried. When I paused at the corner of Pilgrim Street, I knew he had done exactly the same, that he had looked at these same gaunt, unlighted buildings against this same black sky. I knew what his thoughts had been that night—he had been possessed by the strange discrepancy between his private and his public life.

The most celebrated Englishman of his time, victor of Cape St. Vincent and the Nile, scourge of the hated French, destroyer of Bonaparte's designs on Egypt and India. From the moment of his arrival in Yarmouth, squads of cavalry escorted him throughout the county. In Ipswich the crowd took the horses from their traces and drew his carriage in triumph through the town. In London he was cheered wherever he went, admiring throngs followed his every step. If it was known that he intended to go to the theatre, every seat in the house would be instantly sold; he would enter his box to the strains of "See the Conquering Hero Comes" from the theatre orchestra. By day there was business at the Admiralty and the Navy Office; the evenings were occupied with banquets, presentations, receptions in his honour. He had taken his seat in the House of Lords—he was a peer now, Baron Nelson of the Nile.

Such adulation has seldom befallen mortal man. But at home within the walls of number 17 Dover Street, there was tension and distress. This same evening of our lonely walk, or so I believe, he had earlier insisted that the Hamiltons be invited to dine. He could never accept defeat, it was not in his nature. Emma was advanced in pregnancy, a fact that may or may not have been known to Fanny. During the meal she felt ill and left the table. Rebuked by Horatio for neglecting their guest, Fanny went after her. There followed a painful parody of that mutual good will he must still have been hoping for: the dutiful wife held the basin while the pregnant mistress vomited into it.

Had he witnessed this scene before he set out? As I crossed Ludgate Circus, I felt suddenly convinced that he had. Harrison does not give us the date, but I believe it was on that same night, after the Hamiltons had returned home to Grosvenor Square, after Fanny had gone to bed. It was this grotesque episode that threw him into despair, set him walking the night streets. He expected the fear and antagonism of the women to melt in the warm breath of his enterprise, as the odds had melted at Cape St. Vincent and would again at Trafalgar. Sure mark of the hero, this believing so completely in the transforming power of his desire.

It was well after ten now, and Ludgate Hill was all but deserted. The banks and business houses were darkly cavernous within their Corinthian porticoes, waiting for the next day's tide. I felt footsore—I was not used to so much walking—but I was happy to be so close to him in understanding and sympathy. I stood looking up at the dome of St. Paul's, followed the struggling white of pigeons caught up there in some remote alarm, fluttering in the milky shafts of the floodlights. I had the brief impression that they were trapped in the light itself, the rays were like bars.

In the crypt of this great church he lies entombed—this is where they brought him, after the Painted Hall at Greenwich where he lay in state, after the room in the Admiralty where he rested overnight before the funeral service. No-one before him in the whole history of England ever had such a splendid funeral. Thinking of this, and of his nearness and farness, I felt the air around and above me thicken with mourning; that massed cry of lamentation I experienced in my dreams came raining down from the cathedral and the buildings all around— it came like gentle rain, not sound, enveloping, all-pervasive, like rain.

How long this grief endured I could not tell. It was broken by an unkempt man who appeared from some dark place beyond the churchyard and came up to me and asked me for money. He was old and smelled very bad and he did not look at me. I put a pound into his hand, taking care not to touch him.

I walked the whole way back with Horatio, all the way to Dover Street. I was afraid of the streets so late, but I did it. I was tempted briefly to give it up when I reached Trafalgar Square, and take a taxi home. I was tired out and, as I say, afraid. Moreover, it seemed fitting to leave him there with his pigeons and lions, standing on his tremendous column at the farthest reach of the light, too high to be really seen from the common level, endlessly scanning the Thames, keeping his eye on Big Ben. But the parallels had to be kept up. I went on; I went all the way back with him.

8

*M*iss Lily's attitude towards me had changed significantly in the two weeks since our disagreement over Horatio's treatment of Fanny, as had mine towards her. She had survived something that night and it had brought her into a privileged zone. I could not think of her now merely as someone I was employing, not when I had looked with such passionate interest at the back of her skull. She registered the change, of course, though she could hardly have known the reason, and it made her bolder. She became somehow more personal, she felt free to interject, to express opinions. To the danger of her sleuthing was now added this irritant of her judgements. Then on Tuesday, March 11, she came bearing a circular tin with a design in tartan around the top. Her manner seemed less positive than usual. "These are for you," she said.

The weather was still cold, and Miss Lily presented her usual chilled appearance. It was an accident, the date; she didn't know or had forgotten that this was Horatio's wedding day. Or so she was to maintain. I opened the tin and found to my astonishment that it was full of biscuits.

"Shortbread," Miss Lily said. "They are home-made." She was looking at me in a way that seemed almost apprehensive. Miss Lily is not pretty, but she has unusual eyes, a deep, soft brown and very steady, somehow undefended-looking, like a cow's—they seem to have no means of concealment or retreat. But they are not timid, far from it; they do not flinch away. Miss Lily notes things. This gaze of hers, helpless and perceptive at the same time, makes it difficult to know whether what you see there is a disturbance of her feelings or a reflected disturbance of your own. "I put them in that tin," she said. "Just to have something to carry them in, nothing to do with Scotland."

I was sure at this point that she had schemed to make an effect by timing this gift of biscuits to coincide with his wedding day. I was on the point of handing back the tin, telling her I never ate biscuits, which was actually true, since it never occurred to me to buy them. I almost began to say this, then held back at the last moment. The fact is that I hate people giving me things under any circumstances; it is demeaning, it subjects you. But to show this openly looks like weakness. Something of an impasse. So I held back, I said nothing, I just looked at her.

This I was able to do as she was for the moment distracted, she was burrowing in her capacious handbag for something, a hankie as it turned out, so I had a short period of grace in which to regard her undetected. Tonight she was wearing her hair loose and she had on a dark blue woollen jumper and a rather narrow-fitting grey skirt which came down to just above the knees. She usually wore loose, smocky sorts of things, but the jumper, without being very tight, showed Miss Lily's straight shoulders and the shape of her breasts. There was something I recognized as characteristic in her movements as she searched in the bag, a sort of total intensity of purpose, as if for these few moments nothing else existed in the world. She looked up and caught my eye on her. "I made a good lot," she said, "and I thought, you know, why not take some round, he probably doesn't get home-made shortbread all that often."

"Well, that is quite true, he doesn't," I said. "The right day for gifts, in any case, on the anniversary of his wedding day."

"I didn't know you had been married."

"Two hundred and ten years ago today he married Frances Nisbet at Nevis in the West Indies."

"Oh, you were talking about him." A silence followed, during which Miss Lily seemed to be considering or absorbing something. Then she said, "I didn't know."

"The whole thing is in my book. You have typed it out at my dictation and we have revised it at least once since then. Perhaps you knew subconsciously?"

Miss Lily had flushed, though this might have been owing to the warmth of the room. "People use that word a lot, don't they?" she said. "In my opinion, you either know something or you don't, and I didn't. I knew they were married on Nevis, but I had forgotten the date."

Of course, if she truly hadn't known, it made the symbolism of the timing stronger. This gift to me, Horatio's sharer . . . "Easy to forget dates," I said. "He met her first in the May of 1785, when he was commander of the twenty-eight-gun frigate *Boreas* and posted to the West Indies."

She was some months his senior, widow of a surgeon, with an infant son, Josiah. Slender and delicate, a daughter of colonial society, her father a senior judge on the island, her uncle president of the council. A product of her time and class, parasol-wielding, tea-dispensing, intensely proper. Not original or forceful or very clever but loyal and devoted. The other woman, who was not proper at all, was waiting in the wings. She would wait without knowing for thirteen years to release the joys and torments lacking in his marriage and to share in his fame. Seven years younger than the victim-wife, outstandingly beautiful, the daughter of an illiterate blacksmith named Henry Lyon, London maidservant at the age of thirteen, then some years of modelling and occasional whoring. At sixteen she was the mistress of a wealthy young baronet who cast her out when she got pregnant. When Horatio met Fanny on the island of Nevis, Emma Hart, as she called herself then, was living in a house on the Edgware Road, installed there by Charles Greville, second son of the Earl of Warwick and the nephew of Sir William Hamilton, at that time British ambassador to Naples. Later, wanting to marry well and recoup his fortunes, Greville passed Emma on to this elderly uncle, who had seen her on a visit to London and been smitten.

The graphs of these lives are fascinating to me, the parallels, the convergences and collisions. In the centre the glittering thread of Horatio's life, with these others running alongside, above and below, some lightly touching the thread, some giving it a twitch, some clinging. That May, when Horatio met his wife-to-be, Emma was sitting for portraits to Romney, who painted her in a bewildering variety of attitudes; Hardy, who was to give the dying Horatio his last kiss, was a sixteen-year-old midshipman in the Channel Fleet; Arthur Wellesley, later Duke of Wellington, had just been taken out of Eton on grounds of invincible stupidity; Napoleon Bonaparte was a sulky cadet at the Military School in Paris.

I did not speak to Miss Lily of these presences hovering over his wedding day. In fact, we did not talk much more about Horatio's wedding. I mentioned—still clutching the tartan tin—that his "people," the crew of the *Boreas*, gave him a silver watch, which they had clubbed together to buy. "A very handsome gift," I said. "They didn't have much money, you know. But then, he was always greatly loved."

Miss Lily made no reply to this. She had never seemed much impressed by this quality of Horatio's. Charisma, we would call it today, the devotion he inspired in crew after crew, the way his men would follow him wherever he led and be ready to lay down their lives for him. This great gift—for we must call it that—which I so much admired and which so moved me, seemed to leave Miss Lily quite cold. Perhaps a question of gender. All the same, in some obscure way I was disappointed. I wanted her to see how wonderful Horatio was. She smiled now, but it was not a smile that occupied much of her face. "Well," she said, "it's his wedding anniversary, not yours. You can't expect silver watches."

I could have said much to that: nothing that ever happened to Horatio did not also happen to me. I had stood with him that Sunday morning in the great drawing room of Montpelier House, the president's mansion, where they were married; I had stood beside Fanny, who wore a gown of Irish lace. She was given away by Prince William Henry, son of King George III, a personal friend. Toasts and speeches, to which we replied with grace and wit and a likable sincerity. Arm in arm down the steps of polished teak, out into brilliant sunshine. Behind us the immaculate house with its white wood gables and verandahs. Arm in arm on the flawless lawns, kept trim and vivid by generations of faithful blacks. We assemble in the shade of the great silk-cotton tree. Popping corks. We are surrounded by well-wishers, all dressed in light colours, the men in satin suits, the ladies in summer dresses, smiling in the tinted shade of parasols. Beyond the terraced gardens and the parkland, as far as the eye can see, the smooth green sweep of the sugarcane fields . . .

"Nothing left of it now," I said. "Someone was talking about it at the club."

"Left of what?"

"The house they got married in, where Fanny lived with her uncle. Nothing left but a pair of stone gateposts. Thank you very much for the biscuits, I look forward to having them with my tea in the mornings." I resolved as I spoke to find some way of reciprocating this gift and so cancelling it out, something on my part stronger, more lordly. For the moment, however, no ideas came to me.

I remember some degree of tension developing between us later on, during our session of work. I sensed that Miss Lily was dissatisfied, or disappointed rather, because I was proposing to bypass, for the time being, Horatio's sojourn in Naples and Palermo, the period between September 1798 and June 1800. I told her I was not ready to deal with it; there were so many revisions of one sort or another, I could not even dictate it, I would have to make a fair copy. The real reason was that I could not yet determine the part Horatio had played in the surrender of the Neapolitan republicans, could not yet find a path for him out of that marsh. I knew that Miss Lily, though it was not in her character to admit it, had been looking forward to dealing with this period of his life. She did not care so much about Horatio's triumphs at sea—to my mind the most essential part of him—but she took a close interest in his life on land. And of all Horatio's land experience, his stay in the Kingdom of the Two Sicilies was by far the most colourful and dramatic, comprising his hero's welcome in Naples, the love affair with Emma blossoming in the hothouse of the Bourbon court, the *ménage à trois* that resulted, the flight of the royal family as the French closed in, Horatio's dealings with the republican rebels, and much else besides. And here was I, proposing to go round it and resume in the June of 1800, date of Horatio's recall to England.

As I say, I could not tell her the true reason, could not explain how important it was for me to preserve his name and reputation, how the remotest suggestion of deceit on his part filled me with a sort of dread, as if it called my own existence into doubt, as if my being depended on his truth. However, we were able to go as far as the triumphant arrival, one of my favourite passages so far in the book. He anchored in the bay on September 22, just a week from his fortieth birthday, after a voyage of 1300 miles from the mouth of the Nile. I had decided to include extracts from Horatio's letter of September 25, written to Fanny, in which he describes his arrival and the meeting with the Hamiltons. My own comments were interspersed with these extracts, so the whole thing had to be dictated.

Alongside came my honoured friends: the scene was terribly affecting; up flew her ladyship, and exclaiming, "Oh God, is it possible?" she fell into my arm more dead than—

"Did you say *arm?*" Miss Lily said. "Oh yes, I see, he only had one by this time, didn't he?" She giggled a bit. "Sorry."

I made no reply to this but observed a pause before continuing in order to mark my disapproval of the interruption. *I hope some day to have the pleasure of introducing you to Lady Hamilton, she is one of the very best women in this world. How few could have made the turn she has. She is an honour to her sex . . .*

I paused again here, as I wished to insert some speculations that I had written the evening before about Fanny's reactions to these words. It was typical of Horatio's frank and enthusiastic nature that he should write in such terms to a wife so conventional, so far away and lonely, who must have known Emma's fame as a beauty, must have known too about her earlier career as mistress to the rich.

"One wonders," I began, "what Lady Nelson would privately have made of—"

But Miss Lily was not typing. She was sitting inactive at the keyboard. After a moment she turned to me with an expression of perplexity I knew at once to be false. She said, "What does that mean, an honour to her sex?"

Now this was not, strictly speaking, a legitimate question for Miss Lily to ask; it did not arise from any difficulty in carrying out her task of typing. That she should ask it at all—and even more that I should attempt to answer it—was a mark of the changed relations between us and her talent for taking over the ground.

"He was paying her a compliment," I said. "He thought she did credit to her sex."

"No, but what does it *mean?*" Her face wore the same expression as when she had talked about Scott of the Antarctic.

I tried again. "He thought her a fine example of womanhood."

"Nelson was a fine example of manhood, I suppose."

The grotesqueness of this understatement almost made me laugh aloud. "Only the finest this nation has ever produced or ever will."

"Could someone writing about him say he was an honour to his sex?"

I thought for a moment, Miss Lily's eyes intently on me. "Well, not in so many words."

"It is words we are talking about, isn't it? Could it mean he was brave or had a good character or that there was something special about him, like he was very strong or . . ." Miss Lily's indignation wavered a bit. "Something physical," she said. "Could it be that?"

"No, I don't think so." I was growing weary of this conversation, for which, after all, I was paying at the rate of fifteen pounds an hour.

"It isn't what you would call logical, that's all I am saying," Miss Lily said.

"It meant something to Horatio, and that is the point at issue, in my opinion. You have to think historically." But this was something, I had already discovered, that Miss Lily never did. She used the past tense, but she had no sense of the past at all. Everything and everybody lived in a perpetual present in her mind.

She looked at me now in silence for a moment or two, compressing her lips as if considering how to reply. The expression gave an unaccustomed severity to her face, slightly increasing the prominence of her cheekbones, thinning out the rather full lower lip. "Well," she said, "instead of talking about honour to her sex and so forth, he should have had the sense to see that she was just making a big scene of it. How long had she known he was on the way—three or four weeks, wasn't it? She had plenty of time to get the act together."

"Perhaps we could move on?" I said. I spoke rather coldly. It was true, of course, that Horatio was simple-hearted and devoid of guile, but I didn't like Miss Lily's tone; it reflected on his intelligence. She was not much taken with Emma, that was obvious—but I didn't want to lose more time discussing the matter, I was keen to make the two-year hop, to reach the haven of June 1800, the departure from Naples.

All the same, we had not proceeded far when there was another interruption. I was dictating a passage very much altered and revised, describing the return to England of Horatio and the Hamiltons. A strange trio they must have seemed to those who met them at this time: the admiral so wizened, so decked with stars and medals, re-turning to popular applause and establishment disfavour; Sir William not far from his end, his face like parchment, his liver in ruins after thirty-six years at the Naples court; Emma large and flaunting and noisy, heavier now but beautiful still, facing an uncertain future in England, on affectionate terms with both husband and lover, as were these with each other. *Tria juncta in uno*, they called themselves: three joined in one. The motto of the Order of the Bath, to which both men belonged. Emma's phrase, perhaps. Horatio could never have said it; he was joined with no-one, ever, he was unique. He travelled with them, yes; so much is true. As a trio they did not make a good impression, at least not on their compatriots. I was obliged to admit this, though it pained me that he could be so misjudged. It was not

any fault of his. He was on land, he was in travesty. And he was envied. In my book I was intending to quote a passage from General Sir
John Moore's diary as typical of this prejudice against him. In the
summer of 1800, in Leghorn, Moore made a brief note: *Sir William
and Lady Hamilton were there attending the Queen of Naples. Lord Nelson was there attending on Lady Hamilton. He is covered with stars, ribbons and medals, more like a Prince of the Opera than the Conqueror of
the Nile. It is really melancholy to see a brave and good man, who has deserved well of his country, cutting so pitiful a figure.*

Moore did not remark on the strangest fact of all: Rear-Admiral
Lord Nelson of the Nile and of Burnham Thorpe was returning home
overland. It was a decision that had always perplexed me. An admiral
recalled after famous victories, his flagship waiting in the bay . . . I was
arriving at this point now in my dictation.

"In Nelson's life, as in all lives, there were concurrent paths, lines
running in parallel, each characterized by a cluster of attributes particular to itself, appearing simple in stated form but complex and
subtle in suggestion. The obvious broad division in Nelson's case
was between sea life and land life. At sea he was himself, he was per-
forming the task for which he was gloriously fitted; on land he sometimes faltered, his faculties lost the concentration of genius they
possessed at sea. Why then, in that June of 1800, did he choose to return home by land? Was it for the pregnant Emma's sake, because she
was unwilling to face the long voyage? Had Sir William some business
to see to on the way? Or was it that Nelson himself was anxious to
postpone—"

But Miss Lily had paused again. Without looking at me—she was
regarding the screen of her computer—she said, "I have a good idea
why they went by land."

I became aware of needing patience, a considerable store of it.
"Have you?"

"It was the obvious choice, really. I mean, they were a travelling show by this time, weren't they?"

"What on earth do you mean?"

"Everybody knew about them in advance, wherever they went. So the more places they went to, the better, that's all I am saying. From the point of view of the spectacle, that is. It was like a tour. I mean, they took risks going by land, didn't they? Napoleon had just defeated the Austrians at the Battle of Marengo. He was invading Italy again. Their carriage passed within a mile of the French outposts. It would have been much safer by sea, but that way they wouldn't have been able to put on the show, would they? Trieste, across Slovenia, then through the Alps to Klagenfurt and Vienna, then Prague and Dresden, then all those little courts in Germany, all the way to Hamburg. Everywhere they went, fireworks, bands playing, spectators by the thousand. I mean, it's obvious, isn't it? It was a show, they were stars—that's all I am saying."

For some moments, hearing her say these things about Horatio, hearing her compare this greatest of men to a travelling player, I felt a mixture of fury and distress that I was afraid might have drained the blood from my face. I turned away from her in a pretence of looking at the shelves of books, as if in search of some reference. I could not read the titles; agitation blurred my sight. But I felt no urge to move round behind her, no impulse to renew that terrible scrutiny. All I wanted was to hide my feelings. She was immune, and somehow she knew it. I cannot describe my sense of this more exactly. It was as if she had got inside my guard.

However, something else came now into mind, the disturbance in my feelings settled into a kind of curiosity. Still with my face turned away, I said, "How is it that you know so much about the circumstances of the journey, the route they took and so forth? We haven't done this part before."

"I got a book out of the library."

At this I turned to face her. She was sitting quite composed, her hands resting quietly on either side of the keyboard. "What book?" I asked her.

"It's about the three of them, Nelson and the Hamiltons. It's by a man called Russell."

"I know the book. I've got it here." I made a gesture towards the shelves. I was touched, deeply, inordinately, that Miss Lily had shown this interest, had taken the trouble to borrow this book from the library. My rage was forgotten. "Quite good," I said. "A bit on the chatty side."

"That's what I like about it." She smiled suddenly, her first real smile of the whole evening. It occurred to me now that her sharpness of tone, her tendency to interrupt, those disrespectful remarks about Horatio, might have been due simply to wounded feelings at my seeming to doubt her word in the matter of his wedding date. (I was wrong about this, as it turned out. She continued to argue and interrupt on a regular basis.)

I don't know how it happened—an accidental combination of circumstances, the smile, this moment of perception coming after my rage, a desire to trump the shortbread biscuits: before I knew it, I was asking Miss Lily if she would like to go to Portsmouth one of these days to visit HMS *Victory*, Horatio's flagship, now permanently docked there.

"Well, that would be nice." Miss Lily's eyes were bright and helplessly steady and somehow relentless. "Get a bit of sea air," she said. "It would have to be a Saturday."

9

Almost as soon as Miss Lily had gone I fell prey to doubts about the wisdom of this Portsmouth offer. The typing sessions were one thing—they were limited in duration, specific in function, easily controllable, though Miss Lily was showing alarming signs now of breaking through the fences. The trip to Portsmouth was a very different matter. It involved a whole day; we would be thrown together, obliged to converse, to look at each other, in a train, in a café, without the protection of the desk, the bookshelves, my dictating voice. The prospect made me feel nervous.

On the other hand, there was a certain excitement in the idea and an element of self-congratulation—I had acted spontaneously, I had taken a leap. As I thought more about it, this aspect came uppermost. All in all, I decided, it had been a Nelsonian gesture, putting me, albeit briefly, on a plane with him. Of course, he was an angel, he was a creature of free, untrammelled action; in him, impulse and decision were fused together, sheathed in the same fire. But for him too there were periods of monotony, of a constricting sameness—the weeks and months of blockading duties, the long pursuit of an elusive enemy over immensities of ocean.

And there were the periods on land, that time of travesty in Naples and Palermo, the long years of enforced inactivity on half-pay in Norfolk. I thought about these Norfolk years now as I sat on in my study, which was still somehow not quite empty of Miss Lily. How you must have hated it. Twenty-eight years old, just married, distinguished service in home waters, the West Indies, North America. Clear already that you were a commander of no ordinary gifts. Zealous, energetic, fearless in combat, a superb seaman. You had influential patrons—essential for any rapid advancement in the navy at that time. And yet you found yourself placed on half-pay and living with your wife in your father's parsonage in the village of Burnham Thorpe in Norfolk, where you were born, which you left at twelve to go to sea. And you remained there, beached up, for more than five years.

Who the ill-wishers were, the nature of the enmity—presumably it was among the lords of the Admiralty—are questions difficult now to determine. In fact, no-one will ever answer them fully, though I had tried to address them in my book. Of course, it was a period of relative peace and low naval employment. The War of American Independence was over; the French Revolutionary War had not yet begun. A brief lull in the almost incessant fighting of the century. All the same, lesser men got ships. He himself never understood the matter. While stationed in the Leeward Islands he had made enemies; he had insisted on enforcing the Navigation Act, by the terms of which American ships could not trade in the British colonies. He had ordered the seizure of ships attempting to break the embargo, and this had caused financial loss to a number of influential people and led to quarrels with the governor, Sir Thomas Shirley. Perhaps his friendship with Prince William did him harm; the prince had enemies in high places and was not always on good terms with his father, George III. However this may be, when Horatio, that devoted servant of kings, applied for help to Lord Hood, whose patronage had been promised, he was told that no request could be made to the Admiralty on his behalf for a ship, *as the King was impressed with an unfavourable opinion of him.*

This was in 1790, halfway through your exile. It must have been a heavy blow, this royal disapproval. Worse was to befall you ten years later on your return to London after what Miss Lily so perversely referred to as the travelling show, when you were deep in disfavour. At a royal levee, King George snubbed you publicly, addressing a brief remark to you, then turning his back when you started to reply. On that occasion, ironically, you had arrived decked out with the gifts of kings: the gold medal for Cape St. Vincent, the Star of the Bath, the Sicilian order conferred by King Ferdinand, and a resplendent aigrette, or plume of triumph, from the grand signior of Turkey, which had thirteen strands of diamonds, one for each of the French warships taken or destroyed at the Nile, and in the middle a radiant star turning on its centre by means of concealed clockwork. This glittering plumage, with its spinning centre, you wore in your hat . . .

Unkindness from kings cut you deeply. You needed a higher power, divinely appointed, to seal and sanctify your courage and achievement, to bestow the decorations that you hung about your person, signs of favour, marks of status. Perhaps that is why you detested rebels and revolutionaries so much—they had violated the principle of authority and authentication that gave your whole existence its meaning. And I was with you there, as in all else, every inch of the way. Without recognized authority, there is no concept of the sacred, a Nelson cannot be born.

You hated the French even before they rose in revolt, even

before they killed their king. You got that from your mother. Catherine Nelson talked fiercely against the French. For the whole of your infancy, the two nations were locked in bitter combat from Quebec to Bengal. Was it this fierce mother that made you believe so in legality, in vested powers? I believe in these things too, but my mother wasn't fierce; she admired Gandhi, she practised yoga, a word that disturbed my childhood with painful questions, not fearful. Nothing about her inspired fear in me; she was always gentle, she touched things as if to avoid hurting them, even things that couldn't feel. But I could not discover what this yoga was and never saw her do it; the door was always locked. I knew the rug she used, she left it there on the floor, it was thin and made of cotton and had a twining pattern of dark pink and pale blue tendrils. When she left us, she took it with her. Now I have a clearer mental picture of this rug than I have of her face. There were no photographs, they disappeared overnight, my father destroyed them all. I thought for years he had put them away somewhere, but when I went through things after his death, there were none to be found.

A total belief in constituted authority—that's how you made enemies. You were applying the law, you were doing your duty; how could you be at fault? I would have done the same, absolutely.

It was very quiet in my study as I sat there, thinking these thoughts, communing with him. In that short terrace where my house is, just off England's Lane, the sound of traffic is barely audible, more like a graining of the silence than a sound, something you easily get used to. I felt very close to him that night, I had the feeling of *confirmation*, like a current of power.

He was innocent and open-hearted. Miss Lily did not understand this when she criticized his letter. Only an innocent man could have written to an insecure wife in the terms he did, extolling the virtues and attractions of a famous beauty and former courtesan who was there on the spot, swooning in his embrace. The swoon was real enough—I forgot to tell Miss Lily that; Emma was quite bruised by the fall.

No, you were innocently set on describing the nature of your triumph, of your glory . . . or didn't you care?

This thought, intensely disagreeable, swooped on me before I could block it. Of course he would have cared; that was not the point. But did he *see*? Enthusiasm, generosity of judgement—these are merely terms, they can mean more than one thing. Was it that Horatio didn't see other people as existing in a space separate from his own, that he couldn't admit into his mind the possibility of different minds? Not opinions, he was used to differing over the conduct of battles, but sensibilities, other ways of feeling things.

The silence in my room had lost its comfort, it had become stark, there was no refuge in it. So often lately, since my father's death, I had been undermined by unworthy thoughts of this kind, proof not of any defect in Horatio but of my own corrupted nature. It was a poison that spread, and the centre of the discharge was Naples. I was struggling against darkness now, this madness of judgement that opened the gulf between us, broke the current of power. I felt that constriction in my breathing and the throbbing somewhere behind the eyes that always accompany my agitation. Then the room was again bright and clear about me. I could feel the beat of my heart, but my breathing came easier. I had realized my error. I had been upsetting myself over irrelevant issues. You had every virtue that could be reconciled with the mission and destiny of a hero. Probably, too, I had been unconsciously confusing your physically impaired sight with moral blindness, a great blunder—there was no doubt, of course, that your eyesight was deteriorating; even before the wound, while you were still "on the beach" in Norfolk, from the inner corner of each eye, a membranous substance was beginning to cover the ball. If you had lived to be old, you would have died blind.

Released from the nightmare of doubt, I turned my mind to the January of 1793, which was when the call came. This was one of my favourite episodes in his career; I used often to dwell on it. On the twenty-sixth the news comes from Paris: Louis XVI has gone to the block before a jubilant populace. Even as the royal head rolls into the basket, life changes for Horatio—his long exile is over, his days as petty squire draw to a close. It is the beginning of that twelve-year struggle with revolutionary France which was to take him to the heights of achievement and renown. That same day there is a despatch from the Admiralty: he is appointed to command HMS *Agamemnon*, sixty-four guns. At the beginning of February, France declares war on Britain. Four days later, Horatio leaves Burnham Thorpe for London, never to return.

What an amazing change of fortune. As yet no-one knows his name. All his great battles are before him. He is thirty-four years old, emerging from obscurity with all his energy and ambition, still whole and unmutilated, at the height of his powers and in the prime of life. The ship they have given us is in the prime of life too, twelve years old. She is sheathed in copper to reduce the drag of accumulated weed and shellfish. Standard practise by then. But the *Agamemnon* is one of the first ships to have her plating secured by copper bolts in-stead of iron to avoid electrolysis. Technically, her sixty-four guns are too few for a rating of ship of the line, but her sailing qualities more than make up for this. That February, as he sets about commissioning her at Chatham, Horatio is taking possession of a warship that for her size is one of the fastest and strongest in the world.

Thinking of this, the power and promise of it, the mettle of the man and the ship, I felt again the prickle of tears, companion of my solitude. I was with him as he trod a quarterdeck for the first time in five years, amid the odours of river water and tar and raw hemp and wet planks, with him as he went down to his cabin, opened the new logbook with its binding of black leather, saw in its unmarked pages his days of opportunity ahead.

There is a lot to be done before we are ready for sailing: the hold has to be trimmed, a new foremast and bowsprit have to be fitted, stores to be loaded, working clothes and hammocks to be issued to the crew. By the middle of April she is ready. She waits in the Downs Roadstead for a convoy she is to escort down-Channel to Portsmouth. I see her swinging at her anchor, tugging at her cables—the ship as impatient to be gone as her captain. The ancestral foe across the water . . . It was the beginning of his true life, the phase of glory.

With this image, the slim figure pacing the deck, the scent of battle borne to his nostrils through the Channel mists, I took myself off to bed. A few pages of Keegan's *Battle at Sea* and I was ready for sleep. I passed into first sleep easily enough in those months but almost always woke in the early morning and then could not sleep again. Waking me this time was one of my sorrow dreams, as I was in the habit of calling them. The ground floor of an old house, ruinous and empty, with wooden floors that echoed to the steps. From somewhere above me a voice raised in lamentation—high-pitched, throat-formed sounds, overwhelmingly lonely and desolate, as if from some far edge of the world. As always, the sorrow seemed tangible, physical, like rain, and the rain had a light of its own, whitish, slightly phosphorescent. It came down through the house, enveloping but not touching me. The voice was known to me, but I resisted the knowledge. Then the divisions between the levels of the house melted away and I saw in a sort of sliding diagonal vista the slope of attic ceilings and a figure with its back to me, sitting on a bed. High-collared coat, narrow shoulders, some suggestion of a wig. Then I was in the same room, the figure had fallen silent, the head was beginning to turn slowly towards me. I made a clattering escape downwards and away, a sensation like running downhill in a landslide, a debris of metal or wood moving under my feet. I slid and scrambled down, away from the turning head, the terrible prospect of meeting the eyes. This clattering descent drowned other sounds. However, it was not the panic of being pursued that I woke to but the anguish of that screaming grief and the fear that lay below it, a fear that kept me lying rigidly there, as if waiting for an assault in the dark—fear of grief itself, fear of the loss foretold.

I 0

J slept again when the light came. But all next day and the one following I felt the shadow of that dream over me, a sense of foreboding and at the same time a sort of restlessness, a feeling of impending change. This mood was broken on the thirteenth of the month, when—as always—I celebrated the engagement known as Hotham's Action. March 1795—an important date, I had always considered it. Though hardly more than a skirmish compared to his great battles of later, it was the occasion when Horatio first showed signs of angelic promptings, his capacity for breaking free, breaking the line.

Two years and some weeks have passed since Horatio was treading the decks of his new ship at Chatham and just over eight months since the injury to his right eye at Calvi during the Corsican campaign. On this side by now he is virtually blind; he can distinguish light from darkness but not much more than that. Still in command of the *Agamemnon*, he is with the Mediterranean Fleet under Admiral

William Hotham, engaged in the blockade of Toulon—there is a danger that the French may break out and attempt to retake Corsica.

Difficult to say precisely when a sea battle begins. There is the vast arena, the seeking out, the sighting, the chase, the first shots. I date Hotham's Action from March the eighth, a Sunday evening, six days before fighting was joined. Horatio is at anchor at Leghorn, writing home to Fanny. He is interrupted; there is no time for more than a hasty close: *I have only to pray God to bless you.*

This interruption can only have been the order to put out to sea. Hotham had received intelligence that the French under Rear-Admiral Pierre Martin had left Toulon with fifteen sail of the line. Their intention: to cover a troop convoy bound for the invasion of Corsica. Two days later, on the morning of the tenth, the French ships are sighted. Hotham, with fourteen British warships and one Neapolitan, gives the signal for a general chase. It is the first fleet engagement of Horatio's career, but he has to wait for the action he craves; the enemy is elusive and the weather fickle.

Impossible here, of course, in this unvarying light, on this glinting sea of my table, to reproduce that uncanny weather, mists that lifted and fell, dwindling breezes, shifting hazes on a horizon of phantom clouds and phantom sails. It is during this time that the ardent Horatio, on fire to get to grips with the foe, adds a postscript to his letter: *My character and good name are in my own keeping. Life with disgrace is dreadful. A glorious death is to be envied.*

I quoted those words to Miss Lily one evening—I think it was after this. They had always been important words for me. I first heard them from my history teacher when I was fourteen. "Not very reassuring for Fanny," she said. That was her only response. A perfect statement of the heroic creed, and that was all she could find to say. *Not very reassuring for Fanny.* She reduced the whole thing to the reactions of a limited person like Fanny Nelson. I tried to point this out to her at the time, how absurd it was, but she wouldn't see it. Not couldn't, wouldn't. "Well, he was writing to her, wasn't he?" she said. "I mean, he was writing to *her*, not one of his mates. She would have been worried enough already. Did he have to talk about dying?"

I felt a sort of pity for Miss Lily as I was setting out the ships, because in uttering these words she had shown herself to be just as limited as Fanny. But I soon forgot this as I began to concentrate on the action. It was a brush rather than a full-scale engagement, though the French losses were high, at least eight hundred dead. I did not set out the whole line, only the ships immediately concerned—on the French side, the *Ça Ira*, *Censeur*, *Sans Culotte*, and *Jean Bart*; on the English side, the frigate *Inconstant*, Horatio in the *Agamemnon*, and Hotham's flagship, the *Britannia*.

Seven forty-five by my watch. In anxiety not to fail with the timing, I had set the alarm for seven that morning, but I had not needed it; I had been awake since four. It was 8 A.M. when Horatio saw his chance, and that is for me the beginning of the action. At daybreak the enemy have been sighted three or four leagues to the southwest, approximately a yard on my table here. The French are refusing battle; they are running southward with the wind, pursued by the English fleet on a parallel line. Hotham, in the *Britannia*, breaks the red flag for action stations. The sound of drumming is heard on all the English ships, bulkheads and screens and movable furniture are stowed away, the galley fires are doused, the gundecks watered and sanded. The ship's companies bind their heads, cast off their shoes, strip to the waist—cooler working at the guns and easier for the surgeons to operate on wounds not infected by dirty cloth. The surgeons themselves wait with their knives and saws and swabs down in the orlop, below the water line. Sleeves rolled up well above the elbows . . .

Six minutes from the first drumbeat to readiness for battle. Now, exactly now, 8 A.M. on this morning of the thirteenth, Horatio, well ahead in the speedy *Agamemnon*, sees a French eighty-gun ship, afterwards identified as the *Ça Ira*, fall foul of another, sees them collide, draw apart again, sees that the *Ça Ira* has had her fore and main topsails carried away; they lie trailing over her starboard side. At once she begins to lose way, she is detached from the main body. Here she is, here I place her, lying astern of the French line.

For all their stateliness and the beauty of their sail, these fleets were like fierce hunting packs, constantly famished. To fall out, to be isolated, to be sick or disabled, meant mortal danger. First to go for her is the leading frigate, the *Inconstant*, at the head of the English line. But the *Ça Ira* is a heavily armoured ship; she can't run, but she can still bite. The frigate is savaged, she reels away. Now comes Horatio's moment. He swings out of the line and stands towards the disabled ship. She has now been taken in tow by a frigate, which is attempting to draw her away westward. The *Sans Culotte* and the *Jean Bart* have come in to protect her. I place them here, on her weather bow, at gunshot distance.

Horatio bears down on her. Still in tow, she gives him a raking fire as he approaches. He is intending to wait till the ships touch before ordering the broadside, but this fire from her stern is so accurate and damaging that he cannot wait so long. At a distance of one hundred yards, less than an inch on my table, he gives the order: the helm of the *Agamemnon* is put astarboard, and as she falls off he gives the *Ça Ira* a full broadside, raking her from stern to stem, each gun double-shotted. Almost every shot goes home. Immediately the broadside is discharged, he puts the helm aport and stands after her again. For the best part of two hours this manoeuvre is repeated. He stands after her, falls away to starboard, pounds her with a broadside, stands after her again. The French ship, big enough to put the *Agamemnon* in her hold, is still under tow; she cannot get round to return the broadsides. The carnage among her crew is terrible; her masts and rigging are in ruins, but most of her guns are still serviceable.

Now the towing frigate succeeds in getting her round; at last she can bring her broadside to bear, use her heavier guns to pulverize her tormentor. But their setting is misjudged, they are too much elevated. Horatio runs on boldly; the enemy shots fly over him. He is ready to fight the Frenchman broadside to broadside. And it is now, at this crucial stage, that the cautious Hotham hoists the signal of recall.

Nothing could better illustrate the difference in temper between these two commanders: the angelic extremist and the prudent half-measures man. Believe me, I know what you must have felt that day, I understand your frustration.

Next day, March 14, after a brief but violent action, the wrecked *Ça Ira* and the seventy-four-gun ship that was now attempting to tow her to safety, the *Censeur*, were both taken by the British. As soon as the French ships struck their colours, Horatio—always prompt to seize the occasion—went aboard the admiral's flagship to urge an immediate pursuit. They could leave their prizes under a guard of frigates; with bold action, they could destroy the French fleet altogether . . .

I saw them in fancy that March morning, as I had seen them often before, in private colloquy together on the quarterdeck of the *Britannia*: the stolid Hotham, not much heat there despite the name, and the slight, eager Horatio with his strange dead eye. The pupil of the right eye was much enlarged now, diffused in shape and immovable, almost covering the blue of the iris. When another life is closely knit into the fabric of one's own, certain pictures are favoured by the frequency with which they occur to the mind, though this frequency seems arbitrary and is impossible to explain. From boyhood I have seen those two pacing together as the firing grows slacker and the French ships crowd all possible sail to westward, making for the shelter of Toulon. Hotham is looking straight before him; Horatio is gesturing, glancing from time to time at his commander's face. The cursed French—they could still be cut off, they are demoralized; what a victory it would be for the Crown. He is vehement—too much so, probably, in view of the difference in rank. And the admiral's measured reply: "We must be contented, we have done very well."

This in its way was true. Corsica was temporarily saved; two French warships had been captured. But Horatio expressed his feelings privately in a letter home some two weeks later. If we had taken ten sail, he said, and allowed the eleventh to escape, I could never have called it well done. Here, in a nutshell, is the whole thesis of my book, the ultimate statement of heroic ambition. Always reaching higher, seeking greater achievement, always wanting the odds to be greater . . . In that same letter, words printed on my mind for many years now: *My disposition cannot bear tame and slow measures.* Neither can mine. In spite of all appearances to the contrary, in spite of my obscure life, I knew that he and I were at one, we were like diamond and carbon.

The moment is all; he knew that, none better. Circumstances had favoured him in this brush with the French, giving him the opportunity to distinguish himself, to be the only commander to go singly into action, a thing very rare in fleet engagements. And he had a fast ship, he was well ahead in the line. But it was he, and he alone, who seized the moment, made it his own. Hotham's Action, they call it, but it will always ring with Horatio's name.

Again the words of the letter came back to me, first heard from the man who taught us history when I was in the fifth form, the man I had talked about in my sessions with Penhas. His name was Grigson. He was broad and short, and he had wiry reddish hair that would not lie back; it stood up straight from his forehead like bristles. He wore rimless glasses, behind which his eyes were a warm orangy colour, like marmalade. I remember him well. He was a Nelson lover too, the first I had ever met. Also, he was a brilliant teacher. Coppernob, his nickname among us. He had a habit of rather tense-seeming gesture, quick cutting or chopping motions of the hands. He would sit before us and talk, not from behind the desk—he brought the chair and sat in front of us, almost among us. Grigson had no problems with discipline; he was strong-voiced and challenging in his gaze, and there was a suggestion of contained violence about him, in those abrupt movements of his hands. No-one dared to show a flicker of derision, even when he fell into the moralizing vein, which was fairly often—it was moralized history he gave us, a course of events determined by character, good or bad. If Napoleon had been a different kind of man, if he had been a true patriot, as Horatio Nelson was, and not set on personal glory, he would have struck at England's heart in 1798, when the way was open, by landing an army in Ireland, which was in revolt and ready to welcome him with open arms, instead of sacrificing that same army to his grandiose dreams of oriental conquest. Genius, perhaps. But what price genius in a mere adventurer? And he was Corsican into the bargain, which, Grigson implied, was in moral terms a grave disadvantage to start with. Nelson, in that situation, would have put king and country first; he would have gone for the jugular.

I thought then that Grigson was right, and I think so now. He had notes in a quarto-size red folder, which rested on his knees as he sat there. There was a gesture he made, both hands brought sharply down, a foot or so apart, in a sort of double chopping motion, to indicate the red file in his lap. *Here is your grade A in O-level history.*

He kept the flame alive. I was already making my model ships by then—I had started that at thirteen—and I kept a scrapbook in which I put anything to do with fighting ships before the age of steam. But Grigson gave my passion for Horatio an adult endorsement. In a certain way this was fortuitous; it depended on the power he was able to exert. Had it been possible to make fun of Grigson or disrupt his lessons or behave disrespectfully towards him, his view of Nelson and the importance of character would have gone up in smoke along with everything else about him. Inconceivable now, of course, but then . . . In adolescence we are easily swayed. If Grigson had been a different kind of man, I might have lost Horatio. But he sat among us and controlled us and drove the message home. *This great Englishman—I use that word advisedly, boys, no admixture of the Celt there, generations of Norfolk yeomen, he was English to the core . . .*

And a mind knifelike in its penetration, a heart inspired by selfless devotion to duty, a spirit that knew no fear. The embodiment of the genius of his country. How I drank in those words. Grigson was the most stimulating and exciting teacher I ever had. He quoted from Horatio's letters and despatches and sometimes dictated short extracts for us to memorize and reproduce in essays. *My character and good name are in my keeping . . . Remember that, boys, always remember that.*

He was wonderful on the battles; he went through every phase on the blackboard. But there was nothing in all he said that could help me now in my quandary over Naples and the part Horatio played there. Grigson made no reference at all to this episode, nor to the involvement with Emma Hamilton, nor the separation from Fanny, nor anything to do with his domestic existence. Grigson was a devotee; for him, Horatio was an ethereal being, all fire and air, no nether parts.

Quite suddenly thinking of this, I was swept by despair at the protracted hold-up with my book and my problems with the business in Naples. Somewhere, I was convinced, there was the clinching piece of evidence that would set everything to rights. But supposing I could not find it? We would both be left floundering there, in that quagmire. *My disposition cannot bear tame and slow measures.* On an impulse, standing there in the quiet of my operations room, with Hotham's Action over and only the dead to dispose of and the decks to swab clear of blood, I uttered these words of his aloud. My voice sounded hollow to me, quite unreal. How would he have pronounced them? I knew nothing of his voice, whether it was harsh or soft, high-pitched or deep. He would have kept the burr of rural Norfolk; people did not try to gentrify their accents in those days. East Anglian, then, but softer than the urban southeast, perhaps a bit slower. I tried the same sentence again. It sounded more like Essex than Norfolk. I needed more text; only by some more continuous reading could I get any closer.

I left the ships there on the table and went upstairs to my study. I took down Laughton's edition of the letters and despatches, opened it at random, and began to read aloud.

As to myself, upon the general question, that if a man does not do his utmost in time of action, I think but one punishment ought to be inflicted. Not that I take a man's merit from his list of dead and wounded . . .

I was self-conscious at first, but I persisted. I wanted to find his voice. Then, as I settled into the reading, my intentions of mimicry were somehow cancelled out. The sounds I began to make were not a stranger's, but they were not mine either. And they were not the accents of rural Norfolk. The voice that came was slightly metallic, with a slur on the dental consonants caused by the tongue being held too close to the roof of the mouth.

It was not his voice—how could it be? It was not a friendly voice at all. It ended by frightening me.

I I

I could not stay in the study after this. I thought of going back down to the basement and perhaps rearranging some of the cabinets—always a soothing occupation. But I suddenly felt enormously weary, so much so that I could hardly keep on my feet. I was averaging no more than four hours' sleep at night during all that period. For some time now I had been sleeping at odd times of the day, a habit quite new to me.

I went along the passage to the living room and sat in the big old armchair, the one I always used, dark green in colour and very capacious. I wrapped myself in the patchwork rug that my mother made, which I always kept over the back of the chair. I saw her making this rug. I suppose I was three years old, or perhaps four. She had her own room where she did this kind of work, and I was allowed in there. She used odds and ends of different-coloured wool to make the squares, any colour at all, it didn't seem to matter. Use enough colours and they will not clash, she said. The table was heaped with bright remnants.

I found this rug some time after she was gone. It was in a spare bedroom, rolled in a cotton bag, in the big drawer at the bottom of the wardrobe. I think my father put it away there, or told the house-keeper to do so. There was a housekeeper then, a Mrs. Bryce. I suppose I was eleven when I found it, one day during the summer holidays. In those August afternoons I would sometimes go to the bedroom, get out the rug, and spread it on the bed. I would take off my clothes: shoes, jacket, trousers, shirt, underclothes—socks always last, for some reason. It always had to be in the same order. When I was naked I would creep under the rug until it came over my head, but in such a way that I did not disturb the edges at the sides or foot. If I failed in this, I would have to spread the rug out and try again. I would lie there on my back, quite still, in the dimness under the rug. I would feel the warmth spread over me, and with the warmth there seemed to come the scent of my mother. No-one ever found out about this, and after the beginning of the new term I never did it again. Now, when the rug was warm, I still sometimes imagined I could catch the scent of her in it.

I slept long, perhaps two hours. When I woke it was late after-noon; the light was already fading. I was not conscious of having dreamed, but I had woken with some vague feeling of horror, and as I sat there this became clearer and colder and I knew it had concerned the *Ça Ira* and the terrible damage she had suffered, a disabled beast, cut off from the pack, wallowing there with her heavy cannon that she could not bring to bear while Horatio savaged her hindparts, rent her, and bled her. Images of the slaughter on her decks came to me, the sounds of it, always the same sounds: crash of shot in the timbers, keening of shrapnel, shrieks of the men on the raked decks, cheers from our English lads as they gave the crappos a good drubbing. Shrieks and cheers again mingling . . .

I sat there as the room grew darker around me, trying to break free from these thoughts. After all, war was war; it had been a triumph, Horatio had acted with great gallantry and panache. It was the next day that the *Ça Ira* was taken. She was too much hurt to repair her masts in the night and make good her escape. She waited there, bleeding into the sea. All through the night her surgeons worked in the after cockpit, sweating in the close heat, fighting to win the race against gangrene, sawing and slicing on the improvised operation table in a stench of blood and sawdust and rum, with buckets for the amputated parts and a brazier to warm the blades, lessen the shock of the cold steel.

And then, with her masts gone and most of her guns out of action, at five minutes past ten next morning, she surrendered. Andrews, the name of the lieutenant that Horatio sent aboard her to take possession. He would have needed a strong stomach, walking about on those decks. Three hundred and fifty dead and wounded, getting on for half her total complement. And on the *Agamemnon*, in the whole engagement, thirteen men slightly wounded, no dead. We were right to hail it as a triumph, to thank the Almighty for his manifold favours, as we did that following Sunday, holding services on the decks of the ships. Horatio did his duty and came out with credit. *Thank God I have done my duty.* His last words . . .

Upon this thought, quite unbidden, there again came into my mind the verdict of the poet laureate of the day, Robert Southey, most famous of all his biographers, on the events in Naples in 1799—the sticking point of my book. *A stain upon the memory of Nelson and the honour of England.* I had always discounted this judgement. Southey was influenced by the views of Charles James Fox and the

Whig politicians; he listened to the malicious innuendos of republican sympathizers; he actually allowed himself to believe that Horatio had tricked the Neapolitan Jacobins into quitting their forts under promise of safe conduct, only to have them arrested and handed over to the vengeance of Ferdinand and Maria Carolina.

Horatio could never have stooped to such a thing. His nature was too noble; he was the incarnation of the spirit of fair play, that profoundly British virtue, for which we are known far and wide. But the slanders had persisted, maintained an evil life on their own, in spite of his many champions. Buried somewhere in this great heap of argument, two centuries old by now, was the bright fragment that would clear his name. How glorious to be the one to find it, to see it glint like gold among the husks of old polemic. My name would be joined with his for as long as his deeds were remembered. Charles Cleasby, the vindicator of Horatio Nelson.

I got up to put on the standard lamp behind the chair. But Southey's unjust words remained in my mind, despite the light that came flooding. I decided to check the reference once again. Pointless— I was completely familiar with the words—but there was a semblance of purpose in it, and anything was better than sitting on there, a passive prey to his vilifiers. I was worried about returning to my study so soon, because of that inimical voice. I entered the room somewhat apprehensively, but everything seemed quiet and accustomed in there. I found the passage almost at once: *To palliate it would be in vain; to justify it would be wicked: there is no alternative, for one who will not make himself a participator in guilt, but to record the disgraceful story with sorrow and with shame.*

Strong words indeed, and beautifully put, however misguided. The most robust response I had so far found was J. K. Laughton's in the preface to his selection of Horatio's letters and despatches, which came out in 1886: *Southey was wrong. There is another alternative. We neither palliate, nor justify, nor record; we deny. The story is a base and venomous falsehood.*

My heart warmed to this sturdy and patriotic rebuttal by the then professor of modern history at King's College, London. Historians were more personal and more passionate in those days. I was sure that Laughton was in the right of it, but unfortunately he calls no witnesses, he refuses to admit any evidence outside of Horatio's own words, as contained in his letters and despatches. The reasoning is therefore circular. Of course it is right, in a way, that it should be circular. After all, Nelson is in a special category as our quintessential hero and quintessential national representative. We British do not extol cunning as a virtue, but courage and honour. Horatio is the soul of honour, he tells the truth under all circumstances, therefore his own reports of the business are to be believed without reservation, therefore Southey's verdict is false.

Certainly Horatio's words are there and he never wavered in them. There is his letter to Alex Stephens written nearly four years later, in the February of 1803: *I very happily arrived in Naples and prevented such an infamous transaction from taking place; therefore when the rebels surrendered, they came out from the castles as they ought, without the honours of war and trusting to the judgement of their sovereigns.*

This is clear enough but lacking in detail. The transaction he was referring to is the treaty with the rebels signed before his arrival. The crux of the thing is in the last few words. Did these people, when they came out of their forts, think that they were going to be shipped to France in accordance with the treaty, or did they think they were going to be handed over to their Sicilian majesties? That is the argument, that is the form it has taken; but for me there was no argument at all. To believe that they didn't know what they were coming out to is to believe that Horatio was first a party to fraud and afterwards covered it up by lying. No-one could believe that who knew him as I did. The difficulty lay not in knowing what to believe but in finding the proof of his innocence.

He is not helped by those of his defenders who try to gloss over the business or even, in their generous sympathy, actually misrepresent the facts. Carola Oman is a case in point. A surprising thing, to my mind, that it should be a woman to write one of the best lives of Horatio this century. First published in 1947, containing much new material, it is a detailed and vivid picture of the man. Yet coming to his dealings in Naples on the morning of June 26, 1799, this is what she writes: *Sir William Hamilton sent the Cardinal a hasty assurance that Lord Nelson would do nothing, pending instructions from Palermo, to break the Armistice, a statement which Nelson . . . later confirmed in his own hand.*

This confirmation in Horatio's own hand I had not so far found, nor, as far as I knew, had anyone else. The ambassador's note, however, does exist: *Lord Nelson begs me to assure your Eminence that he is resolved to do nothing that can break the Armistice which your Eminence has accorded to the Castles of Naples.*

That is the whole text. Nothing about pending instructions, nothing about Palermo. Palermo, of course, was where the king and the queen were, having fled to Sicily from the advancing French. What led Carola Oman, so generally scrupulous, to insert that phrase into her text as if it were an integral part of Hamilton's note? She would have had that note before her, as did I. It is hard not to conclude that she was taking for granted the very thing she should have been trying to prove: that these people knew when they came out of the forts that the fulfilling of the treaty depended on the endorsement of their offended sovereigns—an endorsement not yet received.

A being of such shining honesty as Horatio is not to be defended by sleight of hand. Nor is it to be done by glaring omission. In the most recent biography I had read, that of Christopher Hibbert, published in 1994, in a total of almost five hundred pages, only five lines are devoted to June 26, 1799, surely one of the most important dates in Nelson's entire life. Hibbert refers to the rebel garrisons emerging under the treaty as refugees, which suggests that they were already outside the forts before the intention was formed to arrest them, which completely begs the question of why they left the forts in the first place. As I sat there that March evening, as darkness settled over the stricken *Ça Ira*, I was swept once again by the ardent desire to clear him, free him forever from the bungling of his friends as well as from the malice of his foes. Everything lay there, in those few days of June. The clue was there if I could find it. I fell to pondering the sequence of events yet again.

Already by the twenty-fifth, relations between Horatio and Cardinal Ruffo are breaking down. For hours the two of them argue, face to face in Horatio's cabin on the *Vanguard*, in the hot June weather, the cardinal speaking French, the admiral English, and the ambassador interpreting. Emma in the background, dressed in white, with a broad-brimmed hat. Perhaps she throws in the occasional few words in her mixture of Lancashire and Neapolitan. She peers through the bay window of the cabin to see if anyone she knows is in the pleasure boats out in the bay.

The dispute continues. Horatio does not hate Italians in the way he hates the French, but he regards them as immoral and lacking in the military virtues. He distrusts Ruffo as a devious and probably treacherous cleric. To Ruffo he seems irascible, overbearing, ignorant of the real situation in Naples. Horatio refuses to accept the treaty that Ruffo, as commander of the royalist forces, has signed in King Ferdinand's name. The rebels are traitors; they must surrender unconditionally and be delivered to the justice of their sovereign. Ruffo insists that the treaty to which he has put his name should be honoured.

The people in the forts are misguided patriots. The best way to heal the wounds of civil war is to be lenient with the vanquished.

This treaty, the heart of the dispute, has been signed not only by Ruffo but, in the name of George III, by Captain Foote, the senior British officer in Naples at the time, and by the representatives of the Russian and Turkish detachments—in other words, by the whole allied command. By its terms the castles are to be handed over to the allied troops and the people composing the garrisons are to take their choice of being carried with their property under safe conduct to Toulon or remaining unmolested in the city.

Neither will give way. Horatio works the stump of his arm—a habit of his when irritated or impatient. Ruffo displays an amazing virtuosity of gesture. Voices rise and tempers fray. Ruffo quits the ship in disgust. Horatio writes a declaration, which is handed in to the forts at daybreak on the twenty-sixth: *Rear-Admiral Lord Nelson, K.B., Commander of his Britannic Majesty's Fleet in the Bay of Naples, acquaints the rebellious subjects of his Sicilian Majesty that he will not permit them to embark or quit those places. They must surrender themselves to His Majesty's royal mercy.*

This they show no smallest sign of doing. Noteworthy, this use of the word *embark*. It seems here to mean depart, sail, leave for Toulon. Later it came to bear a more restricted meaning.

By now the situation is extremely dangerous. The English fleet is drawn up in line of battle in the bay, ready to bombard the forts. The guns of the French garrison in the Castle of St. Elmo are ready to reply. The republican rebels in their forts lack cannon and shot, but they are desperate, and there is enough explosive in the magazines to blow themselves sky high and half the city with them. Ruffo has made it clear that if Horatio breaks the armistice, he will give no assistance with either men or guns. Not only that: he will withdraw his forces from the positions they have occupied, leaving the English to conquer the enemy with their own forces.

In spite of all this, Horatio sends in his declaration. Thereupon the cardinal, believing that the English are preparing an assault, sends in a note warning the garrisons that the allied troops will now retire to their original positions. This sudden withdrawal causes immediate consternation and terror in the city. People stream out of Naples in their thousands, fearing that a general bombardment is about to begin. Rumours circulate that the besieged Jacobins have torn up the steps over the powder magazines so as to be able, in the last extremity, to throw in a match. This seems to suggest, if it is true, that they were not thinking of surrender—not yet, at least.

Now, at this most critical of moments, there occurs that sudden change in Horatio's attitude which no documents have yet been found to explain. By ten o'clock on the morning of the twenty-sixth, Ruffo had in his hands that hasty note of Sir William Hamilton's to which Carola Oman so misleadingly refers. It is brought by two of Horatio's captains, Troubridge and Ball. In the cardinal's presence, these two either write or dictate a further declaration: *Captains Troubridge and Ball have authority on the part of Lord Nelson to declare to his Eminence that his Lordship will not oppose the embarkation of the rebels and of the people who compose the garrison of the Castles of Nuovo and dell'Ovo.*

There it is again: *embarkation.* They were embarked—so much is certain. That same afternoon they came out of their forts, carrying with them the personal effects they were intending to take to France. But they did not sail. They waited there in the harbour, under the eyes of the English ships, crowded together on the small transports, men, women, and children—for many of the men had been joined by their families. Then, on the morning of the twenty-eighth, the expected letters were received from Palermo: Horatio was officially authorized to act. The transports were brought under the English guns and the people aboard them made prisoners.

You detested the French, that much is beyond doubt. I remembered your solemn words of advice to a young midshipman: *You must hate a Frenchman as if he were the devil.* You also detested rebels, and these were rebels doubly detestable: they had leagued themselves with the French. But you would never have allowed that to sway you from the path of honour. You, more than any other Englishman who ever lived, epitomize our great past, you are the standard-bearer to this more tarnished age, you gave your life, you cleared the seas of our enemies for a century to come. Was there a distinction in your mind between embarking and sailing? Could you have thought those people in the forts would come out only to be embarked and not to sail? That hasty note—it was written by Sir William Hamilton and sent by him to Ruffo. It was written in French, a language of which you were largely ignorant. Could this foxy diplomat have deliberately omitted something you intended him to include, something to make that crucial distinction clear? But if so, where was the proof? And how can one explain the subsequent declaration, made in your name by Captains Troubridge and Ball, in which you repeated the undertaking not to oppose the embarkation? Was it possible for Ruffo to take this document in any other sense than as an agreement on your part to allow the treaty to be put into effect?

I was now at the heart of the problem that had held up my book and exhausted my mind for more than two months by that time. And I was no nearer a solution that March evening than I had been at the outset. I was beginning to feel the usual nausea of defeat, that slackening and slipping away of the mind which seemed like a foretaste of death. Always worse, compounded by all the previous failures . . . Quite suddenly I remembered Miss Lily's words: *It was a show, they were stars.* Ludicrously inappropriate to talk about Horatio in that way. But perhaps, in the absence of any other sort of evidence, some clue to the truth of those June days could be found in the personages involved, in the interplay of character. A cast of six: the two protagonists in conflict, Horatio and Ruffo; the diplomatic go-between, Hamilton; the confidante and messenger of the queen, Emma; and their Sicilian majesties, Ferdinand IV and Maria Carolina, in whose names these actions were taken. I could make a brief sketch of each in turn and see what light was cast, if any. Not a course of events, a maze of personality. There can be more than one way into a maze, and which you have chosen doesn't matter once you are in it. I started with the diplomat.

Sir William Hamilton. Sixty-eight-years old at this time, tall and lean, slightly stooped, from either scholarly activities or the many years of elaborate courtesies at the Neapolitan court; a man of distinguished appearance, with an aquiline nose and an air of intelligence and refinement. Son of Lord Archibald Hamilton, grandson of the third Duke of Hamilton, he had served for some years as an officer in the Third Foot Guards and had been—very briefly—member of Parliament for Midhurst. Younger son of a younger son, he had no money of his own, a state of things he remedied in 1758 by marrying an heiress, through whom he obtained an estate in Wales worth about £8000 a year. In 1764 he joined the Diplomatic Service, a career for which by background and manners he was well fitted. The delicate state of his wife's health made Naples, with its sea air and warm climate, a natural choice. The marriage by all accounts was happy. The first Lady Hamilton died in 1782, and in the following year, returning to England with her embalmed body for burial, he met the extremely beautiful young woman who was his nephew's mistress. She called herself Emma Hart at this time and was to become the second Lady Hamilton and Horatio's great love. (I had been fascinated to learn that he met her at the same hotel, Nerot's in St. James's, where eighteen years later Fanny and Emma were to endure the mutual dislike of their first encounter.)

That September of 1798, when Horatio, the victor of the Nile, came sailing into the bay, Hamilton had been British envoy extraordinary and minister plenipotentiary to the court of Naples for thirty-six years. A man of elegant manners, all were agreed. A keen sportsman, hunting companion of King Ferdinand—they slaughtered thousands of quail and woodcocks together. A more than competent musician. He played the cello and kept his own band of musicians. He made experiments with electricity, kept a tame monkey, and planted an English garden in the grounds of the royal palace at Caserta. William Beckford said of him: "The first of connoisseurs—not only in the fine arts, but in the science of human felicity." *The best dancer at the Neapolitan court, it was said, though his dancing days were drawing to a close by then, must have been—he was feeling his age, his liver was in bad shape. Too many banquets. The wild and voluptuous Sicilian dance, the tarantella, which was all the rage, was probably beyond him. Emma, still only thirty-three, danced it wonderfully well . . . From February of the following year, the year of the Jacobins, Horatio and Emma were sleeping together, as regularly as Horatio's duties would allow.*

I paused at this point to pace about the room for a while. No clue in the bare facts of anyone's life. A typical product of his time and class. He seems not to have believed in anything much. Prejudices and opinions, yes, but no very firm principles. He wanted to pass his days agreeably. And yet in one or two important ways he wasn't typical at all. What really distinguished him was his very refined taste. Connoisseur, collector of classical antiquities, expert vulcanologist . . . He had one of the best collections of antique vases in private hands. And he was tolerant to an extraordinary degree. Victorian biographers deny that he knew of the adultery, deny that there was any adultery.

But all the evidence goes to show that there was and he did. Not only knew, but fully accepted it, lived in the knowledge of it, unruffled and benign. All three lived under the same roof, they saw each other every day. Emma had been passed on to him; perhaps he was ready to pass her on in his turn, feeling himself too old, too tired? A woman, of whatever class, was always a commodity. And for a collector, of course, anything could be passed on, people as well as objects. Just a matter of rearrangement. I remembered reading somewhere that when he returned to London in 1800, his days of foreign service over forever, the house he took in Piccadilly had garden statuary that outraged his taste. It gave him a headache just to look at it. He could not live in the house until he had got rid of it all and put there in its place an antique statue of the Nile.

Nowhere any evidence that this exquisite sensibility suffered through thirty-six years at the corrupt and devious court of Naples. Presumably there was nothing in this to outrage him—moral outrage was probably not much in his line. A collector acquires things, sets them out, finds the right arrangement. If it doesn't look good here, we shift it there. I had quoted in my book some lines from a letter of his that very well illustrated this readiness to shift things. Written to Sir John Acton, prime minister in the Neapolitan court, the queen's adviser and rumoured former lover, perhaps the most powerful man in the kingdom: *However, after good reflection, Lord Nelson authorized me to write to his Eminence yesterday morning early to certify to him that he would do nothing to break the Armistice . . . That produced the best possible effect . . . If one can't do exactly what one wishes, one must act for the best; and that is what Lord Nelson has done; I hope therefore that the result will be approved by their Sicilian Majesties . . .*

That is a shifty letter. What does it mean? Acton would have known, presumably. This was June 27, when the rebels had already been embarked. *If one can't do exactly what one wishes, one must act for the best.* In what way did you act for the best? What you wanted is clear enough: you wanted unconditional surrender. And all the rest of your life you maintained that that was what it had been. What can Hamilton be talking about? The assurance was given, Naples was restored to calm, the Jacobins came out and embarked on their transports. Two days later they were seized; the transports were converted into floating prisons.

Yes, there is no doubt that Hamilton was shifty. Highly diplomatic, to call it by a gentler name. He even, in a later despatch to Lord Grenville at the Foreign Office, says that the Jacobins were already on the transports on June 14, already there before you arrived, and that there was an urgent need to arrest them because they were about to set sail! No question of subterfuge, no question of what the garrisons were led to believe. So he became the first in that long line of obfuscators that extends to the present day, those who have smirched you, who were all truth, by their lack of it. Grenville could not have believed it, in any case. His view of Hamilton's conduct comes out clearly enough in his letter to the new ambassador in Palermo, asking him to explain to Sir William, *without reserve,* the utter impossibility of his going back to Naples in any public situation. Though this, of course, may be due more to disapproval of an ambassador's sharing his wife with an admiral at a foreign court.

In the stress of these thoughts, I fell to pacing from bookshelf to wall. Approach the bookshelf, choose a book. This evening it was Harold Acton's *The Bourbons of Naples.* Choose a word in the title. You can choose any word, but once you have chosen, you must keep to it. I chose *Bourbons.* Forefinger of the right hand, touch the word, then straight across, six paces, touch the wall with both palms flat against it, thumbs horizontal but they mustn't touch. Then six paces back to the shelves, touch the word again. Very soothing. The only other thing about Hamilton that came to my mind that evening, as I went through my paces, was the fact that he had recently suffered a grievous loss. Earlier that year he had heard that the *Colossus*, bound for England with his entire collection of classical treasures aboard her, the cherished hoard of a long career, had been wrecked off the Scilly Isles. Nothing of the cargo was saved but the corpse of Admiral Lord Shouldham, preserved in spirits. The kind of thing to break the heart of an elderly aesthete—a dead admiral pointlessly rescued, his precious collection lost in the depths. Did he somehow hold the Jacobins responsible? Habitual cynicism, embittered by such a loss, might have made him vindictive . . .

I went back to my desk, settled down to write again. Who next? Who but the detested adversary, the man behind the treaty?

Cardinal Fabrizio Ruffo. Fifty-five years old at the time of these events, active and vigorous. Member of an ancient, princely family, inheritor of vast feudal estates in his native Calabria. In his younger days a prominent member of Roman high society. (He was descended from the Roman family of Colonna on his mother's side.) For a while he was the lover of the marchesa Girolama Lepri, notorious for her promiscuity. This was a profligate, licentious, profoundly corrupt society. By all accounts Ruffo was entirely at home in it. Horatio calls him a "swelled-up priest," but he had never taken orders. His cardinal's hat had been bestowed on him when he retired from the post of treasurer-general to the Vatican— some say in order to get rid of him after a suspected misappropriation of funds. Slander, probably; a man like that would not have lacked for enemies . . . Of all the nobles and court hangers-on that fled with their majesties to Palermo, he is the only one to show spirit. With the blessing of Ferdinand and Maria Carolina—though without their material assistance—he leaves Sicily on January 27, 1799, four days after the proclamation of the republic in Naples. His declared object: to promote and lead a counter-revolution, drive out the French, suppress the republican rebels, restore the kingdom of Naples to Ferdinand.

At the beginning of February he lands in Calabria with only eight followers and proclaims a holy war to rid the kingdom of foreign atheists. Within a few weeks, 17,000 fierce and undisciplined irregulars have flocked to his standard. This horde—the Christian Army of the Holy Faith, as Ruffo calls it—sets off from Naples bearing the Sicilian royal standard and spreading terror as it advances. Their numbers are swelled by bands of brigands and by some thousands of convicts released from Sicilian jails.

Success is rapid. By the beginning of June the French have withdrawn, leaving only a garrison in the castle of Sant'Elmo. On the fourteenth, Ruffo lets loose his Christian army on Naples. No, that is to misrepresent him; he can no longer hold it back. The Jacobin rebel militia take refuge in their two forts of Nuovo and dell'Ovo. Ruffo's troops give themselves up to slaughter and pillage. They are joined by the street people of Naples, called the lazzaroni, *a ragged army many thousand strong, fiercely loyal to the king. Anyone suspected of Jacobin sympathies—and it is enough to be respectably dressed—is hauled off to the main square and butchered on the spot.*

I paused at this point to consider the situation now facing the victorious Ruffo. The city is in chaos. His troops openly defy his attempts to restrain them. A visiting German author, August von Kotzebue, describes the terror of those days in his *Travels through Italy.* One or two extracts were there in my book.

The lazzaroni *roasted men in the streets and begged money of the passers-by to purchase bread to their roast meat. Many of them carried in their pockets fingers, ears, etc. which they had cut off; and if they met a person they looked upon as a patriot, they triumphantly exhibited their bloody spoils . . . All who wore cropped hair fell victim to the mob. False tails were procured but the people ran behind anyone that passed, pulling him by the tail, and if it came off, it was all over with the wearer . . .*

Touch the word, six paces, palms against the cool wall. Naples given over to a festival of blood. People dragged out of their houses, on any pretext or none, men, women, and children, and hacked to death on the streets. The slaughter went on through the night, lit by the flames from buildings set on fire by the looters or by incendiary bombs from the besieged republicans in their forts.

What was Ruffo to do? He was not burdened by principle, any more than Hamilton—in fact, these two had a great deal in common. The aesthete and the pragmatist, both deep-dyed. Not much difference. The cardinal's main purpose in all this, from the very beginning, had been to secure Bourbon gratitude and the rewards he hoped would follow. He was cynical, opportunistic, completely egotistical. His whole career goes to show this. But above all he was very, very realistic and therefore entirely unheroic, light-years away from an angelic nature like Horatio's.

This was the main difference, but there was another. I wanted to be fair to Ruffo, to try to see things as he would have seen them that afternoon as he sat arguing there and the rage mounted. Otherwise there was no point in assembling these people, there could be no exit from this maze of personality, I would just go walking round and round in it. Ruffo was a royalist because the power of the great families was guaranteed by the monarchy. But he had no devotion to the Bourbon cause or to any other. The thing that really marked him out was that he was an Italian, and Calabrese at that; Naples was his city. He cared what happened to her and to her people. A Spanish king, an Austrian queen, a prime minister half English and half French, a British ambassador . . . So he makes the treaty, knowing it will not be welcomed in Palermo but believing himself to be authorized, as vicar general and Ferdinand's accredited representative, to act on his own initiative. The objective is gained; he sees no point in further bloodshed. But the others do; they are intent on punishment, especially the fearful and vindictive Carolina, from whom in one way or another they all take their tone. Yes, even you, Horatio.

Then, on that morning of the twenty-sixth, after all the quarrelling, there comes the volte-face. Ruffo finds in his hands first Hamilton's hasty assurance, then the declaration delivered by the captains—which they refuse to sign. *His Lordship will not oppose the embarkation.*

And in fact you did not. Now comes the question: if on someone's part there was an intention to deceive, who in fact was deceived? Was it Ruffo? Domenico Sacchinelli, the cardinal's secretary, in his account of the events of that morning, says that his employer suspected something was wrong: *The Cardinal, although he suspected there might be here some treachery, not wishing to wrangle with those two captains, took no further measure beyond deputing the Minister Micheroux to accompany those two captains to the Castles to arrange with the republican commanders the execution of the articles agreed upon.*

Why should he suspect treachery? Not because the captains refused to sign; there was no reason for them to sign, they were the transmitters, not the authors. Surely, then, because of the equivocal tone. In that case, why didn't he demand further clarification? Why, above all, did he send to Micheroux, together with the ambiguous documents he had received, a letter in his own hand stating that Lord Nelson *had consented to carry out the capitulation,* a clear exaggeration of their import? Did he believe what he wrote or merely pretend to believe it? Perhaps he didn't suspect anything at all? Sacchinelli was writing many years later, working from notes and memories. He was on a pension from the Bourbon court; he wanted to shift the blame to the English for the terrible things that happened afterwards.

In this business, wherever one pressed, a dark syrup of treachery came oozing round the edges. But whose? Whose was the mind, whose were the glances? The rebels came out to atrocious deaths. Was it Emma? The thought sent me back to my desk again. Difficult to write briefly about Emma; there was so much of her, and so much of it was folly. Her beauty, her vulgarity, her extraordinary spelling, her capacity to absorb and deal out flattery . . . However, there was no play without her; the attempt had to be made.

Emma, Lady Hamilton. Born in 1765 to a colliery blacksmith and his wife on the Wirral Peninsula in Cheshire. Baptized in the name of Emy Lyon. No birth certificate yet found. Father signed his marriage certificate with a cross. The hamlet where she was born one of the most wretched and squalid in the land, a collection of hovels lived in by the colliers who worked in the nearby pit. Difficult to imagine, even in those times, more miserably deprived beginnings to life.

Emma was spirited and notably beautiful and she got out. At twelve she was employed as an under-housemaid in the home of a Chester surgeon. A year or two later she found a place in London as a maidservant. At the age of sixteen she gave birth to an illegitimate child, having been abandoned in pregnancy by the young baronet who was keeping her. She subsequently fell into the hands of the Hon. Charles Greville, whose mistress she became. She loved and admired this cold-eyed young man, second son of the Earl of Warwick, and was deeply hurt when, wanting to marry money, he packed her off to Naples, into the hands of his uncle, Sir William.

She was stricken, yes—she had thought Greville returned her love. But she must have known already, must have known from her earliest years, that she was a commodity. And the move turned out lucky for her. There wouldn't have been much for her in England, once her looks had gone. In Naples, beauty and spirit again combining, she first captivated the aging ambassador, then became indispensable to him. In 1791 he made her his wife. So she got out twice—she was an escapee. (Her third

*great escape, drunk and destitute in Calais, ten years after Trafalgar, was
out of this world altogether.)*

*When Horatio's sails appeared on the horizon that September day,
he was nearly forty, she was thirty-three. For eight years she had been a
celebrated figure at the Bourbon court, intimate friend of the queen, hostess to a wealthy and glamorous international society.*

I paused on this. Thoughts of Emma excited me almost always.
She was fond of dressing up, and in my imaginings she had worn
many kinds of attire and often none at all. But I wanted that evening
to control all stirring in the loins. I was intent not on putting her
beauties together in that synthesis of touch upon touch until only the
last, the lightest touch is needed, a patient and precarious process that
I knew well. No, I was set on analysis, I wanted to isolate some element in her that might help me to understand the part she had
played in those June days.

She had become flaunting and splendid and in a way powerful,
with many favours in her gift. But to have known want and degrada-
tion, to have known yourself for a commodity—these are things that
can never be effaced. Kindness will seem like love; love will get confused with gratitude. I remembered an early letter of hers to her
benefactor, Sir William, and I got up from my desk to find it.

*My friend, my All, my Good, my kind Home in one, you are to me
eating, drinking and cloathing, my comforter in distress. Then why shall I
not love you?*

It is all there. This was what lay behind her habit of flattery, both
the practise and the appetite. The mutual assurance of being safe, being necessary, being admired. Like preening among birds that have
come to a sheltered place in the course of some perilous migration.
For full effect, it had to be reciprocal . . .

Finger on the gilt letters. *Bourbons.* Six paces, palms against the wall, thumbs mustn't touch. Miss it once and you have to start all over again with a different book. Emma's love for Greville was not reciprocated, though she thought it was. Sir William was kinder but not much different in spirit. Besides, he was drying out. The queen, she loved the queen; they wrote to each other every day, even when they were both in Naples. Emma would write to Maria Carolina in moments of exaltation, with no intention of sending the words to her. It was a form of praying. Like the words she wrote on the envelope of one of the queen's letters: *Yes, I will serve her with my heart and soul. My blood if necessary shall flow for her. Emma will prove to Maria Carolina that a humble-born Englishwoman can serve a Queen with zeal and true love, even at the risk of her life.*

There was no risk to Emma's life. She always saw herself as the heroine; Miss Lily had been right in that. But once again she believed that her love was reciprocated. She was surely mistaken in this. Maria Carolina was a member of the great Hapsburg dynasty, rulers of Austria-Hungary, allied by blood or marriage with practically all the crowned heads of Europe. She would have grown up in the art of self-preservation and the exercise of power. Monarchs rarely reciprocate devotion from commoners. They take it for their due and use it for their ends. Emma was the deputy and mouthpiece of this woman, who hated the French and all liberal sentiment, who feared the loss of her life and throne, who needed Horatio's total support in eliminating opposition in Naples, and who knew that Horatio was deeply in love with her devoted messenger.

She was there with them that day, in the cabin of the *Foudroyant*, while Horatio and the cardinal argued together, while the differences between them widened and the dislike grew. As I continued to pace back and forth, never faltering, never missing, soothed by the simple but exact repetition of gestures and steps, I could see them there, in their particular places.

Horatio walks up and down, working the stump of his arm. Such a poor remnant; it seems strange it could move at all. The cardinal sits at one end of the table; he is richly dressed and wears a black velvet skull-cap. He interrupts, he gestures. The treaty must be respected. Horatio raises his voice. He is being contradicted aboard his own ship, in his own cabin. He stops to slam his left hand down on the table. The treaty must be scrapped. Hamilton stands midway between them in close-fitting white trousers and a cutaway coat, peering down that high-bridged nose of his, softening the tones as he translates. Emma takes no direct part, but she is very much there, she is the queen's special agent. She is constantly on the move—she could never keep still for long. She listens to everything. How she hates this wily priest who wants to offer terms to the vile republicans. She is in a dress of white muslin with a fringed sash. Her hat, broad-brimmed, trimmed with red ribbons, and crowned with ostrich plumes, lies discarded on the table.

Through the great bay window of the cabin, stretching the whole width of the ship, they can see the lights of Naples and the flames and smoke of riot; they can hear the occasional crash of shots; perhaps the screams of raped or mutilated victims carry across the bay. Among the warships, the bobbing lamps of dozens of small boats, offering to sell fish to the sailors. The barges of the nobility have seen a hasty change of flag since Horatio's arrival. The tricolour of the republic has been hauled down; they fly the white standard of the Bourbons now. From these barges, through the soft summer air, come the strains of "Rule Britannia"—the fiddlers have played it so often in these two days that they know it by heart.

Emma moves constantly against the lamplight in her fever of duty and importance. That perfect molding of the brows and mouth. She passes from one side to the other, across the whole width of the window. Between the lamps of the cabin and the deepening indigo of night outside, her limbs glow through the thin stuff of the dress. With every movement, every slightest turn, the muslin touches and defines her—the beautiful shoulders, deep breasts, strong hips. The dress is high-waisted, in the fashion of the time, emphasizing the long thighs, the curve of the abdomen as it dips to the shadowed cleft below, the exquisite concavity in the small of the back, the swell of the buttocks. Back and forward, wall to wall she goes; she cannot keep still. She leans to look through the window, she waves, she has seen someone she knows on one of the gilded, high-prowed barges. Her dress at the front falls away from her body, only a little, enough to see the sway of her breasts, to know they are unconfined. She is wearing only the lightest of garments underneath. Stripped away, thrown aside easily.

We know, even in the rage that possesses us at the cardinal's obduracy, we know she is waiting. Back and forth, between the lamplight and the lights of the murderous city, waiting for us. She is entirely ours, entirely ready. When this discussion ends, as it will, in frustration and ill-temper, she will still be there for us, she will wash the cramp away in a gush of love. What greater pleasure than the sureness of love waiting? Across the window, from side to side, a promise in every movement . . . Later, when the yellow-looking Sir William has retired to his chamber, she will come to ours. She will still be in the same dress, she will kneel, she will lift it up over her head, she is wearing nothing under it. She kneels above us. She will take us in her hand, she will lower her warm mouth to us . . .

I 2

I wrote no more character sketches that evening; Emma's visit drained me. I slept better for it, however. Next day was a Friday. I spent most of it examining what information I had been able to collect as to Horatio's state of health during those Naples days. He had received a bad wound at Aboukir Bay; a piece of shrapnel had opened his forehead above the right eye, blinding him with blood, so that he thought at first the sudden darkness was a presage of death. This came after weeks of intense uncertainty and strain while he ranged the Mediterranean trying to find the pusillanimous French and bring them to battle. After the victory he suffered from headaches and nausea and had frequently the sensation of a metal belt being tightened across his chest, constricting his breathing. When he arrived at Naples, he had been continuously at sea for six months.

Could a case be made for temporary disturbance of personality, some medical condition that made him peculiarly vulnerable—to

Naples, to Emma? A blow to the forehead, almost certainly concussive, might damage the frontal lobes of the brain, disturb the judgement, loosen inhibitions . . .

I grew absorbed in this and did not ask myself until much later in the day—halfway through the afternoon—what I was really engaged in, what I was trying to do. Immediately I did so, I felt hot with shame. I had vowed to clear his name, not to seek excuses for him, not to explain everything away on spurious medical grounds.

I had forgotten about lunch and now began to feel hungry. There was not much to eat, however. I had by this time lost all system in my shopping. I could no longer be bothered to make lists. Sometimes there was too much and things went bad; sometimes there was hardly anything. Bread and cheese was all there was that afternoon, and half a Mars Bar. There was a cauliflower in the plastic box at the bottom of the fridge, but it was half liquefied; I had to throw it away. The bread needed to be thawed out in the oven. In those days I used to buy sliced loaves, several at a time, and keep them in the freezer. The cheese tasted all right, perhaps slightly stale. In any case, by this time I was feeling depressed and not in a mood to register gastronomic subtleties. Afterwards I tried to sleep under my mother's rug, but I was too tense. The same questions revolved in my mind, scraps of quotations asserted their terrible familiarity, the usual clusters of doubts and misgivings forming immediately round them like scavenger fish converging on scraps of offal cast into the sea.

To make things worse, I was beginning now to feel distinctly nervous about my forthcoming talk at the Nelson Club, due to be delivered on the evening of April 9—the day, incidentally, on which Horatio, not yet eighteen, passed his examination for lieutenant and was appointed to HMS *Lowestoffe* for service in the West Indies. I wanted my talk to be a success, to have impact, to be something people remembered and talked about afterwards, an important contribution to the understanding of Horatio's life. I intended subsequently to submit it for publication in *Mariner's World*.

At seven in the evening Miss Lily arrived, punctual to the minute as always. She was carrying a large bunch of daffodils. In the rather dim light of my hall, the trumpets of flower and the fleshy stems looked strange and savage.

"Dad put the bulbs in, years ago now," she said, with that sort of slight irrelevance, or excess of information, which was somehow typical of her, as if she were disarming some protest in advance. "We have a bit of a garden at the back, they keep coming through year after year. It doesn't matter what the weeds are like, they push up through, nothing stops them."

She paused, looking at me solemnly over the nodding heads of the flowers. Her mouth was different. Then I saw she was wearing lipstick, something I had not known her to do before—I would have noticed it sooner but for the flowers. "Nothing is stronger than a daffodil," she said. "I think they would find their way through concrete."

"Your father is keen on gardening, then?" I was constrained to keep on with the conversation, not knowing how to greet these clamorous intruders, afraid of a pause in which I would have to make some response. A distant memory of some similar gift tugged at my mind, a memory of helplessness and dismay.

"Dad died eight years ago—that's what I am getting at. He died eight years ago and he put the bulbs in, I don't know, maybe nine or ten years before he died. That's seventeen years or so these daffs have been coming out, and they've spread, they're all over the place now. No, we live with my mum. Or she lives with us, rather—it's my house."

I had noticed the *we* and wondered, not for the first time, if Miss Lily shared her bed with someone. Was there someone who watched her move about, back and forth, with that absolute trust in her love?

She wore no ring, but that meant nothing. "Well," I said, "it is really very kind of you."

"I thought they might brighten the place up a bit. You know, now that the weather is better." While I was still puzzling over this, she said, "I'll just go and get something to put them in."

Barely pausing to deposit her computer, still in its case, against the wall, asking for no directions, she went rapidly down the passage and turned without hesitation into the kitchen, where to the best of my knowledge she had never set foot before. I was left standing there in the hall, in the narrow space between the door and the tall oriental jar I used for my umbrella.

I felt I should join her in the kitchen but hesitated. It seemed a risky thing to me. Too intimate, searching together in that small space for something to put the flowers in. More to the point, I thought, to look for something to put Miss Lily in; it was she that needed containing, far more than the daffodils. I still could not quite believe she had gone marching in like that. There was, however, in spite of my incredulity, a strange feeling of peace at the idea of being in the kitchen with her. I remained where I was—not for long, perhaps a minute or two. The silence seemed intense. I was aware of the small complex of cracks in the wall above the door, like a delta, and the shiny black handle of my umbrella, leaning out of the jar. I began to make my way down the passage. Faint sounds of movement came from the kitchen. I made no sound at all as I approached. I was wearing slippers, but this was an accidental circumstance—I had no intention of creeping up on her. At the doorway I stopped short. Miss Lily had taken one of the kitchen chairs and was standing on it with her back to me, reaching up into one of the overhead cupboards. She did not know I was there. Her black skirt ended some way above the knee, and as she reached into the cupboard the hem rose an inch or two. I saw that her legs, though sturdy, were well shaped, even beautiful, full at the calf and narrow at the ankle; also that she had on black tights decorated with a sort of diamond pattern; also that she had no shoes on, she had slipped them off before climbing onto the chair, but for the thin integument of the tights she was barefoot.

I did not stay there longer than the time needed to register these impressions. I retreated to the sitting room and waited there, near the open door, so I would know when she passed. She saw me as she came down the passage, stopped at the threshold for a moment, then came through. She had the flowers in a green glass vase with fluted edges, which I knew from my childhood days when my mother used to put flowers in it. It had not been used for a long time—I would not have remembered where it was.

"I had to stand on a chair," Miss Lily said. She was smiling with pleasure as she bore the daffodils before her, holding the vase chest-high. She moved about the room with complete assurance, not as if it were strange to her at all. She set the vase down on a small round table in one corner. "There," she said. "They look nice there, don't they?"

All this had taken up some time. "They do, yes," I said. "Shall we go along to the study and sort of get started?" There might have been some edge to my voice, I don't know. I had felt a sudden impatience at this dalliance.

Miss Lily looked at me more closely. "You are very pale," she said. "You don't look well to me. You should try and get out more."

"Get out more?" I said. "I've been in Naples all day."

She did not smile much at this. "There is such a thing as too much studying," she said as we made our way towards the study. She looked round at me and nodded seriously. "A bit of fresh air and a good brisk walk never did anybody any harm." She sounded as if she might at any moment thrust a cap on my head and wrap me in a scarf and send me out for a turn round the block. It was really too much.

I am not a child, I felt like saying. *Secretarial services are what I need.* But of course that would have hurt her—I did not want to hurt Miss Lily.

And so, a good quarter of an hour late, we began the evening's work. As I have said, I was getting nervous about my talk. I had decided to set my book aside for the time being so as to prepare the talk well in advance. I hate being hurried—it always results in the neglect of something essential—and it was a relief, in a way, to suspend work on the book, postpone the problems of Naples. I had already written a first draft in pencil and corrected this in black ink, my invariable procedure: pencil, correct in black, dictate, typescript, correct in red, dictate. Already, even at this early stage, my pages were a mass of alterations and insertions. I was eager to dictate it all to Miss Lily so that I could then start revising on the typescript. Type gives us a whole new experience of the text, refreshing the eye, stimulating the critical faculty. Those who don't first labour in longhand never get this boost.

I intended to base my talk upon two episodes in the early life of Horatio, absolutely crucial, in my view, to his development as a hero, as *the* English hero, *no slightest admixture of the Celt there, he came from generations of Norfolk yeomen.* These episodes took place in 1771 and 1775, respectively. The earlier one concerned the first days of his naval career, when he joined the *Raisonnable*, a sixty-four-gun ship taken from the French twelve years before and captained now by his uncle, Sir Maurice Suckling. Wanting to render this episode as vividly as possible, I had decided to recast parts of it in the present tense. I began my dictation as soon as Miss Lily was ready.

"It is March 1771. His father, the Reverend Edmund, has accompanied him from Norfolk to London, to the inn from which the coaches leave for Chatham. There, in the yard of the inn, father and son say good-bye, with sage advice on one side and earnest promises on the other. Now the boy is quite alone. He is twelve years old, small for his age, delicate in appearance.

"The coach goes jolting along—it is a six-hour journey to Chatham, time enough to ponder the future. Perhaps he wonders if he has after all made a mistake. But to admit the possibility of mistake was not much in his nature, nor is it in the nature of heroes generally. They know they have been singled out; in the furnace of their destiny, mistakes are either consumed or transmuted to the intentions of providence.

"When he arrives at Chatham, he asks people at the staging inn for directions, but no-one has so much as heard of the ship. Carrying his baggage, he makes his way down cobbled streets to the docks . . ."

By a coincidence that to my mind far transcended chance, the *Victory* was also lying in the Medway at this time. In seeking his first ship Horatio passed close to his last, his death-ship, which had been commissioned in the year of his birth. I was tempted to include mention of this pattern of timings, in which I too, as his parallel walker, was involved. But I decided against—it could not be done briefly; it would have disturbed the balance.

"Still lugging his valise, he asks passing sailors if they know where the *Raisonnable* lies. One of them points. The boy strains his eyes. Across the grey, wind-scourged water of the Medway, he makes out the ship lying at her moorings. But now comes the real problem: how can he get to her? There are no boats. The ship is too far away for him to attract the attention of anyone on board. For a time that seems endless he waits there in the icy wind, completely helpless and forlorn."

At this point, as I was dictating my text to Miss Lily, there came to me a sensation not altogether unfamiliar but more pronounced that evening than ever before: my voice, the quality and sound of it, had become more present to my mind than the words it was saying, the meaning it was seeking to convey. From being a strand of sound edged with silence, it was filling the whole room, there were no borders to it; it was not my voice at all but someone else's, someone whose borders of silence lay elsewhere. I saw Miss Lily's hands pause, move away from the keys, and come to rest at either side of the keyboard. I looked at her hands—this was an evening for noticing things about Miss Lily. Strong hands but not ill shaped. Like the rest of her. I came back to myself at the sight of them, and in the momentary blankness of this return I felt a sudden rush of pity for Horatio and myself and all the lost children. But pity for him was wrong; I had never felt it before, he was not to be pitied. In that lonely moment, under that hostile sky, the steel of resolution had entered the child's heart. It was an essential moment in the heroic career. Miss Lily had not looked up. With a sense of having got away undetected, I resumed my dictating.

"Finally a passing officer takes pity on him and arranges for a boat to carry him across the river. For the first of many times, he climbs aboard a warship. Step by step, as he climbs the companion-ladder, he is entering a new world. He is a child—it is natural that a sort of dread should descend on him, he does not know what will be required. However, the captain is his uncle, after all. Uncle Maurice will guide and advise him.

"But Uncle Maurice is not on board; he is not expected for some days. No-one has heard of the new midshipman, no-one shows the slightest interest in him. He waits for someone to take notice of him, tell him where he should go, what he should do. Eventually he is told to carry his luggage down the two steep ladders that lead to the midshipmen's berth on the orlop deck. Here all seems chaos and confusion to him. It is dark down here, below the water line. The beams are low, and there is a smell of tar and damp rope. Someone shows him how to sling a hammock, how to stow away his things.

"For the rest of that day and all the next he walks the deck. The weather could hardly be worse—'fresh gales with squally weather and snow,' according to the ship's log. No-one pays any attention to him. He walks about on the tilting deck, he looks across the choppy waters towards where London lies, and beyond that, Norfolk.

"Then at last, to much ceremony of saluting and a great shrilling of bosuns' whistles, Captain Suckling comes on board. With his appearance everything changes, the ship takes on life and purpose. He summons his nephew aft to the great cabin. This is on the upper deck, where only the captain can have his quarters. The tallest man can walk upright here, and it is flooded with light. The wide bow windows occupy the whole width of the ship, beautifully framed in scrolled wood, elegantly curving, giving broad views across the river. From the dark, cramped, malodorous place where he has been peering and creeping below, the boy mounts into space and light . . ."

I paused here, and Miss Lily paused with me, and for some while there was silence. I was not yet satisfied with this passage. I wanted to convey the contrast somehow more vividly, as vividly as it was present to my own mind. For in this contrast lay the whole meaning. The chintz and mahogany of that beautifully appointed cabin, furnished in masculine style but with great elegance, the great swaths of light, the order and the calm. The strangely different uncle, metamorphosed from the country squire the boy knew, resplendent in his blue, gold-trimmed uniform. Uncle Maurice was transfigured, he was a god, he had come aboard and breathed life, he lived up here in the pure ether. As the diminutive Horatio listened to his uncle explaining the workings of the ship, he understood the meaning of power and godhead. It was the first lesson of his naval career and one he never forgot.

I was about to resume when Miss Lily spoke, breaking the silence. "That was really interesting, if you don't mind me saying so. I could just see that poor lonely boy, walking about in the chilly wind, not having the least notion what to do with himself. My brother used to live near Gravesend, it can get bitter down there. I hope he had a good coat on."

Her imagination, as usual, had been stirred by the drama of weather. But had she got the essential point, I wondered, the being summoned into light, that crucial early experience of the privilege that went with command? It irked me that she should seem so sorry for him—it reminded me of my own earlier moment of weakness.

"They took hardship better in those days," I said. "They were tougher, more enduring. They didn't expect to be cossetted, as people do now. There was no Granny State to shelter them from the cradle to the grave."

"Cradle to the grave? You been on the South Bank lately, round Waterloo Bridge? You won't see much of Granny there, unless it is her that gives them the cardboard boxes. Anyway, I wouldn't have liked it, I do know that." She grimaced in saying this and wrinkled her nose, a sign of serious emphasis. I didn't know if she meant the period as a whole or just Horatio's experience. "Why didn't he just go and find some corner where he could sit down?" she said. "Somewhere out of the wind?"

"He didn't want to appear idle. Character was character in those days."

"I can't see the point of suffering for nothing. If he had kept out of the wind, I would have thought more of him. They cut pieces off him, didn't they?"

"Well, the surgeons had to take off his arm after the failure of the attack on Tenerife, and then there was the eye, but that—"

"I don't mean pieces of his body, I mean pieces of himself as a person."

"I don't understand what you are getting at."

"He was an orphan, wasn't he? His mother died when he was nine, and he was only twelve when he went away to sea. After they parted that day in London, his father never knew him again as a child—it was years before they met again, he was grown up by then. You can't take a boy away from home and the world he has grown up in without him losing some bits of himself. I don't know whether you'd call it cutting pieces off or just sort of putting him in a narrow place where he couldn't grow."

Miss Lily paused. I saw the rise and fall of her breathing. She was impassioned. "He was hemmed in, that's all I am saying," she said.

Avon Secretarial Services, from Camden, were remarking on the narrowness of Horatio Nelson's life. It was so absurd that I could not feel angry. In fact, I think I smiled. "A narrow place, was it? Horatio served five months as a midshipman on the *Raisonnable*, then he sailed as captain's servant on a West Indiaman bound for the Caribbean archipelago. He went from Florida and Yucatán to Venezuela, then to the Bahamas and the Antilles Islands. He saw birds of paradise and coral snakes and armadillos. He saw forests of palm. When he returned, still only fourteen, he piloted a longboat on the Thames, transporting stores from the Pool to the Delta, learning to deal with crosscurrents and shoals. In the following year he took part in an expedition to the Arctic, where he saw polar bears and fields of ice and the sun at midnight. Then he joined HMS *Seahorse* and went to the East Indies with her, from Bengal to Bushire. And he was still only sixteen. Would you really call that a hemmed-in life, Miss Lily?"

I had become excited in my turn, stirred as always by these gorgeous travels. "If he was hemmed in, what are we?"

"What was it you called me?" Miss Lily was smiling slightly but looked at the same time rather perplexed. I realized then that I had made a slip.

"I'm sorry," I said. "That's what I call you when I think about you. It just came out."

"When you think about me?"

"You know, when you need to think about someone or something, you generally give it a name. Might be Socrates or dialectical materialism or Manchester United. Your name in my mind was always Miss Lily." As I was saying this, I realized in a confused kind of way why I wanted her to see what a wonderful person Horatio was, how marvellous his life had been. He and I were so close, she could not admire Horatio without admiring me.

Miss Lily's expression changed; her smile faded. I had the impression that my confusion of feeling was reflected in her eyes, which continued to look steadily at me. Not experienced on her part, simply reflected. "Well," she said, "I'm not going to call you Mr. Charles."

"Charles will do."

My face felt hot. I could not remember when I had last invited anyone to call me by my first name. It was Miss Lily who brought things back to order. "What he didn't have was a normal life, that's all I am saying," she said. "By the way, I meant to ask you, what is a midshipman exactly?"

I was aware that this was a sort of diversion, but I was grateful for it. I explained that midshipmen were junior ratings, mainly intending to be officers, that they lived together in the cramped and crowded quarters of the orlop, that they were of all ages from children of ten or eleven to full-grown men, the raw material of the officer class.

Miss Lily listened carefully enough, but her comments, when they came, only served to prove how tenacious she was in argument. "That's exactly what I was getting at," she said. "I didn't mean narrow in the physical sense. I meant emotional. He was narrowed down in his emotions. Stands to reason, really, doesn't it? If you are pushed out too soon, certain kinds of feelings aren't much use to you anymore, so they sort of get lost. Must have been the same with all those boys, those that went to the midshipman—it just isn't normal."

"That's how the navy got its officers—the ship was the school. That was the system and it worked—it gave us Camperdown and the Battle of the Saints and the Glorious First of June. Above all, it gave us Trafalgar, it gave us supremacy at sea into the twentieth century."

"Be that as it may," Miss Lily said, "I can't help thinking it sort of blunted them. I am glad my Bobby doesn't need to go through it."

"Your Bobby?"

"That's my little boy. He is just twelve. The same age Nelson was when he went to sea."

"I didn't know you had a child."

Miss Lily glanced away as if momentarily distracted. "It didn't come up before."

I was quite staggered by this news, which was somehow completely unexpected. "You must have been very young when you had him."

"I brought him up myself," she said, as if this fully solved the question of youth. "Me and Mum. His father pushed off at an early stage, which was just as well, in my opinion—and I even thought so at the time. I was wondering—Bobby is ever so interested in ships and battles. He has been doing a project on Nelson at school. When I told him, you know, that we are going to Portsmouth to see the *Victory*, I could tell he really wanted to go. He didn't say much, but I could tell. It would be so good for him to have a man to show him round . . ."

And so it was decided. Still in a state of mild shock at the news of Bobby's existence, I agreed on a date for the Portsmouth trip. We would go—the three of us—on the first Sunday after my talk.

13

During those years my Aprils always began with a battle, third in that great quartet of his victories I enacted on my table: April 2, 1801, the Battle of Copenhagen, last of his triumphs before Trafalgar. He had been appointed second-in-command of the Channel Fleet at the beginning of the year, with the rank of vice-admiral. Tempting to think there was some motive of humanity on the part of the lords of the Admiralty in this appointment, which cut short the misery of his marital break-up, allowing him to escape—without seeming to be running away—from the public scandal of his affair with Emma and the cruel caricatures by now so frequently appearing in the London papers, where the trio were depicted together, Sir William the desiccated connoisseur, surveying the world through his lorgnette, Emma fat and billowing and given to dramatic attitudes, Horatio grizzled and thin, with one eye and one arm missing. *Travel-*

ling players . . . He was grotesque, Horatio was grotesque in that company. I accepted it, I had accepted it for years, it had never made any difference between us; I set it down to his angelic disorder on land. What else would an angel seem, out of his element, portrayed by mediocre men, but grotesque?

A great relief it must have been to escape from these devastating lampoons. But there was reason enough in the appointment without looking for kindness in it. England by now was fighting for her life, for her very existence. With Napoleon's defeat of the Austrians at Marengo, the anti-French alliance had collapsed; we stood quite alone, with a great fleet preparing against us in the Baltic ports and a new army of invasion gathering across the Channel. Not until 1941 was this country again to be in such danger.

Once more he comes to the rescue, so slight, so maimed—what an overwhelming debt he has laid on us! At the beginning of February, he learns that he will be sailing for the Baltic in an operation designed to discourage the Scandinavian states from allying themselves with France and Russia and closing their ports to English shipping. These are not traditional enemies, but the crazed Czar Paul, shortly to be assassinated, is besotted with Napoleon and has leagued Russia with him. And he, the scoundrelly Corsican, diabolical bogeyman to generations of our ancestors in infancy, has come to a logical conclusion—the cursed French, they are never short of logic. England rules the seas, yes, well then, we will make the seas useless to her, we will close the Baltic ports to her trade. Grain and timber: without the one she cannot feed her people, without the other she cannot build masts for her ships.

Our first move is to threaten the Danes. Perhaps a show of force will be enough. The commander-in-chief, Admiral Sir Hyde Parker, who has played safe all his life, is a good enough man for that; but they have Horatio as second-in-command, knowing—as everyone in the service knows—that where he goes, victory goes with him. A fortunate appointment, because the show of force is not enough; the Danes reject our terms, they are set on resistance, they prepare to defend their city.

I had to start quite early in the morning. The first shots were not fired until shortly after 10 A.M., but the signal was given at 9:30 and there was a long approach before that. The battle in any case took quite a while to lay out, because it involved the Danish land defences. I was slower even than usual that morning because I had laid awake most of the night, then fallen asleep at about 5:00. The alarm went off as usual, but I could not come to the surface; I lay between sleeping and waking till after 8:00, then panicked at the idea of being late for the battle and went down to the basement carrying my coffee with me. I did not even stop to heat the milk.

I had everything I needed. I had modelled the Danish shoreline years before in compressed paper, exactly to scale—the inlet into the harbour of Copenhagen, the headland with the formidable Trekroner battery defending the approaches. I had the shore guns too, small-scale models made in lead, which I had bought at Wrights in Holborn. The shape of the Middle Ground I had first traced and then cut out of thick cardboard, which I had left its natural sand colour.

It is this tapering lozenge of sand-coloured cardboard, this Middle Ground, that constitutes the main difficulty for the attackers. I take care to place it in exact position. It lies here, sharp end to the south, between the Danish shore batteries and the Swedish coastline, dividing the strait into two channels, the western or inner one narrower and shallower, heavily defended by the floating batteries, which I put in place now to the south of the city. Here they are, one after the other, moored broadside on. Formidable obstacles to any approach from the south. However, to approach by the outer, more easily navigable channel means bringing the English ships under devastating fire from the guns of the Trekroner fortress guarding the harbour.

Horatio is all on fire to attack; his superior hesitates, prevaricates— he will not risk the heavier ships in those shallow waters. Once again that classic combination of prudent principal and risk-taking second; only at Horatio's last battle will this conflict be resolved and all power rest in the hands of the risk-taker. But he has more on his mind now than impatience with Sir Hyde Parker. He has received word from London that Emma has been delivered of a baby daughter, whom she will call Horatia. He is a father for the first time and wild with joy. Also, and at the same time, he is tormented by jealousy. The Prince of Wales has ogled Emma at a reception, and Horatio fears she may fall prey to the wiles of this practised lecher. He even suspects Sir William, his devoted friend, of acting the pander out of deference to royalty.

Sir Hyde Parker continues irresolute. He summons one conference after another. He cannot decide whether to fight or not. Horatio sums up his feelings in a letter home: *If a man considers whether he is to fight, when he has the power in his own hands, it is certain that his opinion is against fighting . . .*

Finally he has his way: they will attack from the south, approaching by the narrower channel, avoiding the Trekroner guns. He shifts his flag into the shallower-draft *Elephant* and takes command of about half the fleet: twelve sail of the line with shallow draft, a squadron of frigates, some bomb ketches and fireships. He will make a direct attack on the city. Hyde Parker remains with his heavy ships here, six miles to the north, eighteen inches on my table.

The wind turns fair, veers to the south. On this day 196 years ago, at just this time in the morning, the first signal flew from the *Elephant*'s halyards: weigh anchor and make sail. With this order, the action begins. The English ships under topsails move majestically into the attack. I place them in their order of sail, the *Edgar* leading. The plan is simple: they will pass down the enemy line, concentrating their fire, battering the moored gunships into silence one by one.

The opening phase is disastrous. The *Agamemnon*, which should have followed the *Edgar*, fails to do so; she cannot weather the shoals. Here she is at the entrance to the channel, signalling her inability to proceed. Then the *Bellona* goes aground on the east side of the Middle Ground. The *Russell*, mistakenly following her in the smoke of battle, suffers the same fate. I place them together here, one just south of the other, almost touching. Horatio's twelve ships are reduced to nine. However, he keeps the signal to advance flying, the remaining ships take up position, the action becomes general. It is a static, murderous battle now, with great slaughter on both sides, a series of thunderous, half-blind duels at cable-length range. On the main deck of the *Monarch*, immediately ahead of Horatio, not a man is left standing the whole length of the ship. Our gun crews, as always, are superbly trained and disciplined, but the ships are on the light side because of the shoals, and the Danish floating batteries are strongly built, low-lying; some of their guns are forty-four-pounders, heavier than anything on our side. A thousand dead and wounded on the English side in the first three hours of fighting.

My *Monarch* rested on her glinting artificial sea, with no sound, no motion other than what I gave her. As far from the bloody pandemonium of those decks as my body was from risk of wounds . . .

Just at this moment, in the midst of these thoughts, I had a terrible sensation of having been wounded myself, somewhere low in the leg or in the foot. There was no pain, but I could feel the wetness of the blood. For a moment I braced myself for the pain to come. But the wetness was cold, too cold for blood. When I looked down, I saw that I was standing with one slippered foot in water, the other just out of it. A stream about two feet wide was running from under the door.

I was forced to abandon Horatio in the midst of the battle, the issue still in doubt, something I had never done before. The water was flowing in a shallow stream down the basement passage, fortunately not spreading much, as the floor slanted slightly towards the skirting board. It was coming from above, shining and murmuring in a sort of ecstasy as it dropped down the stairs. When I went up, I found the kitchen floor completely submerged; water was brimming over the sink and splashing down. In my sleepy haste I had left the cold tap running, and somehow the sink had got clogged.

Slippers and socks and trouser bottoms were now completely soaked. I splodged my way to the sink, turned off the tap, scrabbled to clear the paste of bread crumbs and coffee grounds from the plughole. A bucket and mop were the only answer. For some nightmarish moments I waded here and there, trying to remember where Mrs. Watson kept them. I found them in the cupboard adjoining the pantry. Then I began swabbing—a task that was to take up all my afternoon and most of my evening.

Mop and squeeze, mop and squeeze. I was still in the kitchen at 1 P.M., when Sir Hyde Parker began to grow alarmed—or rather, when the state of alarm he had been in from the beginning began to intensify—and sent his historic signal of recall. Quite understandable, in a way. From six miles off he couldn't see much—a thick pall of smoke lay over the battle. He could hear the thunder of the guns, apparently unabated. He could make out the distress signals flying from the grounded ships. He was an old man, and he subscribed to the old maxims, one of which said that ships could not stand and fight against fortifications. In his heart, he did not believe Horatio could carry the day. So he sent signal number 39, the signal of recall.

At this historic moment, one of the highlights of Horatio's career, I was still miserably mopping and squeezing. I hadn't even got as far as the basement stairs. My feet were soaked. Nevertheless, on this day of his triumph I fixed my mind on him, I gave him his due of homage. He sees the signal, of course. What is his first reaction? He asks if his own signal is still in place, his favourite, the signal for close action. He is told that it is. *Mind you keep it so.* Then he turns to Captain Foley at his side—Foley, superb seaman and pilot, his battle companion at the Nile. *You know, Foley, I have only one eye—I have a right to be blind sometimes.* He puts the telescope to his blind eye. *I really do not see the signal!*

This is the moment when legend is born. The path of the hero cannot be smooth; he must show disregard for all restraints of prudence, he must not stop short; he must always struggle to thrust aside impediment, to break through into pure freedom, absolute success. Those around him on board the ship never forgot this moment: the lieutenant who brought him the news of the signal; Foley, to whom the words were said; Colonel Stewart, the commander of marines, who recorded them for posterity. And so they have come to generation after generation of British schoolchildren, as they came to me. The quintessential act of heroic insubordination, the ultimate rejection of half-measures. And he, the hero—he understood completely the value of that gesture, the moment when acting the part and realizing the self meet and blend together. And to use his infirmity to reinforce his strength! *I really do not see the signal.* Wonderful, wonderful. At 1:40 P.M., when these words were uttered, I stood with mop suspended, quite still there in the kitchen, observing a minute's silence.

However, fear somehow entered this silence, or foreboding rather, making it difficult to sustain: I had not been properly present in these moments of his triumph, I had failed in my role of witness and shadow. There would be a price to pay. Again that yearning for freedom came to me. I thought then it was *his* freedom I wanted—all fear conquered. Someday, and perhaps soon, I would prove worthy of him. I vowed it as I stood there. But then I began to worry about my wet feet; I was afraid I might catch cold and be unable to deliver my talk, only a week away now. The kitchen floor was still wet but no longer awash. I went to my bedroom and changed my socks. I had no idea which of my shoes might be waterproof or whether any of them were, but I put on the stoutest I had. Then I went back to my mopping.

It was nearly eight in the evening before I got things back in some sort of order, and by that time I was tired out. In my anxiety to deal with the flood I had neglected to eat. The Italian takeaway on Haverstock Hill had a delivery service, and I phoned them and ordered a pizza margherita, which came very promptly—it took twenty-two minutes from the phone call to the ring at the door. I had some claret with it. Sitting in my study afterwards, I felt reasonably at peace—to begin with, at least.

I was thinking about the battle as it had developed after Horatio's inspired disobedience. The firing had begun to slacken off after an hour or so. By about four in the afternoon, most of the Danish gunships were smoking wrecks. Their dead and wounded amounted to more than two thousand. But they still had not capitulated, still maintained a sporadic fire on our ships. It was then that Horatio showed the other essential side of the untrammelled angel; to courage and panache is added the ruthless will to victory. He sent for writing materials. Spreading the paper on the wooden casing over the rudder head, he wrote a message to Crown Prince Frederick. He would spare the Danes if they no longer resisted, but if resistance were continued, he would be obliged to set on fire all the floating batteries he had taken, *without having the power to save the men who had defended them.*

And he would have done it! He would have sent his fireships in among the defenceless hulks and burned the whole line, men and ships together. And if this had not been enough to bring them to a cease-fire, he would have pounded into ruins the beautiful city of Copenhagen, whose steep-pitched roofs and copper-green spires were clearly visible to him.

The Danes knew it was no bluff; their remaining guns fell silent. After a week of negotiations, an armistice was signed; Denmark was detached from her alliance with Russia. By an irony of history, one of those parallel courses I always found so fascinating, none of all this was necessary; none of those thousands of dead and maimed need have received a scratch. Unknown to either Danes or English at the time, an event had taken place that made the bloodshed and the bargaining equally superfluous. A week before the battle, a group of Russian officers who had dined rather too well made their way to the Mikhailovsky Palace and strangled the lunatic Czar Paul, choking the life out of the Scandinavian alliance at the same time.

But this, in a sense, was beside the point. Horatio would have done it—he would have burned Copenhagen to the ground if necessary. There was only one portrait of him I had seen which reflected this capacity for extreme measures, that painted by Heinrich Füger, court painter of Austria. Both Emma and Horatio sat to him in his Vienna studio in the course of their return from Naples to England in 1800. By training he was a miniaturist, but failing eyesight had obliged him to take up the larger scale.

I felt an urge to look at this portrait again. The only form in which I had it was as a colour plate in the *Nelson Companion*. I found the book on the shelf and took it over to my table. This was covered with papers—notes about Horatio in Naples in 1799, discarded sheets from my forthcoming talk at the club. I pushed them aside, feeling distaste at these reminders of my labours. I felt again that longing for freedom, for the removal of my doubts. To be his chronicler was not enough, it never had been . . .

I found the portrait, brought the arm of the lamp closer down to it. He is in full-dress uniform and encrusted with silver and gold: gold collar, gold facings and epaulettes, the silver rays and gold suns of his three orders—the Bath, St. Ferdinand, the Turkish Crescent—pinned to his breast on the left side, with the three gold discs of his naval medals one below the other down his front.

I stared at his face, under the strong light. Füger had caught something no other artist had, perhaps because of his training as a miniaturist, a technique that requires close observation. Not caught, *detected:* there was a ruthlessness here, a capacity for intense concentration. But it was a borrowed face, it was not his . . . Eyes a greenish brown, an expression cold, pitiless, but not as though native to him—it was induced, laid on his face. The cruelty was something he was bleakly resigned to, as he was resigned to his role. Not the travelling player now. This was Horatio in the part of killer.

Always a mistake to look at anything too long. Already in childhood I knew this. In the days of my illness it was a kind of frightening game. Any object can become dangerous when detached by the violence of the eyes from everything else in the world. A pencil, an elastic, a light switch. And how much more the pictured human face—and his, of all faces! I looked too long at this face of a necessary killer and I felt my being dissolved in his stronger one, I felt the terror of this necessity, there was a darkness at the edges of my vision. I raised my hand to my face, but I could feel nothing that made this face my own. I shut my eyes and clutched at the front of my jacket and felt the rough tweed and knew it was mine. I closed the book without glancing again at the picture. I stood there at the table for a time that seemed short but may not have been, striving to keep my eyes unfocused. By degrees I came to myself again, a self that was clammy: I had been sweating all over my body, and the sweat was cold.

14

s I have said, Miss Lily had broken through into a zone of immunity; she had crossed the line. I still felt hostility when she spoke against Horatio, but there had been no impulses of violence after that first. She had changed too in these few months. She had taken to reading about him, she argued, she stayed on longer than the two hours without charging me extra. Her hair was longer, and she wore it in a softer style, with a fringe over the forehead. Now that the weather was milder, she had lost that shiny look and her skin seemed paler. I looked forward now to the evenings when she came. I even looked forward to getting her view of things, limited as this invariably was. By that time I had begun to neglect my appearance rather, but on Tuesdays and Fridays, knowing she was coming in the evening, I made a point of washing and shaving and cleaning my nails.

However, she seriously annoyed me that Friday evening, two days after Copenhagen, by what she said about his conduct during the battle. Where she had got it from I don't know. I had been repeating the story of how he clapped the telescope to his blind eye. One of the great moments in our island story. The impulse, the improvisation—

"Well," she said, "there are them that say the importance of this incident has been very much exaggerated."

"Exaggerated? How can it be exaggerated?" She sounded as if she had lifted the words straight from some book; they were not like her words at all.

"There is reason to believe that this Parker had a private understanding with Nelson that if he hoisted the signal at a certain point, it was to be considered optional."

"Are you saying it was all arranged in advance?"

"I am not saying anything, I am just remarking."

"And Foley and the others?"

"They were all in the know."

By this time I had begun to experience the usual symptoms of rage: a sense of impaired vision, a feeling that the skin of my face was too tight. But the unusual and surprising thing was that I did not try to hide this from Miss Lily, did not turn away or make any diversionary gesture. That evening, with Miss Lily, I broke my lifelong habit of concealment.

"And the telescope?" I said. "That putting the telescope to his blind eye? Just playing to the gallery, according to you."

I saw her eyes widen, become somehow more alert, more watchful. But she went on looking at me steadily enough.

"It's not according to me. That is what they say about it—that he knew beforehand."

Whatever blood had been left in my face must have drained away at this. "What they say? *What they say?* How can you repeat such lies? Do you realize what you are doing? You are adding to the slanders about him, you are joining the ranks . . ."

I had to pause to control my voice. My vision was narrowed to her face, the dark hair over the brows, the soft, undefended-looking, obstinate eyes, the wide mouth with its sharp corners.

"You are joining in the conspiracy against him," I said, too loudly for that small room. "Two hundred years it's been going on. It's the same people that talk about his conduct in Naples in 1799, trying to make out that he committed a fraud there."

"What people are those?"

Her tone had not changed; she was still looking closely at me. This steadiness had a chastening effect; my voice was more under control when I answered. "Those who cannot bear to think that anyone so great could ever have existed, who always have to undermine him, to take the lowest view of everything he did. This man who saved our country from the vile French, who had a lion's heart inside his frail body . . ."

Uttering this praise of him, my voice broke a little. I turned away from Miss Lily and began to shuffle with the papers on my table, but stopped almost at once because my hands were trembling.

There was silence for some moments. Then she said, "You only say the French are vile because you know he didn't like them. I know it means a lot to you, Charles, and it's a very good thing to have a hobby, but he was only a man, that's all I'm saying. Don't take offence, but I think myself that you are too wrapped up in him. As far as I can see, nobody knows the truth of that telescope business and nobody ever will. You can think one thing or another. I mean to say, there are lots of things like that, aren't there? I know it isn't my place to say it, but you really need a bit more variety in your life."

Variety, when I had his life to look at!

"I know we are going out on Sunday," she said. "But it is still Nelson, isn't it?"

When I turned back towards her, I found her eyes fixed on me with a serious and quite unmistakable solicitude. That she was in her own way concerned about me I had sometimes felt before. Misguided, of course; I was managing well enough. But I understood now for the first time that the way she expressed this concern was by undermining Horatio. She wanted me to think less of him, but this did not put her among the ranks of his slanderers, because she did it for my sake. In this brief moment of humility I saw—glimpsed, rather— how much less selfish Miss Lily was than I, who had wanted her to admire Horatio, not for her sake but my own, so I could share the glory with him, bask in the same sunshine.

The mood, as I say, did not last long, but a certain obscure prospect of change had come with it, and the last of my anger was cleared away. And then I broke my second rule—I told a story detrimental to myself. I told her of my frantic mopping while Horatio thundered at the gates of Copenhagen, and she laughed. I laughed too—I remember that I laughed too.

She was not much interested in his battles, not even Trafalgar. She seemed to see no more in them than a perverse expenditure of human life; all the courage and patriotism and fighting spirit counted for nothing, or she turned it into a cause for pity. As I say, her view was limited. She hadn't much in the way of idealism. But she took a great interest in Horatio's private life and particularly in his relationship with Emma Hamilton, whom most of the time she didn't really care for.

"That woman," she said, "she played on his jealousy. She didn't care that he was about to risk the lives of all those men."

I could not help smiling at this. I had been telling her about Horatio's state of mind on the eve of Copenhagen, that strange mixture of feelings: impatience for battle, joy of fatherhood, torments of jealousy. "The risk to his men's lives was not the foremost consideration," I said.

"If it wasn't, it should have been. What was there in it for them?"

"Horatio didn't ask them to take any risk he wasn't prepared to take himself."

"We have had this conversation before. He shared the risks, I don't say he didn't. But he didn't share the rewards. If he lived, he got richer and more famous. If they lived, they stayed the same."

I felt my smile wearing thin. It was always the same problem with her; she simplified the issues to such an absurd degree that there was no way of explaining anything to her.

"You can't say there is not a difference there," she said. "Anyway, she exploited his love, this woman he thought such an honour to her sex."

How did she know about it? We hadn't got to that point yet in my book. A question not worth asking—I knew by now that my book was no longer her sole source of information.

"I've been reading their correspondence," she said, as if after all I had asked. "They go to a reception in London, the three of them, the Hamiltons and him. The Prince of Wales is there, he sees her and he fancies her—he always liked them on the large side. So he makes eyes at her. Nelson notices this, and afterwards he takes it up with her. She tells him there is nothing in it—she can't help it if the Prince likes the look of her, but that's as far as it goes."

Her face was settling already into the expression, dogged and ex-alted at the same time, that it always wore when she was giving vent to feelings of disapproval.

"Strange to think," I said, "that William Pitt the Younger was also there, together with most of his cabinet. Horatio came face-to-face with him that same evening."

This was an attempt to sidetrack Miss Lily, but of course it failed, because she had no idea of the significance this meeting had in my mind; she did not know the story of the chess game and the two figures side by side in my father's book. It came to me now, with the force of some exciting, illicit impulse, that I could actually tell Miss Lily this story, as I had once told it to Penhas; I could try to explain how important it had been to me, that wound I had received in the moment of victory, the choice between the statesman and the sailor, the early lesson in concealment. I hesitated; the moment passed. But temptation once admitted leaves us never quite the same; I was to remember that urge to confide in her and how it came to me like something sinful. For the moment, I contented myself with a statement of fact: "It wasn't a reception exactly. It was a very grand dinner party at the house of Alexander Davison, in St. James's Square."

"Who was he?"

"He was Horatio's prize agent."

"What is a prize agent?"

"That is the man who managed the prize money falling due to the people who fought in a battle. Some of the enemy ships taken might be carrying valuable cargoes. Occasionally they might be carrying hugely valuable cargoes. There was a system of prizes. The total value was divided in strict proportion. The commander of the ship got one quarter, the lieutenants got one eighth, and so on."

"So they just sort of shared out the booty?"

"You could put it like that, I suppose."

"How much did the men get, the ordinary seamen?"

"It depended on how many there were. There was always one quarter left after all the rest had been shared out."

"Sounds like blood money to me."

"Horatio didn't fight for money. He fought for his country."

"Be that as it may, it wouldn't have come amiss on top of his pay, that's all I am saying. Anyway, where the party took place is neither here nor there. The Prince of Wales takes a fancy to her and she makes sure her lover knows it. As soon as he goes to sea again, she starts tormenting him. The Prince keeps cropping up in her letters. She is taking care not to go where the Prince is likely to be. The Prince is doing his best to seduce her, but so far she has managed to escape him. Then, against her will, Sir William invites him under their roof. She has her duty as hostess, what can she do? And so on. Letter after letter. That reception or dinner party or whatever it was happened in November, and she is still keeping it warm the following March. He is sitting in his boat, miles from anywhere, going through hell."

"Ship, not boat."

"I can read her like a book."

"Well, she wasn't young anymore, her looks were going, she was worried about the future."

"Who isn't? I mean, if we made that an excuse for everything . . ."

Miss Lily was obviously not herself destined to be a fading beauty, and I privately thought this was why she was so unsympathetic towards Emma, but naturally I did not say so. Instead I suggested it might be time we got on with some work.

My talk was only five days off now, and I was still not satisfied with what I had written. I crossed out and rewrote and crossed out again in a progression that was beginning to seem infinite. Everything took longer than expected. Miss Lily grew weary of these endless corrections. "I know you are a perfectionist," she said, "but there is a limit."

A limit was precisely what I couldn't reach, there being virtually no limit to the ways in which words can combine. Under the stress of all this, an old nervous habit had reasserted itself—a tendency, slight and I hoped unremarkable, to gulp a little, to make from time to time a sort of involuntary swallowing, the teeth meeting in a very faint click, I think audible only to me. It was a strange reflexive motion of the throat, perhaps belonging to the remote diluvian past of the species, like snapping at some wavering insect that had come too close.

I had rewritten part of the second of my two episodes in "The Making of a Hero," the one that occurred in 1775, when Horatio was seventeen, and marked the real end of youth for him. He had been serving as midshipman on board the *Seahorse* on a voyage to the East Indies, a voyage of marvels—they had rounded the Cape, stood along the northern edge of the Roaring Forties, steered north for Madras and Calcutta, then up the Persian Gulf to Basra and back to Tricomalee in Ceylon.

From boyhood, from my first interest in Horatio, I had followed every step of the way in my school atlas, imagining the brilliant light, the sea tilting up to meet a voracious moon, deserts of red sand, the swollen waters of great rivers, stork-legged people who lived in flooded places, fiery tigers, crocodiles like floating logs. The scattered fragments of my reading and imagining all came together in that voyage of the *Seahorse*. Thoughts of my mother too. It was for India that she left us. Somewhere on that continent, my mother is or was. Just as I was Horatio's witness and his shadow over this wide gap of time, so the process could work in reverse. Perhaps Horatio saw a woman in a blue robe on temple steps across wide muddy waters against the sky of swooning whiteness . . .

All my childish knowledge of brutality was in that voyage too. Horatio had been to the Arctic and the tropics, but this was his first fighting ship on active service, and the captain, George Farmer, was a noted disciplinarian. On three hundred occasions, each meticulously recorded in the ship's log, a man was stripped to the waist, lashed to the gratings, and flogged with the thonged whip known as the cat-o'-nine-tails. Two or three times a week. Horatio would have witnessed these floggings.

The voyage ended for him in December 1775 somewhere south of Bombay, with an attack of malaria. It was his first, and it nearly killed him. He was transferred to the *Dolphin*, the only available ship, to be carried home—England was thought to be his one chance of recovery. But the *Dolphin* didn't sail till the following March, with Horatio still confined to his hammock, still at death's door.

"His famous luck," I said to Miss Lily. But *luck* was the wrong word; I knew that, even if she didn't. "If they had sailed immediately he would have died. The voyage would have taken five or six months—he could not have lasted out."

It was a storm that saved him. The first days were calm; the ship made slow way, with light breezes puffing her sails. I wanted to convey the quality of this calm, the slow heave of the sea, the sick boy's hammock swaying with the sway of the ship, the moaning complaint of the timbers, the moving shadows of the rigging, the shadow of death on him as he lay there. A famous ship, the *Dolphin*, though he would not have cared just then: the first ship ever to sail twice round the world.

Then, in early April, the storm struck with tremendous violence, choking the scuppers so that the decks flooded, splitting sails, carrying away the lighter yards and springing the heavier ones from their slings. Already enfeebled and sick, helpless in this nightmare tumult, the young Horatio came very close to his end. But now, just in time, Table Mountain is sighted across the surging waters, they reach the shelter of the Cape, the *Dolphin* anchors at Simon's Town for repairs. These take a month, a month of fresh air and wholesome food for Horatio after the stifling humidity of the Indian coast—a month that saved his life.

All these preliminaries I wanted to include, as being essential to the drama. But the formative experience came afterwards, somewhere in the Atlantic on the way home. He was returning to health by this time, but still extremely weak and listless. He thought much of the future, and in this depressed state his prospects seemed bleak.

"I've decided to put it all in the first person," I said to Miss Lily. "I want to use his own words as far as possible. I don't know why I didn't think of it to begin with."

Miss Lily turned to me a face of concern. "You are changing it again, for the umpteenth time. You are making yourself ill over it. There comes a point when you have to say enough is enough, it's as good as I can make it."

"I have to do it justice. I have to quote him in his own words. This was a conversion experience, a call to vocation." I gulped, lowered my head in an attempt at concealment, heard the tiny click of my teeth. "There he is," I said, "standing on deck or perhaps in his quarters below. He has been in the valley of the shadow. Then the long convalescence—the body is recovering, but there is still that darkness in the mind. The future seems to hold nothing for him. What does he say? *I could discover no means of reaching the object of my ambition* . . . Then comes the deliverance, the vision—he sees a radiant golden orb suspended in the air before him, actually there before him physically. In that moment he understands his destiny, he is a boy no longer. I want to put it in his own words. *A glow of patriotism was kindled within me and presented my King and country as my patron. My mind exalted in the idea. Well then, I exclaimed, I will be a hero! And confiding in Providence I will brave every danger.*"

I paused on this. I felt suddenly exalted myself. It seemed to me that some streaming of that radiance, a fainter impression of that shining orb, lay now between Miss Lily and me. "There you are," I said. "There you have it. The vocation of hero, solemnly vowed and undertaken. That radiant vision stayed with him all his life—it must be stressed in my talk."

However, I saw no slightest look of exaltation on Miss Lily's face.

"I don't believe in this orb," she said. "It was a long time afterwards when he wrote about it—twenty years, something like that. I mean, things get embroidered, don't they? Besides, your country can't be a patron, it has to be a person. And King George III was off his head, and the Prince of Wales turned out to be nothing but a playboy and overweight with it. Nelson thought he was after Emma, but he probably wasn't at all. *God strike him blind if he looks at you,* that's what Nelson wrote to her."

It was the first time she actually quoted his words to me. Of course I ought to have known that she would be incapable of seeing the meaning of this transcendent moment in his life, patriotism experienced as religious impulse in this clergyman's son. She was unable, constitutionally unable, to shift from the concrete to the abstract, unable to see that it was not this or that embodiment of kingship that mattered but the dedication to an ideal of service. It was really so obvious that it wasn't worth arguing about. I said, "I want to follow it up with some general remarks about the symbolism of the orb. Held in the hand of a monarch, it signifies his sovereignty over the world. It was first used by the Roman emperors. In religious art, it is held by Christ as *Salvator Mundi,* the Saviour of the World."

"He must have been lonely, that's all I can say."

"Who?" I was bewildered by this interjection, which seemed not to relate to anything I was saying. "Do you mean Christ?"

"I mean him, Nelson. He must have been terribly lonely. It wasn't natural."

There was pity in her voice—she was presuming to pity him. Even worse, when I glanced at her face, I had the impression I was being included in the same intolerable embrace.

15

The night before I was due to give my talk I slept very little. I lay awake for hours in the dark, thinking of the April deaths. In our calendar, Horatio's and mine, April is the month of deaths. It was in April 1802 that Horatio's father died, the Reverend Edmund Nelson, pride in his son's career darkened by distress at the wreck of the marriage, Fanny's unhappiness, the scandal of the affair with Emma. A year later, again in April, Sir William Hamilton breathed his last, desiccated and sad, in his house in Piccadilly. In Emma's arms, holding Horatio's hand, he faded away "like an inch of candle." The trio was dissolved, the pretence of Horatio as a sort of permanent guest went with it, there were just the two lovers; they could not stay under the same roof after his death. Horatio's own end was not far away; it was in April two years later that he set out on his death-chase, the pursuit of the French fleet that would culminate in Trafalgar.

It was in April that my father died, last April, a year ago. On a hospital bed in a private room, his life haemorrhaged away. It was a process he would have condemned as illogical if he had been able to gather himself; the tumor was not a killer by nature but became so in effect when they removed it.

Where did the blood go? There was no outward mark of it on him, no slightest spot or faintest smear. Again, as I lay there in the dark, the question returned; I felt the same horrified incredulity at thoughts of the blood pooling slowly within the wasted vessel of my father's body. And again, to fend off the horror, I thought about the light on the April afternoon when he died. It was that impartial light that comes through thinly curtained windows on dull or cloudy days and lies without discrimination over everything. I tried again to re-member where the windows were in that room and where the bed lay, and again it seemed strange and in a way outrageous that a scene so stamped on my mind in its essence should be in its particular de-tails quite beyond recall. Perhaps it was my own blankness of memory that made the light that afternoon seem in retrospect so blank, so unselective. There was a fan-shaped window over the door, glazed white . . .

Periodically my father's eyes would open and his hands would pluck at the coverlet, the white coverlet, yes. For perhaps half a minute he would keep this up. Then the eyes would close and the hands would be still again, as if halted by some abrupt reflection, something occurring behind the mask of the face, something that needed to be processed carefully, in utter impassivity and stillness. Whatever the conclusions arrived at, they were not communicated to Monty and me as we sat there on either side of the bed. Chairs with chrome frames, yes, their gleaming softened in that light. After some minutes the eyes would open and stare upward, the little fretting movements of the bloodless hands would begin again, as if in search of some fresh food for thought.

It was strange, and I was tempted afterwards to mention it to Monty but never did, how in these intervals of ambiguous stillness, which seemed like grave reflection but might have been something else altogether, heralds of his death in any case, how then, at the edge, our father seemed most himself, most in command. He had always ruled us by not demonstrating anything, and he kept it up to the end, almost to the end. But it was not the kind of thing Monty and I could ever have talked about.

He takes after our father in looks, the same long face and prominent square chin, the same straight cast of brow, eyes dark and rather deep-set. Perhaps this was what made him the preferred one—a doubtful blessing: more was expected. Such a resemblance is a good start, Father possibly reasoned; a boy with those looks may do something. Monty was not thought clever at school, but he is hard-working and he understands about money—like Father in this too. He makes a fair amount of it working in the City as an investment consultant for the Japanese. He likes men. My looks are different, I am fair and blue-eyed, more like my mother, at least as I remember her. I have no photographs; all likenesses of her vanished, it seemed overnight, after she left.

Awkwardly, in that flat light of mid-afternoon, on the edge of our chairs on either side, we watched him dying. We were not told he was dying, no-one there in the hospital said so. An Irish nurse bustled in from time to time to check the suspended bottle. She must have known, all of them must have known, that his life was leaking away.

For a few minutes, not long before he died, there was a change. He became feverish; a certain warmth—not colour—came to his face. He set up a sort of muttering, accompanied by fumbling movements of one hand, his right hand, yes, he attempted to point at the air before him or at the opposite wall. He was indicating something or asking for something, but we could not understand at first what it was. He struggled to raise himself, and we helped him. His eyes were wide open and full of urgency. He was staring across the room at the curtained recess in the white wall. "Trousers," he said, in a voice that was clear but quite unrecognizable as his. "Get them for me."

He paused for a moment, still pointing. Then his hand moved up to his face in a gesture of secrecy and caution. "Don't tell *her*," he said. "She won't see, do it now, get my trousers."

He wanted to escape from his death, which without trousers he could not attempt. He had not asked us for help ever before; appropriate, of course, that it came in the form of an order. My brother and I both made a movement to obey. Even then, in his weakness and delirium, his notion of reality was stronger than ours, his vision of himself as trousered escapee impressed itself on us. "Quick," he said in that stranger's voice. "You must be quick."

We started up, both of us, momentarily ready to be his means of escape. And it came into my mind then, in that briefest of moments before I remembered the limits of his power—the question forced itself on me: did I want him back in trousers, home again, back beside the billiard table, which I was already envisaging with its glinting cover of baize and glass as our ocean, Horatio's and mine?

This pang of hesitation was terrible; the moment of it has haunted my mind ever since. Did I want him to die? I saw Monty settle back in his chair and wondered whether he too had been blighted by this doubt. I wonder still.

When we made no move to get his trousers, my father's face became sorrowing and then quite blank. He lay back, and soon afterwards he died. The moment was quite undetectable. We had been looking at the lifeless face for several minutes when the nurse came in, touched him, went out again, and came back with a doctor, who told us he had passed over.

There was a strange element of reversal in it, this command of my father's to be rescued from hospital. It echoed a distant time when he had come to a hospital to rescue me. I did not think of the connection on that afternoon of his death, but it came often to my mind in the months following, and it came again that night as I lay sleepless in a darkness that was filling with voices.

I was six years old. Before my chess days, before the pictures in the book, long before I knew that Horatio and I were the same age when we lost our mothers. I had been in hospital for two weeks, after an operation to remove my appendix. I hated the hospital and wanted terribly to go home. However, adept at concealment even then, I had shown no sign of these feelings to anyone there, any of the nurses, any of the other children on the ward. I was washed and combed and ready, but they had not made me dress in outdoor clothes; I waited for him in pyjamas and dressing gown—a new, smart one, I remember it still. I was without trousers, in other words. Probably because of the car, I think now; I was to be taken home in the car. But at the time this did not occur to me. The notion of betrayal came early to me. The fact that I was still in hospital clothes made me suspect that they didn't really mean to let me go.

He seemed from another world when he came for me, god-like. In that place of pale walls and floors, glazed and glimmering to my memory, he was alien and somber with his dark hair and eyes, his long navy-blue overcoat and maroon scarf. The clothes he wore that day made an impression on me that has never faded. He was triumphantly trousered then. His long, big-chinned face with the sociable smile on it . . .

Some words with the nurses while I stood waiting. They were impressed—there was a flutter of interest round him. Then he looked at me. "Ready to go?"

How I responded to this I don't know. No more than a nod perhaps, or some shy assent—in company he made me shy. Response enough, in any case, to reveal my state of mind to him. He was always very noticing of troubled states.

"Perhaps you'd rather stay?" He looked at the nurses. "You would keep him, I dare say, wouldn't you?"

"Only too pleased. Quite a little charmer. He has made conquests everywhere. Won't you stay with us, dear?"

I didn't know, I was too young to see, or perhaps my precocious suspicion of treachery prevented me from seeing, that this was not meant seriously, that grown-ups bait children in a pretence of joking, with words not really addressed to the child at all but to themselves, to one another, to celebrate their superior worldliness and wisdom. I thought they meant it. I thought he would go away again without me, leave me in that awful place. I did not know what I could say to stop him without betraying my fear, without hurting the nurses' feelings. And on my father's face that same expression when he glanced at me, the one I knew already—not really amused, I never saw amusement on his face, but alert, interested; he was *studying* me. Perhaps it was born then, my fear of eyes.

Only a moment or two, I suppose, the time that I stood there, speechless and lost, in my new dressing gown, dark blue with silver stitching round the pockets and a silver cord belt. Then the tone of the laughter changed, my father picked me up and carried me in triumph out to the car—his triumph, not mine. Thirty-six years later, in the indifferent light of a hospital room, he mutters and points and yearns for his trousers.

My brother and I have met only once since the funeral, and that
was to settle some matters arising out of the plan we had made together for me to buy him out of his half of the house. I was arranging
to do this by using some of my share of the money placed in trust for
us by our mother's father, who died when I was ten and Monty thirteen. The balance of the capital was still enough for me to live on,
more than enough.

He came on a Sunday afternoon, the eighteenth of May. I was
down in the basement when he rang the bell, drinking red wine and
rearranging some of the cabinets. I had lost no time in having cabinets
fitted to house the pieces I valued most, the nineteenth-century long-
case clock with a picture of HMS *Victory* on the face, the set of
Wedgwood vases in coloured jasper made in 1905 to celebrate the
centenary of Trafalgar, a Liverpool creamware soup tureen with tinted
portraits of him in the panels. The other pieces I kept on open shelves
set round the walls. What a joy it had been to get these things out of
the boxes they had lived in so long, set them out where they could
be seen.

I remember the date of Monty's visit quite well—it was on the
eighteenth of May, 1803, that Horatio, newly appointed commander-
in-chief Mediterranean, hoisted his flag in the *Victory*. I was having
a glass of claret down there in the basement to mark the occasion. I
was working my way through a stock of it that my father had been
obliged to leave behind.

I got a terrible shock when I opened the door. I thought for a
moment that it was my father walking in, come back to resume residence, take over the basement. Monty had grown a narrow moustache
on the exact model of Father's, he had parted his hair near the middle in just the same way. He was wearing an old-fashioned brown
tweed suit with broad lapels, which I recognized as having belonged

to Father. The shirt looked old-fashioned too. Monty had kept all his clothes, down to socks and underwear, or so I now suspected, and in a final bid for approval he was dressing up in them.

The strangest thing of all was that I made no comment about this and neither did he. We had not been in the habit of confiding in each other, not of late years, not since my illness. Seeing him impersonating our father like that made me seriously doubt his mental balance. Certainly not a person to show one's Nelson collection to. I had never shown it to anyone, as a matter of fact. I kept the basement always double-locked.

Penhas was at the funeral, rather surprisingly—no personal invitation had been sent to him. A notice had been sent to his and my father's club, the Atheneum; he might have seen that, or perhaps been told of it—he was not really a viable club member any longer, though I did not realize this until we talked together.

He was sitting towards the rear of the church with a woman in a stiff-looking black hat beside him. After the first surprise, it seemed somehow natural that he should have come. I had not seen him in the years since my illness, but I had always thought of him as belonging to my life rather than my father's; I don't think they had ever been particularly close. To me he had been, if not a friend exactly, for a while, in a way, a fellow twenty-year-old. In his efforts to help me he had told me stories about his youth, brought himself to an age with me. It was he, after all, who had put me back on the rails, held out to me the lifeline of Horatio. I felt sure he had come to the funeral for my sake, out of professional concern, to see how I was bearing up.

This feeling was confirmed afterwards, after the delivery of my father's body to the flames, when I found them both waiting outside in the uncertain spring sunshine, the woman still beside him, taller than he and straight as a ramrod. We shook hands. He did not introduce the woman, she introduced herself—her name was Elizabeth

White. It was she, not he, who expressed their condolences. Even before he spoke, it was clear that Penhas was greatly changed. The short imperial beard was still in place, quite grey now. The eyes were as I remembered them, dark and depthless—the first eyes I was able to sustain when I was beginning to recover. But the rest of the face had departed, so to speak, from the sombreness of the eyes. The features were relaxed and oddly puffy; the mouth looked softer and thicker and it wore a half-smile, inappropriate for a funeral. The whole face was blurred somehow, as if it had been sponged over.

"He wanted to come," Mrs. White said. "He wouldn't take no for an answer."

"Well, nothing is forever," Penhas said. His voice still had the careful modulations of a foreigner, but it was slower and thicker than I remembered. "There was the *poule de luxe*, do you remember her? Living on the earnings of a highball lady. *Born, worn.* She kept us in funds for nearly . . . How long was it?" Very swiftly and adroitly, almost imperceptibly, he winked at me. "She has a most amazing repertoire, that woman, she is a professional contoonist, made of india-blubber. *Rubber.* God, the things she gets up to."

"Now then, keep the party clean," Mrs. White said. She gave me a look of grim patience. I had thought for a wild moment that Penhas might be referring to her, though her appearance made this improbable. Then I understood that she was a nurse or attendant of some kind.

"That was in Stralsburg," Penhas said. "No, wait a minute . . ." The smile disappeared and his face became anxious and intent. "*Salzburg, Stralsburg, Strassburg . . .*"

There were other people I should speak to. Monty had already gone back to the house to receive those of my father's relatives and closer acquaintances due to forgather there. I was beginning to express my thanks, beginning to withdraw, but Penhas—who I don't think had a total sense of where he actually was—began to tell me the story of the bicycles, how somewhere in a hilly region north of Bolzero or Bulzano, footsore and penniless, on his way to Spain, he had seen two bicycles standing outside a lonely farmhouse, one very old and battered, the other brand-new. He had stolen one of them. Which one, did I think?

"No idea," I said. I didn't want to spoil his story.

"I took the old one. I was not a high-trade thief, you see. *Grade.*"

"Sanity depends on making distinctions," I said, couldn't help saying.

Penhas nodded, his smile broadened, and little webs of saliva stretched at the corners of his mouth. He seemed to be attempting, with that sponged-over face, the same expression, ironic and sly, that he had worn twenty years before when he told me the story of the bicycles.

I spoke on an impulse, a thing very rare with me. "You are not someone who steals, Mr. Penhas, you are a giver. You gave me Horatio, you brought me back to normal life."

"Horatio?"

"Horatio Nelson."

There was no faintest look of recollection on his face. He had no idea at all what I was talking about. Whatever had brought him, it was not the professional follow-up to an interesting case. I thought I knew now what it was. He had not come here for me at all but for himself, to grope through the mist that was descending on him for the self he had been when he told me the stories, bold and adventurous in a way I had never been, with Spain and the world before him.

"Horatio?" he said. "Sheer affectation. Why not Horace?"

Mrs. White took him by the arm. "Time to call it a day." She smiled for the first time, a smile incongruously cheerful. "Homeward bound."

Penhas gave me a look, perhaps of complicity, the fathomless eyes seeming to cast sadness over the ruins of the face and mind. Then, obediently, without farewells, he allowed himself to be led away. I watched them walk down the path to the chapel gate. He had a walk that was at once shambling and quick. Mrs. White kept close beside him, a head taller, regimental-looking in her black hat.

I was left with my memories of the story, the theft of shirts and knickers from a clothesline, the binding of the bare rims of the wheels with them, the epic journey on this rattling steed. Somewhere south of Avignon, in difficult terrain, it finally gave up the ghost.

Perhaps after all I was wrong, I thought now; perhaps Penhas had told these stories to scores of people since . . . Such questions occupied me as I lay through the hours of darkness thinking of the April deaths, actual and foreshadowed. Towards dawn I heard the resident blackbird strike up in the small drenched garden behind the house. It sang the story of faces, Penhas's spongy and sly, my father's transfigured by eagerness for his trousers, Horatio's pale and noble in the allegorical painting by Benjamin West, where the dead hero's body, unmarked by blood or wounds, is raised by Neptune and Victory into the arms of mourning Britannia.

Other birds joined in; the song became a chorus of lamentation, like the rain of grief I sometimes experienced in my dreams, which was both sound and touch. I felt something of the oppressive sorrow that comes on waking from such dreams and then a return of the terrible restlessness that afflicted me all through that spring and summer, the sense that my life was changing, that something would be required of me. My body had tensed—with resistance, with acceptance, with a kind of fear. Then, quite casually, with a typical absence of fuss, Miss Lily came into my mind and I remembered a conversation we had had about April, how I had quoted to her the lines of T. S. Eliot, in which he says that April is the cruellest month. Quoting poetry to Miss Lily! Three months ago I would not have dreamed of such a thing. I thought of the lines again now; they come, appropriately enough, at the beginning of *The Burial of the Dead* in *The Waste Land*:

> April is the cruellest month, breeding
> Lilacs out of the dead land, mixing
> Memory and desire . . .

Famous lines. Miss Lily considered for a while, compressing her lips and slightly tilting her head, as she did when focusing on something dubious. Then she made a quick, decisive movement of the shoulders. "No," she said, "he's got it quite wrong. I know poets have to follow their inspiration, but if he had stopped to think, he would have seen that the cruellest month is November, because you know that winter is just round the corner."

Accusing that most sober and cerebral poet of ill-considered haste! All her hatred of cold weather in those words, and something more: a literalness of mind that now, remembering it, seeing her convinced face, made me smile broadly in the dark. Poor Miss Lily.

I 6

J spent most of the next day going over my talk, resisting the temptation to make further changes—it was too late for that now. The day began fine, but in the afternoon the sky clouded over and towards five o'clock it started to rain, something less than a downpour but much more than a drizzle, very steady and remorseless.

When I left the house, it was still raining at the same steady pace. I thought briefly of a taxi, but my habit of economy prevailed. Armed with raincoat and umbrella, I walked to Belsize Park station, took the tube to Russell Square, and cut through behind St. Pancras to the club premises.

In my anxiety not to be late I had left home earlier than necessary, and it was still not quite seven when I arrived, a good half-hour before the talk was due to begin. Ample time for a drink, a glass of red wine to steady me, give poise to my body and timbre to my voice. Only one, however . . .

Hugo was there as usual and gave me good-evening in his thin, rather nasal tones. He is conscious, I think, that his voice lacks natural bonhomie and tries to make up for this, infusing warmth into it by drawing out the vowels, which makes him sound stagy at times, to me at least.

There were only three people in the bar, but I thought nothing of this at the time; no premonition came to me. It was early, after all. Afterwards it was to occur to me that there was cause for misgiving right from the start, not so much in the small number of people but in who they were. Kismet Walters was there, and Robbins, the expert on naval signals in the age of sail, and a pallid man named Summerfield, a great admirer of Admiral Cornwallis, the commander of the Channel Fleet at the time of Trafalgar. Now the point about these three was that despite being very different one from the other in their personalities and opinions, they were all absolute regulars, people who passed probably the greater part of their leisure time on the club premises, invariably present at talks and slide shows, snoozing away odd hours in the reading room or browsing through the compilations of the Naval Records Society and back numbers of the *Mariner's Mirror*. In short, they were people who would have been there *in any case*.

As I say, the significance of this did not come home to me at first. Having decided in advance against a second glass, I took this one slowly. I had to be careful not to cloud my mind; I needed clarity for the numerous questions I was sure my talk would provoke. I encountered Horatio's regard in the Abbot portrait up on the wall behind the bar, that face of suppressed pain. Something about the eyes I had never noticed before: they seemed to look inwards, as if in search of a self that was deserting, absconding, leaving him to the pain of his wounds and the loneliness of the stars on his chest. *They cut pieces off him, didn't they?*

It was anxiety about my approaching talk that gave me these negative thoughts about him. I knew that a bright angel never looks inwards, though dark angels may. Introspection makes for hesitation and divided counsels. No, consistency of word and deed, magnanimity, fearlessness, self-command—these are the heroic virtues. Honour, in a word . . . A shaft of anguish struck me. Naples, 1799. Just one week from your arrival in the city to the embarkation of the rebels. Just one week in a lifetime. *The violation was at sea.* Of course, Sacchinelli was biased, Ruffo was his employer, he wanted to show him in a good light . . .

I could feel that my palms were sweating. I had the folder containing the pages of my talk held closely under my left arm. I saw Hugo's movements duplicated in the mirror behind the bar. He caught my eye and gave me his slightly rabbity smile.

It was twenty past seven. I had again the impression that time had somehow accelerated, gone ahead of me. These thoughts, which had seemed of the briefest, had occupied twenty minutes. Naples, it was Naples that had slowed me down . . . There were six people in the bar now. Summerfield came over to me and said he was looking forward to my talk, but this was just a prelude and a pretext; he wanted to tell me about a talk that he himself was due to deliver on the subject, inevitably, of Cornwallis.

"The point is, you see," he said, "and it can't be repeated often enough, that without Cornwallis, Nelson's victories would not have been possible. Nelson gets all the credit. No-one ever praises Cornwallis, he is the unsung hero, but if it hadn't been for the blockade of Brest between 1803 and 1805, Napoleon would have been landing troops in Kent long before Nelson got to grips with Villeneuve at Trafalgar." Summerfield's eyes, so pale as to be almost colourless, were wide with sincerity. "In my talk I intend to set the record straight," he said.

As always, I sprang to Horatio's defence. "Wars are won by winning battles."

"Listen, what was the navy trying to do from 1803 onwards? Basically, I mean basically, what were we trying to do?"

"Destroy the French fleet, break French naval power, drive them from the seas."

Summerfield shook his head. "You are talking in Nelsonian terms. You are conditioned, like everyone else in this club. What we were doing was trying to prevent a French invasion. The true hero of Trafalgar is therefore Cornwallis, who kept them bottled up in Brittany for the best part of two years."

Even in my growing agitation at the poor turnout, I could not help thinking it strange that a man would join the Nelson Club and spend much of his time on its premises when the main focus of his interest was not Nelson at all but an obscure admiral named Cornwallis, an effective blockader no doubt, but that was about all—no glamour, no hint of the angelic. Not for the first time, it occurred to me that the club numbered too many cranks among its members. "Well," I said, "the obvious thing to do is go off and found a Cornwallis club."

The club president, Pratt-Smithers, now came in, accompanied by a man with a short white beard and an abstracted way of looking about him, as if he were not quite sure of being in the right place. This was the guest for the evening. Members were allowed to bring guests, but quite often someone was invited in the name of the club as a whole; and Pratt-Smithers, who knew nothing much about Horatio but liked running things, tried to bring in people who might be good for some publicity or might help to increase the membership. This one, it seemed, was a writer who had just published a long novel about the eighteenth-century African slave trade. I hadn't read it. Until that moment I hadn't heard of it, or him. I am not a man for fiction.

"Absolutely monumental," Pratt-Smithers said now, apparently referring to this novel.

The novelist had a slightly crooked smile and large grey eyes behind thin-rimmed glasses. The eyes were mournful in spite of the smile, and the glasses were very old—the metal of the frame was tarnished green here and there. I didn't much take to this man; he didn't look the sort who would take pride in our country's great past, and that's a fundamental division of categories with me, those capable of patriotism and those not.

"Scotch, please, no ice, no nothing," he said to Hugo in a voice that contained traces of northeast England. Waiting for it, he squinted vaguely round the bar. "This all the audience?" Not tremendously tactful. I had a feeling it wasn't his first drink of the evening.

"Oh, there'll be others," Pratt-Smithers said. "Not everyone comes to the bar, you know, some people wait in the auditorium." He smiled at me, and I knew what the smile was saying: *This is the most miserable turnout for any talk in the history of the club.* "It's a rainy night," he said. "Puts people off, some people."

"Auditorium?" Summerfield looked bewildered. "We were just talking about Cornwallis."

"Friend of yours?" the novelist said.

Summerfield is a solitary character, easily thrown out. First there had been the unusual word, then this dreadful ignorance. Looking if possible paler than ever, he made a rather abrupt movement of the head, jerking it sideways, then back to the front again. The novelist followed this jerking motion with his eyes. Summerfield had seemed to indicate the area behind the bar.

"That's him, is it?" The novelist was looking at the Abbot painting. "Naval man, I see, yes."

"Good God, man," I said, "that's Nelson." It was all I could do to keep my voice steady. I couldn't yet quite believe, not altogether, that the membership as a whole could have boycotted my talk. I knew it, yes, but I resisted the knowledge. Perhaps I had slipped out of parallel again, gone too far ahead somehow . . . The sounds in the bar seemed to die away, and a sort of ringing hush came to my ears. I was still clutching my file, pressing it close against my side, under my left arm. I felt some pain at this pressure now from the hard edges of the folder.

"Time we were going in, I think," Pratt-Smithers said. "Ah, you're having another."

This was said to the novelist, who it seemed had asked for another whisky, which Hugo was now passing to him. He disposed of it with a fair turn of speed, but it was twenty minutes to eight by the time we got into the lecture room.

Not until I was there at the table, facing my audience of seven scattered persons in a room with seating for seventy, with the carafe of water and the clean glass before me and Pratt-Smithers's introductory remarks sounding in my ears, not until then did I finally accept it: they had deliberately stayed away. The rain was not the reason, though of course it was the reason they would give.

In that moment, while I was still arranging my papers before me, everything came together, everything made sense. I knew this was a plan that had been concerted against me. They had been waiting several weeks, for this occasion of my talk, to deal the blow. A faint feeling of sickness accompanied this realization, but there was no surprise in it. Ever since joining the club, I had known that my better understanding of Horatio was resented by the common run of the members. Brilliance of any kind infuriates the mediocre. It was the same with Horatio. When he broke the line at Cape St. Vincent and so secured the victory, there were those who urged Jervis to reprimand him for disobeying orders.

If this was a plot against me—and I now felt certain it was—then the people who had actually come were obviously suspect too; among them there must be spies whose sole purpose it was to observe my reactions and report back. Otherwise, where would be the satisfaction? There and then I made my resolution, and it was one worthy of him: I would show no sign of disappointment, I would give my talk, I would deliver it with clarity and force, I would speak to this small, spy-riddled group as I would have done if the room had been packed to overflowing. I owed it to him, I owed it to myself. *Never show what you feel.* My father's lesson.

And I kept to it. I redeemed the occasion for us both, I made it my own and his. I relaxed my shoulders, I lightened my glance. I heard my voice in that almost empty room, reading the sentences I had put together with such careful toil. The two essential elements, vision and conversion. The lonely boy at the dockside, his vision of divinity in the person of his metamorphosed uncle, in that light and spacious cabin of his first warship; then the conversion, the radiant orb, the culminating phrase: *Why then, I will be a hero.*

As I spoke I glanced at the faces, wondering who were the spies. No-one could be excluded, not the president or the guest, not Hugo, who had left the bar and come to sit at the back of the room, not even Summerfield or Kismet Walters. Any or all of them might be in the enemy camp. But I did not falter. I was defending him as well as myself, I was saving his dignity with my own. The hero carries human dignity for all those who cannot. Horatio's role and mine—I felt closer to him that evening than perhaps I had ever felt before.

Of course, such exertions take their toll. When I sat down again at the table and reached for the water glass, I saw that my hand was shaking and realized that this would be obvious to anyone who saw me try to drink. I retracted the hand with studied slowness, as if I had thought again.

Pratt-Smithers was now on his feet, inviting questions. There was a short interval of silence, and then the visiting novelist raised his hand. "It would be interesting to know," he said, "whether Nelson ever had a black woman?"

This was the question, this was the level of interest my talk had aroused. Contempt for question and questioner steadied me now; the trembling ceased. I poured out water and drank, without a clink or a spill. I allowed myself a slight smile. "You are suggesting that that would be a third stage in the making of a hero?"

"No, no." He sounded on the defensive—I had scored a hit with this counter-question. "No, but he spent a lot of time in the West Indies in his younger days, didn't he? I mean, I know he was a hero and all that, but youth will have its fling—he was only about twenty. The climate favoured it. There was an abundance of woman slaves, a hundred thousand or so in Jamaica alone—no shortage of choice . . ."

I remembered it now, his novel was about the slave trade. Clearly an obsessive type. "There is no evidence for anything of the sort," I said. "One can always speculate, if that is what one likes doing." In the midst of saying this, it came into my mind, with the force of a decision already made, that I would resign from the club.

There were no more questions. Pratt-Smithers uttered some thanks, and I was released. I made at once for the door but not in any abrupt or unceremonious manner. Appearances had to be kept up. Pratt-Smithers suggested a drink with himself and guest, who it seemed wanted to pursue the question of Horatio's sexual activities in Jamaica. This was more than I could stomach, and I declined, though politely enough, as I hope and think. Naturally I said nothing about my decision to resign, otherwise it might have seemed I was acting out of pique rather than responding to a mortal insult. I was eager to get away. Kismet Walters was bearing down, doubtless intent on telling me about his latest researches into Horatio's secret links with the world of Islam.

"I thought your talk was really good, first-rate," Hugo said to me as I was passing through into the corridor that led to the stairs. He came close to me in the manoeuverings at the door. He moved his narrow shoulders as if uneasy in the confined space. I saw his eyes, moist blue and full of seeming sympathy, quite close to my own. "I am ever so sorry at the poor attendance," he said. "Shame it is such a rainy night."

I could not be sure whether this was meant sincerely, so I said nothing, merely nodded. Next moment I was out and down the stairs, into the street. Once I was on the pavement, however, under cover of night and anonymity, my composure began to crack. It was something like the experience of having drunk too much and been constrained to conceal it, show no sign; then the release into solitude, the cooler air—one begins to stagger and lurch.

This I did now in spirit, so much so that I went the wrong way, turning left into Doughty Street. Without quite knowing how, I found myself in the unfamiliar region south of St. Pancras. The rain had stopped, but the pavements were still wet, they gleamed in the reflected lights of cars and streetlamps. I must have lost the best part of an hour wandering here, but I was not much aware of time passing. Then, quite by chance, I found myself back in Mecklenburgh Square, which was quite deserted.

I knew the way now, but I did not want to turn towards home. Nothing awaited me there but the evening's end, the final acknowledgement of failure and fiasco. I walked round the small square several times, past the locked gates and the spiked railings. From the darkness on my left, beyond the railing, came the smell of wet leaves and mould and some vague fragrance of flowers. But the trees and bushes inside were indeterminate, massed together in the dark. I had the sense, frequent in nighttime London in these regions of quiet squares, of walking at the limits of the light, as if I were on the bright rim of a dark bowl and the light merely served the essential darkness, made it denser, less accessible, created a territory separate enough, extensive enough—or so it seems at night—for rapine or oblivion.

An impulse came to me to climb the railings, get through somehow into the darkness beyond, enter that darkness and stay in it forever, absorbed, annihilated, unseen and unseeing in the thickest part of the bushes. All my persecutors I could escape in that way, all my problems with Horatio in that nightmare city. In fact, even Horatio would be extinguished, in that darkness beyond the railings he would die with me. For some terrible moments I wanted this, wanted to climb in there and put an end to us both. Then a car went round the square, making a soft hiss on the wet road, a small sound but it startled me, like a reminder or a warning. I turned and began to walk back towards Guilford Street. With calmer feelings came a renewed sense of my isolation. It was impossible to pretend to myself that I was unhurt. From time to time as I walked, the smart of tears came to my eyes.

I heard my name called, and when I stopped and turned I saw, but not immediately, that it was Hugo, unfamiliar in a macintosh. I had only ever seen him in the rather skimpy clothes he wore when behind the bar—tight waistcoats, shirts with narrow collars, that sort of thing. We had passed each other, it seemed, and he had recognized me at the last moment and called after me.

"You don't usually go this way," he said.

"Well, no. I felt like a bit of exercise, so I decided to take a turn or two round the square before making for home."

We stood there a moment or two without saying anything more, and I was about to resume my way before the silence grew too protracted, and in fact may even have taken a step or two, preliminary to bidding Hugo a cheery good-night, when he said, "I live quite near, just round the corner. Would you like to come for a coffee or something?"

I had actually started to refuse this offer, I think, when something—perhaps no more than a renewed wish to postpone my lonely and defeated homecoming—made me change my words in mid-career, shape them to a stumbling acceptance. And so we went together back to the square again and along the western side of it.

"Very handy, living so near the club," Hugo said as we went along. "Ten minutes after leaving home I can be behind the bar."

He had a basement flat just off Great Ormond Street, not far from the hospital. He took my coat and umbrella and hung them up in the narrow hallway. I sat on a sofa with pink and white stripes while Hugo made the coffee, a process I could watch from moment to moment as the tiny kitchen was built on an open plan with only a counter separating it from the room where I was sitting. The lower part of Hugo was cut off by the counter; his head and shoulders were sometimes visible, sometimes not, depending on whether he was standing straight or reaching down for something.

A sense of wonder possessed me as I sat there, conversing intermittently, glimpsing Hugo in sections, his glinting earring, his furry-looking hair—he wore his hair very close-cropped—his rust-coloured pullover, narrow-fitting and short, as all Hugo's clothes seemed to be.

"I think it is a real shame so few people came to your talk," he said through the hatchway as he put the coffee things on the counter. "They missed something, they missed an experience."

It irked me, this further reference to the fiasco of my talk; it brought back my earlier doubts as to where Hugo stood in the matter. Was he probing the wound to elicit winces and whimpers so he could then carry tales back? It was important to give nothing away.

"Well, it was a rainy evening," I said. "Besides, the talk is what it is. I mean, it is as good or bad as it was before I gave it, irrespective of the audience."

I wasn't quite sure what I meant by this, but Hugo widened his eyes at me and nodded seriously. He was sitting opposite in an arm-chair upholstered in some velvety red material—there was a lot of red in this room. A faint, sweetish smell like incense hung in the air, and on the wall behind him there was a poster, a picture of a man with fine-drawn features, rather androgynous-looking. His hair was matted with some silvery dust, and his suit glittered with tiny spangles like coarse sugar. In the background, a dark sky thickly scattered with stars.

"Well, my word," Hugo said, "I call that a really mature attitude."

Away from the softer lighting of the bar, Hugo looked older, nearer my own age, rather than in his middle twenties as I had thought. The earring and the short bristle of the hair and the clothes like those of an adolescent growing too fast had all contributed to this impression, as did his habit of twitching his shoulders from time to time, as if in some impatience with his own body.

"Take your jacket off if you feel too hot," he said now. "I keep the heating full on, it's my only extravagance."

"I'm all right like this," I said. It was indeed very hot in the room, and the predominance of red made it seem hotter still. I felt a wave of nostalgia for that cold breath that had reached me through the railing of the square and the promise of oblivion that had come with it.

"I love the heat," Hugo said. "I should have been born in the tropics. I like to go round, you know, just light clothes. Sometimes in the summer I don't bother with clothes at all. It is very private here, no-one can see in."

I said nothing to this. Hugo waited some moments, then said, "Rise above it, that is what we've got to do. Like he did."

"Who's that?"

"Him, Lord Nelson."

This seemed a very strange thing to say about Horatio, who did not need to rise above anything, because he was above already. What could Hugo mean, what could he be referring to? I was about to ask him when he started speaking again.

"Rise above it, that's the only way. Take my case now. I have only got these two evenings at the bar, and on Saturdays and Sunday afternoons I work in a bookshop in Covent Garden. I have to manage on that for the time being. There was someone sharing with me, but he walked out two weeks ago. Just up and left without a word and took a looking-glass that used to belong to my grandmother, framed in silver and mother-of-pearl—a family heirloom, you might say."

"Can't you get it back from him?"

"He didn't leave a forwarding address, did he?" Hugo gave a twitch of his right shoulder. "What a creature," he said. "After two years and a bit. I don't know why I am talking to you like this—I just feel you are a very understanding person."

He paused on this and again seemed to wait. Silence lengthened in the room. My eyes were confused by the heat, the pink sheen of the sofa, the spangled figure on the wall. I was troubled by the blank television screen on my right, a lurking presence whose gaze I could only avoid encountering by being careful not to glance that way.

Hugo shifted in his chair. "Well, anyway," he said, "one has one's value as a human being, they can't take that away, can they? I am a bit of a psychologist, and working behind a bar gives you scope for it, if you know what I mean. Of course, you have to have intuition. I am very rarely wrong about people. You always struck me as a free spirit. First time I saw you, I thought to myself, here is someone who knows his way about, someone who has seen a thing or two, been in some odd corners. Someone not easily shocked. A man of the world in the true sense of that term. Some of those others, you would think they had spent their entire lives with only Nelson for company."

I was conscious now of the beginnings of a headache. "Who is that chap with the silver hair and spangly suit?" I asked.

"Who do you mean?"

"The man on the wall behind you."

Hugo smiled a little, as if he thought I was joking. Then, as he looked at me, his face lost all expression. "You don't know who that is?"

"No idea, I'm afraid."

"That is David Bowie."

"He's a pop star, isn't he?"

Hugo shook his head slightly, as if seeking to dislodge some small object. "I don't believe we are having this conversation," he said. "David Bowie is much more than a pop star, he is a wonderful actor and a superlative singer, he is the media star of our time, he is the person I would most have wanted to be. He is just like me—he has the same attitudes that I have, he is nonaggressive, he believes in cosmic harmony and animal rights."

"You can't really tell whether he is a man or a woman, can you? Why is he wearing that sugary, shiny stuff all over him?"

"That is stardust. David Bowie belongs among the stars."

This was a fairly sickening thing to say in any case, but there was something in the inflection that brought about a return of my suspicions. I thought back quickly over his earlier remarks, and it seemed to me now that I could see a pattern in them. What had he meant by saying that Horatio had to rise above it? *Rise above what?*

"I've got everything of his." Hugo gestured towards a low, open-fronted cabinet against the wall near the sofa where I was sitting. "Would you like to hear something?"

"Are you trying to make a convert of me?"

Hugo seemed not to hear this. He got up, crossed to the wall beside me, and crouched before the cabinet. "What shall it be?" he said, crouching there at the side of the sofa, close beside me, tilting his head and stretching his neck to see along the row of CDs. His pullover had ridden up over his narrow waist, showing some inches of dark red shirt. His eyes were invisible to me. There was the back of his head, his neat ears, the left one with its gold band; there was the pale, undefended nape of his neck. Higher, up towards the crown, a glaze of pinkish skin showed through the sparse hair. Hugo was balding.

Pity for his early baldness, for the pathetic inadequacy of his starry icon, made this dwelling on him more terrible, more monstrous. He was too close to my eyes. Sensation, sound, the hot colours of the place, the lingering smell of joss-sticks, all merged in that helpless scrutiny of the frail skull. I was impaled on my own regard; my eyes were pierced to an even narrower focus, the slight bump above the hairline, just before the more pronounced convexity of the occipital bone. A ridge rather than a bump. It had the dull shine of an eggshell under the hair . . .

Then he straightened up, moved away. "Got to begin somewhere," he said. "Let's try this." He put in the disc, then turned towards me. He was smiling, I suppose in anticipation of the music. But it seemed to me that his face changed when he met my eyes. A moment later a sound of lamentation filled the room, a voice that resonated with shuddering falls, as if the recording had been made in some remote and echoing cavern far from human eyes. It was like all the sorrow of my dreams. I was sweating heavily and I felt giddy. I spoke loudly through the music, explaining to Hugo that it was late, that I had to leave. He seemed not to understand.

I went quickly into the hallway, found my coat and umbrella, and fled up the steps into the street.

17

*M*iss Lily came as usual on Friday evening. She was hardly through the door when she began asking me about the talk. "I was thinking about you," she said. "How did it go?"

"Very well."

"I saw that it was raining and I wondered, you know, if it would put people off."

"No, no, they came all the same." A modest smile. "The place was pretty packed."

"Did you get some good questions?"

I had a brief recollection of the novelist's raised hand. "One or two, yes. It was a mixed bag, you know. But there was a fair degree of interest, I think I can say that."

"And so there should have been."

Miss Lily said this with considerable emphasis. I looked at her, not for long—I never look long at faces—but long enough to see that she really meant it, she really was glad at the thought of my success. Her face was bright with pleasure. And I thought, if the talk is a success in her mind, then so am I and all that work is rewarded—rewarded by the look on her face. I felt a certain impediment in my throat and tried to swallow it down, but it stayed. I busied myself with papers for some moments. Then I said, "I couldn't have got it together without your help."

It was an effort to say this, to overcome the humiliation of gratitude. When I glanced at Miss Lily again, the pleasure was still there on her face but it was different, more serious; there was that deepening of expression I had noticed before. It came to me that there was beauty in her face, and something more—she possessed without effort the dignity I strove to protect in Horatio and in myself. It was disturbing, that I should see myself as striving to protect what he possessed so that I could possess it too. Hugo's face came into my mind, rabbity-looking somehow, with the eyes wide apart, rather protruberant. His look that changed as the music began. *You have to rise above it.* Only the evening before, but it was remote already, like something in somebody else's life.

"We'd better get going," I said. I was still trying to circumvent the problems of Naples 1799, at least temporarily, by jumping ahead to the following year, when Horatio and the Hamiltons, after their long journey home, with the cruises, the sittings to painters, the sojourns at foreign courts—the roadshow, as Miss Lily persisted in calling it—had finally arrived in London.

In a way she was right, I had to admit that. They were performers whether they wanted to be or not. Even when they were back in England, the show went on—it had to, because the spectators were always waiting, the theatre was always crowded. The maimed admiral, the antiquated ambassador, the beautiful, corpulent dame they shared, the suffering, unoffending Fanny—fame and scandal made them players. Everywhere they went, reporters followed; every move they made was recorded in the daily press.

The rift between Fanny and Horatio was past mending now, but they still appeared together in public. I wanted not merely to catalogue the events of those days but to convey the essence, catch the highlights and the low. However, the main job that evening was to correct a mistake I had made, a confusion between two separate visits to the theatre by the Nelson party in the same week. In fact, it was difficult to be certain about Horatio's activities during this period. Many of the newspaper reports of his attendance at public events were apocryphal; the managers of every show in London, from Pidcock's Zoo to the Sans Souci in Leicester Square, had found out that they could fill the house at short notice by putting it about that Lord Nelson would be in the audience that evening.

The first occasion was on November the eighteenth, at the Covent Garden Theatre, where the comedy *Life* was playing, followed by the spectacle *The Mouth of the Nile*, celebrating Horatio's victory. The theatre was packed to overflowing, and Horatio's appearance in his box was greeted by prolonged applause. He had to take repeated bows before the curtain could go up. The cast sang "Rule Britannia"; the Reverend Edmund, Horatio's father, burst into tears; the hero then seated himself, with Emma on his right and Fanny on his left, and the play began.

"He had the mistress on his right, you notice, his disarmed side," I said, by way of a joke, but Miss Lily did not think it funny.

"What a fuss, all that jumping up and down and bowing," she said. "I am sorry for Fanny, that's all I can say. Why did he have to put her through all that?"

I made no reply to this typical piece of parochialism; I knew that if we started arguing now, we would never get the passage corrected that evening. I had ascribed to the second occasion the dresses that the ladies had worn on this one. I wanted to put it right but still keep the description, because it seemed exactly to convey their different temperaments and situations, Emma flamboyant in a blue satin gown, fashionably high-waisted to conceal her pregnancy, and a headdress with a great plume of flowers, Fanny in simple white with a violet turban and one small white feather.

After the comedy and before the spectacle, Munden came forward and sang a song specially written for Horatio:

> May peace be the end of the strife we maintain,
> For our freedom, our king, and our right to the main!
> We're content to shake hands; if they won't, why, what then!
> We must send out brave Nelson to thrash 'em again.

Prolonged and deafening applause. Horatio jumps up again to bow his thanks. It takes two more choruses of "Rule Britannia" to restore order for the next piece, which, being in Horatio's honour, naturally brings the audience to its feet again with cheers and huzzas.

In short, a totally successful evening. The second occasion, which took place six days later, was less so. This was at the Theatre Royal in Drury Lane, the last occasion when Fanny and Horatio appeared together in public. The play was *Pizarro*, a melodrama by Kotzebue touched up by Sheridan, with the celebrated John Kemble in the part of Rolla. It had been a great hit. Pizarro hats were in fashion for a whole season. In the box with the Nelsons were Emma and Sir William, the Reverend Edmund and a certain Princess Castelcicala. The party was greeted with loud cheers from every part of the house and a spirited rendering of "Rule Britannia." Emma had been disappointed to learn that Mrs. Siddons was not playing Elvira, but Mrs.

Powell was generally accounted a success in the part. Horatio appeared to be enjoying the play; he applauded vigorously throughout the first two acts.

"How did he applaud?" Miss Lily said, and she giggled a little. "I mean, he couldn't clap, could he?"

"I've no idea. Probably he cheered or shouted." This was said stiffly; I hated his being laughed at.

"Perhaps he just jingled his medals. I'm sorry, I shouldn't have said that, should I? The truth is, he brings out the worst in me."

I looked at her in absolute amazement. The man who established British supremacy at sea for a century to come, who secured for us the tea gardens of India, the sugar islands of the Caribbean, one of the principal founders of the greatest maritime empire that the world has ever known, who made this country great and died for her in the end—this man brought out the worst in Miss Lily! I couldn't say anything, I could only stare—yes, stare. I even forgot my antipathy for the mutual regard. There were still the traces of laughter on her face.

"I'm sorry," she said. "I won't interrupt again."

I took a deep breath and resumed.

"At the end of Act Three, Elvira, her pleas rejected by the cold and inhuman Pizarro, breaks into her impassioned vow of vengeance. *How a woman can love, Pizarro, thou hast known . . . How she can hate thou hast yet to learn.* Elvira is alone on the stage. The audience is spellbound. Her voice rises. *Thou, who on Panama's brow . . . wave thy glittering sword . . . Come fearless man! Now meet the last and fellest peril of thy life, meet and survive—an injured woman's fury . . .*

"A piercing scream from the box. Lady Nelson has fainted. She has to be taken home. The curtain falls, but applause is hushed. All eyes are fixed on the box where the admiral sits immobile—"

"Do you mean to tell me," Miss Lily said, "that he just went on sitting there when his wife—I mean, she was his wife, wasn't she?—

had just given a shriek and passed out? He had the use of his limbs, didn't he, those that were left? I mean, he could jump up and take his bow quick enough."

"The trouble with you, Miss Lily," I said—she drove me to frankness—"the trouble with you is that you have no historical sense, none at all. As far as you are concerned, everything is happening in a sort of eternal present. Horatio was a great hero, a great public figure. It was an age that valued decorum. He had always to think of the figure he was cutting."

"Well, he cut a bad one there, that's all I'm saying."

"There was a French word much in use at the time among the upper class—*bienséance*, propriety. You had always to keep up appearances."

"That's what I am saying—the appearance he kept up was a bad one. Besides, I think you go too far in the opposite direction."

"What do you mean?"

"Well, I dare say you have got this historical sense, but you don't join up the past with the present. I mean, the present is where we are now, isn't it? If you did join it up, you would see that Nelson is one of those people who think they are above everything. Whatever they do is all right because they are so popular. Like these footballers who play for England, or that punk group that smashed up the hotel, the Sex Pistols, gone without trace now thank God, or someone like Woody Allen, who goes and marries his adopted daughter when he is old enough to be her grandfather and does it in the middle of a film festival. Then he complains that the journalists won't leave him alone. If enough people think you are great, you can do anything, but it doesn't make you a better person."

These comparisons were so absurd, it was all I could do to keep from laughing. "We are in the Nelson decade," I said. "In a few years we will be commemorating the great victory of Trafalgar. The whole nation will remember Horatio with gratitude. There will probably be a two-minute silence for him at Plymouth. Do you really think that in two hundred years' time the nation will be remembering with gratitude the goals scored by some footballer or the films of Woody Allen?"

"They'll be cheering someone else. Some last longer than others, but it comes to the same thing in the end. Anyway, there was something wrong with him. He must have known it was humiliating for Fanny, he wasn't stupid. Yet he insists on bringing her, he sits between them. I mean, it's pretty obvious why she fainted, isn't it?"

"Well, yes, she was an injured woman, but—"

"And that is what he couldn't forgive her," she said triumphantly. "She put him in the wrong, and he couldn't be wrong, could he? That's why he was so cruel to her. I mean, think what she must have felt in that theatre. What happened after she fainted?"

"She was helped out by the Hamiltons and old Mr. Nelson."

"Did they come back?"

"No, it seems not."

"So he sat there on his own till the end of the play? Charles, don't you think there is something terribly wrong with that?"

"No, I don't, as a matter of fact. You persist in looking at him as if he were any Tom, Dick, or Harry. He was the idol of the people. Do you think that the break-up of his marriage was the only thing he had on his mind? He had money problems as well. He had lived far above his means in Naples. When he came back, he had to sell half his holdings in stocks to pay off his debts. So he lost half of the interest. And he was involved in a court case with Lord St. Vincent. Do you remember who he was?"

"I'm not likely to forget *him*. He was the one who called for an orange in the middle of a battle, when a soldier beside him had his head shot off."

"That's him, yes. Two Spanish frigates had been taken the year before, and the prize money had gone to St. Vincent—fourteen thousand pounds, a lot of money in those days. Horatio thought it should have gone to him, as he was senior officer in the Mediterranean at the time—St. Vincent was in London. So you see, he had quite a lot on his mind besides Fanny."

"We all have our troubles," Miss Lily said. "But we still have to try to do the right thing."

"He was in the situation, there was nothing else he could have done."

Miss Lily looked at her watch, something she did openly only when she had decided that the session was over. "That's what is so terrible about it," she said. "That's why he had to do all that fighting and killing, isn't it? That's how people come to get their heads blown off."

A typical non sequitur on her part, though I lacked the energy by this time to take her up on it. When she had gone, I stayed where I was in the study, thinking about the conversation. It had followed the form of nearly all our talks about Horatio. Miss Lily generally started by joking, then worked herself into a state of indignation and ended on a softer, more sympathetic note, which contained, however, some quality of darker hinting. For my part, I always tried to be indulgent, to make allowances for her obvious inability to appreciate Horatio's genius. My closer understanding made me—as it made him—impervious to the sort of criticisms that she brought to bear. All the same, there was something troubling to me in the note of pity she struck so frequently these days. Troubling too, even more so, was the fact that I looked forward to Tuesdays and Fridays, looked forward to breathing the air Miss Lily brought with her . . .

As a refuge from these thoughts, I turned back to Horatio, to the December of that same year, when he and the Hamiltons were guests of William Beckford at his country estate in Wiltshire. Strange guests, a strange host—the incongruities of this visit had intrigued me for years, ever since I first read about it. Beckford had inherited great wealth from his merchant father, something like £60 million in equivalent value today. At the age of five he had been given piano lessons by the child prodigy Mozart, aged eight. He was the author of the celebrated *Vathek*, classic among Gothic novels, a tale of gloomy splendour and bizarre invention. Eccentric, romantic, increasingly reclusive, he devoted most of his energies—and vast sums of money—to the construction of a Gothic "abbey" on his estate, all turrets and crenellations, with an octagonal central tower that rose eventually to a height of nearly three hundred feet.

He invited them because they were celebrities—it is difficult to see what else they could have had in common. They were escorted from Salisbury by a detachment of cavalry. As they made their way up the drive to Beckford's mansion, a thirty-piece band played "Rule Britannia." Beckford waited for them on the steps, accompanied by his pet monkey and a dwarf he had acquired in Portugal.

The highlight of the stay was a visit to the abbey, which took place after lunch on the twenty-third. Also in the party were Madame Banti, the opera singer; Benjamin West, the American painter; John Wolcot, a composer of satirical verses; and an architect named Wyatt, who was helping Beckford in the design of his amazing folly. Darkness was already falling when they climbed into their carriages and set off across the park through the gloomy avenues of trees. Their way was shown by lanterns hung from the branches. As they came in sight of the vast building, a hidden orchestra struck up a solemn march. The massive walls rose above them, and the great tower, still incomplete, was half lost in the darkness.

Once through the portals of the place, we walk across the hall, a room so high that the lights in the sconces do not reach the ceiling, then into the Cardinal's Room, hung with purple damask, where hooded servants silently take our cloaks and hats. We sit down to eat at an enormous refectory table covered with golden baskets of sweetmeats and flagons of spiced wine. Solemn music sounds from the gallery. But where is Emma? She is not there beside us.

Some moments of anxiety—her presence is necessary, indispensable. But Sir William does not seem perturbed. Then, from the far end of this vast, dim room, glimmering and vague at first, dressed in a simple white robe, she advances, very slowly. She is bearing a golden urn. Urbane, knowledgeable Sir William whispers behind his hand: "Agrippina bearing the ashes of Germanicus." We nod, as being well acquainted with this episode in Roman history.

Emma passes from pathos to pride, from sorrow to scorn, from rage to final triumph as she rouses the Romans to revenge the death of her husband. It is one of the most successful and memorable of her Attitudes. Her fellow guests, sitting in that strange room with its yellow hangings and candlelit statues and reliquaries, are moved to tears as they watch. Above them in the darkness rises the great tower. It is nearing completion—it will reach an amazing 276 feet. Seven years later it will collapse, destroying most of the building.

Scholars, poetasters, opera singers, journalists—you were the odd one out in that company, as you always were in any company on land. Sir William was a collector and bookish. His taste did not run to the Gothic, but he would have had much in common with Beckford. Emma was a natural actress and a talented singer, she won applause with her Attitudes, she sang duets with Madame Banti. But you? Victor of the Nile, saviour of your country—your brightness was eclipsed among them. Better so, better you were dimmed. As an angel, you could not have endured such company. It was much like what you had come from in Naples. *A country of fiddlers and poets, whores and scoundrels.* That is how you wrote of Naples on the morning after your fortieth birthday. Those were the early days, before you were caught in the toils of the city.

As always, I had returned to Naples. Whatever the point of departure, I always ended there. I had solved nothing by leaping with Horatio to a London theatre or a Gothic folly. The doubts kept pace with me, however far ahead I went in his life—and only five years remained for him now. He took the city with him wherever he went, and so did I, and so we both would until I could clear him.

I 8

Perhaps it was fear of drowning in the poisonous flower-trap of Naples that was responsible for the dream I had that night. Fear was my inseparable companion in one form or another—and it has many forms.

A pervasive presence in this dream was a woman called Pat, whom I did not see but knew to be living in the desolate aftermath of an unhappy love affair with the president, he too invisible. I was approaching Pat's ruined cottage, which I knew in my dream represented her ruined life. In the abandoned garden was an old Morris Minor, half submerged in water. The garden itself had sunk and flooded, and I found myself standing chest-high in black water, tepid, not unpleasant. A woman who was not Pat appeared beside me and told me to look at my legs. I succeeded somehow in getting one leg out of the water. It was naked and covered with black centipede shapes printed on the skin. I felt a horrified repugnance and knew that I had stayed too long in the water. Rising before me was a sort of stone column, not very tall. If I could climb that, I could get out of the water. I had to embrace the column in order to climb. But the stones were loose, they crumbled in my hands, I kept slipping back. Surmounting the column, outlined against the sky, a figure leaning towards me, a shimmer of light on his chest. He leans towards me, but he does not offer to help. He is leaning to watch me, not to help me. He is faceless, some suggestion of wispy hair. He is wearing the same cocked hat, I feel the same terror as he brings his face nearer.

I woke from this sweating profusely, and for some time afterwards I groaned to myself in the darkness. Thoughts of my dead father came into my mind, and I was stricken with a sense of irreparable loss, as if something immensely valuable, irreplaceable, had slipped from my grasp and shattered beyond mending. It was myself I grieved for, what I might have been to him; I suppose I knew that then. It was the same grief that coloured my dreams, all-enveloping, too pervasive to be contained, an element of weather, like mist or dew.

Memories spring without warning or bidding into the mind, near and far, real and fabricated, all weeds in the same garden. There was no definite moment of transition, no moment when you saw him cross the great divide. There should be a moment, there must be a moment. The one detectable change was when his face lost that cruelty of keenness, of questioning. He died then.

So many things realized too late, understood too long after. I thought he was concerned with truth. A May afternoon, late May, I was seven years old—it was the year after my stay at the hospital. Another of those country walks, but this time my mother was with us and it was in Cambridgeshire, where her parents lived.

Childhood memories are so helplessly subject to tampering. So difficult not to take a chisel to them, or a brush. Sure memory of it is only sunlight, of being first high up as we walked, then low down between the hawthorn bushes, my mother in a light blue summer coat, no hat, her hair loose, blown sometimes across her face. Later days of similar weather must have got into the picture, but to me the essence of May is concentrated in that afternoon of broken cloud and hazy sunshine, the silver gleam of the birches, the hawthorn blossom everywhere in profusion, pink and white, accompanying us along the path like a prodigal bridal.

We had driven out to Devil's Dyke, to where the road crosses the dyke on the Newmarket Downs, not far from the racecourse. The footpath ran along the top of the dyke and it was high at first, you could see a long way across the downs on either side. To children from London the openness was exhilarating, the broad views, the vast sky crisscrossed with singing larks. The larks were stitching up the sky, so my mother said, that day or another. Who had torn it? Some giant, I imagined. I am not sure, she said; perhaps it tears itself. But the larks are busy stitching it up. Smiling, flushed with the sun, her reddish brown hair falling sometimes across her face. Blue eyes, like mine.

Then the dyke flattened down into wooded gullies, with clumps of alder and scrub willow. Names not belonging to that day, learned later. The path was more winding, less clearly defined, there were possibilities of detours and shortcuts. My father set Monty and me on to a game of his own devising, in retrospect totally characteristic of him, a game of observing and competing and reporting. Perhaps he had seen that we were flagging. In any case, a good way of getting rid of us for a while. We were to go on ahead, take careful mental note of everything, and return to make a full report.

It was seductive, to be an explorer, to break new ground before the adults, to be able, just for once, to tell them something they didn't know, couldn't know. I remember the excitement of running ahead. I kept close to Monty at first, thinking that if I looked where he looked I would see what he saw, a tactic wholly mistaken—I could not know what messages were being conveyed to him, and he, wanting to outshine me, offered no clues.

So I developed ambitions of my own, and from the very beginning they were enormous. I wanted to have something outstanding to report. I wanted to find another pathway, one that nobody else knew about, a sort of secret alternative to the one we were on. Did it start there, the fascination with the parallel track, the private access, a life to run alongside my own life?

Down into those wooded hollows, plunging down, looking for the big scoop. Cardinal error, looking for what you hope to find rather than looking at what is there before you. My father would not have made that error, nor did Monty. I was lost in the confusion of detail, not knowing the names of things. Flowers, birdsong, broken sunlight.

Meanwhile my brother, sober and methodical, three years older, not distracted by grand designs, pursued his observations. When I saw him run back I ran after him, wanting somehow to share in the credit, but then I had nothing to report, I stood silent under a blank sky. Monty had seen tracks of a dog, a big dog, in a place where the ground was soft; he had seen a colony of ants in a dead tree; he had seen briar roses in the hedge. He brought back, concealed till the moment of presentation, a pheasant's tail feather, a piece of the chalk on which the downs rested. *Good work, Monty. Try again, Charles—use your eyes, boy, you must learn to use your eyes.*

But my eyes were clotted with failure. My mother was smiling, but she knew what I was feeling, she knew my distress. Did I know hers? So difficult, across this ocean of time, to see her, to know. She spoke very quietly to me, a little aside. Perhaps you will see some oxlips. The yellow flowers with leaves like primroses. Not among the trees, they grow on the banksides. They like the chalk, you know. My father could not hear, but he saw, he guessed. *No special treatment, Dorothy. The boy must learn to use his eyes.* But I knew that with my eyes I could not win.

I knew there were creatures called moles, and they fascinated me because they were black and blind and had a mysterious alternative life under the ground. What more triumphant thing than to see one in broad daylight? I reported that I had seen a mole.

My father's face at once took on a certain gleam. I think he understood from the beginning that I had made it up, but he didn't say so, he expressed no hint of scepticism, offered me no joking way of escape. That was not his way. No, he led me on with questions, friendly questions.

Gracious me, a mole. Did you hear that, Dorothy? What was it like?

I said it was little and velvety-black and explained that it kept its nose close to the ground as it went along because it couldn't see very well.

What was it doing when you saw it?

I said it was just walking along; it was enjoying the sunshine after being in its dark burrow underground.

Is that all it was doing, just walking along?

Some hint of disappointment in my father's voice. My report was not dramatic enough. I said that I had seen it eating something.

Really? Now that is really interesting. What was it eating?

I think my mother attempted to intervene at this point. I have a vague memory of some words, an expression of remonstrance on her face as she looked at my father. But he was enjoying the game too much.

No, no, fair play. The boy must be allowed to make his report. What was it eating?

I said it was eating a piece of sandwich. It seemed reasonable—I had seen scraps of old picnics blown down there.

The trap was closed. My father's face lost its smile. *Moles don't eat sandwiches. Look me in the eye, Charles. You didn't see any mole at all, did you?*

I didn't see any mole, Monty said. I was in the same place that he was and I didn't see any mole.

You know how imaginative he is, my mother said. Don't be hard on him, he got carried away.

You told us a deliberate lie, didn't you? The whole thing was a lie.

Still that gleam of alertness about his face. Not anger, not reproach. He was *interested*, he was waiting for my confession. Then the moment of inspiration. No, I said, it wasn't a lie, it was a trick. His face changed as I spoke. This was unexpected, it was not part of the entertainment.

Come, you must learn to face up to things. Admit it was a lie and we'll say no more about it.

Not a lie, a trick, it was a TRICK.

I was afraid of him in all his moods, but that afternoon I was afraid of humiliation more. This was the fear that made me obstinate, that gave me one of the few triumphs of my childhood. For I did not retract.

He was enraged. He had been ready to put the rabbit out of its misery, but if I would not admit to being a liar, where was the rabbit? He made me walk back on my own, behind the others, in disgrace. *Until you own up, until you learn to face the music.* But I never did own up.

It was not that I thought him in the wrong or myself in the right. At the time I believed his anger was due to outraged principle, my failure to face the music and so on. Only much later did I come to understand the true nature of my offence: I had spoiled his game. But

I knew even then, as I trailed behind the others, forlorn but unrepentant trickster, knew that I had held out against an adversary immensely more powerful on his own ground and I had done it by not yielding, not admitting—I had done it *by not showing*. I began to learn the lesson then: reveal yourself and you are lost, you are crushed. It is by concealment that we avoid the fate of the rabbit under the boot.

19

*T*he following Sunday was the day of the Portsmouth trip, a prospect which had been troubling me intermittently ever since Miss Lily and I had made the arrangement several weeks before. The whole thing had been complicated further by the inclusion of this son of hers, Bobby, whose existence I had not suspected when I first suggested the outing.

As I got ready that morning, the same feeling descended on me that used to descend when I was returning to school at the close of the holidays. I had a special style of dressing then. Everything had to be done in a certain way so as to compensate for loneliness, disarm threats, make sure things would be all right. The basic principle was to do everything contrary to habit—right sock first, left sleeve first, shoelaces left over right. The more custom could be violated, the safer you would be. Sometimes in the years since then I had been able to muffle my fears and doubts in this way. I did it again now, socks before trousers, trousers before shirt, left hand first into the shirtsleeve.

I was there ten minutes early under the big clock at Waterloo Station. Exactly at eleven I saw them coming towards me, Miss Lily in a dark brown beret and a long suede coat, the boy in a padded anorak with various badges stitched to it and a red cap with a long peak. She smiled when she saw me, as if in relief. She looked quite unfamiliar, like a stranger at first, and I realized after a moment that this was be-cause I had never seen her out of doors before—my top step could hardly be called out of doors. This was the world where people caught trains, had drinks together, looked in shop windows.

"This is Bobby," she said. "Bobby, this is Mr. Cleasby."

"Charles," I said.

He was a pale boy, quite tall, with a bony face. He had his mother's wide mouth and a gaze just like hers, very clear and steady, but the eyes were lighter, rather an unusual colour, somewhere be-tween green and hazel.

"I am glad you were able to come along," I said. I smiled at him. I was managing this meeting really rather well.

"But you are not wearing a coat," Miss Lily said to me, a remark that certainly belonged to the new, outside person she was now rather than to Avon Secretarial Services. "Not so much as a scarf," she added in accents of dismay.

"I don't wear scarves, I don't possess one," I said, answering the smaller matter first. It was true that I had omitted to bring a coat with me, but I was wearing a woollen pullover and a tweed jacket and flan-nel trousers. And the morning had seemed mild enough. "I am quite all right as I am," I said.

Miss Lily seemed to doubt this—there was a tendency to a pursing of the lips. "You really don't take enough care of yourself. It might be chilly there, beside the sea. I mean, it's only April."

I could not help feeling the irony of it. Horatio walked the decks in all weathers, enduring everything that sky and sea could visit upon him, from the tropics to the North Pole, and here were we, discussing the perils of an April day in Portsmouth. I made a sort of face at Bobby. "Does your mother go on about scarfs to you too?"

"She does, yeah. Coats and hats as well. She feels cold, so she thinks everyone else does."

He spoke as if he were my age, or I were his.

"Don't you be cheeky," Miss Lily said. She smiled at him and he smiled back, and I saw that these were two people who got on well together.

"Well, we are made of sterner stuff, aren't we?" I said, man to man. I saw now that he was wearing a scarf, a blue and white one, tucked inside the collar of his anorak.

While I was waiting to get the tickets, I fell to wondering what it really signified, that expression—to take care of yourself. Of course Miss Lily had meant nourishing food and wrapping yourself up. But that is not the self, only the body. Harm is done to the self before we have a say in it; after that the choices are limited. It was in order to help me take care of myself that poor Penhas steered me back to Horatio.

When I turned back to them, I seemed to notice Miss Lily all over again. In that great glass hangar of a station, with its strange, bleak plenitude of light and strains of vaguely martial music, she looked bright-eyed and ready for anything in her jaunty beret. The other people I saw moving through those light-filled spaces seemed faint and somehow glaucous, leached of colour, but she was deepened. Bobby stood close beside her, solemn and still. For some reason he had turned his cap back to front—the long peak lay over the back of his neck. His eyes were on a dishevelled pigeon that had found its way in and was strutting about among the feet of passers-by.

Nothing much was said in the train. There were others in our compartment, and the presence of strangers imposed a constraint on us, who were not much more than strangers ourselves. She was sitting opposite, and sometimes our eyes met. Bobby fished out a folded magazine from his anorak pocket. It had a picture of a dinosaur on the outside and seemed to be mostly pictures inside too. We got sand-wiches and tea and a Coke for Bobby from a trolley that passed down the corridor.

Portsmouth was distinctly chilly. A cold wind straight from the sea met us as we stepped from the station, striking through the poor defences of my jacket and pullover. My eyes watered. Naturally I de-nied any slightest discomfort when Miss Lily—inevitably—remarked on this nasty wind and asked me if I didn't feel perished. No, no, very bracing, very refreshing. It got even colder as we approached the har-bour. Miss Lily tucked her chin into the collar of her coat; Bobby took some quick steps forward and then back, as if casting for a scent. He was still wearing his cap the wrong way round.

It is not possible to go aboard HMS *Victory* and wander about as and when you want; you have to go in a group with a guide, and these tours take place at regular times through the day. We had an hour to wait before the next one, and I suggested a visit to the Naval Museum on the quayside. This houses the whole splendid story of our wars at sea, from the timbers of Henry V's flagship, the *Grace Dieu*, to maps of naval operations in the Gulf War. But in view of the limited time, we naturally made for the Nelson Gallery.

It was warmer in here, but the sea light followed us, striking through the walls of glass that ran round the gallery on three sides—the same desolate light he must have seen on so many days, the light that lay around him as he waited that March day at Chatham to join his first ship. We mounted to the upper gallery, where the figureheads and pendants and cannon are displayed. I pointed out the ensigns and flags hanging there and explained to Miss Lily and Bobby what they stood for, whom they had belonged to. They always stirred my blood and quickened my imagination, not these naval standards only but all flags, all insignia of battle, the tattered banners of obscure regiments collecting dust in country churches, the monuments to the fallen in quiet squares, with their scrolled lists of the dead, the poignancy of these symbols wreathed in sacrifice and mourning.

Overhead and on the walls all round, the emblems hung motionless. I pointed out the ensigns on their poles, the white ones and the red, some with the Union Jack set in the upper left-hand corner, some without. "Do you know why that is?" I asked Bobby. He shook his head. His eyes seemed dazed, perhaps from the flooding of light through the huge plates of glass that surrounded us. "They started to include the Union Jack after 1707," I said. "That was the date of union with Scotland."

I felt cheerful and happy explaining these things. The gallery was empty; we had it for the moment to ourselves. The things that had been plaguing me, my restlessness and foreboding, my failure so far to extricate him, haul him free from the swamps of Naples 1799, all this receded and I felt at peace. Moreover, the light had changed; a thin sunshine had struck through the cloud and through our glass walls, and it fell here and there among the objects on show. Faint and pallid in itself, it brought brilliance to the painted figureheads, the pitted snouts of the cannon, the pink-faced uniformed effigies lining the gallery. I pointed out the broad pennant Horatio would have flown, as commander of a squadron, when he went into action at Cape St. Vincent, and the two flags, one below the other, that made up his favourite signal, the first in vertical stripes of red, white, and blue, the second a blue cross on a white background: *Engage the enemy more closely.*

"He was a great believer in close engagement." I looked at Miss Lily as I said this, wanting her to share my feeling for the impetuous genius of Horatio, for the scenes of heroism that had taken place beneath these vivid emblems. However, she seemed no more than politely interested.

It was when I glanced at Bobby that I saw where my true audience was. He was chewing some substance now, very slowly. There was no mistaking his interest in these flags. In that pale face of his, with its thin ridges of bone at the temples and cheeks, the greenish eyes were serious and intent. "How close could they get?"

"They could still go on firing broadsides when they were practically touching."

"But it is better to avoid fighting altogether," Miss Lily said. "Things can generally be settled by a bit of common sense, and nobody gets hurt."

"We couldn't have settled Napoleon's hash by any amount of common sense."

"There's always somebody's hash to settle, isn't there? That's one thing that never changes. Might be the French, might be the man next door. It's the Bedouin syndrome."

"What on earth is that?"

"Me against my brother, me and my brother against our cousin, my family against the rest of the tribe, my tribe against everyone who isn't Bedouin. That sums it all up for me, all these flags and things."

"Common sense is the virtue of the common man," I said, "and that is one thing Horatio Nelson wasn't." I was rather vexed with Miss Lily for these inappropriate remarks of hers among the emblems and engines of battle. "Where did you pick up this Bedouin business?" I asked her.

"Heard it on the radio. Years ago now." She was looking from Bobby to me with the expression of mild obstinacy that characterized her. "It stayed in my mind," she said. "Because it's true, that's why."

"We had a different style of fighting," I said to Bobby. "The French gunners preferred to fight at long distance, cutting away our masts and rigging and so disabling our ships. Our tactic was always to get in close, taking the enemy's fire at first, until we were near enough to do massive damage. *Lay a Frenchman close enough and you will always beat him.* One of our favourite sayings. And by God, it is true. I got that saying from Locker."

Bobby was still chewing, even more slowly now. "Who is Locker?"

I looked, smiling, at Miss Lily, expecting her to answer. But she said nothing at all. Her face wore a slight frown, as if she were puzzled about something. This silence on her part struck me as distinctly odd. She must know who Locker was; I had referred to him several times in the earlier sections of my book. At this moment of uncertainty, I was again aware of the sunlight but now as a source of confusion; my mind wavered among real and fabricated things, the staring figureheads, the stiff models of midshipmen and marines, the woman and boy before me. I knew I had to be careful how I answered. "Horatio's friend and mentor," I said. "He was captain of the frigate *Lowestoffe*, thirty-two guns, which Horatio joined in April '77 as an eighteen-year-old lieutenant. Locker was forty-six, and they became lifelong friends. Horatio had a great gift for friendship." I was aware of the difference as I said this; I had no friends at all. But of course it was the price one paid for being on the shadow side.

The time for our visit to the *Victory* was drawing near. We left the museum, walked back along the quay, and joined the party waiting to go aboard, about a dozen people loosely grouped in the shadow of the mighty hull. No sign of a guide as yet.

She towered above us, fresh-painted in black and pale gold, stripped of sail but fully rigged, the Union Jack at her bow, the white ensign at her stern. I had seen her a number of times over the years, but the sight thrilled me again now: the exact intervals of her gun-ports, the scarlet and gilt of her figurehead, the fretted window frames of the captain's cabin—his, Horatio's, cabin. In this splendid ship the nation honours the time of her greatness, now gone forever, when she was mistress of the seas; honours too her greatest hero, a man fashioned for heroism just as this great wooden ship with its tiers of guns was fashioned for destruction. Instruments both . . . *They cut pieces off him, didn't they?* Miss Lily's question came at me again, uninvited, deeply unwelcome. I was turning to her, perhaps with some vague idea of expunging the offence by the sight of the offender, when the guide appeared at the top of the companion-ladder—he had been lurking within all this time—and beckoned us to come up, recommending caution as he did so.

A motley crew we clearly were, now that we converged on the ladder and I was able to take more note. Two couples who looked married; a younger couple who might or might not have been; two stout elderly ladies with identical-looking grey perms in company with a younger, talkative man, perhaps a son or nephew; a woman, short and whiskery, with notebook and pencil at the ready; and a silent tall man on his own. In anoraks and overcoats and hats and scarfs they had come together on this cold day to pay their respects to Horatio. However, we were unfortunate in the constitution of this group; I sensed it from the start.

"Up you go," the son or nephew said in jovial tones to the ladies he was escorting. He glanced behind and gave the rest of us a wink. I hate these self-appointed jokers and professional jolly chaps. Urged on by him, the unwieldy permed ladies started up the ladder. They mounted with excruciating slowness, making the rest of us wait. At the top, in the confined space of the upper gundeck, we reassembled in a ring round our guide. Some members of the group made exaggerated sounds of exertion, especially one of the older couples, who had already been infected by the joker. "Mind your head, dear," the husband said as we ducked under the beams. "You never know when you might need it." It is always the case; you start off with one fool, then the spirit of emulation sets in and you end up with several.

The guide was a sandy-haired, square-faced man in a buttoned-up double-breasted blazer with coronet and shield stitched in blue and red on his breast pocket. "Well, here we are on HMS *Victory*, Lord Nelson's flagship," he said. "I am intending to conduct the tour in English, if that is okay with everyone."

"We was sort of hoping you would do it in French," one of the perms said. Everyone laughed at this except me and serious Bobby and the lady with the notebook. Miss Lily laughed with the others, and I was sorry to see this.

This laughter, in which she shared, was the real beginning of my suffering that day, because the guide too, as we descended to the bowels of the ship from deck to deck, stooping lower and lower as headroom diminished—he too turned out to be a comedian, delivering his commentary in a stale mix of joke and drama, no doubt derived from a hundred past tours. The joking was blasphemy, the drama was superfluous. On this ship where Horatio fought his last battle and took his last breath, all the imagination needs is the stimulus of facts.

In regard to these, the guide was competent but not wholly reliable. He said Horatio was "just turned twelve" when he joined the *Raisonnable* as midshipman, whereas in fact he was twelve years and three months when he was entered on the muster-roll and nearly twelve and a half when he actually joined the ship. Then he told us that the firing rate on board the *Victory* was a shot a minute, whereas in fact our gun crews at their best could deliver a broadside every seventy-five seconds, the French needing almost twice as long—a crucial element in the ultimate victory.

Nor did he succeed very well in conveying to his audience, accustomed to central heating and refrigerated food and the privacy of bathrooms, the nature of daily life on board a ship like this, the suffocating promiscuity of the lower gundeck, where several hundred men, among them a good number of disturbed or violent persons, lived in a proximity from which there was no escape, sleeping in hammocks slung from the beams and eating at mess tables put up between the guns. At sea, with the gunports closed, it would be dark and hot, the air would be thick with the stench of unwashed humanity. And the latrines, only six of them, out in the open, in the bows, six "seats of ease" for upwards of five hundred men . . .

In spite of the guide's shortcomings, I did nothing to interrupt him but now and again shook my head at Miss Lily. At one point, my forbearance growing thin, I drew her and Bobby a little apart, in a darker space between the guns, and began to mutter some of the essential facts. But Miss Lily was only half listening to me; she was trying at the same time to hear what the guide was saying. He was telling them about the procedure for burial at sea.

"They put two cannonballs at the foot to weigh the body down. Then the tailor is brought in and he stitches the corpse into the hammock, beginning with the feet. When he gets to the face—"

"Excuse me, how many guns were there on the ship?" This was the lady with the notebook; she was in a world of her own. It was the third time she had interrupted the guide with a question, severely factual, quite unrelated to the discourse of the moment and always timed to ruin some high point in the narrative.

"One hundred and four, madam. The *Victory* was a first-rate, and a first-rate ship of the line had to have a hundred guns as minimum."

She wrote this down, peering at her notebook in the light from the open gunport, just as she had peered a short while previously when writing down the cost of the ship's construction, £63,000 in the money of the time, about £50 million today. What could she want with this information? She wore thick glasses, and there was a whiskery glint about her jaws. It was pathetic, really.

I began my muttering again, trying to secure Miss Lily's interest, divert her attention from the guide. "That piece of rope there, you see it is blackened at one end—it has been dipped in tar in order to harden it."

"Why did they do that?" Bobby asked. In the half-light I saw his eyes fixed on me. Miss Lily had moved away. She was listening to the guide, who was still rambling on about sea burial.

"When he gets level with the nose, he puts his needle through it as a final test of life before stitching the canvas over the face. If the face twitches or the eyes water . . . I can give you a practical demonstration if you like. The hammock is here before us. I'll be the tailor. Any volunteers?"

Laughter. Again I see Miss Lily laughing among the others. She belongs in the crowd . . .

The laughter is cut short by the lady with the notebook, who this time performs a service. "How much canvas was used in the sails?"

"Madam, roughly four acres of canvas were needed to make the *Victory*'s sails."

General expressions of astonishment. Bobby was still standing close, and he was looking at me, not the guide. On an impulse hardly understood at the time, I drew him farther from the group, away from the light of the gunport. I began in low tones to tell him about the loading procedure, illustrating with gestures in the dimness the action of pushing a charge into the bore, then ramming it home, then jabbing a stiff wire down the vent to pierce the flannel cartridge before priming and firing.

It was strange—I forgot myself completely, acting this out for

Bobby. I explained, in no more than a murmur, the mechanism of the flintlock, the spark that ignited the priming.

"Flintlock." He lingered on the word. I saw the gleam of his eyes in the dimness. He was still wearing his cap back to front in that ridiculous fashion. "Did the flint always make a spark? What happened if the flint didn't make the spark?"

"They used a piece of hemp as a match. There is a piece of it over here."

We moved a little farther away. We were standing close together, speaking very quietly so as not to disturb the others. His face was turned up to me, very pale, glimmering slightly. He was looking towards the source of light, the open gunport and the thirty-two-pounder cannon within it, resting massively there on its blocked wheels. It suddenly seemed to me that I knew Bobby's face from somewhere long ago; it was the face of someone I had once known well. I felt a certain threat to my balance as I stood there on that motionless deck, then something more, a feeling of urgency, an impulse to raise my voice, speak a loud warning. I had to go on talking, I could not look away from his face.

"This is a kind of shrine now. You must try to picture it as it was when the ship was in action—the heat and the din, the deck heaving, the guns roaring, the crews barefoot so as not to slip in the blood, the powder monkeys running up with cartridges from the magazines."

"They were boys, weren't they?"

"Boys like you. Younger than you. They had to be small and light to get up and down the ladders quickly. Men and boys alike wore bands around their heads to keep the sweat—"

"Protect their ears."

"What?"

"I put it in my project. The teacher told us. They wore the bands over their ears instead of earplugs."

"Quite right, your teacher is quite right. Not that cotton head-bands were much good—the men would bleed from the ears after the battle, quite copiously, yes, gushes of blood, did your teacher tell you that? No? Well, you can put something in your project that he doesn't know or at any rate doesn't say."

"He says our sailors were the best in the world and we had better officers."

I could not remember when I had last looked into another human face for as long as I had now looked into this boy's. Again I felt the impulse of warning; again I blunted it, held it off with speech, but in a voice not like my own.

"And then there are the types of shot—cannonballs for damage to the body of the ship, chains to cut through the rigging, grapeshot for killing the crews . . ."

I could feel my larynx working and was aware of my mouth stretching and contracting, but it was as if I were listening to someone else on a bad line. Then I suppose I stopped talking altogether; there was a sort of resonant hush, faint and steady, like a distant sea. Through this the guide's voice came, from somewhere behind me. I wrenched my gaze from the boy's face, looked again at the tarred rope's end, the hemp match, the grapeshot in cloth bags, strangely like testicles, lying on their racks behind the thrusting black muzzle of the cannon: things placed here for display, for devotion. It was true what in my agitation I had said to Bobby. This was a shrine, a memorial to forms of warfare long superseded. Here, in the still heart of the ship, one knew it. The *Victory*, so painted and burnished, so scrupulously maintained, was dead.

"Three tons of metal on wheels," the guide said behind me. "Imagine the recoil of it, imagine what happened to the men in its way if once it got free."

How much time had passed in this talk with Bobby I had no

definite idea; not very much, I suppose. No-one paid any attention to us when we moved back to rejoin the group. Miss Lily glanced at us and smiled. After some minutes more we went down to the cockpit in the orlop, where the dying Horatio was carried. And now at last there was unity among us and harmony of feeling, an absence of that coarse human propensity to belittle things, bring them down to our own mediocre level. No-one was so grossly insensitive as to make jokes down here, not even that clown of a nephew or son.

He was carried down to die among the dying. Space was made for him in a narrow corner. The pallet he died on is still there, and a low lamp is kept burning. He received his wound while the issue was still in doubt, but he was alive when they came to him with the news of the victory, the greatest British naval victory in history, the annihilation of the enemy that he had hoped for, prayed for. Some of the words of that last prayer he wrote before the battle ran through my mind: *May the great God, whom I worship, grant to my country and for the benefit of Europe in general a great and glorious victory . . .*

The prayer was answered. The Franco-Spanish fleet was destroyed, their dead and wounded five times ours—the French lost twice as many men by drowning alone as we lost in the whole action. A triumph to ease the pains of his wound, the approach of death. *Thank God I have done my duty.* As we stood there in silence, the spirit of devotion rose in me, as it always had in this place, finally setting to rest the disturbance I had felt earlier, whispering to Bobby on the dark gundeck. I knew in that moment that I had been foolish and perverse to think this great ship was dead. Our small group, standing in awkward silence at the place where the hero died, was part of a vast annual pilgrimage. Millions of people had stood where we were standing in this obscure corner of the ship, far below the water line. Millions . . . That was hardly to be called a death. He had not died, he never will, not while our country's great past is still remembered.

The tour finished on the quarterdeck, at the point where he received his wound. How vast the world seemed after the closeness and darkness belowdecks, how vast it must have seemed to them on that morning of Trafalgar as they prepared for battle. We stood round the polished brass plaque flush with the deck, marking his exact position when the ball struck him.

"Captain Hardy was walking with him," the guide said. "Hardy was a big man, a good foot taller than Nelson. More of a target, you might say. It's the luck of the draw, isn't it? They were walking side by side here on the quarterdeck. Ten paces forward, ten paces back."

He took a few stiff paces to dramatize the event.

"They turned here, at the ladderway. Then they started out towards the stern . . ."

With a sudden gesture he opened the palm of his right hand and showed us what he had been holding there: a lead ball, looking too small to do much harm, like a small marble that a child might play with.

"The admiral was struck by one of these."

I thought this was a pretty cheap piece of showmanship, but there was no doubt it impressed the others, except the woman with the notebook, who was, as I have said, in a world of her own and about to prove it yet again. My feeling of hostility towards the guide returned when I saw them riveted on him, Miss Lily included. Paunchy, undistinguished-looking, not totally reliable as to the facts, he yet could command attention, hold the stage. He had seduced her away from me. But not Bobby . . .

"Entered by the left shoulder," the guide said. He was still displaying the ball in the palm of his hand. "Passed through one lung and lodged in—"

"Excuse me," the woman with the notebook said. "How much rope went into the rigging?"

A muttered exclamation from someone, I think the tall, lonely man, at this crassly inopportune question. The guide looked a bit glassy, as if he had taken a punch. However, he behaved well, I had to admit it. His big moment had been ruined, but he showed no more than a laborious politeness.

"Twenty-seven miles of rigging, madam, on HMS *Victory*. It lodged in the admiral's spine."

On this anticlimactic note and with a chorus of thank-yous, the guided tour came to an end. I remember little more about the day. Bobby wanted a hamburger, so we went to a McDonald's and all had one. I enjoyed mine, but I did not say much. I felt ill at ease and over-exposed among the shiny surfaces and bright colours. Miss Lily was chatty—it seemed she had enjoyed herself. But it was the other members of the group she talked mainly about, not Horatio; she had noticed all sorts of things about them that had quite escaped me, and formed opinions as to their occupations, material condition in life, character, and degree of personal fulfilment. Bobby, I remember, ate with gusto, pale face intent over his plate, cap still back to front.

We had the compartment to ourselves during the train journey home. Miss Lily was still quite talkative. She had been affected by the drama of Horatio's last moments, but it was not so much the heroic sacrifice that moved her as the sad cutting short of a promising love.

"They could have had another twenty years together," she said. "He would have retired—they had already bought a house in the country. I haven't all that much time for Emma Hamilton, I mean she wasn't my sort, too much of a show-off. But think what she must have felt when the news came. She had no friends in England, she had no secure income, she had a young child to bring up on her own."

Her mouth had thinned with feeling as she spoke. I could see that she was acknowledging something she felt she shared with Emma. I personally felt the situations to be distinctly different, but this was not the moment to say so, not with Bobby sitting there.

"If they had really thought so much of him, they would have carried out his last wishes for her," Miss Lily said. "I read all about it before we came here to Portsmouth. One of the last things he said was that he left Lady Hamilton and their daughter as a legacy to his country. He said it with his dying breath. It was the only thing he asked them for. And what did they do? They left her to die abroad, completely penniless."

"She was a very extravagant woman," I said. "Her life in Naples hadn't exactly taught her restraint. She was addicted to gambling, and in her later years she had what we would now call a drink problem."

"And so?" She had flushed a little and was looking at me with that particular sort of steadiness that I recognized as the prelude to indignation.

"Well," I said, "she was a difficult woman to help."

"Charles, don't mind me saying this, but you can be really dodgy sometimes when it comes to discussing things. What's the point of saying she was difficult to help when you know perfectly well that they didn't even try to help her? It was his dearest wish, and they just let her go to the dogs and the child with her. They were ready to give him a big funeral and put up statues to him but not to recognize the woman he loved, the mother of his child. It was the same thing when he was dead as when he was alive. They went on cutting pieces off him. Don't you think there's something terribly wrong with that?"

Asking me to share a sense of wrongness was one of Miss Lily's favorite ploys in argument, and I generally resisted on grounds of principle. But here, in the enclosed space of the compartment, with her earnest face so close before me, it was more than usually difficult. She had made progress in debate in these months, I had to admit that; she had become formidable.

"But really, don't you think so?" she said now. "They didn't want to honour him as a man, that's all I am saying. I mean, they didn't even let her attend his funeral, did they?"

It was Bobby who saved the day for me, relieved me from the need to answer, showing again that reverence for facts as opposed to sentiments that I had noticed in him earlier. "What did they do with him?" he asked.

"Do with him?"

"How did they get him back? I mean, the *Victory* took a long time to get back home, didn't she? Did they put him in a coffin?"

"They had to preserve the body," I said. "They stripped him and put him in spirits."

"What spirits?"

"Brandy, I think it was."

I saw that a smile had appeared on Miss Lily's face, the curving smile I liked, with her mouth just sufficiently open to show the white edges of her teeth. Her indignation was forgotten.

"Cognac," she said. "Must have been French. There you are now, that's what you call a turn-up for the books. He hated the French so much and he was brought home pickled in a barrel of French brandy."

Bobby's stare, its solemn character unaffected by his mother's levity, came back into my mind that night, when I was alone again at home. He was a boy for facts. One fact that the notebook woman had not elicited and the guide had forgotten to tell us, to my mind the most staggering of all, was that more than two thousand oak trees had gone into the making of the *Victory*'s hull; she was a floating forest. On that scale, the British fleet at the battle of Trafalgar must have represented something like fifty thousand oaks, roughly two million years of oak tree life. Bobby was twelve; his sense of scale and number would be developed enough. I resolved to impart these facts to him when I saw him again so that he could incorporate them in his project.

This resolution made me think of his face and particularly his eyes, his awe in that dim place, my recognition of him as someone I had known, and that strange paralysis of faculties that had descended on me. I had wanted the world to continue, I had wanted to shout a warning. But the memory of this was easy and calm now, it was like recalling an anecdote. Miss Lily had glanced at us when we rejoined the group, with an expression difficult to read—approval, perhaps; two men getting together. Perhaps something else altogether.

The faces, mother's and son's, thinned away and I was left with a memory of that drab and disparate group standing round the memorial plaque. They saw Horatio as a being expressing their own humanity and aspirations. Totally wrong, of course. He was not an ordinary man translated into greatness by particular circumstances; he was a bright angel. He is unaccountable, unjudgeable by the standards of those who gather at the place of his death—except for me, except for me.

At 1:25 P.M. on October 21, 1805, a French sharpshooter perched aloft in the topmast of the *Redoubtable* drew a bead on your starred and medalled breast. The ball struck you as you were about to take your third step from the companion-ladder towards the stern. It pierced your lung and broke your back, and you fell silently to the deck. At that precise moment, all around you on the upper deck and on the gundecks below, men were screaming and dying. Only half an hour before, at almost exactly the same point, your secretary, John Scott, had been cut in two by a round shot. But it is your death that we commemorate; there is only one plaque. Many were crucified, but there is only one cross.

2 0

I let six weeks go by before resigning from the club—time enough, I thought, for the decision to seem considered, deliberate. They were weeks of waiting, for what exactly I didn't know—certainly not for the moment when I would be writing to inform Pratt-Smithers of my decision to cancel my subscription. That had been my intention, worthy of Horatio himself in its unswerving firmness, from the moment I realized the implications of those empty seats.

I didn't attend the club in the interval. I didn't want to see any of them again, and certainly not Hugo—I wanted no deepening of acquaintance there. A man who could work behind the bar in the Nelson Club, have Horatio's image constantly before him for two nights every week, and then go and pin up an effeminate pop star on his wall. He and I had survived something that night. It was enough.

No, the waiting went on, it continued after my resignation, though taking on some extra quality afterwards, some quality of dread, some-thing that disturbed my nights rather than my days—these were still absorbed in the close study of that June week in Naples in 1799. I had not lost hope of being the one to clear his name. I was reading A. T. Mahan's account of those days, contained in his 1897 life of Nelson and in his subsequent articles in the *English Historical Review* defend-ing Horatio from charges of fraud. Mahan is the great champion of Horatio's honour and argues the case very strenuously and forcibly. Chief opponent among his contemporaries is F. P. Badham, a waspish close reasoner, dangerously precise in the matter of dates and times. These two, with names so similar, the impetuous and patriotic Mahan and the lucid, sardonic Badham, had come to seem like allegorical fig-ures to me, Virtue and Vice personified.

This, as I say, kept my days busy. My paper had failed, I was re-signing from the club, but there was still my book. Miss Lily came as usual on Tuesday and Friday evenings. A week after our visit to Portsmouth she brought me a burgundy-coloured woollen scarf, which she had knitted herself. "I had a lot of wool left over," she said, "just lying around, taking up space." Bales of it, she implied. All her gifts were the result of some surplus, or so she said, and all described in the same way, hasty but not shy—she always looked straight at me when she spoke, and I was finding myself, as time passed, more able to look firmly back at her, meet her eyes. Nowadays we looked at each other when we spoke together.

"You said, you know, that you hadn't got one."

As always, I found thanks difficult. Besides, some part of me re-sented this attempt to change my habits. What I had actually said was that I never wore them. The scarf lay there, over the back of a chair, till the following Monday. Then, noticing it again, on an impulse I picked it up and held it against my face.

I was thinking at that time about suggesting a trip to the Maritime Museum at Greenwich one Sunday afternoon. They have a whole section devoted to Horatio there. With the days getting warmer now, it would be a pleasant outing. We could walk across the park or along the river and have tea somewhere in Greenwich. She could bring Bobby too, now that a precedent had been set. In any case I had a certain feeling of tenderness for him after those moments of communion between us on the lower gundeck. But the days passed and I did not ask her, I found reasons for delay. Instead of taking the plunge, I made more and more elaborate plans for a time when the plunge had been taken. We could go to Burnham Thorpe in Norfolk, Horatio's birthplace, and stay at the village inn, the Nelson Arms. On that occasion Bobby could be left with his gran. It would mean a weekend together . . .

With all this to occupy my mind, the general election and the Labour landslide went over my head. I did not know of it till the Friday evening, when Miss Lily told me. I had forgotten altogether it was voting day, impaled as I was on the twin prongs of Mahan and Badham, trying to establish to my own satisfaction whether Cardinal Ruffo had indeed withdrawn the Russian troops from their advanced positions on the morning of June 26, 1799, as the acerbic Badham maintained, whether he had merely threatened to do so, or whether there had been neither the act nor the threat, as generous Mahan appeared to be asserting. It was a crucial point; if there had been no threat, Horatio had been under no pressure, would not have needed to mask his purposes, trick the rebels into surrender so as to hand them over to their Bourbon king.

She was elated by the election results, but I didn't want to talk about it, I didn't find it interesting, I didn't know what any of them looked like. I still had the horror of blank screens that had been with me since my illness, so there was no television set anywhere in the house, and for some months now I had not been bothering with newspapers. Miss Lily, of course, could not forbear to comment.

"Well, you are strange in some ways, Charles, that's all I'm saying. You wouldn't know Tony Blair if you passed him in the street, but you would know an admiral that fell off his perch two hundred years ago."

"He never fell off anything, he is immortal," I said, but it was a waste of breath. She used habitual phrases and did not think beyond them; it did not occur to her that she was speaking of Horatio as if he were a dead canary.

That was about the sum of our political conversation. After that we resumed work. But the book was giving me less pleasure now. It is from around this time that I date the real beginnings of the dissatisfaction that would lead me in the end to suspend work on the book altogether. The further I went ahead with his life, the more my failure to clear up the Naples business weighed on me. It was in the May of 1803, on the sixteenth, that the Napoleonic War began, after the brief interval of peace afforded by the Treaty of Amiens, signed the previous March. Two days later, as commander-in-chief Mediterranean, he hoisted his flag in HMS *Victory* and the run-up to Trafalgar began. How could I take him through these days of unparalleled glory while leaving unresolved in his wake the question of his conduct in Naples? It was not a question of some violent excess or tempestuous love, such as could easily be accommodated in the heroic life. It was a question of cold-blooded falsehood and fraud. This would never do for the British. A wily hero might suit the Greeks, but we are a straightforward people, detesting perfidy in all its forms. No, he had to be cleared.

As the weeks passed and the anniversary of the events themselves came closer and closer, I dashed myself repeatedly against these

rocks of the past, made up of truth and lies and unsupported assertions, and fell back bruised. Mahan and Badham, allegorical twins,
stalked mouthing and gesturing through my days and nights. Whether
Ruffo had actually moved the troops was in a way immaterial; it
would have been enough that Horatio believed he intended to do so.
In fact, to withdraw them would have been the proper thing if Horatio was offering to break the treaty, because they had been moved to
this favourable position on the twenty-third at the request of the
rebels themselves, in anticipation of their coming out, to protect
them from the vengeance of the populace, the savage *lazzaroni*, one of
the bloodthirstiest mobs in history, passionately faithful to King Ferdinand, murderously disposed towards his republican enemies. Natural and honourable, then, if the treaty was to be abrogated, to restore
the status quo ante. And Horatio *was* threatening to abrogate the
treaty. There is his Declaration, sent into the forts on the morning of
the twenty-fifth, signed by his own hand, in which he acquaints the
rebels that he will not permit them to embark or quit those places,
that they must surrender to His Majesty's royal mercy.

The following morning the cardinal despatched his ultimatum
to Horatio that he would withdraw the Russian troops and leave the
English to conquer the enemy on their own. Or so Badham asserts;
Mahan denies it. On that morning, the twenty-sixth, a Thursday, I
woke at daybreak and the questions fastened on me again, buzzed in
my ears like flies. Why would Ruffo write thus if he didn't believe
Horatio was about to break the treaty? Even if, as Mahan maintains,
there was no document at all, even if there was no more evidence
than the résumé of the cardinal's intentions made in retrospect by his
secretary, Sacchinelli—even so, would it not have put Horatio under
pressure to seek some less direct way of repossessing the forts? There
was a change of attitude on his part between the twenty-fifth and the
twenty-sixth, no-one denies that. He gave an assurance to Ruffo on

the twenty-sixth that he would not oppose the embarkation of the rebels. This document exists. In Badham's view, this was tantamount to an endorsement of the treaty as a whole, or so the rebels would have understood it—they would have believed they would be allowed to sail for France. In Mahan's view, the document referred only to the embarkation and nothing further, and the rebels knew this perfectly well. The crux of the thing was there. *What were they given to understand?* Would they have come out only to sit and wait in the crowded transports? Wait for what?

His Majesty's royal mercy . . . It occurred to me now that I had not completed the cast of players. There was still the royal couple, Ferdinand and Maria Carolina. The prospect of some action came as a relief. I got out of bed, dressed in the dimness, and went along to the kitchen, where I made tea, observing each stage in the process carefully. I took the teapot and my special mug with the double C on it into the study. Clean sheet, carefully sharpened pencil.

Ferdinand IV, king of Naples and Sicily. Born in 1751, the third son of Charles III of Spain. The eldest son was mad—he had to be restrained from assaulting any woman on sight; the second was feeble-minded, quite incapable of rule. Ferdinand was not mad, but from childhood on he was kept ignorant and simple so that the government of Naples could continue to be directed from Spain through Charles III's ministers. He grew up without any call being made on his mind or judgement; his companions were people of the lowest sort, and his speech was like theirs, the street language of Naples. At the age of seventeen he married Maria Carolina of Austria, a woman far more intelligent and forceful than himself.

He was strong and active and his cramped energies found release in rough games, practical jokes, above all in hunting and fishing. Hunting was his ruling passion, but it was hunting without risk. He would drag his ministers with him for dawn-to-dusk sessions of slaughter. Standing in a brick-built shooting box, he would wait for his keepers to drive the game to him. *He was a crack shot—a visiting diplomat recorded that in a hundred shots, the king only missed once. An expert fisherman and sailor, he delighted in running races with boatmen out in the gulf. Dressed as a fisherman, he would sell his catch on the market, haggling over the price in Neapolitan dialect. The common people loved him, they thought of him as one of them. Unprepossessing in appearance, with a low forehead, a huge nose, and a pendulous lower lip.*

He had a rough good humour when things were going smoothly, but he hated anything to be required of him, any opposition or difficulty, any mental effort. He avoided the trouble of having to sign documents by giving one of his ministers, the Marquese Tannucci, a stamp with his signature on it. He was never required to consult anything but his own pleasures. His manners were gross, even for that age. Sir William Hamilton, who was often in attendance on the king, relates in a letter how Ferdinand, after a hearty meal, would lay a hand on his belly and remark that having eaten well, he now needed a good easing of his bowels. He would choose some of those around him for the privilege of keeping him company during the performance. Infantile, cowardly, vindictive when crossed, totally lacking in conscience or compunction . . .

Attacked by restlessness at this point, I got up and fell to my usual pacing from bookshelves to wall. The title this time was *The Wooden World*, by N.A.M. Rodger, and the word was *Wooden*. Finger on the letters, six paces, palms against the wall, thumbs mustn't touch. This was the king of Naples and Sicily, this the man who came out across the bay in his royal barge, sweating in his black velvet and gold lace, to thank his one-armed, one-eyed saviour, the hero of the Nile, on that September day in 1798, while the bands played and the white birds flew up from their cages into the sky. Infantile. That was the key. It was a ruined child that clambered aboard to make you that speech of welcome and thanks. It was a ruined child to whom you delivered the Neapolitan Jacobins. The past is littered with ruined children. *His Majesty's royal mercy . . .* But that was not it either: it was not to him but to the queen that they were really delivered. Her turn now, the last member of the cast.

Maria Carolina. Born 1752, daughter of the Austrian empress Maria Theresa. At sixteen she was married to Ferdinand, who was one year older. She bore him eighteen children, of whom eight survived. Her sister Marie Antoinette married Louis XVI of France and went to the guillotine some months after him, in October 1793, confirming Maria Carolina's fear and hatred of republicanism and all forms of liberal dissent, especially if they came with a French stamp on them. They had this in common, she and Horatio . . .

Devout and superstitious—she wrote prayers on scraps of paper and tucked them into her stays or sometimes swallowed them. In marked contrast to Ferdinand, she had regal manners, a grasp of European politics, and the will to rule. On the birth of her first son, in 1775, she claimed her right to sit in the Council of State and within a few months was the effective ruler of the kingdom. She was subject to violent swings of emotion. On the few occasions that Ferdinand attempted to oppose her will, she screamed and raged at him and drove him to flight. On that day of your triumphant arrival in the Bay of Naples, she was forty-five years old. She had never been regarded as a beauty. A glassy eye, a frozen look, the long Hapsburg jaw, a figure at once massive and gaunt. But she had a grand manner. You were impressed with her, touched by her dignity and her distress at the danger from France, the common enemy. Truly a daughter of Maria Theresa, you said. What did you mean by that? You were moved because she placed her trust in you, the one man who could save her kingdom and her person. And she, what did she think of you, what did she really think?

The question gave me pause. There was no way of knowing. She needed the ships and the guns, the backing of Britain. Horatio was a hero; she flattered him—he was always susceptible to flattery, she would have known that. And in those June days of the following year, which were giving me so much trouble, she would have known something more. The admiral was deeply in love with the lady ambassadress, who was also her private ambassadress—a flatterer too and a hater of the French. Love, trust, flattery—not easy to disappoint the expectations of two such women, not when you share the hatred too.

Truly a daughter of Maria Theresa. Somewhere in my notes I had an extract of a letter of Hamilton's in which he spoke of this inheritance. After some minutes I found it: *It is well to own, and indeed the Emperor Joseph told me so himself when at Naples, that all the daughters of Maria Theresa had very tender hearts susceptible to sudden and violent impressions.*

A hysteric married too young to a ruined child, putting it in basic terms. This was the royal couple who enlisted your services and gained your devotion, to whose mercy the rebels were delivered. However obscure the circumstances in which they were prevailed upon to surrender, there is no doubt at all about what happened to them subsequently. They were embarked on the transports and kept there in the bay. On the twenty-eighth, the letters Horatio had been waiting for arrived from the court at Palermo, conferring full powers on him. Who had these powers before? A question raised by Badham. Presumably it was Ruffo.

Your first move was to order the boats with the rebels on board to be hauled under the guns of the warships. Some of the leaders were taken off and put in irons. The people who had left the forts during the truce were summoned to give themselves up on pain of death. Ruffo protested, then backed down, and with this all hopes for the rebels were at an end.

The king sailed in with his suite on July 10 and established his court aboard your flagship, the *Foudroyant*. He held levees on the quarterdeck and amused himself by shooting passing seagulls. In the balmy evenings, Emma would dress as Britannia and stand on the poop to sing to the assembled company, beginning, naturally, with "Rule Britannia."

The picture came irresistibly into my mind as I sat there. The warmth of the evening, the aromatic hillsides and the stinking city blending their scents together, wafting them across the bay; the shifting reflections in the water, with here and there dead floating gulls attesting to the king's marksmanship; Emma resplendent on the poop in helmet and trident and billowing robe.

> When Britain first, at heaven's command,
> Arose from out the azure main,
> This was the charter of the land,
> And guardian angels sung this strain . . .

The swelling notes must have filled the hearts of those on board and carried far across the bay—to the sailors of the British fleet in their hammocks; to the republicans in the cramped and unsanitary prison ships, where they had been confined for two weeks now; perhaps to the city itself, where the faithful *lazzaroni* were continuing to cut up, roast, and eat suspected French sympathizers.

The royal justice began to operate soon after this. All through the summer the executions continued. Some went to the block; others, women as well as men, were hanged. It was these public hangings that were dreaded most, because of the hideousness of the method. Thoughts of this fascinated and appalled me; I could not keep still, I had to get up and start my pacing again. This time the book was John Keegan's *Battle at Sea* and the chosen word was the first one, *Battle*. But now, quite naturally and without being conscious of any choice, I found myself varying the procedure, touching the word with the forefinger of my *left* hand.

Most of the executions took place in the Piazza del Mercato, which I had never seen but imagined as vast and desolate, on a scale somehow with the number and manner of the deaths. The gallows was a tall post with one arm, which was reached by means of a ladder. The hangman bound the arms of the prisoner, blindfolded him, and placed the rope round his neck. This done, he went first up the ladder, leading the prisoner by the rope. Blind, the rough hemp at your neck, tugged upward step by step, mounting to the sky, the terrible shouts of the populace in your ears. *Battle.* White word on a black spine. Left forefinger, six paces, arms against the wall, thumbs mustn't touch . . . Step by step, mounting the ladder. Close behind, bringing up the rear, the hangman's nimble assistant, known as *tirapiedi*, pull-feet. The hangman scrambles onto the crossbeam and makes the rope fast. He then makes a sign to his assistant, who pushes the prisoner off the ladder, adroitly catches him by the feet as he falls, and swings with him into space. At the same moment the hangman lowers himself from the crossbeam and straddles the shoulders of the prisoner, and the three of them swing back and forth like a circus act, applauded by the vast crowd. Back and forth, back and forth. Thumbs mustn't touch. This time, however, I stop, lean forward, lay my forehead against the cool wall, close my eyes. In my mind the picture of that dangling, three-headed beast, all in struggling movement. One riding above, one swinging below, the middle one choking, dying. Eleonora Pimentel Fonseca, the poetess, died like this, and Domenico Cirillo, the biologist, fellow of the Royal Society, and Michele Natale, bishop of Vico, and the philosopher Mario Pagano.

You never faltered in the belief that you had acted justly, that their punishment was deserved. At least you did not falter in asserting this, and with you there could be no discrepancy between assertion and belief. You could not, surely you could not, have had any slightest sense that those who went to their deaths had been deceived, betrayed.

Six times back and forth and I could return to my desk. I wanted to look again at a letter you wrote to Lord Spencer that same July, in which you sum up your own sense of what you had achieved in Naples: *It will be my consolation that I have gained a kingdom, seated a faithful ally of His Majesty firmly on his throne, and restored happiness to millions* . . .

Certainly Ferdinand was grateful. On August 13, the Duke of Ascoli, one of the gentlemen of the bedchamber, came bearing a truly regal gift: the king's own sword. Made of gold, its hilt and blade set with diamonds, it is the sword Ferdinand was given by his father, Charles III, as a token of his duty to defend the kingdom, the same that Louis XIV gave his grandson Philip V when he succeeded to the throne of Spain. On the same day, Prince Lucci writes to inform us that we have been created Duke of Bronte, with an estate at the foot of Etna worth £3000 a year. Now we can sign ourselves Nelson and Bronte.

Then, not long after, there is the *fête champêtre*, held by the court in Palermo, to celebrate the first anniversary of the arrival in Naples, on September 3, of the news of our great victory at the mouth of the Nile. This is the last and most splendid of the court's tributes to us.

Evening; the garden of the royal palace lit with fairy lights; a select company of courtiers, foreign ministers, and their suites, officers from the allied navies, British, Turkish, and Russian. We are greeted on our arrival by the king and queen and young Prince Leopold in his midshipman's uniform. I am wearing the new sword; Emma is breathtaking in a white gown with aigrette, earrings, and bracelet of diamonds.

We begin with a magnificent firework display representing the battle of the Nile, culminating in the blowing up of the French flagship, *L'Orient*, and the ceremonial burning of the tricolor. This we watch from a balcony, with Emma on one side of me and Queen

Maria Carolina on the other. In attendance are also the Turkish and Russian admirals. To the former, Cadir Bey, the queen speaks a few words, pointing out to him how by this glorious victory I have saved his country and hers and all Europe. Cadir Bey smiles and bows. Then follows a cantata, specially composed for the occasion.

> Long live the British hero!
> Long live great Nelson!
> It is he who drove far from us all affliction.
> It is he who gave peace to our troubled hearts.

Preserving a modest impassivity, I take my bow. Then come the refreshments, ices and sweets. We saunter through the lamplit lanes of the garden, Maria Carolina on my arm. Now comes the climax of the evening. We pass between elegant pavilions. Before us rises a Greek temple, magnificently illuminated. A flight of steps leads up to a vestibule supported by columns. Inside, in a blaze of light, three life-size wax figures: myself, Sir William, and Emma. I am in full dress, the ambassador in Windsor uniform, and Emma in white, with a blue shawl embroidered with the names of all the captains who took part with me in the battle. Beyond, within the temple itself, is an altar surmounted by the allegorical figure of Glory. There before it, in the centre of the place, standing upright in a golden chariot, the figure of King Ferdinand. Picked out in lamps, running all round the inside of the temple above the columns, BRITANNIA RULES THE WAVES.

The orchestra plays "God Save the King." Little Prince Leopold places a laurel wreath on my waxwork figure. He has to stand on tiptoe to do it. I run forward up the steps. I kneel and kiss the prince's hand. The boy throws his arms round my neck, he embraces me. I look into his face—it is a face I know, a face I have seen somewhere, long ago. I try to shout a warning but can make no sound . . .

The shock of this half-recognition brought me back from that spectacular evening to the daylight of my room, the littered desk before me. Why did he do it? It was not part of the programme, it was an impulse, nobody expected it. The people cheered and wept to see the maimed hero, so slight in frame, so haggard, kneel before the boy. It was a sight no-one there would ever forget—this man who had saved the kingdom, kneeling.

No mention of it in the *Times* report. The fireworks, yes, the paean of praise, the wax figures, Ferdinand in his chariot. All in that tone of solemn satire the newspaper had made its own: the be-ribboned admiral among the waxworks in the Temple of Fame. But no smallest reference to this one action, which brought warmth and spontaneous feeling to the pomp of the proceedings, broke the mould. That was it—you shattered the programme, you found again the grace you had found at Cape St. Vincent, *you broke the line.*

Leopold was wearing midshipman's uniform. Was it because you saw yourself in the child? On the quayside at Chatham that cold March day, staring across the grey water at your first ship?

It was too young. You acknowledged as much four years later, at a dinner aboard the *Victory* celebrating the anniversary of the battle of Cape St. Vincent. A young midshipman named Parsons finds himself, as the youngest present, seated on the right side of the withered admiral. He will write about it later: the stateroom flooded with Mediterranean sunshine, the gleam of silverware on the table, his awe at the proximity of his famous commander. He is too shy to look up during the meal, but when the cloth has been removed you turn to him, as custom demands. "A glass of wine with you, Mr. Parsons." By way of opening the conversation, you remark on his youth: "You entered the service at a very early age to have been in the action off Cape St. Vincent." Parsons speaks his first words: "Eleven years, my lord." He sees the smile vanish from the admiral's face and hears the muttered words: "Too young, much too young."

That September evening when they cheered and wept to see you kneel, plaudits of a different sort were rising heavenwards in Naples. There on the lamplit square they were celebrating the three-headed beast that dangled and swung below the arm of the gallows. One after the other, day after day, week after week, republicans of a short-lived republic.

You never doubted that right was with you. Perhaps sometimes privately? How can we know? Publicly you never wavered. *When the rebels surrendered, they came out from the castles as they ought, without the honours of war and trusting to the judgement of their sovereigns.* You wrote that in 1803, four years later. I know what Miss Lily would say—she would say you couldn't forgive them, that you dealt with them in the same way that you dealt with Fanny, you were still sitting up there, immobile, in your theatre box, while she suffered and they died. *He couldn't be wrong, could he?* Strange how her remarks, which I generally at first thought flippant or ill-informed, lingered in the mind, persisted and strengthened, took over the ground, just as she herself, her whole person, had done in my thoughts of her.

2 I

J continued my wrestling with the facts of those Naples days, or
versions of the facts rather, though there was a growing sickness
now in this travail, the sickness of anticipated knowledge or anticipated defeat. I think I must already have known then, as June drew to
a close and summer green thickened the hedges of the gardens,
known in my heart, that this issue would not be listed among the victories, for Horatio or me. I was trying to set him securely in bluff and
hearty Mahan's embrace, save him from the clutches of spiteful
Badham, who addressed the preface to his *Nelson and Ruffo* from the
Reform Club in Pall Mall in October 1904, a creature for whom preserving Horatio's honour mattered little.

When Miss Lily arrived on Friday evening, June the twenty-
seventh (the day Ruffo, under the illusion or in the pretence that the
treaty was to be honoured, celebrated his mass of thanksgiving at the
Carmine church in Naples), I was utterly weary with all these specu-

lations. Moreover, I had neglected to eat that day, although, knowing she was coming, I had shaved and made an effort to tidy myself up. The house was not in good order. Mrs. Watson, perhaps demoralized by the fact that I avoided communicating with her except in the form of notes, was not doing such a thorough job as she had in my father's time; there was a dustiness and unkemptness about the place, which I was sure Miss Lily noticed, though so far she had not remarked upon it.

This evening she took one look at me and asked whether I felt all right. "You look exhausted," she said.

"No, I am quite all right." However, I stood up rather too suddenly in order to get some papers. A blackness came before my eyes; I staggered slightly and put a hand against the wall to support myself. I felt her hand under my forearm, had the sense of a strong support.

"What is it?" she said. There was alarm in her voice.

"Just a dizzy spell. I'm all right now."

"Are you sure?" Her hand was still there under my arm. I felt the warmth of it. "Why don't you sit down for a while?"

"I tell you, I'm all right." Her hand was gone, but I felt the warmth of it still. "Can we get on?" I said.

But of course I had reckoned without her obstinacy. "I do think you ought to just sit down and take it easy for a bit. You would have fallen just now, if it hadn't been for the wall and me holding you up."

Once you have shown weakness, it is very hard to resist advice of this kind; there is somehow a psychological weight against you. She was trying to get power over me, I knew that. All the same, I capitulated; I made for the armchair and sat down in it. She remained standing before me, inquisitorial.

"Does it happen often, dizzy spells like that? I was frightened for a moment, I thought you were going to fall."

"Just lately, now and again."

Black specks before the eyes, sparse in the first moments, massing swiftly to form the darkness that threatened my balance. I did not go into these details with Miss Lily—the less you give away, the better. But about Horatio's ailments I could talk.

"He suffered from something similar," I said, "in Naples and Palermo, after the Battle of the Nile. Giddy spells. Also palpitations and attacks of breathlessness. As if a girth were buckled tight over his breast, as he described it. These are all symptoms of Da Costa's syndrome."

"And what may that be?" Miss Lily spoke in the tone she reserved for abstract concepts.

"It's a disordered action of the heart. Sometimes called soldier's heart, because there were so many cases during the First World War."

"Are you telling me you've got a heart condition?" Her voice had sharpened; it sounded like reproach, strangely comforting to me.

"No, no. Horatio was afraid it was heart disease at the time, but modern medical opinion gives it out as disorder of the heart due to prolonged anxiety and physical strain. Don't forget, it was only five months after the Battle of the Nile. That was a great victory, but it had taken weeks to find the French and bring them to action. His hours of sleep were short during all that time. He got a bad head wound in the battle; he thought at first his end had come. Then there was the affair with Emma—he was still under the Hamiltons' roof, he was still writing home to Fanny, there must have been a lot of guilt. And think of the responsibility. He was the commanding officer. Napoleon was already in Egypt with an army, en route for India. The fate of our empire was in the balance, everything hung on this one man, thin, slight, maimed already in the service of—"

"He probably wasn't very used to the food," Miss Lily said. "I mean to say, southern Italy. The food is very rich, isn't it? Especially in those days. They hadn't been alerted to the danger of animal fats. Ignorance is bliss, you might say, but it can't have been good for them, can it?"

"Good God," I said, "we are talking about his heart and mind, not his stomach."

"They are all pretty well tied up together. Anyway, you can't have this Costa thing, you haven't been in any wars. I don't suppose you have been hobnobbing with any ambassadors' wives, either."

In saying this, Miss Lily looked at me with the teasing expression that had been more and more common with her lately. I was at a disadvantage, sitting there—I did not know how to reply. Her words constituted another proof, if one were needed, of her pedestrian way of looking at things. Had I not gone with Horatio every step of the way? I had felt his anguish at the cowardly tactics of the French. I had suffered his head wound, felt the warm blood slide over my eyes, blinding me. I had lived through his hero's welcome, his rescue of the royal pair, the love of the motherless boy for the sensual, ample woman. Was I not during these very days living through the terrible temptations of power, his negotiations with Ruffo and the Neapolitan Jacobins?

"I expect you haven't been eating so well yourself," she said now. "What did you have for lunch?"

I did not want to reply to this, not thinking it her business; but she waited, with her eyes fixed on me. It was only then I realized that I had omitted to eat anything that day.

"A sandwich," I said. "Cheese sandwich." It was the first thing that came into my head, and at once I was carried back to the time before my mother left, that distant May afternoon, the walk along the dyke, the splendid profusion of the hawthorn flower. *Moles don't eat sandwiches. Look me in the eye, Charles* . . .

But I didn't fear Miss Lily's eyes. "Cheese and cress," I said.

"You are so absent-minded, you could be talking about yesterday or the day before or last week. I've known Bobby to have them, dizzy spells, when he skimps on his lunch at school, but he's still growing, and I don't think you are, are you? Well, we'll just have to see what there is."

Her expression had softened talking about Bobby, but I could see that she was fixed on some purpose. "What do you mean?" I said.

She gave two or three brisk nods. "I'll just go and have a look."

I asked her where she was going, but she went out of the room without replying. After a few minutes she was back again.

"Must have been a bought sandwich if you had one at all—there is not a scrap of either cheese or bread anywhere to be found. Cress I didn't bother to look for."

"Well, it was a bought one."

She looked at me with a scepticism that she took no trouble to conceal. "All I can find," she said, "in the way of foodstuffs, is four eggs that are not in a carton, so we don't know their date of birth, a cauliflower that has seen better days, and some potatoes in a string bag. Oh yes, and a bit of margarine."

She paused on this. I understood now that she was proposing to do something with these poor remnants. She was waiting for me to agree or object or perhaps even to suggest, as an alternative, that we should go out to eat. But I did not want to be with other people; I wanted the two of us to be together quietly. So sudden and strong was the attraction of this idea that I was afraid to speak, afraid of giving myself away. But I think silence betrayed me just as much, or else it was something in my face. After a moment she said, "Well, it will have to do, won't it?"

The upshot was that instead of going ahead with the book, that evening we ate together in the kitchen. The eggs were all right still. Miss Lily broke them one by one into a cup to make sure. The central parts of the cauliflower were eatable, the potatoes virtually pristine;

we had them steamed. There was just enough margarine to make an omelette. I still had a stock of claret, and I fetched a bottle up from the basement passage where I kept it.

She sat opposite me across the kitchen table. As we ate and drank, I felt glad and relieved to be released from the book for a while. It was a kind of holiday, and I knew I could not have had it on my own, could not have had it without her. There was no-one else. Monty was no good, we had not been on close terms for years—not since we were children, in fact. And now that he was dressing up in our dead father's clothes . . . There was something wrong with him, he needed some central interest in his life.

No, there was no-one else. I was aware that this gratitude I felt was illogical in a way. She was kind, but it was a constant kindness, not just for me. She was merely existing, being herself. I looked across the table at her; I was able, though briefly, to look into her eyes. The June weather had brought an olive tint to her face and throat—not that the days had been so sunny, but she had the sort of complexion that is deepened by warmth. She was wearing a white shirt, open at the neck. She was in that moment the sum of all the moments of her being as these had gathered for me, as I had known her, from the first time she had come to my door, Avon Secretarial Services in person. Her jokes, her rages, the perennial surplus from which she made her gifts, the limited sympathies that made her fail to understand Horatio, her championing of dim Fanny, her belief in wrapping up well . . .

As we ate and the wine went down, she talked about the circumstances of her life, something she had done rarely before and then only briefly. I had grown unused to conversation, and there seemed to me an extraordinary immediacy in everything she said; they were the things on her mind, the things that affected her from day to day. She had been overcharged for repairs to her car and intended to take it up with them, they might think women didn't know much about engines but they would learn better, she had done a car-maintenance course at evening class. Bobby was something of a problem at school, not that he was a bad boy but he was dreamy, half the time he was in a world of his own, sometimes his teachers got cross with him, he answered a different question from the one they were asking, they thought he was trying to be funny. She had been to the school; the class teacher said it was only a phase. He was very good at designing things and drawing, where he got that from she didn't know, she wasn't any good at it.

"Perhaps from his father?" I said—a bold stroke, but I was curious.

Miss Lily did not seem to be put out. "Not him," she said. "He might have been interested in someone behind a bar drawing him a pint. Actually he wasn't so much of a beer drinker, as far as I remember. Scotch would have been more his style, malt of course, and a choice of wines with dinner. He had a lot of money. This will sound funny, but he was a totally ideal person to me. For a while."

"How was that?"

"He was fifteen years older, divorced, rather good-looking. He was used to running the show. Like I say, he always had plenty of money. He had his own firm and he employed quite a lot of people. I suppose he told me how many—it was the sort of thing he would have told me—but I can't remember now. The boyfriend I had at the time worked for him, that's how we met, I was waiting for my boyfriend outside the office. I was just turned eighteen. I used to watch a lot of soaps, especially the ones where everybody seemed rich. All those glamorous people with such eventful lives. I used to love those programmes, I never missed. There was one called *Dynasty*, which I specially liked. My own life wasn't glamorous or eventful, I was working in an office, typing out invoices. Then when I met this man, he seemed to belong to that other world. It wasn't that I thought *Dy-*

nasty was the real world, but I thought there was a real world that was like *Dynasty*. Know what I mean?"

"I think so, yes."

"His name was Alex. Perfect, isn't it? I was never a beauty, but I was attractive—I spent more time on myself in those days. I was lively too. He sent me flowers all the time. He had a Porsche. He took me to expensive places. He was like a hero to me."

"Like a knight in shining armour."

"Shining Armani, more like it. I thought, you know, this is it, this is the real thing, this is what I was meant for. When I got pregnant, the flowers stopped coming. He told me to get an abortion. If I didn't, I would have to go it alone—he wouldn't help. An abortion would have been the reasonable thing, but I couldn't do it, I just couldn't. I mean the reasonable thing then, at the time. When I look at my Bobby now, it's just unthinkable. I had the baby on my own—Mum and Dad helped, they were great. Then when Bobby was born, this man had a change of heart. He'd be ready to help if I'd sign papers acknowledging him as the father. He would pay the rent on a flat. He was full of enthusiasm and paternal pride—it was a boy, you see. He was going to be a beautiful parent. 'I'll buy him a speedboat,' he said to me. That was what did it for him. A speedboat! There was the little kid, a tiny baby, with all his need for care and love, and there was this fool who was his father talking about speedboats. See what I mean? It was just what somebody in *Dynasty* would have said. But things were different now. This was a real baby and I was a real mother. I told him to make himself scarce. I never took a penny from him, and I never watched *Dynasty* again. I never watch soaps now, except for *Coronation Street*."

I listened spellbound to this story, which Miss Lily told without rancour or bitterness of any kind. She didn't mention any man currently in her life, though perhaps there was one. I didn't want to think about that. She lived in a world different from mine, not more eventful exactly—after all, I had Horatio—but somehow more spacious and hazardous. I wanted to reciprocate, find something from my own experience that might engage her interest. For some time nothing came to mind; then I hit upon it.

"It is really quite extraordinary," I said, "the shift there has been in the course of this century in the tone of Nelson biographies. Right up to the 1930s there was a concern to show him as he was, a truly noble character. Not all his biographers, of course, but nearly all." I was thinking here of bilious Badham.

"How do you mean?"

"Well, there was a concern to show him as *good*. Not only brave, not only a naval commander of genius, but virtuous too. The Victorians denied the adultery with Emma because they didn't think it proper behaviour for the hero of Trafalgar. That's going too far—we haven't got the hang-ups they had—but I take the old-fashioned view myself. His modern biographers don't seem to care one way or the other. Here we have the national hero and they skate over the question of whether he was good or not, in the sense of truthful and honourable. They simply don't seem to care."

"Well, we have gone down in the world, haven't we? Nelson has gone down with us, I suppose. We don't think we are so great anymore, so we don't need to make him out to be so great."

"But that is terrible, it is degenerate." I felt the usual distress at this belittlement of him, this abject surrender of a glorious past. "You would think it would work the other way," I said. "Here is someone who should make us proud to be British. Where has the pride gone?"

"It hasn't gone anywhere, as far as I am concerned. It was never there in the first place. I'm not proud to be British any more than I would be proud to be a Hottentot. There's such a thing as luck, I grant you that. Hottentots might have less going for them in the way of secondary education and supplementary benefits. But I honestly don't see where the pride comes in. How can you be proud of an accident?"

This was so wrong-headed and even perverse that for some moments I could not find the words to reply. "Where you are born is a matter of chance," I said at last. "No-one would deny that. But from that moment onwards, you accumulate impressions, form attachments, grow familiar with certain habits of thought and speech, certain great events in the past of your people. Horatio Nelson looms large in our past—he established our supremacy at sea for a century to come, he saved us from the vile French. Imagine what would have happened if it had gone the other way at Trafalgar and that rabble had come sailing up the Thames. That is what I meant by saying he should make us proud to be British."

Miss Lily paused a moment, then said, "Charles, I know you would like me to admire him as much as you do, and I take that as a compliment, but I can't. It's no good pretending. I can see he had his good points, but I wouldn't like my Bobby to turn out the way he did, just shaped for one purpose. There is more to life than shooting broadsides at the French, that's all I'm saying. As I see it, they took him away at twelve and sort of processed him. That midshipman business was a way of processing people. As far as I can see, they've been processing him ever since. Why couldn't they say, Well, yes, he was a great admiral and a very brave man, and yes, he was generous and warm-hearted, and he won a sweeping victory in the hour of his country's need, but he was narrow-minded and eaten up with vanity and could never admit he was in the wrong? He was a person, in other words. But no, they had to make him into a great man."

"You can't talk about him as an ordinary man. He wasn't an ordinary man. He was a great hero. And I don't believe he was processed, either. You are seeing things in the light of the present. As usual. You are ignoring the nature of eighteenth-century society. You talk as if he had a lot of choice. He was well connected on his mother's side, but he couldn't expect much help there—on land, at least. He inherited no fortune. He wasn't bookish, he didn't want to be a parson like his father. One step down and it would have been minor civil servant or farm bailiff."

"But that is the whole point. That made it easier for them."

"How do you mean?"

"The less choice he had, the easier they could brainwash him."

"Who on earth are the *they* you keep talking about?"

"Them that stood to gain. Anyway, we were talking about being proud, and he really doesn't make me proud at all. Being proud means not lowering yourself. Same thing applies to me and you and Nelson and everybody. I was left with Bobby, but I kept my head up. I've had to bring him up on my own, trying to make ends meet, working free-lance so I could be home when he got in from school. If he turns out well, maybe I can be proud of that. No, I've said it before, I can't help it, he puts my back up—Nelson, that is. He was always so ready to get people killed. If you look at it one way, he was a sort of serial killer. I like men who are gentle and kind and try not to hurt anyone. Women too, for that matter."

She paused again, then said in a deeper tone, "People like you, Charles. You can put it down to the wine if you want, but there's something I've been meaning to say to you for a long time now. I mean, I know you are very bound up with him and it's a good thing for a man to have a hobby, but I have to say that you are just about as different from Admiral Lord Horatio Nelson as a person could possibly be."

I was quite unprepared for this. She had spoken with such conviction, it was almost like a blow. My first impulse was to get up, move to where she could not see me. She was wrong, of course, I was

Horatio's other self, the shadow side, the reverse of the medal; I could not lose him without losing myself. But she was saying that she liked me, that I belonged among the people she liked. It came to me in my confusion that perhaps these contradictions were only apparent. After all, Miss Lily had nothing much in common with theatrical, beautiful, self-deluding Emma, but sometimes, in my thoughts and dreams, their bodies had blended . . .

I sat there in silence, without looking at her. I wanted to say that I liked her too, liked the sort of person she was, liked her looks and the way she talked to me, even when it made me angry. But I could not frame the words.

Into this silence came more words from her, words I hardly took in at first, in the confusion of my feelings. She had meant to tell me as soon as she arrived, but with one thing and another and me taking that funny turn . . . Just out of the blue, the offer had come. She would have to leave Bobby with his gran to begin with, she couldn't take him out of school.

On her face the look of a person in serious argument, wanting to convince. "I'm hoping they will let him come up for the holidays—it would be so good for him to get out of London for a bit."

I had the strange, familiar feeling of blood leaving the face. "You can't go away. There is the book," I said, as if it were something she had overlooked.

"It's only for ten weeks," she said.

"But you can't." Even to myself I sounded like a child.

"I've been thinking about it. If you like, I could find someone to replace me while I am away."

"No," I said, "I don't want anyone else."

"I have to fend for myself, you know, Charles. I always have had to. I can't afford to refuse a thing like this, the money is so good and everything found."

"When are you going?"

"July the seventh, a week on Monday. It's a residential course in business management at Matlock, in Derbyshire. I'll be doing the secretarial work—I was recommended for it. I can come next week as usual if you like."

"No, you'll have things to do, preparations to make and so on. We'd better say good-bye tonight."

I had spoken on impulse, but I knew it was best. I could not bear the thought of passing another week in the shadow of her leaving. Seeing her, talking to her, knowing all the time . . .

"It's not good-bye," she said.

"Of course I'll pay for next week's sessions anyway."

"I wasn't thinking of that."

"It's only fair—I'm the one who says you shouldn't come."

The week in question was the first week of July, and as I paid by the month, I had to make a cheque out. This gave me time to gather myself together. I had accepted now that she was going away; the thing was to find some sure means of bringing her back.

"I have enjoyed it so much," she said, "working together on the book. It is one of the most interesting jobs I have ever had. It has started me off reading about him and that whole period, I never thought I would get so interested in history, I didn't take to it much at school. And it is entirely because you talked to me, Charles—you weren't just the employer, you asked my opinion."

I couldn't really remember asking her opinion all that often; she had never much needed to be asked. There must be some way I could make sure she would come back, something I could tempt her with. Then in a flash it came to me: *Francesco Caracciolo.*

"We have to deal with Caracciolo next," I said. "When you come back, that is. I am beginning to believe he will provide some essential clues to the problem of Horatio's dealings with the Neapolitan Jacobins in 1799."

This was calculated to please her. She had always been more interested in Horatio's doings in this murky city than in any other period of his life whatever, and had been distinctly put out when we sidestepped it.

"I don't think we have mentioned him yet in the book," she said.

"No." In fact I had been delaying his introduction because he showed Horatio in what some—especially Badham—had thought to be a bad light.

"Who was he?"

"He was an admiral in the Neapolitan navy who went over to the Jacobin side and took part in the rebellion against King Ferdinand. They set up a republic—the Parthenopean Republic, it was called— very short-lived, it was born and died within a few months in 1799. It came into being when the king and queen fled to Sicily, and it was propped up by the French—they occupied Naples for a few weeks. When they withdrew, the republic collapsed. We haven't dealt with this period in the book yet because I can't quite get it straight in my head. Horatio played a very important part in negotiating the surrender of the rebels, but this Caracciolo wasn't among them when they came out from their forts. He had gone into hiding on his uncle's estate. He was arrested and brought in handcuffs to the *Foudroyant*."

"What had he done exactly? I'll just wash up these few things while you're talking. No, there's hardly anything—you just stay where you are."

So I went on sitting there at the table and watched her wash up the things and talked about Francesco Caracciolo, raising my voice a little to compete with the clatter.

"What had he done? What hadn't he done? He had rebelled

against his lawful sovereign and accepted command of a rebel fleet. He had made gunboat attacks on British and royal Neapolitan ships. He had fired on the frigate *Minerva* and damaged her. The *Minerva* had been his own flagship—he was firing on his own colours, enough in itself for a capital charge."

"What did they do with him?"

She had her back to me, standing there at the sink. She reached to put the dishes in the rack overhead and I saw the arch of her back. An inch or so of shirt had escaped from the waistband of her trousers. Some strands of brown hair had worked loose from the coil at the back of her head; the light brought out glints of copper in them. She was going away. A feeling of grief rose within me, like a slow tide. I did not believe she would come back.

"He was arrested by Ruffo's men and handed over to Horatio, who convened a court martial that same morning. It took them two hours to bring in a death sentence, by a four-to-two majority. The verdict was reported to Horatio, and he ordered the execution to be carried out at five that afternoon. Caracciolo was hanged in full view of the fleet from the yardarm of the *Minerva*, which he had once commanded. He remained hanging there till sunset. Then they cut the rope and let him fall into the bay."

Miss Lily turned towards me. The washing-up was finished. "Who ordered that to be done?"

"Horatio. He wasn't present at the trial, though."

"He didn't need to be, did he? Do you mean to say he had this man tried, condemned, and executed all in the course of a few hours?"

"He was absolutely right, in my opinion. Naples was still full of unrest. He wanted to make an example."

"Well, he certainly did that. But what was it an example of?

How to hang people in a hurry? He was supposed to believe in God, wasn't he?"

This was one of the fairly frequent occasions when the precise import of Miss Lily's words was not immediately clear to me. But she seemed to need no answer to her question. Perhaps I had succeeded in interesting her in Caracciolo, I couldn't really tell; but it was clear that she didn't view Horatio any more favourably than before.

It was nearly eleven by the kitchen clock. She was getting ready to go. I could think of nothing now to delay it. In silence I followed her to the study, watched her collect her bag with the computer, accompanied her to the door.

She smiled up from the lower step as she had so often done before. "It's been a nice evening, hasn't it?" she said. "Don't work too hard, and don't worry. Take some time off in the summer, go for a trip somewhere. We'll catch up on the book when I get back."

"I thought we might go to the Maritime Museum at Greenwich when you get back," I said. "They've got a whole section devoted to Horatio. We could walk through the park and maybe have tea somewhere in Greenwich. Bobby could come too, if he liked the idea."

"That sounds nice," she said. She sounded as if she meant it. She was going away. I sensed she was sorry for me, sorry to be leaving me alone in the house. I had a momentary, desolate sense of advantage. This would be a good time to mention the trip to Burnham Thorpe, Horatio's birthplace, a weekend together and Bobby left at home. But before I could speak, while I was still gathering my nerve, Miss Lily did something she had never done before: she came back up the steps and kissed me on the cheek, the right cheek. I felt the brief warmth of her lips and the warmth of her face against mine.

2 2

J tried for a while to go on with the book, but I added nothing of
significance after she had gone. I had come to depend on these
dictating sessions more than I realized, and not only for the material
help: I had come to take her interest, though generally expressed in
interruptions, as a gauge of the interest of the book, a sort of guarantee. Without her, almost at once, I began to falter, lose confidence. In-
sensibly, without my being aware of it, Miss Lily had insinuated
herself into the very grain and texture of the work; her presence, her
voice, were everywhere in it, winding and coiling through. I knew by
the middle of July that I would not be able to continue until she came
back. I still hoped she would come back.

I spent my days reading and rereading the conflicting versions of
Horatio's conduct in Naples in 1799. As I had remarked to Miss Lily,
the more closely argued of these dated from late Victorian times, concern for his honour having declined more or less to zero level in this

cynical age of ours. On the defending side there was a phalanx of robust, deep-voiced males: A. T. Mahan, naval historian, forty years' service in the American navy, his staunch supporters Professor J. K. Laughton of London University and H. C. Gutteridge, late scholar of King's College, Cambridge, a more Jesuitical type. The other side was more feline in character: F. P. Badham, about whom I knew only that he addressed his prefaces from the Reform Club in Pall Mall; Constance Giglioli, née Stocker, who was married to an Italian botanist and lived many years in Italy; and various Italian sources, not translated and therefore out of my reach—out of the reach too, as it appeared, of Mahan, Laughton, and Gutteridge.

This controversy, at once passionate and remote, was a maze that I entered and wandered about in every day after the ritual making of the tea. I would pour out the tea in the kitchen into my monogrammed mug and carry it through on the black-and-red japanned tray I always used, together with six biscuits, always six. I had taken to buying the sort of biscuit called wholemeal digestive, as being a convenient form of food and also pleasant to dip into the tea.

I could feel myself getting slower and slower. Everything took longer. I often felt impelled to stop what I was reading and start again from the top of the page or the beginning of the chapter. Somewhere, embedded in the texts I was reading, lay the glinting nugget that would clear his name, set him beyond the snipings of malice forever. I was dogged by the appalling fear that I would miss it, somehow skim over it. Hours went by in the contemplation of a paragraph, sometimes only a sentence. This one of Gutteridge's, from the introduction to his *Nelson and the Neapolitan Jacobins*, occupied a whole morning: *The chief object of the present volume is not to continue the controversy, but rather to bring together the mass of evidence which deals with the point, and to reduce it to a form in which it will be accessible to the English reader, who may therein find the refutation of these charges.*

I sought refutation too, but this sentence, from whatever direction I approached it, had a strange opacity about it, almost mystical in nature. The original pile, the mass of evidence, could obviously not be assembled within the covers of a single book; there was simply too much of it. So the reduction had been carried out beforehand. How could I know by what means it had been done? Abridgement, summary, excision, exclusion? And what particular attributes could a form have, by whatever means reduced, that would make it accessible to an English reader rather than a Chinaman, say? He was writing in English, of course, but he surely couldn't mean that. Was he implying that the English have some faculty of understanding denied to others? Or was he implying the opposite, that the English are so dense that only simplified forms can be accessible to them? Was it simply an appeal to shared prejudice? Could he really hope to put an end to controversy in such a way? What, in short, did H. C. Gutteridge *mean?*

He gave me headaches, but he was merely a satellite. It was the two protagonists, Mahan and Badham, that stalked through my days and nights. By now they had acquired definite physical characteristics. Touch by touch, detail by detail, these two long-dead Nelson scholars, so opposed in their views and the tone of their discourse, had assumed form and shape in my mind. Mahan was bluff and hearty, large of frame, with blue eyes; he had sandy-coloured hair, rather bushy at the temples, and those wrinkles around the eyes that come from scanning far horizons. He had a slightly shambling, careless gait and a sprawling fashion with his legs when he sat down; he was expansive and open-handed, always the first to pay for the round. Badham was thin and sparse and yellowish and he wore rimless glasses that reflected the light; his mouth was like a cut in a lemon and he had a prominent Adam's apple; he was neat and precise in all his movements and very quick-stepping, and he spoke Italian and wore thin black leather gloves. Their voices too were quite different. Mahan's was manly and energetic, interspersed with easy laughter; Badham's was metallic, slightly nasal, and though he sometimes showed a malignant glee, he never laughed.

Mahan's view of the Naples episode accorded fully with his generous nature. Basically, he took Horatio's word for it. Incapable himself of treachery and falsehood, he could not believe it of a man he admired so much, any more than I could. He accepted Horatio's declaration that the rebels came out in the full knowledge that the treaty was annulled. Badham, on the other hand, subjected to close analysis—he was generally a disagreeably analytical character—Horatio's assurance that he would not oppose the embarkation of the rebels, maintaining that the distinction between embarking and sailing was never made clear to them and that this was a deliberate fraud on Horatio's part, designed to winkle them out.

The whole moral world was here, in these two pure, irreducible representatives of the polarity that haunts our lives. Every day that July, in the silence of my study, good and evil did battle. Good was steadier, less coherent; evil more flickering, more lucid. I thought at the time they were contending for Horatio . . .

They disagreed about Caracciolo also—natural enough, they disagreed about everything. In Mahan's view, he was a traitor to his king under circumstances of particular flagrancy and richly deserved his fate. Badham, seconded by Constance Giglioli, pointed to the unseemly haste of the proceedings and to irregularities in the trial, the fact that no witnesses were called for the defence. An absurd objection, stout Laughton says; what need witnesses when his guilt was so patently clear?

I had not told Miss Lily about the grisly aftermath of Caracciolo's hanging, whether to spare her or myself I didn't know. Since the age of fourteen or so I had been troubled by the horror of it. At sunset the rope was cut and his body was allowed to fall into the bay. Two days later King Ferdinand returned to Naples, but the city was still in turmoil, so he took up his quarters on Horatio's flagship and amused himself by shooting seagulls. Early one morning a fisherman reported that Prince Caracciolo had risen from the sea and was coming home to Naples. The king went up on deck, scanned the horizon with his telescope. Midshipman Parsons, standing nearby, saw him turn white and drop the telescope and heard him utter an exclamation of horror. Looking in the same direction, Parsons saw the corpse of Caracciolo standing upright, half out of the water. His face was turned towards them, swollen and discoloured, the eyes started from their sockets by strangulation. He was bobbing up and down on the current and seemed to be heading for the shore. One among the retinue of priests on board, quicker-witted than his fellows, said that Admiral Caracciolo knew he had offended the king and could not rest. This helped Ferdinand to rally from his fear, and after a while he began to joke about it and say that the corpse had come to beg his forgiveness.

Whether the staring, bobbing, hideously bloated corpse stayed long in the king's mind or Horatio's, no-one can say. It had certainly stayed in mine over the years, pegged there by a single astounding fact: the admiral had risen and floated with a weight of 250 pounds attached to him. There was no doubt of this. A boat was sent to tow the corpse ashore, where it found a shallow grave in the sand. The boat brought back the shots that had been tied to him, and Captain Hardy weighed them. The ropes by which they had been fastened still had scraps of the admiral's skin on them . . .

Perhaps I was more than usually prone at this time to dwell on such thoughts. July is the month of maimings and disfigurements and outrages to the body. It was on July 12, 1794, when Horatio was thirty-five, that he suffered the wound to his eye. On land, not at sea. Seven o'clock in the morning. I always made sure I was up and about well before this on the twelfth, so I could give him his due of silent remembrance before I started with the tea.

I sat at my desk and made the shape of the island with my left hand—it helped me to concentrate. Corsica is shaped like a pointing hand; I had first seen this on my school atlas. The index finger is the peninsula of Cape Corsica, and it points northwards. At the base of this pointing finger, on opposite sides of the knuckle, are Bastia to the east and St. Florent to the west, twelve miles apart. And thirty miles away, roughly corresponding to the knuckle of the little finger, lies Calvi. Blockaded by the British and harassed by the Corsicans on land, the French occupying troops had retreated to these three strongholds.

A combined sea-and-land attack was decided on. Having lost Toulon, we needed an alternative base, and Corsica answered the purpose. Bastia had a good harbour, and it was well placed for attacks on French shipping and for the defence of Italy. However, St. Florent had to be taken first. One night in February, lying off Bastia, you saw the mountains behind the town lit up with a red glow, and you knew then that St. Florent had been taken and the ships in the harbour set ablaze. You had both your eyes still when you saw these fires of victory . . .

As always, you were eager to attack. You were set on taking Bastia by storm. But General Dundas, commander of the land forces, would not give you troops. Visionary and rash, he called the enterprise. Once again prudence and daring were confronted. So you landed with 250 of your faithful crew from the *Agamemnon* and hoisted twenty-four-pound cannon to the rocky ridges above the citadel, dragging them from rock to rock with the ship's tackle, a labour of enormous, almost superhuman difficulty. The men would not have toiled so for anyone but you.

We did this together, Miss Lily and I—it is all in the book. While still making the shape of the island with my hand, I remembered her voice, her face. I had expected her to be impressed by the devotion of these men. It was a labour of loyalty and even love, hauling up the heavy guns by means of great straps fastened to the rocks. But she didn't see it. She didn't see the point of it. What did they get out of it? she said. Except for ruptures. The comradeship, the pride of achievement—she didn't see it. Mahan expresses warm admiration, quoting the words of Horatio himself: *A work of the greatest difficulty which in my opinion would never have been accomplished by any other than British seamen.*

I quoted this too in the course of my dictation; it was important for the understanding of him, that pride in his men. But she was unmoved. One of the earliest of her interruptions. I was surprised at the time—I wouldn't be so surprised now. She didn't see the point. What was it *for?* I could hear her voice in the quiet room, that edge of impatience or slight annoyance in it that what she felt to be unreasonable always induced in her. *If it had been to help someone. You know, rescue someone. Even a cat. But just dragging guns up a cliff . . .*

This voice came to me from the walls, as voices often did. Not faces, not then. Mahan's reply came almost at once, jovial and easy. He didn't really want to argue with a lady. *To get men to do that, you need leadership qualities of the highest order. You would not expect them to be employed in rescuing a cat now, would you?*

A different voice, a different direction. *What did they get out of it?* Nasal, metallic—it was Badham. And the answer: *A pat on the back and a rupture.* But this was not Badham's voice, it had changed to Miss Lily's. The terrible suspicion came to me: were Miss Lily and Badham on the same side, were they in league? *We are talking about inspiration,* Mahan said, but no-one paid him any attention. And that voice of Badham's was familiar, I recognized it now, it was the voice that sounded in my ears when I read aloud from Horatio's despatches . . .

This was frightening. I had to get up, do a bit of pacing. This time I chose *Trafalgar*, by Alan Schom. Only one word in the title, no problem of choice. Unerring forefinger on the middle letter. Six paces to the silenced wall. These voices had broken my concentration, taken me away from Horatio and the morning when he lost his eye. It was getting on for seven.

Bastia was taken in May, thanks to Horatio and his faithful Agamemnons. Now there remained the third citadel, Calvi, difficult of access—there were no landing places nearer than four miles. Again guns had to be hauled up, this time by soldiers and sailors working together. Then, at daybreak on the twelfth, the enemy opened a heavy fire. You were watching from a flat-topped rock that gave a view over the besieged fort when a shell burst on the sandbags on the ramparts, sending out a hail of stone splinters and sand, cutting and bruising you on the right side of the face.

At first you made light of it. In a letter to Fanny you said it was only a scratch. But it proved more serious. As I continued to pace back and forth, touching the *a*, spreading my palms against the wall, I pictured you alone in your cabin on the *Agamemnon*. It is a month after the surrender of Calvi and the expulsion of the French. You are bound for Leghorn to refit. You are still weak and tremulous from the malaria that returned to you in the fierce heat of that Corsican summer. You look in the mirror, clapping a hand first over the left eye, then the right. It is no longer possible for you to deceive yourself: the right eye is useless to you, always will be. The pupil is irregular, immobile, it has spread to cover almost all the iris; it knows the difference between darkness and light, nothing else.

I was moved yet again by this testing, childlike and lonely. I was passing the glass-fronted bookcase on my right, where I keep the books I particularly value—Nicolas's monumental edition of the letters and despatches, some of the earlier biographies. The light was reflected from the glass as I passed. On an impulse I broke off my pacing, advanced my face to the glass, and placed a hand over my left eye. The eye that looked back at me was dazed and disabled by the shine of the glass, but I saw it reflected: vague, cloudy, strangely shapeless and amorphous. It was not mine, and I recoiled from it with a fear that for some moments seemed to stop my heart.

I did not stay longer in my study that day. I remember that an immense weariness descended on me; my limbs felt heavy, and it seemed hard for me even to hold my head up. I went to the big armchair in the sitting room, got under my mother's rug, and dozed away the rest of the morning.

This sort of daytime sleeping fit grew frequent as the days passed. I think it was a sort of subterfuge, a means of escape from Mahan/Badham, perhaps a way of bringing Miss Lily's return nearer. Ten weeks, she had said. That would take us to Monday, the fifteenth of September. I had decided to phone Avon Secretarial Services that day to see if she was back.

In the midst of all this, I did not neglect Horatio's calendar. I was ready well in advance to commemorate his second maiming, which took place early in the morning of July 25, three years later. With three ships of the line and a frigate, he had been ranging from Lisbon to the coast of North Africa, hoping for a favour from the gods, a sight of the legendary Spanish treasure fleet, returning from South America. Now the rumour came that they had arrived, loaded with bullion, in the Canary Islands, Tenerife. What a prize!

Grigson was very good on the Tenerife engagement. I have never forgotten his lessons. The big map, glossy and smelling of hot glue, draped over the blackboard, Grigson stocky and nimble, a creature of fire with his reddish hair and the glinting pelt of his sports jacket, wielding a billiard cue, his own property, pointing out the routes, the distances. *Here is your grade A in O-level history.* The pointer hovering, tracing, pausing, and pouncing, keeping always to the rhythm of his voice and his movements before us. *Boys, we stood alone, the French had twice our population* . . .

Cadiz to Tenerife, a thousand miles. According to intelligence reports, Santa Cruz de Tenerife was ill defended. Reports also mentioned Spanish merchant ships in the harbour. A thousand miles, six days running before the wind, while the crews trained at the guns and the carpenters made scaling ladders for the assault. Then, faintly outlined against the sky to the southwest, the volcanic peaks of Tenerife, where Grigson's cue came to rest.

The intelligence reports were false; the fortifications were formidable. The sea approaches below the town were commanded by powerful batteries. Should they have attacked at all? *Boys, you must try to imagine the times they lived in and the men they were. In 1797, as in 1940, we stood alone. Any measure, any prospect of success, anything that could force the allies of France out of the war* . . . Grigson had a sense of the past—he should have talked to Miss Lily.

The plan depended entirely on surprise. Under cover of darkness, a combined force of seamen and marines would put ashore in boats with muffled oars. Without warning, they would attack the batteries on the heights to the north of the town. Grigson rolled up the map at this point and used coloured chalks on the blackboard. Red for the French batteries, blue for our ships, dotted white for the planned line of attack. Here is the bomb ship ready to open fire on the town; here are our three ships of the line, anchored out of range. At dawn they will close in, ready to bombard the town. But that won't be necessary. With the guns taken by storm and the town threatened with destruction, the governor will capitulate, all bullion or treasure belonging to the Spanish will be handed over.

But it is not to be. Grigson shakes his head, the cue is grounded, the blue ships stay where they are. Strong offshore currents make it impossible for the frigates to land the men, and in their battle with the tides they are sighted by the enemy; the advantage of surprise is lost. The attack has failed. But when did you ever accept defeat? What did you say? *Thus foiled in my original plan, I considered it necessary for the honour of our King and country not to give over the attempt.*

Heat rose through Grigson's wiry reddish hair, warming the air around him. The gestures of the hand not holding the cue were brief and strong, cutting or chopping motions. No-one could long sustain his gaze. He approved of your words; we knew he approved by the tone in which he quoted them—I think it was the first time I ever heard your words spoken aloud. They came to me in Grigson's voice that July evening, while I waited. It was late, nearly midnight. I was waiting for one o'clock, the time of the wound.

The walls and ceiling of the study were shadowed. The only light came from the lamp on my desk. Your words, as spoken by Grigson, were in my mind. Then a surprising thing happened. After all these years of recalling the wound, remembering Grigson and his billiard cue and coloured chalks, it came to me that there had been one boy in that class at odds with the rest of us. Strange that I had not remembered him before. A picture of him came now into my mind, gradually, detail by detail. It was like peering at something under water that has been stirred, waiting for the tremors of the surface to subside. A sallow boy, large but not athletic. Heavy brows. Rather adenoidal. The nature of his questions came similarly slowly to my mind. A nasal voice. I think he wore rimless glasses. At that moment, when Grigson's theme was honour, this boy actually asked if it hadn't been wrong of Nelson to try again. This to Grigson, whose bristles of hair seemed to issue sparks, who perhaps misunderstood the question, not thinking any boy could be so lacking in *esprit de corps*. Well, certainly it was wrong of him to lead this second attack in person, he was a rear-admiral and commander of the whole squadron, he was wrong to risk himself, but of course it was gallant too . . .

But no, that was not what this boy meant. I could not remember his name. What about the thousand officers and men Nelson took with him, only half of whom returned? This boy had been reading other texts than those furnished by Grigson. We were all against him, we shared our teacher's disdain for this insinuating outsider.

But he would not be silenced. The sea was rough, there were powerful batteries on the heights above the shore, the chances of success were almost nil. Is that what honour means? Was it the hope of Spanish gold that made you throw those lives away? *A kind of serial killer.* No, he didn't say that, the Badham boy didn't say that, Miss Lily said that. This boy had a limited existence. Why couldn't I remember his name? Why had I no memory of him in any other class, questioning any other teacher?

Wiped off the slate for all these years between. I tried not to think of him anymore, but only of that doomed, gallant second attempt. Quarter to one now, fifteen minutes to go, you are already pulling for shore, you and the thousand others. Shortly before you have written a hasty letter to Sir John Jervis. *Tomorrow my head will probably be crowned with either laurel or cypress.*

Grigson approved of this too, but I was not in his class now, I was alone in my study, the class had gone, that boy had gone, who could tell where Grigson was? As the moment of the wound drew nearer, I was quite alone. Laurel or cypress. You knew, you must have known, how expensive in lives it would be, how slight the chances of success. Even to get ashore under fire like that, let alone to storm the heights. A thousand men, all with a hope of life, and you wrote to Jervis as if there were only one. What was it for? Miss Lily's favorite question. No use as a base, too far away—the Mediterranean was the vital zone.

The point was the treasure. You were the commander of the squadron, you were entitled to one quarter. *No, boys, personal greed did not enter into it; the objective was to cripple the Spanish by depriving them of the means to continue the war.* Yes, he was right, the times were desperate, the Spanish could not be brought to a battle, it was the only way. Think of the times they lived in, think of the men they were.

Three minutes to one. A heavy sea running. The boats are too crowded, many of them do not reach the shore, they capsize, and the men in them are drowned. The Spaniards have seen us; the shore batteries open up while the boats are still hundreds of yards from land. However, you reach the harbour mole, you draw your sword, prepare to leap ashore. At that moment, as you raise your sword, your right arm is shattered by grapeshot. You make an attempt to pick up the sword with your left and continue, but your strength fails and you fall. Bleeding heavily, you are laid in the bottom of the boat, and they begin to row you back to the ships. But you will not allow them to return in an empty boat. Half fainting as you are, you will not let them proceed, you order as many men as possible to be gathered into the boat from the sea.

Thinking of this, I felt the familiar smart of tears. Tears always came to restore my feeling for him. That stoicism, that forbearance, that care for others. The same man, the author of the letter to Jervis . . .

The first ship they came up with was the *Seahorse*, commanded by your friend Fremantle, still out there in the night somewhere, taking part in that disastrous landing. But his wife, Betsey, is still aboard—she has been given special permission to accompany her husband. By now your arm is pumping blood in spite of the tourniquet, but you refuse to quit the boat. *I would rather suffer death than alarm Mrs. Fremantle by her seeing me in this state, when I can give her no tidings whatever of her husband.* You order them to go on, to find your own ship, the *Theseus*. At last they do so, but you will not be helped aboard. *Let me alone. I have yet my legs left and one arm. Tell the surgeon to make haste and get his instruments.*

You were magnificent. And to think that the later progeny of Badham have set this fortitude down to the effects of shock. No memory of that rotten apple in our class daring to say anything about it. Grigson would have come down on him heavily. *We stood alone against a powerful continental aggressor. To the generations born since 1940 the situation is difficult to imagine.*

Long afterwards, in a Greenwich bookshop, perched on the top of a ladder to get at the dusty top shelf, I came upon a monograph: *Eye-witness Accounts of Nelson's Battles*, by H. C. Grigson, M.A. (Leeds). It was the same man. I bought it and have it still. There is a brief biographical note at the back. Grigson was born in 1927. He was twelve when the war broke out; he would not have seen any fighting. That sense of crisis, of heroic isolation, he would have got it from others—parents, teachers . . .

The arm was cut off high up, near the shoulder. It was thrown overboard, on your orders. More terrible than the pain of the cut, or perhaps it was the expression itself of this pain, was the bitter coldness of the surgeon's blade. Always, afterwards, on any of your ships, you made sure that the surgeons warmed their blades before operating. It took them half an hour to sever the arm and bind the stump. Then—only then—they gave you opium to ease the dreadful pain.

I have on one wall of my study a framed facsimile, enlarged to double size, of the first letter written with the left hand. This was two days after the loss of his arm. I got up now and went to look at it again, trying as I did so to avoid looking towards the glass-fronted bookcase, which I was now rather nervous of. Wavering, very variable as to the size and the slant of the letters, all the same it is not bad for a first attempt, when one considers that he was still sick and suffering and in a mood of deep discouragement. *I am become a burden to my friends and useless to my country.*

This on the eve of his great victory at Aboukir Bay, with the triumphs of Copenhagen and Trafalgar to follow! He rose from the ashes of defeat like the fabulous bird. So could I too, I resolved there and then. I would rise with him, above failure and discouragement, above my psychic mutilation. I would fight on. My battle would be Naples 1799, and I would win it for him. In the glow of this determination I took a new exercise book from my drawer, one of my specials, with strong covers and good, smooth paper. This would be my left-handed journal. I would not begin it yet; I would begin when he began, two days after the wound.

23

*T*he July of mutilations and maimings gives way to glorious August, the Battle of the Nile on the first day of the month, in 1798. Of all his battles before Trafalgar, this was the one I looked forward to most.

A night battle, his only one. I was at my table in the ops room by 5 P.M., laying the ships out, a bottle of my father's claret ready-opened at my elbow. I never drank before his battles, only after he had hoisted the order for close action.

Forty minutes to go. The long hoped-for, long sought-for engagement about to begin. Since April, Horatio has been scouring the Mediterranean in search of the French fleet. His squadron has been brought up to a strength of twelve seventy-four-gun warships and three frigates. The situation is desperate. We have no base east of Gibraltar; the Mediterranean is a hostile sea. On land the French are everywhere dominant. We know they are about to leave Toulon with a fleet of transports and escorting warships commanded by Bonaparte in person. But we don't know where he is intending to strike. It could be anywhere in the region. An attack on Portugal from the east, through Spain? A breakthrough into the Atlantic and a descent on Lisbon that way? A landing in Ireland, now in open revolt against us?

It is our task to find out. A heavy responsibility on that great stretch of water, in those slow ships. In May we learn from a captured French corvette that the expedition is about to set sail. Fifteen enemy sail of the line and twelve thousand troops are already embarked. The warships are under the command of Vice-Admiral François de Brueys, whose flagship is the gigantic *Orient*, 120 guns.

Still no-one knows where they are going. They are sighted north of Corsica, steering southeast. An attack on the Two Sicilies? But that would be easier by land. Or Malta, which dominates the central Mediterranean? But thirty-five thousand men, which Bonaparte's strength is now believed to be, would be far more than needed for this. Some altogether more ambitious attempt it must be . . .

Late in July, from a Genovese brig hailed off Cape Passaro, we learn that the French have been in Malta, that the Knights Templar have surrendered to them, that they have filled the army's coffers with the treasures of the churches and then left again, destination unknown.

In the solitude of the great cabin of our flagship, the *Vanguard*, with maps covering the table before us, we try to work it out, try to enter the mind of the enemy. Unlikely they have gone west; the prevailing winds of the season would make it difficult with transport ships. East, then. Corfu? Constantinople, where the Ottoman Empire could be smashed at the heart? But Bonaparte's great enemy now is Britain, and the greatest threat to British interest lies farther east. We have detailed information about the French force now; in addition to troops and artillery it includes naturalists, astronomers, mathematicians. What would be the destination for specialists such as these? It could only be countries with ancient, esoteric civilizations. Egypt, the Red Sea ports. Then India, and a crippling blow to this most vital of our colonies. That must be it.

We set off for Alexandria. But what if we are wrong? What if the slippery crappos have doubled back behind us, taken Sicily? Then the failure would be complete. Not a gallant failure, as Tenerife was regarded, but a failure of judgement with disastrous consequences for the whole conduct of the war. Mistakes like that are never forgotten, never forgiven. If we are wrong, our career is at an end. And we are handicapped, we are half blind in the metaphorical sense also—we have only three frigates, only three ships fast enough to scout ahead for information.

We are not wrong, but for some terrible days it seems that we are. No sign of them at Alexandria when we get there; they are still on the way, we have outsailed them, but of course we do not know this at the time. Back to Sicily; no sign there either. Egypt again, but now there is no doubt: the French have been sighted from Greece, heading southeast for Egypt.

Four days later, at ten o'clock on the morning of August 1, we sight once again the lighthouses and minarets of Alexandria. The harbour is crammed with empty transports, but there are no warships. Napoleon has landed. He is on his way to the destruction of the Mamelukes at the Battle of the Pyramids, and the conquest of Cairo.

Some minutes of terrible disappointment. Then we give the order to steer east along the coast, towards the delta of the Nile. At two in the afternoon, roughly three and a half hours ago, we see at last, with joy and relief, the masts and yards of the French fleet at anchor. On the halyards of the *Zealous*, second ship in the British line, the signal is hoisted: *Enemy in sight.*

You knew then that decisive action was a certainty. *Before this time tomorrow, I shall have gained a peerage or Westminster Abbey*. That is what you said. Why does it trouble me so now, after all these years? Is it because of her? Like the cypress-and-laurel remark before the attack on Tenerife. That was traditional, death or glory, the genuine heroic impulse. But this . . . All those men, all the blood and rending of the flesh that awaited only a few hours away. A peerage or a state funeral. If I were talking to Miss Lily, I would not mention this remark of yours; she would call it monstrous. Still theatre, she would say, but a one-man show now, the others lining the decks to kick their legs, make up the chorus. Why I had begun to subject you to her opinion at all, that was the mystery. She was miles away in Derbyshire; why did I give her so much say? How could Avon Secretarial Services be expected to appreciate your heroic sense of destiny, the patriotic identification of Britain's interests with your own? Her face with that little frown on it, the slight flush that came to her cheeks when she was indignant about something.

The French ships are set out now, all thirteen of them, anchored in their curving line. Their commander, Admiral de Brueys, whose last day of life this is, is an experienced seaman, a former royalist officer, reinstated by Napoleon. He has fought the British before, during the American War of Independence. He has three 80-gun ships, the *Franklin*, the *Tonnant*, and the *Guillaume Tell*, and one of 120 guns, his flagship, the *Orient*. For ships as big as this, Alexandria Harbour is rather too narrow; he is afraid of jamming at the harbour mouth. So he has brought the ships eastward, here to Aboukir, and anchored them in a tight defensive line protected behind by the shoals and sandbanks of the bay.

I always used the top left-hand corner of my table for this battle, a triangular space taking up almost half of the total surface. The right angle formed by the sides of the table represents the arms of the bay, with the peninsula of Aboukir to the north and the Nile delta to the south. The French line curves shallowly outwards toward the open sea, with the *Guerrier* in the van, the *Timoléon* in the rear, and the mighty *Orient* in the exact centre. They are anchored, *but only by the bow*; they swing with the current, there are spaces between them. An error on the part of de Brueys, yes, but who would have supposed Horatio would try to pass through, risk the shallows inside the bay, notoriously treacherous? And at night, in darkness, without maps!

Other errors the French admiral has made, all springing from the assumption that his rear is secure. Believing that the attack must come from seaward, he has placed his strongest ships in the centre, his weakest and oldest in the van. And he has failed to ensure that his leading ship, the *Guerrier*, is anchored right up against the shoals, so as to prevent our ships from passing inside, between his line and the shore.

Five twenty-two by my watch. There has been time to prepare for battle since that first sighting of the French, ample time—that leisurely preparation for mortal risk; as always I was troubled and excited by it as I set out the British ships in their rough grouping on the seaward side. Rarely can men have prepared to face death with more deliberation, more knowledge of it in every heart. The port lids are opened and the guns run out; hammocks are rolled up and packed in nets along the bulwarks as a shield against splinters and musket shot; the furled sails are wetted to reduce risk of fire; damp sand is strewn on the gundecks to prevent bare feet from slipping on blood. The gun crews, stripped to the waist, stand by the lines of cannon; the surgeons wait in the cockpit; the marines, in full uniform, troop with their muskets to the upper deck, watched by their lieutenants with drawn swords.

Our ships are fortunate in the wind; a brisk northwesterly fills their sails as they bear down from the north. As they approach, they form a line in obedience to your general signal, number 31: *Form line of battle ahead and astern of the admiral as most convenient.*

At a distance, from the open sea, the French line looks impregnable, set in a convex curve outward from the shoals, the sea behind seething white as it breaks against the sandbanks. The ten British seventy-fours, hauled sharp to the wind, are already in the shallower water, sounding as they go, fifteen fathoms, thirteen, eleven, nine . . . One is out of action already; Troubridge, in the *Culloden*, has run aground. Here he is, in a frenzy of frustration, at the tip of the shoal stretching east from the bay. I try not to think further of Troubridge; thoughts of him distress me, renew that sickness of doubt, inappropriate on the eve of such a glorious victory. Troubridge was one of the two captains—Ball was the other—that you sent to Cardinal Ruffo in Naples the following July, with your assurance that you would not oppose the embarkation of the rebels . . .

But now you are innocent still. You scan the French line with the eye of a commander set on immediate attack. Landwards, behind them, the sun is setting in the magnificent summer dustglow of the Levant. Their masts and yards are fiery, they ride on a molten sea. You see their weakness together with their beauty. You will throw your whole weight on their van and crush it before help can come. But the shoals are dangerously close. The *Zealous* is still in the lead, sounding as she goes—eight fathoms, seven . . .

The last moment for choice is approaching. You can stay outside, order your captains to anchor two by two opposite the enemy ships. This is what de Brueys expects. You can break through the gaps in the French line and attack from the inside. But how can you be sure there is enough water?

It is exactly 5:40 P.M. You give the signal for close action. I pour out my first glass. Now it comes, the moment of pure and perfect opportunity. Can we outflank the French by rounding his line and attacking from inside? From our flagship, here in the centre of the line, we shout across to Hood in the *Zealous*. Can he take his ship round the end of the enemy line? Hood shouts back that he will try. So to the *Zealous* falls the honour of being the first to round the point of the shoals. But I have been too hasty—it is still only six minutes to six; I must wait six more minutes before taking her round. I have been rather hasty with the wine too, in my excitement; the glass is almost empty, and I am not due for another till 6:28, when the battle is joined.

These are the last moments of the day, before the swift descent of that southern darkness. I have turned off the overhead light, left on only the lamps at the ends of the table. This is the poised moment—everything is at risk; we are entering a strange bay at nightfall, without pilots, without reliable charts, moving in narrow waters among invisible reefs and shoals. The progress of the *Zealous* is slow because of her need to take continual soundings. She is overtaken now by Captain Foley in the *Goliath*. Foley has made a deduction and acted on it with a boldness worthy of his great commander. If the French have anchored their ships by the bow only, there must be water enough to allow for the swing. If there is water enough to allow for the swing, there must be water enough for another ship to pass inside.

Impeccable logic. The *Goliath* sweeps into the lead. Here she is. It is 6:28, time for another glass. The enemy have hoisted their colours and opened fire. Foley has crossed the bows of the *Guerrier*, raking her with a broadside as he does so, then passing on to anchor here, on the inner quarter of the *Conquérant*, next French ship in line. Hood takes up his station opposite the *Guerrier*. Our ships follow round in order of sail—the *Orion*, the *Theseus*, the *Audacious*. As the fires of that sunset are quenched in the sea, the five leading British ships are all inside and at closest possible quarters, bringing a concentrated fire to bear on the enemy van, the more deadly as the French can make no adequate reply. Their guns on the shoreward side have not been cleared for action, they are cluttered with rope and tackle and mess furniture—another disastrous consequence of the French assumption that attack was bound to come from the open sea.

Our flagship, the *Vanguard*, is the sixth ship to come into action, the first to anchor on the seaward side. Here she is, abreast and within pistol shot of the *Spartiate*. Now she is hard pressed, fired upon by both the *Spartiate* and the *Aquilon*, next ship in the French line. The *Minotaur*, Captain Louis, relieves us, ranging up to draw off the *Aquilon*'s fire.

Seven P.M. Night has fallen in a thunder of guns. In a pall of smoke, lit only by gunfire, the five seventy-four's of the French van, undermanned and able to fire only on the starboard side, are being beaten into helplessness by eight of ours settled like a swarm about them. My lamps cannot match the glimmer and flicker of the gunfire and the lurid flaring of the smoke, and my room is hushed, only the slight sounds of my miniature hulls scraping on the glass; but my table is beautiful, reflections glinting on the dark surface, changing with the movements of my hands and arms as I direct the ships.

The eighth and ninth in our line, coming into position opposite the enemy centre, sustain the heaviest damage. In the smoke-hung confusion, the *Bellerophon* misses her chosen foe, the *Franklin*, first of the French eighties—at present being very gallantly attacked by one of our frigates, the fifty-gun *Leander*—and fetches up abreast of the mighty *Orient*, a ship with double her armament. Within fifteen minutes her masts have been entirely shot away. She veers out of the line, completely disabled. I leave her here, over on the lee side of the bay. The *Majestic* also suffers heavy loss, her captain, Westcott, being fatally wounded in the throat by a musket ball.

But we are gaining. Our ships are like a swarm—it is as if they are feasting on carcasses. No, not carcasses, bodies still twitching. Always the same tactic: pass along the line, gather on either side, concentrate the fire.

Now, with battle fully joined, comes the wound. You are standing on the quarterdeck with Berry by your side when a flying piece of scrap shot slashes your brow to the bone. A flap of flesh falls over your good eye, and the blood flows thickly down, blinding you. Berry catches you as you fall. *I am killed*, he hears you say. *Remember me to my wife.*

I see you as you are carried down to the cockpit, I see the lamps down there, swaying with the roll of the ship and thud of the gun carriages. There are seventy or so men already waiting there, in that shuddering heat, many of them gravely injured. You do not allow the surgeons to be told you are among them. Still blinded, your face a mask of blood, you wait your turn.

The surgeon probes the wound, pronounces the damage not serious—the visible damage, that is. You are in total darkness; you send for the chaplain and dictate messages for Lady Nelson and for Louis, the captain of the *Minotaur*, who relieved your flagship from the dual fire of the enemy. *Your support prevented me from being obliged to haul out of the line.* This was before your wound had been dressed, while you lay waiting for the dressing. You could not see. That you should think of Fanny at such a time was natural enough. But a message of thanks to one of your captains . . .

Once again, as I thought of you lying there, that familiar prickle of tears came to my eyes. How could this behaviour of yours be named? It was something more than courage or endurance. It was *grace*, springing like a flower from the hard ground of duty.

Still blind, you hear cheering from above. The youthful Berry enters with what he announces as a "pleasing intelligence"—one of the great understatements of history, this must be regarded, considering that he brings news of the most notable British victory at sea since the defeat of the Spanish Armada. The French fleet is shattered. The *Spartiate* has altogether ceased to fire; the *Aquilon* and the *Peuple Souverain* have struck their colours; the *Orient*, the *Tonnant*, and the *Heureux*, though not yet captured, are no longer able to make effective reply to our shot.

News to bring you back to life. Time for my third glass. Your brow stitched and bandaged, you are settled in the bread room in the hold, below the water line, as far removed as possible from the din of battle. You send for your secretary to take down a despatch to Earl Spencer, the first lord of the Admiralty. But the secretary is in a state of nervous collapse; at the sight of you, blinded by bandages and working the stump of your arm in a fury of impatience, he loses his nerve altogether and cannot write. There and then I dismiss him from my service. I push up the bandage, take the pen myself. *My Lord, Almighty God has blessed His Majesty's arms in the late Battle . . .*

I am interrupted again by Berry, this time to report that the *Orient* is on fire. The surgeon has ordered me to stay quiet, but with the usual disobedience I demand to be helped up on deck. The night is soft and warm, thickly hung with smoke. A reddish glow is creeping over the expanse of the bay. My head throbs and aches, it hurts me to focus my eye, but as the glow strengthens I can distinguish the colours of the ships, make out the situation of the battle, see the leaping flames on the poop of the French flagship. I tell Berry to do what he can to save as many as possible of the crew. At the same time I give orders that our shot should be concentrated on the blaze so as to hinder the enemy from bringing it under control. Many of the *Orient*'s guns are now disabled, but some on the lower deck are still firing, the French gun crews serving them until the fire gets too close and they are driven off. I see the flames begin to race up her tarred rigging, flare blue along her newly painted sides. I know that the flames will be seeking paths downward, towards her powder magazine.

What I do not see—what no-one in the British fleet sees—is the appalling fate of the French wounded, trapped belowdecks with their surgeons, all burned alive together. Or Admiral de Brueys, who had made all the wrong assumptions, with both his legs shot away and tourniquets tied around the stumps, seated on a chair on his blazing deck, still facing his tormentors, still shouting orders to maintain fire, until another shot cuts him in two and puts him out of his misery.

A competent commander—not brilliant, not like you. The end he made has been a recurrent nightmare since I first read of it at the age of fifteen. Thoughts of it now wrenched me from the action. I was here, this was me in the basement, reaching for my glass. You were there on the deck of the *Vanguard*, pushing up your bandages for a sight of your beautiful, desolate victory.

The cannonade continues. Our ships aim their guns at the heart of the blaze. Swarms of sparks fly over the face of the water and in among the anchored ships. The British captains nearer the blaze cut their cables to get clear. At five minutes past ten, just at this moment, with a stunning detonation and a great flash of light, the *Orient*'s powder magazines explode. A fiery wreckage is flung high into the night sky, hangs in its own light for some moments, then descends in a rain of masts, yards, red-hot ammunition, charred fragments of corpses, thudding on the decks of the neighbouring ships or falling back into the sea in a hiss of mingled smoke and steam.

This mighty bang is heard in Alexandria, fifteen miles away. After it, for several minutes, an utter silence lies over the bay. Then the guns start up again. The French van and centre have been destroyed, it is now the turn of their rear. By sunrise, the full extent of our victory is apparent. Of the thirteen French warships lying at anchor the day before, ten have been captured, one has been blown up, and two have escaped. Aboukir Bay is a scene of utter desolation, with listing, smoking ships and scorched bodies drifting in the shallows. As you truly said, *Victory is not a name strong enough for such a scene.* Once again we rule the waves, control of the Mediterranean is restored to us. Bonaparte is stranded on shore, the threat to India is removed, the French losses are six times ours. The remains of the *Orient* are in the depths of the bay, together with her butchered admiral and her treasure—the enormous sum of £600,000 in gold bars and diamonds wrested from the Swiss republic and the Roman state to finance Bonaparte's eastern expedition, along with the irreplaceable treasures of the Knights of St. John.

A great action, demonstrating yet again the truth of Grigson's words to us so long ago and those of Bobby's teacher so recently. He would be with his mother now, in Derbyshire. I thought of the boy's face looking fixedly at me in the dim light of the *Victory's* gundeck, a light similar to that here in my ops room, where shadows lay on all sides beyond the arena of the table. *He says our sailors were the best in the world and we had better officers.* Quite right, my boy, quite right. It wasn't the ships, it was the men. They were better trained, more disciplined; they had superb morale. They cheered when they saw the *Orient* go up. What would Miss Lily say to that? She would go round it, she would find a question to which there was no answer. Something outside the records. Did a single one of them, officers or men, at the time or later, express pity for the crew of the *Orient?* Not as far as we know. The men cheered. The officers of course did not cheer, but they did nothing to check the men.

I couldn't help it. All these years of celebrating the Battle of the Nile and now I had to listen to questions from Avon Secretarial Services, try to understand the way this woman associated things together. She had soured his great victory with this talk about pity. Now, because of her, I was obliged to remember the way he talked about the battle himself in Palermo a few months later, as related by Captain Gordon, a Scot who was there as travelling tutor to the invalid Lord Montgomerie. I could not remember the words in detail, but Gordon's memoirs were up there in my study, on the shelf. It was only twenty to eleven, much too early to go to bed. I slept badly at night in any case, and I was stimulated now by the battle and the wine. I decided to go up and check the reference.

I was moving towards the wall, towards the light switch. I think I had begun to reach towards it, actually extended my arm. I glanced aside—some sense had come to me that I was being watched, that my movements were being noted, registered. I looked to the right, where I sensed this interest lay—looked through the open door of the ops room to the larger room beyond, my gallery of Nelsoniana so lovingly assembled over the years.

All the light there was came from the lamps at either end of my table. The farther of these cast a white pool, fringed by the pattern of the raffia lampshade, over the threshold of the door. The fringes seemed to shift, to eddy very slightly, as if prey to some remote disturbance. Beyond the door they drew together, made a narrow, wavering shaft into the next room, touched the straight outer side of the porcelain tankard commemorating Trafalgar, slid round the convex curve of the Copeland loving cup with the handpainted full-face portrait of him in one of its panels.

At the dim limits of this faint plank of light was the huge papier-mâché bust of him, roughly twice life-size, that stood in the centre of the floor. The face was turned directly towards me. Despite the dimness I was aware of the features, though I did not know whether I was seeing or remembering the yellowish complexion, the look of moisture given by the pulped and oiled paper, the heavy sweep of the cocked hat, the garish emblems painted on the breast. Whether seen or remembered, tonight he had a different, crueller face. That thick curl of the mouth . . . He looked like a god glutted with sacrifice. The eyes were not visible, they were shadowed by the hat as they always were in my dreams, but I knew that they would soon be levelled at me, that they would contain a deadly reproach. *You have let me down,* the eyes would say, *you have failed to clear my name.* An angel's displeasure is horribly dangerous. I knew I had to get out before he showed his eyes.

I put the light on now, and that helped. My heart thumped and my breath caught as I passed him. I felt a feverish heat in the glands at the sides of my neck. But I did not look. At the top of the stairs I remembered that I had left the lamps on in the ops room, but I could not look behind me, let alone go back.

24

*T*he lights in the basement burned for three days before I could bring myself to go and switch them off. And then I went almost at a run and didn't look at him, not at the bust, not at the portraits on the wall. If Miss Lily had been there, I would have asked her to do it, on some pretext or other. She would not have been afraid.

I told myself I needed more time. But the time did not come. The basement stayed locked. Those few hours at the table moving my ships about, celebrating our victory, drinking perdition to the damned French, before I felt him watching me—they were the last I could remember with any pleasure, and they left me only bad dreams. Soundlessly the *Orient* went up again. Fiery fragments rained through my nights. A featureless figure in a cocked hat bobbed on the tide, then dived and sported like a dolphin among the spars and corpses, still with his hat on. de Brueys sat bolt upright in his chair among the flames, the stumps of his legs sticking out before him. His face was melting in the heat . . . I would wake to find my whole body rigidly braced, as if in expectation of some blow.

Habit is strong, however. It can hold you against terror, at least for a while; it can run parallel, a parallel track. In that time of my nightmares I made another trip to Seldon's in Sloane Street to buy a Staffordshire group depicting the moment of the fatal wound. No date on it, but typical of the mid-nineteenth century. Horatio has fallen, his lung pierced and his back broken. He is supported by Doctor Scott, the chaplain, and Hardy, both very pink in the face to contrast with the stricken admiral's pallor. A curiosity, no value much, crudely made, with Horatio wearing an eyepatch, something he never did. But I had an open-fronted cabinet in the basement containing a small collection of such pieces, and I thought I would add this one to it.

Strange to relate, while I was buying this piece and all the time I was bringing it home, my purpose remained clear: I would put it with the other things in the cabinet. I was sustained by the years of happy acquisition, by the prospect of that healing peace that used to descend on me when I was down there, moving about among my exhibits.

It was only when I got home and the piece was on my study table that the first doubts came to me. However, I tried. I tried to pretend, to trick myself. I went with it in my hands to the basement stairs. I went halfway down, more than halfway. The door was there, deeply familiar, varnished brown, with the brass knob and the neat little slot of the lock waiting for my key. But already I was gulping and sweating. I began to feel that same hotness at the sides of my neck. Almost before I knew it, I was back at the top of the stairs.

I never tried again. I remember sitting for a long time, back there in my study, looking closely at pale Horatio with his eyepatch, at his florid, tight-trousered helpers. He was not frightening here, he had no gaze. But down below there, in the basement . . . You, who rescued me from fear!

So it was that in the days following the Battle of the Nile, I was obliged to face the fact that the basement was effectively out of bounds—that picture gallery, exhibition cabinets, ops room, were all closed to me. I was reduced to the bedroom, the armchair in the sitting room with my mother's rug, the desk and walls of my study. Added to this was the fact that I could not get on with my book and could not believe Miss Lily would come back.

These were terrible days. I neglected to eat. I neglected to wash. I left a note for Mrs. Watson asking her not to come anymore and enclosing a cheque for a month's money. Without her ministrations the spiders thrived, the dust collected, the sink got clogged, and little balls of fluff began to creep about in the passages. There was one hope, and it kept me moving through the hours. If I could solve the problem of Naples 1799, if I could show how wrong they were who accused you of treachery and falsehood, everything would fall into place again, everything would start functioning. You would look kindly at me; you and I would be together again as always before, the bright and the dark. Miss Lily would come back, we would work on the book, we would go for outings to the Maritime Museum at Greenwich and further afield to Burnham Thorpe, your birthplace, perhaps even someday abroad—Palermo, for example, where you and Emma became lovers. I would not worry about being among so many foreigners; she would keep everything safe in her handbag.

I tried to write my thoughts in the left-handed journal. My writing had improved by now, it was much firmer. But no thoughts of my own ever came to me when I took up the pen in my left hand. The pages were covered by your words, not mine, snippets from the letters and despatches, written at different times and in different circumstances. They came to me without any searching, any effort of recollection. Vacant, pen in hand, I would let my eyes and my mind skim over them.

It was my good fortune to have under my command some of the most experienced officers in the English Navy, whose professional skill was seconded by the undaunted courage of British sailors . . . I have brought home a faithful and honourable heart . . . I shall return—if it please God—a victor; and it shall be my study to transmit an unsullied name . . .

An unsullied name—that was his wish, his dearest wish. Tears came into my eyes at the simplicity of it, at my failure so far to deliver it to him. I had been clinging during these last few days to the Fatal Misunderstanding Theory, which has been advanced by various of his biographers over the years. According to this, on that morning of June 26, both parties were labouring under a misapprehension: the rebels came out believing in the treaty, Horatio believed they had understood that the treaty no longer applied. Could this be possible? The trouble with it as a theory is that only the rebels' view of things had any circumstantial support. They had come out with their belongings packed and ready—books, linen, plate. They had embarked. Surely this meant they believed in the treaty. For what Horatio believed, there is only the evidence of his own statements, and these are sometimes confusing. His letter to Lord Spencer some fortnight later, for example: *The rebels came out of their forts with this knowledge, without any honours, and the principal rebels were seized and conducted aboard the ships of the squadron.*

The knowledge that they were surrendering unconditionally, you meant. But it looks from your words as if the seizure followed immediately on the surrender, whereas the rebels were allowed to

embark before the ringleaders were seized. Haste? A careless over-
sight? How could one know? I was in chase of meanings and motives
gone forever, fishing in the past with nets always too coarse for the ag-
ile fish I was after, never getting more than the flash of a tail. It
seemed like an ocean to me, and I went down into it with my crude
equipment day after day. Ruffo and Hamilton, the subtle priest and
the wily diplomat—could they have contrived between them to keep
you in ignorance? But it must have struck you as odd. You saw the
rebels come out. Through your telescope, from the deck of the *Vanguard*, you saw them come out through the sea gates of their forts.
You must have thought it was odd that people who knew they were
going to be seized, put in irons, and handed over to the tender mer-
cies of Ferdinand and Maria Carolina would embark *with their luggage*.
The real trouble with the Fatal Misunderstanding Theory was that it
made you seem incredibly dense.

Such problems did not trouble Mahan, of course. He did not see
them as problems at all. His view of things was admirably clear. Ruffo
was the trickster; he had taken advantage of the sailor's simplicity. A
man such as Nelson, totally honourable and honest, does not suspect
duplicity in others. He had promised not to hinder the embarkation
and he did not do so; but he had never wavered in his refusal to accept
the treaty. He would not stand by and see those miscreants go unpun-
ished. They were traitors, friends to the cursed French, vapid theorizers,
full of airy-fairy ideas, not an ounce of true grit among them.

Irish accent, faint but attractive. A bluff and likable fellow, Mahan. He flings his long legs out before him when he sits. Nothing
mean or cramped about him. Laughter lines in that weather-beaten
face. A man whose conversation is frank and far-ranging, who exacts
nothing from you. A man to repose in, have a drink with.

Badham comes into view, skulking behind, narrow-shouldered
and dark-suited. A bitter smile of disbelief. *Nelson wasn't that stupid,*

nobody could be. Those conflicting signals, all the confusion—it worked in his favour. Armistice and treaty, embarking and sailing—these are words we play with when vagueness suits us. He wanted them out of the forts, he wanted them hanged, let them think what they liked. Badham's glasses shine, he is wearing a wing collar, he raises one evil, black-gloved hand. I wait for Mahan to get up and give him a straight right to the jaw, but he seems not to have heard. If I could get round to the other side, get within range of that narrow skull . . . I found myself looking round the room for a weapon. It was at that moment of desperate impulse that the idea came, a kind of call. And it was associated from the first with the name of a man I had never met but whose five-year-old notepaper I still had, a man named E. L. Sims, a resident of Naples.

It was appalling, but it was undeniable. There was nothing more that I could do here. If I wanted to keep Horatio with me, I would have to go in person to that city. Naples must contain him still, must contain the truth of those June days. The rooms he ate in, slept in, the streets and buildings he knew—they were still there. Take a trip, Miss Lily had said—advice I had never intended to act on. Dread mounted within me. I was going to act on it now.

breakfast aboard ship on the Sunday morning, when he was host to a distinguished company, including Lord Grandison and the bishop of Winchester and family; the sudden request, shortly before 11 A.M., that his guests should quit the ship because a French man-of-war had been sighted off Sardinia and he intended to sail immediately to intercept her.

Nothing new in this, but by following the timing so closely and cross-cutting between events, Sims had succeeded very cleverly in conveying the drama of Horatio's life at this time—the glitter of high society, the political manoeuvring, the looming death-struggle with France for supremacy at sea, which was not to end until twelve years later, at Trafalgar. Sims was a man with a sense of the clock, so much was clear; a man with a feeling for parallels. After several weeks of painful indecision I had written to him, and he had replied with thanks, courteous though brief. Whereupon I had proposed to the committee that Sims should be invited to become an honorary overseas member. He had accepted the invitation. No more had been heard from him, but somewhere I still had the single sheet of his notepaper with at the head his address in Naples and—or so I hoped— the telephone number.

Of course, he might well have moved since that time. It was Friday afternoon on the fifth of September when I had the impulse to inflict grievous bodily harm on Badham. I knew that if I hesitated much or launched on any sort of debate with myself, I would never make the call. As if under the duress of a dream, I opened drawers, fumbled among papers, finally found Sims's note. There was a telephone number at the head. Then it came to me that my passport might be out of date. I had not been out of the country since the trip to Tenerife with my father. After more minutes of search I found it: still seven months to run. I did not know the code for Italy—I had to look it up in the phone book.

2 5

The salient facts about Sims were that he was an
member of the Nelson Society and that he had lived
for a good many years and so must know the city well. He
just the person to give me some tips, set me on the right trac
was an honorary member was largely due to me, which
might give me some claim on him. Five years before I had s
cle of his in the *Historical Review* entitled "Four Days
which dealt with Horatio's first brief visit to the city in the
of 1793, when he was thirty-four years old, a mere captai
faithful husband, and had both eyes and all his limbs and v
command of his spanking new ship, the *Agamemnon*.

I had been impressed by Sims's meticulous scholar
tailed way in which he charted Horatio's movements:
with the Hamiltons and the prime minister, Sir John A
ner at the royal palace, when he sat at the king's ri

In the course of these harassing preliminaries, the protection of dream wore off and my hands became unsteady. However, I did not dare to pause. A peevish, waspish sound to the ringing tone, foreign and far away. Could he be there, at the back of such a sound? Five years . . . Then a voice, without discernible accent but in some way familiar.

"Sims."

The hiss of his identity seemed to hang in the air between us. There was an agitation in my throat, but I contained it. I explained to him who I was.

"Yes," he said, after a considerable pause, "I remember that you wrote to me. Some years ago, yes. Where are you now? Are you in Italy?"

"No," I said. "No, I am here."

There was what sounded like a thin clearing of the throat at the other end of the line. "Here is always where we are," the voice said.

"Here in London," I said. "I am planning to visit Italy, Naples in fact, and I wondered if we could . . . It would give me great pleasure if you could spare some time for me. I thought we might meet for a drink. Compare notes."

"Notes?"

"As you know, I greatly admired your article about Horatio's first visit to the city."

There was again a pause, this time rather briefer. "Horatio, yes," Sims said. "Well, it would have been very pleasant, Mr. Cleasby, but I am leaving Naples soon and I'll be away until the end of the year, so I am afraid—"

I showed a promptness now I had not known I was capable of. "When?" I said. "When are you leaving?"

"At the end of next week."

"I was planning to come more or less at once. You will still be there in the early part of the week?"

In a tone that I thought indicated resignation, he said, "Yes, in the early part of the week, certainly, I will still be here."

And so it was all arranged. I would telephone Sims from my hotel on the evening of my arrival. We would meet and have a drink together.

Reaction set in immediately. I had some moments of giddiness moving away from the phone, and then I experienced a sort of twitching behind the knees, distinctly alarming. It might have been an obscure symptom of hunger; nothing had passed my lips since the tea and digestive biscuits of the morning. Despite this weakness, I was pleased with myself. I had acted with decision, I had not allowed myself to be fobbed off. Something like Hotham's Action, when we nobbled the *Ça Ira*. I decided to celebrate by phoning the takeaway for a pizza.

There was a shadow over things, however, and it grew darker while I waited for the pizza to arrive. I would not be here for Miss Lily's return. She was due back at the end of the following week—I had been ticking off the days. Now, after all this time of waiting, I would not see her before I left. It couldn't be helped, I knew that. Sims might hold the vital clue, perhaps even something he wasn't himself aware of. Armed with it, I would return. Miss Lily would commend my initiative, we would complete the book together, it would revolutionize Nelson studies . . . All the same, I felt heavy-hearted at the thought of missing her, and when the pizza arrived I no longer wanted it. I had some red wine instead.

They were anxious days that followed. There were things I had not foreseen, not being an experienced traveller. It was short notice for early September, still the holiday season. I succeeded in getting a flight to Rome for the following Monday afternoon, but no connecting flight to Naples was available. I would have to go by train. I could have got the train ticket through the agency, but it didn't occur to me.

The whole thing bristled with difficulties. What should I pack, what should I wear for the journey? I had been shuffling around in old clothes for months, not changing very often. My shirts had been folded away too long; they had grubby marks along the folds. My trousers had horizontal crease marks made by the hangers. Before I could become a traveller, before I could present myself to Sims, I had to clean myself up, go to a barber, buy some socks.

I felt almost distraught, locking the front door, locking myself out, hoisting my case down to the waiting taxi. However, this state of nerves subsided, eclipsed by the different order of stress involved in finding my way about at Heathrow. On the whole I acquitted myself well there, I think. I lost some minutes waiting in the wrong queue, among people who were travelling business class, but I soon realized the mistake and moved on down to the right counter.

I got the train from Rome Airport to the central railway station without mishap, but I had a bad time at the station itself. I was confused by the crowd and the jostling movement, by the need to be constantly stepping out of the way. Untrustworthy-looking people in white caps with plastic peaks repeatedly asked me if I wanted a hotel. However, I found the ticket office, joined the queue. When I got up to the counter and met the dark, indifferent gaze of the clerk—eyes that had seen so many other eyes, so close; horrendous thought—at this last moment I asked for a single ticket, not a return, asked for it in English and with a sudden loud insistence, as if it might be denied me.

It wasn't, of course; the clerk's expression did not change by the slightest flicker. When I tried to ask about train times, he shook his head, raised one hand in a gesture that seemed to take in the entire station. Information was to be sought out there; his job was selling tickets.

Clutching my little oblong of pinkish card, I walked away. I had a sense, exhilarating and alarming, that I was burning my boats behind me. This single ticket was a mark of my determination, my commitment. Without the truth, I would not return. However, I had first to get to Naples. I still did not know the time of departure. The information office was full of people waiting and there was only one woman behind the counter to answer their questions. Here and there along the station concourse there were large illuminated screens, but these did not show times of arrivals and departures, as I was expecting, only a series of images fleeting and diverse, quite soundless: a woman undressing, drifting autumn leaves, oddly angled faces.

Anxiety fastened on me almost unawares. I found myself breathing open-mouthed, as if I had been running. It was quarter past two. The heat of the day outside had flowed in, struck through the girders of the roof high above. I felt it pressing down on my head. I was still lugging my case. I thought of finding a left luggage office, but what if I had to leave in a hurry? There was no friendly-looking buffet where one might have hoped to get tea and a jam doughnut in total anonymity; there was only a sort of glassed-in café, where waiters hovered about. You would have to sit down, catch the waiter's eye, struggle to make your wants known, worry about how much to tip. I could not meet the hazards of such a place until I knew the time of my departure, and probably not even then.

I was not far from total anguish and immobility when I came upon a poster at the far end of the station that had details of intercity connections. There was a train to Naples at 2:46. A little star was printed after the time, and I saw from the foot of the poster that this was a Eurostar train, distinguished with a note in both Italian and English, *Alta velocità, High speed*. There would almost certainly be an extra charge on a train like this. It was now 2:27 by my watch. A man in a railway uniform was passing close to me. I stepped in front of him, swinging my case. "Eurostar ticket?" I said to him loudly. He regarded me without much expression but not unkindly. I tried again. "Euro-star ticket?"

He raised a forefinger as if testing the wind. "*Uno,*" he said. "*Binario uno.*"

Platform one. We were then alongside platform twenty-two. Hastily back the full length of the station, humping my case. Sure enough, there it was, clearly marked, the Eurostar ticket counter. A strip of red digital lettering above stated that all seats had to be booked in advance. Five or six people were already queueing there. It was 2:35. Minutes ticked away. I was sweating heavily, unable to prevent myself from gasping. I have always, from childhood, practised open-mouthed breathing as a relief from all manner of stress, and now it has become quite involuntary. I felt that people were looking at me, but I did not return these glances. It had become immensely important, symbolical, not to miss this special high-speed train. I understood now that the train itself was a part of the design, that I was being tested. A failure at this point could put my whole enterprise at risk.

At last my turn came. I paid the supplementary charge, received the white card that recorded my booking. Where did the train leave from? Platform twenty-two, naturally. It was now exactly 2:43. I had three minutes to traverse the whole length of the station again. In a panic of haste I set off. The blood throbbed at my temples, my vision was clouded, I heard my panting progress through the crowd. I made it with half a minute to spare. The brand-new train was there, towering above me, in all the gleam of imminent departure. I found my seat, collapsed into it, waited for the moment of drawing away.

We remained where we were, without explanation, for the next seventeen minutes, while my breathing returned slowly to normal, my heart quietened, the perspiration cooled on my body. I understood the whole thing now: there had been no need for haste, no need for fear, a period of error had been allowed for, *the train had been scheduled to wait.* This thought brought no ease of mind; it merely increased my sense of responsibility. It came to me now, in these moments of restored calm, came to me like a folding of wings, that it had not after all been fear of missing the train that had agitated me so but fear of what I was doing, of the mission itself, a fear no doubt quickened by the distress I had just been put through, but already there, already existing—I had brought it with me from Belsize Park. Miss Lily's face came into my mind, that flushed look of hers and her indignation when she met with something that seemed contrary to common sense. I was swept with a desolate sense of her absence and I seemed to hear her voice saying, "But what does it mean, Charles, what does it *mean?*"

Her smile when she heard about the brandy—I hadn't minded it somehow. And Bobby's solemn stare . . . The progress of the train was smooth, almost silent. I felt weary but safe from harm for the moment, quite relaxed. The countryside south of Rome slipped by unheeded. I began to think again, in a wandering, sleepy kind of way, of that last voyage in the battered flagship, that long return to gratitude and grief. They took every care to keep you fresh, repeatedly draining the spirits off from below, topping them up from above. But the sentinel who was on guard beside your barrel got a bad fright one morning—he saw the lid lifting up and gave the alarm. Nothing supernatural in it; your body had absorbed most of the brandy, and a pressure of gas had built up.

It was early in December when you arrived at Spithead, two weeks later when you made your way round to the Nore. When you were taken from the cask and inspected, you were found to be in a perfect state of preservation. An autopsy revealed that your heart and liver and lungs were free of all trace of disease; all your vital parts were perfectly sound. You might have lived to a great age, the doctors said. But your remaining eye was going; in a few years you would have been completely blind.

They took you and put you in a plain coffin, one that had been waiting for you ever since 1798, made from the timbers of the *Orient*, the French flagship destroyed at Aboukir Bay. This was cased in lead and then enclosed in an outer coffin encrusted with heraldic devices, your coat of arms, the stars of your orders, a crocodile representing the Battle of the Nile. In this you lay in state in the Painted Room at Greenwich. Here the Prince of Wales came alone to pay his respects, that same prince who had once caused you torments of jealousy. Next day the doors were thrown open to the people, who came in such enormous numbers that the governor of the hospital panicked and called for extra troops. They were not needed, there was no disturbance, the people were docile with grief.

Three days later the grand river procession from Greenwich to London, the stately City barges with the black and gold of their cabins and the brocaded liveries of the oarsmen, your funeral barge towering above them with its huge canopy and its plumes of dyed ostrich feathers tossing in the wind off the river, the silent crowds lining the riverbanks. There was a moment which I had always felt to be significant, ever since first reading about it. I couldn't remember when— perhaps in the Grigson days. As your barge was brought alongside Whitehall Stairs, the sky darkened and there was sudden violent squall of rain, lashing the bearers as they struggled to raise the coffin and place it on the waiting funeral car. This intervention of the sky was remembered and retold, those darkened moments when you quitted forever the element that had seen your triumphs.

A vast procession had been assembled to escort the body to St. Paul's, but there were too many soldiers, it was a river of red, the blue naval uniforms were almost overwhelmed. Just forty-eight men, seamen and marines from HMS *Victory*. The crowd roared its approval of them—they were cheered continuously as they marched past, proudly displaying the flags of their ship, two huge Union Jacks bearing the marks of the enemy shot and the St. George's ensign, which they held up to view, ripped and shattered, amid the sobs and plaudits of the crowd. But silence fell at the passing of the funeral car. As it went by, with its tall four-posted canopy and nodding plumes, bearing the gilded coffin high above the heads of the people, its progress was accompanied by a great rustling noise like the sound of waves on the seashore, as the thousands of male onlookers removed their hats.

The burial service was performed after the office of evensong. The coffin made its slow way up the aisle to the haunting music of William Croft's "Burial Sentences": *I am the resurrection and the life, saith the Lord.* But the piece most people remembered and spoke about came at the end of the service, just before the coffin was lowered to its final resting place in the crypt: the music composed by Handel for the funeral of Queen Caroline in 1737, with its ringing assertion *But his name liveth evermore!*

Precisely at thirty-three and a half minutes past five, the coffin was lowered into its grave and disappeared from public view. It was the garter king at arms—I tried to recall his name but could not—who proclaimed the style and the titles of the dead lord: *Thus it hath pleased Almighty God to take out of this transitory life, unto his divine mercy, the Most Noble Lord Horatio Nelson, Viscount and Baron Nelson of the Nile, and of Burnham Thorpe, in the County of Norfolk, Knight of the Most Honourable Order of the Bath, Vice-Admiral of the White Squadron of the Fleet . . .*

I drifted into sleep before getting to the end of the list. I roused myself to produce my ticket when the inspector came, but for most of the journey I was comatose. I didn't take much notice of the surroundings until we were approaching Naples and I saw the tawny, crumpled summit of Vesuvius, familiar to me from a hundred illustrations. There were glimpses of the coast, a glitter of sea, a strip of bright sand, a vivid cluster of beach umbrellas, swallowed up almost at once by the ugly and haphazard jumble of buildings stretching up from the shore. On the other side, to my left, a constant rippling line of mountains, bare, bluish in this afternoon light, rank on rank of them.

I took a taxi from the station to my hotel, the Santa Lucia, closing my eyes on the anarchic disorder of the traffic. This improved when we reached the wide seafront road where the hotel was. All the same, I was glad to climb out from the taxi into the flooding sea light that came off the bay, glad to be able to understand the driver's English, work out the liras, give him a tip that seemed acceptable. Glad, in short, to have survived thus far. My visit was already assuming the characteristics it was to have all the way through, almost till the end: a surviving of encounters, a sense of having—only just—kept a step ahead. Horatio was in this city. I had to keep going till I found him. More than that: I had to keep on the lookout, keep my mind open for the truth when it came. I kept on, I was careful—almost till the end.

All the details of my arrival at the hotel were attended by this same sense of obstacles ovecome: checking in, ascending in the lift, following the porter down the quiet corridor, finally finding myself alone, still all in one piece, in my distinctly handsome room—they had given me one overlooking the bay.

Only now, in this first solitude achieved in Naples, about to reach for the phone, only now did I register the address of this hotel—such a famous name, it had not been necessary to mention the street. But I noticed it now on the brochure lying beside the phone: Via Partenope 46. Parthenopean Street. It was named after that short-lived republic whose fate had tormented me for months, named after those Neapolitan Jacobins whom Ruffo and his Calabrian irregulars defeated and drove into their forts, to whom the promise of safe conduct was made and not kept, who came out in the end to cast themselves—you said—on the mercy of their notoriously unmerciful sovereigns. Did you believe it? Did you? It was that botched attempt at liberty, those heart-sickening deaths, that the street commemorated, not your loyal support of the Bourbon monarch . . . I felt a chill, something like premonition, as I took out my wallet, found the card on which I had written Sims's number, made the call.

"Ah, it's you," he said without particular expression. "So you have arrived."

"Minutes ago," I said. "You see I lost no time in phoning."

"No, you didn't."

"I am very much looking forward to—"

"Did you have a good journey?"

The conventional politeness of this took me quite by surprise. The journey had nothing to do with it; I was on a mission. "Yes," I said. "Quite uneventful."

"Uneventful is always good," Sims said. "Especially on aeroplanes."

"I was wondering if tomorrow we might meet . . ."

"During most of the day I am busy, unfortunately. There are so many things to see to before I go away. But late in the afternoon I would have some time, if that suits you. Or perhaps you would prefer the day after?"

"No," I said. "No, tomorrow would be fine."

So it was arranged. Sims would come to the Santa Lucia at 5:30; we would have a drink together at the hotel bar. It was a great relief to me to have definitely fixed this appointment. Sims was a resident of this city, he would know Italian, he was a knowledgeable, scholarly fellow, he might put me on to something, new material, a line to follow up. I would have to be on the alert—it might be small, something Sims himself might not think was important. Something to establish

your good name forever and join mine to it. Entwined together, inseparable, vindicated and vindicator, the bright and the dark.

In the glow of hope these thoughts afforded me, I went over to
my window and looked across the bay. Your eyes saw this when you
looked out from the balcony of your room in the Palazzo Sessa, residence of the Hamiltons, where you stayed. Not perhaps the immediate foreground lying just below me, the little harbour with its moored
launches and yachts, the gently glimmering water warmed by the reflections of the boats to shades of ochre and pale orange. No, but you
would have seen the more distant view, the open sea, the island of
Capri with its ridged head and long jaw. Like some fabulous dragon.
Perhaps you too made just that comparison in your mind, looking out
from your room that September of your second visit, when you were
falling in love with Emma Hamilton. Some warm evening like this
one. Languid and feverish after your great victory at the Nile, still suffering from the strain of it and the shock of the wound. She moves
quietly about in the room behind you, preparing something for your
comfort. What you need most for your comfort is the enfolding of her
lovely thighs, but this is five months away still, in Palermo, on a cold
day of February. No heating to speak of, chilly marble everywhere in
those Sicilian palaces; Miss Lily would not have liked it, she feels the
cold. In the tent of the blankets a warm refuge, a mingling of breaths.

A white cruise liner was crossing the bay from right to left, in
the direction of Sorrento. Immediately below me a policeman in a
white helmet and pale blue uniform was directing the traffic. To the
north, barely a hundred yards beyond the marina, was the Castel
dell'Ovo or Castle of the Egg, from which, under the eyes of the British fleet, some of the Jacobins, clutching the belongings they would
never need again, were embarked on their transports. A massive, squat,
square-topped building, windowless on the shore side. I could make

out a poster on the façade, brightly coloured, with a figure on it that looked like Donald Duck but of course couldn't be. This castle was so close, only minutes away, I could leave it to the last.

It was after seven. Already there was some gathering of darkness in the air; strings of coloured bulbs on the café fronts and along the harbour railings had been lit while I watched. After the trials of the day I was tired. I would eat at the hotel, go early to bed. In this new place a nightmare might give me some respite. I would be fresh next day, ready to search for him, ready to face Sims. I had high hopes of Sims.

2 6

J slept fitfully but better than usual. I had a strange dream, different from any I could remember. I was walking on smooth sand,
gleaming wet, giving slightly to the weight. I was looking for something, stones of some kind that might be concealed in the sand, but I
found nothing. The sand became more shining and softer; my feet
made oily swirls in it, like oil spreading on a wet film. A white goat
approached me, very shyly. I tried to encourage the goat to come
nearer, and it did so, finally. I put my hand out to caress the goat but
found that it had turned so that its rear was towards me. I felt my
hand caught in a warm dry clamp. I thought at first it was the goat's
prehensile anus but saw after a moment that he had a very long tail
with a thick, fleshy bump at the end like a bullrush and this contained
a kind of mouth, in which my hand was imprisoned. For some moments I tried to withdraw it, not violently but discreetly. I felt some
disgust, some fear, but mainly a desire that no-one should witness my

humiliating predicament. No-one did. Still politely tugging, I rose to wakefulness in the pale light of early morning. Slowly the sense of mystery and beauty and repugnance caused by this dream faded away, to be replaced by an uneasy question: why was there no reference to Palazzo Sessa in my guidebook, otherwise so packed with information? Why was it not marked on any of the maps?

Even later, setting forth, fortified by coffee and various pastries, the question still exercised me. I knew the way, of course. I had traced it in imagination a hundred times: your triumphant coach ride up from the waterfront, after the salutes of the guns; the swooning of Emma; the welcoming speech of King Ferdinand, sweating in his velvet suit.

Every detail of my walk that day has stayed with me. The glittering sweep of the bay, Vesuvius mild-looking in the early sunshine, the cindery tracks of its eruptions clearly visible, a group of policemen with gleaming revolver-holsters laughing and joking together at a streetcorner. Across the broad Via Marina, up to Largo di Castello, then steeply up again into the side of the Pizzofalcone hill. I was out of condition and had to take it slowly. The streets were narrow, paved with dark stone, the houses tall and close together. Full daylight had not arrived here yet; some residue of darkness still grained the air between the houses. There was a short alley ending in a cobbled yard with on one side a small church and on the other a vaulted passage opening onto the courtyard of the palazzo.

There it stood before me, Palazzo Sessa, official residence of the British ambassador, rented by him from the Marchese di Sessa for £150 a year, a high rent for the time; before that, home to monastic orders for something like seven centuries. Here Emma arrived on her twenty-first birthday, in the full flower of her beauty, cast off by Sir William's nephew, though not yet knowing it, soon to be the mistress, then the wife, of the elderly uncle. Here exhausted Horatio was brought after his great victory at the Nile, to be tended by Emma, to lie and watch her as she moved about the room, her full figure under the loose drapes. Here began their celebrated love.

I scanned the façade, every inch of it. I looked carefully at the arched entranceway. It was incredible: there was nothing whatever to record or commemorate the fact that the greatest hero in our national history had spent months of his life here at a time of crucial importance, when the fate of the city was hanging in the balance. Standing there on the dark cobbles of the courtyard, I looked up to the first floor, where your room was. A line of washing obscured the tall windows. Another went across from one side of the courtyard to the other. Somewhere inside the place a baby was crying with a blind, persistent woe, hardly pausing for breath. Across from me, at the foot of the stone steps that you must have mounted to reach your apartment, two women were standing together. They had been talking but fell silent when I appeared and looked closely at me. The place was a tenement, in multiple occupation. There was no way it could be entered, no way of finding that room of your fever and dawning desire, the room I had shared with you, as I had shared thoughts of Emma's body. With a sensation of bewilderment, I raised my head to the clear blue of the day above me, clouds moving slowly in it, swifts wheeling high up. There was a sudden silence, or so it seemed. I thought I could hear the thin shrieks of the swifts, distant as they were, some message contained in them important for me to know. But it was the sound of mourning, it fell on my upturned face, it touched my face like rain. His words printed on my mind, his courage that supplied my lack . . . The sky was blank, the birds were silent. I became aware again of the wailing baby, the glances of the women, the lines of washing. From somewhere behind me came music from a radio, thin notes, slightly distorted.

I turned away, went back through the vaulted passageway, past the church, back down towards the water. Everything I looked at seemed improbable, insubstantial. You saved their Bourbon majesties, you delivered Naples from the cursed French . . . Perhaps in the two forts where the Jacobins held out against you I might discover something that would save the day.

Castel Nuovo was the nearer, just across from the Royal Palace, on the seaward side. It took me not quite half an hour to walk there. Round, crenellated towers in dark stone, an incongruous triumphal arch in white marble, celebrating the taking of the city by Alfonso I of Aragon. I got my ticket from the small office adjoining the courtyard. Somewhere here, in a corner, royalist hostages were shot by the rebels, panicking as their time ran out. Perhaps over against the steps the killing was done, where now a group of schoolchildren clustered and chatted. Or against the wall, below the chapel—mass shootings generally seemed to take place up against something. Was this the deed of blood that determined you to deal harshly with the rebels, to regard them as beyond the pale, people to whom promises need not be kept? You see, I was still trying to find reasons. But the outrage was small compared to what the royalist mob was doing in the streets of the city. No, you were against them from the start, you loathed their libertarian rhetoric, all that claptrap, that parroting of the bombastic, bloody French.

It was a question of getting up to the top of the castle, up to the ramparts, so I could look down over the sea gates that the rebels came out of, see the view towards Sorrento as they must have seen it on that last day of their liberty, as they were embarked on the transports that became their floating prisons.

A flight of stone steps led upwards. I mounted quickly, a sort of excitement possessing me, a sense of possible revelation up there on the heights. I would see where the rebels came out along the mole; I would see them, by a stretch of imagination, as he would have seen them, waiting in his anchored flagship out in the bay, telescope to his eye, noting with approval that they were not being accorded honours of war. Perhaps in this violation of the parallels, in this splicing of viewpoints, some essential clue might be vouchsafed me . . .

But on the broad stone landing of the second floor my way was barred by two attendants, who pressed with their palms at the air between us and uttered words I did not understand. I heard the slam of heavy doors closing. It seemed I was required to go down to the courtyard again. What had happened? It couldn't be closing time, it wasn't eleven yet. The attendants were shouting among themselves. A different sort of shouting came from the street outside, a heavy, reiterated chant. And from some invisible source high above, other voices, thinned by distance.

The man behind the counter at the ticket office knew some English. Things were finally explained to me. A mass demonstration by the unemployed of Naples was going on outside; some of the demonstrators had infiltrated the fort, occupied the battlements. Theirs were the voices I had heard shouting down. They were armed with clubs, the man said—he gestured with his hands to show the formidable nature of these. His face took on a look of painful sincerity. They were very bad people, he said, not genuine unemployed at all. There was fear of some violent assault on the picture gallery, the frescoes in the chapel. Everything had to be locked and barred.

There didn't seem much point in hanging about waiting. It might take a long time to expel these intruders. I thought it likely that the riot police would have to be brought in. I made for the exit gates but found these barred too. Two attendants in hot blue suits, one on either side. Please open this gate. I made gestures of unbarring and opening. The attendants shook their heads, miming in their turn: more people with clubs just outside, waiting for a chance to break in. How long will this go on? Tapping my watch, raising my eyebrows.

Shrugs all round; nobody knew. I was caught there, trapped between occupied battlements and barred gates.

It was hot, even in the shade of the courtyard wall. The remote harangues from the men on the battlements still came floating down. Straining my eyes against the glare, I made out two gesturing figures. One of them raised and waved what looked like a staff or short pole, thicker at one end than on the other. Besiegers or besieged? Beyond them, the sky was glazed white, painful to look at. A moment of giddiness came to me and I felt in danger of falling. I stepped back, groped for the support of the wall, remembering as my vision cleared how Miss Lily had supported me the evening I had staggered, remembering the warmth of her hand under my arm.

There were other visitors, drifting round the courtyard or standing in the ticket office. A gaunt American couple; an Italian family, man and wife and two small, fractious girls; a mixed group of young people, probably students. Hostages all, fellow victims of circumstance, we avoided one another's eyes. After something more than an hour the gate was unbarred, we were allowed to leave. There were no demonstrators in the street outside, but a number of helmeted policemen waited there, standing in silent groups near the vans that had brought them.

It was quarter past twelve when I emerged. The sun swooped down as if it had been waiting in ambush just for me. Nothing looked the same. The street seemed wider than before, it was a river flowing with cars; looking across it was like straining to see a far shore. It was too far, there was too much glare. I felt the eyes of the police on me.

Lunchtime was approaching, but I felt no smallest desire to eat. I set off walking, keeping the water on my right, stopping every now and again to consult my map. It took me nearly forty minutes to get within sight of the Carmine church. I had to cross the road—a hazardous business, this, as there were side lanes as well as the main ones and no-one took any notice of the traffic lights. I had to make a dash and only narrowly avoided being run over. This made my temples throb and I felt the beginning of a headache, a dull, persistent pain along the ridges of the brows. But it was cool and dim inside the church, all a harmony of variously coloured marbles. There was no-one else there. I stood still for some moments absorbing the peace and silence of the place, the inlaid pilasters at their exact intervals, the stone heads of seraphim decorating the arches. Nothing much had changed since Ruffo's time, since that morning of June 27, 1799, when the cardinal had come here in state to celebrate a mass of thanksgiving for the fortunate outcome of the treaty negotiations.

He was happy that day—or so he gave it out. *Full of contentment that the English had not only recognized but themselves executed the treaty.* Sacchinelli again, the diligent secretary, writing after his employer's death. The words sounded now like an echo in the cavern of my mind, in this sumptuous, cavernous church. What was in the cardinal's mind as he intoned the *Te Deum*, raised the host that day? The rebels were already out of the forts; they had been jostled to their transports by Horatio's marines. How much did Ruffo know, how much did Ruffo suspect? Did he really think the Jacobins would be allowed to sail for France? Or was that mass a piece of ornate and solemn hypocrisy, designed to exculpate him, throw the odium of betrayal on the British?

The same questions. I was no nearer the answers here than I had been in my basement in Belsize Park. Standing there with that dull band of pain along my brows, I felt the same sorrow, the same helplessness that I had so often felt at home in my study. Whatever one made of the documents, the truth of the past was beyond grasping—it lay in the looks exchanged, the tones used, and the eyes and voices had left no trace.

Out again, into the blinding sun. A walk of five minutes took me from the scene of thanksgiving, whether genuine or not, to the site of the indisputably genuine hangings that shortly followed. Piazza del Mercato, where the executions were carried out, where public executions had been carried out for many hundreds of years. A vast and desolate square between the dock area and the district of Forcella, with a few nondescript stalls round the edges. Along the eastern side an open-air market for cheap leisure goods—plastic garden chairs, inflatable dinghies and ducks and paddling pools, brightly coloured beach umbrellas, all set out on the cobbles. Some small boys listlessly kicking a ball around in a far corner. A Baroque church with a lead-coloured dome and eroded saints on the façade.

Somewhere here, in the middle . . . Whatever the rights and wrongs, the promises kept or broken, this is where it ended for the leaders of that short-lived republic. Day after day through those summer months of 1799, they were brought here in batches to combine with hangman and pull-feet and make that triple-headed, dangling beast that had so haunted my imagination.

I squinted across the vast square. The flat light of afternoon lay over everything—there were no shadows. I found myself longing for the cool of night, for the dark, as they must have done as they were led out to die. The agony would be over, they would have found their own darkness. The troops withdrew at nightfall; their only purpose was to ensure that the executions were carried out. The corpses were stripped by the hangman and left hanging, sport of the populace. If they were not citizens of Naples, no-one would claim them; they would remain there. The *lazzaroni* would push and pull them this way and that. Cruelty, like other motions of the heart, needs time to warm up. With time they went from jeers to knives, slashing at the bodies, cutting off the ears, the nose, the testicles, hacking through the ribs. After that came the feast. The livers were roasted, eaten, here on the square, perhaps just where I was standing. It is related that a passer-by who refused to partake of this meal was killed on the spot.

You saw none of this, you saw none of the executions, you came nowhere near the contagion of the mob. You were . . . elsewhere. On board ship or in Sicily or dozing through the hot afternoons in the Palazzo Sessa. You heard it, you must have heard it—no-one in Naples could escape it, that great roar of jubilation as the victim was launched into space.

The dome of the church opposite was clear in every detail. I had the impression of some quivering or disturbance in the air, like the single swing of an invisible pendulum. Then the square was blank again, drab, dusty, featureless, pressed down under the flat light. The garish beach goods, the occasional voices of the children, the squat little church . . . That great sum of terror and pain—I had somehow expected to find it reflected here, but there was only this bleakness and ugliness of the present.

Turning away, quitting the square, was attended by a curious sense of effort. No more than tiredness, I suppose, but I felt I could have stayed there a long time without moving, one of the derelict props of the place. It was twenty past two; Sims was coming to the hotel at five-thirty; there would be time to see the other fort, Castel dell'Ovo, but I had omitted to find out whether it was open to visitors in the afternoon. Probably not, I thought. It was near the hotel, in any case. I was exhausted, but the thought of resting or stopping to eat something did not come into my mind. I did not want to take a taxi, shrinking from the human encounter it would involve. Only Sims I wanted to see; I had hopes of Sims.

I was walking more slowly now; it took me more than an hour to get to the fort. I was relieved to find the gate open; but as I approached, I was astonished to see that the figure on the poster over the entrance, which I had observed at a distance from my hotel room and which had so much resembled Donald Duck, was in fact Donald Duck, complete with jaunty sailor's cap and chortling beak and clumpy webbed feet. Above his head in bright red letters, *Il Mondo dei Paperi*. Ripples of light moved over the poster, cast up by the jiggling reflections of the harbour water. *Mondo* was world—the World of Donald Duck. After some moments of incredulity, I understood: there was a Donald Duck exhibition taking place inside this venerable building.

It might be possible to bypass Donald, get a ticket for the fort only. I went through the vaulted tunnel of the entrance and spoke to the man inside the little glassed-in ticket office. I spoke carefully through the grid. *Not Donald, please.* But you couldn't have one without the other. I didn't like the man's eyes, they were small and black, I didn't like the way he stared through his glass wall, as if there were something wrong with me, something strange about wanting to give Donald a miss. It occurred to me now that I could ignore the exhibition altogether, go straight on past. I would walk past, make my way up to the sunlit bastions, inspect the cannon, still in their emplacements, look out from those heights over the water to where your ships lay at anchor.

But at the entrance to the exhibition I came upon two young people, a boy and a girl; they were wearing Donald Duck T-shirts; they had spotted the brightly coloured ticket in my hand, it too bearing Donald's image. They smiled in greeting; they held out catalogues; they thought I had come for him. I was too tired, too confused, the smiles and T-shirts were impossible to disappoint; I could not simply slink past, keeping my head down so as not to see their expressions change. I tried to smile, tried to assume the look of someone looking forward to a rare treat, and passed inside.

Once in, there was no quick way out again. It was a one-way system, arrows pointed from room to room. The exhibition was enormous; it occupied three floors, all of them strangely resonant with voices. Voices and echoes of voices, in the cavernous rooms; but no faces of people, none that I can remember, so terrible was the impact of the faces on the walls. All Donald's relatives were there, grotesquely blown up, staring down. Everywhere I looked I met their eyes, enormous, unshaded by lashes, horribly intent. The primary colours shrieked from the walls. The glands at the sides of my neck felt hot, I felt the run of sweat on my chest and back. Twice I tried to go back, to retrace my steps, but the way was barred by more young people in Donald Duck T-shirts. They smiled, they pointed at the arrows; I had to follow the arrows. The second floor was worse than the first, with the Scottish branch all represented and named in glaring capitals, Jack McDuck and Dirty Dingus and Sir Quackly, huge and terrifying in a top hat and spats. There was nowhere in the room to look, nowhere my eyes could take refuge from them. A moment came when I doubted my ability to walk across the room, expose myself to the barrage of those eyes, reach the stairs to the third and final floor, the only way out. I wanted to hide, to press back against the doorway. I was aware of my own noisy breathing. I made it to the slit of a window, peered out at a sudden, brilliant section of sea, the broken crest of Vesuvius, the mole of the fort along which the Jacobins made their way to be embarked. Here, finally, was the view I had wanted. Turning back, I encountered with an irrepressible leap of terror the enormous, baleful eyes of old Scrooge McDuck, the collective stare of a boatload of jowly dog-pirates in black masks.

How long I stayed here, how I found the resolution to get out, I cannot clearly remember. In the end, keeping my eyes down, I forced myself to walk across to the foot of the stairs and mount upward. The third floor was better. There were no more monstrously enlarged and malignant ducks, only a few of Donald's milder-eyed cousins, Molly Mallard, Cuthbert Coot, Luke Goose.

The last gallery was quite different from the others, devoted to copies of well-known paintings, faithful in every particular except that the human subjects had been replaced by Disney characters. I stayed here some time, waiting for my breathing to come back to normal, for that flush of panic to subside—fear with me was a fever, not a chill; the chill came now as the sweat cooled on my body. There was the Arnolfini Betrothal by Jan Van Eyck, with the Happy Hippos, Horace and Clarabella, as the engaged couple, and Caravaggio's celebrated Lute Player, with Minnie Mouse plucking the strings.

As I stood before these travesties in the blankness of mind that followed upon fear, through my weariness, my headache, my strained sight, there came to me some dawning hope of revelation. These images imposed on images, this simpering Minnie, these toothy hippos— perhaps here, not outside on that sunlit sea, was the secret, the key I was looking for. This Vermeer, with a pinafored Snow White in the kitchen among hanging fowl and the utensils of an alien culture . . . If one could peel the layers away, find the truth below the image, before the original painter found it, before the first, deceiving brushstrokes . . . A memory came to me of the coloured stamps I had so loved as a small child—transfers, as they were called, about the size of a matchbox top, backed by some thin adhesive tissue. You peeled the tissue away, you pressed the stamp on a blank sheet, and there, clearly printed, was the image. Angelfish, flamingos, a boat on a blue sea, a huntsman in a red coat. It would work on your skin too, particularly where the skin was pale and hairless, like the inside of the forearm. A transfer could be used only once, but one could be superimposed on another, and this was always a temptation and always regretted, resulting in botched shapes, blurred colours. Perhaps my earliest experience of sorrow, that remorse for the blighting of the pristine image, the knowledge that it could never be recovered.

I was driven away by the arrival of a chattering group of children shepherded by an elderly lady—their teacher, as I supposed. Finally there was an escape route—stone stairs led down and away. Too late now to see more of the fort. I was due to meet Sims at half past five in the bar of my hotel. If I wanted to be there before him, there was time only to find my way out of this place, walk back past the little harbour, cross the broad road that ran along beside the bay.

I reached the air-conditioned haven of the bar with six minutes to spare. I felt sticky and dishevelled, but there was no time for a shower if I wanted to be in place first. The bar was long and darkly shining. Pale lights were already on behind the counter, but shaded sunlight still lay over the wicker chairs and glass-topped tables at the nearer end. Hobnobbing on the bar stools was quite out of the question; I knew my disabilities, I did not want to sit too close to Sims, I would not have been able to talk to him or meet his eyes. I went to the bar and asked for red wine. I took my glass over to the corner table farthest from the bar and sat with my back to the wall so as to observe the approaches. At this early hour I was alone there, among the tables. I drank some of the wine, which was good, full-bodied, dark ruby in colour—from Sardinia, the barman had said. Almost at once, with the first taste of it, my headache receded, my weariness disappeared, and I felt entirely alert.

He came at twenty-three minutes to six. I knew him at once, before he had reached the table, before he had broken into the smile, signal of uncertainty, apology in advance for possible mistake. I had never set eyes on him before, but I experienced a pang of delighted recognition. That large, loose-knit figure, the careless, slightly shambling gait, the light hair, tanned face, the lines round the eyes that came from scanning wide horizons—it was Mahan to the life.

As he drew near and I stood up to answer his smile, the impression grew stronger and stronger. He corresponded in every detail. So much so that when he held out his hand and said, "Sims, Ernesto Sims," I was momentarily at a loss for his meaning.

"Charles Cleasby," I said. "So kind of you to find the time for me." Somewhere between the beginning of this sentence and the end of it, the incongruity, the foreignness of his first name struck me. He seated himself opposite my chair, at the farthest remove, and I was pleased by this, it seemed like a mark of tact. I asked him what he wanted to drink—a waiter had materialized at his elbow. He asked for something called *carpano*, which I had never heard of but took to be a sort of apéritif. This again seemed slightly incongruous—I had set Mahan down as a whisky-and-soda man, whether on foreign verandahs or by the hearth of home. I asked for another glass of the Sardinian wine. "Good of you to give up your time," I said, shyness causing me to repeat myself.

"Not at all. It is good to meet a fellow member of the Nelson Club."

There was something in the tone of this that made me glance quickly at him. Nothing showed on his face. Did he know I was no longer a member? Why had I thought his eyes were blue? They were dark, almost black. But his long legs were thrust out before him, carelessly sprawled, just as they had been that day in my study. He was wearing a linen jacket, rather crumpled. A dark blue handkerchief fell in loose folds from his breast pocket.

"How are you liking Naples?" he said.

An odd question, I thought it. How could I tell him that Horatio's Naples and mine was a sticky trap, a smeared web? He lived in Naples. I could not risk giving him offence; he might withhold his help.

"Well," I said, "I'm not really here as a tourist, you know, I am here to try and pick up his traces."

"Excuse me, whose traces are we talking about?"

"Why, his, you know. Nelson's. I have rather drawn a blank so far."

I suspected nothing. In that first flush of confidence I began to tell him about my book, about the problem I had run into. "I wondered whether you might be able to put me on to something," I said.

I had spoken in a light tone, not wanting Mahan to think me stumped but merely casting around. He had leaned forward in his chair. The red-brown stuff in his glass was hardly touched.

"A plaque?" he said. "Did you expect to find a plaque commemorating Nelson on the wall of the Palazzo Sessa? One of those blue ones that they put on houses in London?"

This was not the tone I had expected; there was something harsh in it, something derisive, setting me on the defensive. "Perhaps not a plaque," I said, "but something at least, something to mark his stay there." *Ernesto.* And the eyes, dark, fathomless . . .

He looked down for a moment, and his shoulders slumped in what seemed a long release of breath. "My dear man," he said, "you have had a disappointing day, but you could walk round in this city every day for a year and you wouldn't see the slightest sign of Nelson anywhere, neither hide nor hair of him. Not a syllable. The Palazzo Sessa looks down over the Piazza dei Martiri. Did you look at the monument there?"

"No."

"The martyrs in question are the Neapolitan Jacobins who went to the scaffold in the name of liberty in 1799, sent there through the good offices of Lord Nelson. This hotel is on a street named after the republic that Nelson helped to bring down."

"Yes, I know that."

"And do you know that if you went out of here and turned right you would come before long to the Via Caracciolo, a broad and beautiful avenue that runs along beside the sea towards Vomero? Or that if you went a little way up Via Santa Lucia, which is just behind us here, you would arrive at the little church of Santa Maria in Catena, which contains Caracciolo's tomb? That same Caracciolo, the Neapolitan admiral whom Nelson, on doubtful authority, had court martialled for treason and condemned and hanged in the course of a few hours—he was already hanging there from the yardarm when Nelson sat down to dinner. It was Caracciolo's corpse that rode the waves, you remember? Yes, of course, you will have read Parsons's account. The local fishermen recovered his body from the scrape in the sand where the English had left it, without even protection from the dogs. Now he lies there in state, one of Italy's most honoured sons."

He paused here and took a sip of the syrupy-looking liquid in his glass. He had been careful otherwise, but ordering that drink had been a false move on his part. I knew now that he was not what he seemed. I knew I'd have to be very careful.

"You have come for the wrong hero," he said. "Caracciolo is the hero here. Heroes are always local."

I saw the sudden, ironic twist of his lips as he said this. Thin lips. It was clear that heroes meant little to him, whether English or Italian. Mahan would never have said a thing like that. This was a person without ideals. A change had come over him while he spoke. He seemed narrower somehow in his chair; even his face seemed narrower, and the hairline more receding. He was an impersonator, a dangerously clever one. But his disguise was slipping away.

"After all," he said, "they would not be likely to honour the memory of someone they consider responsible for the destruction of the one of the most cultivated societies in Europe. Between the July of Ferdinand's return and the following March, a hundred and twenty were put to death in Naples and the islands and two hundred twenty-two were sentenced to life imprisonment. To say nothing of the hundreds given shorter sentences who died in Ferdinand's filthy jails. Very few of these were men of the populace—perhaps two or three. All the rest were nobles, officers, lawyers, doctors, professors, and men of science and letters. In the exercise of his royal mercy, Ferdinand strangled or decapitated or shut away the whole of the Neapolitan intellectual class. Do you appreciate the gravity of a loss like that? They cut off the head and left the trunk to the mob and the church and the Bourbon tyranny. The whole south of Italy still feels the effect of that today." He was shaking his head. "And you come here to look for Nelson."

"He was not responsible," I said. "How could he have known what would happen to them?"

These words of mine served only to give the person opposite me more power, I knew that. I was afraid of him, but I could not prevent myself from inviting more harm, from putting my head on the block. It was why I had arranged the interview, I understood it now. I looked away from him, summoning resolution. There were more people at the bar, and three men in business suits were sitting at one of the tables, but too far away to hear us. People were passing through the swing doors that gave onto the street outside, people entering and leaving. Rapid shapes of light were made by the swinging of these doors, flexing, spiralling shapes, gone as soon as glimpsed. This light had a reddish tinge—the awning outside the hotel was red, I suddenly remembered. The reception area lay beyond the doors, beyond the passing people and the play of light. It seemed strangely distant, and the air looked thicker there, opaque and still, like cloudy water in a glass tank. It was suddenly quite clear to me that I had not come here to find Horatio at all: I had brought him here to be killed, and myself with him. "I intend to clear his name," I said.

"Clear his name?" Even the voice seemed different now, thinner, more nasal. I nerved myself to meet the dark eyes. He was smiling, that same uncertain smile he had worn as he approached me, as if not sure of my identity. "Have you read the Italian sources?"

"Those that have been translated."

"But most of them haven't. I work at the National Library here in Naples, you know. It is one of the best in Italy—we like to think it is the best. I am in charge of the European history department. It contains the most extensive collection of local materials—chronicles, journals, eyewitness accounts—anywhere to be found. They don't leave you in any doubt as to what the rebels themselves believed. Even in early July, when they had been embarked for more than a week, they still believed they would be sailing for France. Gaetano Rodinò, in his *Racconti Storici*, tells us that Mario Pagano, who was subsequently executed, was still planning as late as the fifth to set up a fencing academy when he got to Toulouse. Rodinò, as you will know, was a fellow prisoner of his on board one of the transports."

"It is not a question of what they believed. Horatio acted in good faith—he needn't have had any knowledge of what they believed. How can he be held responsible for what went on in their minds?" It was my last attempt to fight back. I straightened myself, I looked the fellow in the face. "There is no evidence," I said. "None whatever." It is a terrible thing to face a cynic and put all your hope in a negative. "Not a scrap," I said, and I pressed my lips together to keep them from trembling.

I had looked away, but his voice came over to me, unhurried, unmistakably nasal now, slightly metallic. "This is a case where the search for evidence complicates the issues and obscures the truth, as it has been doing now for two hundred years. You say there is no evidence, therefore we cannot know. That is false reasoning, Mr. Cleasby. We should look first at what we already know, because it often precludes the need for evidence. If we know the painter's work, we don't need his signature on the painting—not necessarily. Don't you agree?"

"We do if we have to prove it."

"But we are talking about knowledge, not proof. What do we know about Horatio Nelson? A gifted naval commander, certainly, but that does not help much. A hero, yes. Heroes never admit mistakes, let alone wrongdoing. Heroes need to succeed gloriously—it is obligatory, at least until the moment comes for them to die gloriously, and this was not his moment. We know he was inordinately vain, we know he could gobble up flattery by the cartload, we know he took in hatred of the French with his mother's milk, we know he was a lifelong devoted servant of monarchs, we know he was totally ignorant of Naples except for where it lay on his charts, we know he was besotted with Emma Hamilton, who was besotted with Queen Maria Carolina, who wasn't besotted with anyone but had a lively desire to save her kingdom from the French and avoid the fate of her sister Marie Antoinette. She was just as set on winning as the admiral but a lot more adaptable. Or perhaps I mean intelligent. *My saviour,* she said to him. Devoted Lady Hamilton said the same. The queen and the mistress. Do you not see what this comes to, the irresistible conclusion? Look at the picture. Do you really need a signature?"

I could not answer him. His loquacity amazed me: deliberate, unfaltering, with a constant edge of malice in it. Those wrinkles round his eyes that I had thought due to scanning far horizons came from squinting over books in his library. He was shortsighted, of course. He would have his glasses in a case in one of the pockets of his jacket. Rimless glasses.

"In order to satisfy his appetite for victory, in order not to disappoint those who hailed him as their saviour, in order to punish those who had dared to desire a republic on French lines . . . Do you not see? He could not fall short in any particular. In his way were a few hundred men and women who thought they were protected by a treaty, and an intractable warrior-priest named Ruffo, who had made the treaty with them and wanted to save his face. So a way was found, a form of words. The appearance of good faith was preserved. And lo and behold, the rebels come walking out into the arms of the British marines."

So far I might have resisted; it was still, after all, in the realm of argument. But he had foreseen everything, even this vestige of resistance. He had planned everything in advance. He kept the killing stroke for the end.

"What does it matter, after all?" he said. "Why should it matter?" That thin smile was on his face again. "He was a man in a tight corner, wasn't he? We were at war with France—it was a struggle for survival, great issues were at stake. A spot of fraud, a few hundred expendable people, the statutory cover-up afterwards. Fairly standard for our times, isn't it? Or any other times, for that matter. Look at this century of ours, the things that have been done. Churchill made shadier deals and he is thought a great Englishman, whatever that means."

"He was a politician."

He leaned forward—he hadn't heard me. "What was that?"

"Churchill wasn't a hero."

"Oh, I see. It's because Nelson was a hero that they have been trying so long to keep the taint of falsehood from him. That's why he couldn't be allowed to do anything underhand. Well, heroes are useful, there is no denying that. Nelson was useful at the time, and he has been useful ever since. The Royal Navy keep a silence for him on Trafalgar Day, don't they, and fly the flags at half-mast? Stirring stuff, especially now that most of the glory has departed."

"He was a rebel too. He broke the line . . ."

My voice was again reduced to little more than a whisper. He gave no sign of having heard me. "Don't you know it yet?" he said. "Heroes are fabricated in the national dream factory. Heroes are not people."

He was looking at me as he spoke, but I could not meet his eyes. I looked down at his hands. One lay palm down on the table, the other was loosely curled round his almost empty glass. The nails were immaculate. The pads on the knuckles looked soft.

"You know," he said, "*dulce et decorum*, sweet and fitting. Not to die for one's country exactly, not necessarily, but to dream of it and be proud. To deal with our fears by dreaming. There are no heroes out there, Mr. Cleasby, there are only fears and dreams and the process of fabrication."

He knew me, somehow he knew me. I was still looking at his hands.

"No heroes," he said. "Surely you know that?"

Soft indoor hands. Quite hairless on the backs. *Of course.* The hair had been worn away by gloves, kid gloves, black . . . Why hadn't I seen it before? He was Badham.

I stood up quickly. "Another drink?"

He made as if to rise from his seat. He didn't want me to get away. "No," I said, "it's on me."

"The waiter will come," he said, but I didn't answer, I turned and walked over to the bar. There were more people there now, someone was asking for a drink, I had to wait, and this was a good thing because it enabled me to gather myself together. Some sort of a plan had to be made. I had to prevent him from realizing that I knew his true identity.

I glanced towards him. He was sitting in the same position, with his back to the bar. Across the few yards that separated us I took in the details of his appearance, seen thus from behind: the slightly ridged line of his jacket collar, the strip of shirt above, a cream or pale yellow colour. The shirt seemed too tight; it creased the flesh of his neck into folds at the sides. Above this the hair on his nape grew in loose thin curls like delicate shavings of some pale wood. The bar had hushed around me, all sound had drained into this closeness of sight. But I must have shifted my position, moved a little closer to the counter of the bar. I met Badham's eyes! There was a narrow panel of mirror set in the angle of the wall behind my chair, and he was watching my face in the glass. His own seemed to change now as he met my eyes, and I knew he had understood I was on to him.

There was no time to lose. There were no lifts on this side of the hotel, so I could not follow my first escape plan, which was to mount to the first floor and then come down by the stairs past the reception desk and out to the street. I would have to walk past him—there was nothing else for it. My heart was beating heavily and my throat had gone dry. He would assume I was going to the gents, or so I hoped. When I got opposite the swing doors I darted suddenly sideways, bumping into a porter with a luggage trolley and knocking my shin on one of the cases. And so I made it out into the street.

The sun was low over the sea now but still strong; I felt the heat of it as I stepped out from the shade of the awning. I must have crossed the road directly and gone down the steps, because I was suddenly there in the little marina where the white boats rested in their moorings, side by side. The boats didn't move, but the surface of the water was shivering all over, and this seemed strange, unaccountable, the masts and mooring ropes quite motionless, their reflections wriggling in the water like snakes, there was blood in among them too, a shuddering of red, as if the snakes were bleeding as they writhed. The cruelty that Badham had used against me came to my mind. A lump formed in my throat and my eyes filled with tears. The surface of the water glimmered and blurred and it seemed to me that the ripples of blood were gaining, spreading, soon they would cover the whole surface of the harbour. I had to get away from this. I went back again, onto the pavement. The white rocks on the foreshore below me were dazzling in the sunlight. There was the gleaming sweep of the bay, the softly glowing crests of the promontories beyond. In this luminous moment the message came to me, like a pulse beat in the softness of the evening: *Villa Emma*. The little house that Hamilton built for her at Posillipo. Where we went to escape the foul city, where we walked hand in hand through the gardens above the sea. I would go there now, at once. She would be waiting. I would get a taxi or a bus.

I began to walk across the pavement. I was still almost directly opposite the hotel. I saw Badham come through the swing doors, pass under the awning, and emerge onto the pavement. I saw him hesitate, look this way and that. I had the impression that he might be going to cross the road towards me. I went rapidly back down the steps. One of the boats had a black rubber guard tied to the bow, and I saw this stretching and contracting in the water like a lung. I waited some minutes, then I went up again, holding myself in readiness for flight. There was no sign of him on the opposite pavement, but this meant nothing in itself, he could easily have been hiding somewhere.

A man dressed in a dark suit and carrying a briefcase was approaching along the pavement. I moved into his path. "Villa Emma," I said. He raised his eyebrows and moved his head a little to one side. He had not understood, or so I thought at the time. "Villa Emma, Posillipo," I said. At this he smiled and made a sort of pointing gesture over his shoulder. There was a bus stop not far behind him, twenty yards or so, and he seemed to be indicating this. I think he was about to say something more, but then his expression changed completely; a cheeping sound had come from somewhere in the region of his heart. He thrust a hand inside his jacket and brought out the cheeping thing and spoke to it as if he wanted to soothe its alarm. At this moment a bus pulled into the stop and one or two people began to descend from it. I was still afraid that Badham might be somewhere near. I ran the distance at an unsteady jog and clambered up.

The driver started up again as soon as I was on board. He did not look at me or ask for any money. I had to stand to begin with; the bus was full. It jerked and shuddered and swayed heavily on the corners. I found a rail near the door and clung to it. I could not see where we were going. It was very hot inside the bus; I could feel the sweat gathering on my scalp and in all the concave places of my body. Some of the people inside the bus struggled to a yellow box attached to the rail near the entrance. They thrust white slips at this and it made a ringing sound. I understood that they were stamping tickets that they must have had before boarding the bus.

People got on and off, and after a while I found a seat. We had left the sea and turned inland—I only noticed it now. The street ascended steeply; the sounds of the engine were guttural and grinding. It was now that the pair of them got on, a woman and a girl, the woman bulky and matronly with a red canvas shopping bag, the girl with a face from a nightmare bestiary, wedge-shaped, with a hideously elongated nose like the proboscis of an anteater.

I suspected nothing at first. All I felt was a sort of dread. The seats on this bus did not all face the same way; they were in two lanes separated by an aisle, and the four at the front faced towards the others. I was sitting in the most forward of these four. For the moment there was no-one sitting opposite. What I was dreading came about. The two of them chose to sit side by side directly in front of me, face-on, the square-faced matron with the shopping bag on her knees and the monstrous girl with her staring green eyes and flexible snout and chin receding to nothing. And both of them looked fixedly at me.

It was this fixity of regard that alerted me. I could feel their eyes on me all the time. Things began to fall into place. Badham emerging from the hotel, looking to right and left—that had been a signal. The man with the telephone, receiving instructions. The bus that drew up so opportunely, the driver who did not ask me to produce a ticket. And now these two, keeping me under observation.

They were cunning; every time I glanced at them, they were looking somewhere else. The girl sat hunched forward. She was continually wrinkling the loose skin on her nose and opening her mouth in a snarling expression. She had on a white T-shirt with *Louisiana Country Club* inscribed across the bosom. What did that mean? They could have been notified that I would be on this bus, but how could Badham have known I would get on it in the first place? Could he have watched me? I had not actually seen him walk away.

The girl was looking about her, still wrinkling her nose and snarling. She was looking at the other people on the bus. Suddenly I realized: it was an outing, she was enjoying herself, this was her best T-shirt. She was retarded, to say the least, and this woman was looking after her. Surreptitiously, I scanned the woman's face. I was afraid, but I had to do it. Broad cheeks, small deep-set eyes, an expression of placid resignation. Not the mother—a nurse of some kind, the girl's keeper . . . She had taken some trouble to change her appearance, but I knew her now, I recognized her, I had last seen her leading away poor Penhas on the occasion of my father's funeral. Nothing to do with Badham. Her name was Mrs. White. I felt a great rush of relief. I caught her eye and nodded slightly to show that I had understood, and she blinked twice in reply.

We were on a level now, far above the sea, moving between large buildings with identical balconies. The roads were wider and there were pockets of greenery here and there, scattered groups of trees and clumps of brightly flowering bushes. There were not many people on the bus now, but a man was sitting opposite me on the other side of the aisle. I leaned forward and spoke to his averted face: "Posillipo?" He turned and looked at me for some moments in silence. Then he shook his head and pointed in the direction the bus had come from. He called forward to the driver, who merely shrugged. Some minutes afterwards the bus stopped. "*Capolinea,*" the man said. He again pointed behind him, the way the bus had come. The bus driver got down from his seat and came towards us. "*Capolinea,*" he said.

Everyone was getting off; we had come to the end of the line. I understood now. They had wanted to keep me away from Villa Emma at all costs. Misled by the man with the telephone, I had boarded the bus on the wrong side of the road. Posillipo was in the other direction. The driver showed me his watch and made a little circle above it with his forefinger. One hour. I would have to wait an hour before I could get a bus back. The driver smiled; his moustache lifted. He made little chopping motions in the direction from which we had come. "Posillipo." He was in it too, of course.

Everyone else was off the bus by now. I followed them. The driver got back into his seat and the bus drew away, gathered speed, disappeared in the distance. If this was the end of the line, where was he going? I thought I knew the answer to that. Mrs. White and her charge had got off with the others. They were someway off, walking along together by the side of the road. I had no idea where I was or what I should do. It was ten minutes to seven. The sun was setting in silver cloud over a sea invisible from here. I was not proposing to stay where I was, in that empty place, alone and exposed, without cover of any kind. I was not such a fool as that. While I was still hesitating, the signal came. Mrs. White glanced slightly over her shoulder. I immediately began to follow, taking care to keep a distance between us.

The road curved away; I lost them from view. When I came round the curve, there was no sign of them. But there was an unsurfaced road going off at right angles, with houses on one side and a stone wall on the other, bordering what looked like private grounds. After a while the road narrowed, the houses were less frequent. It was no more than a footpath. There was no sign of Mrs. White or the girl. I had made a mistake somehow, I had misread the signal. I stopped at the edge of the road and stood still. Immediately, with this ceasing of movement, I became aware that I was being watched. I was in a trap. I could not simply go back the way I had come, it was too dangerous, it was what they expected. Then I saw that there was a gate in the wall on the other side, a little way farther along, a metal gate, painted green.

There was no padlock on the gate, just a simple bar. It opened quite easily. I was planning to make a detour, keeping within the shelter of the wall, until I could get back to the dirt road again at a point somewhere near where it joined the main road, find a hiding place where I could wait for the bus. But I was too much in fear of the open, I stayed in the shelter of the wall too long. When I finally hoisted myself over it and dropped down on the other side, bruising my elbows and jarring my legs in the process, there was no sign of the road. I was in what I took to be the grounds of some large house or perhaps hotel. A gravel path wound away through thick shrubbery. All I could do was follow this—I had lost all sense of direction now.

I came out onto an asphalt driveway and an empty car park with white lines marking the spaces. On the other side of this were some single-storey brick buildings that looked like offices and then a large white house with balconied windows. I crossed the car park, passed round the nearer of the brick buildings. Through a window I saw two men in long white coats talking together. They stared at me as I passed.

I began to walk more quickly. There was a pavement now, leading in the direction of the white house. A man appeared suddenly from a side turning and walked towards me. He was passing a hand over his face, down and up again, with rapid repeated movements. As we drew opposite he stopped doing this, but he kept his hand stretched over his nose and peeped at me over the top of it.

Someone called out, perhaps in greeting, someone hidden by an angle of the building. From an upper room I heard the sound of a woman's laughter, strangely sustained, as if she were laughing also on the intakes of breath. A uniformed nurse came round a corner of the building with a very old man in a wheelchair. His face was tilted back and his eyes were closed, his sharp nose pointed up towards the sky. From the frame of his wheelchair there dangled a teddy bear and a black monkey with glass eyes. The bear and the monkey jerked and danced—they were on strings of elastic. The old man's eyes were not closed, they were white slits, he was watching me. The nurse said some words I did not understand. She left the wheelchair and came round towards me.

I understood everything now. Mrs. White and the girl were in it too, they had led me here. The men with white coats, the hand signals, the laughter . . . They had anticipated everything. There was no time to lose. I jumped over the low hedge that bordered the pavement, ran back across the car park and into the shrubbery. There was great power and freedom in this running at first. I ran in a wide circle, crashed through another low hedge, climbed a wooden fence, and found myself behind the house on ground that led upwards through a straggle of bushes and bare earth and patches of burned-out grass.

That sense of freedom did not last. I was breathing hoarsely, open-mouthed, lungs straining as I climbed higher. A thin screen of trees, cluttered with ivy. I pushed through them and half scrambled, half fell down a bank on the other side into a deep-sided cutting, broad and flat enough at the bottom to walk along—it looked as if there might once have been a single rail track here. There were grassed-over mounds of stones at intervals along the way.

Down here the night had begun to take over, there was an advance of darkness between the banks. After a while I stopped and listened, but there was no sound of pursuit. When I judged the distance to be safe, I climbed up the bank on the farther side. I had to get up on hands and knees and I was torn by brambles and thorny scrub. But when I reached the top of the bank, I forgot my hurts. I was looking down over the distant lights of streets and houses and the vanishing gleams of traffic, looking beyond this to the glimmering radiance of the bay. The sun had gone, but the sea still held the last of the light in a luminous solution of silver.

This was what you climbed up to as a boy, climbing from the sheltered glebeland, from the riverside meadows where the parsonage lay, mounting the bridle path towards the high ground above the village, high above, between the shoulders of the downs, from where we could look down over sand and saltmarsh, strands of gold and strips of shallow pool and at the verge the real sea, the mass of it, seamed white or silvered over. Behind us great rafts of bright cloud and the soft gleam of the sun on wet sand ripples and mudflats and the glitter of dried pebbles and shingle up the beach. Curlews whistling above the marshes, the terns with their wild cries and plunging flight.

How often we had seen it together. But now I was alone and the light was fading and I knew I had been brought here only for this, brought here alone to see the line of the sea as you saw it that evening in March when you were twelve years old, the evening before you left. It was the only point in all the countryside around from which to get a view of the sea. You came here in the fading light and looked at the sea and you walked away to spend your life with the sea and when you did that you took my life with you.

What I would have done, how long I would have stayed there, I don't know. I thought everything was at an end. But then the miracle happened, the boy appeared. For some moments I could not believe it. Only a dark shape at first, surmounted by the pale glimmer of the face. There below me, in the last of the light he came walking. Between the crest of the cutting where I crouched and the lights of the houses below, neither fast nor slow—it was a path well known to him. On his back a sort of bump, which I made out to be a small rucksack.

Of course, his provisions would be there, his provisions for the journey. He was not going home to the parsonage, he was leaving, he was going away to spend his life with the sea, he was taking my life with him.

Down the slope again, through the thorns and scrub. I found a stone big enough, not too big. Panting now with the fear of being too late, I kept along the cutting out of hearing, out of sight. When I clawed myself up again, he was still there below me, a diminutive figure, walking at the same pace, looking ahead of him. And now, when I had to get behind him, he started singing!

Incomprehensible words in a child's treble—your voice had not broken yet. A blunder of the first order, preventing you from hearing me as I drew closer behind you, my step uncertain in this difficult light. Perhaps at the last moment you heard or sensed something. But then it was too late, too late to turn on me the terror of your eyes. I struck downward at the small head, once, twice. The figure sank to its knees, half turning towards me, raising an arm. A sound came from it, not very loud, like sobbing but more liquid—as though there were some liquid in the throat. I struck again and he fell forward. I heard the crash of his fall.

Then I walked away, continuing the boy's path, keeping the lights below me. There was no need to hurry now. I had nothing to fear. I had done it, I had broken the line. Dark and bright angels meet at twilight, it is the only time. And when they meet they join. We can never lose each other now.

Barry Unsworth won the Booker Prize in 1992 for *Sacred Hunger;* his next novel, *Morality Play,* was a Booker nominee and a best seller in both the United States and Great Britain. His other novels include *After Hannibal, The Hide,* and *Pascali's Island,* which was also short-listed for the Booker Prize and was made into a feature film. He lives in Umbria with his wife and recently held the position of Visiting Fellow at the University of Iowa Writers' Workshop.